BIBLIOGRAPHY
of
DISCOGRAPHIES

BIBLIOGRAPHY
of
DISCOGRAPHIES

Volume 2
JAZZ

by
Daniel Allen

R. R. Bowker Company

New York and London, 1981

Published by R. R. Bowker Company
1180 Avenue of the Americas, New York, N.Y. 10036
Copyright © 1981 by Xerox Corporation
All rights reserved
Printed and bound in the United States of America

Library of Congress Cataloging in Publication Data
Main entry under title:
    Bibliography of discographies.
    Includes indexes.
    CONTENTS: v. 1. Gray, M. H. and Gibson, G. D.
Classical music, 1925–1975.—v. 2. Allen, D. Jazz.
    1. Music—Discography—Bibliography. I. Gray,
Michael H., 1946–   . II. Gibson, Gerald D.,
1938–   . III. Allen, Daniel.
ML156.2.B49   016.0167899'12   77-22661
ISBN 0-8352-1342-0 (v.2)   AACR1

825349

LIBRARY
ALMA COLLEGE
ALMA, MICHIGAN

Contents

Preface

This second volume of *Bibliography of Discographies*, encompassing discographies of jazz, blues, ragtime, gospel, and rhythm and blues music published between 1935 and 1980, continues a series of works that will eventually number five volumes devoted to discographies in all subject areas. The first volume, covering discographies of classical music published between 1925 and 1975, was compiled by Michael Gray and Gerald Gibson and published by Bowker in 1977. Subsequent volumes will survey popular music, ethnic and folk music, and general discographies of music, as well as label lists, speech, and animal sounds.

In compiling this bibliography pioneering efforts in this field were consulted, especially the Discographical Index, published in early issues of *Discographical Forum* (1960); indexes of discographies by John Godrich and Bob Dixon published in *Vintage Jazz Mart* (1959–1960); and the *Bibliography of Jazz Discographies since 1960* by Pete Moon (London: British Institute of Jazz Studies, 1972).

As in Volume 1 of this series, a definition of "discography" will not be attempted in spite of the efforts of many others to do so; instead, the selection of citations has been guided primarily by the self-designation of the work and by its potential usefulness to the user. Effort has been made, however, to exclude from this bibliography the following types of works:

1. Record company catalogues.
2. Works that are exclusively of a critical nature, such as guides to recommended records, record reviews, and critical discussions of a musician's recorded output.
3. Those "discographies" that are actually only discographical references to works discussed in an accompanying text.
4. Record lists selected on basis of popularity.

It is realized that many discographies included in this bibliography, especially those published before 1960, do not give any more information than can be found in the various general discographies of jazz and related music, notably Rust's *Jazz Records 1897–1942*; Godrich and Dixon's *Blues and Gospel Records*; Jepsen's *Jazz Records 1942–1962*; and Bruyninckx's *Fifty/Sixty Years of Recorded Jazz*. However, such discographies are included both for their historical interest and their potential usefulness to those lacking the general discographies previously mentioned.

RESEARCH METHOD

In gathering citations, there has been a reliance almost exclusively on examination of the discographies themselves. Those not seen by me or my correspondents, but taken from various secondary sources, have been enclosed in double brackets [[ ]]. Citations of monographs are taken as closely as possible from the title page, with interpolations or other alterations enclosed in single brackets. Because of this method, some citations will differ in form from those found in other bibliographies and reference sources. A number of secondary citations that could not be clarified in the time allotted to the research have been omitted.

As part of the examination process, a nine-number annotative code has been adopted to identify elements believed to be of special importance to users. These coded elements appear in double parentheses (( )) included in or following the citation. The symbol ((—)) is used to signify that no coded elements appear in the discography. The elements and their symbols are:

    1 Noncommercial recordings
    2 Personnel
    3 Matrix number
    4 Index:
        4c Composer index
        4p Personal name index
        4r Record number index
        4t Title index
    5 Release dates
    6 Take numbers
    7 Place and date of recording:
        7d Date only
        7p Place only
    8 Composers
    9 Musicological information, such as: tune structure, key, soloists, tempo, length and/or sequence of solos, duration, musical notation of solos, and description of difference between alternate takes.

ORGANIZATION

The bibliography is divided into two sections: the body, which contains personal names and other subjects arranged in a single-numbered alphabetical sequence, and the index, encompassing names of authors, editors, series titles, and distinctive discography titles. Surnames of authors and editors in the body have been capitalized to facilitate identification and to make scanning entries easier. Filing of multiple listings under a given heading is by either name of the compiler of the discography or the title of the discography.

Headings for citations that are not names of musicians, composers, or musical groups are shown in the list of subject headings that follows the Preface. (See the back of the book for names and addresses of small

publishers and periodicals cited.) Forms of personal names in the body
are based on standard usage as found in general discographies of jazz
and related music (for example, Duke Ellington is standard usage over
the given name Edward Kennedy Ellington); where appropriate, cross-
references linking variant subjects or name forms to those used have
been made. Filing in the main text and in the index follows American
Library Association filing rules.

Discographies appears in the following forms:

	ELLINGTON, DUKE (Edward Kennedy Ellington), 1899–1974 piano, composer
(Journal article) →	E40 AASLAND, Benny H.: Duke och piraterna; rovarpressade godbitar for discofilen in Orkester Jour- nalen, Vol. 24 (January 1956): 24–25 ((1, 7, 9))
(Title entry) →	E59 Discographie de Duke Ellington et son orchestre (disques parus en France) in Jazz Hot, No. 43 (April 1950): 8–9, 18 ((2, 7d))
(Monograph) →	E73 JEPSEN, Jorgen Grunnet: Duke Ellington 1947–1958; a discogra- phy [Vanløse, Denmark]: 1959, 14 pp. ((2, 3, 7))
(Label entry) →	KEYNOTE label
(Additions/corrections → *cited with discography* *being corrected)*	K31 MORGAN, Alun: Keynote label list- ing in Jazz Monthly, No. 186 (August 1970): 27–28; No. 187 (September 1970): 28–31; addi- tions and corrections in Jazz Monthly, No. 190 (December 1970): 27–29 ((2, 3, 6, 7))

There are similar forms for other types of subject headings. Where the
title of a discography is incomplete or misleading as to content, a brief
note has been added in brackets between the citation and the (( )) code.
The expression *name discography* (appearing in many British discographies of musicians) means a "discography of recordings made under
that musician's own name."

Because no work of bibliography can ever be complete, readers are
invited to submit their additions or corrections to the compiler in care of
the publisher. For discographies published after this publication, readers
are urged to consult the ongoing annual Bibliography of Discographies—
Annual Cumulation, published approximately yearly in issues of the
Journal of the Association for Recorded Sound Collections (available
from the executive secretary, Les Waffen, Box 1643, Manassas, VA
22110).

Acknowledgement is gratefully made to the help and assistance
provided by the following persons and institutions: the late Walter C.
Allen; the Association for Recorded Sound Collections; Coda Publications, Toronto; Harold Flakser, Brooklyn, NY; Michael Gray, Voice
of America, and Gerald Gibson, Library of Congress, Washington, DC;
Franz Hoffman, West Berlin; Steve Holzer, Indianapolis, IN; the Institute

of Jazz Studies, Newark, NJ; the New York Public Library, especially the Rodgers and Hammerstein Archives of Recorded Sound and the Schomburg Collection; Norbert Ruecker, publisher of *Jazz Index*, Frankfurt, West Germany; Ron Sweetman, Ottawa; the Metropolitan Toronto Central Library; the University of Toronto Music Library; and Barry Witherden, British Institute of Jazz Studies.

January 1981   Daniel Allen

Subject Headings Used in This Book

This list contains only those headings that are not names of musicians, composers, or musical groups. Forms of headings follow those used by the Library of Congress if such forms are reasonably consistent with normal usage among jazz enthusiasts. Subject headings not covered by the Library of Congress have been formulated according to such normal usage. Explanatory notes have been added to some headings in this list to help those unfamiliar with certain terms. These notes are not repeated in the main text. The subject headings included in this list have been classified into the following categories:

General categories of music
Styles of jazz
Instruments and orchestral types
Subheadings under names of musicians
Tune titles
Types of recordings
Record company producers or executives
Record labels and companies
Miscellaneous

General Categories of Music

Note: The subheading Additions and Corrections (under Blues Music, Jazz Music, and Rhythm and Blues) refers to works consisting entirely of additions and corrections to several discographies, discographies in general, or unknown discographies (the annotative code (( )) is not used with such entries). Works adding to and/or correcting *specific* discographies or discographies of specific musicians will be cited along with the discography or musician being corrected.

Blues Music
Blues Music—Additions and
  Corrections
Blues Music—California
Blues Music—Chicago
Blues Music—Cincinnati
Blues Music—Memphis
Blues Music—Netherlands
Classical Music—Influence
  on Jazz

Fugues
Gospel Music
Jazz Dance
Jazz Music
Jazz Music—Additions and
  Corrections
Jazz Music—Australia
Jazz Music—Austria
Jazz Music—Belgium
Jazz Music—Canada

General Categories (cont.)

Jazz Music—Czechoslovakia
Jazz Music—Denmark
Jazz Music—Europe
Jazz Music—Europe, Eastern
Jazz Music—Finland
Jazz Music—France
Jazz Music—Germany
Jazz Music—Germany, Eastern
Jazz Music—Great Britain
Jazz Music—Greece
Jazz Music—Italy
Jazz Music—Japan
Jazz Music—Netherlands
Jazz Music—New Orleans
Jazz Music—New York City
Jazz Music—Newport, Rhode Island
Jazz Music—Norway
Jazz Music—Poland
Jazz Music—St. Louis
Jazz Music—Scandinavia
Jazz Music—Sweden
Jazz Music—Switzerland
Jazz Music—West Coast (U.S.)
Jazz-Rock Music
Ragtime Music
Ragtime Music—Great Britain
Ragtime Music—Orchestrations
Rhythm and Blues
Rhythm and Blues—Additions and
  Corrections
Rhythm and Blues—Cleveland
Rhythm and Blues—Detroit
Rhythm and Blues—Michigan
Rhythm and Blues—Ohio
Serial Music and Jazz

Styles of Jazz

Jazz Music—Avant-Garde
Jazz Music—Bebop
Jazz Music—Chicago Style
Jazz Music—Modern Style
Jazz Music—New Orleans Style

Instruments and Orchestral Types

Accordion Music (Jazz)
Big Bands
Brass Bands
Clarinet Music (Jazz)
Drum Music (Jazz)
Electronic Musical Instruments
  (Jazz)
Guitar Music (Jazz)
Jug Bands
Percussion Music (Jazz)
Piano Music (Jazz)

Saxophone Music (Jazz)
Trombone Music (Jazz)
Trumpet Music (Jazz)
Vibraphone Music (Jazz)
Vocal Music (Jazz)

**Subheadings Under Names
  of Musicians**

Arrangements
Compositions
Influences (i.e., used in the case of a
  discography of recordings or
  musicians who influenced another
  musician)
Piano Rolls
Sidemen (i.e., used for discographies
  of musicians who played with
  another musician)
Soundtracks (See **Types of
  Recordings**)
Transcriptions (See **Types of
  Recordings**)

Tune titles

Bugle Call Rag
Cold in China
Darktown Strutters Ball
Dipper Mouth Blues
High Society
How High the Moon
I Wish I Could Shimmy Like My
  Sister Kate
Jazz Me Blues
Jazzin' Baby Blues
Love with a Feeling
Maple Leaf Rag
Milenburg Joys
My Baby It's Gone
Panama
Ragging the Scale
St. Louis Blues
San
Star Dust
Sugar Foot Stomp
Sweet Georgia Brown
That's a Plenty
Tiger Rag
Tin Roof Blues

Types of Recordings

Airshots (i.e., recordings made from
  broadcasts)
Cylinder Recordings
Piano Rolls
Private Recordings (i.e., recordings

not made for commercial issue,
often without the musicians'
consent)

Soundtracks (i.e., recordings on
motion-picture film)

Test Pressings (trial copies of
recordings made for possible
commercial issue)

Transcriptions (i.e., recordings made
for the sole use of broadcasters)

Record Company Producers
or Executives

Bolletino, Dante
Granz, Norman
Hammond, John
Khoury, George
London, Mel
Rose, Boris
Toscano, Eli

Record Labels and Companies

Note: Nationality of the label or
company is indicated if not U.S.

A-1 Dud
ABC Paramount
ACO (British)
Acquarian
Actuelle
Ajax
Aladdin
All Points
Allegro
Alto
American Music
American Record Corporation
American Record Society
Ampersand (Australian)
Apex (Canadian)
Argo
Armed Forces Radio Service
Artistic
Atlantic
Audiophile
Aurora (Canadian)
Autograph
Bango
Banner
Baronet
Bay-Tone
Beka (German)
Bethlehem
Biltmore
Birth (German)
Black and Blue (French)

Black and White
Black Patti
Black Swan
Blue Ace
Blue Horizon (British)
Blue Note
Blue Rock
Blue Star (Australian)
Blue Star (French)
Bluebird
Blues Unlimited
Bluesville
Bluesway
Bobbin
British Rhythm Society
Broadway
Brunswick
Brunswick (Australian)
Brunswick (British)
BVHaast (Dutch)
Byg (French)
CBS Sony (Japanese)
CJ
Cadet
Candid
Capitol
Carousel
Cat
Century
Cetra (Italian)
Champion
Chance
Chariot
Checker
Chess
Chiaroscuro
Chief
Circle
Circle (Australian)
Clarion
Clef
Cobra
Colt
Columbia
Columbia (British)
Commodore
Compo Corporation (Canadian)
Constellation
Cosmopolitan
Creole
Crescent
Crimson
Crown
DC Sound
Dakar

Labels and Companies (cont.)

Dan (Japanese)
Debut
Decatur
Decca
Decca (British)
Decca (Dutch)
Dee Gee
Delmar
Delta (British)
Deluxe
Dial
Dig
Disc
Diva
Dixi (Swedish)
Dooto
Dragon (Swedish)
Dud Sound
Duophone (British)
Durium (British)
Dynamo
ECM (German)
E-Disc
ER (Swedish)
ESP
Eastern
Edison
Egmont (British)
Ekophon (Swedish)
Elite
Emarcy
Empire
Empirical
Enja (German)
Esquire (British)
Evergreen (Swedish)
Excello
FM
Fay
Feature
Federal
Fine Art
Folkways
Friendly 5
Futura (French)
GHB
Gazell (Swedish)
Gennett
Glory
Golden Crest
Good Time Jazz
Gotham
Groove
Groovy

Guardsman (British)
HJCA
HMV (British)
HMV (Swedish)
HRS
Harmony
Harvey
Herald
Herwin
Hit
Hit of the Week
Holiday
Hollywood
ICP (Dutch)
Imperial (British)
Impulse
Incus (British)
Interlude
Invictus
Italian Jazz Stars Series (Italian)
Jay
Jazz Archive Series (British)
Jazz Classics
Jazz Collector
Jazz in Italy Series (Italian)
Jazz in the Troc Series
Jazz Information
Jazz Record Society
Jazz Society (French)
Jazz Star (Swedish)
Jazz Studio Series
Jazz West Coast
Jazzart
Jazzology
Jewel
Job
Jolly Roger
Josie
Jump
KRC
Kas-Mo
Keymen
Keynote
King
Knight
Lasalle
Library of Congress
Lindstrom (German)
Loma
London (British)
London Jazz (British)
Lucky (Japanese)
Luniverse
Lyric
MJR

M-Pac
Macgregor Transcriptions
Macy's
Majestic
Maltese
Marterry
Mar-V-Lus
Mel/Mel-Lon
Melodisc (British)
Melotone
Melrose
Mercer
Mercury
Meritt
Metronome (Swedish)
Mikim
Minit
Mirwood
Mo Soul
Mode
Moonsong
Mouldie Fygge
Musicraft
Muza (Polish)
National
A Natural Hit
Nocturne
Norgran
North Bay
OFC (Argentine)
Odeon (German)
Odeon (Italian)
Okeh
Onyx
Oriole
Ozone
Pacific Jazz
Palm (French)
Palm Club (French)
Panachord (British)
Paradox
Paramount
Parlophon (German)
Parlphone (British)
Parrot
Pathe
Pax
Peacock
Perfect
Phantasie Concert
Philips (British)
Pick-Up
Pirate (Swedish)
Planet
Plaza Music Company

Plymouth
PM (Canadian)
Polydor (Australian)
Post
Prestige
Progressive
Project (British)
Purist (British)
QRS
RCA Victor
Rampart
Regal
Regal (British)
Regal Zonophone (British)
Reprise
Revelation
Revue
Rex (British)
Rhythm
Ric Tic
Ristic (British)
Riverside
Rocko/Rocket
Roost
Royale
SABA/MPS (German)
Sabre
Sandman
Saravah (French)
Savoy (Chicago)
Savoy (Newark, NJ)
Scala (British)
Scala (Swedish)
Selmer
Sensation
Sepia
Sesac
Session (Chicago)
Session (New York)
Sew City
Shandar (French)
Signature
Silver Fox
Silverton (Swedish)
Silvertone
Sincopa y Ritmo (Argentine)
Sonata (Swedish)
Sonora (Swedish)
Soul
Soul City
Soundcraft
Southland
Special Editions
Specialty
Spring

Labels and Companies (cont.)
Starr Gennett (Canadian)
States
Stateside
Stax
SteepleChase (Danish)
Steiner-Davis
Summit
Sun
Sunset
Superior
Supraphon (Czech)
Sussex
Swaggie (Australian)
Swan
Swing (French)
TDS
Tailgate
Talent
Tamla
Telefunken (Swedish)
Televox (German)
Temple
Tempo (British)
Tiger
Tower (British)
Transition
Triple B
Trix
Trusound
Twin Stacks
UHCA
Ultra
Ultraphon (Swedish)
United
V Disc
Vanguard
Varsity
Vee Jay
Veep

Velvet Tone
Verve
Victor
Victory (British)
Vinylite Jazz Reissues
Vocalion
Vocalion (British)
Vogue
Vogue (French)
Wax Shop
Weathers
Wheelsville
Whirlin' Disc
Wingate
World Program Service
X
XX (Australian)
Yambo
Zynn

Miscellaneous
Association for the Advancement
   of Creative Musicians
Chocolate Kiddies (musical revue)
Esquire Jazz Concert
Jazz at the Asahikodo
Jazz at the Philharmonic
Jazz Scene (British broadcast series)
Montreux Jazz Festival
Newport Jazz Festival
Territory Bands (commonly used to
   refer to jazz orchestras of the
   1920s and 30s, based in the
   midwest and southwest, who
   toured throughout that area and
   never, or seldom, went to the major
   U.S. recording centers)
This Is Jazz (radio broadcast series)
Village Vanguard (night club, New
   York City)

BIBLIOGRAPHY
of
DISCOGRAPHIES

AACM
  See ASSOCIATION FOR THE ADVANCE-
  MENT OF CREATIVE MUSICIANS

ABC PARAMOUNT label
  See WHITE, JOSH (Coller, Derek:
  Josh White on ABC-Paramount)

A-1 DUD label
  See DUD SOUND label

AALTONEN, JUHANI
  tenor saxophone

A1 Selected Juhani Aaltonen discog-
    raphy in Jazz Forum (Poland), No.
    42 (April 1976): 52 ((—))

ABCO label

A2 TURNER, Bez: A crap shooting
    fool; Eli Toscano's labels in
    Blues Unlimited, No. 134 (March-
    June 1979): 9-11 [ABCO, Cobra,
    and Artistic label listings]
    ((3))

ABERCROMBIE, JOHN, 1944–
  guitar

A3 Plattenhinweise in Blues Notes,
    No. 3/79 (1979): 43 ((—))

A4 Selected Abercrombie discography
    in Down Beat, Vol. 43 (Febru-
    ary 26, 1976): 18 ((—))

A5 Selected Abercrombie discography
    in Down Beat, Vol. 46 (Febru-
    ary 22, 1979): 42 ((—))

ABRAMS, IRWIN
  violin

A6 LANGE, Horst H.: Irwin Abrams; a
    discography of Irwin Abrams' Okeh

recordings in Discophile, No. 47
(April 1956): 8, 12 ((2, 3, 7))

ABRAMS, RICHARD, 1930–
  piano

A7 BERNARD, Marc: Richard Abrams et
    l'AACM in Jazz Magazine (France),
    No. 209 (March 1973): 21 ((2, 9))

ACE, JOHNNY, 1929-1954
  piano, vocal

A8 MOHR, Kurt: Discographie de
    Johnny Ace in Jazz Hot, No. 272
    (May 1971): 16-17 ((2, 3))

A9 MOHR, Kurt, and Bernard NIQUET:
    Discographie de Johnny Ace (1952-
    1954) in Soul Bag, No. 41 (Sep-
    tember 1974): 21 ((2, 3))

ACCORDION MUSIC (JAZZ)

A10 BERGQUIST, C. H.: Swedish accor-
     dion jazz discography in Metro-
     nome, Vol. 71 (August 1955): 37
     ((2))

ACO label (British)

A11 BADROCK, Arthur, and Derek
     SPRUCE: Aco (a label listing) in
     R.S.V.P., No. 2 (June 1965) to
     No. 15 (August 1966); No. 17
     (October 1966) to No. 25 (June
     1967); No. 27 (August 1967) to
     No. 31 (December 1967); No. 34
     (March 1968); No. 35 (April
     1968); No. 38 (July 1968); No. 40
     (September 1968) to No. 42
     (November 1968); with additions
     and corrections in No. 43 (Decem-
     ber 1968); No. 47 (April 1969);
     and No. 52 (January/February
     1970), various paginations
     [G15000 series] ((3))

1

ACQUARIAN label

A12 KUDLACEK, Kerry: [listing] in his
     I was born under Aquarius in
     Blues Unlimited, No. 50 (October
     1968): 12 ((3))

ACTUELLE label

A13 BADROCK, Arthur: Actuelle Pathe;
     a Collecta label listing in
     Collecta, No. 2 (October 1968) to
     No. 10; No. 13; No. 18 (September
     1972), various paginations (dis-
     cography has own page-numbering
     system, different from the maga-
     zine's) ((3, 5))

ADAMS, GEORGE, 1940–
tenor saxophone

A14 Selected George Adams discography
     in Down Beat, Vol. 46 (November
     1979): 34 ((—))

ADAMS, MARIE
vocal

A15 CHOISNEL, Emmanuel; Kurt MOHR;
     and Jacques PERIN: Marie Adams
     discography in Soul Bag, No. 48
     (June 1975): 13-14; additions and
     corrections in Soul Bag, No. 51
     (January 1976): 32 ((2, 3, 7))

ADAMS, WOODROW, 1917–
guitar, harmonica

A16 ROTANTE, Anthony: Woodrow Adams
     in Record Research, No. 33 (March
     1961): 14 ((3))

ADDERLEY, JULIAN "CANNONBALL," 1928–
1975
alto saxophone

A17 ADKINS, Tony: Private recordings
     in Discographical Forum, No. 11
     (March 1969): 10 ((1, 2, 7, 9))

A18 EYLE, Wim van: Cannonball Adder-
     ley discografie in Jazz Press,
     No. 37 (April 29, 1977) to No. 40
     (June 10, 1977), various pagina-
     tions; additions and corrections
     in Jazz Press, No. 43 (September
     2, 1977): 6 ((1, 2, 3, 7))

A19 Farewell Cannonball in Swing
     Journal, Vol. 29 (October 1975):
     248-255 ((2, 7d))

A20 JEPSEN, Jorgen Grunnet: Discog-
     raphy of Cannonball Adderley/John

Coltrane. [Brande, Denmark: Debut
Records, c1961], 31 leaves ((2,
3, 7))

A21 Sélection de disques de "Cannon-
     ball" Adderley publiés en France
     in Jazz Hot, No. 157 (September
     1960): 14 ((—))

ADDERLEY, NAT, 1931–
trumpet

A22 FLUCKIGER, Otto: Nat Adderley; a
     name discography in Jazz Statis-
     tics, No. 1 (April 1956): 6-7;
     additions and corrections in Jazz
     Statistics, No. 3 (August 1956):
     9 ((2, 3, 7, 9))

A23 Selected Adderley discography in
     Down Beat, Vol. 43 (November 18,
     1976): 14 ((—))

AGE label

A24 BAKER, Cary: Age label listing in
     Shout, No. 82 (December 1972):
     3, 4 ((3, 5))

AIRSHOTS
     See also ALTO label; ARMSTRONG,
     LOUIS (Norris, John); ELLINGTON,
     DUKE (Aaslund, Benny H.: Duke och
     piraterna); HOLIDAY, BILLIE
     (Millar, Jack: Billie Holiday--a
     selected discography of air-
     shots...); LUNCEFORD, JIMMIE
     (Dutton, Frank: Jimmie Lunceford;
     the broadcasts and transcrip-
     tions) and (Hall, Bill: Jimmie
     Lunceford broadcasts-transcrip-
     tions & filmtracks); OZONE label;
     SESSION label (New York); YOUNG,
     LESTER (Schroeder, Harry)

A25 FLUCKER, Jack: "Jazz Scene" at
     the Ronnie Scott Club in Disco-
     graphical Forum, No. 27 (November
     1971) to No. 28 (January 1972),
     various paginations ((1, 2, 7, 9))

A26 LITCHFIELD, Jack: A listing of
     the radio series This Is Jazz in
     Matrix, No. 99/100 (April 1973):
     3-19 ((1, 2, 9))

AIRTO, 1941–
percussion

A27 STIX, John: Airto and Flora in
     Different Drummer, Vol. 1 (Decem-
     ber 1974): 17 ((—))

AJAX label

A28 ALLEN, Walter C.: [listing of all known issues, nos. 17005 to 17133] in his Discomania column in Jazz Journal, Vol. 9 (July 1956): 26, 36; (August 1956): 30, 36 ((3, 5, 6))

A29 ALLEN, Walter C.: [revised version of previous entry] in Record Research, No. 45 (August 1962); No. 50 (April 1963); No. 53 (July 1963); No. 62 (August 1964), various paginations ((3, 7, 8))

AKIYOSHI, TOSHIKO, 1929-
   piano

A30 Akiyoshi-Tabackin discography in Down Beat, Vol. 44 (October 20, 1977): 14 ((—))

A31 Selected T.A.L.T. discography in Jazz Forum (Poland), No. 64 (1980): 34 ((—))

A32 Toshiko Akiyoshi discography in Swing Journal, Vol. 28 (October 1974): 76-79 ((2, 7))

ALADDIN label
   See also YOUNG, LESTER (Lester Young on Aladdin)

A33 ROTANTE, Anthony: Aladdin records in Record Research, Vol. 1 (December 1955): 9-10 ((3))

ALBANY, JOE, 1924-
   piano
   See also PIANO MUSIC (JAZZ) (Edwards, Ernie)

A34 TARRANT, Don, and Chris EVANS: Joe Albany discography in Journal of Jazz Discography, No. 4 (January 1979): 2-7 ((1, 2, 3, 7))

ALBERT, DON, 1908-
   trumpet

A35 A Don Albert discography in Storyville, No. 31 (October-November 1970): 25 ((2, 3, 6, 7))

ALEMAN, OSCAR, 1905-
   guitar
   See CHRISTIAN, CHARLIE (Evensmo, Jan)

ALEXANDER, TEXAS (Alger Alexander), ca. 1880-ca. 1955?
   vocal

A36 BAKKER, Dick M.: Alger "Texas" Alexander in Micrography, No. 8 (January 1970): 10 ((7d))

A37 McCARTHY, Albert, and Ralph VENABLES: Discography of Texas Alexander in Jazz Music, Vol. 3, No. 1 (1946): 20-22 ((2, 3, 7d))

ALEXANDRIA, LOREZ, 1929-
   vocal

A38 CHAUVARD, Marcel, and Kurt MOHR: Discography of Lorez Alexandria in Jazz Statistics, No. 25 (March 1962): 4-5 ((2, 3, 6, 7))

ALL POINTS label
   See LONDON, MEL

ALLEGRO label
   See ROYALE label

ALLEN, HENRY "RED," 1908-1967
   trumpet

A39 BAKER, Frank Owen: Jazz biographies 4--Henry Allen Jr. in Jazz Notes (Australia), No. 80 (January 1948): 12 [Australian releases] ((—))

A40 DAVIES, John R. T., and Laurie WRIGHT: The Allen Victors in Storyville, No. 34 (April-May 1971): 131-132 [1929-1930 recordings] ((2, 3, 6, 7, 8, 9))

A41 EVENSMO, Jan: The trumpet and vocal of Henry Red Allen 1927-1942. [Hosle, Norway: 1977], 54 pp. (Jazz solography series, Vol. 8) ((1, 2, 3, 6, 7, 9))

A42 GERDEAU, Maurice: A list of Australian releases featuring Henry Red" Allen in Jazz Notes (Australia), No. 69 (December 1946): 6-7 ((7d))

A43 HAGUE, Douglas: Complete discography in Jazz Journal, Vol. 8 (August 1955): 2, 31-33; additions and corrections in letter from Eric Townley in Jazz Journal, Vol. 8 (October 1955): 33 ((2, 7))

ALLISON, LUTHER, 1939–
    guitar, harmonica, vocal

A44 [[LIBERGE, Luigi, and Daniel
    BELLEMAIN: Luther Allison disco
    in Jazz, Blues & Co., No. 15
    (March 1978): 12–13; additions
    and corrections in Jazz, Blues &
    Co., No. 16 (April 1978): 14]]

A45 SVACINA, Fritz: Discographie:
    Luther Allison in Blues Life, No.
    5 (1979): 9–11 ((2, 7))

ALLISON, MOSE, 1927–
    piano, vocal

A46 JEPSEN, Jorgen Grunnet: Mose
    Allison diskografi in Orkester
    Journalen, Vol. 27 (February
    1959): 50 ((2, 3, 7))

A47 Mose Allison; can a white man
    sing the blues? in Different
    Drummer, Vol. 1 (May/June 1974):
    30 ((—))

A48 Selected Allison discography in
    Down Beat, Vol. 43 (September 9,
    1976): 15 ((—))

ALTO label
    See also ROSE, BORIS

A49 DAVIS, Brian; Bill MINER; and Don
    TARRANT: Alto—a complete listing
    in Discographical Forum, No. 37
    (1976) to No. 40 (spring 1978),
    various paginations; additions
    and corrections in Discographical
    Forum, No. 41 (1978?): 2 ((1, 2,
    7))

A50 WINTHER-RASMUSSEN, Nils: Alto
    records in Orkester Journalen,
    Vol. 41 (June 1973): 19, 35 ((1,
    2, 7))

ALTSCHUL, BARRY, 1943–
    drums

A51 Altschul discography in Down
    Beat, Vol. 42 (February 13,
    1975): 15 ((—))

A52 Selected discography in Coda, No.
    168 (August 1979): 13 ((—))

AMERICAN MUSIC label
    See also DODDS, BABY (The Baby
    Dodds LPs); JOHNSON, BUNK
    (Bakker, Dick M.); LEWIS, GEORGE
    (Bakker, Dick M.); NICHOLAS,
    WOODEN JOE (Bakker, Dick M.)

A53 ALLEN, Walter C.: American Music
    long-playing records in Disco-
    phile, No. 22 (February 1952):
    13–14; supplemented in his Alter-
    nate masters on American Music
    LP; some notes in Discophile, No.
    33 (December 1953): 19; and in
    CAREY, Dave; Paul B. SHEATSLEY;
    and J. Ernest STORK: Alternate
    masters on "American Music" LP;
    some notes in Discophile, No. 38
    (October 1954): 16–17 ((2, 3, 7,
    9))

A54 HULME, George: The American Music
    catalogue; a listing of the 78
    rpm. issues in Matrix, No. 5
    (March 1955): 3–5, 9; additions
    and corrections in Matrix, No. 7
    (July 1955): 6, 17; No. 8 (Sep-
    tember 1955): 3; No. 13 (August
    1956): 15; No. 55 (October 1964):
    16 ((3, 7d))

A55 HULME, George: American Music
    records; a discographical survey
    of the microgroove issues in
    Matrix, No. 13 (August 1956):
    12–14; No. 14 (December 1956):
    17–18; No. 15 (February 1957):
    6–8; additions and corrections in
    Matrix, No. 17 (April 1958): 11;
    No. 18 (July 1958): 19–20; No. 28
    (April 1960): 16; No. 34 (June
    1961): 19; No. 35/36 (September
    1961): 38; No. 55 (October 1964):
    16 ((2, 3, 7))

A56 KING, Bruce: Discography in Jazz
    Monthly, Vol. 5 (April 1959):
    10–11 [nos. 638 to 648] ((2, 3,
    7))

A57 SHEATSLEY, Paul B.: Sorting out
    "American Music" in Discophile,
    No. 41 (April 1955): 12–13; ad-
    ditions and corrections in
    Discophile, No. 45 (December
    1955): 13 [July 1949 and May 1945
    sessions] ((2, 3, 6, 7))

AMERICAN RECORD CORPORATION
    See also LEADBELLY (Chmura,
    Helene F.) and (Wyler, Mike);
    WELDON, CASEY BILL (Godrich,
    John)

A58 BEATON, Josephine, and Howard
    RYE: More on the ARC TO-series in
    Storyville, No. 75 (February-
    March 1978): 102–103 [supplements
    Storyville No. 38; covers ma-
    trices 1125–1671] ((3, 7d))

AMERICAN RECORD SOCIETY label

A59   JEPSEN, Jorgen Grunnet: Disko-
      filspalten in Orkester Journalen,
      Vol. 26 (February 1958): 25;
      (March 1958): 19 ((2))

AMMONS, ALBERT, 1907-1949
      piano

A60   EWERT, Hans W.: The Albert Ammons
      discography in Jazz Bazaar, No.
      11 (September 1971): 51-52; No.
      12/13 (December 1971-January
      1972): 30-32 ((1, 2, 3, 6, 7))

A61   HOPES, Jimmy: Boogie woogie man;
      a bio-discography of Albert
      Ammons in Jazz & Blues, Vol. 1
      (September-October 1971): 5-7
      ((1, 2, 3, 6, 7))

A62   OLDEREN, Martin van: Albert
      Ammons in Boogie Woogie & Blues
      Collector, No. 15 (April 1972):
      3; No. 16 (May 1972): 3 ((3, 6,
      7))

AMMONS, GENE, 1925-1974
      tenor saxophone

A63   COOKE, Ann: Eugene "Gene"
      Ammons: discography in Jazz-
      Disco, Vol. 1 (July 1960): 5-8
      [to ca. 1949-50] ((2, 3, 6, 7))

A64   PORTER, Bob, and Frank GIBSON:
      Gene Ammons; a discography in
      Discographical Forum, No. 6 (May
      1968): 11-14; No. 7 (July 1968):
      10-12 ((1, 2, 3, 7))

A65   PORTER, Bob: Great Chicago jazz!
      Gene Ammons in Different Drummer,
      Vol. 1 (October-November 1973):
      15 ((—))

A66   WALKER, Malcolm, and Tony
      WILLIAMS: Private recordings in
      Discographical Forum, No. 5
      (March 1968): 11-12; additions
      and corrections in Discographical
      Forum, No. 13 (July 1969): 2;
      No. 16 (January 1970): 2 ((1, 2,
      7, 9))

AMPERSAND label (Australian)

A67   BAKER, Frank Owen: Ampersand
      records in Music Maker, Vol. 46
      (May 1951): 38 ((—))

ANDERSEN, ARILD, 1945-
      bass violin

A68   Arild Andersen discography in
      Jazz Forum (Poland), No. 37 (May
      1975): 39 ((—))

ANDERSON, BUDDY (Bernard Hartwell
      Anderson), 1919-
      trumpet, piano

A69   HOEFER, George: Buddy Anderson
      discography in Down Beat, Vol. 30
      (December 19, 1963): 45 ((2, 3, 7))

ANDERSON, CAT (William Alonzo
      Anderson), 1916-
      trumpet

A70   MOHR, Kurt: Discography of Cat
      Anderson in Jazz Statistics, No.
      28 (December 1962): JS-3 ((2, 3,
      7, 9))

ANDERSON, FRED, 1929-
      saxophones

A71   Fred Anderson discography in Down
      Beat, Vol. 46 (March 8, 1979): 21
      ((—))

ANTHONY, RAY, 1922-
      trumpet

A72   [[LANGE, Horst H. [Discography]
      in Jazz Podium, Vols. 8-9 (1959-
      1960), issues and paginations
      unknown (part 4 in February 1960,
      part 5/6 in April 1960 issues)]]

ANTIGUA JAZZ BAND

A73   Antigua Jazz Band in Anuario de
      Jazz Caliente 1972: 12 ((2, 7))

APEX label (Canadian)
      See also GOTHAM label

A74   ROBERTSON, Alex: The Apex 8000
      numerical. [Montreal]: 1974, 58
      leaves ((3, 6))

ARCADIAN SERENADERS

A75   LOPOSER, Avery, and George
      HOEFER: Discography of the Ar-
      cadian Serenaders in JONES,
      Clifford, ed. Black and white,
      part 1. London: [ca. 1945], 10
      ((2, 3))

ARGO label

A76   RUPPLI, Michael, and Bob PORTER:
Marterry/Argo/Cadet label listing
(later titled Argo/Cadet label
listing) in Hot Buttered Soul,
No. 37 (January/February 1975?);
No. 39 (July 1975?) to No. 41
(October 1975), various paginations [matrix numbers 5249-5700]
((3))

ARGO SINGERS

A77   [[Discography in Soul Bag, No.
7/8]]

ARIGLIANO, NICOLA, 1924-
vocal

A78   [[BARAZZETTA, Giuseppe: [Discog-
raphy] in Musica Jazz, Vol. 16
(July 1960)]]

ARMED FORCES RADIO SERVICE
See CONDON, EDDIE (Rippin, John
W.); ELLINGTON, DUKE--Trans-
criptions (Valburn, Jerry);
GOODMAN, BENNY (Teubig, Klaus)

ARMOUR, WILLIE
See WEE WILLIE

ARMSTRONG, LIL (née Lillian Hardin),
1898-1971
piano

A79   TOSCANO POUCHAN, Mario A.:
Brevísima sinópsis de Lilian
[sic] Hardin, más conocida como
Lil Armstrong in Hot Jazz Club,
No. 22 (June 1949): 3, 9-10
[recordings as leader] ((2, 3, 7d))

ARMSTRONG, LOUIS, 1900-1971
trumpet
See also HENDERSON, FLETCHER
(Bakker, Dick M.: Henderson-
Armstrong recordings)

A80   BAKKER, Dick M.: Louis and the
females in Micrography, No. 18
(February 1972): 4; additions
and corrections in his Louis and
the females and males in Micrography, No. 27 (September 1973):
2-3; No. 29 (December 1973): 1
((7d))

A81   BAKKER, Dick M.: Louis Armstrong
Decca's [sic] 1934-1946 in Micrography, No. 32 (1974): 2-3 ((7d))

A82   BAKKER, Dick M.: Louis Armstrong
'25-'32 in Micrography, No. 7
(November 1969): 2-4; corrections
in Micrography, No. 8 (January
1970): 1 ((7d))

A83   CALVER, V. C.: A short survey of
Armstrong records in Swing Music,
Vol. 1 (June 1935): 102-103
((7d))

A84   CHILTON, John: Louis LPs available in Britain in JONES, Max;
John CHILTON; and Leonard
FEATHER: Salute to Satchmo. London: IPC Specialist and Professional Press [c1970], 132-140
((—))

A85   CHOLINSKI, Henryk: Louis Armstrong on LP's in Jazz Forum
(Poland), No. 17 (June 1972); No.
18 (August 1972), various paginations ((—))

A86   [[DELAUNAY, Charles: Discographie
complète in PANASSIE, Hugues:
Louis Armstrong; l'homme--le
style--l'oeuvre. Paris: Belve-
dere: 1947]]

A87   DELAUNAY, Charles: Discographie
complète in PANASSIE, Hugues:
Louis Armstrong; l'homme--le
style--l'oeuvre. rev. ed. Paris:
Nouvelles Editions Latines, 1969,
219-220 ((—))

A88   Discographie française in Jazz
Hot, No. 263 (July-August 1970):
28 ((1, 2, 3, 6, 7))

A89   Discographies in Jazz Hot, No. 37
(October 1949): 30 [also of
Johnny Dodds] ((—))

A90   GODRICH, John, and Robert M. W.
DIXON: Louis Daniel Armstrong as
an accompanist; a simplified
listing of records made between
1924 and 1930. Liverpool: A. R.
Webster, 1968, 5 leaves ((2, 3,
4p, 6, 7))

A91   GRAS, Pim, and Simon KORTEWEG:
Armstrong's muzikale erfenis in
Jazz Wereld, No. 35 (September-
October 1971): 10-12 ((—))

A92   HILBERT, Bob: Louis Armstrong
research in Record Research, No.
65 (December 1964); No. 68 (May
1965); No. 69 (July 1965), various paginations [additions and
corrections to various discog-
raphies]

A93   HOEFER, George: Louis Armstrong discography in Down Beat, Vol. 17 (July 14, 1950-September 8, 1950), various paginations, in 5 parts ((3, 6, 7))

A94   IKEGAMI, T.: The Louis Armstrong discography covering all his records issued in Japan in Jazz Hot Club Bulletin, Vol. 4 (January 1951): 1-4; (February 1951): 2-3 ((3))

A95   JEPSEN, Jorgen Grunnet: Discography of Louis Armstrong [Brande, Denmark: Debut Records, c1959], 3 v. ((1, 2, 3, 6, 7))

A96   JEPSEN, Jorgen Grunnet: A discography of Louis Armstrong, 1923-1971 [Rungsted Vyst, Denmark]: Knudsen [c1973], 102, 6 pp. ((1, 2, 3, 6, 7))

A97   JEPSEN, Jorgen Grunnet: Louis Armstrong 1947-1957; a discography [Copenhagen: 1959], 17 leaves ((1, 2, 3, 7))

A98   Louis on records in Metronome, Vol. 66 (April 1945): 18-19, 35 ((—))

A99   LOVE, William C.: Louis Armstrong's discography in Jazz (US), Vol. 1 (December 1943): 18-21 ((2, 3, 6))

A100 McCARTHY, Albert: Discography in Record Changer, Vol. 9 (July-August 1950): 37-42 ((1, 2, 3, 6, 7))

A101 MILLER, Paul Eduard: Complete Louis Armstrong discography in Down Beat, Vol. 6 (June 1939-September 1939), various paginations, in 4 parts, [to late 1930] ((2, 3, 6, 7, 8))

A102 MOHR, Kurt: Nachtrag zur Discographie von Louis Armstrong in Jazz Bulletin, Vol. 2 (May 1953): 4-5 [1951-1952 recordings] ((2, 3, 6, 7))

A103 NEVERS, Daniel: Louis Armstrong; un essai de discographie 1923-1971 in BOUJUT, Michel: Pour Armstrong. Paris: Jazz Magazine, 1975, 103-124 ((1, 2, 3, 6, 7))

A104 NORRIS, John: The other side of Louis Armstrong; a discography of privately recorded film sound tracks, concerts, and broadcasts in Coda, Vol. 11 (July-August 1973): 40-46 ((1, 2, 7))

A105 SIMONS, Sim: Louis Armstrong and the All-Stars Nice recordings in Micrography, No. 41 (May 1976): 20 ((7))

Soundtracks
See also ARMSTRONG, LOUIS
(Norris, John)

A106 DELAUNAY, Charles: Filmographie in Jazz Hot, No. 263 (July-August 1970): 29 ((—))

A107 ENGLUND, Bjorn: A Louis Armstrong filmography in Coda, Vol. 12 (January 1975): 5-6; additions and corrections by Klaus Stratemann in Coda, No. 145 (March 1976): 32-33 ((2))

A108 HAGGLOF, Gosta: Snatches of Satch in Orkester Journalen, Vol. 36 (June 1968): 9-10 ((5))

109   NEVERS, Daniel: Filmographie; musicien et acteur in BOUJUT, Michel: Pour Armstrong. Paris: Jazz Magazine, 1975, 127 ((—))

A110 Satchmo à Hollywood in Jazz Magazine (France), No. 191 (August 1971): 35-36 ((—))

A111 STRATEMANN, Klaus: Louis Armstrong; a filmo-discography in IAJRC Journal, Vol. 10 (fall 1977) to Vol. 11 (fall 1978), various paginations, in 5 parts ((2, 5, 7, 9))

ARNOLD, BILLY BOY (William Arnold), 1935-
vocal, harmonica

A112 MOHR, Kurt: Billy Boy Arnold; disco in Blues Unlimited, No. 22 (May 1965): 7 ((2, 3, 7))

A113 MOHR, Kurt: Discography of William "Billy Boy" Arnold in Discographical Forum, No. 2 (July 1960): 11 ((2, 3, 7))

ARNOLD, HARRY, 1920-
leader

A114 BORG, Christer: Harry Arnold and his Swedish Radio studio orchestra; a discography; Metronome recordings only in Jazz-Disco, Vol. 1 (April 1960): 3-4, 8 ((2, 3, 6, 7, 9))

ARNOLD, KOKOMO (James Arnold), 1901–
1969
guitar, vocal

A115 PARSONS, Jack H.: Kokomo Arnold
discography in Jazz Monthly, Vol.
8 (May 1962): 15; (June 1962): 7
((2, 3, 6, 7))

ARODIN, SIDNEY, 1901–1948
saxophones

A116 PERRY, Don: Up the lazy river;
Sidney Arodin: his life and
records in Jazzfinder, Vol. 1
(March 1948): 11–12 ((2, 3, 7))

ART ENSEMBLE OF CHICAGO

A117 [[DUTILH, Alex: Discographie: Art
Ensemble in Jazz Hot, No. 356/357
(December 1978/January 1979):
29]]

A118 Selected Art Ensemble discography
in Down Beat, Vol. 46 (May 3,
1979): 16 ((—))

ARTISTIC label
See ABCO label

ARVANITAS, GEORGES, 1931–
piano

A119 Discographie sommaire d'Arvanitas
in Jazz Magazine (France), No. 57
(March 1960): 46 ((—))

ASHBY, IRVING, 1920–
guitar

A120 Discographie d'Irving Ashby in
Jazz Hot, No. 50 (December 1950):
33 ((2))

ASMUSSEN, SVEND, 1916–
violin

A121 [[[Discography] in HENIUS, Bent:
Swend Asmussen. Copenhagen:
Erichsen, 1962]]

ASSOCIATION FOR THE ADVANCEMENT OF
CREATIVE MUSICIANS
See also ABRAMS, RICHARD

A122 AACM in Swing Journal, Vol. 29
(July 1975): 231–237 ((2, 7d))

A123 TEPPERMAN, Barry: The new music
from Chicago; a discography of
the A.A.C.M. in Pieces of Jazz
(1970): 52–54 ((2, 7))

ATLANTIC label
See also: COLEMAN, ORNETTE
(Raben, Erik); COLTRANE, JOHN
(Raben, Erik: Coltrane on At-
lantic)

A124 ADLER, Eddie, and Mike MILLER:
Atlantic discography in The Big
Beat [[No. 8 (1965?)]]; No. 9
(March 1965): 3–4 [and possibly
other issues; No. 9 covers nos.
898–1000] ((7d))

A125 GRENDYSA, Peter A.: Atlantic
master book #1. Milwaukee: c1975,
44 pp. ((3, 7d))

A126 GRENDYSA, Peter A.: Atlantic 78
rpm albums and microgrove [sic]
records, 1949–1954 in Goldmine,
No. 13 (November–December 1976):
4 ((—))

A127 GRENDYSA, Peter A.: Atlantic's
early groups in Record Exchanger,
Vol. 4 (August 1975): 12–13 ((3,
7))

A128 GRENDYSA, Peter A.: Atlantic's
gospel series in Record Exchanger, Vol. 4 (May 1975): 21
((3, 7))

A129 GRENDYSA, Peter A.: Atlantic's
minor series in Goldmine, No. 14
(January–February 1977): 14 ((7))

A130 RUPPLI, Michael: Atlantic records; a discography. Westport,
CT: Greenwood, [c1979], 4 v. ((2,
3, 4p, 7))

AUDIOPHILE label

A131 WEST, Robert D.: Jazz on the
"Audiophile" label; a complete
listing in Discophile, No. 37
(August 1954): 15–16, 7 ((2, 7))

AULD, GEORGE, 1919–
tenor saxophone

A132 EDWARDS, Ernie: George Auld
(1940–1962); a name listing in
Matrix, No. 57 (February 1965):
3–13; additions and corrections
in Matrix, No. 68 (December
1966): 15–16; No. 69 (February
1967): 13 ((2, 3, 6, 7))

AURORA label (Canadian)

A133 BEDOIAN, James, and Will Roy
HEARNE: The complete Canadian
Aurora catalog in The Discog-
rapher, Vol. 1 (first quarter

1968): 1-223 to 1-226; additions by Jim KIDD in The Discographer, Vol. 1 (first quarter 1969): 1-319; index in Vol. 2 (second quarter 1970): 1-22 ((3, 4p))

AUSTIN, LOVIE (née Cora Calhoun), 1887-1972
piano

A134 Lovie Austin; a revision of the section under this name in "Jazz Directory" in Discophile, No. 24 (June 1952): 15-16; additions and corrections in Discophile, No. 25 (August 1952): 9; No. 26 (October 1952): 9; No. 27 (December 1952): 14 ((2, 3, 6, 7))

A135 STEWART-BAXTER, Derrick: Lovie Austin discography in Playback, Vol. 2 (August 1949): 14-18; additions and corrections in his Afterthoughts on Austin in Playback, Vol. 3 (January 1950): 13 ((2, 3, 6, 7d))

AUSTRALIAN JAZZ QUARTET/QUINTET

A136 JEPSEN, Jorgen Grunnet: Diskofilspalten in Orkester Journalen, Vol. 32 (October 1964): 23, 35 ((2, 7d))

AUSTRIAN ALL STARS

A137 The Austrian All Stars; a brief history and a short but complete discography in Jazz Studies, Vol. 1, No. 1 (1967): 8-9 ((2, 3, 6, 7))

AUTOGRAPH label
    See also MORTON, JELLY ROLL (Bakker, Dick M.: Jelly Roll Morton on the labels Gennett & Paramount...)

A138 HENRIKSEN, Henry: Autograph; an unfinished discography of an important early 1920s label in Record Research, No. 153/154 (April 1978): 5-7 ((2, 3, 7, 8))

AVANT-GARDE JAZZ
    See JAZZ MUSIC--Avant-Garde

AYLER, ALBERT, 1936-1970
    tenor saxophone
    See also JAZZ MUSIC--Avant-Garde (Raben, Erik)

A139 BURKE, Patrick: Albert Ayler; a preliminary checklist of concert/ club, etc. appearances in Discographical Forum, No. 12 (May 1969) to No. 15 (November 1969), various paginations ((1, 2, 7))

A140 COWLYN, Martin: Discography; Albert Ayler in The Professional, No. 2 (February 1974): 3 ((—))

A141 Discographie in Jazz Hot, No. 268 (January 1971): 26 ((1, 2, 7))

A142 KORTEWEG, Simon: Albert Ayler discografie 1962-1968 in Jazz Wereld, No. 24 (June-July 1969): 18 ((2, 7))

A143 RABEN, Erik: Albert Ayler in Musica Jazz, Vol. 21 (July 1965): 36-37 ((1, 2, 3, 7))

A144 RABEN, Erik: Ayler diskografi in Orkester Journalen, Vol. 35 (May 1967): 8 ((1, 2, 6, 7))

A145 RABEN, Erik: I dischi di Albert Ayler in Musica Jazz, Vol. 22 (August-September 1966): 37 ((1, 2, 7))

A146 RABEN, Erik: Diskofilspalten in Orkester Journalen, Vol. 39 (January 1971): 19, 31; (March 1971): 22 ((1, 2, 6, 7))

A147 [[RISSI, Mathias: Albert Ayler; discography. Adliswil, Switzerland: 1977, 9 pp.]]

BABS, ALICE (Alice Nilsson Sjoblom), 1924-
vocal

B1 Discography in HEDMAN, Frank: Alice Babs; berattelsen om artisten Alice "Babs" Nilsson Sjoblom [Stockholm]: Raben & Sjogren, 1975, 195-202 ((—))

B2 ENGLUND, Bjorn: Alice Babs diskografi jazzinspelningar in Orkester Journalen, Vol. 40 (December 1972): 48-49; Vol. 41 (January 1973): 30-31 ((2, 3, 6, 7))

BABY FACE LEROY
    See FOSTER, LEROY

BABY HUEY, 1944-
vocal

B3 NIQUET, Bernard: Discographie de Baby Huey in Soul Bag, No. 45

(January 1975): 36; additions and corrections in Soul Bag, No. 46 (February 1975): 6; No. 47 (March 1975): 1; No. 51 (January 1976): 32 ((2, 7))

BAILEY, DEREK, 1932–
    guitar

B4   PIACENTINO, Giuseppe, and Veniero RIZZARDI: Discografia di Derek Bailey in Musica Jazz, Vol. 32 (February 1976): 17 ((—))

BAILEY, MILDRED, 1907–1951
    vocal

B5   A selective discography in Record Changer (January 1952): 13 ((1))

BAILEY'S LUCKY SEVEN

B6   WHYATT, Bert: Bailey's Lucky Seven in Collecta, No. 8 (January–February 1970): 18–27 ((3, 6, 7d))

BAKER, CHET (Chesney H. Baker), 1929–
    trumpet

B7   GAUTHERIN, Gilles, and Alain TERCINET: Discographie de Chet Baker in Jazz Hot, No. 327 (May 1976): 12–15 ((2, 7))

B8   MORGAN, Alun: A Chet Baker discography in Jazz Monthly, Vol. 9 (May 1963): 24–27; additions in Jazz Monthly, Vol. 9 (September 1963): 26 ((2, 3, 6, 7))

BAKER, LAVERN, 1929–
    vocal

B9   MOHR, Kurt: Discographie de Lavern Baker in Soul Bag, No. 35 (February 1974): 34–38 ((2, 3, 7))

BAKER, LEE
    See BROOKS, LONNIE

BALL, KENNY, 1930–
    trumpet

B10 BIELDERMAN, Gerard: Kenny Ball since the compilation of Jazz Records 1942–1962 in Matrix, No. 92 (April 1971): 5–7; corrections

in Matrix, No. 105 (November 1974): 15 ((2, 7))

BALLARD, FLORENCE
    vocal

B11 HUGHES, Rob: Florence Ballard discography in Hot Buttered Soul, No. 47 (August–September 1976): 5 ((3, 7, 8))

BALLARD, HANK
    See ROYALS (musical group)

BANGO label
    See FINE ART label

BANKS, BILLY, 1908–1967
    vocal

B12 BAKKER, Dick M.: The Rhythmakers in Micrography, No. 3 (May 1969): 9 ((7d))

B13 BAKKER, Dick M.: The Rhythmakers in Micrography, No. 4 (June 1969): 2; additions and corrections in Micrography, No. 5 (August 1969): 12 [rev. ed. of previous entry] ((7d))

B14 Discography of the Rhythm Makers in Jazz Music, Vol. 11 (April 1960): 31 (reprinted from Podium, unknown issue) ((2, 7d))

B15 DOYLE, Mike: The Rhythmakers in Discographical Forum, No. 19 (July 1970): 19–20 ((2, 3, 6, 7))

B16 SILVESTRI, Edgardo M.: Discografia de "The Rhythmakers" in Jazz Magazine (Argentina), No. 37 (January–February 1953): 18–19 ((2, 3, 6, 7d))

B17 WHYATT, Bert: Billy Banks' Rhythmakers and Jack Bland; a summary of the four sessions in Jazz Journal, Vol. 1 (December 1948): 8 ((2, 3, 6, 7))

BANNER label

B18 Complete numerical of Banner Melotone Oriole Perfect Romeo, 1935–1938 in Playback, Vol. 3 (February 1950) to Vol. 4 (March–April 1952), various paginations, in 5 parts ((—))

B19 HEARNE, Will Roy: The Banner 7000
     series; a note in Matrix, No. 78
     (August 1968): 9-10 ((3))

BARBARA AND GWEN/BARBARA AND THE
    UNIQUES

B20 MOHR, Kurt: Barbara & Gwen/
     Barbara & the Uniques in Soul
     Bag, No. 45 (January 1975): 29-30
     ((2, 3, 7))

BARBER, CHRIS, 1930-
    trombone

B21 BIELDERMAN, Gerard: Chris Barber;
     corrections to the listing in
     Jazz Records 1942-1962 in Matrix,
     No. 81 (February 1969): 9-11
     [part 2, titled Chris Barber
     since Jepsen]; No. 83 (June
     1969): 3-5; additions and cor-
     rections in Matrix, No. 90
     (December 1970): 13 ((2, 7))

B22 [[BIELDERMAN, Gerard: Chris
     Barber discography 1949-1975.
     Zwolle, Netherlands: 1976? 38
     pp.; supplemented in his Chris
     Barber discography; additions
     1976 to June 1977. Zwolle,
     Netherlands: 1977, 1 sheet]]

B23 HULME, G. W. George, and Karl
     Emil KNUDSEN: Discography of
     Chris Barber in Matrix, No. 14
     (December 1956): 3-16; additions
     and corrections in Matrix, No. 15
     (February 1957): 15-14; No. 17
     (April 1958): 13-14; No. 18 (July
     1958): 19; No. 21 (January 1959):
     22; No. 33 (March 1961): 14-15
     ((2, 3, 6, 7))

B24 [[RUST, Brian A.: Chris Barber; a
     biography, appreciation, record
     survey and discography. London:
     National Jazz Federation [1958],
     20 pp.]]

BARBIERI, GATO (Leandro J. Barbieri),
    1934-
    tenor saxophone

B25 Gato Barbieri discography in Jazz
     Forum (Poland), No. 36 (April
     1975): 38 ((—))

B26 Selected Barbieri discography in
     Down Beat, Vol. 44 (April 21,
     1977): 16 ((—))

B27 [[VINCENT, B.: Gato Barbieri,
     discographie in Jazz Hot, No. 242
     (August-September 1968): 20]]

BARGE, GENE
    vocal, tenor saxophone

B28 MOHR, Kurt: Gene Barge in Soul
     Bag, No. 45 (January 1975): 24
     ((2, 3, 7))

BARKAYS (musical group)

B29 [[[Discography] in Soul Bag, No.
     2]]

BARNARD, LEN, 1929-
    piano

B30 KENNEDY, John: Jazz...Australia,
     a discography of Len Barnard in
     Matrix, No. 1 (July 1954): 18-20,
     18a-18b [latter 2 pages not bound
     in issue, but supplied along with
     No. 2]; additions and corrections
     in Matrix, No. 7 (July 1955): 1;
     No. 26 (December 1959): 18; No.
     35/36 (September 1961): 37 ((2,
     3, 7))

BARNES, EMILE, 1892-1970
    clarinet

B31 STENBECK, Lennart: Emile Barnes
     diskografi in Orkester Journalen,
     Vol. 31 (January 1963): 34 ((2,
     7))

BARNET, CHARLIE, 1913-
    alto saxophone

B32 CROSBIE, Ian: Clap hands, here
     comes Charlie, part 2 in Jazz
     Journal, Vol. 26 (July 1973):
     26-28 ((1, 2, 3, 6, 7))

B33 EDWARDS, Ernie; George I. HALL;
     and Bill KORST, eds.: Charlie
     Barnet and his Orchestra.
     Whittier, CA: Jazz Discographies
     Unlimited, 1965, 36 leaves (Dance
     band series, B-2) ((1, 2, 3, 6,
     7))

B34 EDWARDS, Ernie; George I. HALL;
     and Bill KORST, eds.: Charlie
     Barnet and his Orchestra. Whit-
     tier, CA: ErnGeoBil, 1967, 39
     leaves (Dance band series, B-2R)
     ((1, 2, 3, 6, 7))

B35 GARROD, Charles: Charlie Barnet
     and his Orchestra. Spotswood,
     NJ: Joyce Music, 1973, 53, 5
     leaves ((1, 2, 3, 4t, 6, 7))

B36 HALL, George I., ed.: Charlie
     Barnet and his Orchestra. rev.

ed. Whittier, CA: Jazz Discographies Unlimited, 1970, iv, 47 leaves ((1, 2, 3, 6, 7))

B37   HOEFER, George: Barnet discography in Down Beat, Vol. 18 (September 21, 1951): 16 ((—))

BARONET label

B38   KNUDSEN, Karl Emil, and Allan STEPHENSON: Baronet; a label listing in Discophile, No. 60 (June 1958): 13-15, 7 ((2, 3, 7))

BARRETT SISTERS

B39   NIQUET, Bernard: Essai de discographie des Barrett Sisters in Soul Bag, No. 45 (January 1975): 37 ((2, 7))

BARRETTO, RAY, 1929–
conga

B40   Selected Barretto discography in Down Beat, Vol. 43 (April 22, 1976): 17 ((—))

BARRON, KENNY, 1943–
piano

B41   Selected Barron discography in Down Beat, Vol. 42 (November 6, 1975): 18 ((—))

B42   Selected Kenny Barron discography in Down Beat, Vol. 47 (June 1980): 27 ((—))

BARTHOLOMEW, DAVE, 1920–
trumpet, vocal

B43   MOHR, Kurt: Discography of Dave Bartholomew in Jazz Statistics, No. 28 (December 1962): JS-4 to JS-6 ((2, 3, 6, 7))

BARTKOWSKI, CZESLAW, 1943–
drums, piano

B44   Czeslaw Bartkowski's selected discography in Jazz Forum (Poland), No. 47 (1977): 57 ((—))

BARTZ, GARY, 1940–
saxophones

B45   Plattenhinweise in Jazz Podium, Vol. 25 (February 1976): 8 ((—))

BASCOMB, PAUL, 1910–
tenor saxophone

B46   HARTMANN, Dieter: Paul Bascomb on States in Jazz + Classic No. 1 (February–March 1979): 20 ((2, 3, 6, 7))

BASIE, COUNT (William Basie), 1904–
piano

B47   BAKKER, Dick M.: Count Basie Decca's [sic] 1937-1939 in Micrography, No. 31 (1974?): 6 ((—))

B48   BAKKER, Dick M.: Count Basie Vocalion-Okeh's [sic] 36–42 in Micrography, No. 44 (May 1977): 5-6 ((6, 7d))

B49   BAKKER, Dick M.: Count Basie's Decca band-recordings complete 1937-1939 on 4 lp's in Micrography, No. 21 (September 1972): 11 ((—))

B50   Basie discography in Down Beat, Vol. 17 (November 17, 1950): 14; reprinted in Bouquets to the living [Chicago: Down Beat, 195?: 5] ((—))

B51   Count Basie big band in Swing Journal, Vol. 32 (May 1978): 284-291 ((2, 7d))

B52   DANCE, Stanley: Selected discography in his World of Count Basie. New York: Scribners [c1980], 357-370 [also includes selective discographies of his sidemen] ((—))

B53   [Discography, 1965-1968] in Jazz Monthly, No. 173 (July 1968): 15-17 ((2, 7))

B54   GELLY, Dave: [Discography of octet recordings] in Jazz Monthly, Vol. 9 (July 1963): 11; additions and corrections in Jazz Monthly, Vol. 9 (September 1963): 26 ((1, 2, 3, 7))

B55   HARTMANN, Dieter: Count Basie–– different takes in Jazz + Classic, No. 3 (June–July 1979): 5 [1936-1952 recordings]

B56   JEPSEN, Jorgen Grunnet: Count Basie 1947-1958; a discography. [Copenhagen, 1959?], 11 leaves ((2, 3, 7))

B57   JEPSEN, Jorgen Grunnet; François POSTIF; and G. KOPELOWICZ: Discographie (1950-1957) Count Basie in Jazz Hot, No. 126 (November

1957): 10-11; additions and corrections by Jacques PESCHEUX in
Bulletin du Hot Club de France,
No. 74 (January 1958): 34 ((2, 3,
6, 7d))

B58   JEPSEN, Jorgen Grunnet: Discography of Count Basie [Brande, Denmark: Debut Records, c1959], 32
leaves ((1, 2, 3, 6, 7))

B59   JEPSEN, Jorgen Grunnet: Discography of Count Basie. rev. ed.
[Brande, Denmark: Debut Records,
c1960], 43 leaves ((1, 2, 3, 6,
7))

B60   JEPSEN, Jorgen Grunnet; Bo
SCHERMAN; and Carl HALLSTROM: A
discography of Count Basie. Copenhagen: Knudsen [c1969], 2 v.
((1, 2, 3, 6, 7))

B61   JEPSEN, Jorgen Grunnet: 1950-
1957; a discography of the Count
Basie Orchestra in Jazz Journal,
Vol. 10 (April 1957): 10-11;
additions and corrections from
Frank DUTTON in Jazz Journal,
Vol. 10 (June 1957): 35 ((2, 3,
6, 7))

B62   MOHR, Kurt: Orchestre Count
Basie; discographie partielle in
Hot Revue, No. 4 (1947): 22-23
[1941-1947 recordings] ((2, 3,
7))

B63   MORGAN, Alun: A Count Basie dis-
cography in HORRICKS, Raymond:
Count Basie and his Orchestra;
its music and musicians. London:
Gollancz, 1957 (also New York:
Citadel, 1957; London: Jazz Book
Club, 1958; Westport, CT: Green-
wood, 197?), 282-304 ((2, 3, 7))

B64.   REHNBERG, Bert; Ernie EDWARDS;
and Jorgen Grunnet JEPSEN: Count
Basie; a selective discography
1949-1954 in Jazz Music, Vol. 9
(May-June 1958): 10-13 ((2, 3,
7d))

B65   REHNBERG, Bert: The new Count
Basie Orchestra; a selective
discography in Jazz Statistics,
No. 2 (June 1956): 2; No. 3
(August 1956): 3, 9 [1952-1954
recordings] ((2, 3, 6, 7))

B66   RICHARD, Daniel: Les Basie de
base in Jazz Magazine (France),
No. 251 (January 1977): 44-45
((—))

B67   A very selective Count Basie
discography in Down Beat, Vol. 46
(September 6, 1979): 26 ((—))

Soundtracks

B68   LELOIR, Denis, and Jacques LUBIN:
Les écrans de Basie in Jazz Magazine (France), No. 251 (January
1977): 46-47 ((—))

BASS, FONTELLA
       vocal

B69   Discographie de Fontella Bass in
Soul Bag, No. 51 (January 1976):
18-20 ((2, 3, 6, 7))

B70   MOHR, Kurt; Peter GIBBON; and
Derek BRANDON: Fontella Bass
discography in Soul, No. 4 (June
1966): 14-15 ((2, 3, 7))

BATES, L. J.
       See JEFFERSON, BLIND LEMON

BAY-TONE label

B71   CHOISNEL, Emmanuel; Brad TAYLOR;
and Kurt MOHR: Listing Bay-Tone
in Soul Bag, No. 22/23 (January-
February 1973): 44 ((5))

BEALE STREET SHEIKS
       See STOKES, FRANK

BEALE STREETERS

B72   PERLIN, Victor: The Beale
Streeters in Paul's Record Magazine, Vol. 2 (November 1975): 9-
10 ((3))

BEBOP
       See JAZZ MUSIC--Bebop

BECHET, SIDNEY, 1897?-1959
       soprano saxophone
       See also MEZZROW, MEZZ (Phythian,
       Les)

B73   BAKKER, Dick M.: Sidney Bechet
part 1 in Micrography, No. 2
(February 1969): 4 ((—))

B74   BAKKER, Dick M.: Victor recording: Sidney Bechet in Micrography, No. 25 (March 1973): 10
((7d))

B75   Bechet's Blue Notes in Jazzology
(UK), No. 7 new series (July
1946): 17 ((2, 3))

B76 [[BERG, Arne: Sidney Bechet.
Stockholm: 196?]]

B77 Discographie des disques de Sidney Bechet parus en France in
Jazz Hot, No. 33 (May 1949): 7
((2, 3, 7d))

B78 HOEFER, George: Bechet discography in Down Beat, Vol. 18 (December 14, 1951): 18 ((—))

B79 JEPSEN, Jorgen Grunnet: Sidney
Bechet in Les Cahiers du Jazz,
No. 10 (1963?): 103–111; No. 11
(1963?): 120–142 ((1, 2, 3, 6,
7))

B80 JEPSEN, Jorgen Grunnet: Sidney
Bechet discography. Lübeck,
W. Germany: Uhle & Kleimann, 1961,
37 leaves ((1, 2, 3, 6, 7))

B81 [[JEPSEN, Jorgen Grunnet: Sidney
Bechet 1947–1957. Copenhagen:
1957]]

B82 [[LAFARGUE, Pierre: Complete discography in MOULY, Raymond: Sidney Bechet, notre ami. Paris: La
Table Ronde, 1959 [48 pages of
discography]]]

B83 MAUERER, Hans J.: A discography
of Sidney Bechet. Copenhagen:
Knudsen, 1969, 86 pp. ((1, 2, 3,
4p, 4t, 6, 7))

B84 McGARVEY, Robert: Bechet's records in Playback, Vol. 2 (September 1949): 5–15; additions and
corrections in Playback, Vol. 2
(December 1949): 18 ((2, 3, 6,
7d))

B85 MYLNE, David: A catalogue of the
recordings of Sidney Bechet in
BECHET, Sidney: Treat it gentle.
London: Cassell, 1960 (also New
York: Hill & Wang, 1960; London:
Jazz Book Club, 1962; London:
Transworld, 1964; New York:
DaCapo [1975]), 221–240 ((1, 6,
7))

B86 MYLNE, David, and Ron DAVIES:
Discography of Sidney Bechet in
Jazz Music, Vol. 3, No. 10
(1948): 9–17; additions and cor-
rections in Jazz Music, Vol. 4,
No. 2 (1949): 23–24; continued in
Sidney Bechet 1949 and 1950
recordings in Jazz Music, Vol. 8
(July–August 1957): 9–13; addi-
tions and corrections in Jazz
Music, Vol. 8 (November–December
1957): 14–15 ((2, 3, 6, 7d))

B87 MYLNE, David: A latter-day discography of Sidney Bechet in

Melody Maker, Vol. 28 (January
26, 1952); (February 16, 1952);
(February 23, 1952); (March 8,
1952); (March 15, 1952), various
paginations; additions and corrections in Melody Maker, Vol. 28
(February 9, 1952): 9 [from Erik
WIEDEMANN] (April 19, 1952): 9
[recordings since 1947] ((1, 2,
3, 7))

B88 NIQUET, Bernard: Discographie
Blue Note in Jazz Hot, No. 240
(April 1968): 13 ((2, 7d))

B89 REID, John D.: Discography of
Sidney Bechet in Jazz Information, Vol. 2 (November 22, 1940):
11–21 ((2, 3, 7))

BECK, GORDON, 1936-
piano

B90 Gordon Beck selected discography
in Jazz Forum (Poland), No. 41
(March 1976): 50 ((—))

BEIDERBECKE, BIX (Leon Bix
Beiderbecke), 1903–1931
cornet

B91 BAKKER, Dick M.: Bix Beiderbecke
1924–1936 in Micrography, No. 34
(December 1974): 4–8; No. 35
(March 1975): 12 ((6, 7d))

B92 BAKKER, Dick M.: Bix Beiderbecke
on Victor's [sic] in Micrography,
No. 5 (August 1969): 8 ((7d))

B93 BAKKER, Dick M.: Bix on Victor
1924–1930 in Micrography, No. 30
(April 1974): 6–7 [revised version of previous entry] ((7d))

B94 CASTELLI, Vittorio; Evert
KALEVELD; and Liborio PUSATERI:
The Bix bands, a Bix Beiderbecke
bio-discography. Milan: Raretone, 1972, 223 pp. ((2, 3, 4p,
4r, 4t, 6, 7, 9))

B95 DEAN-MYATT, William: Bix Beider-
becke; a discography in Matrix,
No. 10 (February 1956): 3–17;
additions and corrections in
Matrix, No. 13 (August 1956):
15–16; No. 17 (April 1958): 11;
No. 18 (July 1958): 20; No. 29/30
(August 1960): 35 ((2, 3, 6, 7))

B96 Discographie de Bix et Trumbauer
in Jazz Hot, No. 1 (March 1935):
21 ((2, 3))

B97   Discography; Leon Bismarck (Bix) Beiderbecke in Recordiana, Vol. 1 (June–July 1944): 3–4; (October 1944): 3–5 [other parts announced in part 2, possibly in later issues] ((2, 3, 6, 7))

B98   EVANS, Philip R., and William DEAN-MYATT: Bix Beiderbecke on record; a comprehensive discography in [EVANS, Philip R., with Richard M. SUDHALTER]: Bix: man & legend. New Rochelle, NY: Arlington House [1974] (also London: Quartet Books, 197?; New York: Schirmer Books, 1975 [c1974]), 401–472 ((1, 2, 3, 4p, 4t, 5, 6, 7, 8, 9))

B99   HESS, Jacques B.: Bix Beiderbecke; sélection discographique in Jazz Magazine (France), No. 190 (June–July 1971): 35 ((—))

B100 HIBBS, Leonard: Records by Bix in Swing Music, Vol. 1 (August 1935): 166; corrections in letter from Juan Rafael GREZZI in Swing Music, Vol. 1 No. 9 (November? 1935): 262 ((2))

B101 HOEFER, George: Here is a complete listing of all Bix records! in Down Beat, Vol. 7 (February 15, 1940): 6, 20; (March 1, 1940): 12; (March 15, 1940): 12 [title varies; reprinted with the title Beiderbecke discography complete in Bixography, Nos. 1–4 (1943), various paginations; for revised version of this entry see B103] ((2, 3, 6, 7))

B102 JAMES, Burnett: Selected discography in his Bix Beiderbecke. London: Cassell, 1959 (also New York: Barnes, 1961), 78–88 [possibly same discography also in Stockholm: Horsta, 1959 and Milan: Ricordi, 1961 with different pagination] ((2, 7))

B103 LOWEY, Hal: Discography in Recordiana, Vol. 1 (June–July 1944): 2–3; (October 1944): 2–4 [parts 1 and 2, to 1929; possibly in other issues] ((2, 3, 6, 7))

B104 TEALDO ALIZIERI, Carlos L.: Discografia de Bix Beiderbecke in Jazz Magazine (Argentina), No. 15 (August–September 1950) to No. 17 (November 1950), various paginations [issues mentioned cover February 1927 to April 1928; other parts of this discography are probably in earlier and later issues]; additions and corrections in Jazz Magazine (Argentina), No. 25 (August 1951): 25 ((2, 3, 6, 7))

B105 VENABLES, Ralph G. V.: Bix Beiderbecke discography in his Bix. London: Clifford Jones [194?], 10–16; additions and corrections in Corrections and additions to the Bix discography in JONES, Clifford, ed.: Black and white, part 1. London: [ca. 1945], 6–7 ((2, 3, 7))

B106 WAREING, Charles H., and George GARLICK: Discography in their Bugles for Beiderbecke. London: Sidgwick and Jackson [1958] (also London: Jazz Book Club, 1960), 299–333 ((2, 3, 6, 7))

BEKA label
      See LINDSTROM label (Lange, Horst H.)

BELGIANETTES

B107 MOHR, Kurt: The Belgianettes in Soul Bag, No. 45 (January 1975): 20 ((2, 3, 7))

BELL, GRAEME, 1914–
      piano

B108 HARRIS, H. Meunier, and Derrick STEWART-BAXTER: Graeme Bell in Europe; a discography in Jazz Notes (Australia), No. 87 (September 1948): 8–10 ((1, 2, 3, 7))

B109 HULME, G. W. George: A discography of Graeme Bell in Matrix, No. 2 (September 1954): 3–17; additions and corrections in Matrix, No. 4 (January 1955): 16–18; No. 16 (May 1957): 17; No. 17 (April 1958): 13; No. 21 (January 1959): 21; No. 26 (December 1959): 18–19 ((2, 3, 6, 7))

B110 HULME, G. W. George: A discography of the Graeme Bell band in Discophile, No. 21 (December 1951): 7–10; additions and corrections in Discophile, No. 22 (February 1952): 10; No. 24 (June 1952): 11; No. 25 (August 1952): 9–10; No. 26 (October 1952): 9; No. 34 (February 1954): 11–12; No. 38 (October 1954): 11 ((2, 3, 6, 7))

B111 VENABLES, Ralph G. V., and H. Meunier HARRIS: Discography of the Bell band in Europe in Jazz

Music, Vol. 3, No. 9 (1948): 12-
15; additions and corrections in
Jazz Music, Vol. 4, No. 1 (1949):
13 ((1, 2, 3, 7))

BELL, ROGER, 1919-
trumpet

B112 HARRIS, H. Meunier: Roger Bell; a
name listing in Discophile, No.
23 (April 1952): 9; additions and
corrections in Discophile, No. 29
(May 1953): 8 ((2, 3, 7))

B113 HULME, G. W. George: Roger Bell...
a discography in Matrix, No. 3
(November 1954): 8; additions and
corrections in Matrix, No. 21
(January 1959): 21 ((2, 3, 7))

BELLSON, LOUIS, 1924-
drums

B114 Selected Louie Bellson discography in Down Beat, Vol. 43 (June
3, 1976): 13 ((—))

BENNINK, HAN, 1942-
drums

B115 EYLE, Wim van: Han Bennink disco
in Jazz Press, No. 31 (February
4, 1977): 8-9; correction in Jazz
Press, No. 32 (February 18,
1977): 6 ((1, 2, 7))

B116 Han Bennink's selected discography in Jazz Forum (Poland), No.
47 (1977): 53 ((—))

BENSON, GEORGE, 1943-
guitar

B117 [Discography] in Swing Journal,
Vol. 31 (May 1977): 284-287 ((2,
7d))

B118 Selected Benson discography in
Down Beat, Vol. 43 (September 9,
1976): 17 ((—))

BENTON, WALTER, 1930-
tenor saxophone

B119 [[DEVOGHELAERE, Mon: Walter Benton: discografie (additions and
corrections) in Swingtime (Belgium), No. 22 (June-July 1977):
33]]

BERGER, KARL, 1935-
vibraphone

B120 Selected Berger discography in
Down Beat, Vol. 43 (June 3,
1976): 19 ((—))

BERGIN, SEAN, 1949-
flute

B121 LEEUWEN, Frans van: Discografie
in Jazz Nu, Vol. 2 (March-April
1980): 247 ((—))

BERIGAN, BUNNY (Rowland Bernart
Berigan), 1908-1942
trumpet

B122 BAKKER, Dick M. Bunny Berigan in
Micrography, No. 23 (January
1973): 6 ((7d))

B123 CROSBIE, Ian: Bunny Berigan in
Jazz Journal, Vol. 27 (September
1974): 14 ((2, 3, 6, 7))

B124 CROSBIE, Ian: Selected discography in Pieces of Jazz (1971): 8-
12 ((2, 3, 6, 7))

B125 DANCA, Vince: Bunny; a bio-discography of jazz trumpeter Bunny
Berigan. [Rockford, IL: c1978],
66 pp. ((2, 3, 6, 7))

B126 GLUCKMANN, Helmut: Bunny Berigan
broadcasts 1936-1942 in Micrography, No. 43 (March 1977): 6-7
((1, 7d))

B127 GLUCKMANN, Helmut, and Dick M.
BAKKER: Bunny Berigan 1934-1940
in Micrography, No. 41 (May
1976): 10-13 ((6, 7d))

B128 KINKLE, Roger D.: Bunny Berigan--
his records as a sideman in his
Check sheet (project #4). [Evans-
ville, IN?: n.d.], 21-32 ((9))

B129 McCARTHY, Albert J.: The Bunny
Berigan reissues in Discophile,
No. 30 (June 1953): 12; additions
and corrections in Discophile,
No. 33 (December 1953): 15 ((3,
7))

B130 [REID, John D.?]: Bunny Berigan
discography; Victor records.
n.p., n.d., 7 leaves ((2, 3, 7))

B131 TONKS, Eric: Bunny Berigan in
Pickup, Vol. 2 (February-March
1947): 2-4 ((2, 3, 7))

BERNARD, CLAUDE
tenor saxophone

B132 Discographie in Jazz Magazine
(France), No. 253 (April 1977):
42 ((—))

BERNARD, MIKE
    piano

B133 LOVE, William C.: Discography in
    his Original Dixieland not 1st
    hot records in Record Changer
    (February 1945): 48 ((5))

BERNHARDT, CLYDE, 1908–
    trombone

B134 STEWART-BAXTER, Derrick, and
    Bernard NIQUET: Discographie L.P.
    de Clyde Bernhardt in Jazz Hot,
    No. 278 (December 1971): 23 ((1,
    2, 3, 6, 7))

BERRY, CHU (Leon Berry), 1910–1941
    tenor saxophone
    See also SAXOPHONE MUSIC (JAZZ)
    (Evensmo, Jan: The tenor saxo-
    phonists of the period 1930–1942)

B135 EVENSMO, Jan: The tenor saxophone
    of Leon Chu Berry [Hosle, Norway:
    1976], 36 pp. (Jazz solography
    series, Vol. 1) ((1, 2, 3, 6, 7,
    9))

B136 JEPSEN, Jorgen Grunnet: Discogra-
    phie Leon "Chu" Berry in Les
    Cahiers du Jazz, No. 4 (August
    1960?): 118–126 ((2, 3, 7))

BERTONCINI, GENE, 1937–
    guitar

B137 [Discography] in Different Drum-
    mer, Vol. 1 (February 1974): 9
    ((—))

BERTRAND, JIMMY, 1900–1960
    drums, xylophone

B138 FLUCKIGER, Otto: Jimmy Bertrand
    xylo-discography in Jazz + Clas-
    sic, No. 2 (April–May 1979): 3
    ((7d))

BETHLEHEM label
    See CBS SONY label (Bethlehem
    jazz series)

BIG BANDS

B139 EDWARDS, Ernie: Big bands.
    Whittier, CA: Jazz Discographies
    Unlimited [Vols. 1–3] or ErnGeo-
    Bil [Vols. 4–7], 1965–1968, 7 v.
    ((1, 2, 3, 6, 7))

B140 SIMON, George T.: Selective dis-
    cography in his The big bands.

New York: Collier-Macmillan
    [c1964], 553–560 ((—))

B141 WILSON, John Steuart: Big band
    jazz in High Fidelity, Vol. 5
    (October 1955): 114–120, 122,
    124, 126–132 ((—))

BIG BILL
    See BROONZY, BIG BILL

BIG MACEO (Major Meriweather), 1905–
    1953
    piano, vocal

B142 [[MOODY, Peter: Big Maceo. Bris-
    tol: 1968, 21 leaves]]

B143 PANASSIÉ, Hugues: A name discog-
    raphy of Big Maceo in Discophile,
    No. 45 (December 1955): 21, 23;
    additions and corrections in
    Discophile, No. 47 (April 1956):
    1 ((2, 3, 6, 7))

BIG MAYBELLE
    See SMITH, MAYBELLE

BIG THREE TRIO
    See DIXON, WILLIE

BIGARD, ALEX, 1898–
    drums

B144 Discography of Alex Bigard in
    Eureka, Vol. 2, No. 1 (n.d.):
    9–10 ((2, 7))

BIGARD, BARNEY (Albany Leon Bigard),
    1906–1930
    clarinet

B145 [[KOECHLIN, Daniel: Discography
    of Barney Bigard. Darnetal,
    France: 1980, 55 pp.]]

BILK, ACKER, 1929–
    clarinet

B146 Acker Bilk's confusing days in
    Matrix, No. 63 (February 1966):
    8–9 ((2, 7))

BILTMORE label

B147 A checklist of the issues on the
    Biltmore label in Matrix, No. 80
    (December 1968): 3–8; No. 81
    (February 1969): 3–7; additions

and corrections in Matrix, No. 87
(February 1970): 14 ((3, 6))

BIRMINGHAM JUG BAND

B148 McCarthy, Albert J.: [Discography] in Discographical Forum,
No. 3 (September 1960): 9 ((2, 3,
6, 7))

BIRTH label (German)
See HAMPEL, GUNTER

BISHOP, WALTER, 1927-
piano

B149 GARDNER, Mark, and Frank GIBSON:
Walter Bishop Jr. discography in
Jazz Journal, Vol. 17 (September
1964): 29; (October 1964): 24, 44
((1, 2, 3, 6, 7))

B150 Selected Bishop discography in
Down Beat, Vol. 44 (March 24,
1977): 17 ((—))

B151 THOMPSON, Vern: Walter Bishop,
Jr. in Different Drummer, Vol. 1
(November 1974): 12 ((—))

BLACK AND BLUE label (French)

B152 RUPPLI, Michel: Black and Blue LP
listing in Discographical Forum,
No. 29 (March 1972): 3-6 ((2, 7))

BLACK AND WHITE label

B153 WHYATT, Bert: The "Black and
White" label; fifty sides in the
matrix series commencing at
"BW-1" in Discophile, No. 7 (August 1949): 10-11; additions and
corrections in Matrix, No. 9
(December 1949): 14-15; No. 12
(June 1960): 11 ((3, 7d))

BLACK PATTI label

B154 DAVIS, Bruce: Black Patti catalogue in Jazz Digest (New
Orleans), Vol. 1 (January 1966):
14-16 ((3))

B155 WYLER, Michael: Black Patti label
listing in Storyville, No. 1
(October 1965): 13-17; additions
and corrections in Storyville,
No. 4 (April 1966): 11 ((3, 6,
7))

BLACK SWAN label

B156 KUNSTADT, Len, ed.: Black Swan
catalogue in Record Research,
Vol. 1 (October 1955); (December
1955); Vol. 2 (May-June 1956);
(July-August 1956); (January-
February 1957); Vol. 3 (August-
September 1957); (October-November 1957); (January-February
1958), various paginations ((3,
5, 6, 8))

BLACKNELL, EUGENE
arranger, guitar

B157 CHOISNEL, Emmanuel: Eugene Blacknell in Soul Bag, no. 22/23
(January-February 1973): 21 ((2,
3, 7))

BLACKWELL, ED, 1940-
drums

B158 Biodiscographie in Jazz Magazine
(France), No. 213 (July 1973): 13
((—))

BLAKE, BLIND (Arthur Phelps), ca.
1895-ca. 1932
guitar, vocal

B159 BAKKER, Dick M.: Blind Blake 26-
32 in Micrography, No. 2 (February 1969): 10; additions and
corrections in Micrography, No.
5 (August 1969): 12 ((—))

B160 BAKKER, Dick M.: Blind Blake
1926-1932 in Micrography, No. 31
(1974?): 11 ((7d))

B161 VREEDE, Max E.: A discography of
Blind Blake in Matrix, No. 19
(September 1958): 6-11; additions
and corrections in Matrix, No. 33
(March 1961): 18; No. 35/36 (September 1961): 35 ((2, 3, 6, 7d))

BLAKE, CICERO
vocal

B162 MOHR, Kurt: Cicero Blake in Soul
Bag, No. 45 (January 1975): 33
((2, 3, 7))

BLAKE, EUBIE (James Hubert Blake),
1883-
piano

B163 Currently available recordings/
recordings in preparation in Sin-

cerely Eubie Blake; 9 original
compositions for piano solo,
transcribed by Terry Waldo. Mel-
ville, NY: Belwyn Mills/Marks
Music, c1975, 3 ((—))

B164 Discography in ROSE, Al: Eubie
Blake. New York: Schirmer Books
[c1979], 174-197 ((2, 7d, 8))

B165 Eubie Blake discography in Record
Research, Vol. 1 (February 1955):
7-10; additions and corrections
in Record Research, Vol. 1 (April
1955): 19; (June 1955): 1, 9;
(August 1955): 11, 22; (December
1955): 11; Vol. 2 (February
1956): 14; (May-June 1956): 23
((2, 3, 5, 6))

B166 MONTGOMERY, Michael: Exploratory
discography of Noble Sissle,
Eubie Blake, and James Reese
Europe in KIMBALL, Robert, and
William BOLCOM: Reminiscing with
Sissle and Blake. New York:
Viking [c1973], 247-254 ((2, 3,
6, 7))

B167 Selected discography in Eubie!;
arranged by Danny Holgate. New
York: Warner Bros., c1979, 6
((—))

Piano Rolls

B168 MONTGOMERY, Michael: Eubie Blake
piano rollography/Piano roll reissues on records in KIMBALL,
Robert, and William BOLCOM:
Reminiscing with Sissle and
Blake. New York: Viking [c1973],
245-247 ((2, 5, 8, 9))

B169 MONTGOMERY, Michael: Eubie Blake
piano rollography (revised) in
Record Research, No. 159/160
(December 1978): 4-5 [rev. ed. of
previous entry] ((5, 8, 9))

B170 MONTGOMERY, Michael: Eubie Blake
rollography in Record Research,
No. 27 (March-April 1960): 19
((5))

B171 MONTGOMERY, Michael: Revised
Eubie Blake rollography in Record
Research, No. 33 (March 1961): 16
((5))

Soundtracks

B172 MONTGOMERY, Michael: List of
Sissle and Blake films in
KIMBALL, Robert, and William
BOLCOM: Reminiscing with Sissle
and Blake. New York: Viking
[c1973], 254 ((—))

BLAKE, RAN, 1935-
piano

B173 Selected Ran Blake discography in
Down Beat, Vol. 47 (February
1980): 25 ((—))

BLAKEY, ART, 1919-
drums

B174 Art Blakey & the Jazz Messengers
in Swing Journal, Vol. 33 (February 1979): 224-229 ((2, 7d))

B175 COOKE, Ann: Art Blakey; a discography in Matrix, No. 24 (July
1959): 3-10; No. 25 (October
1959): 3-15; No. 26 (December
1959): 3-14; additions and corrections in Matrix, No. 34 (June
1961): 19; No. 35/36 (September
1961): 36-37; No. 37 (November
1961): 18; No. 45 (February
1963): 13 ((2, 7))

B176 JEPSEN, Jorgen Grunnet: Art
Blakey's Jazz Messengers diskografi in Orkester Journalen, Vol.
27 (November 1959): 46-47 ((2,
3, 7))

B177 LITWEILER, John: Selected Blakey
discography in Down Beat, Vol. 43
(March 25, 1976): 17 ((—))

B178 RICHARD, Daniel: Disques de Jazz
Messengers actuellement dispon-
ibles en France in Jazz Magazine
(France), No. 254 (May 1977): 50
((—))

B179 Selected Art Blakey discography
in Coda, No. 173 (June 1980): 19
((—))

B180 Selected Blakey discography in
Down Beat, Vol. 46 (November
1979): 22 ((—))

BLAND, BOBBY, 1930-
vocal

B181 MOHR, Kurt, and Emmanuel
CHOISNEL: Bobby Bland in Soul
Bag, No. 41 (September 1974):
6-12; additions and corrections
in Soul Bag, No. 44 (November-
December 1974): 9 ((2, 3, 7))

BLAND, JACK, 1899-
guitar
See BANKS, BILLY (Whyatt, Bert)

BLANTON, JIMMY, 1918-1942
bass violin

B182 HOEFER, George: Jimmy Blanton discography in Down Beat, Vol. 29 (February 1, 1962): 36-37 ((2, 3, 6,7))

B183 [[KANTH, Ingvar: A discography of Jimmy Blanton. Stockholm: Swedish Jazz Federation, 1970, 8 pp.]]

BLEY, CARLA, 1938–
composer, piano

B184 BUNLES, Gunter: Diskographie in Jazzforschung, Vol. 8 (1976): 37-38 ((—))

B185 Diskographie in Jazz Podium, Vol. 28 (February 1979): 11 ((—))

B186 Selected Bley discography in Down Beat, Vol. 45 (June 1, 1978): 18 ((—))

BLEY, PAUL, 1932–
piano

B187 [Discography] in Swing Journal, Vol. 31 (July 1977): 288-291 ((2, 7d))

B188 PETERSON, Ib Skovgaard; Laurent GODDET; and Paul BLEY: Discographie de Paul Bley in Jazz Hot, No. 332 (November 1976): 26-28; reprinted in Coda, No. 166 (April 1979): 9-11; additions and corrections in letter from Len DOBBIN in Coda, No. 168 (August 1979): 38-39 ((2, 3, 7))

B189 RENSEN, Jan, and Han SCHULTE: Paul Bley discografie in Jazz Press, No. 44 (October 1, 1977): 15-16 ((1, 2, 3, 7))

B190 WILBRAHAM, Roy J.: Paul Bley; a discography in Jazz Studies, Vol. 1, No. 3 (1967): 2-6; additions and corrections from Victor SCHONFIELD in Jazz Studies, Vol. 1, No. 4 (1967): 65 ((2, 3, 7))

BLIND BLAKE
See BLAKE, BLIND

BLIND PETE
violin, vocal

B191 RUSSELL, Tony: Blind Pete in Jazz & Blues, Vol. 2 (February 1972): 25 ((2, 3, 6, 7))

BLUE ACE label

B192 WHYATT, Bert: Catalogue of Blue Ace label in Discophile, No. 22 (February 1952): 3-6 ((—))

BLUE HARMONY BOYS (RUFUS QUILLAN AND BEN QUILLAN)

B193 Discography in Blues Unlimited, No. 123 (January-February 1977): 25 ((2, 3, 6 7d))

BLUE HORIZON label (British)

B194 TAYLOR, Roy: Blue Horizon: label listing in Sailor's Delight, No. 4 (1979): 2 unnumbered pages ((—))

BLUE MOUNTAINEERS

B195 BADROCK, Arthur, and Ted LAMONT: The Blue Mountaineers (a first listing) in Matrix, No. 50 (December 1963): 15-17; additions and corrections in Matrix, No. 55 (October 1964): 10 ((2, 3, 7))

BLUE NOTE label
See also BECHET, SIDNEY (Bechet's Blue Notes); and (Niquet, Bernard); DePARIS, SIDNEY (Sidney DeParis and James P. Johnson Blue Note sessions); HALL, EDMOND (Edmond Hall Blue Note sessions); HODES, ART (Art Hodes Blue Note sessions)

B196 DOYLE, Mike: Blue Note 12" 78s label listing in Journal of Jazz Discography, No. 1 (November 1976): 16-18; additions and corrections in Journal of Jazz Discography, No. 2 (June 1977): 4 ((3))

B197 FRESIA, Enzo: I dischi della "Blue Note" della serie 4000 in Musica Jazz, Vol. 20 (November 1964): 43-46; (December 1964): 37-40; Vol. 21 (January 1965): 43-46; additions and corrections in Musica Jazz, Vol. 21 (March 1965): 43 ((2, 7d))

B198 MANKTELOW, R.: Unissued Bluenotes in Jazz Monthly, Vol. 12 (October 1966): 29-30 ((2, 7))

B199 SHERA, Mike, and Malcolm WALKER: Blue Note BLP5000 Series (10 inch) in Discographical Forum, No. 36 (1976) to No. 41 (1978?),

various paginations; additions and
corrections in Discographical
Forum, No. 41 (1978?): 20 ((2, 7))

BLUE ROCK label

B200 [[[Listing] in Soul Bag, No. 7]]

BLUE SMITTY label

B201 Discography in Living Blues, No.
45/46 (Spring 1980): 55 ((3, 7))

BLUE STAR label (Australian)
See CIRCLE label (Australian)

BLUE STAR label (French)

B202 PASCOLI, Daniel: Blue Star chronology from nos. 1 to 100 in
Playback, Vol. 2 (April 1948): 18-
19 ((2, 3, 7d))

BLUEBIRD label
See also ELLINGTON, DUKE (Reid,
John D.); WELDON, CASEY BILL
(Panassié, Hugues)

B203 PARRY, William Hewitt: The Bluebird 34-0700 race series in
Discophile, No. 15 (December 1950):
12-16; additions and corrections
in Discophile, No. 16 (February
1951): 9; No. 17 (April 1951): 14;
No. 19 (August 1951): 10; No. 22
(February 1952): 10-11 ((2, 3, 6,
7d))

BLUES MUSIC
See also JAZZ MUSIC (Bruyninckx,
Walter) and (Carey, Dave) and
(McCarthy, Albert: Jazz discogra-
phy 1); PIANO MUSIC (JAZZ)
(Disques de piano-blues) and
(Kriss, Eric)

B204 BASTIN, Bruce: Test exists [part
1, A to Jackson] in Storyville,
No. 82 (April-May 1979): 128-129;
corrections from John COWLEY in
Storyville, No. 83 (June-July
1979): 164 ((3, 6))

B205 Blues lexicon; blues, cajun,
boogie woogie, gospel [Antwerp]:
Standaard [1972], 480 pp. ((—))

B206 COLTON, Bob, and Len KUNSTADT:
Race artist Vocalion red records
in Record Research, No. 31 (November 1960): 9, 20 ((3, 6, 7d))

B207 EAGLE, Bob: The neglected men
[column] in issues of Alley Music
((2, 3, 7))

B208 GODRICH, John, and Robert M. W.
DIXON: Blues and gospel records,
1902-1942. Hatch End, Middlesex:
Brian Rust, 1963/64, 766 pp.; additions and corrections in
GODRICH, John: Blues and gospel
records--amendment service in
Blues Unlimited, No. 14 (August
1964) to No. 55 (August 1968),
most issues, various paginations;
GODRICH, John: Blues and gospel
records 1902-1942; omissions in
Blues Unlimited, No. 12 (June
1964): 20; GODRICH, John: John
Godrich's survey of pre-war blues
artists reissued on E.P. and L.P.
1951-1964. Bexhill-on-Sea, Sussex: Blues Unlimited, 1965, 16
pp.; GODRICH, John: Talking the
blues; blues book addenda in
Blues Unlimited, No. 11 (April-
May 1964): 20; KENDZIORA, Carl:
Behind the cobwebs in Record Research, No. 86 (September 1967);
No. 88 (January 1968); No. 91
(July 1968); No. 92 (September
1968), various paginations ((2,
3, 4t, 6, 7))

B209 GODRICH, John, and Robert M. W.
DIXON: Blues and gospel records
1902-1942 [London]: Storyville
[c1969], 912 pp.; additions and
corrections in their I believe
I'll make a change in Storyville,
No. 24 (August-September 1969) to
date, various paginations.

B210 GROOM, Bob: Story of a blues in
Blues World, No. 44 (fall 1972):
2 [recordings of the tunes Cold
in China, My Baby It's Fine, and
Love with a Feeling] ((7d))

B211 GURALNICK, Peter: Selected discography in his Feel like going
home; portraits in blues and rock
'n' roll. New York: Outerbridge
& Dienstfrey, 1971, 213-217
[covers Muddy Waters, Johnny
Shines, Skip James, Robert Pete
Williams, Howlin' Wolf, Chess and
Sun labels] ((—))

B212 LEADBITTER, Mike, and Neal
SLAVEN: Blues records 1943-1966.
London: Hanover, 1969 (also New
York: Oak, [c1968]), 381 pp.; ad-
ditions and corrections in EAGLE,
Bob: Corrections to Leadbitter &
Slaven in Alley Music, Vol. 1

(May 1970): 22-23 and possibly other issues; LEADBITTER, Mike: Post-war discographical comment in Blues Unlimited, No. 24 (August 1965) to No. 40 (January 1967); No. 45 (August 1967); No. 55 (July 1968), various paginations; LEADBITTER, Mike: Post war discography in Blues Unlimited, No. 64 (July 1969): 15 ((2, 3, 6, 7))

B213 LEADBITTER, Mike: Those "one-record" country bluesmen in Blues Unlimited, No. 36 (September 1966): 10 ((3, 7))

B214 MORGAN, John P., and Thomas C. TULLOSS: The jake walk blues; a toxicologic tragedy mirrored in American popular music in Annals of Internal Medicine, Vol. 85 (1976): 806; reprinted in JEMF Quarterly, Vol. 13 (fall 1977): 126 [blues and hillbilly recordings on subject of Jamaica ginger paralysis] ((7))

B215 PARTH, Johnny: Country blues regional in Blues Notes, Vol. 3 (Nos. 10 & 11, 1971): 35-57 ((4p))

B216 RIJN, Guido van: Prewar blues re-issues in Boogie Woogie & Blues Collector, No. 24 (January 1973): 4-5; No. 25 (1973): 6; No. 30/31 (August 1973): 15-18 ((7))

B217 ROTANTE, Anthony, ed.: Blues research. Brooklyn, NY: distributed by Record Research, issue Nos. 1 to 16, May 1959 to January 1970 [each issue consists entirely of label listings of small jazz-blues-R&B labels] ((3))

B218 RUSSELL, Tony: Discography in his Blacks, whites and blues. New York: Stein & Day [c1970], 105-109 ((—))

B219 STEWART-BAXTER, Derrick: Discography in his Ma Rainey and the classic blues singers. London: Studio Vista (also New York: Stein & Day) [c1970], 106-110 ((—))

B220 STRACHWITZ, Chris: A guide to the postwar blues singers in Coda, Vol. 2 (November 1959-March 1960); Vol. 3 (May-July 1960); (September 1960); (October 1960); (January 1961), various paginations, in 11 parts [covers A to B only] ((2, 3, 7))

B221 STRACHWITZ, Chris: Postwar "down-home" blues in Jazz Report (California), Vol. 1 (April 1961): w-11 to w-13 [covers W only] ((2, 3, 7))

Additions and Corrections

B222 BOAS, Gunter: Chirpin' the blues; a selection of items from my collection, which may offer discographers additions to their files and reference books in Discophile, No. 39 (December 1954): 21; No. 45 (December 1955): 13

B223 COLLER, Derek: Blues discography [column] in Rhythm and Blues Panorama, various paginations [in No. 22, 1963, and probably others]

B224 COLLER, Derek: Recording the blues; a column about blues singers and their records in Vintage Jazz Mart, Vol. 5 (January 1959-September 1966), various paginations.

B225 New discographical comment [column] in Blues Unlimited, No. 51 (March 1968) to No. 53 (May 1968), various paginations

B226 ROTANTE, Anthony: Blues & rhythm in Record Research, Vol. 1 (February 1955 to July-August 1956); No. 20 (November-December 1958); No. 32 (January 1961) to No. 37 (August 1961); No. 60 (May-June 1964); No. 62 (August 1964) to No. 70 (August 1965); No. 72 (November 1965); No. 76 (May 1966); No. 78 (August 1966) to No. 137/138 (February-March 1976), most issues, various paginations

California

B227 LEADBITTER, Mike: The cats from Fresno--discography in Blues Unlimited, No. 35 (August 1966): 7 ((2, 3, 7))

Chicago

B228 Record listing in ROWE, Mike: Chicago breakdown. London: Eddison [c1973], 219-222 ((—))

Cincinnati

B229 Selected LP discography; prewar blues in Cincinnati in Living

Blues, No. 38 (May-June 1978): 25 ((7d))

Memphis

B230 LEADBITTER, Mike: "Memphis" (discographically!) 1950-1953 in Blues Unlimited Collectors Classics, No. 13 (1966): 5-14 ((2, 3))

B231 OLSSON, Bengt: Discography in his Memphis blues. [London]: Studio Vista (also New York: Stein & Day) [c1970]: 110-112 ((—))

Netherlands

B232 WISSE, Rien; 10 jaar nederlandse bluesgroepen in Jazz Press, No. 25 (October 29, 1976): 7-10; No. 26 (November 12, 1976): 7-10 ((—))

BLUES UNLIMITED label

B233 BASTIN, Bruce: Discography of the Blues Unlimited (no relation) label in Blues Unlimited, No. 122 (November-December 1976): 17 ((—))

BLUESVILLE label

B234 ROTANTE, Anthony: Prestige/Bluesville in Record Research, No. 73 (January 1966): 5; additions and corrections in Record Research, No. 74 (March 1966): 8 ((—))

BLUESWAY label

B235 [[Listing in Soul Bag, No. 4]]

BLYTHE, ARTHUR, 1940-
saxophones

B236 Selected Arthur Blythe discography in Down Beat, Vol. 47 (April 1980): 26 ((—))

BLYTHE, JIMMY, ca. 1901-1931
piano

B237 [[BERG, Arne: Jimmy Blythe including piano-rollography, Earl Bostic, Graeme Bell, Dave Brubeck. Stockholm: 196?]]

B238 DAVIES, Ron: Discography of Jimmy Blythe in Jazz Music, Vol. 3, No. 4 (1946): 15-19; additions and corrections in Jazz Music, Vol.

3, No. 7 (1948): 17-21; No. 8 (1948): 18-19 ((2, 3))

B239 HAESLER, William J.: Discography of James Blythe--pianist in Matrix, No. 4 (January 1955): 3-15; additions and corrections in Matrix, No. 5 (March 1955): 15; No. 7 (July 1955): 7-9; No. 13 (August 1956): 16-17; No. 35/36 (September 1961): 38; No. 45 (February 1963): 13 ((2, 3, 6, 7))

B240 KUNSTADT, Len: James Blythe piano-rollography in Record Research, Vol. 2 (February 1956): 9; additions and corrections in Record Research, Vol. 2 (January-February 1957): 23 ((5))

BO DIDDLEY (Ellas McDaniel), 1928-
guitar, harmonica, vocal

B241 Bo Diddley discographie in Soul Bag, No. 61 (June 1977): 11-15 ((2, 3, 7))

B242 ROBERTON, Paul, and Mike LEADBITTER: Discography in Blues Unlimited Collectors Classics No. B-3 (April 1964): 8-10 ((2, 3, 7))

BOB AND EARL (musical group)

B243 [[Discography in Soul Bag, No. 5]]

B244 GIBBON, Peter: Bob and Earl disco in Soul, No. 3 (April 1966): 10 ((—))

BOBBIN label

B245 [[Listing in Soul Bag, No. 5]]

B246 PEARLIN, Victor: Bobbin Records in Blues Unlimited, No. 119 (May-June 1976): 16 ((3, 6))

BOGAN, LUCILLE, 1897-1948
vocal

B247 [Discography] in Collectors Items [column] in Jazz Information, Vol. 2 (February 7, 1941): 20 ((2, 3))

B248 [[Discography in Living Blues, No. 44 (1979): 28]]; additions and corrections from Guido van RIJN in Living Blues, No. 45/46 (spring 1980): 5

BOLAND, FRANCY, 1929–
    piano, leader
    See CLARKE–BOLAND BAND

BOLDEN, BUDDY, 1877–1931
    cornet

B249 Discography in MARQUIS, Don: In
    search of Buddy Bolden; first man
    of jazz. Baton Rouge: Louisiana
    State University Press [c1978],
    177 ((—))

BOLLETINO, DANTE
    record producer

B250 The Dante Bolletino labels:
    British Rhythm Society, Carousel,
    Cosmopolitan, Jolly Roger, Para-
    dox, Pax, Wax Shop in Matrix, No.
    58 (April 1965): 3–29; additions
    and corrections in Matrix, No. 69
    (February 1967): 13; No. 71 (June
    1967): 19 ((4p, 5))

BOLLIN, ZU ZU
    guitar, vocal

B251 MOHR, Kurt: Zu Zu Bollin in Blues
    Unlimited, No. 30 (February
    1966): 19 ((2, 3, 7))

BONANO, SHARKEY (Joseph Bonano), 1904–
    1972
    trumpet

B252 HABY, Peter R.: Sharkey Bonano; a
    discography in Footnote, Vol. 9
    (June–July 1978): 9–13; (August–
    September 1978): 4–8 ((2, 3, 6,
    7))

BONNER, JUKE BOY (Weldon H. Philip
    Bonner), 1932–1978
    guitar, harmonica, vocal

B253 LOBSTEIN, Patrick: Discographie
    de Juke Boy Bonner in Soul Bag,
    No. 71 (1979): 22–27 ((2, 3, 7))

BOOKER T AND THE MGS

B254 [[Discography in Soul Bag, No.
    14]]

BOP
    See JAZZ MUSIC––Bebop

BORNEMANN, CHARLES
    trombone

B255 POWELL, Robert H.: The discogra-
    phy of Charles Bornemann––trom-
    bone in The Jazz Blast (July–
    August 1970): 4–7 ((2, 7))

BOSE, STERLING, 1906–1958
    trumpet

B256 VENABLES, Ralph G. V.: The story
    of Sterling Bose in New Orleans
    and Chicago jazz; a pamphlet pub-
    lished for the Discographical
    Society. London: Clifford Jones,
    1944, 12, 14 ((—))

BOSTIC, EARL, 1913–1965
    alto saxophone

B257 Disques d'Earl Bostic parus en
    France in Jazz Hot, No. 91 (Sep-
    tember 1954): 9 ((—))

B258 FRIEDRICH, Heinz: A Earl Bostic
    (Parlophone) discography in Jazz
    Statistics, No. 4 (November
    1956): 3–6; No. 14 (January
    1960): 2–5; additions and correc-
    tions from Michel VOGLER in Jazz
    Statistics, No. 17 (1960): 8 ((2,
    3, 6, 7))

BOTHWELL, JOHNNY, 1919–
    alto saxophone
    See also RAEBURN, BOYD (Edwards,
    Ernie)

B259 EDWARDS, Ernie: Johnny Bothwell;
    a discography in Matrix, No. 62
    (December 1965): 9–11; additions
    and corrections in Matrix, No. 63
    (February 1966): 10; No 74 (De-
    cember 1967): 10 ((2, 3, 6, 7))

BOYD, EDDIE, 1914–
    guitar, piano

B260 Discographie Eddie Boyd in
    Anschlaege, No. 3 (September
    1978): 76–104 ((2, 3, 4p, 4r, 4t,
    6, 7))

B261 Eddie Boyd discography in Living
    Blues, No. 37 (March–April 1978):
    16–17 ((2, 3, 7))

B262 ROTANTE, Anthony, and Marcel
    CHAUVARD: The records of Eddie
    Boyd in Record Research, No. 42
    (March–April 1962): 12, 19 ((2,
    3, 7))

BRACEY, ISHMON, 1901–1970
    guitar, vocal

B263 BAKKER, Dick M.: Ishman [sic] Bracey in Micrography, No. 9 (February 1970): 7 ((—))

BRACKEEN, JOANNE, 1938–
piano

B264 Plattenhinweise in Jazz Podium, Vol. 28 (March 1979): 7 ((—))

BRADFORD, PERRY, 1893–1970
piano

B265 ALLEN, Walter C.: [Discography] in Jazz Journal, Vol. 10 (August 1957–October 1957), various paginations, in 3 parts ((2, 3, 6, 7))

BRADIX, CHARLEY
piano, vocal

B266 LEADBITTER, Mike: Big Charley Bradix in Blues Unlimited, No. 33 (May-June 1966): 6 ((3, 7))

BRADLEY, WILL, 1912–
trombone

B267 CROSBIE, Ian: The Will Bradley-Ray McKinley orchestra in Jazz Journal, Vol. 26 (February 1973): 17 ((2, 3, 6, 7))

BRADSHAW, TINY (Myron Bradshaw), 1905–1958
drums, piano, vocal

B268 MOHR, Kurt: Discography of Tiny Bradshaw in Discophile, No. 30 (June 1953): 6-8 ((2, 3, 7))

B269 MOHR, Kurt: Discography of Tiny Bradshaw. Reinach, Switzerland: Jazz-Publications, 1961, 16 + 1 pp. ((2, 3, 6, 7, 9))

BRAFF, RUBY (Reuben Braff), 1927–
cornet

B270 HALL, George I.: A discography of Reuben "Ruby" Braff in Matrix, No. 54 (August 1964): 3-12; additions and corrections in Matrix, No. 63 (February 1966): 12 ((2, 3, 7))

B271 HALL, George I.: The Ruby Braff discography. Laurel, MD: Jazz Discographies Unlimited, 1965, 14 leaves (Spotlight series, Vol. 2) ((2, 4p, 7))

B272 LINDEROTH, Lars: Skivor in Orkester Journalen, Vol. 32 (September 1964): 15 ((—))

B273 [[McCARTHY, Albert J.: Ruby Braff; a biography, appreciation, record survey and discography. London: National Jazz Federation, 1958, 20 pp.]]

B274 McCARTHY, Albert J.: Ruby Braff discography in Jazz Monthly, Vol. 3 (February 1958): 24-25; Vol. 4 (March 1958): 26-27, 32 ((2, 3, 7))

B275 Plattenhinweise in Jazz Podium, Vol. 28 (November 1979): 17 ((—))

B276 [RACE, Steve]: Braff on record in Jazz News, Vol. 6 (May 16, 1962): 7 ((—))

BRAND, DOLLAR (Adolph Johannes Brand or Abdullah Ibrahim), 1934–
piano

B277 Abdullah Ibrahim (Dollar Brand): a selected discography in Contemporary Keyboard, Vol. 6 (May 1980): 32 ((—))

B278 BAGGENAES, Roland, and John W. NORRIS: Discography in Coda, Vol. 11 (February 1973): 5-6 ((1, 2, 7))

B279 LUZZI, Mario: Discografia Dollar Brand in Musica Jazz, Vol. 31 (April 1975): 46 ((2, 7))

B280 RABEN, Erik: Diskofilspalten in Orkester Journalen, Vol. 40 (November 1972): 17; addition in Orkester Journalen, Vol. 41 (April 1973): 19 ((2, 7))

BRASS BANDS

B281 SCHAFER, William J.: Discography in his Brass bands and New Orleans jazz. Baton Rouge: Louisiana State University Press [c1977], 102-105 ((2, 7d))

BRAXTON, ANTHONY, 1945–
saxophones

B282 CONLEY, George, and John W. NORRIS: The Anthony Braxton discography in Coda, Vol. 11 (April 1974): 10-11 ((2, 7))

B283 Discography in Swing Journal,
    Vol. 27 (November 1973): 167 ((2,
    7d))

B284 DUTILH, Alex: Discographie
    d'Anthony Braxton in Jazz Hot,
    No. 329 (July 1976): 46-49 ((2,
    7))

B285 JACCHETTI, Renato: Discografia
    Anthony Braxton in Musica Jazz,
    Vol. 36 (April 1980): 50-53 ((2,
    7))

B286 [[RISSI, Matthias: Anthony Brax-
    ton; discography. Adliswil,
    Switzerland: 1977, 16 pp.]]

B287 Selected Braxton discography in
    Down Beat, Vol. 43 (August 12,
    1976): 15 ((—))

BRECKER BROTHERS

B288 Selected Brecker Brothers discog-
    raphy in Down Beat, Vol. 46 (June
    21, 1979): 25 ((—))

BRENSTON, JACKIE, 1927-1979
    baritone saxophone, vocal

B289 CHAUVARD, Marcel, and Kurt MOHR:
    Discography of Jackie Brenston in
    Jazz Statistics, No. 25 (March
    1962): 3-4 ((2, 3, 7))

BREUKER, WILLEM, 1944-
    alto saxophone

B290 Discographie sélective de Willem
    Breuker in Jazz Hot, No. 347
    (March 1978): 15 ((—))

B291 EYLE, Wim van, and Jan MULDER:
    Willem Breuker discografie in
    Jazz Press, No. 41 (May 8, 1977):
    10-11; reprinted with title
    Willem Breuker discography in
    Coda, No. 160 (April 1978): 8-10
    ((1, 2, 7))

BRIDGES, HENRY, 1908-
    tenor saxophone
    See SAXOPHONE MUSIC (JAZZ)
    (Evensmo, Jan: The tenor saxo-
    phones of Henry Bridges...)

BRIGGS, ARTHUR, 1901-
    trumpet

B292 [[DELDEN, Ate van: [Discography]
    in Doctor Jazz, No. 64 (February-
    March 1974)]]; additions and cor-
    rections from Herman OPENNEER in

Doctor Jazz, No. 81 (1977): 4; in
LOTZ, Rainer: Some comments on
Arthur Briggs in Doctor Jazz, No.
82 (December 1977): 17-19; from
Ernst GROSSMAN in Storyville, No.
87 (February-March 1980): 107-108
((3))

B293 [[GROSSMAN, Ernst: Polydor &
    Briggs; the Australian Polydor
    issues of Arthur Briggs in Doctor
    Jazz, No. 90 (December 1979):
    5-6]]

BRIGNOLA, NICK, 1936-
    baritone saxophone

B294 Selected Brignola discography in
    Down Beat, Vol. 45 (May 18,
    1978): 22 ((—))

BRIM, JOHN, 1922-
    guitar, vocal

B295 PATERSON, Neil: John Brim discog-
    raphy in Blues Unlimited, No. 21
    (April 1965): 6-7 [excludes re-
    cordings with Big Maceo] ((2, 3,
    7))

B296 ROTANTE, Anthony, and Paul
    SHEATSLEY: A discography of John
    Brim in Blues Research, No. 9
    (September 1962): 14 ((2, 3, 7))

BRITISH RHYTHM SOCIETY label
    See BOLLETINO, DANTE

BROADWAY label

B297 MACKENZIE, John K., and John
    GODRICH: The Broadway race series
    in Matrix, No. 48 (August 1963):
    3-13; additions and corrections
    in Matrix, No. 57 (February
    1965): 20; No. 59 (June 1965):
    19; No. 61 (October 1965): 14;
    No. 63 (February 1966): 10 ((3,
    6))

BROOKMEYER, BOB, 1929-
    trombone
    See TERRY, CLARK (Adkins, Tony)

BROOKS, LONNIE, 1933-
    guitar

B298 CHOISNEL, Emmanuel, and Kurt
    MOHR: Guitar Junior in Soul Bag,
    No. 38 (May 1974): 26 ((2, 3, 7))

B299 LEADBITTER, Mike: Discography of Guitar Jr. (Lee Baker Jr.) in Blues Statistics, No. 2 (March 1963): 4 ((2, 7d))

BROONZY, BIG BILL, 1898-1958
    guitar, vocal

B300 COLLER, Derek: Big Bill Broonzy; the following is a discography of the records made by the late Bill Broonzy since the publication of the discography in "Big Bill blues" in Matrix, No. 33 (March 1961): 3-6; additions and corrections in Matrix, No. 40 (April 1962): 19 ((2, 3, 7))

B301 ISETON, Bill: Selected discography in Jazzology (UK), Vol. 2 (January 1947): 7 ((—))

B302 McCARTHY, Albert J.: Discography in Big Bill blues; William Broonzy's story as told to Yannick Bruynoghe. London: Cassell [c1955], 119-135; additions and corrections in Jazz Report (St. Louis), Vol. 5 (February 1957): 6; see also B300 ((1, 2, 3, 6, 7))

B303 McCARTHY, Albert J.; Ken HARRISON; and Ray ASTBURY: Discography in Big Bill blues; William Broonzy's story as told to Yannick Bruynoghe. New York: Oak [1964, c1955]: 153-175 ((2, 3, 6, 7))

B304 McCARTHY, Albert J.: Discography of Big Bill Broonzy in Jazz Forum (UK), No. 4 (April 1947): 25-30 ((2, 3, 7d))

BROTHERS OF SOUL (musical group)

B305 BRYANT, Steve, and Alan ELSEY: Makin' up for lost time--try it baby--the Brothers of Soul in Hot Buttered Soul, No. 42 (November 1975): 4 ((3))

BROWN, BOYCE, 1910-1959
    alto saxophone, clarinet

B306 MILLER, Bill, and Ralph VENABLES: Discography in Jazz Music, Vol. 2 (March-April 1944): 130 ((2, 3, 7d))

BROWN, CHARLES, 1920-
    piano, organ, vocal

B307 Albums by Charles Brown in Living Blues, No. 27 (May-June 1976): 27 ((—))

BROWN, CLARENCE "GATEMOUTH," 1924-
    guitar, harmonica, vocal

B308 MOHR, Kurt: Clarence "Gatemouth" Brown, discography in Blues Unlimited, No. 33 (May-June 1966): 10-11 ((2, 3, 7))

B309 MOHR, Kurt: Clarence "Gatemouth" Brown on Peacock in Jazz Statistics, No. 9 (March 1959): 5; additions from Jorgen Grunnet JEPSEN in Jazz Statistics, No. 12 (September 1959): 8 ((2, 3, 7))

BROWN, CLEO, 1909-? (deceased)
    piano, vocal

B310 BALLARD, Eric: Records by Cleo Brown in Swing Music, No. 14 (fall 1936): 52 ((2))

B311 NELSON, John R.: Discography of Cleo Brown in Record Exchange, Vol. 2 (July 1949): 8 ((2))

BROWN, CLIFFORD, 1930-1956
    trumpet
    See also NAVARRO, FATS (Jepsen, Jorgen Grunnet: Discographie Fats Navarro et Clifford Brown) and (Jepsen, Jorgen Grunnet: Discography of Fats Navarro/Clifford Brown); ROACH, MAX (Luzzi, Mario)

B312 Clifford Brown discography in Swing Journal (1977 annual): 194-197 ((2, 7d))

B313 Clifford Brown Oct. 30, 1930-Jan. 26, 1956 in Swing Journal, Vol. 34 (July 1980): 180-183 ((2, 7d))

B314 Discographie de Clifford Brown in Jazz Hot, No. 100 (June 1955): 12-13 ((2, 7))

B315 JEPSEN, Jorgen Grunnet: Clifford Brown; a complete discography in Down Beat Music 15th yearbook (1970): 109-113 ((2, 3, 7))

B316 [[JEPSEN, Jorgen Grunnet: Clifford Brown; a discography. Copenhagen: 1957, 9 leaves]]

B317 JEPSEN, Jorgen Grunnet: Clifford Brown; a discography in Jazz Journal, Vol. 12 (March 1959): 6-8; corrections from Mike SHERA in Jazz Journal, Vol. 12 (May 1959); from Carlos de RADZITSKY and Frank DUTTON in Jazz Journal, Vol. 12 (July 1959): 34-35 ((2, 3, 7))

B318 JEPSEN, Jorgen Grunnet: Clifford Brown discography in Orkester Journalen, Vol. 24 (December 1956): 39; Vol. 25 (February 1957): 50 ((2, 3, 7))

B319 MONTALBANO, Pierre: Clifford Brown: a discography in Discographical Forum, No. 17 (March 1970) to No. 19 (July 1970), various paginations; additions and corrections in Discographical Forum, No. 21 (November 1970): 20; No. 22 (January 1971): 2, 20 [rev. ed. of next entry] ((1, 2, 3, 6, 7))

B320 [[MONTALBANO, Pierre: Clifford Brown: biography & discography. Marseille: Jazz Club Aix-Marseille, 1969, 12 pp.]]

B321 POSTIF, François: La discographie française de Clifford Brown in Jazz Magazine (France), No. 20 (September 1956): 31, 33 ((2, 3, 7))

B322 [[RUPPLI, Michael: Discographie: Clifford Brown in Jazz Hot, No. 347 (March 1978): 24-27]]

B323 ·We remember Clifford; Clifford Brown discography in Swing Journal, Vol. 27 (August 1973): 266-271 ((2, 7d))

BROWN, GABRIEL, ca. 1910-ca. 1972
   guitar

B324 STEWART-BAXTER, Derrick: Gabriel Brown--a listing in Jazz Journal, Vol. 28 (June 1975): 15 ((2, 7d))

BROWN, GARNETT, 1936-
   trombone

B325 Selected Brown discography in Down Beat, Vol. 42 (May 22, 1975): 20 ((—))

BROWN, GATEMOUTH
   See BROWN, CLARENCE "GATEMOUTH"

BROWN, HENRY, 1906-
   piano, vocal

B326 HENRY, Tom: Henry Brown discography in Record Changer, Vol. 3 (June 1944): 47 ((2, 3))

BROWN, JOHN T., ca. 1920?-
   tenor saxophone

B327 EAGLE, Bob: J. T. Brown in Alley Music, Vol. 1 (August 1969): 18 ((2, 3, 7))

BROWN, LES, 1912-
   leader, clarinet

B328 CROSBIE, Ian: That band of renown in Jazz Journal, Vol. 24 (February 1971): 26-27 ((2, 3, 6, 7))

B329 EDWARDS, Ernie: Les Brown and his band of renown. Whittier, CA: Jazz Discographies Unlimited, 1965, 52 leaves (Dance band series, B-1) ((1, 2, 3, 6, 7))

B330 EDWARDS, Ernie: Les Brown and his band of renown. Whittier, CA: ErnGeoBil, 1966, 53 leaves (Dance band series, B1-R) ((1, 2, 3, 6, 7))

B331 GARROD, Charles: Les Brown and his Orchestra 1936-1952. Spotswood, NJ: Joyce Music, 1974, 44, 6 leaves ((1, 2, 3, 4t, 6, 7))

BROWN, LILLYN, 1885-1969
   vocal

B332 KUNSTADT, Len: Lillyn Brown discography in Record Research, Vol. 2 (November-December 1956): 12 ((2, 3, 6))

BROWN, MARION, 1935-
   alto saxophone

B333 Marion Brown in Swing Journal, Vol. 29 (September 1975): 238-241 ((2, 7d))

B334 Marion Brown in Swing Journal, Vol. 32 (November 1978): 322-325 ((2, 7d))

B335 TEPPERMAN, Barry: Marion Brown discography in Jazz Monthly, No. 187 (September 1970): 19-21 ((1, 2, 7))

BROWN, MEL, 1940-
   guitar, vocal

B336 NIQUET, Bernard: Discographie de Mel Brown in Jazz Hot, No. 257 (January 1970): 26 ((2, 7))

BROWN, RAY, 1926-
   bass violin

B337 Selected Brown discography in Down Beat, Vol. 43 (January 29, 1976): 13 ((—))

BROWN, ROY, 1925–
vocal

B338 MOHR, Kurt: Discographie de Roy Brown in Soul Bag, No. 61 (June 1977): 25-28 ((2, 3, 7))

B339 MOHR, Kurt: [Discography] in Jazz Statistics, No. 11 (July 1959): 2-3; additions by M. VOGLER in Jazz Statistics, No. 17 (1960): 2; No. 22 (June 1961): 1 ((2, 3, 6, 7))

B340 Roy Brown and his mighty men; a discography in Discophile, No. 50 (October 1956): 2-4; additions and corrections in Discophile, No. 51 (December 1956): 14-15 ((2, 3, 7))

B341 TOPPING, Ray, and Mike LEAD-BITTER: Discography in Blues Unlimited, No. 124 (March-June 1977): 19-21; additions and corrections in Blues Unlimited, No. 126 (September-October 1977): 17 ((2, 3, 7))

BROWN, SANDY, 1929-197?
clarinet

B342 MORGAN, Alun: Sandy Brown--a discography in BROWN, Sandy: The McJazz manuscripts; a collection of the writings of Sandy Brown, compiled and ed. by David Binns. London: Faber & Faber [c1979]: 151-164 ((1, 2, 3, 7))

B343 Sandy Brown's Jazz Band; a discography in Discophile, No. 47 (April 1956): 6-7; additions and corrections in Discophile, No. 52 (February 1957): 11 ((2, 3, 6, 7))

BROWN, WILLIE
harmonica

B344 MOHR, Kurt: Discography of Little Willie Brown in Blues Unlimited, No. 19 (February 1965): 11 ((2, 3, 7))

BRUBECK, DAVE, 1920–
piano

B345 D'ANGELO, Bruno: [Discography] in Jazz Magazine (Argentina), No. 56

(September-October 1955): 6 ((—))

B346 Dave Brubeck in Swing Journal, Vol. 34 (February 1980): 164-169 ((2, 7d))

B347 [[[Record list] in HENTOFF, Nat: Dave Brubeck. New York: BMI [c1961] ((2))]]

B348 Selected Brubeck discography in Down Beat, Vol. 43 (March 25, 1976): 19 (—))

BRUCE, JACK, 1943–
guitar

B349 Selected Bruce discography in Down Beat, Vol. 45 (January 26, 1978): 18 (—))

BRUNIS, GEORGE (George Clarence Brunies), 1900–
trombone

B350 GAZE, Richard: A discography of George Brunies in Reprints and Reflections, No. 12 (February 1946): 4-6 ((2, 3, 7p))

B351 STRASSBURGER, Arturo J.: Su discografia in Jazz Magazine (Argentina), No. 8 (May 1946): 5, 27 ((—))

BRUNSWICK label
See also ELLINGTON, DUKE (Bakker, Dick M.: Ellington-Brunswick-Vocol listing 1926-35) and (Bakker, Dick M.: Ellington Brunswicks 1936-40); HOLIDAY, BILLIE (Bakker, Dick M.); NICHOLS, RED (Bakker, Dick M.: Red Nichols Brunswick-recordings 1926-32); OLIVER, KING JOE (Bakker, Dick M.: King Oliver 1926-1931 Voc/Br)

B352 McCARTHY, Albert J.: Brunswick race series in Jazz Forum (UK), No. 4 (April 1947): 24-25 [to no. 7040] ((—))

BRUNSWICK label (Australian)

B353 WANSBONE, Ernie: An Australian Brunswick listing in Matrix, No. 5 (March 1955): 17-19 ((—))

BRUNSWICK label (British)

B354 DARKE, K. Peter, and Jim HAYES: English Brunswick 10" 78 rpm

RL200 series in R.S.V.P., No. 20 (January 1967); No. 24 (May 1967) to No. 29 (October 1967); No. 31 (December 1967); No. 32 (January 1968); No. 35 (April 1968); No. 38 (July 1968); No. 40 (September 1968); No. 43 (December 1968); No. 47 (April 1969); No. 49 (August 1969); No. 52 (January-February 1970); No. 53 (March-April 1970), various paginations ((3, 4p, 4r, 4t))

B355 DUTTON, Frank: Brunswick modern rhythm series in Matrix, No. 50 (December 1963): 3-12; additions and corrections in Matrix, No. 55 (October 1964): 17; No. 57 (February 1965): 20 ((—))

B356 GRAY-CLARKE, G.F.: The Brunswick muddle in Jazz Record (UK), No. 12 (April 1944): 6-8 [KP series and special pressings] ((—))

B357 HAYES, Jim: Brunswick special series in Matrix, No. 74 (December 1967): 3-4 ((—))

B358 [[HAYES, Jim: English Brunswick artist catalogue 02000 series (02000 to 02999). Liverpool: 1969, 30 pp.]]

B359 HAYES, Jim: Numerical catalogue listings number E 1; English Brunswick 78/45 RPM (0) 1000 series. Part 1: 1000 to 2000 (Dec. 1930 to May 1935). Southhampton: 1967, 50 pp. ((—))

BRYANT, RAY, 1931–
piano

B360 EYLE, Wim van: Ray Bryant discography in Jazz Nu, Vol. 1 (July 1979): 451 ((—))

B361 JEPSEN, Jorgen Grunnet: Ray Bryant diskografi (skivor under eget namn) in Orkester Journalen, Vol. 29 (May 1961): 34; additions in Orkester Journalen, Vol. 29 (September 1961): 21 ((2, 3, 7))

B362 Ray Bryant discography in Swing Journal, Vol. 27 (November 1973): 280-287 ((2, 7d))

B363 Sélection de microsillons enregistrés avec le concours de Ray Bryant in Jazz Hot, No. 158 (October 1960): 23 ((—))

BRYANT, RUSTY, 1929–
alto and tenor saxophones

B364 ROTANTE, Anthony and Len KUNSTADT: Rusty Bryant in Record Research, No. 78 (August 1966): 9 ((2, 3, 6, 8))

BRYDEN, BERYL, 1926–
vocal

B365 [[BIELDERMAN, Gerard: Beryl Bryden discography. Zwolle, Netherlands: 197?, 8 pp.]]

B366 BIELDERMAN, Gerard: A discography of Beryl Bryden in Matrix, No. 101 (August 1973): 3-8 ((2, 3, 6, 7))

BUE, PAPA
See PAPA BUE

BUFFALODIANS

B367 BACKENSTO, Woody: The Buffalodians in Record Exchange, Vol. 3 (August 1950): 1-2; Vol. 4 (February 1951): 1 ((3, 7))

B368 BACKENSTO, Woody: Who were the Buffalodians? in Record Changer (January 1954): 7, 14 ((2, 3, 6, 7))

BUFORD, MOJO (George Buford), 1929–
harmonica, vocal

B369 LECUYER, Claude; Emmanuel CHOISNEL; and Jacques PERIN: Discographie de Mojo Buford in Soul Bag, No. 27 (June 1973): 6 ((2, 3, 7))

BUGLE CALL RAG (tune title)

B370 RUGGLES, Happy: Bugle call rag in Jazz Discounter, Vol. 2 (January 1949): 15-16 ((—))

BULLOCK, CHICK, ca. 1905–
vocal

B371 KINKLE, Roger D.: Numerical list of Chick Bullock recordings in his Check sheet (project #2): [Evansville, IN?]: n.d., 1-6 ((9))

BUMBLE BEE SLIM
See EASTON, AMOS

BUNN, TEDDY, 1909–
guitar

B372 TANNER, Peter: A discography of
Teddy Bunn in Jazz Journal, Vol.
24 (November 1971) to Vol. 25
(January 1972), various paginations in 3 parts ((2, 3, 6, 7))

BURBANK, ALBERT, 1902–
clarinet

B373 HILLMAN, J. C.: The issued recordings of Albert Burbank in
Jazz Journal, Vol. 21 (May 1968):
27, 29; additions and corrections
[from Tom STAGG] in Jazz Journal,
Vol. 21 (July 1968): 26 and [from
Marek BOJUR] (September 1968): 19
((2, 7))

B374 VAN VORST, Paige: An available
discography of Albert Burbank in
Mississippi Rag, Vol. 4 (October
1976): 3 ((—))

BURKE, RAYMOND, 1904–
clarinet

B375 BURKE, Don: Raymond Burke--dis-
cography in Jazz Notes (New Orleans), No. 2 (October 1951): one
unnumbered sheet ((2, 3, 7))

BURKE, SOLOMON, 1936–
vocal

B376 MOHR, Kurt: Solomon Burke in Soul
Bag, No. 35 (February 1974): 20-
25; additions and corrections in
Soul Bag, No. 38 (May 1974): 46;
No. 45 (January 1975): 34 ((2, 3,
7))

BURNETTE, JOHNNY

B377 KOCKS, J. C.: Discographie de
Johnny Burnette in Jazz, Blues &
Co., No. 25/26 (January 1979):
19; additions and corrections
from Albert BOUYAT in Jazz, Blues
& Co., No. 27 (February 1979): 15
((—))

BURNS, EDDIE, 1928–
guitar, harmonica, vocal

B378 LEADBITTER, Mike: Eddie Burn's
biography/discography in Blues
Unlimited, No. 13 (July 1964): 9;
additions and corrections in
Blues Unlimited, No. 22 (May
1965): 10 ((3, 6, 7))

BURNS, TITO
accordion

B379 MOON, Pete: Tito Burns and his
sextet; a discography in Jazz
Studies, Vol. 2, No. 2 (1968):
19-20 ((2, 3, 7))

BURRAGE, HAROLD
vocal

B380 MOHR, Kurt: Harold Burrage in
Soul Bag, No. 45 (January 1975):
17-18 ((2, 3, 7))

BURRELL, DAVE, 1940–
piano

B381 Selected discography: Dave
Burrell in Coda, No. 175 (October
1980): 18 ((—))

BURRELL, DUKE
See MERCURY label (Seroff, Doug)

BURRELL, KENNY, 1931–
guitar

B382 Kenny Burrell discography in
Swing Journal, Vol. 29 (April
1975): 234-241 ((2, 7d))

BURTON, GARY, 1943–
vibraphone

B383 Gary Burton in Swing Journal,
Vol. 33 (July 1979): 226-229 ((2,
7d))

B384 Gary Burton selected discography
in Jazz Forum (Poland), No. 46
(1977): 55 ((—))

B385 RUPPLI, Michel, and Erik RABEN:
Discographie de Gary Burton in
Jazz Hot, No. 342 (October 1977):
26-30 ((2, 3, 7))

B386 Selected Burton discography in
Down Beat, Vol. 42 (November 20,
1975): 12 ((—))

BUTLER, BILLY, 1945–
leader

B387 MOHR, Kurt: Billy Butler in Discographical Forum, No. 6 (May
1968): 18 ((3, 6, 7))

BUTLER, GEORGE "WILD CHILD," 1936–
guitar, harmonica, vocal

B388 LEISER, Willie: Disco Wild Child Butler in Soul Bag, No. 38 (May 1974): 33; additions and corrections in Soul Bag, No. 43/44 (November-December 1974): 44 ((2, 3, 7))

B389 Wild Child Butler discography in Blues Unlimited, No. 131/132 (September-December 1978): 30 ((2, 3, 7))

BUTTERFIELD, BILLY, 1917-
trumpet

B390 EDWARDS, Ernie: Billy Butterfield; a name listing in Matrix, No. 53 (June 1964): 3-13; additions and corrections in Matrix, No. 63 (February 1966): 10 ((1, 2, 3, 6, 7))

B391 ENDRESS, Gudrun: Von der Polka zum Dutch Swing: Billy Butterfield in Jazz Podium, Vol. 23 (March 1974): 13 ((1))

BVHAAST label (Dutch)

B392 EYLE, Wim van: BVHaast discografie in Jazz Press, No. 52 (June 1, 1978): 6 ((2, 7))

BYARD, JAKI (John A. Byard), 1922-
piano

B393 Selected Byard discography in Down Beat, Vol. 46 (March 8, 1979): 16 ((2))

B394 WALKER, Malcolm: Jaki Byard in Jazz Monthly, No. 159 (May 1968): 29-31; No. 160 (June 1968): 30-31; No. 161 (July 1968): 30-31 ((2, 3, 7))

BYAS, DON, 1912-1972
tenor saxophone

B395 MOHR, Kurt: Discographie provisoire de Don Byas in Hot Revue, No. 11 (1946): 24-25; No. 12 (1946): 23-25 ((2, 3, 7d))

B396 MOHR, Kurt: Don Byas on "Vogue" records; a listing in Discophile, No. 45 (December 1955): 11-12 ((2, 3, 7))

B397 WILKIE, David B.: A Don Dyas discography 1938-1972 in Micrography, No. 46 (April 1978): 17-20 ((1, 6, 7))

BYERS, BILLY, 1927-
trombone

B398 Selected Byers discography in Down Beat, Vol. 42 (November 20, 1975): 16 ((—))

BYG label (French)

B399 RABEN, Erik: Diskofilspalten in Orkester Journalen, Vol. 40 (January 1972): 15, 26; (February 1972): 19 ((2, 7))

BYRD, DONALD, 1932-
trumpet

B400 Donald Byrd discography in Swing Journal, Vol. 13 (December 1974): 248-255 ((2, 7d))

B401 JEPSEN, Jorgen Grunnet: Donald Byrd diskografi (skivor utgivna under eget namn) in Orkester Journalen, Vol. 26 (October 1958): 50 ((2, 3, 7d))

B402 [[JEPSEN, Jorgen Grunnet: Donald Byrd; a discography. Copenhagen: 1957, 13 leaves]]

B403 WALKER, Malcolm: Donald Byrd discography in Discographical Forum, No. 30/31 (1972) to No. 38 (1977), various paginations; additions and corrections in Discographical Forum, No. 36 (1976): 1; No. 40 (spring 1978): 2; No. 41 (1978?): 20 ((2, 3, 6, 7))

BYRD, ROY, 1918-
piano
See also MERCURY label (Seroff, Doug)

B404 JONES, Tad: Discography in Living Blues, No. 26 (March-April 1976): 28-29 ((2, 3, 6, 7))

B405 LEADBITTER, Mike: Discography of Professor Longhair (Roy Byrd) in Blues Unlimited, No. 29 (January 1965): 20 ((3, 6, 7))

B406 MOHR, Kurt: Professor Longhair discography in Soul Bag, No. 26 (May 1973): 16, 15 ((2, 3, 7))

B407 OLDEREN, Martin van: Professor Longhair in Boogie Woogie & Blues Collector, No. 30/31 (August 1973): 19-20 ((3, 7))

B408 POSTIF, François: Professor Longhair in Jazz Hot, No. 299 (November 1973): 19 ((2, 3, 7))

B409 ROTANTE, Anthony: [Discography] in Record Research, Vol. 1 (April 1955): 4 ((2, 3))

C & THE SHELLS
    See SANDPEBBLES

C B S SONY label (Japanese)

C1 Bethlehem jazz series in Swing Journal, Vol. 30 (April 1976): 192-195 ((2, 7))

C2 Mainstream jazz series in Swing Journal, Vol. 30 (May 1976): 190-195 ((2, 7))

C J label

C3 BAKER, Cary: The C. J. Records story in Goldmine, No. 15 (March-April 1977): 7 ((—))

C4 C. J. Discography in Blue Flame, No. 12 (n.d.): 18-19 ((—))

CADET label
    See ARGO label (Ruppli, Michel)

CAIN, JACKIE, 1928-
    vocal

C5 BROWN, Wilson H.: A discography of Jacqueline Ruth Cain and Roy Joseph Kral, 1948-73 in Jazz Journal, Vol. 29 (June 1976): 20 ((2, 7))

CALHOUN, EDDIE, 1921-
    bass violin

C6 MOHR, Kurt: Eddie Calhoun in Jazz Statistics, No. 7 (ca. 1958): 6-8 ((2, 3, 7))

CALIFORNIA RAMBLERS

C7 BACKENSTO, Woody, and Perry ARMAGNAC: Ed Kirkeby's California Ramblers in Record Research, No. 47 (November 1962) to No. 49 (March 1963); No. 55 (September 1963); No. 56 (November 1963); No. 58 (February 1964); No. 66 (February 1965); No. 74 (March 1966), various paginations ((2, 3, 6, 7))

C8 BAKKER, Dick M.: California Ramblers in Micrography, No. 10 (May 1970): 6 ((7d))

C9 BAKKER, Dick M.: California Ramblers etc. 1924-1929 in Micrography, No. 12 (January 1971): 6-7; additions in Micrography, No. 13 (February 1971): 4 ((7d))

CALLOWAY, CAB, 1907-
    leader, vocal
    See also GILLESPIE, DIZZY (Dizzy with Cab); MISSOURIANS (Fluckiger, Otto)

C10 BAKKER, Dick M.: Cab Calloway 1930-1932 in Micrography, No. 31 (1974?): 3 ((7d))

C11 BAKKER, Dick M.: Cab Calloway 30-41 in Micrography, No. 7 (November 1969): 6 ((7d))

C12 BAKKER, Dick M.: Cab Calloway 35-42 in Micrography, No. 26 (1973): 7 ((7d))

C13 BAKKER, Dick M.: Cab Calloway-- Victors in Micrography, No. 38 (October 1975): 8 ((6, 7d))

C14 FLUCKIGER, Otto: Cab Calloway discography and solography in Jazz Journal, Vol. 14 (May 1961): 1-4; (June 1961): 13-14; (July 1961): 11-12 ((1, 2, 3, 6, 7, 9))

C15 FLUCKIGER, Otto: [Discography] in Jazz Statistics, No. 19/20 (1960): 1-16 ((1, 2, 3, 6, 7, 9))

C16 FLUCKIGER, Otto: Discography and soligraphy of Cab Calloway and his orchestra. Reinach, Switzer- land: [Jazz-Publications], 1960, ca. 30 pp. ((1, 2, 3, 4p, 4t, 6, 7, 9))

C17 POPA, Jay: Cab Calloway and his orchestra. Zephyrhills, FL: Joyce Music, 1976, 36, 10 leaves ((1, 2, 3, 4t, 6, 7))

CANDID label

C18 Candid & Transition in Swing Journal, Vol. 31, No. 6 (June 1977 special issue): 52-57 ((2, 7d))

C19 WILBRAHAM, Roy J.: Candid label listing in Discographical Forum, No. 11 (March 1969): 2, 7-8; No. 12 (May 1969): 7-8; No. 13 (July 1969): 3-5 ((2, 7))

CANE AND ABLE (musical group)

C20   MOHR, Kurt: Discographie de Cane & Able in Soul Bag, No. 20 (July-August 1972): 13-14 ((2, 3, 7))

CANNON, GUS, 1883-1979
       guitar, jug, vocal

C21   MILLER, Manfred: Frühe amerikanische Berufsmusikanten--1: Gus Cannon in Anschlaege, No. 4 (December 1978): 68-115 ((2, 3, 6, 7, 9))

CANNON'S JUG STOMPERS
       See also MEMPHIS JUG BAND (Allen, Walter C.)

C22   BAKKER, Dick M.: Cannon's Jug Stompers in Micrography, No. 8 (January, 1970): 11 ((7d))

CAPITOL label
       See also DAILY, PETE (Edwards, Ernie); DAMERON, TADD (Evans, Chris); ELLINGTON, DUKE--Transcriptions (Bakker, Dick M.: Duke Ellington's Capitol transcriptions); GOODMAN, BENNY (Benny Goodman ... some revisions); KENTON, STAN (Venudor, Pete, and Michael Sparke: Kenton on Capitol)

C23   NEU, Robert J.: Classics in jazz on Capitol in Discophile, No. 26 (October 1952): 5-8; additions and corrections in Discophile, No. 30 (June 1953): 5 ((2, 3, 7))

CAPLAN, DAVE
       leader

C24   MILLER, Gene: Canadian band records in Europe in IAJRC Journal, Vol. 6 (January 1973): 7-8; (summer 1973): 13-14 ((2))

CARL, RUDIGER
       tenor saxophone

C25   Discographie in Jazz Hot, No. 359 (March 1979): 24 [also of Hans Reichel] ((2))

CARMICHAEL, HOAGY, 1899-
       piano, composer

C26   VENABLES, Ralph: Hoagy Carmichael discography in Melody Maker, Vol. 25 (July 9, 1949): 11; (July 16,

1949): 11; (July 23, 1949): 11, and at least one other issue; additions and corrections in Melody Maker, Vol. 25 (September 3, 1949): 11 ((2, 7d))

CAROUSEL label
       See BOLLETINO, DANTE

CARR, IAN, 1933-
       trumpet

C27   Plattenhinweise in Jazz Podium, Vol. 25 (August 1976): 21 ((—))

C28   PRIESTLEY, Brian: Discography in Jazz Monthly, Vol. 12 (October 1966): 4-5; additions and corrections in Jazz Monthly, Vol. 11 (December 1966): 27; [from David GELLY] Vol. 12 (January 1967): 29 ((2, 7))

CARR, LEROY, 1905-1943
       piano, vocal

C29   BAKKER, Dick M.: Leroy Carr in Micrography, No. 8 (January 1970): 9 ((7d))

C30   BAKKER, Dick M.: Leroy Carr 1928-1935 in Micrography, No. 31 (1974?): 12 ((7d))

C31   HARRIS, H. Meunier: From the race lists--Leroy Carr in Jazz Notes (Australia), No. 64 (May 1946); additions and corrections from Ron DAVIES in Jazz Notes (Australia), No. 70 (January 1947): 17-19 ((2))

C32   McCARTHY, Albert J.: Leroy Carr in Record Changer, Vol. 6 (May 1947): 8 ((2, 3, 7))

C33   RANKIN, Bill: Leroy Carr in Jazz Reprints, Vol. 1, No. 2 (n.d.): 36-40 ((2, 3, 7))

CARROLL, ROBERT, ca. 1905-1952
       tenor saxophone
       See SAXOPHONE MUSIC (JAZZ) (Evensmo, Jan: The tenor saxophones of Henry Bridges ...)

CARTER, BENNY, 1907-
       alto saxophone, arranger
       See also HAWKINS, COLEMAN (Bakker, Dick M.: Coleman Hawkins and Benny Carter in Europe 1934-1939)

C34   Benny Carter in Swing Journal,
      Vol. 33 (June 1979): 222-227 ((2,
      7d))

C35   Discographie de Benny Carter
      (disques publiés en France) in
      Jazz Hot, No. 52 (February 1951):
      10 ((7d))

C36   JEPSEN, Jorgen Grunnet: Benny
      Carter diskografi 1949-1959 in
      Orkester Journalen, Vol. 27 (De-
      cember 1959): 56-57; Vol. 28
      (January 1960): 34; (February
      1960): 38-39 ((2, 3, 6, 7))

C37   Selected Carter discography in
      Down Beat, Vol. 44 (February 24,
      1977): 21 ((—))

      Arrangements

C38   BERGER, Edward: Benny Carter's
      arrangements; recordings by other
      artists in Journal of Jazz
      Studies, Vol. 5 (fall-winter
      1978): 36-80 ((1, 7d))

CARTER, BETTY, 1930-
      vocal
      See also PLEASURE, KING (Discog-
      raphy, King Pleasure & Betty
      Carter)

C39   Selected Carter discography in
      Down Beat, Vol. 43 (August 12,
      1976): 24 ((—))

C40   Selected Carter discography in
      Down Beat, Vol. 46 (May 3, 1979):
      14 ((—))

CARTER, BO
      See CHATMAN, BO

CARTER, CHARLIE
      See JACKSON, CHARLIE

CARTER, CLARENCE

C41   [[Discography in Soul Bag, No.
      2]]

CARTER, KENT, 1939-
      bass violin

C42   Discographie in Jazz Magazine
      (France), No. 262 (February
      1978): 31 ((—))

CARTER, LEROY
      piano, vocal

C43   McCARTHY, Albert J.: [Discogra-
      phy] in Discographical Forum, No.
      3 (September 1960): 8 ((3, 7))

CARTER, RON, 1937-
      bass violin

C44   [Discography of Ron Carter and
      Tony Williams] in Swing Journal,
      Vol. 31 (October 1977): 290-293
      ((2, 7d))

C45   Ron Carter in Swing Journal, Vol.
      29 (June 1975): 242-249 ((2, 7d))

C46   Selected Carter discography in
      Down Beat, Vol. 42 ((March 27,
      1975): 13 ((—))

CARY, DICK, 1916-
      trumpet

C47   Plattenhinweise in Jazz Podium,
      Vol. 25 (June 1976): 22 ((—))

CASEY BILL
      See WELDON, CASEY BILL

CASH, ALVIN

C48   MOHR, Kurt: Alvin Cash discogra-
      phy in Hot Buttered Soul, No. 13
      (December 1972): 10-11 ((3, 7))

CAT label

C49   GRENDYSA, Pete: Cat in R and B
      Magazine, Vol. 1 (November 1970-
      February 1971): 35-36 ((3, 5))

CBS SONY label
      See C B S SONY label

CELESTIN, OSCAR, 1884-1954
      trumpet

C50   Chronology of Celestin recordings
      in Jazzfinder, Vol. 1 (April
      1948): 13 ((2, 3, 7))

C51   Discography in Second Line, Vol.
      6 (January-February 1955): 11
      ((2, 3, 6, 7))

C52   HULME, George: Oscar "Papa"
      Celestin in Matrix, No. 47 (June
      1963): 3-5; additions and correc-
      tions in Matrix, No. 53 (June
      1964): 18 ((1, 2, 3, 6, 7))

CENTURY label

C53 Century originals in Discophile, No. 19 (August 1951): 8-9; additions and corrections in Discophile, No. 22 (February 1952): 11 ((2, 3, 7))

C54 The Century 3000 series in Matrix, No. 63 (February 1966): 4-6 ((—))

CERRI, FRANCO, 1926-
bass violin, guitar

C55 [[BARAZZETTA, Giuseppe: Discography in Musica Jazz, Vol. 16 (July 1960)]]

CETRA label (Italian)

C56 FRESIA, Enzo: Discografia: la serie "Jazz in Italy" della Cetra in Musica Jazz, Vol. 18 (November 1962): 47-48 ((2, 7))

CHA-PAKA-SHAWEES (musical group)

C57 HITE, Richard: Mini-discography number 1 in R and B Collector, Vol. 1 (January-February 1970): 5 ((2, 3, 6, 7))

CHAIX, HENRI, 1925-
piano

C58 WIDEROE, Arild: Discography in Coda, Vol. 9 (July-August 1970): 8; additions and corrections from Hans J. MAUERER in Jazz Bazaar, No. 5 (March 1970): 46 ((2, 7))

CHALOFF, SERGE, 1923-1957
baritone saxophone

C59 MOON, Pete: Serge Chaloff discography in Discographical Forum, No. 38 (1977) to No. 41 (1978?), various paginations; additions and corrections in Discographical Forum, No. 40 (spring 1978): 1-2; No. 41 (1978?): 20 ((1, 2, 3, 6, 7))

C60 MORGAN, Alun: Discography in Jazz Monthly, Vol. 3 (October 1957): 26-28, 31 ((1, 2, 3, 6, 7))

CHAMBERS, PAUL, 1935-1969
bass violin

C61 Discographie de Paul Chambers in Jazz Hot, No. 248 (March 1969): 35 ((2, 7))

C62 Discographie (enregistrements sous son nom) in Jazz Hot, No. 159 (November 1960): 21 ((2))

CHAMBLEE, EDDIE, 1920-
tenor saxophone

C63 MOHR, Kurt: Eddie Chamblee records in Jazz Statistics, No. 1 (April 1956): 3, 5, 7 ((2, 3, 7))

CHAMPION label

C64 ALLEN, Walter C.: Champion 50000 series in Jazz Journal, Vol. 11 (July 1958): 23-24; (August 1958): 6; (October 1958): 32 [to no. 50077] ((3))

C65 BLACKER, George: George Blacker's parade of Champions in Record Research, No. 169/170 (January 1980) to date, various paginations [No. 175/176 (September 1980) reached no. 15990, to be continued] ((3, 6))

CHANCE label
See also LITTLE WALTER (Rotante, Anthony)

C66 ROTANTE, Anthony: Chance and Sabre catalogues in Record Research, Vol. 3 (October-November 1957): 12 ((4p))

CHANDLER, GENE, 1940-
vocal

C67 BAKER, Cary: Discographies; Gene Chandler, the Duke of Earl in Blue Flame, No. 14 (n.d.): 10-11 ((2, 3))

CHARIOT label

C68 BRYANT, Steve: Chariot label listing in Hot Buttered Soul, No. 35 (November 1974): 4 ((3))

CHARLES, RAY, 1932-
piano, vocal

C69 MOHR, Kurt, and Marcel CHAUVARD: Discographie de Ray Charles in Jazz Hot, No. 176 (May 1962): 8-9; No. 177 (June 1962): 37; No. 178 (July-August 1962): 44, 46 ((2, 3, 6, 7))

C70 Ray Charles discography in Billboard, Vol. 78 (October 15, 1966): RC10 ((—))

C71   RITZ, David: Discography and
      notes in Brother Ray; Ray
      Charles' own story. New York:
      Dial [c1978], 318-340 ((—))

C72   RUPPLI, Michael: Discographie in
      Jazz Hot, No. 329 (July 1976):
      11 ((—))

C73   Selected Charles discography in
      Down Beat, Vol. 44 (May 5, 1977):
      15 ((—))

CHARLES, TEDDY (Theodore Charles Cohen),
      1928-
      vibraphone

C74   EDWARDS, Ernie: A "name" discogra-
      phy of Teddy Charles "New Direc-
      tions in Jazz" in Discophile, No.
      39 (December 1954): 8-9; additions
      and corrections in Discophile, No.
      40 (February 1955): 14 ((2, 3, 7))

CHARLESTON CHASERS

C75   BAKKER, Dick M.: Charleston
      Chasers 25-30 in Micrography, No.
      5 (August 1969): 5 ((7d))

C76   BAKKER, Dick M.: The Charleston
      Chasers 1925-31 in Micrography,
      No. 43 (March 1977): 4 ((7d))

CHARLIE PARKER label
      See EGMONT label

CHARMS (musical group)

C77   Charms discography in R and B
      Magazine, No. 9 (March 1972): 20
      ((—))

CHATMAN, BO (Armenter Chatmon),
      1893-1964
      guitar, violin, vocal

C78   BAKKER, Dick M.: Bo Carter in
      Micrography, No. 26 (1973): 11
      ((7d))

C79   MOORE, Dave: Discography and re-
      issue listing in Blues Magazine,
      Vol. 5 (June 1979): 19-22 ((—))

CHATMAN, PETER
      See MEMPHIS SLIM

CHECKER label
      See LITTLE WALTER (Rotante,
      Anthony)

CHENIER, CLIFTON, 1925-
      accordion, vocal

C80   LEADBITTER, Mike, and Chris
      STRACHWITZ: Clifton Chenier--a
      discography in Blues Unlimited,
      No. 25 (September 1965): 4-5 ((2,
      3, 7))

C81   LOBSTEIN, Patrick: Discographie
      de Clifton Chenier in Soul Bag,
      No. 71 (1979): 17-20 ((2, 3, 7))

C82   TANNER, George: Clifton Chenier:
      disco in Blues Life, No. 3 (1978);
      additions in Blues Life, No. 5
      (1979): 42 ((—))

CHENIER, MORRIS, 1929-
      guitar, vocal

C83   LEADBITTER, Mike: Big Morris
      Chenier discography in Blues Un-
      limited, No. 25 (September 1965):
      6 ((2, 3, 7))

CHERRY, DON, 1936-
      trumpet
      See also JAZZ MUSIC--Avant-Garde
      (Raben, Erik)

C84   [[Discography in Musica Jazz, Vol.
      27 (1971)]]

C85   Don Cherry discography in Swing
      Journal, Vol. 28 (April 1974):
      252-255 ((2, 7d))

C86   IOAKIMIDIS, Demetre: Leurs en-
      registrements [i.e., Don Cherry,
      Freddie Hubbard, Richard Williams]
      in his Trois trompettistes de la
      nouvelle vague in Jazz Hot, No.
      169 (October 1961): 25 ((—))

C87   RABEN, Erik: Diskofilspalten in
      Orkester Journalen, Vol. 34 (No-
      vember 1966): 21; (December 1966):
      31 ((2, 3, 7))

C88   RABEN, Erik: Don Cherry--1958-1964
      in Musica Jazz, Vol. 21 (February
      1965): 43; additions and correc-
      tions in Musica Jazz, Vol. 21
      (March 1965): 43 ((2, 3, 7))

C89   Selected Cherry discography in
      Down Beat, Vol. 42 (October 9,
      1975): 13 ((—))

C90   Selected Cherry discography in
      Down Beat, Vol. 45 (July 13,
      1978): 22 ((—))

CHESS label
      See also BLUES MUSIC (Guralnick,
      Peter)

C91   Chess numbers 1425 to 1945 in
      Blue Flame, No. 14 (n.d.): 15
      ((—))

C92   [[HEERMAN VAN VASS, A.J.: De Chess
      LP's in Boogie Woogie & Blues
      Collector part 8 in No. 30/31
      (August 1973) ((—))]]

C93   [[RUPPLI, Michael. Chess label
      listing in Hot Buttered Soul, No.
      11 (October 1972) to No. 14 (Janu-
      ary 1973), various paginations]]

CHESTER, BOB, 1908–
      leader

C94   GARROD, Charles: Bob Chester and
      his orchestra/Teddy Powell and his
      orchestra. Spotswood, NJ: Joyce
      Music, 1973, 1, 15, 7, 1, 9, 4
      leaves ((1, 2, 3, 4t, 6, 7))

CHI-LITES (musical group)

C95   MOHR, Kurt: The Chi-lites in Soul
      Bag, No. 45 (January 1975): 21-22;
      additions and corrections in Soul
      Bag, No. 46 (February 1975): 6
      ((2, 3, 7))

CHIAROSCURO label

C96   LAING, Ralph: The specialist la-
      bels; a listing--Chiaroscuro in
      Jazz Journal, Vol. 29 (June 1976):
      22-23 ((2, 7))

CHICAGO FOOTWARMERS

C97   BAKKER, Dick M.: Chicago Foot-
      warmers in Micrography, No. 3
      (May 1969): 4 ((7d))

CHICAGO STYLE JAZZ
      See JAZZ MUSIC--Chicago Style

CHIEF label

C98   BAKER, Cary: Chief label listing
      in Hot Buttered Soul, No. 11
      (October 1972): 11-12 ((3))

CHISHOLM, GEORGE, 1915–
      trombone

C99   [[CLUTTEN, Michael N.: A George
      Chisholm discography. Leicester,
      England: 1978, 50 pp. Supplement
      by GALLICHAN, Syd R.: Supplement
      one, 1980, 13 pp.]]

C100 GALLIMORE, Denis, and Syd R.
      GALLICHAN: Chisholm discography in
      Discography (January 15, 1944):
      15-16 ((7, 9))

CHOCOLATE DANDIES (musical group)

C101 DELAUNAY, Charles: Extraits
      empruntés à "Essais de discogra-
      phie hot" in Jazz Hot, No. 3 (May-
      June 1935): 4-5 ((2, 3))

CHOCOLATE KIDDIES (musical revue)

C102 ENGLUND, Bjorn: Discography of
      recordings of tunes from Chocolate
      Kiddies in Storyville, No. 62
      (December 1975-January 1976): 50
      ((—))

CHRISTENSEN, JON, 1943–
      drums

C103 Jon Christensen selected discogra-
      phy in Jazz Forum (Poland), No.
      47 (1977): 45 ((—))

CHRISTIAN, CHARLIE, 1916-1942
      guitar

C104 BAKKER, Dick M.: Charlie Christian
      with Benny Goodman sextet/septet
      in Micrography, No. 35 (March
      1975): 4, 9 ((6, 7d))

C105 CALLIS, John: Charlie Christian
      1939-1941; a discography. [London:
      Tony Middleton, c1978], 41 pp.
      ((1, 2, 3, 6, 7))

C106 Discographie française de Charlie
      Christian in Jazz Magazine
      (France), No. 27 (May 1957): 25
      ((—))

C107 [Discography] in booklet with
      [phonodisc], CBS-Sony SOPZ 4-6.
      Tokyo: CBS-Sony [c1972], 8-11
      ((1, 2, 3, 6, 7))

C108 EVENSMO, Jan: The guitars of
      Charlie Christian, Robert Normann,
      Oscar Aleman (in Europe). [Hosle,
      Norway: 1976], 29, 4, 6 pp. (Jazz
      solography series, Vol. 4) ((1, 2,
      3, 6, 7, 9))

C109 HOEFER, George: Charlie Christian
      on records in Down Beat, Vol. 28
      (November 9, 1961): 40-42 ((2, 3,
      7))

C110 JEPSEN, Jorgen Grunnet: Charlie
      Christian diskografi in Orkester
      Journalen, Vol. 29 (December 1961):

50; Vol. 30 (January 1962): 34;
(February 1962): 34 ((2, 3, 6, 7))

C111 JEPSEN, Jorgen Grunnet: Discographie Charlie Christian in Les
Cahiers du Jazz, No. 3 (May
1960?): 108-112 ((1, 2, 3, 6, 7))

C112 [[TERCINET, ALAIN: Discographie:
Charlie Christian in Jazz Hot, No.
355 (November 1978): 25-29]]

CINQ BOOGIES (musical group)

C113 RADO, Alexandre: Les Cinq Boogies
in Jazz Hot, No. 250 (May 1969):
31 ((2, 3, 7))

CIRCLE label
See LEWIS, GEORGE (Hulme, George);
MORTON, JELLY ROLL (Pautasso,
Oscar)

CIRCLE label (Australian)

C114 MITCHELL, F. J.: Circle & Blue
Star in Australia in Matrix, No.
53 (June 1964): 14 ((3))

CIRILLO, WALLY, 1927–
piano

C115 EYLE, Wim van: Wie was Wally
Cirillo? in Jazz Press, No. 42
(August 5, 1977): 8; additions
and corrections in Jazz Press, No.
44 (October 1, 1977): 6 ((2, 7))

CJ Label
See C J label

CLAES, JOHNNY
trumpet

C116 [[VISSER, Hein: Discography in
his Johnny Claes & the Hot Sparts
in Doctor Jazz, No. 84 (June 1978):
20-23]]

CLAPP, SUNNY, 1899–
leader

C117 RANDOLPH, John: A Sunny Clapp
discography in Jazz Journal, Vol.
7 (December 1954): 16; additions
and corrections in WHYATT, Bert:
Some notes on the Sunny Clapp
discography in Jazz Journal, Vol.
8 (September 1955): 8 ((2, 3, 7))

CLARINET MUSIC (JAZZ)

C118 TEPPERMAN, Barry: Suggested
listening in his Little big horn;
an assessment of the clarinet and
baritone saxophone in the new jazz
in Coda, Vol. 9 (May-June 1970):
11 ((—))

CLARION label

C119 The Clarion checklist; a numerical
sequence of the Clarion label from
5001-C to 5477-C in Discographer,
Vol. 2 (second quarter 1970): 2-83
to 2-110 ((3))

CLARK, SONNY (Conrad Yeatis Clark),
1931-1963
piano

C120 GARDNER, Mark: Sonny Clark in Jazz
Monthly, Vol. 13 (February 1967):
21-22; (March 1967): 28-30; (April
1967): 28-29; additions and corrections in Jazz Monthly, Vol. 13
(June 1967): 28; (September 1967):
31 ((2, 3, 6, 7))

CLARKE, KENNY, 1914–
drums
See also CLARKE–BOLAND BAND

C121 HOEFER, George: Kenny Clarke's
early recordings in Down Beat,
Vol. 30 (March 28, 1963): 23 (to
1941) ((2, 3, 7))

C122 RABEN, Erik: Diskofilspalten in
Orkester Journalen, Vol. 32 (June
1969): 17 ((2, 7))

CLARKE, STANLEY, 1951–
bass violin

C123 Discographie de Stanley Clarke in
Jazz, Blues & Co., No. 36/37 (January-February 1980): 13 ((—))

C124 Selected Clarke discography in
Down Beat, Vol. 42 (March 27,
1975): 15 ((—))

CLARKE–BOLAND BAND

C125 FRIDLAND, Hans: [Discography] in
Orkester Journalen, Vol. 37
(September 1969): 9 ((—))

C126 RABEN, Erik: Diskofilspalten in
Orkester Journalen, Vol. 37
(June 1969): 17 ((2, 7))

C127 SCHULZ, Jurgen: Kenny Clarke, Francy Boland and the bands; a discography in Jazz Bazaar, No. 4 (December 1969) to No. 6 (June 1970); No. 9 (March 1971) to No. 11 (September 1971), various paginations ((1, 2, 7))

CLASSICAL MUSIC--INFLUENCE ON JAZZ
See also SERIAL MUSIC AND JAZZ

C128 BROWN, Robert L.: Selective annotated discography in his A study of influences from Euro-American art music on certain types of jazz with analyses and recital of selected demonstrative compositions. Dr. Ed. dissertation, Columbia University Teachers College, 1974 (available from University Microfilms, Ann Arbor, MI: order no. 75-28928), 260-268 ((9))

C129 BROWN, Robert L.: Selective annotated discography in Journal of Jazz Studies, Vol. 3 (spring 1976): 32-35 ((9))

C130 STUESSY, Clarence Joseph: Discography in his The confluence of jazz and classical music from 1950 to 1970. Ph.D. dissertation, Eastman School of Music at University of Rochester, 1977 (available from University Microfilms, Ann Arbor, MI; order no. 78-5144), 503-512 ((9))

CLAY, OTIS
vocal

C131 MOHR, Kurt: Otis Clay in Soul Bag, No. 45 (January 1975): 23-24; additions and corrections in Soul Bag, No. 46 (February 1975): 6; No. 51 (January 1976): 32 ((2, 3, 7))

CLAY, SONNY (William Rogers Clay), 1899-
drums

C132 Chronology of Sonny Clay recordings in Jazzfinder, Vol. 1 (September 1948): 3-4 ((2, 3, 7p))

CLAYTON, BUCK (Wilbur Clayton), 1911-
trumpet

C133 [[JEPSEN, Jorgen Grunnet: Buck Clayton 1949-1957. Copenhagen: 1957, 15 leaves]]

C134 RUSSELL, Peter: Buck Clayton: a discography of English releases currently available in Jazz Journal, Vol. 12 (September 1959): 5-9; additions and corrections from D.W. SAWYER in Jazz Journal, Vol. 12 (October 1959): 35 ((2, 3, 6, 7))

C135 TOLLARA, Gianni, and Erik RABEN: Discografia: Buck Clayton in Musica Jazz, Vol. 22 (July 1966): 45-47 [1953-1964 recordings] ((2, 7))

CLAYTON, DOCTOR (Peter Joe Clayton), 1898-1947
vocal

C136 Doctor Clayton & related recordings on microgroove in Talking Blues, No. 6 (July-September 1977): 14 ((—))

CLEARWATER, EDDY, 1935-
guitar, vocal

C137 CHOISNEL, Emmanuel, and Kurt MOHR: Discographie de Eddie Clearwater in Soul Bag, No. 38 (May 1974): 27 ((2, 3, 7))

CLEF label
See GILLESPIE, DIZZY (Jepsen, Jorgen Grunnet: Dizzy Gillespie diskografi pa Clef-Norgran-Verve); GRANZ, NORMAN; YOUNG, LESTER (Morgan, Alun)

CLEIGHTON, PETER
See CLAYTON, DOCTOR

CLESS, ROD, 1907-1944
clarinet

C138 Discografia di Rod Cless in Jazz di Ieri e di Oggi, Vol. 2 (June 1960): 11-12 ((2, 7))

C139 MORGAN, Alun: Rod Cless; a personal view in Jazz & Blues, Vol. 1 (May 1971): 7-10 ((2, 3, 6, 7))

C140 TEMPLE, Rita: Rod Cless discography in Jazz Record (US), No. 28 (January 1945): 18 ((2))

CLINTON, LARRY, 1909-
leader

C141 GARROD, Charles: Larry CLinton
and his orchestra. Spotswood,
NJ: Joyce Music, 1973, 1, 19, 3
leaves ((1, 2, 3, 4t, 6, 7))

CLOVERS (musical group)

C142 GOLDBERG, Marv: The Clovers in
Rhythm & Blues Train, Vol. 1
(August 1964): 3 ((7d))

COASTERS (musical group)

C143 Discography in MILLAR, Bill: The
Coasters. London: Star Books,
1975, 189-204 ((3, 7))

C144 ROHNISCH, Claus: Coasters: en Fard
genom Vokalgrupp-Varlden Cireron
in Jefferson, No. 22 (1973): 8-14
((3, 7))

COBB, ARNETT, 1918-
tenor saxophone

C145 DEMEUSY, Bertrand, and Otto
FLUCKIGER: Arnett "the wild man of
the tenor sax" Cobb. Basel: Jazz-
Publications, 1962, 21 pp. ((1, 2,
3, 6, 7, 9))

C146 PANASSIÉ, Hugues: Arnett Cobb et
son orchestre in Revue du Jazz,
No. 6 (June-July 1949): 11 ((1,
2))

COBB, JUNIE, ca. 1896-
piano

C147 DÜRR, CLAUS-UWE: Junie Cobb; a
discography in Matrix, No. 56 (December 1964): 10-12; additions and
corrections in Matrix, No. 68
(December 1966): 15 ((2, 3, 6, 7))

C148 DÜRR, CLAUS-UWE: Junie C. Cobb in
Record Research, No. 75 (April
1966): 4-5; additions and corrections in Record Research, No. 82
(March 1967): 10; No. 83 (June
1967): 5, 9 ((2, 3, 6, 7))

COBBS, WILLIE, 1940-
guitar, harmonica, vocal

C149 LEADBITTER, Mike, and Bruce
BROMBERG: Willie Cobbs; an exploratory discography in Blues
Unlimited, No. 31 (March 1966):
15 ((2, 3, 7p))

COBHAM, BILLY, 1944-
drums

C150 Selected Cobham discography in
Down Beat, Vol. 42 (December 4,
1975): 13 ((—))

C151 STIX, John: Billy Cobham in Different Drummer, Vol. 1 (November
1974): 15 ((—))

COBRA label
See also ABCO label

COHN, AL, 1925-
tenor saxophone

C152 Al & Zoot in Swing Journal, Vol.
32 (October 1978): 308-311 ((2,
7d))

C153 Selected Cohn discography in Down
Beat, Vol. 47 (April 1980): 28
((—))

COLD IN CHINA (tune title)
See BLUES MUSIC (Groom, Bob)

COLE, COZY (William Randolph Cole),
1909-

C154 Discography of Cozy Cole. Basel:
Jazz-Publications, 1962, 8 pp.
(Discographical notes, Vol. 3)
((2, 3, 6, 7))

COLE, NAT "KING," 1917-1965
piano, vocal

C155 Complete discography of Nat King
Cole on Capitol Records in COLE,
Maria: Nat King Cole; an intimate
biography. New York: Morrow, 1971
(also London: W. H. Allen, 1972),
163-184 ((7d))

C156 HALL, George I.: Nat "King" Cole,
a jazz discography featuring the
Nat Cole trio. Laurel, MD: Jazz
Discographies Unlimited, 1965,
18 leaves (Spotlight series, Vol.
1) ((1, 2, 3, 6, 7))

C157 [[Teubig, Klaus: Nat "King" Cole
Discographie, 1936-1953 Hamburg:
1964, 16 pp. ((1))]]

COLEMAN, BILL, 1904-
trumpet

C158 CHILTON, John: Bill Coleman on record; a discography. London: 1966, 18 pp. ((2, 3, 6, 7))

C159 COLLER, Derek: Bill Coleman--discography in Jazzology (UK), No. 1 new series (January 1946): 4-7 ((2, 7))

C160 DELAUNAY, Charles: Discographie de Bill Coleman (extraits empruntés à "Essai de discographie hot") in Jazz Hot, No. 7 (April 1936): 4 ((—))

C161 Discographie Bill Coleman (disques parus en France) in Jazz Hot, No. 51 (January 1951): 24-25 ((2, 3, 7d))

C162 EVENSMO, Jan: The trumpets of Bill Coleman 1929-1945, Frankie Newton. [Hosle, Norway: 1978], 21, 21 pp. (Jazz solography series, Vol. 9) ((1, 2, 3, 6, 7, 9))

COLEMAN, GEORGE, 1935-
tenor saxophone

C163 Selected George Coleman discography in Down Beat, Vol. 47 (March 1980): 27 ((—))

COLEMAN, JESSE
See MONKEY JOE

COLEMAN, ORNETTE, 1930-
alto saxophone
See also JAZZ MUSIC--AVANT-GARDE (Raben, Erik)

C164 Current discography in Different Drummer, Vol. 1 (January 1975): 27 ((—))

C165 Les faces d'Ornette in Jazz Magazine (France), No. 250 (December 1976): 20-22 ((2, 7))

C166 GICKING, Jim: Ornette Coleman's discography in booklet with [phonodisc] Artists House AH6. New York: Artists House Records, c1979, unpaged ((1))

C167 Ornette Coleman in Swing Journal, Vol. 33 (October 1979): 232-235 ((2, 7d))

C168 [[Ornette Coleman Diskografie in Jazz Podium, Vol. 27 (September 1978): 13-15]]

C169 RABEN, Erik: Ornette Coleman on Atlantic in Discographical Forum, No. 22 (January 1971): 19 ((3, 7))

C170 RUPPLI, Michel: Discographie d'Ornette Coleman in Jazz Hot, No. 334 (February 1977): 24-25 ((1, 2, 3, 7))

C171 Selected Coleman discography in Down Beat, Vol. 45 (October 5, 1978): 19 ((—))

C172 [[STIASSI, RUGGERO: [Discography] in Musica Jazz, Vol. 23 (January 1967)]]

C173 WALKER, Malcolm: Ornette Coleman in Jazz Monthly, Vol. 12 (May 1966): 24-25; additions and corrections in Jazz Monthly, Vol. 12 (July 1966): 15; Vol. 13 (May 1967): 28 ((2, 7))

C174 WILD, David, and Michael CUSCUNA: Ornette Coleman 1958-1979; a discography. Ann Arbor, MI: Wildmusic, 1980, 76 pp. ((1, 2, 3, 4p, 4r, 4t, 6, 7, 8, 9))

COLLETTE, BUDDY (William Marcell Collette), 1921-
saxophones

C175 [[BARAZZETTA, Giuseppe: [Discography of Italian recordings] in Musica Jazz, Vol. 17 (May 1961)]]

COLLIE, MAX, 1939-
trombone

C176 HACHENBERG, Friedrich: Max Collie on LPs in Hot Jazz Info, No. 12/75 (1975): 11 ((—))

COLLINS, ALBERT, 1932-
guitar, vocal

C177 Albert Collins discography in Blues Unlimited, No. 135/136 (July-December 1979): 11 ((2, 3, 6, 7))

C178 [[Discography in Soul Bag, No. 6]]

COLLINS, LEE, 1901-1960
trumpet

C179 ALLEN, Walter C.: Lee Collins discography in Hot Notes, Vol. 2 (March 1947): 3-4 ((2, 3, 6, 7))

C180 RUST, Brian A. L., and Frank J. GILLIS: Discography in COLLINS, Lee: Oh, didn't he ramble; the life story of Lee Collins as told to Mary Collins, ed. by Frank J. Gillis and John W. Miner. [Urbana, IL: Univ. of Illinois Pr., c1974], 141-147 ((1, 2, 3, 6, 7))

COLLINS, ROGER
vocal

C181 CHOISNEL, Emmanuel: Roger Collins
discography in Soul Bag, No. 22/23
(January-February 1973): 30 ((2, 3,
7))

COLT label
See C J label

COLTRANE, JOHN, 1926-1967
tenor and soprano saxophones
See also ADDERLEY, JULIAN (Jepsen,
Jorgen Grunnet)

C182 DAVIS, Brian: John Coltrane discography. London: 1976, 43, 6
leaves ((1, 2, 3, 6, 7))

C182 DAVIS, Brian: John Coltrane discography. 2d ed. London: 1976, 58,
6 leaves ((1, 2, 3, 4p, 4t, 6, 7))

C184 FRESIA, Enzo: John Coltrane su
Impulse in Musica Jazz, Vol. 20
(February 1964): 42 ((2, 3, 7))

C185 GODDET, Laurent: Discographie/2;
les enregistrements privés in Jazz
Hot, No. 265 (October 1970): 24-
25 ((1, 2, 7))

C186 JEPSEN, Jorgen Grunnet: A discography of John Coltrane. Copenhagen:
Knudsen [c1969], 35 leaves; additions and corrections in Orkester
Journalen, Vol. 37 (December 1969):
20 ((1, 2, 3, 7))

C187 JEPSEN, Jorgen Grunnet: John
Coltrane; a complete discography
in Down Beat Music 68 (13th yearbook): 106-113 ((2, 3, 6, 7))

C188 JEPSEN, Jorgen Grunnet: John
Coltrane diskografi in Orkester
Journalen, Vol. 26 (March 1958):
42; (April 1958): 46-47 ((2, 3,
7d))

C189 John Coltrane discography in Swing
Journal, Vol. 34 (May 1980 special
issue): 198-215 ((1, 2, 7d))

C190 KORTEWEG, Simon: Discografie John
Coltrane in Jazz Wereld, No. 14
(September-October 1967): 33-35;
additions and corrections in his
Anvulling op discografie John
Coltrane in Jazz Wereld, No. 16
(January 1968): 23; from F. W.
NAUJOKS, No. 19 (August 1968): 3
((2, 7))

C191 NORRIS, John W.: John Coltrane on
record; a discography in Coda, Vol.
8 (May-June 1968): 1D-12D (also

published separately; Toronto:
Coda, 1968, 12 pp.) ((2, 3, 6, 7))

C192 RABEN, Erik: Coltrane on Atlantic
in Discographical Forum, No. 23
(March 1971): 9-10; No. 25 (July
1971): 19 ((3, 7))

C193 RABEN, Erik: Diskofilspalten in
Orkester Journalen, Vol. 35 (October 1967) to Vol. 36 (January
1968); Vol. 38 (June 1970), various paginations, in 5 parts ((2,
3, 7))

C194 RABEN, Erik: Diskofilspalten in
Orkester Journalen, Vol. 39 (February 1971): 15 [private recordings
1961-1965] ((1, 2, 7))

C195 [[RISSI, Mathias: John Coltrane:
discography. Adliswil, Switzerland: 1977, 39 pp.]]

C196 Selected Coltrane discography in
Down Beat, Vol. 46 (July 12, 1979):
20-21 ((—))

C197 [[STIASSI, Ruggero: [Discography]
in Musica Jazz, Vol. 24 (March
1968) to (April 1968)]]

C198 STIASSI, Ruggero: John Coltrane
discography on Impulse in Change,
No. 2 (spring-summer 1966): 69-72
((2, 7d))

C199 [[SWOBODA, Hubert: The John
Coltrane discographie 1949-1967.
Stuttgart: Modern Jazz Series,
1968, 40 pp.]]

C200 TERCINET, Alain: Discographie de
John Coltrane in Jazz Hot, No.
339/340 (July-August 1977): 36-
42 ((1, 2, 3, 7))

C201 THOMAS, J. C.: Discography in his
Chasin' the Trane; the music and
mystique of John Coltrane. Garden
City, NY: Doubleday, 1975 (also
New York: DaCapo [1976]), 233-252
((2, 7d))

C202 WALKER, Malcolm: John Coltrane in
Jazz Monthly, Vol. 12 (August
1966) to (November 1966), various
paginations, in 4 parts [Erik RABEN
added as author in later issues];
additions and corrections in Jazz
Monthly, Vol. 13 (December 1967):
29; (January 1968): 28 ((2, 3, 6,
7))

C203 WILD, David: The recordings of
John Coltrane; a discography. Ann
Arbor, MI: Wildmusic [1977], 72,
16 pp.; additions and corrections
in his Supplements. Ann Arbor, MI:
Wildmusic, 1977-1979, 3 v. ((1, 2,

3, 6, 7, 8, 9)); supplements add ((4p))

C204 WILD, David: The recordings of John Coltrane; a discography. 2d ed. Ann Arbor, MI: Wildmusic [1979]; additions and corrections in his irregular serial Disc-ribe, 1980– ((1, 2, 3, 4p, 4t, 6, 7, 8, 9))

C205 WINTHER-RASMUSSEN, Nils: John Coltrane--private recordings in Discographical Forum, No. 28 (January 1972) to No. 30 (1972), various paginations ((1, 2, 7, 9))

COLUMBIA label
See also ELLINGTON, DUKE (Bakker, Dick M.: Duke Ellington on Columbia/Okeh/Harmony 1927-1930) and (Bakker, Dick M.: Ellington Brunswick-Voc-Col-listing 1926-35); GOODMAN, BENNY (Benny Goodman...some revisions...); GOOFUS FIVE; JACKSON, MAHALIA (Chmura, Helene F.); LUNCEFORD, JIMMIE (Bakker, Dick M.: Jimmie Lunceford Voc/Col 33-40); OKEH label (Rust, Brian); SPECIAL EDITIONS label; WALLER, FATS (Bakker, Dick M.: Thomas "Fats" Waller); WHITEMAN, PAUL (Bakker, Dick M.: Whiteman's Columbia's [sic] 1928-30)

C206 ALLEN, Walter C.: The Columbia "Personal" label in Jazz Journal, Vol. 11 (December 1958): 34 ((2, 3, 6, 7d))

C207 BEDOIAN, James, ed.: Columbia "D" series recordings in The Discographer, Vol. 1 (1967) to Vol. 2 (second quarter 1970), various paginations ((3, 4p))

C208 BROOKS, Tim: Columbia acoustic matrix series 19100 in Record Research, No. 137/138 (February-March 1976) to date, most issues, various paginations ((3))

C209 CHMURA, Helene F. Some oddments on Columbia in Discophile, No. 56 (October 1957): 4, 8 ((2, 3, 7))

C210 COLTON, Bob, and Len KUNSTADT: Columbia tests--research in Record Research Supplement, No. 11 (February 21, 1959): 1-2 ((3, 6))

C211 DAVIS, John, and G. F. GRAY-CLARKE: Columbia race section in Jazz Magazine (UK), Vol. 3, No. 2 (n.d.) to Vol. 3, No. 4 (n.d.), various paginations (maybe also in other issues) ((—))

C212 DAVIS, John, and G. F. GRAY-CLARKE: New Orleans jazz--Columbia New Orleans recordings in Hot Notes, Vol. 2 (May-June 1947): 15-16; (July-August 1947): 12-15; (October 1947): 24-25 ((3, 7d))

C213 DIXON, Robert M. W.: The Columbia 30,000 series in Matrix, No. 35/36 (September 1961): 3-17; additions and corrections in Matrix, No. 45 (February 1963): 9-12; No. 49 (October 1963): 14 ((3))

C214 MAHONY, Daniel L.: The Columbia 13/14000-D series; a numerical listing. Stanhope, NJ: Walter C. Allen, c1961, 80 pp. (Record Handbook, No. 1) ((2, 3, 4p, 4t, 5, 6, 7, 8))

C215 MAHONY, Daniel L.: The Columbia 13/14000-D series; a numerical listing. 2d rev. ed. Highland Park, NJ: Walter C. Allen, 1966, c1961, 80 pp. (Record handbook, No. 1) ((2, 3, 4p, 4t, 5, 6, 7, 8))

C216 MAHONY, Daniel L.: The Columbia 18000D and 56000D series in Matrix, No. 37 (November 1961): 16-17 ((3, 6, 7d))

COLUMBIA label (British)

C217 FRY, John, and Peter SEAGO: English Columbia "Super" Swing Series in R.S.V.P., No. 9 (February 1966) to No. 11 (April 1966), various paginations ((3, 6, 7d))

C218 HAYES, Jim: English Columbia CB 1 series. Liverpool: Discographical Workshop, c1968, 37, iii pp. ((3, 4r, 6, 7))

C219 HAYES, Jim: English Columbia FB1000 series. Liverpool: 1969, 24 pp. ((4r))

COLYER, KEN, 1928-
trumpet
See also CRANE RIVER JAZZ BAND

C220 HULME, George: A discography of Ken Colyer in Matrix, No. 21 (January 1959): 3-13; additions and corrections in Matrix, No. 29/30 (August 1960): 34 ((1, 2, 3, 6, 7))

C221 [[REDDIHOUGH, John: Ken Colyer; a biography, appreciation, record survey and discography. London: National Jazz Federation [1958], 20 pp.]]

COMBELLE, ALIX, 1912–
    tenor saxophone

C222 MOHR, Kurt: The Vogue recordings
    of Alix Combelle in Discophile,
    No. 44 (October 1955): 6–7, 11
    ((2, 3, 7))

COMMODORE label

C223 DUTTON, Frank: Commodore "Star-
    maker" series in Jazz Journal,
    Vol. 15 (November 1962): 34
    ((3))

C224 DUTTON, Frank: Commodore 10-in.
    78 r.p.m. series in Jazz Journal,
    Vol. 13 (January 1960) to (April
    1960); (June 1960); (October 1960),
    various paginations, in 6 parts;
    additions and corrections in Jazz
    Journal, Vol. 14 (April 1961): 25;
    (December 1961): 41–42 ((2, 3,
    6, 7))

COMPO CORPORATION labels (Canadian)

C225 ROBERTSON, Alex: Canadian Compo
    numericals. Montreal: 1978, v,
    82 leaves ((3, 6))

CONDON, EDDIE, 1905–1973
    guitar

C226 BAKKER, Dick M.: Eddie Condon
    1929–1933 in Micrography, No. 25
    (March 1973): 5; No. 26 (1973): 1
    ((7d))

C227 KELLER, Willem: Discografie van
    Eddie Condon's eerste opnamen in
    Doctor Jazz, No. 61 (July–August
    1973): 18–19 ((2, 3, 6, 7))

C228 RIPPIN, John W.: Eddie Condon—
    Armed Forces Radio Service tran-
    scriptions; a draft discography in
    Matrix, No. 6 (May 1955): 3–7; ad-
    ditions and corrections in Matrix,
    No. 8 (September 1955): 3; No. 18
    (July 1958): 19; No. 66/67 (Sep-
    tember 1966): 28–29 ((1, 2, 7))

C229 SWINGLE, John: The Chicago bands:
    Eddie Condon on records, an infor-
    mal discography in CONDON, Eddie:
    We called it music; a generation
    of jazz. New York: Holt [c1947],
    299–328 (also Westport, CT: Green-
    wood Press, 19?? [c1947], same
    pagination; and pages 265–281 in:
    London: Peter Davies, 1948; Lon-
    don: Jazz Book Club, 1956; pos-
    sibly also in (pagination unknown)
    German translation Jazz—wir

nanntens Musik. Munich: Nymphen-
burger, 1960) ((2, 4p, 7))

C230 WHYATT, Bert: Eddie Condon—a
    discography in Jazz Notes (Aus-
    tralia), No. 91 (March 1949): 3–
    10 ((1, 2, 3, 6, 7))

CONFREY, ZEZ, 1895–
    composer, piano

C231 JASEN, David A.: Discography in
    Rag Times, Vol. 5 (September
    1971): 5 ((—))

C232 JASEN, David A.: Zez Confrey,
    creator of the novelty rag; prep-
    aratory research in Record
    Research, No. 111 (July 1971): 5
    ((3, 5, 6))

CONNORS, NORMAN, 1947–
    drums

C233 Selected Connors discography in
    Down Beat, Vol. 42 (March 13,
    1975): 19 ((—))

CONSTELLATION label

C234 MOHR, Kurt: Constellation label
    listing in Soul Bag, No. 66/67
    (March–April 1978): 11 ((3, 5))

COOK, J. LAWRENCE
    piano
    See WALLER, FATS—PIANO ROLLS
    (Montgomery, Mike)

COOKIE AND HIS CUPCAKES

C235 LEADBITTER, Mike: The southern
    blues singers; Cookie and his Cup-
    cakes; discography in Blues Un-
    limited, No. 7 (December 1963):
    11; additions and corrections in
    Blues Unlimited, No. 12 (June
    1964): suppl–5 ((2, 3, 7))

COON-SANDERS ORCHESTRA

C236 COLTON, Bob, and Len KUNSTADT:
    Coon Sanders discography in Record
    Research, Vol. 3 (June–July 1957):
    4; additions and corrections in
    Record Research Bulletin, No. 3
    ((3, 6, 7))

C237 RETTBURG, Harvey: Coon-Sanders
    discography in Second Line, Vol.
    12 (March–April 1962): 20, 22
    ((—))

COOPER, LITTLE SONNY, 1926–
    harmonica, vocal

C238 KENT, Don: Little Sonny Cooper in
    Blues Unlimited, No. 30 (February
    1966): 21 ((3))

COPELAND, MARTHA
    vocal

C239 DAVIS, John, and G. F. GRAY-CLARKE:
    Martha Copeland: a draft discog-
    raphy in Melody Maker, Vol. 26
    (July 8, 1950): 9 ((2, 3, 7d))

COREA, CHICK (Armando Anthony Corea),
    1941–

C240 Chick Corea in Swing Journal, Vol.
    32 (June 1978): 290-297 ((2, 7d))

C241 [Discography] in ENDRESS, Gudrun:
    Gluck des Augenblicks-Forever;
    gesprach mit Chick Corea in Jazz
    Podium, Vol. 23 (June 1974): 21
    ((—))

C242 Selected Corea discography in
    Down Beat, Vol. 43 (October 21,
    1976): 13 ((—))

CORONA DANCE ORCHESTRA (pseud.)

C243 BADROCK, Arthur: The Corona Dance
    Orchestra in Collecta, No. 10 (May-
    June 1970): 17-22; additions and
    corrections from Fred DREW in Col-
    lecta, No. 11 (July-August 1970):
    2 ((3))

CORYELL, LARRY, 1943–
    guitar

C244 Larry Coryell in Swing Journal,
    Vol. 34 (March 1980): 172-175 ((2,
    7d))

C245 Selected Coryell discography in
    Down Beat, Vol. 42 (January 30,
    1975): 18 ((—))

C246 Selected Coryell discography in
    Down Beat, Vol. 43 (February 26,
    1976): 13 ((—))

C247 Selected Larry Coryell discography
    in Down Beat, Vol. 47 (June 1980):
    21 ((—)

COSMOPOLITAN label
    See BOLLETINO, DANTE

COSTA, EDDIE, 1930-1962
    piano, vibraphone

C248 VINCENT, Don: Eddie Costa in Jazz
    Journal, Vol. 25 (July 1972): 7;
    additions and corrections in Jazz
    Journal, Vol. 25 (September 1972):
    13 ((2, 7d))

COTTON, JAMES, 1935–
    harmonica, vocal

C249 CHAUVARD, Marcel; Jacques DEMETRE;
    and Neil PATERSON: James Cotton;
    notes and discography in Blues Un-
    limited, No. 6 (November 1963): 5
    ((2, 3, 7))

C250 James Cotton in Blues Unlimited
    Collectors Classics, No. 8 (July
    1965): 9 ((2, 3))

COTTON PICKERS
    See JAZZ MUSIC (Venables, Ralph
    G.V.)

COUNTRY JIM (Jim Bledsoe)
    guitar, vocal

C251 HANSEN, Barry: Country Jim dis-
    cography in R and B Magazine, No.
    8 (fall 1971): 14 ((2, 3, 7))

COURBOIS, PIERRE, 1940–
    drums

C252 EYLE, Wim van: Pierre Courbois
    discografie in Jazz Press, No. 18
    (May 12, 1976): 8; No. 19 (May 26,
    1976): 11; No. 20 (June 9, 1976):
    5 ((2, 7))

COUSIN JOE (Pleasant Joseph), 1907–
    piano, vocal

C253 MOHR, Kurt: A Cousin Joe discog-
    raphy in Discophile, No. 11 (April
    1950): 7-8; additions and correc-
    tions in Discophile, No. 12 (June
    1950): 8 ((2, 3, 7d))

COUSIN LEROY (Leroy Rozier)
    guitar, vocal

C254 LEADBITTER, Mike: Cousin Leroy in
    Blues Unlimited, No. 37 (October
    1966): 9 ((2, 3, 7))

COVAY, DON, 1938–
    vocal

C255 MOHR, Kurt: Discographie de Don
    Covay in Soul Bag, No. 35 (Feb-
    ruary 1974): 15-19; additions and

corrections in Soul Bag, No. 38
(May 1974): 46; No. 45 (January
1975): 34 ((2, 3, 7))

COX, IDA, 1896-1967
vocal

C256 BAKKER, Dick M.: Ida Cox in Micrography, No. 13 (February 1971):
5 ((7d))

C257 BAKKER, Dick M.: Ida Cox 1923-29
in Micrography, No. 21 (September
1976): 4 ((7d))

C258 Discography of Ida Cox in Jazz
Music, Vol. 3, No. 3 (1946): 17-
19; additions and corrections in
Jazz Music, Vol. 3, No. 6 (1947):
23-24; Vol. 4, No. 2 (1949): 23
((2, 3,))

C259 RAVEN, Reginald C.: Ida Cox--dis-
cography in Jazzology. London:
American Record Society [194?],
12-13. (Note: there are two (or
more) booklets with this same title
and publisher; of the two examined,
this is the one with page numbers)
((2, 3))

CRANE RIVER JAZZ BAND

C260 HULME, George: The Crane River
Jazz Band; a discography in Discophile, No. 23 (April 1952): 3-4;
additions and corrections in
Discophile, No. 24 (June 1952):
4 ((1, 2, 3, 7))

CRAWFORD, RAY, 1924-
guitar, tenor saxophone

C261 [[Discography in Point du Jazz,
No. 12]]; additions by Bernard
NIQUET in Point du Jazz, No. 15
(July 1979): 141

CRAWLEY, WILTON, ca. 1900- (deceased)
clarinet

C262 HULSIZER, Ken, and Walter C.
ALLEN: The Wilton Crawley records
in Playback, Vol. 2 (December
1949): 4-5 ((2, 3, 6, 7))

CRAYTON, PEE WEE (Connie Curtis
Crayton), 1914-
guitar, vocal

C263 Pee Wee Crayton discography in
Whiskey, Women and...; No. 4
(February 1973): 17-19 ((7))

C264 ROTANTE, Anthony: Pee Wee Crayton
in Record Research, Vol. 2 (May-
June 1956): 11 ((3, 6))

CREOLE label

C265 ROTHACKER, Bob: Creole Records
"Special edition for collectors
on vinyl"; a numerical listing in
Matrix, No. 55 (October 1964):
3-5 ((3, 6))

CRESCENT label

C266 BLACKER, George A.: Numerical list
of Crescent records, with their
suspected Pathe counterparts in
Record Research, No. 106 (July
1970): 3-6 ((3))

CRIMSON label

C267 Crimson label listing in Hot
Buttered Soul, No. 45 (April-May
1976): 12 ((3))

CRISS, SONNY (William Criss), 1927-
1977
alto saxophone

C268 GARDNER, Mark: Sonny Criss discography in Discographical Forum,
No. 16 (January 1970) to No. 18
(May 1970), various paginations;
additions and corrections in Discographical Forum, No. 18 (May
1970): 19-20; No. 21 (November
1970): 19 ((1, 2, 3, 7))

C269 Selected Criss discography in
Down Beat, Vol. 44 (March 10,
1977): 20 ((—))

CROOK, GENERAL

C270 MOHR, Kurt: Discography/General
Crook in Blue Flame, No. 15 (n.d.):
9 ((3, 7d))

CROSBY, BOB, 1913-
leader

C271 BAKKER, Dick M.: Bob Crosby and
the Bob Cats in Micrography, No.
19 (April 1972): 3 ((7d))

C272 BAKKER, Dick M.: Bob Crosby 1935-
1942 in Micrography, No. 39 (January 1976): 2-3 ((7d))

C273 CLARK, Clyde, and Arthur SCHAWLOW:
Bob Crosby's Bob Cats; a critical

discography in Record Changer (May 1945): 7, 24-26 ((2, 3, 6, 7d, 9))

C274 CROSBIE, Ian: [Discography] in Jazz Journal, Vol. 23 (March 1970): 15 (2, 3, 6, 7)

C275 HARRIS, Rex; Max JONES; and Albert J. McCARTHY: Complete Bob Crosby discography in Melody Maker, Vol. 21 (August 25, 1945) to (November 10, 1945), various paginations; additions and corrections in Melody Maker, Vol. 21 (December 15, 1945): 6; (December 29, 1945): 6 [from Eric TONKS discography, see next entry]; Vol. 22 (April 13, 1946): 4 [from Art SCHAWLOW] (June 15, 1946): 4 [rev. ed. of C273] ((2, 3, 7))

C276 TONKS, Eric S.: Bob Crosby discography in JONES, Clifford, ed.: Bob Crosby band. London: [1946], 16-27 ((2, 3, 7))

C277 WHYATT, Bert: March of the Bob Cats in Playback, Vol. 3 (January 1950): 14-17 ((2, 3, 6, 7))

Sidemen
See JAZZ MUSIC--ADDITIONS AND CORRECTIONS (Gordon, Jim)

CROWN label

C278 CLOSE, Al: Jazz LPs on Crown in Discographical Forum, No. 6 (January 1961): 2-4 ((2, 3, 7))

C279 McCRANN, Bo, and Wolfgang BEHR: Crown LP listing; part one in Alley Music, Vol. 1 (winter 1968): 12 ((—))

CRUDUP, ARTHUR "BIG BOY," 1905-1974
guitar, vocal

C280 COLLER, Derek: Arthur "Big Boy" Crudup, 1941-1959 in Matrix, No. 51 (February 1964): 3-6; additions and corrections in Matrix, No. 56 (December 1964): 19 ((2, 3, 6, 7))

C281 STRETTON, M. John: Arthur Crudup, 1905-1974 in Blues Link, No. 5 (1974): 28-29 ((—))

The CRUSADERS

C282 The Crusaders discography in Swing Journal, Vol. 28 (September 1974): 256-259 ((2, 7d))

C283 Selected Crusaders discography in Down Beat, Vol. 43 (June 17, 1976): 13 ((—))

CUPPINI, GILBERTO, 1924-
drums

C284 MAZZOLETTI, Adriano: Discografie di musicisti italiani: Gilberto Cuppini in Jazz di Ieri e di Oggi, Vol. 2 (June 1960): 44-48 ((2, 3, 7))

CURSON, TED, 1935-
trumpet

C285 Selected Curson discography in Down Beat, Vol. 44 (January 13, 1977): 19 ((—))

CURTIS, KING (Curtis Ousley), 1935-1971
tenor saxophone

C286 [[MOHR, Kurt: [Discography] in Jazz (Switzerland), January 1974]]

C287 MOHR, Kurt, and Joel DUFOUR: Disco de King Curtis in Soul Bag, No. 65 (January 1978): 17-25 ((2, 3, 7))

CYLINDER RECORDINGS
See RAGTIME MUSIC (Walker, Edward)

CYRILLE, ANDREW, 1939-
drums

C288 RABEN, Erik: Diskofilspalten in Orkester Journalen, Vol. 37 (October 1969): 19, 28 ((2, 3, 7))

D C SOUND label

D1 BRYANT, Steve: D.C. Sound label in Hot Buttered Soul, No. 34 (October 1974?): 7 ((3))

DABNEY, FORD, 1883-ca. 1957
piano, leader

D2 Ford Dabney discography in Record Research, Vol. 1 (April 1955): 7-8 ((3))

DAILY, PETE, 1911-
cornet

D3 COLLER, Derek: A discography of Pete Daily and his Chicagoans in

Jazz Notes (Australia), No. 92 (April 1949): 16; additions and corrections from Bert WHYATT in Jazz Notes (Australia), No. 96 (September 1949): 6 ((2, 3, 6, 7))

D4 EDWARDS, Ernie: Pete Daily; discography of the Capitol sessions in Discophile, No. 53 (April 1957): 14-15; additions and corrections in Discophile, No. 56 (October 1957): 17 ((2, 3, 6, 7))

D5 Pete Daily and his Chicagoans in Discophile, No. 4 (February 1949): 6; additions and corrections in Discophile, No. 5 (April 1949): 11-12 ((2, 3, 6, 7))

D6 SILVESTRI, Edgardo M.: Discografia de Pete Daily in Jazz Magazine (Argentina), No. 23 (June 1951): 16-17 ((2, 3, 6, 7d))

DAKAR label

D7 HEVENT, Jean Claude, and Pierre DAGUERRE: Listing Dakar in Soul Bag, No. 37 (March 1974): 3 ((3))

DALE, LARRY (Ennis Lowery)
guitar, vocal

D8 MOHR, Kurt: Discography Larry Dale in Blues Unlimited, No. 40 (January 1967): 26 ((2, 3, 7))

DAMERON, TADD (Tadley Ewing Dameron), 1917-1965
piano, composer

D9 COOKE, Ann: Tadd Dameron discography in Jazz Monthly, Vol. 6 (March 1960): 24-26 ((1, 2, 3, 6, 7))

D10 Discography of Tadd Dameron. [Basel]: Jazz-Publications, 1962, 8 pp. (Discographical notes, Vol. 6) ((1, 2, 3, 6, 7))

D11 EVANS, Chris: Tadd Dameron on Capitol in Journal of Jazz Discography, No. 3 (March 1978): 5; additions and corrections in Journal of Jazz Discography, No. 4 (January 1979): 2 ((2, 3, 7))

DAN label (Japanese)

D12 STAGG, Tom: Recent record releases in Footnote, Vol. 7 (December 1976-January 1977): 11 ((—))

DANDRIDGE, PUTNEY, 1900-1946
piano, vocal

D13 DEMEULDRE, Leon: Putney Dandridge in Point du Jazz, No. 13 (June 1977): 144-145 ((2, 7d))

DANKWORTH, JOHN, 1927-
alto saxophone
See also LAINE, CLEO

D14 MORGAN, Alun: A Johnny Dankworth discography in Jazz Monthly, Vol. 9 (February 1964): 3-4; Vol. 10 (March 1964): 3-5 ((2, 3, 6, 7))

DANZI, MIKE
banjo

D15 [[LOTZ, Rainer E.: Mike Danzi; his own recording sessions in Doctor Jazz, No. 79 (1977): 6-11; additions and corrections in his Mike Danzi: additional information in Doctor Jazz, No. 81 (1977): 4]]

DARKTOWN STRUTTERS BALL (tune title)

D16 CROSBY, E. Barney: Starter discography of Darktown Strutters' Ball in Good Diggin', Vol. 2 (October 1948): 3-4 ((—))

D17 Darktown Strutters Ball in Oh Play That Thing, Vol. 1 (December 1948): 5 ((—))

DARVELL, BARRY
vocal

D18 MOHR, Kurt: Discographie de Barry Darvell in Soul Bag, No. 34 (January 1974): 4 ((2, 3, 7))

DASEK, RUDOLF, 1933-
guitar

D19 Selected Dasek discography in Jazz Forum (Poland), No. 64 (1980): 43 ((—))

DASH, JULIAN, 1916-1974
tenor saxophone

D20 DEMEUSY, Bertrand: The Julian Dash's [sic] name discography in Jazz Journal, Vol. 17 (April 1964): 13 ((2, 3, 7))

DAUNER, WOLFGANG, 1935–
  keyboard instruments

D21 Wolfgang Dauner selected discography in Jazz Forum (Poland), No. 38 (June 1975): 62 ((—))

DAVENPORT, COW COW (Charles Edward Davenport), 1894–1955
  piano

D22 Discography in Jazz Music, No. 5 (1943): 12, 14; additions and corrections in Jazz Music, No. 10 (1943): 15 [excluding piano rolls] ((2))

D23 MONTGOMERY, Mike: Charles "Cow Cow" Davenport piano rollography in Record Research, No. 53 (July 1963): 11 ((5))

DAVIS, BOBBY, 1937–
  piano, vocal

D24 MOHR, Kurt, and Emmanuel CHOISNEL: Discographie de Bobby Davis in Soul Bag, No. 38 (May 1974): 36 ((2, 3, 7))

DAVIS, CHARLIE, 1899–
  piano, leader

D25 HARDY, Bruce Allen: Charlie Davis and his orchestra––a discography in Storyville, No. 62 (December 1975–January 1976): 66 ((2, 3, 6, 7))

DAVIS, CLIFF
  tenor saxophone

D26 MOHR, Kurt: Cliff Davis in Soul Bag, No. 45 (January 1975): 26 ((2, 3, 7))

DAVIS, DICK
  leader

D27 [Discography] in Jazz Statistics, No. 7 (1958?): 7; additions and corrections from Jorgen Grunnet JEPSEN in Jazz Statistics, No. 12 (September 1959): 8 ((3))

DAVIS, EDDIE "LOCKJAW," 1922–
  tenor saxophone

D28 [[HEIN, Walther: Discography in Jazz Podium, Vol. 12 (November 1963); Vol. 13 (February 1964)]]

D29 MOHR, Kurt: Additions and corrections to the discography of Eddie "Lockjaw" Davis, i.e., in DELAUNAY, Charles: Hot discographie encyclopédique, Vol. 2, page 87–88 in Jazz Statistics, No. 7 (1958?): 5–6; additions and corrections from Jorgen Grunnet JEPSEN in Jazz Statistics, No. 12 (September 1959): 8 ((2, 3))

DAVIS, GARY, 1896–1972
  guitar, vocal

D30 GLADDEN, Kenneth S.: A Gary Davis discography in Record Changer, Vol. 14, No. 8 (n.d.): 9, 15 ((2))

D31 LAUGHTON, Bob, and Cedric HAYES: Reverend Gary Davis––a post–1943 discography in Talking Blues, No. 6 (July–September 1977): 16–18; No. 7 (October–December 1977): 10–13 ((2, 3, 7))

DAVIS, (BLIND) JOHN, 1913–
  piano, vocal

D32 Blind John Davis; a "name" discography in Discophile, No. 50 (October 1956): 9–10; additions and corrections in Discophile, No. 56 (October 1957): 17 ((2, 3, 6, 7))

DAVIS, LARRY, 1936–
  guitar, piano, vocal

D33 Larry Davis discography in Blues Unlimited, No. 134 (March–June 1979): 7 ((2, 3, 6, 7))

D34 MOHR, Kurt: Larry Davis in Soul Bag, No. 51 (January 1976): 23 ((2, 3, 7))

DAVIS, MILES, 1926–
  trumpet

D35 [[[Discography] in HENTOFF, Nat: Miles Davis. New York: BMI, 1961? ((2))]]

D36 Discography: Miles Davis in Swing Journal, Vol. 12 (No. 9 of 1958): 24 ((2, 7d))

D37 EYLE, Wim van: Miles op de plaat in Jazz Press, No. 19 (May 26, 1976): 7 ((1, 7))

D38 JAMES, Michael: Selected discography in his Miles Davis. London: Cassell (also New York: Barnes) [c1961], 81-90 (Kings of jazz, 9) ((2, 7))

D39 JEPSEN, Jorgen Grunnet: Discography of Miles Davis. [Brande, Denmark: Debut Records, c1959], 19 leaves; additions and corrections from Ernie EDWARDS in Jazz Review, Vol. 3 (May 1960): 3 ((1, 2, 3, 6, 7))

D40 JEPSEN, Jorgen Grunnet: A discography of Miles Davis. Copenhagen: Knudsen [c1969], 40 pp.; additions and corrections in Orkester Journalen, Vol. 37 (December 1969): 20; in KERSCHBAUMER, Franz: Supplement zur Diskographie von J. G. Jepsen in his Miles Davis; stilkritische Untersuchungen zur musikalische Entwicklung seines Personalstils. Graz, Austria: Akademische Druck-und Verlagsanstalt, 1978, 135-153 ((1, 2, 3, 6, 7))

D41 [[JEPSEN, Jorgen Grunnet: Miles Davis; a discography. Copenhagen: 1957, 14 leaves]]

D42 JEPSEN, Jorgen Grunnet: Miles Davis diskografi in Orkester Journalen, Vol. 26 (November 1958): 58; (December 1958): 64-65 ((2, 3, 7d))

D43 Komplet Miles Davis diskografi 1969-1975 in MORTENSEN, Tore: Miles Davis--de ny jazz. Arhus, Denmark: 1977, 115-119 ((2, 7))

D44 LOHMANN, Jan, and Nils WINTHER: Discographie des enregistrements inédits de Miles Davis in Jazz Hot, No. 290 (January 1973): 20-21; No. 296 (July-August 1973): 6-7, 34 ((1, 2, 6, 7, 9))

D45 LOHMANN, Jan, and Nils WINTHER: Diskofilspalten in Orkester Journalen, Vol. 39 (May 1971) to (September 1971); Vol. 40 (April 1972), various paginations, in 5 parts [private recordings and airshots] ((1, 2, 6, 7, 9))

D46 Miles Davis discography in Swing Journal, Vol. 34 (May 1980 special issue): 184-197 ((1, 2, 7d))

D47 POSTIF, François: Discographie de Miles Davis in Jazz Hot, No. 115 (November 1956): 14 ((2, 3, 7d))

D48 RUPPLI, Michael: Discographie: Miles Davis in Jazz Hot, No. 358 (February 1979); No. 359 (March 1979): 26-30 ((1, 2, 3, 6, 7))

D49 Selected Miles discography; recorded Miles as leader, with special emphasis on the years 1959-1974 in Down Beat, Vol. 41 (July 18, 1974): 20, 52 ((7d))

D50 [[STIASSI, Ruggero: [Discography] in Musica Jazz, Vol. 23 (August-September 1967)]]

D51 [[STIASSI, Ruggero: [Discography of Prestige recordings] in Musica Jazz, Vol. 22 (July 1966)]]

DAVIS, SAM
harmonica, vocal

D52 LEADBITTER, Mike: Little Sam Davis in Blues Unlimited, No. 36 (September 1966): 18 ((3))

DAVIS, TYRONE
vocal

D53 MOHR, Kurt: Tyrone Davis in Soul Bag, No. 45 (January 1975): 13-15; additions and corrections in Soul Bag, No. 46 (February 1975): 6; No. 51 (January 1976): 32 ((2, 3, 7))

DAVIS, WALTER, 1912-1963
piano, vocal

D54 BAKKER, Dick M.: Walter Davis in Micrography, No. 11 (September 1970): 12 ((7d))

DAVISON, WILD BILL, 1906-
trumpet

D55 WHYATT, Bert: Wild Bill's bands; recordings under the leadership of Davidson [sic] in Playback, Vol. 2 (May 1949): 7 ((2, 3, 6, 7))

DC SOUND label
See D C SOUND label

DEAN, ALAN
vocal

D56 [[Discography in Journal of Jazz Discography, No. 1 (November 1976): 4]; additions and corrections in Journal of Jazz Discography, No. 29 (June 1977): 1 ((3, 6, 9))

DEAN, ELTON
alto saxophone

D57 RENSEN, Jan: [Discography] in Jazz Nu, Vol. 1 (November 1978): 49 ((2, 7d))

DEAN, TOMMY
    piano, leader

D58 MOHR, Kurt: Discography of Tommy
    Dean in Jazz Statistics, No. 29
    (October 1963): JS-7 ((2, 3, 6,
    7))

DeARANGO, BILL, 1921-
    guitar

D59 EYLE, Wim van: Bill "Buddy"
    DeArango discography in Jazz
    Press, No. 36 (April 1977): 4 ((2,
    3, 6, 7))

DEBONAIRES (musical group)

D60 MOHR, Kurt: Debonaires discography
    in Hot Buttered Soul, No. 32 (July
    1974?) 6 ((3, 5, 7))

DEBUT label

D61 COOKE, Ann: The Debut label; a
    listing in Discographical Forum,
    No. 1 (May 1960): 2-5; No. 2 (July
    1960): 18-19 ((2, 7))

D62 COOKE, Jack: [Debut listing] in
    Jazz & Blues, Vol. 1 (August-
    September 1971): 8-9 ((2, 7))

DECATUR label

D63 Catalogue of Decatur reissues in
    Discophile, No. 26 (October 1952):
    19, 18; additions and corrections
    in Discophile, No. 27 (December
    1952): 15; No. 28 (February 1953):
    7 ((—))

DECCA label
    See also ARMSTRONG, LOUIS (Bakker,
    Dick M.: Louis Armstrong Decca's
    [sic] 1934-1946); BASIE, COUNT
    (Bakker, Dick M.: Count Basie
    Decca's [sic] 1937-1939)

D64 EVANS, Norman: The Decca 7000 race
    series in Discophile, No. 2 (Oc-
    tober 1948) to No. 5 (April 1949),
    various paginations [to no. 7127]
    ((—))

D65 FRESIA, Enzo: Jazz Studio in
    Musica Jazz, Vol. 8 (November
    1957): 39 ((2, 3, 7))

DECCA label (British)

D66 WANTE, Stephen; Jack MILLER; and
    Ernest STORK: Decca "J" and Voca-
    lion "C", "S", and "500" series in
    Jazz Music, Vol. 4, No. 7 (1951);
    No. 8 (1952); Vol. 5, No. 5 (n.d.);
    Vol. 5, No. 7 (1954), various
    paginations [[additions and cor-
    rections in Jazz Music, Vol. 6,
    No. 1?]] ((3, 6))

DECCA label (Dutch)

D67 HURLE BATH, Leslie: Postwar Dutch
    Decca in Playback, Vol. 2 (March
    1948): 18 ((2, 7d))

D68 ZWARTENKOT, H. K.: Decca label
    roed--M 32000 in Doctor Jazz, No.
    43 (August-September 1970) to un-
    known issue [goes at least as far
    as No. 45 (December 1970-January
    1971), part 3, to no. 32100] ((3))

DEE, MERCY
    See MERCY DEE

DEE GEE label
    See GILLESPIE, DIZZY (Walker,
    Malcolm)

DeGRAAFF, REIN
    See GRAAFF, REIN DE

DeJOHNETTE, JACK, 1942-
    drums

D69 Selected DeJohnette discography in
    Down Beat, Vol. 42 (February 13,
    1975): 16 ((—))

DELMAR label

D70 ENGLUND, Bjorn: The truth about
    Delmar in Matrix, No. 31 (October
    1960): 26 ((—))

DELTA label (British)

D71 PAYNE, Pete: Delta discography
    in Discophile, No. 6 (June 1949):
    6, 9 ((2, 3, 7d))

DELUXE label

D72 ROTANTE, Anthony, and Dan MAHONY:
    The Deluxe 3200 series in Record
    Research, No. 4 (August 1955): 2
    ((3, 6))

DENGLER, JOHN, 1927-
    baritone saxophone

D73   DENGLER, John Morgan: DiscoDengler
in Record Research, No. 84 (June
1967): 3, 5 ((1, 2))

DePARIS, SIDNEY, 1905-1967
trumpet

D74   ALLEN, Walter C.: Sidney De Paris
discography in Hot Notes, No. 13
(1948): 3-8 ((2, 3, 6, 7))

D75   MILLER, William H.: Sidney De
Paris in Jazz Notes and Blue
Rhythm, No. 51 (April 1945): 5
((7d))

D76   Sidney DeParis & James P. Johnson
Blue Note sessions in Hip, Vol. 7
(April 1970): 3 ((2, 3, 6, 7))

DePARIS, WILBUR, 1900-1973
trombone

D77   MILLER, William H.: Wilbur De Paris
in Jazz Notes and Blue Rhythm, No.
51 (April 1945): 5 ((—))

D78   SIMONE, Rodney: Wilbur deParis; a
discography of recordings made
under his own name in Matrix, No.
23 (May 1959): 9-12; additions and
corrections in Matrix, No. 29/30
(August 1960): 36; No. 33 (March
1961): 15-16; No. 35/36 (September 1961): 36 ((2, 3, 7))

DESANTO, SUGAR PIE
vocal

D79   CHOISNEL, Emmanuel: Discography of
Sugar Pie DeSanto in Soul Bag,
[[No. 2 [part 1]]]; No. 22/23
(January-February 1973): 9-10
[part 2, 1967-1972] ((2, 3, 7))

DESMOND, PAUL, 1924-1977
alto saxophone

D80   [Discography] in Swing Journal,
Vol. 31 (August 1977): 286-289
((2, 7d))

DETROIT JUNIOR (Emery Williams, Jr.),
1931-
piano, vocal

D81   CHOISNEL, Emmanuel: Discographie
de Detroit Jr. in Soul Bag, No. 38
(May 1974): 28-29 ((2, 3, 7))

D82   HATCH, Peter: This is the blues in
Coda, Vol. 9 (July-August 1970):
13 ((2))

The DEVIL'S SON-IN-LAW
See WHEATSTRAW, PEETIE

DIAL, HARRY, 1907-
drums

D83   [[[Discography?] in Doctor Jazz,
No. 40: 5]]; additions and cor-
rections in Doctor Jazz, No. 45
(December 1970-January 1971): 23

DIAL label
See also PARKER, CHARLIE (Bettonville, Andre) and (Charlie Parker
on Dial) and (Fluckiger, Otto:
Charlie Parker alternate masters
on Dial) and (Korteweg, Simon)

D84   EVANS, Chris: Dial; a listing of
the sessions recorded for Ross
Russell's Dial label in Jazz
Journal, Vol. 21 (September 1968):
19, 22; additions and corrections
in Jazz Journal, Vol. 21 (November 1968): 18; (December 1968):
16 ((2, 3, 6, 7))

DICKENSON, VIC, 1906-
trombone

D85   JEPSEN, Jorgen Grunnet: Vic
Dickenson diskografi in Orkester
Journalen, Vol. 26 (February
1958): 50 ((2, 7d))

D86   Selected Dickenson discography in
Down Beat, Vol. 47 (March 1980):
60 ((—))

DICKERSON, WALT, 1931-
vibraphone
See VIBRAPHONE MUSIC (JAZZ)
(Tepperman, Barry)

DIDDLEY, BO
See BO DIDDLEY

DIG label
See ULTRA label

DiNOVI, GENE, 1928-
piano
See PIANO MUSIC (JAZZ) (Edwards,
Ernie)

DIORIO, JOE, 1936-
guitar

D87   TRA, Gijs: Diskografie in Jazz Nu,
      Vol. 2 (January 1980): 145 ((—))

DIPPER MOUTH BLUES (tune title)
      See SUGAR FOOT STOMP

DISC label

D88   WHYATT, Bert: A numerical listing
      of the Disc label in Matrix, No.
      84 (August 1969): 3-10; No. 85
      (October 1969): 3-6 ((3))

DIVA label
      See HARMONY label (Bedoian, Jim)

DIXI label (Swedish)

D89   [[LILIEDAHL, Karleric: Dixi/Sil-
      verton--en diskografi. Trelleborg,
      Sweden: 1972, 93 pp.]]

DIXIE JAZZ BAND (pseud.)

D90   ARMAGNAC, Perry, ed.: Unmasking
      the Dixie Jazz Band in Record Re-
      search, Vol. 3 (August-September
      1957): 3-7 ((3, 6, 7d)

DIXIE WASHBOARD BAND

D91   ALLEN, Walter C.; Bob COLTON; and
      Len KUNSTADT: Dixie Washboard
      Band; a revision in Discophile,
      No. 34 (February 1954): 16-17
      ((2, 3, 6, 7))

DIXIELAND JUG BLOWERS

D92   ALLEN, Walter C.: Discography in
      Jazz Journal, Vol. 9 (March 1956):
      7 ((2, 3, 6, 7))

DIXON BILL, 1925-
      trumpet

D93   THOMPSON, Keith G.: A discography
      of Bill Dixon in Pieces of Jazz
      (1970): 107-108 ((2, 7))

DIXON, FLOYD, 1929-
      piano, vocal

D94   CHAUVARD, Marcel, and Kurt MOHR:
      Discography of Floyd Dixon in
      Jazz Statistics, No. 29 (October
      1963): BS2-BS5 ((2, 3, 7))

DIXON, WILLIE, 1915-
      bass violin

D95   DEMETRE, Jacques: Willie Dixon--
      discography in Blues Unlimited,
      No. 16 (October 1964): 3-4, 11;
      additions and corrections in
      JEPSEN, Jorgen Grunnet: Diskofil-
      spalten in Orkester Journalen,
      Vol. 33 (February 1965): 19 ((2,
      3, 6, 7))

DOCTOR CLAYTON'S BUDDY
      See SUNNYLAND SLIM

DOCTOR FEELGOOD
      See PIANO RED

DODDS, BABY (Warren Dodds), 1898-1959
      drums

D96   The Baby Dodds LPs in Matrix, No.
      56 (December 1964): 15-16; addi-
      tions and corrections in Matrix,
      No. 68 (December 1966): 15 ((2,
      3, 7))

D97   HELLIWELL, George, and Peter
      TAYLOR: Discography of Warren
      "Baby" Dodds in Jazz Journal, Vol.
      4 (March 1951): 3, 19; (April
      1951): 19; (May 1951): 17 ((2, 3,
      6, 7))

DODDS, JOHNNY, 1892-1940
      clarinet
      See also ARMSTRONG, LOUIS (Dis-
      cographies in Jazz Hot, No. 37)

D98   ARX, Rolf von: ,Johnny Dodds in
      Matrix, No. 72/73 (September
      1967): 3-37; additions and correc-
      tions in Matrix, No. 76 (April
      1968): 14; No. 78 (August 1968):
      14; No. 80 (December 1968): 19;
      No. 82 (April 1969): 13; No. 84
      (August 1969): 19 ((2, 3, 6, 7))

D99   ARX, Rolf von: Johnny Dodds Dis-
      kographie in Jazz Rhythm & Blues;
      Schweizerische Jazz-Zeitschrift,
      No. 3? to ? (part 6, covering
      July 12 to September 16, 1926 in
      No. 8 (1968): 10-11) ((2, 3, 6,
      7))

D100 BAKKER, Dick M.: Johnny Dodds
      1923-1940 in Micrography, No. 44
      (May 1977): 7-13 ((2, 6, 7d))

D101 BAKKER, Dick M.: Johnny Dodds
      1924-29 in Micrography, No. 21
      (September 1972): 6-7 ((—))

D102 BAKKER, Dick M.: Johnny Dodds except the Oliver-Hot Five/Seven-
Morton-Dixieland Jug Blowers and
own Victor's [sic] in Micrography,
No. 8 (January 1970): 2-4 ((7d))

D103 BAKKER, Dick M.: Johnny Dodds on
Victor-sessions in Micrography,
No. 3 (May 1969): 5 ((7d))

D104 BAKKER, Dick M.: Johnny Dodds on
Victor-sessions in Micrography,
No. 16 (December 1971): 4 ((7d))

D105 EVANS, Norman: Collectors' column
in Universal Jazz, Vol. 1 (July
1946): 12-22 ((2, 3, 7d))

D106 GOODALL, Douglas, and Charles FOX:
Johnny Dodds discography in Discography (May 1943): 3; (June
1943): 5-6; additions from Charles
FOX in Discography (August 1943):
7 ((2, 3, 6, 7))

D107 LOVE, William C.: Johnny Dodds'
discography in Jazz (US): Vol. 1,
No. 9 (1943): 23-26; additions and
corrections in Jazz (US), Vol. 1
(December 1943): 16; in FOX,
Charles: More about Johnny Dodds
in Discography, No. 4 (April
1944): 8-10 ((2, 3))

D108 TAYLOR, Peter, and Geoffrey
HELLIWELL: A discography of Johnny
Dodds in Jazz Journal, Vol. 2
(May 1949): 8; (June 1949): 15;
additions and corrections in Jazz
Journal, Vol. 2 (November 1949):
8 ((2, 3, 6, 7))

D109 VREEDE, Max E.: A discography of
Johnny Dodds in Matrix, No. 11/12
(June 1956): 3-34; additions and
corrections in Matrix, No. 15
(February 1957): 16-17; No. 22
(March 1959): 22-23; No. 29/30
(August 1960): 36; No. 33 (March
1961): 14; No. 35/36 (September
1961): 38 ((2, 3, 6, 7))

D110 WRIGHT, Laurie, and John R. T.
DAVIES: Dodds in duo in Storyville, No. 41 (June-July 1972):
170-172; No. 43 (October-November
1972): 11-12; No. 45 (February-
March 1973): 109 [covers only
those recordings for which alternate takes were made] ((2, 3, 6,
7, 8, 9))

DOGGETT, BILL, 1916-
organ

D111 Discographie de Bill Doggett in
Soul Bag [[No. 17 (1972?)]]; No.
18/19 (1972?): 17-21, 57 ((2, 3,
6, 7))

D112 MOHR, Kurt: Discography of Bill
Doggett in Jazz Statistics, No. 6
(October 1957): 6-9; No. 12 (Sep-
tember 1959): 5-6 ((2, 3, 7))

DOLDINGER, KLAUS, 1936-
saxophones

D113 Selected Doldinger discography in
Down Beat, Vol. 42 (August 14,
1975): 20 ((—))

DOLLISON, MAURICE
See McCALL, CASH

DOLPHY, ERIC, 1928-1964
alto saxophone, bass clarinet,
flute

D114 ARCANGELI, Stefano: I dischi di
Dolphy in Musica Jazz, Vol. 32
(June 1976): 12 ((1))

D115 Eric Dolphy discography in Swing
Journal, Vol. 28 (June 1974):
250-255 ((2, 7d))

D116 [[The Eric Dolphy discography
1958-1964. Graz, Austria: Modern
Jazz Series, 1967, 16 pp.]]

D117 JEPSEN, Jorgen Grunnet: Eric
Dolphy in Les Cahiers du Jazz,
No. 12 (1965?): 133-143 ((2, 3,
7))

D118 JEPSEN, Jorgen Grunnet: Eric
Dolphy diskografi in Orkester
Journalen, Vol. 29 (November
1961): 34; (December 1961): 48-
49 ((2, 7))

D119 PORTALEONI, Sergio: Discografia:
Eric Dolphy in Musica Jazz, Vol.
33 (March 1977): 46-48; (May
1977): 46-48 ((1, 2, 6, 7))

D120 RABEN, Erik: Eric Dolphy in Musica
Jazz, Vol. 21 (October 1965) to
(December 1965), various pagina-
tions, in 3 parts ((2, 3, 7))

D121 [[RISSI, Mathias: Eric Dolphy:
discography. Adliswil, Switzerland: 1977, 29 pp.]]

D122 RUPPLI, Michel: Discographie:
Eric Dolphy in Jazz Hot, No. 360
(April 1979): 21-26 ((1, 2, 3, 6,
7))

D123 TEPPERMAN, Barry, and Vladimir
SIMOSKO: His recordings in their
Eric Dolphy; a musical biography
and discography. Washington, D.C.:
Smithsonian Institution, 1974
(also New York: Da Capo [c1974]),
89-119 ((1, 2, 3, 6, 7, 8, 9))

D124 [[STIASSI, Ruggero: Discography in Sounds 3, summer 1967]]

D125 WALKER, Malcolm: Eric Dolphy in Jazz Monthly, Vol. 12 (January 1966): 30-31; (February 1966): 30-31; (March 1966): 29-37; additions and corrections in Jazz Monthly, Vol. 12 (October 1966): 28 ((2, 3, 7))

DOMINIQUE, NATTY (Anatie Dominique), 1896-
trumpet

D126 CABLE, Dave: A Natty Dominique discography in Jazz Journal, Vol. 6 (June 1953): 21-22 ((2, 3, 6, 7))

D127 Natty Dominique discography in Hot Notes, Vol. 2 (October 1947): 4-6 ((2, 3, 6, 7))

DOMINO, FATS (Antoine Domino), 1928-
piano, vocal

D128 PERIN, Jacques: Fats Domino "walking to New Orleans" in Jazz Magazine (France), No. 200 (May 1972): 18-19 ((—))

D129 POSTIF, François: Fats Domino-- some recording details in Discographical Forum, No. 4 (January 1961): 19-20 [1953-59 Imperial recordings and reissues] ((2, 3, 7d))

D130 ROTANTE, Anthony: Al "Fats" Domino; a provisional discography in Discophile, No. 37 (August 1954): 17-18 ((3))

DON AND DEWEY (musical group)

D131 Don & Dewey on Specialty in R and B Collector, Vol. 1 (May-June 1970): 11 ((7d))

DONALDSON, LOU, 1926-
alto saxophone

D132 COOKE, Ann: Lou Donaldson discography in Jazz-Disco, Vol. 1 (April 1960): 5-8 ((2, 3, 6, 7))

D133 Lou Donaldson on LP in Different Drummer, Vol. 1 (February 1974): 12 ((—))

DOOTO label

D134 HORLICK, Richard A: Dooto Records in R and B Magazine, Vol. 1 (July-October 1970): 23-28 [nos. 301-477] ((—))

DORHAM, KENNY (McKinley Howard Dorham), 1924-1972
trumpet

D135 JAMES, Michael: Kenny Dorham: soloist extraordinary in Jazz & Blues, Vol. 2 (January 1972): 9 ((—))

D136 Kenny Dorham discography in Swing Journal, Vol. 27 (March 1973): 260-267 ((2, 7d))

DORSEY, JIMMY, 1904-1957
alto saxophone
See also DORSEY BROTHERS

D137 EDWARDS, Ernie; George I. HALL; and Bill KORST, eds.: Jimmy Dorsey and his Orchestra; a complete discography of the Jimmy Dorsey orchestra covering the years September 1935 to November 1956. Whittier, CA: ErnGeoBill, 1966, 28 leaves (Big band series, D-1A) ((1, 2, 3, 6, 7))

DORSEY, LEE
vocal

D138 MOHR, Kurt: Lee Dorsey discography in Soul, Vol. 4 (June 1966): 23-25 ((2, 3, 7))

DORSEY, THOMAS ANDREW, 1899-
guitar, piano, vocal

D139 VREEDE, Max A.: A discography of Georgia Tom (Thomas A. Dorsey) and his associates in Matrix, No. 31 (October 1960): 3-22 ((2, 3, 6, 7, 8))

DORSEY, TOMMY, 1905-1956
trombone
See also DORSEY BROTHERS

D140 [[EDWARDS, Ernie: Discography. Whittier, CA.?: Jazz Discographies Unlimited]]

D141 ROBERTSON, Alastair: Tommy Dorsey, a swinging gentleman in Jazz Journal, Vol. 25 (February 1972): 19 ((2, 3, 7))

DORSEY BROTHERS
See also DORSEY, JIMMY; DORSEY, TOMMY

D142 BAKKER, Dick M.: Dorsey Brothers
1928-36 in Micrography, No. 10
(May 1970): 6-7 ((7d))

D143 Okeh Dorsey in VENABLES, Ralph
G. V., and Clifford JONES, eds.:
Cream of the white clarinets.
London: Clifford Jones [1946?],
9-11 ((2, 3, 7d))

DOTSON, JIMMY
harmonica, vocal

D144 DEMETRE, Jacques: Discography of
Jimmy Dotson in Blues Unlimited,
No. 22 (May 1965): 7; additions
and corrections in Blues Unlimited, No. 23 (June 1965): 9 ((2,
3))

DOUBLE SIX OF PARIS

D145 LAFARGUE, Pierre: Discographie:
Les Double Six in Jazz Hot, No.
345/346 (February 1978): 57-58
((2, 7))

D146 VOLPI, Luciano: I dischi in Musica
Jazz, Vol. 18 (September 1962):
39 ((—))

DOUGLAS, K. C., 1913-1975
guitar, vocal

D147 K. C. Douglas discography in
Living Blues, No. 15 (winter 1973-
1974): 19 ((—))

DOVER, BILL, 1892-
trombone

D148 RUST, Brian Discography in IAJRC
Journal, Vol. 2 (April 1969): 15
((2, 3, 6, 7))

DRAGON label (Swedish)

D149 Dragon records discography in Jazz
Forum (Poland), No. 60 (1979): 54
((—))

DREW, KENNY, 1928-
piano

D150 Kenny Drew discography in Disk in
the World, Vol. 1 (July 1980):
23-25 ((7d))

DRIFTERS (musical group)

D151 [[[Discography] in Soul Bag, No.
12-13]]

DRIFTIN' SLIM or SMITH
See MICKLE, ELMON

DRUM MUSIC (JAZZ)
See also PERCUSSION MUSIC (JAZZ)

D152 BROWN, Theodore Dennis: Selected
discography listed by performer
(compiled from Delaunay, New hot
discography and Rust, Jazz records, 1897-1942) in his A history
and analysis of jazz drumming to
1942. Ph.D. Music dissertation,
University of Michigan, 1976
(available from University Microfilms, Ann Arbor, MI; order no.
77-7881): 509-584 ((—))

D153 Sélection discographique in Jazz
Hot, No. 291 (February 1973): 39
((—))

The DU-ETTES (musical group)

D154 MOHR, Kurt: The Du-Ettes in Soul
Bag, No. 45 (January 1975): 29
((2, 3, 7))

DUBIN, LARRY, 1931-1978
drums

D155 A Larry Dubin discography in Coda,
No. 166 (April 1979): 14 ((2, 7))

DUD SOUND label

D156 BAKER, Cary S.: The Dud Sound
story in Jefferson, No. 17 (1972):
9 ((3))

D157 Discography: Dud Sound Recording
Co. in Blue Flame, No. 17/18
(n.d.): 27 [Friendly 5, FM, Dud
Sound, TDS, and A-1 Dud labels]
((—))

DUDZIAK, URSZULA, 1943-
vocal

D158 Selected Dudziak discography in
Down Beat, Vol. 43 (January 15,
1976): 14 ((—))

D159 Urszula Dudziak selected discography in Jazz Forum (Poland), No.
42 (April 1976): 38 ((—))

DUKE, GEORGE, 1946-
piano

D160 Selected Duke discography in Down
Beat, Vol. 44 (March 10, 1977):
15 ((—))

DUNCAN, HANK, 1894-1968
    piano

D161 OWENS, Frank: A Hank Duncan dis-
    cography in Jazzology (US), Vol.
    18 (May-June-July 1968): 4-7 ((2,
    3, 7))

DUNN, JOHNNY, 1897-1937
    trumpet

D162 ALLEN, Walter C.: Johnny Dunn's
    early records in Record Research,
    No. 76 (May 1966): 7, 10 ((2, 3,
    6, 7, 8))

DUOPHONE label (British)

D163 BADROCK, Arthur: Duophone 4000
    series in Matrix, No. 62 (Decem-
    ber 1965) to No. 64 (April 1966),
    No. 66/67 (September 1966), vari-
    ous paginations, in 4 parts ((3,
    6))

D164 VENABLES, Ralph G. V.: A feature
    for the connoisseur in Discography
    (November 1942): 5-6 ((3))

DUPREE, CHAMPION JACK, 1910-
    piano, vocal

D165 CHAUVARD, Marcel, and Kurt MOHR:
    Discography of Champion Jack
    Dupree in Jazz Statistics, No. 15
    (March 1960): 2-6; additions and
    corrections from M. VOGLER in Jazz
    Statistics, No. 17 (1960): 2-4;
    No. 22 (June 1961): 1, 7 ((2, 3,
    6, 7))

D166 Discography in Hot Jazz Info, No.
    4/75 (1975): 3 [1940-1941 ses-
    sions] ((2, 3, 6, 7))

D167 Revised discography of Champion
    Jack Dupree. Basel: Jazz-Publica-
    tions, 1961, 12 pp. (Discographi-
    cal notes, Vol. 1) ((2, 3, 6, 7))

D168 ROTANTE, Anthony: The records of
    Champion Jack Dupree in Record
    Research, No. 20 (November-Decem-
    ber 1958): 18, 28 ((2, 3, 6, 7))

DURIUM label (British)
    See also HIT OF THE WEEK label

D169 BADROCK, Arthur: EN series English
    Durium in Collecta, No. 5 (May-
    June 1969): 37-41 ((3, 6))

D170 ENGLUND, Bjorn: Durium/Hit of the
    Week. Stockholm: Nationalfonoteket,
    1967, 14 leaves (Nationalfonote-
    kets diskografier, 1) ((7d, 8))

DUTCH SWING COLLEGE BAND

D171 MAK, Jim: The Dutch Swing College
    Band in Discophile, No. 55 (August
    1957): 11-12 ((2, 3, 7))

DYER, WARWICK
    piano, trombone, vocal

D172 KENNEDY, John: A tribute to
    Warwick "Wocka" Dyer in Matrix,
    No. 9 (December 1955): 3-4 ((2,
    7))

DYNAMO label

D173 [[[Listing] in Soul Bag, No. 3]]

E C M label (German)

E1 ECM Records discography in Swing
    Journal, Vol. 28 (September 1974):
    198-203 ((2, 7d))

E2 RABEN, Erik: Diskofilspalten in
    Orkester Journalen, Vol. 39 (De-
    cember 1971): 29 ((2, 7))

E DISC label

E3 E-Disc Records in Discophile, No.
    19 (August 1951): 7 ((2, 7))

E R label (Swedish)

E4 NYSTRÖM, Borje: Discography of
    Er-Records in Discophile, No. 19
    (August 1951): 13 ((2, 3, 7d))

ESP label
    See also SUN RA (Gant, Dave)

E5 ARMSTRONG, Bryan A.: [Discography
    of avant-garde jazz titles only]
    in Jazz Studies, Vol. 1 (No. 3,
    1967): 10-12 [nos. 1002-1030]
    ((2, 6, 7))

E6 RABEN, Erik: Diskofilspalten in
    Orkester Journalen, Vol. 35 (Janu-
    ary 1967): 17, 30; Vol. 37 (March
    1969): 17, 31 [to no. 1033] ((2,
    7))

EAGER, ALLEN, 1927-
    alto and tenor saxophones

E7 DAVIS, Brian: Allen Eager discog-
    raphy in Discographical Forum,
    No. 34 (1976) to No. 38 (1977),
    various paginations; additions
    and corrections in Discographical
    Forum [from Andreas MASEL], No.

36 (1976): 1; [from Hans WESTER-
BERG], No. 40 (spring 1978): 10;
No. 41 (1978?): 2 ((1, 2, 3, 6,
7))

E8   DENIS, Jacques, and Henri ROB-
BERECHTS: Discographie in Point
du Jazz, No. 8 (April 1973): 110-
119 ((1, 2, 3, 6, 7))

E9   REHNBERG, Bert: Modern stars:
Allen Eager in Record Research
Bulletin, No. 5 (October 1958): 7
((2, 3, 7))

EASTER, MONTE
   trumpet, vocal

E10 MOHR, Kurt, and Marcel CHAUVARD:
Discography of Monte Easter in
Jazz Statistics, No. 28 (December
1962): JS2-JS3 ((2, 3, 7))

EASTERN label

E11 SUZUKI, Hiroshi: Eastern label
listing in Hot Buttered Soul, No.
46 (June-July 1976): 2 ((3))

EASTON, AMOS, 1905-
   guitar, piano, vocal

E12 STEWART-BAXTER, Derrick: A discography of Bumble Bee Slim in Jazz
Journal, Vol. 4 (February 1951):
12-13 ((3, 6))

ECKSTINE, BILLY, 1914-
   vocal

E13 EVANS, Chris: Billy Eckstine in
Journal of Jazz Discography, No.
1 (November 1976): 10-11; additions and corrections in Journal
of Jazz Discography, No. 2 (June
1977): 3, 5; No. 3 (March 1978):
2, 21-22 ((2, 3, 7))

E14 MOHR, Kurt: Des septant-huit aux
trent-trois tours in Point du
Jazz, No. 13 (June 1977): 35-39;
additions and corrections from
Henri ROBBERECHTS in Point du
Jazz, No. 15 (July 1979): 149
[1944-1947 recordings] ((1, 2, 3,
6, 7))

E15 NIQUET, Bernard: Discographie
critique de Billy Eckstine in
Jazz Hot, No. 275 (September
1971): 25 [to 1947] ((2, 3, 6, 7))

ECM label
   See E C M label

EDISON, HARRY, 1915-
   trumpet

E16 [[TOLLARA, Gianni: [Discography,
1953-1966] in Musica Jazz, Vol.
23 (November 1967)]]

EDISON label
   See also NICHOLS, RED (Hester,
   Stan: Red Nichols recordings on
   Edison)

E17 MAHONY, Dan, and Harry CRAWFORD:
Edison jazz in Jazz Music, Vol. 4
(No. 3, 1949): 18-23; additions
and corrections in Jazz Music,
Vol. 4 (No. 7, 1951): 13; Vol. 5
(No. 2): 12 ((2))

E18 WILE, Ray: Edison jazz survey in
Record Research, Vol. 4 (September-October 1958): 12-15; additions and corrections in Record
Research Bulletin, No. 7 (December 1958?): 4 ((3, 7))

E19 WILE, Ray: Edison needle cut records in Record Research, Vol. 2
(July-August 1956): 9-10; (November-December 1956): 11 ((3, 6))

E20 WILE, Ray: Laterally last in Record Research, No. 54 (August
1963): 3-9 ((3, 4p, 5))

EDWARDS, CLIFF, 1895-1971
   ukulele, vocal

E21 BACKENSTO, Woody: Cliff Edwards
and his Hot Combination in Record
Exchange, Vol. 5 (April 1952):
3-5 ((2, 3, 6, 7d))

E22 WATERS, Howard J.: Cliff Edwards
and his Hot Combination in Record
Research, Vol. 2 (January-February 1957): 6; also in International Discophile, No. 2 (fall
1955) ((2, 3, 6, 7))

EDWARDS, DAVID "HONEY BOY," 1915-
   guitar, harmonica, vocal

E23 WELDING, Pete, and Mike LEAD-
BITTER: Discography in Blues Unlimited, No. 54 (June 1968): 13
((2, 3, 7))

EGMONT label (British)

E24 HARRISON, Bob: A listing of the
Egmont-Summit AJS series in
Matrix, No. 102/103 (May 1974):
3-13; No. 104 (August 1974): 3-12
((2, 3, 6, 7))

EICHWALD, HAKAN VON, 1908-1964
  leader

E25 ENGLUND, Bjorn: A discography of
     Hakan von Eichwald in Matrix, No.
     50 (December 1963): 13-14; addi-
     tions and corrections in Matrix,
     No. 55 (October 1964): 17 ((2, 3,
     7))

E26 ENGLUND, Bjorn: Hakan von
     Eichwald diskografi in Orkester
     Journalen, Vol. 43 (December
     1975): 58 ((2, 3, 6, 7))

E27 ENGLUND, Bjorn, and Roger
     ALMQVIST: Hakan von Eichwald re-
     search! in Record Research, No.
     129/130 (October-November 1974):
     6 ((2, 3, 6, 7))

EIGHTH DAY (musical group)

E28 HUGHES, Rob: Eighth Day discogra-
     phy in Hot Buttered Soul, No. 46
     (June-July 1976): 7 ((3, 7))

EKOPHON label (Swedish)

E29 ENGLUND, Bjorn: A glimpse into
     the past; Ekophon in Storyville,
     No. 83 (June-July 1979): 230-231
     ((3, 7))

ELBERT, DONNIE
  vocal

E30 MOHR, Kurt: Discographie de
     Donnie Elbert in Soul Bag, No. 46
     (February 1975): 3-5 ((3))

E31 MOHR, Kurt: Donnie Elbert discog-
     raphy in Hot Buttered Soul, No.
     38 (March 1975?): 7-9 ((7))

ELDRIDGE, ROY, 1911-
  trumpet
  See also GOODMAN, BENNY (Discographies de Benny Goodman et Roy
  Eldridge)

E32 BOLTON, Robert: "Little jazz" Roy
     Eldridge in Jazz Journal, Vol. 24
     (August 1971): 10 [1950-] ((—))

E33 DELAUNAY, Charles: Discographie
     de Roy Eldridge (extrait de la
     Hot Discographie 1948) in Jazz
     Hot, No. 26 (October 1948) ((2,
     3, 7))

E34 EVENSMO, Jan: The trumpet of Roy
     Eldridge 1929-1944. [Hosle, Nor-
     way: 1979], 47 pp. (Jazz Solog-
     raphy series, Vol. 10) ((1, 2,
     3, 6, 7, 9))

E35 HOEFER, George: Selected discog-
     raphy of early Eldridge in Down
     Beat, Vol. 30 (January 31, 1963):
     36 ((2, 3, 7)) [1935-1936 record-
     ings]

E36 REHNBERG, Bert: Recordings (Swe-
     den) in Jazz Music, Vol. 7 (Jan-
     uary-February 1956): 14 ((2, 3,
     7))

E37 Selected Eldridge discography in
     Down Beat, Vol. 44 (December 15,
     1977): 25 ((—))

ELECTRONIC MUSICAL INSTRUMENTS (JAZZ)

E38 LOVAS, Rudolf: 4 way stereo in
     Jazz Forum (Poland), No. 18 (Au-
     gust 1972): 65 ((—))

ELGAR'S CREOLE ORCHESTRA

E39 SAGAWE, Harm: Elgar's Creole Or-
     chestra in Storyville, No. 52
     (April-May 1972): 150-151 ((2, 3,
     7))

ELITE label
  See HIT label; ROYALE label

ELLINGTON, DUKE (Edward Kennedy
  Ellington), 1899-1974
  piano, composer

E40 AASLAND, Benny H.: Duke och
     piraterna; rovarpressade godbitar
     for discofilen in Orkester Jour-
     nalen, Vol. 24 (January 1956):
     24-25 ((1, 7, 9))

E41 AASLAND, Benny H.: Glimtar av en
     unik hertig in Orkester Jour-
     nalen, Vol. 42 (July-August
     1974): 8, 28 ((1, 2, 3, 6, 7, 9))

E42 AASLAND, Benny H.: The "wax
     works" of Duke Ellington
     [Daneryd, Sweden: 1954]; ca. 140
     pp.; additions and corrections in
     JACOBS, Irving L.: The waxworks
     of Duke Ellington; some additions
     in Discophile, No. 44 (October
     1955): 14-17, 19; No. 45 (Decem-
     ber 1955): 14-15; No. 46 (Febru-
     ary 1956): 11-12; No. 47 (April
     1956): 10-11; No. 48 (June 1956):
     13 ((1, 2, 3, 4t, 7d, 8))

E43 [[AASLAND, Benny H.: The "wax
     works" of Duke Ellington. Jar-
     falla, Sweden: Duke Ellington
     Music Society, 1978]]

E44   BAKKER, Dick M.; Hans Ulrich
      HILL; and Joe HARPER: Duke El-
      lington 1943-1944 in Micrography,
      No. 47 (June 1978): 9-16; addi-
      tions and corrections in Microg-
      raphy, No. 48 (September 1978):
      19-20 ((1, 2, 4t, 7))

E45   BAKKER, Dick M.; Hans Ulrich
      HILL; and Joe HARPER: Duke El-
      lington 1943-1945 in Micrography,
      No. 41 (May 1976); No. 42 (Octo-
      ber 1976); No. 43 (March 1977);
      No. 47 (June 1978), various pa-
      ginations ((1, 7d))

E46   BAKKER, Dick M.: Duke Ellington
      on Columbia/Okeh/Harmony 1927-
      1930 in Micrography, No. 9 (Feb-
      ruary 1970): 2 ((7d))

E47   BAKKER, Dick M.: Duke Ellington
      on microgroove 1923-1942. Alphen
      aan de Rijn, Netherlands: Microg-
      raphy, 1974, 52 pp.; additions
      and corrections in Micrography,
      No. 35 (March 1975): 3, 5, 8 ((1,
      2, 3, 4r, 4t, 6, 7))

E48   BAKKER, Dick M.: Duke Ellington
      on microgroove volume one--1923-
      1936. Alphen aan de Rijn, Nether-
      lands: Micrography [1977], 83 pp.
      ((1, 2, 4t, 6, 7, 8, 9))

E49   BAKKER, Dick M. Duke Ellington on
      small labels in Micrography, No.
      1 (December 1968): 6-7; additions
      and corrections in Micrography,
      No. 13 (February 1971): 3 ((6,
      7d))

E50   BAKKER, Dick M.: Duke Ellington
      Victor's [sic] in Micrography,
      No. 6 (October 1969): 2-3 ((7d))

E51   BAKKER, Dick M.: Ellington-Bruns-
      wick-Voc-Col-listing 1926-35 in
      Micrography, No. 12 (January
      1971): 2-4; additions and correc-
      tions in Micrography, No. 21
      (September 1972): 5 ((7d))

E52   BAKKER, Dick M: Ellington Bruns-
      wicks 1936-40 in Micrography, No.
      14 (May 1971): 6-8; additions and
      corrections in Micrography, No.
      21 (September 1972): 5 ((7d))

E53   [[BAKKER, Dick M.: Ellington-
      listing from 1924 till March
      1940. Alphen aan de Rijn, Nether-
      lands: Micrography, 1972, 24
      pp.]]; additions and corrections
      in Micrography, No. 24 (February
      1973): 3; No. 26 (1973): 2 ((6))

E54   BAKKER, Dick M.: Ellington on
      Victor 1940-42 in Micrography,
      No. 15 (September 1971): 9 ((7d))

E55   CALVER, V. C.: A chronological
      survey of Duke Ellington's rec-
      ords in Swing Music, Vol. 1
      (April 1935): 50-52; additions
      and corrections from Terence I.
      GILL in Swing Music, Vol. 1 (May
      1935): 75; [from Nan BLOOM] (June
      1935): 107 ((7d))

E56   CARRIERE, Claude: Stomp, look &
      listen; discographie sélective
      des microsillons du Duke in Jazz
      Hot, No. 298 (October 1973): 22-
      23, 38 ((7d))

E57   CHOLINSKI, Henryk: Duke Ellington
      on LPs in Jazz Forum (Poland),
      No. 23 (June 1973) to No. 26
      (December 1973); No. 27 (February
      1974), various paginations ((—))

E58   DELAUNAY, Charles: Discographies,
      extrait de la Hot discographie
      1948 in Jazz Hot, No. 18 (Decem-
      ber 1947): 10-11 ((1, 2, 3, 7))
      [also of J. C. HIGGINBOTHAM]

E59   Discographie de Duke Ellington et
      son orchestre (disques parus en
      France) in Jazz Hot, No. 43
      (April 1950): 8-9, 18 ((2, 7d))

E60   [[FEATHER, Leonard: Duke Elling-
      ton: a selected and annotated
      discography in Contemporary Key-
      board, Vol. 4 (November 1978):
      76-78]]

E61   [[FRESIA, Enzo: Discografia in
      Musica Jazz, Vol. 17 (May 1961):
      41-42 [March 1959 to October
      1960]]]

E62   FRESIA, Enzo: Duke Ellington 1962
      in Musica Jazz, Vol. 19 (October
      1963): 50-51 ((2, 3, 7))

E63   FRESIA, Enzo: Duke Ellington on
      Capitol in Jazz Music, Vol. 8
      (November-December 1957): 7-10
      [reprinted from Musica Jazz, un-
      known issue] ((2, 3, 7d))

E64   FRESIA, Enzo: Ellington su Re-
      prise in Musica Jazz, Vol. 21
      (July 1965): 36 ((2, 3, 7))

E65   GAMMOND, Peter: Record guide in
      his Duke Ellington; his life and
      music. London: Phoenix House,
      1958 (also New York: Roy, 1958;
      London: Jazz Book Club, 1960; New
      York: DaCapo, 1977 [c1958]), 217-
      255 ((2, 7, 8, 9))

E66   HARRIS, H. Meunier: An Ellington
      investigation in Jazz Notes (Aus-
      tralia), No. 93 (May 1949): 12-
      13 [Australian releases] ((3,
      7d))

E67 HODARA, Morris: The Duke on discs; a key to all currently available recordings in High Fidelity, Vol. 24 (November 1974): 79-85 ((4t, 8))

E68 HOEFER, George: A Duke discography in Down Beat, Vol. 19 (November 5, 1952): 17 [1945-1951 recordings] ((1, 7d))

E69 JEPSEN, Jorgen Grunnet: Discography of Duke Ellington [Brande, Denmark: Debut Records, 1959], 3 v. ((1, 2, 3, 6, 7))

E70 JEPSEN, Jorgen Grunnet: Discography of Duke Ellington. 2d ed. [Brande, Denmark: Debut Records, 1960], 3 v. ((1, 2, 3, 6, 7))

E71 JEPSEN, Jorgen Grunnet: Diskofilspalten in Orkester Journalen, Vol. 25 (July-August 1957): 26-27 [1953-1956 recordings] ((2, 3, 7d))

E72 JEPSEN, Jorgen Grunnet: Diskofilspalten in Orkester Journalen, Vol. 30 (December 1962): 29, 48 [1959-1962 recordings] ((2, 3, 7))

E73 JEPSEN, Jorgen Grunnet: Duke Ellington 1947-1958; a discography [Vanløse, Denmark]: 1959, 14 pp. ((2, 3, 7))

E74 JEWELL, Derek: Selected discography and bibliography in his Duke; a portrait of Duke Ellington. New York: Norton [c1977], 251-253 ((—))

E75 LAMBERT, G. E.: Microgroove reissues of rare early Ellington recordings in Jazz Monthly, No. 153 (November 1967): 29-30 ((3, 6, 7d))

E76 MALINGS, Ron: Duke Ellington forum; a new column of comment in Matrix, No. 78 (August 1968); No. 80 (December 1968); No. 82 (April 1969); No. 85 (October 1969); No. 91 (February 1971), various paginations; additions and corrections in Matrix, No. 86 (December 1969): 14 [additions/corrections to various Ellington discographies]

E77 MASSAGLI, Luciano; Liborio PUSATERI; and Giovanni M. VOLONTE: Duke Ellington's story on records. Milan: Musica Jazz (1967-1972) or Raretone (1974 to date) [latest volume, No. 13 (1979) covers 1963-1965]; addi-

tions and corrections in DEBROE, Georges or Andre FONTEYNE: Ellington en question in Point du Jazz, No. 2 (February 1970) to date; and their Ellington or Ellington en question in Point du Jazz, No. 2 (February 1970) to date, various paginations ((1, 2, 3, 4p, 4r, 4t, 6, 7, 8, 9))

E78 [[POPE'S RECORDS, ed.: Duke Ellington discography. Carnegie, PA: n.d., 24 pp.]]

E79 REID, John D.: Duke Ellington discography; Victor and Bluebird records. n.p., n.d., 18 leaves ((2, 3, 6, 7))

E80 SANFILIPPO, Luigi: General catalog of Duke Ellington's recorded music. Palermo: New Jazz Society, 1964, 70 pp. ((1, 2, 3, 7, 9))

E81 SANFILIPPO, Luigi: General catalog of Duke Ellington's recorded music [2d ed.] Palermo: Centro Studi di Musica Contemporanea/New Jazz Society, 1966, 111 pp. ((1, 2, 3, 4t, 6, 7, 9))

E82 SEIDEL, Richard: Duke Ellington; fifty years on records (1924-74), discography in Schwann-1 Record and Tape Guide, Vol. 26 (April 1974): 34-36 ((—))

E83 Selected discography in ELLINGTON, Duke: Music is my mistress. Garden City, NY: Doubleday, 1973, 491-492 ((—))

E84 Selected discography in ELLINGTON, Duke: Music is my mistress. New York: DaCapo [c1973], 491-492 (Note: this is a rev. ed. of the previous entry. Also published in London by W. H. Allen, 1974 [not examined], which may have one of these discographies) ((—))

E85 SILVESTRI, Edgardo M.: Duke Ellington: sus segundas matrices y Jazz directory in Jazz Magazine (Argentina), No. 34 (September 1952): 9, 19 [adds second takes to Ellington listing in Carey's Directory of recorded jazz]

E86 SIMONS, Sim: Transcribed at last; the uncollected Duke Ellington in Swingtime (Belgium), No. 38 (March 1979): 3-11 [Capitol transcriptions 1946-1947] ((1, 2, 3, 6, 7, 9))

E87 THIELE, Bob: Duke Ellington's discography in Jazz (US), Vol. 1

(No. 5 & 6, 1943): 20-28, 31 ((2, 3))

E88   TIMNER, Willie E.: Ellingtonia; a collector's manual; the recorded music of Duke Ellington and his sidemen. [Montreal]: 1976, unpaged ((1, 2, 3, 4t, 6, 7d))

E89   TIMNER, Willie E.: Ellingtonia; a collector's manual; the recorded music of Duke Ellington and his sidemen. 2d ed. [Montreal]: 1979, unpaged ((1, 2, 3, 4t, 6, 7))

E90   TOLLARA, Gianni, and Luciano MASSAGLI: Discografia; gli inediti di Duke Ellington in Musica Jazz, Vol. 18 (June 1962); Vol. 19 (April 1963): 46-47 ((1, 2, 3, 6, 7, 9))

E91   ULANOV, Barry; Albert McCARTHY; and Charles FOX: A complete Duke Ellington discography in ULANOV, Barry: Duke Ellington. New York: Creative Age, 1946 (also London: Jazz Book Club, 1947; New York: DaCapo [c1946], 277-311; and in Spanish transl., Buenos Aires: Estuardo [1946], 343-387 [recordings to 1936] ((2, 3, 7))

Sidemen

E92   Duke Ellington en Europe; les musiciens de son orchestre in Jazz Hot, No. 43 (April 1950): 13-16 ((—))

Soundtracks

E93   BAKKER, Dick M.: Duke Ellington at the movie [sic] 1929-1934 in Micrography, No. 3 (May 1969): 3 ((7d))

E94   TERCINET, Alain: Hollywood hangover; filmographie de Duke Ellington in Jazz Hot, No. 298 (October 1973): 24-26 ((6, 7d))

Transcriptions

See also ELLINGTON, DUKE (Aasland, Benny H.: Duke och piraterna)

E95   BAKKER, Dick M.: Duke Ellington's Capitol transcriptions in Micrography, No. 49 (December 1978): 19 ((1, 7d))

E96   JACOBS, Irving L.: The discographer's corner; Duke Ellington on transcriptions in Jazz Review, Vol. 3 (June 1960): 41-42 [1941 to 1959 recordings] ((1, 2, 3, 7))

E97   VALBURN, Jerry: Date with the Duke; AFRS transcriptions in The Discographer, Vol. 2 (third quarter 1969): 2-13 to 2-32 ((7d))

ELLIS, DON, 1934-1978
trumpet

E98   Album av Don Ellis and his Orchestra i kronologisk ordning in Orkester Journalen, Vol. 44 (December 1976): 17 ((—))

EMARCY label

E99   JEPSEN, Jorgen Grunnet: Diskofilspalten in Orkester Journalen, Vol. 26 (April 1958); (May 1958); (June 1958); (August 1958); (September 1958), various paginations ((2, 3, 7d))

E100   KWIECINSKI, Walter: Emarcy reissues--from Keynote and National in Jazz Statistics, No. 10 (May 1959): 6-7; additions and corrections from M. VOGLER in Jazz Statistics, No. 17 (1960): 2 ((2, 3, 7))

EMERSON, BILLY THE KID, 1929-
piano, vocal

E101   LEADBITTER, Mike, and John J. BROVEN: Billy "The Kid" Emerson in Blues Unlimited, No. 4 (August 1963): 8-9; additions and corrections in Blues Unlimited, undated supplement to Nos. 1-6: 3; No. 12 (June 1964): suppl-4, 6 ((2, 3, 7))

E102   O'NEAL, Jim, and Billy EMERSON: Billy "The Kid" Emerson discography in Living Blues, No. 45/46 (spring 1980): 43 ((2, 3, 6, 7))

EMOTIONS (musical group)

E103   DAGUERRE, Pierre, and Kurt MOHR: Emotions in Soul Bag, No. 66/67 (March-April 1978): 5-7 ((2, 3, 7))

E104   ELSEY, Alan: Emotions--make up for lost time in Hot Buttered Soul, No. 39 (July 1975?): 6; No. 40 (September 1975?): 2-3 ((3, 7, 8))

E105   ENGEL, Ed: The Emotions in Record Exchanger, No. 22 (1976?): 12, 19 ((—))

EMPIRE label

E106 Empire in Quartette, No. 2 (March 1970): 30 ((3))

EMPIRICAL label

E107 HULME, George: The Empirical label; a listing in Matrix, No. 41 (June 1962): 3-6; additions and corrections in Matrix, No. 49 (October 1963): 16; No. 51 (February 1964): 18 ((2, 7))

ENJA label (German)

E108 Enja in Disk in the World, Vol. 1 (July 1980): 6-20 ((2, 7d))

ER label
    See E R label

ERVIN, BOOKER, 1930-1970
    tenor saxophone

E109 WILBRAHAM, Roy: Booker Ervin discography in Discographical Forum, No. 19 (July 1970) to No. 23 (March 1971), various paginations ((1, 2, 3, 7))

ERWIN, PEE WEE (George Erwin), 1913-
    trumpet

E110 EYLE, Wim van: Pee Wee Erwin name-discography in Jazz Press, No. 44 (October 1, 1977): 20 ((2, 3, 6, 7))

ESQUIRE label (British)

E111 KRAHMER, Carlo: A discography of Esquire records in Discophile, No. 5 (April 1949): 2-5; additions and corrections in Discophile, No. 13 (August 1950): 24; No. 14 (October 1950): 1; No. 15 (December 1950): 2; No. 23 (April 1952): 14-19; No. 24 (June 1952): 11; No. 28 (February 1953): 14-16, 6; No. 30 (June 1953): 3-4; No. 35 (April 1954): 3-6; No. 36 (June 1954): 9; No. 42 (June 1955): 6-15; No. 49 (August 1956): 6-9; No. 50 (October 1956): 12; No. 53 (April 1957): 12-13; No. 56 (October 1957): 9-10; Matrix, No. 29 (August 1960): 6; No. 34 (June 1961): 6-8; No. 35/36 (September 1961): 25-26; No. 37 (November 1961): 12-15; No. 46 (April 1963): 13 ((2, 3, 7))

ESQUIRE JAZZ CONCERT

E112 BAKKER, Dick M.: Second Esquire All-American Jazz Concert 17 Jan. 1945 in Micrography, No. 45 (September 1977): 21 ((7))

E113 COLLER, Derek: The Second Esquire Jazz Concert in Matrix, No. 92 (April 1971): 3-4 ((1, 2, 7))

ESTES, JOHN, 1899-1977
    guitar, vocal

E114 Sleepy John Estes 1929-1941; a reissue discography in Hip, Vol. 4 new series (September 1968): 5-7 ((—))

E115 STEWART-BAXTER, Derrick: [Tentative discography] in Jazz Journal, Vol. 3 (January 1950): 3; additions and corrections from Albert McCARTHY in Jazz Journal, Vol. 3 (April 1950): 14 ((3, 5))

EUROPE, JAMES REESE, 1881-1919
    piano, violin, leader
    See also BLAKE, EUBIE (Montgomery, Mike: Exploratory discography of Noble Sissle...)

E116 Lieut. Jim Europe discography in Record Research, Vol. 1 (December 1955): 5 ((3, 6, 8))

E117 STEINER, John: Jim Europe's discography in Jazz Record (US), No. 60 (November 1947): 18-19 ((3, 6))

EVANS, BILL, 1929-1980
    piano

E118 Bill Evans discography in Swing Journal, Vol. 27 (January 1973): 70-77 ((2, 7d))

E119 Microsillons enregistrés avec le concours de Bill Evans in Jazz Hot, No. 161 (January 1961): 17 ((—))

E120 RUPPLI, Michel: Discographie: Bill Evans in Jazz Hot, No. 353 (September 1978): 45-47; No. 354 (October 1978): 14-18 ((1, 2, 3, 7))

E121 Selected Bill Evans discography in Down Beat, Vol. 46 (October 1979): 20 ((—))

E122 Selected Evans discography in Down Beat, Vol. 43 (March 11, 1976): 12 ((—))

E123 Selected Evans discography in
  Jazz Forum (Poland), No. 58
  (1979): 32 ((—))

E124 WALKER, Malcolm: Bill Evans in
  Jazz Monthly, Vol. 11 (June
  1965) to (September 1965), various paginations, in 4 parts;
  additions and corrections in Jazz
  Monthly, Vol. 12 (August 1966):
  14; (November 1966): 27; (February 1967): 24; Vol. 13 (April
  1967): 26; (May 1967): 28; (November 1967): 27; (December
  1967): 29 ((2, 3, 7))

EVANS, DOC (Paul Wesley Evans), 1907-
  trumpet

E125 [Discography of records made
  under his own name] in Jazz Notes
  (Australia), No. 95 (August
  1949): 6 ((2, 3, 6, 7))

EVANS, GIL (Ian Ernest Gilmore Green),
  1912-
  arranger

E126 ENDRESS, Gudrun: Gil Evans in
  Jazz Podium, Vol. 23 (December
  1974): 11 ((—))

E127 Gil Evans in Swing Journal, Vol.
  30 (May 1976): 270-273 ((2, 7d))

E128 Selected Evans discography in
  Down Beat, Vol. 43 (May 20,
  1976): 15 ((—))

EVANS, HERSCHEL, 1909-1939
  tenor saxophone
  See also SAXOPHONE MUSIC (JAZZ)
  (Evensmo, Jan: The tenor saxophones of Henry Bridges...) and
  (Evensmo, Jan: The tenor saxophon-
  ists of the period 1930-1942)

E129 McCARTHY, Albert J.: Basie's
  other tenor; the Herschel Evans
  story in Jazz & Blues, Vol. 1
  (November 1971): 10 ((—))

EVANS, ROY, ca. 1890-ca. 1943
  drums, vocal

E130 PENNY, Howard E.: Roy Evans discography in Good Diggin', Vol. 2
  (December 1948): 14-16 ((2, 3))

EVERGREEN label (Swedish)

E131 ELFSTROM, Mats: Evergreen records
  in Discophile, No. 24 (June
  1952): 14 ((2, 3, 7))

EXCELLO label

E132 GUERRY, Jean: Les disques de
  blues Excello in Soul Bag, No. 16
  (1972?): 17-19 ((—))

E133 TURNER, Bez, and Peter GIBBON:
  The Excello listing in Blues Un-
  limited, No. 131/132 (September-
  December 1978): 20-26 ((—))

EXCELLOS FIVE JAZZBAND

E134 The Excellos Five Jazzband in
  Doctor Jazz, No. 61 (August-
  September 1973): 7 ((2, 3, 7))

EXCITERS (musical group)

E135 MOHR, Kurt: The Exciters in Soul
  Bag, No. 33 (December 1973): 3-4;
  additions and corrections in Soul
  Bag, No. 45 (January 1975): 34
  ((2, 3, 5, 7p))

EZELL, WILL, ca. 1905-
  piano

E136 HENRY, Tom: Will Ezell discography in Record Changer, Vol. 3
  (June 1944): 47 ((3))

E137 RANKIN, Bill: Behind the label in
  Jazz Record (UK), No. 11 (March
  1944): 16 ((3))

FM label
  See DUD SOUND label

FARLOW, TAL, 1921-
  guitar
  See also NORVO, RED (Kraner,
  Dietrich H.)

F1 EYLE, Wim van: Tal Farlow discog-
  rafie in Jazz Press, No. 51
  (May 1, 1978): 16-17; No. 52
  (June 1978): 25-26 ((2, 3, 6, 7))

F2 GARDNER, Mark: Tel est Tal in
  Jazz Magazine (France), No. 188
  (April 1971): 47 ((—))

F3 POSTIF, François: La discographie
  française de Tal Farlow in Jazz
  Magazine (France), No. 19 (July-
  August 1956): 14 ((2, 3, 7))

F4 Selected Farlow discography in
  Down Beat, Vol. 46 (February 22,
  1979): 22 ((—))

F5 Tal Farlow in Swing Journal, Vol.
  30 (September 1976): 272-275 ((2,
  7))

FARMER, ART, 1928–
trumpet

F6   [Discography] in Swing Journal,
Vol. 33 (April 1979): 232–237
((2, 7d))

F7   McCARTHY, Albert J.: Art Farmer
discography in Jazz Monthly, Vol.
6 (July 1960) to (October 1960),
various paginations ((1, 2, 3,
7))

FARRIS, LONNIE, 1924–
guitar

F8   DEMETRE, Jacques: Lonnie Farris
in Blues Unlimited, No. 96 (November 1972): 15 ((—))

FASCINATIONS (musical group)

F9   MOHR, Kurt: The Fascinations in
Soul Bag, No. 45 (January 1975):
26 ((2, 3, 7))

FAY label
See LASALLE label

FAZOLA, IRVING (Irving Prestopnik),
1912–1949
clarinet

F10   Irv Fazola discography in Down
Beat, Vol. 16 (May 20, 1949): 12–
13 ((—))

FEATURE label
See ZYNN label

FEDERAL label
See PHILLIPS, ESTHER (Mohr,
Kurt); WITHERSPOON, JIMMY (Mohr,
Kurt)

FERGUSON, CHARLIE

F11   MOHR, Kurt: Charlie: "Little Jazz"
Ferguson in Jazz Statistics, No.
7 (1958?): 8 ((2, 3, 7))

FERGUSON, MAYNARD, 1928–
trumpet

F12   DOWL, Pat B.: Maynard Ferguson in
Different Drummer, Vol. 1 (October 1974): 20 ((—))

F13   HARKINS, Edwin: Maynard Ferguson;
a discography. Solana Beach, CA:
1976, 73 leaves ((1, 2, 3, 6, 7))

F14   Selected Ferguson discography in
Down Beat, Vol. 42 (June 5,
1975): 11 ((—))

FIELDS, ERNIE
leader, trombone

F15   MOHR, Kurt: Discography of Ernie
Fields in Jazz Statistics, No. 25
(March 1962): 8 ((2, 3, 7))

FILMS
See SOUNDTRACKS

FINE ART label

F16   ROTANTE, Anthony, and Len
KUNSTADT: Exploring "Fine Art"
and "Bango" labels in Record Research, No. 81 (January 1967): 7;
No. 84 (June 1967): 8–9 ((8))

FIREHOUSE FIVE PLUS TWO

F17   JEPSEN, Jorgen Grunnet: Diskofil-
splaten in Orkester Journalen,
Vol. 31 (July–August 1963): 21;
(September 1963): 23 ((2, 3, 7))

FISHER, EDDIE, 1943–
guitar

F18   NIQUET, Bernard: Discographie de
Eddie Fisher in Soul Bag, No. 51
(January 1976): 25 ((2, 7))

F19   NIQUET, Bernard: Eddie Fisher in
Point du Jazz, No. 9 (December
1973): 57 ((2, 7))

FISHER, MARY ANN
See RAELETS

FITZGERALD, ELLA, 1918–
vocal

F20   LANGE, Horst H.: Discophilia;
Ella Fitzgerald mit Begleit-
Ensembles in Schlagzeug, No. 20
(April 1959) [and possibly other
issues; in separate "pull-out"
section, unpaged] ((2, 3, 7))

FLAMINGOS (musical group)

F21   DIEZ, Jerry: Flamingo discography
in R and B Collector, Vol. 1
(March–April 1970): 15 ((3))

FLANAGAN, TOMMY, 1930–
    piano

F22   Tommy Flanagan discography in
      Swing Journal, Vol. 29 (February
      1975): 240–247 ((2, 7d))

FLEMMING, HERB, 1898?–1970
    trombone

F23   BIAGIONI, Egino: Discography in
      his Herb Flemming; a jazz pioneer
      around the world. Alphen aan de
      Rijn, Netherlands: Micrography
      [1978], 81–87 ((2, 3, 6, 7))

FLOYD, FRANK
    See HARMONICA FRANK

FM label
    See DUD SOUND label

FOL, RAYMOND
    piano

F24   SIMONS, Sim: Raymond Fol in
      Swingtime (Belgium), No. 40 (May–
      June 1979): 28–30 ((2, 3, 6, 7))

FOLKWAYS label

F25   BRUIN, Leo W.: "Folkways" in
      Boogie Woogie & Blues Collector,
      No. 30/31 (August 1973): 6–10
      ((—))

FORD, BILLY
    trumpet

F26   MOHR, Kurt: Discography of Billy
      Ford in Jazz Statistics, No. 21
      (March 1961): 7–8; additions and
      corrections from M. VOGLER in
      Jazz Statistics, No. 22 (June
      1961): 1–2 ((2, 3, 6, 7))

FORESYTHE, REGINALD, 1907–1958
    piano, arranger

F27   McCARTHY, Albert: Reginald
      Foresythe discography in Jazz
      Monthly, No. 187 (September
      1970): 26–27 ((2, 3, 6, 7))

FORMAN, JAMES
    piano

F28   [Discography] in Jazz Statistics,
      No. 25 (March 1962): 6 ((3, 7d))

FORREST, JIMMY, 1920–1980
    tenor saxophone

F29   HARTMANN, Dieter: Jimmy Forrest
      on United in Jazz + Classic, No.
      1 (February–March 1979): 20 ((2,
      3, 6, 7))

F30   TARRANT, Don: Jimmy Forrest dis-
      cography in Journal of Jazz Dis-
      cography, No. 3 (March 1978):
      8–21; additions and corrections
      in Journal of Jazz Discography,
      No. 4 (January 1979): 2 ((1, 2,
      3, 7))

FORTUNE, SONNY, 1939–
    alto saxophone

F31   Selected Fortune discography in
      Down Beat, Vol. 43 (February 12,
      1976): 17 ((—))

FOSTER, EDDIE
    vocal

F32   CHOISNEL, Emmanuel: Eddie Foster
      in Soul Bag, No. 22/23 (January–
      February 1973): 20–21 ((2, 3, 7))

FOSTER, GARY, 1936–
    saxophones

F33   Selected Foster discography in
      Down Beat, Vol. 43 (November 18,
      1976): 15 ((—))

FOSTER, HERMAN, 1928–
    piano

F34   NIQUET, Bernard: Herman Foster in
      Point du Jazz, No. 15 (July
      1979): 140 ((2, 7))

FOSTER, LEROY, 1923–1958
    guitar, vocal

F35   LEADBITTER, Mike: Baby Face
      Leroy Foster in Blues Unlimited,
      No. 31 (March 1966): 11 ((2, 3))

FOSTER, POPS (George Murphy Foster),
    ca. 1892–1969
    bass violin

F36   Quelques enregistrements mar-
      quants de Pops Foster actuelle-
      ment disponibles in Jazz Hot, No.
      316 (May 1975): 29 ((—))

F37   RUST, Brian: Pops Foster discog-
      raphy 1924–1940 in Pops Foster;

the autobiography of a New Orleans jazzman, as told to Tom Stoddard. Berkeley, CA: Univ. of California Pr., 1971: 181-197 ((2, 3, 6, 7))

FOSTER, WILLIE, 1922-
harmonica, piano, vocal

F38 MOHR, Kurt: Little Willie Foster; a discography in Blues Unlimited, No. 26 (October 1965): 13 ((2, 3, 7))

FOUNTAIN, PETE, 1930-
clarinet

F39 BEDWELL, Stephen: A Pete Fountain discography, part 1: pre-1959. Halifax, N.S.: 1975, vi, 111 pp. ((1, 2, 3, 4p, 4r, 4t, 6, 7, 9))

F40 Pete Fountain's record albums in FOUNTAIN, Pete, and Bill NEELY: A closer walk; the Pete Fountain story. Chicago: Regnery, 1972, 201-202 ((—))

FOWLER, LEMUEL
piano

F41 MONTGOMERY, Michael: Lemuel Fowler rollography in Record Research, No. 24 (September-October 1959): 2 ((5))

F42 PARRY, W. H.: Lemuel Fowler (a provisional discography) in Discophile, No. 4 (February 1949): 9-12; additions and corrections in Discophile, No. 5 (April 1949): 10 ((2, 3, 7d))

FRANKLIN, BOBBY
guitar, vocal

F43 MOHR, Kurt: Bobby Franklin in Soul Bag, No. 45 (January 1975): 30 ((2, 3, 7))

FREDERIKSSON, BORJE
tenor saxophone

F44 HANSSON, Lars: Borje Frederiksson diskografi in Orkester Journalen, Vol. 36 (November 1968): 30 ((2, 7))

FREE JAZZ
See JAZZ MUSIC--AVANT-GARDE

FREEMAN, ERNIE, 1922-
piano

F45 MOHR, Kurt: Discographie d'Ernie Freeman in Jazz Hot, No. 122 (June 1957): 24 ((2, 3, 7))

FREEMAN, VON, 1922-
tenor saxophone

F46 Selected Freeman discography in Down Beat, Vol. 43 (November 4, 1976): 17 ((—))

FRIENDLY 5 label
See DUD SOUND label

FRISCO JAZZ BAND

F47 VENABLES, Ralph: The Frisco Jazz Band; a discography in Discophile, No. 3 (December 1948): 4 ((2, 3, 7d))

FUGUES
See MODERN JAZZ QUARTET (Owens, Thomas)

FULLER, BLIND BOY (Fulton Fuller Allen), 1908-1941
guitar, vocal

F48 BAKKER, Dick M.: Blind Boy Fuller 1935-1940 in Micrography, No. 3 (May 1969): 11 ((—))

FULLER, CURTIS, 1934-
trombone

F49 Sélection de microsillons enregistrés avec le concours de Curtis Fuller in Jazz Hot, No. 176 (May 1962): 26 ((—))

FULLER, EARL, 1885-1947
piano, leader
See JAZZ MUSIC (Jewson, Ron) and (Lange, Horst H.: The fabulous fives)

FULLER, GIL, 1920-
arranger

F50 HOEFER, George: Selected discography of Gil Fuller arrangements in Down Beat, Vol. 31 (April 9, 1964): 34 ((2, 3, 7))

FULLER, JOHNNY, 1929–
guitar, vocal

F51   CHAUVARD, Marcel; Kurt MOHR; and
Mike LEADBITTER: Discography of
Johnny Fuller, part 1 in Jazz
Statistics, No. 29 (October
1963): BS-6 ((3))

FULLER, ROCKY (Iverson Minter), 1936–
guitar, harmonica, vocal

F52   LEADBITTER, Mike: Rocky Fuller--
discography in Blues Unlimited,
No. 32 (April 1966): 9 ((3, 7))

FULSON, LOWELL, 1921–
guitar, vocal

F53   STRACHWITZ, Chris; Bob GEDDINS;
and Lowell FULSON: Discography in
Blues Unlimited Collectors Classics, No. 9 (December 1965): 3-7
[rev. ed. of next entry] ((2, 3,
7))

F54   STRACHWITZ, Chris: A Lowell
Fulson discography in Jazz Report
(California), Vol. 1 (March
1961): 26-29 ((3))

F55   TONNEAU, Serge: Discographie in
Point du Jazz, No. 1 (September
1969): 36 ((—))

FUTURA label (French)

F56   RABEN, Erik: Futura label listing
in Discographical Forum, No. 27
(November 1971): 7-8 ((2, 7))

GHB label
See JAZZOLOGY label

GADDY, BOB
piano, vocal

G1   CHAUVARD, Marcel, and Kurt MOHR:
Discography in Blues Unlimited,
No. 3 (July 1963): 2; additions
and corrections in Blues Un-
limited, undated supplement to
Nos. 1-6: 3 ((2, 3))

G2   ROTANTE, Anthony: The discography
of Bob Gaddy; exploratory name
listing in Record Research, No.
70 (August 1965): 9 ((2, 3))

GAINES, EARL
vocal

G3   MOHR, Kurt: Earl Gaines' discography in Soul Bag, No. 64 (October 1977): 6, 2 ((2, 3, 7))

GAINES, ROY, 1937–
guitar

G4   CHOISNEL, Emmanuel, and Kurt
MOHR: Roy Gaines discography in
Soul Bag, No. 48 (June 1975):
19-20; additions and corrections
in Soul Bag, No. 51 (January
1976): 32 ((2, 3, 7))

GARBAREK, JAN, 1947–
saxophones

G5   Jan Garbarek discography in Jazz
Journal, Vol. 30 (October 1977):
19 ((—))

G6   Jan Garbarek selected discography
in Jazz Forum (Poland), No. 54
(1978): 34 ((—))

G7   Selected Garbarek discography in
Down Beat, Vol. 44 (November 17,
1977): 17 ((—))

GARLAND, RED (William M. Garland),
1923–
piano

G8   Red Garland in Swing Journal,
Vol. 33 (May 1979): 220-225 ((2,
7d))

GARLOW, CLARENCE, 1911–
accordion, guitar, vocal

G9   LEADBITTER, Mike: The southern
blues singers--Clarence "Bon Ton"
Garlow in Blues Unlimited, No. 10
(March 1964): 6; additions and
corrections in Blues Unlimited,
No. 22 (May 1965): 10 ((2, 3, 7))

GARNER, EMMETT
vocal

G10   MOHR, Kurt: Emmett Garner in Soul
Bag, No. 45 (January 1975): 32
((2, 3, 6, 7))

GARNER, ERROLL, 1923-1977
piano

G11   DELAUNAY, Charles: [Discographie
extraite de Hot discography 1948]
in Jazz Hot, No. 17 (November
1947): 12; continued in BLUME,

M. A. G.: Discographie complémentaire d'Erroll Garner in Jazz
Hot, No. 36 (September 1949): 26;
additions and corrections in Jazz
Hot, No. 38 (November 1949): 31
((1, 2, 7d))

G12   [[[Discography] in Rytmi, No. 11
(1964)]]]

G13   [Discography] in Swing Journal,
Vol. 31 (March 1977): 276-281
((2, 7d))

G14   [[FRESIA, Enzo: Discografia in
Musica Jazz, Vol. 17 (March
1961): 38-40 [recordings issued
in Italy]]]

G15   SACHS, Tom: Erroll Garner discography in Jazz Monthly, Vol. 4
(November 1958): 7-9, 28; (December 1958): 29-32; (January 1959):
24-25; additions and corrections
from Donald HARLEY in Jazz Monthly, Vol. 4 (January 1959): 32
((2, 3, 6, 7))

GARY, SAM, 1917-
   piano, vocal

G16   COLLER, Derek, and Bert WHYATT:
Recordings in Jazz Music, Vol. 7
(March-April 1956): 29 ((2, 3, 6,
7))

GATES, HEN
   See FORMAN, JAMES

GAZELL label (Swedish)

G17   NYSTROM, Borje: Gazell in Discophile, No. 17 (April 1951): 13
((2, 3, 7d))

GENNETT label
   See also MORTON, JELLY ROLL
   (Bakker, Dick M.: Jelly Roll
   Morton on the labels Gennett &
   Paramount...); STARR GENNETT
   label

G18   Gennett discography in Vintage
Jazz Mart (September 1965) to
(March 1966), (September 1966),
(November 1966), (July 1967),
(April 1968) to (June 1969),
(July 1970), (October 1970), various paginations [discography has
its own paging system, separate
from the magazine's; covers 11000
series recordings up to 12080]
((7d))

G19   HENRIKSEN, Henry: Gennet [sic]
research; last hour in Record
Research, No. 94 (December 1968):
3-5 [from 6000-7000 series] ((4p,
7))

G20   ROBERTSON, Alex: Canadian Gennett
and Starr-Gennett 9000 numerical.
Montreal: 1972, iv, 30 leaves
((3, 6))

G21   WHYATT, Bert: Numerical natter;
Gennett in Vintage Jazz Mart,
Vol. 5 (August 1958): 3; (September 1958): 3, 42 [covers 12250 to
12679] ((3, 6, 7p))

GEORGIA MELODIANS

G22   Discography of Georgia Melodians
in Recorded Americana (January
1958): 1-2 ((2, 3, 7d))

GEORGIA TOM
   See DORSEY, THOMAS ANDREW

GEORGIANS (musical group)

G23   SPECHT, Paul: Discographie des
Georgians in Jazz Hot, No. 60
(November 1951): 12, 31 ((2, 3,
6, 7))

GETZ, STAN, 1927-
   tenor saxophone

G24   ADKINS, Tony, and Malcolm WALKER:
Private recordings in Discographical Forum, No. 13 (July 1969):
5-6; additions and corrections in
Discographical Forum, No. 15
(November 1969): 4; No. 18 (May
1970): 2 ((1, 2, 7))

G25   ASTRUP, Arne: The Stan Getz discography. [Texarkana, TX: Jerry
L. Atkins, c1978], 101 pp. ((1,
2, 3, 7))

G26   DELAUNAY, Charles: Stan Getz in
Jazz Hot, No. 56 (June 1951): 9;
additions in WIEDEMANN, Erik:
Discographie de Stan Getz in Jazz
Hot, No. 100 (June 1955): 16 ((2,
3, 7))

G27   EDWARDS, Ernie: Stan Getz in Jazz
Monthly, Vol. 10 (August 1964) to
(November 1964), various paginations; additions and corrections
from Roy J. WILBRAHAM in Jazz
Monthly, No. 153 (November 1967):
28; No. 155 (January 1968): 27-28
((1, 2, 3, 6, 7))

G28   EDWARDS, Ernie: Stan Getz on
       "Roost" in Discophile, No. 55
       (August 1957): 9-10 ((2, 3, 7))

G29   FRESIA, Enzo: Discografia in
       Musica Jazz, Vol. 18 (March
       1962): 41-42 [1961 Verve record-
       ings] ((2, 7))

G30   Selected Getz discography in Down
       Beat, Vol. 43 (August 12, 1976):
       18 ((—))

G31   Stan Getz in Swing Journal, Vol.
       32 (February 1978): 272-279 ((2,
       7d))

G32   [[WALKER, Malcolm: Stan Getz; a
       discography, 1944-1955. London:
       1957, 20 pp.]]

GHB label
       See JAZZOLOGY label

GIBBS, ARTHUR, ca. 1896-1956
       piano

G33   FLUCKIGER, Otto: The late Arthur
       Gibbs in Jazz Statistics, No. 2
       (June 1956): 5; additions and
       corrections in Jazz Statistics,
       No. 3 (August 1956): 10 ((2, 7p))

GIBBS, TERRY, 1924-
       vibraphone

G34   MORGAN, Alun: Discography; a name
       listing in Jazz Monthly, Vol. 11
       (July 1965): 14-18; additions and
       corrections in Jazz Monthly, Vol.
       12 (April 1966): 27; (August
       1966): 17; (November 1967): 29
       ((2, 3, 7))

GILLESPIE, DIZZY (John Birks
       Gillespie), 1917-
       trumpet

G35   BURNS, Jim: Dizzy Gillespie:
       1945-50 in Jazz Journal, Vol. 25
       (January 1972): 14 ((1))

G36   DELAUNAY, Charles: Discographie
       de Dizzy Gillespie (extrait de
       Hot discography 1948) in Jazz
       Hot, No. 16 (1947): 12 ((2, 3,
       7))

G37   Dizzy with Cab--discography in
       Down Beat, Vol. 28 (September 14,
       1961): 38 ((2, 3, 7))

G38   DOCTOR RHYTHM (pseud.): Disco-
       grafia de Gillespie in Jazz Maga-
       zine (Argentina), No. 9 (June
       1946): 18-19 ((2, 7d))

G39   JEPSEN, Jorgen Grunnet: Discogra-
       phy of Dizzy Gillespie. [Brande,
       Denmark: Debut Records, 1961], 33
       leaves ((1, 2, 3, 6, 7))

G40   JEPSEN, Jorgen Grunnet: A discog-
       raphy of Dizzy Gillespie. Copen-
       hagen: Knudsen [c1969], 2 v. ((1,
       2, 3, 6, 7))

G41   JEPSEN, Jorgen Grunnet: Dizzy
       Gillespie diskografi pa Clef-
       Norgran-Verve in Orkester Jour-
       nalen, Vol. 28 (October 1960):
       42; (November 1960): 46 ((2, 3,
       6, 7))

G42   RICHARD, Daniel: Dizzy disco in
       Jazz Magazine (France), No. 259
       (November 1977): 36-37, 50 ((—))

G43   Selected Gillespie discography in
       Down Beat, Vol. 45 (April 20,
       1978): 14 ((—))

G44   WALKER, Malcolm: Dizzy Gillespie
       on Dee Gee in Discographical
       Forum, No. 5 (May 1968): 10-11
       ((2, 3, 7))

G45   WEINSTOCK, Bob: Dizzy Gillespie;
       a complete discography in Record
       Changer, Vol. 8 (July 1949): 8,
       18; additions and corrections in
       Record Changer, Vol. 8 (November
       1949): 23 ((—))

GILLHAM, ART, 1895-1961
       piano

G46   BACKENSTO, Woody: Art Gillham--
       the whispering pianist in Record
       Research, No. 49 (March 1963):
       3-5; additions and corrections in
       Record Research, No. 71 (October
       1965): 8; No. 73 (January 1966):
       8 ((2, 3, 6, 7))

GILLUM, JAZZ (William Gillum), 1904-
       1966
       harmonica, vocal

G47   PANASSIÉ, Hugues: A discography
       of Jazz Gillum in Jazz Journal,
       Vol. 11 (January 1958): 3 ((2, 3,
       7))

GILMORE, JOHN, 1931-
       tenor saxophone

G48   SIMOSKO, Vladimir: John Gilmore
       discography in Coda, No. 139
       (June-July 1975): 9-11; additions
       from Alan WEST in Coda, No. 142
       (October 1975): 34 ((2, 7))

GILSON, JEF, 1926–
    piano, clarinet

G49 GARDNER, Mark: Jef Gilson discog-
    raphy in Discographical Forum,
    No. 5 (March 1968): 16–18; addi-
    tions and corrections from
    Dietrich KRANER and Mark GARDNER
    in Discographical Forum, No. 7
    (July 1968): 13 ((1, 2, 7))

GIUFFRE, JIMMY, 1921–
    clarinet

G50 JEPSEN, Jorgen Grunnet: Jimmy
    Giuffre diskografi in Orkester
    Journalen, Vol. 25 (December
    1957): 72 ((2, 3, 7d))

G51 NELSON, Don: The music in Jimmy
    Giuffre. New York: BMI, c1961,
    5–18 ((2, 8, 9))

GLENN, LLOYD, 1909–
    piano

G52 CHOISNEL, Emmanuel: Discographie
    de quelques séances auxquelles a
    participé Lloyd Glenn in Soul
    Bag, No. 41 (September 1974):
    25–27 ((2, 3, 6, 7))

G53 DEMEUSY, Bertrand: Lloyd Glenn's
    name discography in Jazz Journal,
    Vol. 18 (October 1965): 13 ((2,
    7d))

GLENNY, ALBERT, 1870–1958
    tuba, bass violin

G54 COLYER, Bill: Glenny discography
    in Eureka, Vol. 1 (March–April
    1960): 20–21 ((2, 3, 7))

GLORY label

G55 BRYMER, George: In that Glory
    land; a listing of the Glory
    label in Discophile, No. 33 (De-
    cember 1953): 13–14; additions
    and corrections in Discophile,
    No. 36 (June 1954): 9; No. 39
    (December 1954): 16 ((3))

GOLDEN CREST label

G56 McCARTHY, Albert J.: Jazz on
    Golden Crest in Discographical
    Forum, No. 1 (May 1960): 16–18;
    corrections from Michael SHERA in
    Discographical Forum, No. 2 (July
    1960): 8 ((2, 7))

GOLDEN GATE QUARTET

G57 GRENDYSA, Peter A.: Discography
    in Record Exchanger, No. 23
    (n.d.): 4–9 ((7))

GOLDKETTE, JEAN, 1899–1962
    leader

G58 BAKKER, Dick M.: Jean Goldkette
    1924–29 in Micrography, No. 38
    (October 1975): 9–10 ((6, 7d))

G59 SCHRAM, Ken: Complete Jean Gold-
    kette discography in Good Dig-
    gin', Vol. 2 (July 1, 1948): 5–8
    ((—))

GOMEZ, EDDIE, 1944–
    bass violin

G60 Plattenhinweise in Jazz Podium,
    Vol. 29 (April 1980): 13 ((—))

GONELLA, NAT, 1908–
    trumpet

G61 BAKKER, DICK M.: Nat Gonella in
    Micrography, No. 23 (January
    1973): 7 ((7d))

G62 [[LAMONT, Ted: Nat Gonella; a
    discography. Glasgow: 1957, 13
    leaves]]

G63 LAMONT, Ted: The recorded work of
    Nat Gonella in Jazz Music, Vol. 9
    (May–June 1958): 18–23; (July–
    August 1958): 13–20; additions
    and corrections in Jazz Music,
    Vol. 10 (January–February 1959):
    8, 10 [[also London: Vintage Jazz
    Mart (VJM Tangential Publication,
    No. 1), 1959]] ((2, 3, 7d))

GONZALES, BABS, 1919–
    vocal

G64 DELAUNAY, Charles, and Bernard
    NIQUET: Discographie de Babs
    Gonzales in Jazz Hot, No. 274
    (July 1971): 21 ((2, 3, 6, 7))

G65 GONZALES, Babs: Babs discography
    in his I paid my dues; good
    times--no bread. [East Orange,
    NJ: Expubedience, 1967], 158–160
    ((—))

GOOD TIME JAZZ label

G66 KOENIG, Lester: Good Time Jazz;
    a discography in Discophile, No.

18 (June 1951): 8-10; additions
and corrections in Discophile,
No. 19 (August 1951): 10; No. 23
(April 1952): 10-11; No. 24 (June
1952): 12 ((2, 3, 6, 7))

GOODMAN, BENNY, 1909-
clarinet

G67   BAKKER, Dick M.: Benny Goodman on
Victor 1926-29 in Micrography,
No. 43 (March 1977): 5 ((6, 7d))

G68   BAKKER, Dick M.: Benny Goodman
Victor's [sic] 1935-1939 in Micrography, No. 28 (September
1973): 9-10 ((7d))

G69   Benny Goodman...some revisions
of the section in "Jazz directory" in Discophile, No. 25
(August 1952): 13-16; additions
and corrections in Discophile,
No. 26 (October 1952): 10 [V
Discs, Columbia, Capitol ses-
sions] ((1, 2, 3, 6, 7))

G70   Benny Goodman's Okeh period in
Jazz Panorama, Vol. 1 (December
1947): 8 ((2, 3, 7))

G71   BOSSERAY, Claude: Benny Goodman's
V-Disc on LPs in Point du Jazz,
No. 11 (June 1975): 101-104
((7d))

G72   CONNOR, Donald Russell: BG--off
the record; a bio/discography of
Benny Goodman. Fairless Hills,
PA: Gaildonna [c1958], xiv, 305
pp.; additions and corrections in
KENDZIORA, Carl: Behind the cobwebs in Record Research, No. 27
(March-April 1960): 6; No. 30
(October 1960): 13, 16; CONNOR,
Donald Russell: Goodmania in Record Research, No. 30 (October
1960): 12, 16 ((1, 2, 3, 4p, 4t,
6, 7, 8))

G73   CONNOR, Donald Russell, and
Warren M. HICKS: B.G. on the record; a biodiscography of Benny
Goodman. New Rochelle, NY: Arlington House [1969], ix, 691
pp. ((1, 2, 3, 4p, 4t, 6, 7))

G74   CROSBIE, Ian: Selected discography in Jazz Journal, Vol. 23
(October 1970): 5 [November 7,
1940 to July 30, 1942 recordings]
((2, 3, 6, 7))

G75   Discographies de Benny Goodman et
Roy Eldridge in Jazz Hot, No. 44
(May 1950): 8-9 ((7d))

G76   [[FRY, John G.: Benny Goodman; an
English discography. Bristol:
1957, 33? pp.; with two supplements issued November 1957 and
January 1958]]

G77   HOEFER, George: Goodman discography in Down Beat, Vol. 18 (January 12, 1951): 9 ((—))

G78   IKEGAMI, T.: The B. G. discography covering Japanese releases
(except his own band) in Jazz Hot
Club Bulletin, Vol. 4 (July
1951): 20-21 ((—))

G79   IKEGAMI, T.: Benny Goodman discography in Jazz Hot Club Bulletin, Vol. 4 (March 1951): 1-2
[Japanese releases only] ((—))

G80   KENDZIORA, Carl: Benny Goodman
discography in Record Changer,
Vol. 7 (April 1948) to (October
1948), various paginations ((2,
3, 6, 7))

G81   [[TEUBIG, Klaus: Discographie of
Benny Goodman's Music Festival
concerts (AFRS Radio transcriptions 1946-47). Hamburg: 1963, 6
pp.]]

GOODWIN, BENNY, 1944-
guitar, vocal

G82   CHOISNEL, Emmanuel, and Kurt
MOHR: Benny Goodwin in Soul Bag,
No. 16 (1972?): 8 ((2, 3, 6, 7))

GOOFUS FIVE

G83   RUST, Brian: Okeh-Columbia discography part 5--the Goofus Five
in Jazz Tempo, No. 16 (n.d.):
8-10 ((2, 3, 7d))

GORDON, BOB, 1928-1955
baritone saxophone

G84   JEPSEN, Jorgen Grunnet: Bob
Gordon discography in Orkester
Journalen, Vol. 25 (March 1957):
50; (May 1957) ((2, 3, 7))

GORDON, DEXTER, 1923-
tenor saxophone

G85   BURNS, Jim: Dexter Gordon 1942-
1952 in Jazz Journal, Vol. 25
(April 1972): 39 ((—))

G86 COOKE, Ann, and Johs BERGH: Dexter Gordon discography in Jazz Monthly, Vol. 7 (April 1961): 18-19; (May 1961): 18 ((2, 3, 6, 7))

G87 Dexter Gordon in Swing Journal, Vol. 32 (January 1978): 319-325 ((2, 7d))

G88 [[RABEN, Erik: [Discography of 1960-1965 recordings] in Orkester Journalen, Vol. 30 (November 1962)]]

G89 Selected Gordon discography in Down Beat, Vol. 44 (February 10, 1977): 13 ((—))

G90 SHERA, Michael: Dexter Gordon on records 1960-65 in Jazz Journal, Vol. 19 (June 1966): 8 ((2, 7))

GOSPEL MUSIC
See also ATLANTIC label (Grendysa, Peter A.: Atlantic's gospel series); BLUES MUSIC (Blues lexicon) and (Eagle, Bob) and (Godrich, John); JAZZ MUSIC (Bruyninckx, Walter) and (Carey, Dave) and (McCarthy, Albert J.: Jazz discography I)

G91 Discography in WARRICK, Mancel: The progress of gospel music. New York: Vantage, 1977, 97-99 ((—))

G92 HAYES, Cedric J.: A discography of gospel records 1937-1971. [Copenhagen]: Knudsen [c1973], 116 pp. ((2, 3, 6, 7))

G93 HAYES, Cedric J.; Bob LAUGHTON; and Robert SACRE: Gospel records 1960-1977 in Point du Jazz, No. 15 (July 1979): 112-128 [part 1, letter A; to be continued] ((2, 3, 7))

G94 HAYES, Cedric J.: Post war gospel groups & singers in Blues Statistics, No. 2 (March 1963): 7-8 [A to ANCHORED] ((3, 7))

G95 HAYES, Cedric J.: The postwar gospel records in Blues Unlimited, No. 3 (July 1963) to No. 70 (February-March 1970), most issues, various paginations; additions and corrections in Blues Unlimited, undated supplement to No. 1-6: 7 ((2, 3, 7))

G96 LAUGHTON, Bob, and Cedric HAYES: Post-war gospel records of the '40s & '50s in Blues Unlimited, No. 120 (July-August 1976) to date, various paginations ((2, 3, 6, 7))

GOTHAM label

G97 ROTANTE, Anthony: Gotham 500; Apex 1100 in Record Research, Vol. 3 (June-July 1957): 19 ((3))

GOTHAM STOMPERS
See WILLIAMS, COOTIE (Bakker, Dick M.)

GRAAFF, REIN de, 1940-
piano

G98 EYLE, Wim van: Bio/disco Rein de Graaff en Dick Vennik in Jazz Press, No. 30 (January 21, 1977): 11 ((2, 7))

GRAETTINGER, ROBERT, 1923-1957
composer

G99 MORGAN, Robert Badgett: Discography in his The music and life of Robert Graettinger. DMA (Music) dissertation, University of Illinois (Urbana), 1974, 91-94 (available from University Microfilms, Ann Arbor, MI; order no. 75-375) ((2, 7))

GRAMERCY FIVE
See SHAW, ARTIE (Simosko, Vladimir)

GRANT, COOT
vocal

G100 RANKIN, Bill: Grant and Wilson discography in Jazz Record (UK), No. 10 (February 1944): 14; additions and corrections in Jazz Record (UK), No. 12 (March 1944): 15 ((3))

GRANT EARL
piano, vocal, organ

G101 MOHR, Kurt: Discography of Earl Grant in Jazz Statistics, No. 25 (March 1962): 2-3 ((2, 3, 7))

GRANZ, NORMAN, 1918-
record producer
See also GILLESPIE, DIZZY (Jepsen, Jorgen Grunnet: Dizzy Gillespie diskografi pa Clef-Norgran-Verve); VERVE label; YOUNG, LESTER (Jepsen, Jorgen Grunnet: Lester Young: records for Norman Granz) and (Morgan, Alan)

G102 JEPSEN, Jorgen Grunnet: Norman
Granz jam sessions diskografi in
Orkester Journalen, Vol. 28
(September 1960): 50 ((2, 3, 6,
7, 9))

GRAPPELLI, STEPHANE, 1908–
violin

G103 RUPPLI, Michel: Discographie:
Stephane Grappelli in Jazz Hot,
No. 349 (May 1978): 30-33; No.
350 (June 1978): 19-22 [record-
ings from his lesser-known per-
iods and from after 1953] ((1, 2,
3, 6, 7))

GRAVES, MILFORD, 1941–
percussion

G104 Discographie in Jazz Hot, No. 252
(July-August 1969): 20 ((2, 7d))

G105 Discographie in Jazz Magazine
(France), No. 226 (October 1974):
13 ((—))

G106 RABEN, Erik: Diskofilspalten in
Orkester Journalen, Vol. 38 (May
1970): 19 ((2, 3, 7))

GRAY, HENRY, 1925–
harmonica, piano, vocal

G107 SACRE, Robert: Henry Gray disco
in Soul Bag, No. 61 (June 1977):
35-36 ((2, 3, 7))

GRAY, WARDELL, 1921–1955
tenor saxophone

G108 BYRNE, Don: Discography of Wardell Gray in Discographical
Forum, No. 5 (March 1968) to No.
9 (November 1968), various paginations; additions and corrections in Discographical Forum,
No. 9 (November 1968): 2-4; No.
14 (September 1969): 4; No. 16
(January 1970): 2 ((1, 2, 3, 6,
7))

G109 DELAUNAY, Charles: Discographie
de Wardell Gray in Jazz Hot, No.
68 (July-August 1952): 16 ((2, 3,
7))

GREEN, BENNIE, 1923–
trombone

G110 McCARTHY, Albert J.: Bennie Green
discography in Jazz Monthly, Vol.
3 (March 1957): 27-28; (April
1957): 26-27, 30 ((2, 3, 6, 7))

GREEN, CLARENCE, 1929–
piano, vocal

G111 LEADBITTER, Mike: Clarence Green
in Blues Unlimited, No. 33 (May-
June 1966): 7, 26 ((2, 3, 7))

GREEN, CORNELIUS
See LONESOME SUNDOWN

GREEN, GRANT, 1931–
guitar

G112 PORTER, Bob: Grant Green in Different Drummer, Vol. 1 (January
1974): 22 ((—))

GREEN, L. C., ca. 1920–
vocal (female)

G113 ROTANTE, Anthony: The discography
of L. C. Green in Record Research, No. 69 (July 1965): 8
((3, 8))

GREEN, LIL, 1919–1954
vocal

G114 PARRY, William Hewitt, and Derrick STEWART-BAXTER: Lil Green
discography in Playback, Vol. 3
(February 1950): 13-14 ((2, 3,
7d))

GREEN, URBIE, 1926–
trombone

G115 Selected Green discography in
Down Beat, Vol. 43 (October 7,
1976): 14 ((—))

GREENE, BURTON, 1937–
piano

G116 Selected Greene discography in
Down Beat, Vol. 47 (June 1980):
29 ((—))

GREENE, JAKE

G117 OPENNEER, Herman: Jake Greene's
opnamen in Doctor Jazz, No. 79
(1977): 20-21 ((—))

GREGOR ET SES GREGORIENS

G118 RADO, Alexandre: Discography in
Jazz Hot, No. 249 (April 1969):
38; No. 250 (May 1969): 31 ((2,
3, 6, 7d))

GRIFFIN, BESSIE
vocal

G119 ROTANTE, Anthony: Sister Bessie
Griffin in Record Research, No.
34 (April 1961): 11; additions
and corrections in Record Research, No. 37 (August 1961): 11
((3, 7p))

GRIFFIN, JOHNNY, 1928–
tenor saxophone

G120 Johnny Griffin in Swing Journal,
Vol. 30 (March 1976): 258-261
((2, 7d))

GRIFFIN BROTHERS ORCHESTRA

G121 MOHR, Kurt: Discography of the
Griffin Brothers Orchestra in
Jazz Statistics, No. 13 (November
1959): 2 ((2, 3, 7))

GRIFFITH, EARL
vibraphone
See VIBRAPHONE MUSIC (JAZZ)
(Tepperman, Barry)

GRIMES, TINY (Lloyd Grimes), 1917–
guitar

G122 CHAUVARD, Marcel, and Kurt MOHR:
Discography of Tiny Grimes in
Jazz Statistics, No. 26/27 (June-
September 1962): 8-10 ((2, 3, 6,
7))

GRISMAN, DAVID, 1945–
mandolin

G123 Selected David Grisman discography in Down Beat, Vol. 46 (November 1979): 31 ((—))

GROOVE label

G124 ROTANTE, Anthony: The Groove
catalogue in Record Research,
Vol. 3 (January-February 1958):
10-11 ((3, 4p))

GROOVY label

G125 LYNSKY, Phil: Groovy label listing in Hot Buttered Soul, No. 46
(June-July 1976): 12 ((3))

GROSS, HELEN
vocal

G126 GODRICH, John, and Bob DIXON:
Margin notes no. 10; Helen Gross
in Vintage Jazz Mart, No. 1
(February 1961): 10-11 ((3, 7))

GROSSMAN, STEVE, 1951–
saxophones

G127 PERLA, Gene: A session with Steve
Grossman and Azar Lawrence in
Down Beat, Vol. 40 (September 13,
1973): 18 ((—))

GUARDSMAN label (British)

G128 BADROCK, Arthur, and Derek
SPRUCE: Guardsman issues of jazz
interest in Discophile, No. 49
(August 1956): 14-19; additions
and corrections in Discophile,
No. 52 (February 1957): 18-19
((3))

G129 BADROCK, Arthur: Guardsman 7000
race series in Discophile, No. 56
(October 1957): 21-23 ((3, 8))

G130 Guardsman in Storyville, No. 23
(June-July 1969): 193-194 ((3,
8))

GUARENTE, FRANK, 1893–1942
trumpet

G131 [Discography] in Jazz Podium,
Vol. 7 (November 1958): 19 ((2,
3, 6, 7))

G132 [[LANGE, Horst H.: [Discography]
in Jazz Music, (June 1960)]]

GUESNON, GEORGE, 1907–
banjo

G133 Discography of Creole George
Guesnon in Eureka, Vol. 1 (Janu-
ary-February 1960): 21-22; addi-
tions and corrections from George
HULME in Eureka, Vol. 1 (July-
August 1960): 10 ((1, 2, 3, 7))

GUILAROFF, VERA
piano

G134 KIDD, Jim: Vera Guilaroff recordings in Record Research, No. 76
(May 1966): 6; additions and
corrections in Record Research,
No. 81 (January 1967): 9 ((2, 3,
6, 7))

GUITAR EDDY
See CLEARWATER, EDDY

GUITAR JUNIOR
    See BROOKS, LONNIE

GUITAR MUSIC (JAZZ)

G135 MARZORATTI, Luis R.: Guitarristas
    de hoy; discografia in Jazz Maga-
    zine (Argentina), No. 34 (Septem-
    ber 1952): 13, 19 [Argentine
    issues only] ((—))

G136 PEYNET, Michel: Discographie in
    Jazz Hot, No. 283 (May 1972): 63
    ((—))

G137 Selected discography of contem-
    porary guitar styles in Down
    Beat, Vol. 44 (February 22,
    1977): 16 ((—))

GUITAR SHORTY (David William Kearney),
    1923-1976
    guitar, vocal

G138 MOHR, Kurt: Guitar Shorty; dis-
    cography in Blues Unlimited, No.
    26 (October 1965): 5 ((2, 3, 7))

GUITAR SLIM
    See JONES, EDDIE

GUITARS UNLIMITED (musical group)

G139 POSTIF, François: Guitars Un-
    limited in Jazz Hot, No. 262
    (June 1970): 31 ((2, 3, 7))

GULDA, FRIEDRICH, 1930-
    piano

G140 GEITEL, Klaus: Diskografie in his
    Fragen an Friedrich Gulda;
    Anmerkungen zu Musik und
    Gesellschaft. Berlin: Rembrandt
    [c1973], 53 ((—))

G141 KRANER, Dietrich H.: Friedrich
    Gulda jazz discography in Jazz
    Studies, Vol. 1 (No. 2, 1967):
    5-9; (No. 4, 1967): 56-60 ((1, 2,
    3, 6, 7))

GULGOWSKI, WLODZIMIERZ
    piano

G142 Selected Gulgowski discography in
    Jazz Forum (Poland), No. 61
    (1979): 46 ((—))

GULLIN, LARS, 1928-1976
    baritone saxophone

G143 [[JEPSEN, Jorgen Grunnet: Lars
    Gullin. Copenhagen: 1957]]

G144 JEPSEN, Jorgen Grunnet: Lars
    Gullin discography in Jazz Month-
    ly, Vol. 3 (November 1957):
    26-27; (December 1957): 24-26;
    (January 1958): 26, 32 ((2, 3,
    7))

G145 JEPSEN, Jorgen Grunnet: Lars
    Gullin diskografi in Orkester
    Journalen, Vol. 33 (April 1965)
    to (July-August 1965); (October
    1965) to (December 1965), various
    paginations ((2, 3, 7d))

G146 Lars Gullin on record in Jazz
    Journal, Vol. 30 (October 1977):
    15 (—))

G147 Lars Gullin pa skiva in Orkester
    Journalen, Vol. 44 (June 1976): 7
    ((—))

GUY, BUDDY (George Guy), 1936-
    guitar, vocal

G148 [Discography] in Blues Unlimited,
    No. 3 (July 1963): 2; additions
    and corrections in Blues Unlimit-
    ed, No. 12 (June 1964): suppl.
    3-4 ((2, 3, 7))

G149 [[[Discography] in Soul Bag, No.
    3]]

G150 PATERSON, Neil, and Mike LEAD-
    BITTER: Discography of Buddy Guy
    in Blues Unlimited, No. 19 (Feb-
    ruary 1965): 4-5 ((2, 3, 7))

GUY, VERNON
    See JOHNSON, STACEY

H J C A label

H1 HJCA in Matrix, No. 87 (February
    1970): 3-10; No. 88 (June 1970):
    3-9 ((8))

H M V label (British)

H2 [[HAYES, Jim: English H.M.V. BD
    5000 series (BD 5000 to 6204).
    Liverpool: 1969, 28 pp.]]

H3 HAYES, Jim: HMV B 5000 series—a
    numerical catalogue listing in
    R.S.V.P., No. 29 (October 1967)
    to No. 31 (December 1967); No. 36
    (May 1968); No. 38 (July 1968);
    No. 41 (October 1960) to No. 45
    (February 1969); No. 47 (April

1969); No. 50 (September 1969);
No. 52 (January-February 1970);
No. 54 (May-June 1970), various
paginations ((—))

H M V label (Swedish)
See RAGTIME MUSIC (Englund,
Bjorn)

H R S label

H4 MAHONY, Dan: Hot Record Society;
a numerical catalogue of the HRS
label in Discophile, No. 51 (December 1956): 16-20; additions
and corrections in Discophile,
No. 53 (April 1957): 9-10; No. 56
(October 1957): 18 ((3))

HACKETT, BOBBY, 1915-1976
cornet

H5 HOEFER, George: Hackett discography in Down Beat, Vol. 18 (February 9, 1951): 16 ((—))

H6 HOLZER, Steve: Bobby Hackett:
records under other leaders in
Record Research, No. 159/160
(December 1978): 14; No. 161/162
(February-March 1979): 10; No.
165/166 (August 1979): 15 [to be
continued] ((1, 2, 3, 6, 7))

H7 VENABLES, Ralph G. V.: A feature
for the connoisseur: Bobby Hackett
discography in Discography (March
1943): 5 ((2, 3, 7d))

HADEN, CHARLIE, 1937-
bass violin

H8 Charlie Haden in Swing Journal,
Vol. 34 (June 1980): 162-167 ((2,
7d))

H9 GICKING, Jim: Charlie Haden's
discography in booklet with [pho-
nodisc] Artists House AH6. New
York: Artists House Records,
c1979 ((7d))

HAGAN, CASS, 1904-
violin, leader

H10 BACKENSTO, Woody: The Cass Hagan
bands of the 20's in Record Research, No. 29 (August 1960): 3-5
((3, 7d))

HAIG, AL, 1924-
piano

See also PIANO MUSIC (JAZZ) (Edwards, Ernie)

H11 DAVIS, Brian: Discograpy [sic]
of issued recordings by Al Haig
1974-1978 in Jazz Journal, Vol.
32 (April 1979): 17-19 ((2, 3, 6,
7))

H12 Discographie Al Haig (disques
publiés en France) in Jazz Hot,
No. 54 (April 1951): 12-13 ((7d))

H13 MORGAN, Alun: Al Haig discography
in Jazz Monthly, Vol. 2 (October
1956): 27-28; (November 1956):
24-26 ((2, 3, 6, 7))

HAKIM, SADIK (Argonne Thorton), 1921-
piano
See PIANO MUSIC (JAZZ) (Edwards,
Ernie)

HALL, EDMOND, 1901-1967
clarinet

H14 BAKKER, Dick M.: Edmond Hall 41-
44 in Micrography, No. 7 (November 1969): 7 ((7d))

H15 Edmond Hall Blue Note sessions in
Hip, Vol. 7 (May 1970): 6 ((2, 3,
7))

H16 [[JEPSEN, Jorgen Grunnet: Edmond
Hall. Copenhagen: 1957]]

HALL, JIM, 1930-
guitar

H17 Jim Hall in Swing Journal, Vol.
29 (December 1975): 264-271 ((2,
7d))

H18 Selected Hall discography in Down
Beat, Vol. 43 (December 16,
1976): 14 ((—))

HALLBERG, BENGT, 1932-
piano

H19 REHNBERG, Bert: Jazz in Sweden:
Bengt Hallberg in International
Discophile, No. 3 (spring 1956):
9-10 ((2, 3, 7))

HAMBRICK, BILLY
vocal

H20 MOHR, Kurt: Billy Hambrick discography in Hot Buttered Soul,
No. 41 (October 1975?): 13 ((3,
7))

HAMILTON, CHICO, 1921–
    drums

H21   EDWARDS, Ernie: Chico Hamilton; a
      name discography in Matrix, No.
      59 (June 1965): 3–10; additions
      and corrections in Matrix, No. 70
      (April 1967): 14 ((2, 3, 7))

HAMILTON, JIMMY, 1917–

H22   MORGAN, Alun: Jimmie Hamilton; a
      name listing in Jazz Monthly, No.
      152 (October 1967): 27; additions
      and corrections in Jazz Monthly,
      No. 154 (December 1967): 29–30
      ((2, 7))

HAMILTON, SCOTT, 1955?–
    tenor saxophone

H23   [Discography] in Orkester Jour-
      nalen, Vol. 47 (June 1979): 26
      ((—))

H24   [[EYLE, Wim van: Scott Hamilton
      discography in Swingtime (Bel-
      gium), No. 34 (October–November
      1978): 4–6]]

H25   Plattenhinweise in Jazz Podium,
      Vol. 28 (August 1979): 13 ((—))

H26   Scott Hamilton discography in
      Jazz Forum (Poland), No. 63
      (1980): 40 ((—))

H27   Selected Hamilton discography in
      Down Beat, Vol. 46 (December
      1979): 30 ((—))

HAMMER, JAN, 1948–
    piano

H28   Selected Hammer discography in
      Down Beat, Vol. 43 (March 11,
      1976): 18 ((—))

HAMMOND, JOHN, 1910–
    record producer

H29   Selective discography in HAMMOND,
      John: John Hammond on record. New
      York: Ridge Press, c1977, 404–413
      ((7d))

HAMPEL, GUNTER, 1937–
    vibraphone, clarinet

H30   TEPPERMAN, Barry: Birth in Coda,
      Vol. 11 (September–October 1973):
      11–14 ((—))

HAMPTON, LIONEL, 1913–
    vibraphone

H31   Discographie complémentaire de
      l'Orchestre Lionel Hampton in
      Jazz Hot, No. 38 (November 1949):
      31 [1947–1949 recordings] ((2, 3,
      7d))

H32   DOYLE, Mike: Lionel Hampton in
      Jazz Monthly, Vol. 13 (August
      1967): 30–31 ((3, 6, 7))

H33   FLUCKIGER, Otto: Lionel Hampton.
      Reinach, Switzerland: Jazz-Publi-
      cations, 1961, 2 v. ((1, 2, 3, 6,
      7, 9))

H34   FLUCKIGER, Otto: Lionel Hampton
      selected discography 1966–1968 in
      Jazz + Classic, No. 2 (April–May
      1979): 8–10 ((2, 3, 7))

H35   [[FLUCKIGER, Otto: Selected dis-
      cography 1966–1978, Reinach,
      Switzerland: 1980?, 20 pp.]]

H36   The Lionel Hampton Orchestra
      story in Jazz Statistics No. 9
      (March 1959): 6–8; No. 11 (July
      1959): LH5–LH10; No. 13 (November
      1959): LH11–LH12 ((1, 2, 3, 6,
      7))

H37   RABEN, Erik: Diskofilspalten in
      Orkester Journalen, Vol. 36
      (March 1968) to (May 1968), var-
      ious paginations, in 3 parts
      [1959–1968 recordings] ((2, 3,
      7))

HANCOCK, HERBIE, 1940–
    piano

H38   Herbie Hancock in Swing Journal,
      Vol. 33 (August 1979): 222–227
      ((2, 7d))

H39   Herbie Hancock discography in
      Swing Journal, Vol. 28 (August
      1974): 74–81 ((2, 7d))

H40   Herbie Hancock discography in
      Swing Journal, Vol. 29 (1975
      annual): 170–179 ((2, 7d))

H41   RUPPLI, Michael: Discographie:
      Herbie Hancock in Jazz Hot, No.
      371? (March 1980) to No. 373 (May
      1980), various paginations [pos-
      sibly in other issues] ((2, 3,
      7))

H42   Selected Hancock discography in
      Down Beat, Vol. 44 (September 8,
      1977): 17 ((—))

H43 TOWNLEY, Ray: Hancock plugs in in Down Beat, Vol. 41 (October 24, 1974): 15 ((—))

HANDY, GEORGE, 1920–
    piano, arranger
    See RAEBURN, BOYD (Edwards, Ernie) and (Hall, George I.)

HANDY, (CAPTAIN) JOHN, 1900–1971
    alto saxophone

H44 HERLING, Horst: Discography in his Capt. John Handy. Menden, W. Germany: Jazzfreund [c1978], 23–39 ((1, 2, 3, 7))

HANDY, JOHN, 1933–
    alto saxophone

H45 Selected John Handy discography in Down Beat, Vol. 43 (February 12, 1977): 20 ((—))

HANNA, ROLAND, 1932–
    piano

H46 Roland Hanna discography in Down Beat, Vol. 42 (April 10, 1975): 16 ((—))

HARDEN, WILBUR, 1925–
    trumpet

H47 GARDNER, Mark: Wilbur Harden in Jazz Journal, Vol. 21 (May 1968): 20 ((2, 3, 7))

HARDIN, LILLIAN
    See ARMSTRONG, LIL

HARDWICK, OTTO, 1904–1970
    saxophones

H48 NIQUET, Bernard: Otto Hardwick 1904–1970 in Point du Jazz, No. 10 (October 1974): 44–54, 111 ((2, 3, 6, 7))

HARLEM HAMFATS (musical group)

H49 McCARTHY, Albert J.: Discography of the Harlem Hamfats in Record Changer, Vol. 4 (February 1946): 13–14 ((2, 3, 7))

HARLEMAIRES
    See ATLANTIC label (Grendysa, Peter A.: Atlantic's early groups)

HARMONICA FRANK (Frank Floyd), 1908–
    harmonica, vocal

H50 LAVERE, Steve: Huntin' blues in Blues Unlimited, No. 99 (February–March 1973): 5 ((2, 3))

H51 LEADBITTER, Mike: Harmonica Frank discography in Blues Unlimited, No. 39 (December 1966): 15 ((3, 7))

HARMONIZING FOUR

H52 HAYES, Cedric J.: The Harmonizing Four (provisional listing) in Blues Unlimited, No. 2 (June 1963): 12–13; additions and corrections in Blues Unlimited, undated supplement to No. 1–6: 6–7 ((3, 7))

HARMONY label
    See also ELLINGTON, DUKE (Bakker, Dick M.: Duke Ellington on Columbia/Okeh/Harmony 1927–30)

H53 BEDOIAN, Jim, ed.: The Harmony-Velvet Tone-Diva numerical lists in Discographer, Vol. 2 (third quarter 1970): 2-159 to 2-184; Vol. 2, No. 4 (n.d.): 2-226 to 2-242 ((3))

H54 CHMURA, Helene: Harmony in Discophile, No. 19 (August 1951): 5–6 ((3, 7d))

HARPO, SLIM
    See SLIM HARPO

HARRIOTT, JOE, 1928–1973
    alto saxophone

H55 TEPPERMAN, Barry: Discography in COTTERELL, Roger: Joe Harriott; his life in music. Ilford, UK [1974], 18–26 ((2, 3, 7))

HARRIS, BARRY, 1929–
    piano

H56 Barry Harris in Swing Journal, Vol. 30 (April 1976): 80–85 ((2, 7d))

H57 GARDNER, Mark: Barry Harris in Jazz Monthly, Vol. 13 (September 1967): 28–29; (November 1967): 31; (December 1967): 31; (January 1968): ((2, 7))

HARRIS, BILL, 1916-1973
trombone

H58   EDWARDS, Ernie: Bill Harris
(trombone); a complete discography. Whittier, CA: ErnGeoBil,
1966, 30 leaves (Spotlight
series, Vol. 9) ((1, 2, 3, 4p, 6
7))

H59   NEU, Robert J.: A discography of
Bill Harris in Jazz Journal, Vol.
6 (August 1953): 19-22; (October
1953): 23-24; (November 1953):
24-25 ((1, 2, 3, 6, 7))

HARRIS, EDDIE, 1936-
tenor saxophone

H60   Selected Harris discography in
Down Beat, Vol. 43 (January 15,
1976): 16 ((—))

HARRIS, WYNONIE, 1915-1969
drums, vocal

H61   MOHR, Kurt: Discography of
Wynonie Harris in Discophile, No.
14 (October 1950): 14-15; additions and corrections in Discophile, No. 19 (August 1951): 10;
No. 24 (June 1952): 17; No. 25
(August 1952): 10-11 ((2, 3, 6,
7))

HARRISON, JIMMY, 1900-1931
trombone

H62   BREDANNAZ, Robert J.: Discographie in Jazz Hot, No. 89 (June
1954): 16, 18 ((2, 3, 6, 7))

H63   DELAUNAY, Charles: Discographie
de Jimmy Harrison (extraits
empruntés à Essai de discographie
hot) in Jazz Hot, No. 7 (April
1936): 7 ((—))

H64   PANASSIÉ, Hugues: Discographie de
Jimmie Harrison in Bulletin du
Hot Club de France, No. 59 (July-
August 1956): 8-10; additions and
corrections in Bulletin du Hot
Club de France, No. 62 (November
1956): 32 ((7d, 9))

H65   TANNER, Peter: [Discography] in
his "Big Jim"--the story of Jimmy
Harrison in ROWE, John, ed.:
Trombone jazz. [London: Jazz
Tempo, 1945], 10 ((—))

HARVEY label

H66   TOPPING, Ray: Harvey label list-

ing in Shout, No. 77 (June 1972):
8 ((3, 5))

HASSELGARD, ÅKE, 1922-1948
clarinet

H67   BERG, Arne: Ake "Stan" Hasselgard; complete chronology of his
records in Playback, Vol. 2
(March 1949): 7-8 ((2, 3, 6,
7))

HAWES, HAMPTON, 1928-1977
piano

H68   [Discography] in Swing Journal,
Vol. 31 (August 1977): 290-293
((2, 7d))

H69   MORGAN, Alun: Hampton Hawes discography in Jazz Monthly, Vol. 3
(August 1957): 26-27 ((2, 3, 7))

H70   Selected Hawes discography in
Down Beat, Vol. 43 (December 16,
1976): 23 ((—))

HAWKINS, COLEMAN, 1904-1969
tenor saxophone
See also SAXOPHONE MUSIC (JAZZ)
(Evensmo, Jan: The tenor saxo-
phonists of the period 1930-1942)

H71   BAKKER, Dick M.: Coleman Hawkins
and Benny Carter in Europe 1934-
1939 in Micrography, No. 43
(March 1977): 12-15 ((6, 7d))

H72   DELAUNAY, Charles: Discographie
de Coleman Hawkins (extrait de
Hot discographie 1948) in Jazz
Hot, No. 20 (February 1948): 10-
11; supplemented in Disques de
Coleman Hawkins actuellement en
vente en France in Jazz Hot, No.
39 (December 1949): 9 ((2, 3,
7))

H73   EVENSMO, Jan: The tenor saxophone of Coleman Hawkins 1929-
1942. [Hosle, Norway: 1975], 34
pp. (Jazz solography series, Vol.
3) ((1, 2, 3, 6, 7, 9))

H74   HOEFER, George: Hawk discography
in Down Beat, Vol. 17 (October
20, 1950): 3 ((—))

H75   KEATING, Liam: Coleman Hawkins on
record in Jazz & Blues Vol. 2

(May 1972) to Vol. 3 (July 1973), various paginations (in 12 parts) ((2, 7))

H76 MOHR, Kurt: Discographie Coleman Hawkins in Hot Revue, No. 6 (May 1946): 23; No. 7 (1946); additions and corrections in Hot Revue, No. 8 (1946): 34-36 ((2, 3, 7))

HAWKINS, ERSKINE, 1914-
trumpet

H77 CROSBIE, Ian: Twentieth century Gabriel, part 2 in Jazz Journal, Vol. 25 (August 1972): 16 ((1, 2, 3, 6, 7))

H78 EDWARDS, Ernie: Erskine Hawkins/ Horace Henderson. Whittier, CA: Jazz Discographies Unlimited, 1965, 10 leaves ((1, 2, 3, 6, 7))

H79 MOHR, Kurt: Disques publiés en France in Jazz Hot, No. 120 (April 1957): 15 ((—))

HAWKINS, (SCREAMIN') JAY, 1929-
piano, saxophones, vocal

H80 HESS, Norbert: Discography in Blues Unlimited, No. 121 (September-October 1976): 12-14 ((2, 3, 7))

HAWKINS, JENNELL
organ, vocal

H81 MOHR, Kurt: Discographie de Jennell Hawkins in Soul Bag, No. 36 (March 1974): 6-7; additions and corrections in Soul Bag, No. 38 (May 1974): 46 ((2, 3, 7))

HAWKS, BILLY, 1941 or 1943-
harmonica, vocal

H82 NIQUET, Bernard: Discographie de Billy Hawks in Jazz Hot, No. 257 (January 1970): 26 ((2, 7))

HAYES, EDGAR, 1904-
piano

H83 KUNSTADT, Len: Edgar Hayes rollography in Record Research, No. 47 (November 1962): 11 ((5))

HAYES, HENRY
alto saxophone, flute, drums

H84 MOHR, Kurt: Henry Hayes discography in Blues Unlimited, No. 33 (May-June 1966): 6 ((3, 7))

HAYES, TUBBY (Edward Brian Hayes), 1935-1973
tenor saxophone.

H85 MORGAN, Alun: Tubby Hayes; a name listing in Discographical Forum, No. 6 (May 1968): 7-10; No. 7 (July 1968): 7-8; additions and corrections in Discographical Forum, No. 9 (November 1968): 1, 4; No. 14 (September 1969): 4 ((2, 3, 7))

HAYMER, HERBIE, 1915-1949
tenor saxophone

H86 Herbie Haymer on wax in Down Beat, Vol. 16 (June 3, 1949): 15 ((—))

HAYNES, ROY, 1926-
drums

H87 Selected Roy Haynes discography in Down Beat, Vol. 47 (February 1980): 18 ((—))

HAYWOOD, LEON
piano, vocal

H88 MOHR, Kurt: Discographie de Leon Haywood in Soul Bag, No. 43/44 (November-December 1974): 14-15; additions and corrections in Soul Bag, No. 46 (February 1975): 6 ((2, 3, 7))

HEARTSMAN, JOHNNY
guitar, organ

H89 CHOISNEL, Emmanuel, and Kurt MOHR: Discographie de Johnny Heartsman in Soul Bag, No. 22/23 (January-February 1973): 18 ((2, 3, 7))

HEIGHT, DONALD

H90 TOPPING, Ray: Donald Height discography in Shout, No. 82 (December 1972): 1-3 ((3, 5, 7))

HENDERSON, FLETCHER, 1897-1952
arranger, piano

H91 ALLEN, Walter C.: Hendersonia;
the music of Fletcher Henderson
and his musicians, a bio-discography. Highland Park, NJ: 1973,
xiv, 651 pp. (Jazz monographs,
No. 4) ((1, 2, 3, 4c, 4p, 4r, 4t,
5, 6, 7, 8, 9))

H92 BAKKER, Dick M.: Fletcher Henderson 1923-26 in Micrography, No.
38 (October 1975): 2-4 ((6, 7d))

H93 BAKKER, Dick M.: Fletcher Henderson 1925-1936 in Micrography, No.
30 (April 1974): 2-4((6, 7d))

H94 BAKKER, Dick M.: Fletcher Henderson on Victors in Micrography,
No. 3 (May 1969): 7; additions
and corrections in Micrography,
No. 5 (August 1969): 12 ((7d))

H95 BAKKER, Dick M.: Henderson-
Armstrong recordings in Microg-
raphy, No. 25 (March 1973): 2;
additions and corrections in
Micrography, No. 26 (1973): 1;
No. 28 (September 1973): 1 ((7d))

H96 BAKKER, Dick M.: Henderson on
microgroove 1923-1933 in Micrography, No. 4 (June 1969): 5-8
((7d))

H97 BAKKER, Dick M.: Henderson on
Victor 27-36 in Micrography, No.
26 (1973): 4 ((6, 7d))

H98 HOEFER, George: Henderson discography in Bouquets to the living.
[Chicago: Down Beat, 195?], 20
((—))

H99 IKEGAMI, T.: The Fletcher Henderson in Jazz Hot Club Bulletin,
Vol. 4 (April 1951): 1-3 ((3))

H100 TONKS, Eric S.: Notes on the dis-
cography of Fletcher Henderson in
GRAY-CLARKE, G. F.: Deep Henderson.
[Chilwell, Nottinghamshire: Jazz
Appreciation Society, 1944], 16-
22 [additions and corrections to
Delaunay's Hot discography] ((3))

Arrangements

H101 ALLEN, Walter C.: Fletcher Henderson orch-ography in his Hendersonia; the music of Fletcher
Henderson and his musicians, a
bio-discography. Highland Park,
NJ: 1973, 513-526 ((1, 3, 4p, 4r,
4t, 6, 7))

HENDERSON, HORACE, 1904-
piano, leader
See also HAWKINS, ERSKINE
(Edwards, Ernie)

H102 DELAUNAY, Charles: Horace Henderson (extrait de Hot discographie
encyclopedique) in Jazz Hot, No.
57 (July-August 1951): 27 ((2, 6,
7d))

H103 SCHACHT, John: [List of compositions and arrangements] in Jazz
Hot, No. 13 (Christmas 1936): 25
((—))

HENDERSON, JOE, 1937-
tenor saxophone

H104 GARDNER, Mark: Joe Henderson in
Jazz Monthly, Vol. 13 (May 1967):
29-30; (June 1967): 31 ((2, 7))

H105 Selected Henderson discography in
Down Beat, Vol. 42 (January 16,
1975): 19 ((—))

H106 TERCINET, Alain: Joe Henderson in
Jazz Hot, No. 292 (March 1973):
18-19 ((2, 7))

HENDRICKSON, HENNY (Clarence H.
Hendrickson)
clarinet

H107 [[MYERS, Chet: Louisville Serenaders research in Record Research, No. 157/158 (September
1978): 13]]

HENDRIKS, GIJS, 1938-
saxophones

H108 [[[Discography] in BEETZ, Tom:
Gijs Hendriks en de nationale
misverstanden in Jazz Nu, Vol. 1
(December 1978): 89-93]]

HENDRICKS, MARGIE
See RAELETS

HENKELS, KURT
leader, arranger

H109 [[SCHUTTE, Joachim: Kurt Henkels
Discographie. Menden, W. Germany:
Jazzfreund, 1971, 42 pp.]]

HENRICHSEN, BØRGE ROGER, 1915-
trumpet

H110 [[JØRGENSEN, BIRGER: Børge Roger
Henrichsen. Copenhagen: Erichsen,
1962, 80 pp.]]

HENRY, DOREEN
vocal

H111 EVANS, Chris: Doreen Henry in
Journal of Jazz Discography, No.
1 (November 1976): 2; No. 2 (June
1977): 5-6 ((2, 3, 7))

HENRY, ERNIE, 1926-1957
alto saxophone

H112 RAFTEGAARD, Borje: Ernie Henry
discography in Discographical
Forum, No. 40 (spring 1978): 3-6;
No. 41 (1978?): 1, 3-6 (parts 1
and 2, to be continued) ((1, 2,
3, 6, 7))

HERALD label
See also LITTLE WALTER (Rotante,
Anthony)

H113 KUNZ, Gunther, and Chuck HERMANN:
Label-list: Herald in Rockrevue,
No. 31 (July 1979): 12 ((—)

HERMAN, WOODY (Woodrow Charles
Herman), 1913-
clarinet

H114 ALBERT, Dick: Then & again--Woody
Herman in Different Drummer, Vol.
1 (August 1974): 20 ((—))

H115 EDWARDS, Ernie: Discography of
Woody Herman (1945) in Jazz Statistics, No. 12 (September 1959):
9 ((2, 3, 6, 7))

H116 EDWARDS, Ernie: Unissued Woody
Herman recordings in Jazz Monthly, Vol. 10 (November 1964): 25
((3, 7d, 9))

H117 EDWARDS, Ernie: Woody Herman and
his orchestra; a discography.
[Brande, Denmark: Debut Records,
c1961] (Vols. 1 and 2) or Whittier, CA: Jazz Discographies Unlimited, 1965, 3 v. (Dance band
series, H-5) ((1, 2, 3, 6, 7))

H118 EDWARDS, Ernie: Woody Herman and
the swingin' herd, 1959-1966,
Vol. 3. rev. ed. Whittier, CA:
ErnGeoBil, 1966, 13 leaves ((1,
2, 3, 6, 7))

H119 EDWARDS, Ernie: Woody Herman discography 1944 in Jazz Statistics,
No. 9 (March 1959): 4 ((2, 3, 6,
7))

H120 EDWARDS, Ernie, and Jorgen Grunnet JEPSEN: Woody Herman 1947-
1958; a discography. n.p, n.d.,
15 pp. ((2, 3, 7))

H121 HALL, George I.: [Discography,
part 1]--the early years. [Lau-
rel, MD?: ca. 1971?], 9 leaves
((1, 2, 3, 6, 7))

H122 [[TOLLARA, Gianni: [Discography
1960-1966] in Musica Jazz, Vol.
23 (May 1967)]]

H123 TRACY, Jack: Herman discography
in Down Beat, Vol. 17 (November
3, 1950): 19 ((—))

H124 TREICHEL, James A.: Keeper of the
flame; Woody Herman and the Second Herd, 1947-1949. Zephyrhills,
FL: Joyce Music, 1978, 56 leaves
((1, 2, 3, 4t, 6, 7))

H125 Woody Herman's selected discography in Jazz Forum (Poland), No.
41 (March 1976): 40 ((—))

Sidemen

H126 EDWARDS, Ernie: Woody Herman
alumni Vol. 1. Whittier, CA: Ern-
GeoBil [1969], 60 leaves ((1, 2,
3, 6, 7))

HERWIN label

H127 GODRICH, John: Herwin 92000 and
93000 in Matrix, No. 52 (April
1964): 3-9; additions and corrections in Matrix, No. 61 (October
1965): 14-16; No. 63 (February
1966): 10 ((3, 6))

H128 MACKENZIE, John: Herwin numerical
in 78 Quarterly, Vol. 1, No. 1
(1967): 22-26 ((3))

HEYWOOD, CEDRIC, 1914-
piano

H129 MOHR, Kurt: Cedric Heywood in
Jazz Statistics, No. 5 (April
1957): 8-9 ((2, 3, 7))

HEYWOOD, EDDIE, 1915-
piano

H130 DELAUNAY, Charles: Discographie
du mois: Eddie Heywood in Jazz
Hot, No. 15 (1947): 21 ((2, 3,
7))

HICKMAN, ART, 1886-1930
leader

H131 CAMP, J. H.: Art Hickman ... discography in After Beat, Vol. 1
(October 1970): 5 ((2))

HICKS, OTIS
See LIGHTIN' SLIM

HIGGINBOTHAM, J. C., 1906-1973
trombone

H132 HOEFER, George: Early Higginbotham discography in Down Beat,
Vol. 31 (January 30, 1964): 33
((2, 3, 7))

H133 TONKS, Eric: Discography of J. C.
Higginbotham in J. C. Higginbotham; a pamphlet published for
the Discographical Society.
London: Clifford Jones, 1944,
7-17 ((2, 3, 7d))

HIGH KEYS (musical group)

H134 MOHR, Kurt: High Keys discography
in Hot Buttered Soul, No. 37
(January-February 1975?): 7 ((2,
3, 7))

HIGH SOCIETY (tune title)

H135 MADISON, Joseph: High Society in
Jazz Discounter, No. 10 (October
1948): 3-4 ((—))

HILL, ALEX, 1906-1937
piano

H136 GULLIVER, Ralph: No jubilees for
Alex (the tragedy of Alex Hill)
in Storyville, No. 38 (December
1971-January 1972): 69-72; trans-
lated as Un destin tragique; Alex
Hill in Point du Jazz, No. 9
(December 1973): 22-27 ((2, 3, 6,
7))

HILL, ANDREW, 1937-
piano

H137 Andrew Hill in Swing Journal,
Vol. 30 (July 1976): 272-275
((2, 7d))

H138 Andrew Hill discography in Down
Beat, Vol. 44 (March 10, 1977):
16 ((—))

H139 GICKING, Jim: Andrew Hill's discography in booklet to accompany
[phonodisc] Artists House AH9.
New York: Artists House Records,
c1979, 3 ((2, 7d))

HILL, BERTHA "CHIPPIE," 1905-1950
vocal

H140 HILL, Brian J.: Bertha "Chippie"
Hill in Jazzology (UK), No. 10
new series (October 1946): 7 ((2,
3, 7d))

HILL, HONEY
piano

H141 McCARTHY, Albert J.: Blues pianists: no. 5--Honey Hill in Jazz
Notes (Australia), No. 63 (April
1946): 15, 17 ((2, 3, 7))

HILL, KING SOLOMON (Joe Holmes),
1897-1949
guitar, harmonica, vocal

H142 The complete King Solomon Hill
discography in Kord, Vol. 2 (No.
3/4, n.d.): 27 ((3, 7))

HINES, EARL, 1903-
piano

H143 BAKKER, Dick M.: Earl Hines 1929-
40 in Micrography, No. 24 (February 1973): 4-5; additions and
corrections in Micrography, No.
26 (1973): 1 ((7d))

H144 DAVIES, John R. T.: The alternate
Earl Hines in Storyville, No. 40
(April-May 1972): 127-130 ((2, 3,
6, 7, 8, 9))

H145 Discographie de Earl Hines
(disques actuellement trouvables
en France) in Jazz Hot, No. 44
(May 1950): 16 ((7d))

H146 RABEN, Erik: Diskofilspalten in
Orkester Journalen, Vol. 35
(July-August 1967): 16-17; Vol.
36 (March 1968): 14 [1960-1967
recordings] ((2, 3, 7))

H147 Selected Hines discography in
Down Beat, Vol. 46 (May 17,
1980): 15 ((—))

H148 [[TOLLARA, Gianni: [Discography
1952-1966] in Musica Jazz, Vol.
23 (February 1967)]]

H149 WILTSHIRE, Tony: Earl Hines on
record in the 1960's in Jazz
Studies, Vol. 3, No. 1 (ca. March
1971): 21-28 ((2, 7))

HINO, TERUMASA, 1942-
trumpet

H150 Terumasa Hino in Swing Journal, Vol. 33 (December 1979): 234-239 ((2, 7d))

HIS MASTER'S VOICE label
    See H M V label

HIT label

H151 BLACKER, George: Eli's Hit man in Record Research, No. 161/162 (February-March 1979) to No. 165/166 (August 1979); No. 171/172 (March 1980), various paginations ((3))

HIT OF THE WEEK label
    See also DURIUM label

H152 WATERS, Howard J.: History & discography of "The Hit-of-the-Week record" (condensed version), in KINKLE, Roger D.: Check sheet (Project #1) [Evansville, IN: n.d.], 19-24; additions and corrections in KINKLE, Roger D.: Check sheet (Project #2) [Evansville, IN?: n.d.], 7 ((3, 6, 7, 9))

H153 WATERS, Howard J.: The Hit-of-the-Week record; discography in Record Research, No. 26 (January-February 1960): 8-18, 27-28 ((2, 3, 5, 6, 7d, 8))

HITCH, CURTIS
    piano, leader

H154 KAY, George W.: Discography in Jazz Journal, Vol. 9 (April 1956): 6 ((2, 3, 7))

HJCA label
    See H J C A label

HMV label
    See H M V label

HOBBS, WILLIE
    vocal

H155 MOHR, Kurt: Willie Hobbs discography in Hot Buttered Soul, No. 39 (July 1975): 13 ((3, 7))

HODEIR, ANDRE, 1921-
    composer, arranger

H156 Discographie d'Andre Hodeir in Jazz Hot, No. 162 (February 1961): 16 ((—))

HODES, ART, 1904-
    piano

H157 Art Hodes Blue Note sessions in Hip, Vol. 7 (June 1970): 5-6 ((2, 3, 7))

H158 FAIRCHILD, Rolph: Discography of Art Hodes. Ontario, CA: [c1962], 36 pp. ((1, 2, 3, 4p, 6 7))

H159 HODES, Art: From Nikolaiev to Nick's in ASMAN, James, and Bill KINNELL, eds.: American Jazz No. 1. Chilwell, Nottinghamshire: Jazz Appreciation Society, 1946, 4-5 ((—))

H160 MAHONY, Daniel L.: Discography of Art Hodes in Australian Jazz Quarterly, No. 6 (March 1948): 3-7 ((2, 3, 6, 7))

HODGES, JOHNNY, 1906-1970
    alto saxophone

H161 FOL, Robert: Discographie in Jazz Hot, No. 43 (April 1950): 14-15 [recordings not with Duke Ellington] ((2, 7d))

H162 JEPSEN, Jorgen Grunnet: Diskofilspalten in Orkester Journalen, Vol. 28 (September 1960): 27; (October 1960): 21 [Norman Granz recordings, 1951-1956] ((2, 3, 6, 7d))

H163 Johnny Hodges since "New hot discography," in Discophile, No. 15 (December 1960): 5, 8; additions and corrections in Discophile, No. 16 (February 1951): 9; No. 17 (April 1951): 14 ((2, 3, 7))

H164 [[TOLLARA, Gianni: [Discography, 1965-1967] in Musica Jazz, Vol. 24 (August-September 1968)]]

H165 TOLLARA, Gianni, and Enzo FRESIA: Johnny Hodges 1951-1964 in Musica Jazz, Vol. 21 (March 1965): 42; (April 1965): 37-38 ((2, 3, 6, 7))

HOFF, JASPER VAN'T, 1947-
    piano

H166 ROTTERDAM, Rijk van: Jasper van't Hoff: Association is een geluid

op zich in Jazz Wereld, No. 37
(January-February 1972): 15
((—))

HOGG, ANDREW "SMOKEY," 1908-

H167 ROTANTE, Anthony: Andrew "Smokey"
Hogg in Discophile, No. 31 (August 1953): 5-7; additions and
corrections in Discophile, No. 34
(February 1954): 12; [from George
HULME and John W. NORRIS] No. 59
(April 1958): 9; No. 61 (December
1958): 17-18 ((2, 3, 6))

H168 STRACHWITZ, Chris: Andrew
"Smokey" Hogg in Jazz Report
(California), Vol. 1 (May 1961):
unpaged Blues Report section ((2,
3, 6, 7))

H169 STRACHWITZ, Chris; and Mike LEAD-
BITTER: Andrew "Smokey" Hogg--
discography in Blues Unlimited
Collectors Classics, No. 9 (December 1965): 12-15 [rev. ed. of
previous entry] ((2, 3, 6, 7))

HOLIDAY, BILLIE, 1915-1959
   vocal
   See also WILSON, TEDDY (Bakker,
   Dick M.)

H170 BAKKER, Dick M.: Billie Holiday
Vocalion-Brunswick recordings
1933-1942 in Micrography, No. 28
(September 1973): 5-8; additions
and corrections in Micrography,
No. 29 (December 1973): 1; No. 30
(April 1974): 1 ((7d))

H171 Days by Lady; Billie Holiday
discography in Swing Journal,
Vol. 27 (April 1973): 76-81 ((2,
7d))

H172 Discography of Billie Holiday in
Swing Journal, issue 9 of 1959:
46 ((—))

H173 GALLETLY, Bill: Chronological
discography in HOLIDAY, Billie:
Lady sings the blues. Garden
City, NY: Doubleday, 1956, 230-
250 ((2, 3, 7d))

H174 JEPSEN, Jorgen Grunnet: A discography of Billie Holiday. [Brande,
Denmark: Debut Records, c1960],
29 leaves ((1, 2, 3, 6, 7))

H175 JEPSEN, Jorgen Grunnet: A discography of Billie Holiday. Copenhagen: Knudsen [ca. 1969], 37
leaves ((1, 2, 3, 6, 7))

H176 McCARTHY, Albert J.: Discography
in HOLIDAY, Billie: Lady sings
the blues. London: Barrie & Jenkins [1973, c1956], 208-234 ((1,
2, 3, 6, 7))

H177 MILLAR, Jack: Billie Holiday--a
selected discography of airshots,
concert recordings, and film
soundtracks in Discographical
Forum, No. 32 (1973) to No. 41
(1978?), various paginations ((1,
2, 7))

H178 MILLAR, Jack: Billie Holiday
discographie [sic] in Australian
Jazz Quarterly, No. 12 (March
1951): 3-11; additions and corrections in Australian Jazz
Quarterly, No. 16 (March 1952):
17-20 ((1, 2, 3, 6, 7))

H179 MILLAR, Jack: Take two; a preliminary listing of the alternate
masters featuring vocal by Billie
Holiday in Matrix, No. 96 (April
1972) to No. 98 (November 1972),
various paginations; additions
and corrections in his Further
alternative masters in Matrix,
No. 105 (November 1974) ((3, 6,
7))

H180 [[POSTIF, François: [Discography]
in HOLIDAY, Billie: Lady sings
the blues. Paris: Plon, 1960
(also Paris: Club du Meilleur
Livre, 1960)]]

H181 RUPPLI, Michel: Discographie:
Billie Holiday in Jazz Hot, No.
363 (summer 1979): 51-55; No. 366
(October 1979): 31-34; No. 367
(November 1979): 33-35 ((1, 2, 3,
6, 7))

H182 [[SCHOUTEN, Martin: [Discography]. Utrecht: Zwarte Beetjes,
1968]]

H183 SHERA, Michael G.: Billie Holiday
& Lester Young 1937-1941; a discography in Jazz Journal, Vol. 14
(August 1961): 16 ((2, 3, 6, 7))

HOLIDAY, JIMMY
   vocal

H184 MOHR, Kurt: Jimmy Holiday discography in Hot Buttered Soul, No.
33 (August 1974?): 2-3 ((3, 5,
7))

HOLIDAY label

H185 EAGLE, Bob: The Holiday label in
Alley Music, Vol. 1 (first quarter 1968): 14 ((3))

HOLIDAYS (musical group)

H186 MOHR, Kurt: Discography des Holidays in Soul Bag, No. 30 (September 1973): 11 ((2, 3, 7))

HOLLAND, DAVID, 1946–
bass violin

H187 Selected Holland discography in Down Beat, Vol. 45 (May 18, 1978): 20 ((—))

HOLLERHAGEN, ERNST
clarinet

H188 [[Ernst Hollerhagen; eine Skizze; Bio-Discographie. Wanne-Eickel, W. Germany: Gerhard Conrad, 1964, 21 pp.]]

H189 [[MUTH, Wolfgang: Ernst Hollerhagen, ein deutscher Jazzmusiker. Magdeburg: Jazz im Club, 1964, 28 pp.]]

HOLLYWOOD label

H190 BENTLEY, John, and Ralph W. MILLER: West coast jazz in the 'twenties; record listing in Jazz Monthly, Vol. 7 (May 1961): 7 ((—))

HOLMAN, BILL, 1927–
tenor saxophone

H191 [[[Discography] in HENTOFF, Nat: Bill Holman. New York: BMI, 1961, 16 pp.]]

HOLMES, HORACE, 1901–
cornet

H192 The Horace Holmes story in Jazz Music Vol. 5, No. 4 (n.d.): 14 ((2, 3, 6, 7d, 9))

HOLMES, RICHARD "GROOVE," 1931–
organ

H193 NOLAN, Herb: Groove Holmes in Different Drummer, Vol. 1 (October 1974): 13 ((—))

HOMESICK JAMES
See WILLIAMSON, JAMES

HONSINGER, TRISTAN
cello

H194 Discografia Tristan Honsingen [sic] in Nuova Musica, No. 2 (November 1979): 19–20 ((7p))

HOOKER, EARL, 1910–1970
guitar, vocal

H195 BAKER, Cary: Earl Hooker discography (updated) in Hot Buttered Soul, No. 16 (March 1973): 11–13 ((3, 7))

H196 [[[Discography] in Soul Bag, No. 7]]

H197 Discography: Earl Hooker in Blue Flame, No. 13 (n.d.): 14–15 ((2, 3, 7d))

H198 TONNEAU, Serge: LP's sous le nom de Earl Hooker/avec divers musiciens in Point du Jazz, No. 3 (August 1970): 57 ((—))

HOOKER, JOHN LEE, 1917–
guitar, vocal

H199 CHAUVARD, Marcel, and Kurt MOHR: John Lee Hooker on Vee-Jay in Jazz Statistics, No. 14 (January 1960): 6; additions from Michel VOGLER in Jazz Statistics, No. 22 (June 1961): 2 ((2, 3, 7))

H200 [[Discography in Rhythm & Blues Panorama, No. 37]]

H201 FANCOURT, Leslie: John Lee Hooker; a discography. Faversham, Kent: 1977, 19 leaves ((2, 3, 6, 7))

H202 POSTIF, François, and Anthony ROTANTE: Discographie de John Lee Hooker in Jazz Hot, No. 103 (October 1955): 17 ((2, 3, 7d))

H203 ROTANTE, Anthony; Paul SHEATSLEY; and Mike LEADBITTER: A discography of John Lee Hooker in Blues Unlimited Collectors Classics, No. 2 (1964): 6–16 ((2, 3, 6, 7, 8))

H204 ROTANTE, Anthony, and George BRYMER: John Lee Hooker; a provisional discography in Discophile, No. 27 (December 1952): 11–13; additions and corrections in Discophile, No. 29 (May 1953): 19; No. 32 (October 1953): 13; No. 59 (April 1958): 10 ((2, 3, 6, 7d))

H205 ROTANTE, Anthony, and Paul SHEATSLEY: The records of John Lee Hooker in Record Research, No. 31 (November 1960): 3–5, 20 ((2, 3, 7))

H206 SAY, Dave: Early Hooker discography in The Blues, No. 9 (n.d.): 50-52 ((3, 7))

HOOPER, Louis, 1894-1977
piano

H207 KIDD, Jim: Louis Hooper discography in Record Research, No. 77 (June 1966): 6, 8-9 ((2, 3))

HOPE, BILLY

H208 MOHR, Kurt: Discographie de Billy Hope in Soul Bag, No. 16 (1972?): 23 ((2, 3, 7))

HOPE, ELMO, 1923-1967
piano

H209 EYLE, Wim van: Elmo Hope discografie in Jazz Press, No. 40 (June 10, 1977): 18-19; additions and corrections in Jazz Press, No. 41 (October 1, 1977): 6 ((2, 3, 7))

H210 NIQUET, Bernard: Microsillons de Elmo Hope publiés ou reédités sous son nom in Point du Jazz, No. 14 (June 1978): 39-40 ((7p))

H211 WALKER, Malcolm: Elmo Hope discography in Discographical Forum, No. 8 (September 1968) to No. 10 (January 1969), various paginations; additions and corrections in Discographical Forum, No. 11 (March 1969): 2; No. 20 (September 1970): 2 ((2, 3, 7))

HOPE, LYNN, 1926-
tenor saxophone

H212 MOHR, Kurt: Discographie de Lynn Hope in Soul Bag, No. 16 (1972?): 22-23; additions and corrections in Soul Bag, No. 21 (November-December 1972): 9 ((2, 3, 7))

H213 ROTANTE, Anthony, and Len KUNSTADT: Discography of Lynn Hope in Record Research, No. 79 (October 1966): 9; additions and corrections in Record Research, No. 84 (June 1967): 9; No. 98 (May 1969): 6 ((2, 3, 7d, 8))

HOPKINS, CLAUDE, 1903-
piano

H214 BAKKER, Dick M.: Claude Hopkins in Micrography, No. 23 (January 1973): 9 ((7d))

HOPKINS, FRED, 1947-
bass violin

H215 Discografia di Fred Hopkins in Musica Jazz, Vol. 36 (March 1980): 29 ((—))

HOPKINS, JOEL, 1904-1975
guitar, vocal

H216 McCORMICK, Mack: Joel Hopkins (vocal and guitar); field recordings in Discographical Forum, No. 2 (July 1960): 6 ((2, 7))

HOPKINS, LIGHTNIN' (Sam Hopkins), 1912-
guitar, vocal

H217 [[BERG, Arne: Jazz rhythm & blues; Panorama special Lightnin' Hopkins discography. Stockholm: 196?]]

H218 HOLT, John: Lightnin' Hopkins discography in his Lightnin' Hopkins. [London: 1965], 11-43 ((2, 3, 7))

H219 ROTANTE, Anthony: Sam "Lightin" Hopkins discography in Discophile, No. 45 (December 1955): 3-7; additions and corrections in Discophile, No. 47 (April 1956): 11; No. 56 (October 1957): 18; No. 59 (April 1958): 8-9 ((2, 3, 7))

H220 STRACHWITZ, Chris: Lightnin Hopkins discography in Jazz Monthly, Vol. 5 (November 1959): 25-26; (December 1959): 13-14 ((2,3, 7))

H221 [[TONNEAU, Serge: [Discography] in Rhythm & Blues Panorama (December 1964)]]

HOPKINS, LINDA
vocal

H222 MOHR, Kurt: Linda Hopkins in Soul Bag, No. 34 (January 1974): 1-2 ((2, 3, 7))

HORTON, WALTER, 1918-
harmonica

H223 PATERSON, Neil: Walter Horton; a discography of his singles in Blues Unlimited, No. 20 (March 1965): 8-9 ((2, 3, 7))

HOT JAZZ CLUBS OF AMERICA label
See H J C A label

HOT RECORD SOCIETY label
See H R S label

HOUSE, SON (Eddie James House Jr.), 1902-

H224 BAKKER, Dick M.: Son House 1930-1942 in Micrography, No. 5 (August 1969): 2 ((—))

H225 GODRICH, John, and Rae KORSON: Son House--a discography in Blues Unlimited Collectors Classics, No. 14 (October 1966): 8-9 [reprinted from Broadside of Boston, unknown issues, 1965] ((2, 3, 6, 7, 9))

H226 NAPIER, Simon A.: [Additions to listing in Blues and gospel records 1902-1942] in Blues Unlimited, No. 14 (August 1964): 11 ((2, 7, 9))

HOUSTON, LAWYER
guitar, vocal

H227 LEADBITTER, Mike: Lawyer Houston in Blues Unlimited, No. 32 (April 1966): 9 ((2, 3))

HOUSTON, THELMA
vocal

H228 MOHR, Kurt: Discographie de Thelma Houston in Soul Bag, No. 62 (July 1977): 3-5 ((2, 3, 7))

HOVE, FRED van, 1937-
piano

H229 Beknopte discografie in Jazz Wereld, No. 27 (January 1970): 9 ((2, 7))

HOW HIGH THE MOON (tune title)

H230 FEATHER, Leonard: How high the tune in Metronome, Vol. 63 (September 1947): 20 ((—))

H231 POPESCU, Gene: How high the moon; a suggested complete listing of this great tune in Jazz Discounter, Vol. 2 (April 1949): 17 ((1))

HOWARD, BOB, 1906-
piano, vocal

H232 TONKS, Eric S.: Discography of Bob Howard in Melody Maker, Vol.

21 (December 8, 1945): 6 ((2, 3, 7))

HOWARD, NOAH, 1943-
alto saxophone

H233 Discography in Coda, No. 146 (April 1976): 12 ((2, 7))

HOWELL, PEG LEG (Joshua Barnes Howell), 1888-1966
guitar, vocal

H234 BAKKER, Dick M.: Peg Leg Howell on microgroove in Micrography, No. 20 (June 1972): 11 ((7d))

HOWLIN' WOLF (Chester Burnett), 1910-1976
See also BLUES MUSIC (Guralnick, Peter)

H235 CHAUVARD, Marcel, and Kurt MOHR: Discography of Howlin' Wolf in Jazz Statistics, No. 16 (1960): 13-14; additions and corrections from Michel VOGLER in Jazz Statistics, No. 17 (1960): 8; No. 22 (June 1961): 2 ((2, 3, 7d))

H236 CHAUVARD, Marcel; Kurt MOHR; and John J. BROVEN: A discography of Howlin' Wolf in Blues Unlimited, No. 3 (July 1963): 7-8 ((2, 3, 7))

H237 MOHR, Kurt; John BROVEN; and Mike A. LEADBITTER: A discography of Howlin' Wolf in Blues Unlimited Collectors Classics, No. 4 (December 1964): 6-9 ((2, 3, 7))

H238 NIQUET, Bernard: Discographie L.P. de Howlin' Wolf in Jazz Hot, No. 269 (February 1971): 23 ((—))

HRS label
See H R S label

HUBBARD, FREDDIE, 1938-
trumpet
See also CHERRY, DON (Ioakimidis, Demetre)

H239 BOWER, Roy: Freddie Hubbard in Jazz Monthly, Vol. 11 (October 1965): 28-29; (November 1965): 29-31; (December 1965): 25-26; additions and corrections in Jazz Monthly, Vol. 12 (April 1966): 27 ((1, 2, 3, 7))

H240 Selected Hubbard discography in Down Beat, Vol. 45 (June 15, 1978): 19 ((—))

H241 THOMPSON, Vern: Freddie Hubbard in Different Drummer, Vol. 1 (December 1974): 20 ((—))

HUGHES, SPIKE (Patrick Cairns Hughes), 1908–
bass violin, leader

H242 WHITE, C. W. Langston, and R. G. V. VENABLES: Spike Hughes and his Orchestra; a complete discography in Jazz Journal, Vol. 1 (October 1948): 4 ((2, 3, 6, 7))

HUMPHREY, PAUL
drums

H243 NIQUET, Bernard: Number one soul drums in Soul Bag, No. 46 (February 1975): 5, 7 ((2, 7))

HUNTER, ALBERTA, 1897–
vocal

H244 Alberta Hunter discography in Down Beat, Vol. 47 (January 1980): 23 [recent LPs only] ((—))

H245 STEWART-BAXTER, Derrick, and Ron DAVIES: Alberta Hunter discography in Jazzfinder, Vol. 1 (December 1948): 11-12 ((2, 3, 6, 7d))

HURT, JOHN, 1893-1966
guitar, vocal

H246 BAKKER, Dick M.: Mississippi John Hurt in Micrography, No. 5 (August 1969): 11 ((—))

H247 GODRICH, John, and Bob DIXON: Mississippi John Hurt discography in Blues Unlimited, No. 4 (August 1963): 4 ((2, 3, 6, 7))

H248 KAY, George W.: Mississippi John Hurt discography in Jazz Journal, Vol. 17 (February 1964): 26 ((2, 3, 6, 7))

HUTCHERSON, BOBBY, 1941–
vibraphone

H249 Bobby Hutcherson discography in Swing Journal, Vol. 13 (November 1974): 244-247 ((2, 7d))

H250 Selected Hutcherson discography in Down Beat, Vol. 46 (April 19, 1979): 15 ((—))

H251 WILBRAHAM, Roy J.: Bobby Hutcherson in Jazz Monthly, Vol. 13 (February 1967): 26-28; additions and corrections in Jazz Monthly, Vol. 13 (April 1967): 25 ((2, 3, 7))

HUTTO, J. B. (Joseph Benjamin Hutto), 1926–
guitar, vocal

H252 [Discography] in Living Blues, No. 30 (November-December 1976): 24 ((2, 3, 6, 7))

H253 ROWE, Mike, and Jacques DEMETRE: J. B. Hutto--a discography in Blues Unlimited, No. 37 (October 1966): 15 ((2, 3, 7))

HYDE, ALEX, d. 1956
violin, leader

H254 LOTZ, Rainer E.: Alex Hyde's hot dance recordings for Deutsche Grammophon Gesellschaft in Storyville, No. 74 (December 1977-January 1978): 52-57; additions and corrections in Storyville, No. 74 (August-September 1978): 204-206 ((2, 3, 6, 7, 8))

ICP label (Dutch)

I1 EYLE, Wim van: De I.C.P. discografie in Jazz Press, No. 43 (September 2, 1977): 16 ((2, 7))

I WISH I COULD SHIMMY LIKE MY SISTER KATE (tune title)

I2 PROSPER, Steve, and Allen W. SCHULTZ: I wish I could shimmy like my sister Kate in Jazz Discounter, Vol. 2 (October 1949): 3 ((—))

ILCKEN, WESSEL, d. 1957
drums

I3 EYLE, Wim van, and Jan MULDER: Wessel Ilcken disco in Jazz Press, No. 53/54 (September 1, 1978): 30-31 ((2, 7))

IMPERIAL label (British)

I4 BADROCK, Arthur: Items of jazz interest on the Imperial label in Discophile, No. 33 (December 1953): 2-9; additions and corrections in Discophile, No. 34 (February 1954): 4-5, 8; No. 39 (December 1954): 5-8; No. 40 (February 1955): 15; No. 43 (August 1955): 7-8; No. 45 (December 1955): 22; No. 47 (April 1956): 17-18 ((3, 6))

IMPRESSIONS (musical group)

I5   CHURCHILL, Trevor, and Peter GIBBON: The Impressions—a discography in Soul, No. 3 (April 1966): 6-9 ((3, 7, 8))

IMPULSE label
   See also COLTRANE, JOHN (Fresia, Enzo) and (Stiassi, Ruggero); SHEPP, ARCHIE (Discographie Impulse d'Archie Shepp)

I6   SHERA, Michael: A discography of the Impulse label in Jazz Journal, Vol. 15 (October 1962): 19, 34 [to no. 14] ((2, 7))

I7   STIASSI, Ruggero: I primi 50 dischi Impulse in Musica Jazz, Vol. 20 (July 1964) to (October 1964), various paginations; continued in his Discografia "Impulse" no. 51 al n. 91 in Musica Jazz, Vol. 22 (August-September 1966): 45-47; (October 1966): 44-46 [to no. 101] ((2, 7))

INCUS label (British)

I8   Listing in ROUY, Gerard: Incus ou la force tranquille in Jazz Magazine (France), No. 254 (May 1977): 21 ((2))

INDEPENDENTS (musical group)

I9   MOHR, Kurt: The Independents in Soul Bag, No. 45 (January 1975): 16 ((2, 3, 7))

INSTANT COMPOSERS POOL
   See ICP label

INTERLUDE label
   See MODE label

INVICTUS label

I10 PETARD, Gilles: Invictus label listing in Soul Bag, No. 20 (July-August 1972): 18-19 ((3))

ITALIAN JAZZ STARS series
   See ODEON label (Italian)

IZENSON, DAVID, 1932-1979
   bass violin

I11 RABEN, Erik: Diskofilspalten in Orkester Journalen, Vol. 37 (September 1969): 23; additions and corrections in Orkester Journalen, Vol. 37 (October 1969): 28 ((1, 2, 7))

JACKSON, BESSIE
   See BOGAN, LUCILLE

JACKSON, CHARLIE, d. 1938
   guitar, vocal

J1   HARRIS, Rex, and Max JONES: Papa Charlie Jackson on wax in Melody Maker, Vol. 22 (July 20, 1946): 4 ((2, 3))

JACKSON, DEWEY, 1900-
   trumpet

J2   CHOQUART, Loys: [Discography] in Hot Revue, No. 8 (1946): 32 ((2))

J3   RANDOLPH, John: Dewey Jackson discography in Jazz Report (St. Louis), Vol. 6 (May 1958): 10 ((7))

JACKSON, FRANZ, 1912-
   tenor saxophone

J4   NIQUET, Bernard: Discographie de Franz Jackson and the Original Jass All Stars in Jazz Hot, No. 236 (November 1967): 27 ((2, 7p))

J5   NIQUET, Bernard: Discographie de Franz Jackson and the Original Jass All Stars in Point du Jazz, No. 6 (March 1972): 88-89 ((2, 7))

JACKSON, JOHN, 1924-
   guitar, vocal

J6   SCALA, Gianfranco: Discografia in Blues Power, Vol. 1 (No. 2/3, 1974): 20 ((—))

JACKSON, JUMP
   drums

J7   [Discography] in Jazz Statistics, No. 18 (1960): 5-6; additions from Michel VOGLER in Jazz Statistics, No. 22 (June 1961): 3 ((2, 3, 7))

JACKSON, LEE, 1907–
guitar, vocal

J8   BAKER, Cary: Lee Jackson discography in Hot Buttered Soul, No. 15 (February 1973): 5 ((3, 7))

J9   MOHR, Kurt, and Niel PATERSON: Lee Jackson--discography in Blues Unlimited, No. 26 (October 1965): 13 ((2, 3, 7))

J10   O'NEAL, Jim: Lee Jackson discography in Living Blues, No. 34 (September-October 1977): 16 ((2, 7))

JACKSON, LIL SON (Melvin Jackson), 1916-1976
guitar, vocal

J11   ROTANTE, Anthony: Lil Son Jackson (Melvin Jackson) in Record Research, Vol. 1 (October 1955): 2, 12 ((7d))

J12   STRACHWITZ, Chris; Kerry KUDLACEK; and Mike LEADBITTER: Discography in Blues Unlimited Collectors Classics, No. 9 (December 1965): 10-11 [rev. ed. of next entry] ((2, 3, 7))

J13   STRACHWITZ, Chris: Lil Son Jackson in Jazz Report (California), Vol. 1 (February 1961): 23-25 ((2, 3, 7))

JACKSON, MAHALIA, 1911-1972
vocal

J14   CHMURA, Helene F.: The Columbia recordings of Mahalia Jackson in Discophile, No. 43 (August 1955): 9; additions and corrections in No. 45 (December 1955): 15 ((2, 3, 7))

J15   HAYES, Cedric J.: Mahalia Jackson; a discography in Matrix, No. 60 (August 1965) to No. 62 (December 1965), various paginations; additions and corrections in Matrix, No. 70 (April 1967): 14; No. 71 (June 1967): 12; No. 72/73 (September 1967): 33 ((2, 3, 6, 7))

J16   HOUGHTON, Tony: Queen of the gospel singers is dead in Collecta, No. 17 (May 1972): 7-8 [recordings to 1950] ((2, 3, 7))

J17   [[KAYSER, Erhard: Discography in Jazz Podium, Vol. 12 (Nos. 3, 5, 7, and 11, 1963)]]

J18   Mahalia on records; selected discography in JACKSON, Mahalia, and Evan McLeod WYLIE: Movin' on up. [New York]: Avon [c1966], 219, 222-224 ((—))

J19   [[UYLDERT, Herman: Vorstin van de gospel: Mahalia Jackson. Tielt den Haag, Netherlands: Lannoo, 1962, 96 pp.]]

J20   WIEDEMANN, Erik: Discography of Mahalia Jackson in Discophile, No. 12 (June 1950): 10, 6; additions and corrections in Discophile, No. 13 (August 1950): 11; No. 19 (August 1951): 11 ((2, 3, 6, 7))

J21   WIEDEMANN, Erik: Mahalia Jackson on records in Melody Maker, Vol. 28 (November 8, 1952): 8 [to be concluded in later issue(s), unknown dates] ((2, 3, 6, 7))

JACKSON, MELVIN
See JACKSON, LIL SON

JACKSON, MICHAEL GREGORY, 1954–
guitar

J22   Précis discographique in Jazz Hot, No. 366 (October 1979): 21 ((—))

J23   Selected Jackson discography in Down Beat, Vol. 47 (March 1980): 30 ((—))

JACKSON, MILT, 1923–
vibraphone

J24   [[JEPSEN, Jorgen Grunnet: Milt Jackson; a discography. Copenhagen: 1957, 13 leaves]]

J25   JEPSEN, Jorgen Grunnet: Milt Jackson discography in Jazz Monthly, Vol. 4 (July 1958): 30-31; (August 1958): 22-24; (September 1958): 24-25 ((1, 2, 3, 7))

J26   Modern Jazz Quartet & Milt Jackson discography in Swing Journal,

Vol. 26 (December 1972): 264-269
((2, 7d))

J27 [[MOHR, Kurt: Discographie.
Paris: Jazz Hot, 1958?]]

J28 Selected Jackson discography in
Down Beat, Vol. 42 (May 8, 1975):
15 ((—))

J29 [[WIEDEMANN, Erik: Milt Jackson
diskografi in Orkester Journalen,
Vol. 23 (May 1955): 43]]

J30 WILBRAHAM, Roy J.: Milt Jackson;
a discography and biography (including recordings made with the
Modern Jazz Quartet). London
[c1968], 40 + 2 pp.; additions
and corrections [from Dieter
SALEMANN] in Discographical Forum, No. 12 (May 1969): 2; [from
Erik RABEN] No. 18 (May 1970):
17-19; [from Roy J. WILBRAHAM] in
Jazz Journal, Vol. 22 (May 1969):
22 ((1, 2, 3, 6, 7))

JACKSON, PRESTON 1904-
trombone

J31 HAESLER, William J.: Preston
Jackson, a draft discographie
[sic] in Australian Jazz Quarterly, No. 17 (June 1952): 15-18;
additions and corrections in Australian Jazz Quarterly, No. 18
(September 1952): 21 ((2, 3, 6,
7))

JACKSON, WILLIS, 1932-
tenor saxophone

J32 Discographie de Willis Jackson in
Soul Bag, No. 65 (January 1978):
11-12 ((2, 3, 7))

JACOBSON, BUD (Orville Kenneth
Jacobson), 1906-1960
clarinet, piano

J33 SCHENCK, John T.: Bud Jacobson
discography in Jazz Session, No.
10 (November-December 1945): 8
((—))

JACQUET, ILLINOIS (Battiste Illinois
Jacquet), 1922-
tenor saxophone

J34 [[WILBRAHAM, Roy J.: [Discogra-
phy]. London: 196?]]

JAFFE, NAT, 1918-1945
piano

J35 EYLE, Wim van: Nat Jaffe--een
onbekende pianist in Jazz Press,
No. 34 (March 18, 1977): 6 ((1,
2, 3, 6, 7))

JAMES, BOB, 1939-
arranger, leader

J36 Selected James discography in
Down Beat, Vol. 42 (October 23,
1975): 17 ((—))

JAMES, ELMORE, 1918-1963
guitar, vocal

J37 BAKKER, Dick M.: Elmore James
titles, now available on LP in
Micrography, No. 2 (February
1969): 11; additions and corrections in Micrography, No. 5 (August 1969): 12 ((—))

J38 Discography in Blues Unlimited,
No. 5 (October 1963): 4-6 ((2, 3,
7))

J39 Discography in Blues Unlimited
Collectors Classics, No. 7 (May
1965): 4-6 ((2, 3, 7))

J40 [Discography] in Jazz Statistics,
No. 18 (1960): 3-4; additions
from Michel VOGLER in Jazz Statistics, No. 22 (June 1961): 3;
[from Wolfie BAUM] No. 24 (December 1961): JS8 ((2, 3, 6, 7))

J41 ROHNISCH, Claus: Elmore James discography in Jefferson, No. 21
(1973): 38-42 ((3, 7))

J42 ROTANTE, Anthony: Elmore James in
Vintage Jazz Mart, Vol. 6 (October 1959): 4, 34; additions and
corrections from Tony STANDISH in
Vintage Jazz Mart, Vol. 6 (December 1959): 4 ((2, 3, 7d, 8))

JAMES, FRANK
piano, vocal

J43 SMITH, Francis: Frank/Springback
James discography in Blues Unlimited, No. 4 (August 1963):
8-9; additions and corrections in
Blues Unlimited, undated supplement to Nos. 1-6: 3 ((2, 3, 7d,
8))

JAMES, HARRY, 1916-
trumpet

J44 BAKKER, Dick M.: Harry James with
Basie bandmembers 1937-1938 in
Micrography, No. 33 (1974): 5
((7d))

J45   GARROD, Charles, and Peter JOHN-
      STON: Harry James and his Orches-
      tra. Zephyrhills, FL: Joyce Music,
      1975, 2 v. ((1, 2, 3, 4t, 6, 7))

J46   HALL, George I., ed.: Harry James
      and his Orchestra, Volume 1,
      1937-1950. Laurel, MD: Jazz Dis-
      cographies Unlimited, 1971, 56
      leaves ((1, 2, 3, 6, 7))

J47   HOEFER, George: James discography
      in Down Beat, Vol. 18 (February
      23, 1951): 18 ((—))

J48   STACY, Frank: Harry James' dis-
      cography in his Harry James pin-
      up life story. New York: Arco,
      1944, 22-23 ((—))

JAMES, HOMESICK
      See WILLIAMSON, JAMES

JAMES, JESSE
      piano, vocal

J49   LEADBITTER, Mike: Jesse James in
      Blues Unlimited, No. 36 (Septem-
      ber 1966): 18 ((3, 7d))

JAMES, McKINLEY, 1935-
      guitar, harmonica, vocal

J50   ALLINSON, John G.: The McKinley
      James story in Blues Unlimited,
      No. 134 (March-June 1979): 7; No.
      135/136 (July-December 1979): 13
      ((2, 3, 6, 7))

JAMES, SKIP (Nehemiah James), 1902-
      1969
      guitar, vocal
      See also BLUES MUSIC (Guralnick,
      Peter)

J51   BAKKER, Dick M.: Skip James in
      Micrography, No. 19 (April 1972):
      12 ((—))

J52   BAKKER, Dick M.: Skip James 31-67
      in Micrography, No. 4 (June
      1969): 10 ((7d))

J53   Platen in Jazz Wereld, No. 19
      (August 1968): 11 ((—))

JANIS, CONRAD, 1928-
      trombone

J54   STAMM, Bill V.: A discography of
      Conrad Janis in Discophile, No.
      22 (February 1952): 15; additions
      and corrections in Discophile,
      No. 24 (June 1952): 12 ((2, 3,
      7))

JARRETT, KEITH, 1945-
      piano

J55   [Discography] in Swing Journal,
      Vol. 31 (December 1977): 300-303
      ((2, 7d))

J56   Keith Jarrett discography in
      Swing Journal, Vol. 28 (January
      1974): 294-299 ((2, 7d))

J57   LUZZI, Mario: Discografia Keith
      Jarrett in Musica Jazz, Vol. 30
      (May 1974): 54-56 ((2, 7))

J58   PALMER, Bob: The inner octaves of
      Keith Jarrett in Down Beat, Vol.
      41 (October 24, 1974): 46 ((—))

J59   POSTIF, François: Discographie in
      Jazz Hot, No. 256 (December
      1969): 20 ((2, 7))

J60   RABEN, Erik: Diskofilspalten in
      Orkester Journalen, Vol. 40 (May
      1972): 19 ((2, 3, 7))

J61   RUPPLI, Michael: Discographie de
      Keith Jarrett in Jazz Hot, No.
      348 (April 1978): 22-25 ((2, 3,
      7))

J62   STEIN, Bob: Keith Jarrett in
      Different Drummer, Vol. 1 (Novem-
      ber 1974): 20 ((—))

JASPAR, BOBBY, 1926-1936
      saxophones

J63   DEVOGHELAERE, Edmond: Bobby
      Jaspar; a biography, apprecia-
      tion, record survey and complete
      discography. Heist-op-den-Berg,
      Belgium: Labris, 1967, 124 pp.;
      additions and corrections in his
      Bobby Jaspar disco in Swingtime
      (Belgium), No. 24 (October 1977):
      10-13 ((1, 2, 4p, 7, 9))

JAY label

J64   JACOBS, Irving L.: The Jay cata-
      logue in Discophile, No. 12 (June
      1950): 12; additions and correc-
      tions in Discophile, No. 16
      (February 1951): 9 ((—))

JAZZ ARCHIVE SERIES (British)
      See LONDON label (British)

JAZZ AT THE ASAHIKODO

J65   Ni Hon no jazz discography;
      J A T A concert in Swing Jour-
      nal, Vol. 31 (January 1977): 315
      ((2, 3, 7))

JAZZ AT THE PHILHARMONIC

J66   [[McCARTHY, Albert J.: A discography of JATP in Melody Maker, Vol. 29 (March 7, 1953): 8]]

JAZZ CLASSICS label

J67   SHARP, Richard: Jazz Classics in Discophile, No. 21 (December 1951): 20-22 ((—))

JAZZ CLUB HOT BAND

J68   Jazz Club Hot Band in Matrix, No. 97 (September 1973): 3-5 ((2, 3, 6, 7))

J69   NELSON, John R.: Jazz Club Hot Band in Matrix, No. 90 (December 1970): 8-9 ((2, 3, 6, 7))

JAZZ COLLECTOR label

J70   [[CAREY, Dave: [Complete numerical list] in Swing Shop Magazine, No. 1 (August 1952)]]

JAZZ CRUSADERS
      See The CRUSADERS

JAZZ DANCE

J71   [[[Discography] in TRAGUTH, Fred: Modern Jazz Dance. Bonn: Verlag Dance Motion, 1977, 219]]

J72   Schallplatten in FISCHER-MUNSTER-MANN, Uta: Vonder Jazzgymnastik zum Jazztanz. Celle: Pohl, 1977, 130-131 ((—))

JAZZ IN ITALY series
      See CETRA label

JAZZ IN THE TROC series

J73   COLLER, Derek, and Jim SHACTER: Jazz in the Troc; from the "Nine greats of jazz" to the "World's Greatest Jazz Band"; a discography in Matrix, No. 105 (November 1974): 3-6 ((2, 7))

JAZZ INFORMATION label

J74   GODRICH, John: Jazz Information; a listing of the reissues in Matrix, No. 82 (April 1969): 3; additions and corrections in Matrix, No. 88 (June 1970): 13;

No. 90 (December 1970): 12 ((3, 6))

JAZZ ME BLUES (tune title)

J75   RUGGLES, Happy: Jazz me blues in Jazz Discounter, No. 11 (November 1948): 20 ((—))

JAZZ MUSIC
      See also BLUES MUSIC (Rotante, Anthony)

J76   ANDERSON, Andy: Jazz men and their records in his Helpful hints to jazz collectors; combined with Jazz men and their records. Baraboo, WI: Andoll, c1957, 37-92 ((9))

J77   BARAZZETTA, Giuseppe: Discografia in Musica Jazz, Vol. 15 (December 1959): 39; Vol. 16 (July 1960): 41-42

J78   Bielefelder Katalog; Verzeichnis der Jazzschallplatten. Bielefeld, W. Germany: Bielefelder, No. 3, 1961-to date (annual; Nos. 1-2, 1959-1960 titled Jazz Katalog; Katalog der Jazzschallplatten; Bochum, W. Germany: Musikhaus Kuhl) ((2, 7d)); No. 15 or 16-to date, also has ((4p)); Nos. 16 and 17 also have ((4t)).

J79   BLACKSTONE, Orin: Index to jazz. Fairfax, VA: Record Changer [1945?-1948], 4 v. (also Westport, CT: Greenwood, 197?, 4 v. in 1); additions and corrections in his Index to recent records in his Jazzfinder '49. New Orleans: [1949], 65-104; in his Jazzfinder new releases in Jazzfinder, Vol. 1 (January 1948) to (December 1948), various paginations (continued as The jazzfinder around the world in Playback, Vol. 2 (January 1949) to Vol. 3 (March 1950) and as This month's records in Playback, Vol. 4 (January 1952) to (March-April 1952), various paginations); in his Looking backward in Jazzfinder, Vol. 1 (January 1948) to (December 1948), various paginations (continued as Discology in Playback, Vol. 2 (January 1949) to Vol. 3 (March 1950) and as Jazz research information in Playback, Vol. 4 (January 1952) to (March-April 1952), various paginations); and in BAKER, John H.: Hot discana in Jazzfinder, Vol. 1 (July 1948):

23; Miscellaneous hot discana in Playback, Vol. 2 (April 1949): 21-23; and in PARRY, William Hewitt: Race research department in Discophile, No. 5 (April 1949) to No. 59 (April 1957), most issues, various paginations ((2, 3, 7d))

J80   BRUYNINCKX, Walter: Fifty years of recorded jazz, 1917-1967. Mechelen, Belgium: 1968?- unpaged looseleaf edition ((1, 2, 3, 6, 7))

J81   BRUYNINCKX, Walter: Sixty years of recorded jazz. Mechelen, Belgium: 1977?, unpaged looseleaf edition, ca. 1000 pages per volume; publication not yet complete ((1, 2, 3, 6, 7))

J82   CAREY, Dave, and Albert J. McCARTHY: The directory of recorded jazz and swing music. Fordingbridge, Hants., England: Delphic Press (Vols. 1 to 4), 1950-1952 or London: Cassell (Vols. 2 to 4, 2d ed.; Vols. 5 and 6), 1955-1957 [subtitle varies: Vol. 3 to 5: including gospel and blues; Vol. 6: including blues, gospel, and rhythm and blues]; additions and corrections in BENECKE, Werner: Miscellaneous corrections and additions to Jazz directory in Matrix, No. 19 (September·1958): 16; No. 23 (May 1959): 13-14; FAIRCHILD, Rolph: Discographical data in Jazz Report (California), Vol. 1 (January 1961); (February 1961); (June 1961) to (August 1961); Vol. 2 (September 1961), various paginations; in Record ramblings [column] in Discophile, various issues and paginations; REHNBERG, Bert: Some additions to Jazz directory in Jazz Music, Vol. 8 (March-April 1958): 18-19; SHEATSLEY, Paul B.: Some notes on volume five of Jazz directory in Discophile, No. 46 (February 1956): 15-16; VREEDE, Max E.: Nothin' but the blues; data with special emphasis on the blues in Matrix, No. 15 (February 1957) to No. 40 (April 1962), various paginations; in [[Swing Shop Magazine, No. 1 (August 1952) to ?]]; The V file in Discophile, No. 57/58 (December 1957), whole issue [about musicians beginning with the letter V]. [Covers A to LONGSHAW; commonly known as Jazz directory] ((1, 2, 3, 7))

J83   CHERRINGTON, George: Discography 1959/60 in TRAILL, Sinclair, and Gerald LASCELLES, eds.: Just jazz 4. London: Souvenir Press, c1960 (also London: Jazz Book Club, 1961), 131-159 ((—))

J84   COLLER, Derek, and Eric TOWNLEY: Jazz discography 1956 in TRAILL, Sinclair, ed.: Just Jazz, Vol. 1. London: Peter Davies [1956], 1-224, blue section ((2, 3, 6, 7))

J85   COLLER, Derek, and Eric TOWNLEY: Jazz discography 1957 in TRAILL, Sinclair, ed. Just Jazz, Vol. 2. London: Peter Davies [c1958], 7-256, blue section; additions and corrections in TOWNLEY, Eric: Jazz information in Jazz Journal, Vol. 11 (December 1958): 41; Vol. 12 (January 1959): 28 ((2, 3, 6, 7))

J86   [[DELAUNAY, Charles: Hot discography. Paris: Jazz Hot, 1936, 272 pp.]]; additions and corrections in: BRYCE, Owen: Diggin' discs column in Jazzology (UK), various issues and paginations; Collectors corner column in Melody Maker, Vol. 19 (December 25, 1943): 19; Vol. 21 (September 1, 1945): 4 and probably other issues; Hot discography in Theme, Vol. 1 (October 1953): 13; in Jazz Information, various issues and paginations; McCARTHY, Albert: Collectors notes [column] in Jazz Music, Nos. 6, 8, and 9 (1943); (September 1943); (October 1943), various paginations ((2, 3))

J87   DELAUNAY, Charles: Hot discography. 2d ed. Paris: Jazz Hot, 1938, 408 pp. (corrected and reprinted, New York: Commodore Music Shop, 1940, 416 pp.); additions and corrections in: BRYCE, Owen: Diggin' discs column in Jazzology (UK), various issues and paginations; Collectors corner column in Melody Maker, Vol. 19 (December 25, 1943): 19; Vol. 21 (September 1, 1945): 4 and probably other issues; Hot discography in Theme, Vol. 1 (October 1953): 13; in Jazz Information, various issues and paginations; McCARTHY, Albert: Collectors notes [column] in Jazz Music, Nos. 6, 8, and 9 (1943); (September 1943); (October 1943), various paginations ((2, 3, 4p))

J88 [[DELAUNAY, Charles: Hot discography. 3d ed. New York: Commodore
Music Shop, 1943 (also Paris:
ABC, 1943), 416 pp. (also Paris:
Collection du Hot Clubs de
France, 1943, 538 pp.)]]; additions and corrections in: BRYCE,
Owen: Diggin' discs column in
Jazzology (UK), various issues
and paginations; Collectors corner column in Melody Maker, Vol.
19 (December 25, 1943): 19; Vol.
21 (September, 1, 1945): 4 and
probably other issues; Hot discography in Theme, Vol. 1 (October
1953): 13; in Jazz Information,
various issues and paginations;
McCARTHY, Albert: Collectors
notes [column] in Jazz Music,
Nos. 6, 8, and 9 (1943); (September 1943); (October 1943), various paginations ((2, 3))

J89 DELAUNAY, Charles, and Kurt MOHR:
Hot discographie encyclopédique.
Paris: Editions Jazz Disques,
1951-1953, 3 v. (A to HEFTI) ((1,
2, 3, 7))

J90 DELAUNAY, Charles: Walter E.
SCHAAP; and George AVAKIAN, eds.:
New hot discography; the standard
directory of recorded jazz. New
York: Criterion, 1948, xviii, 608
pp.; additions and corrections in
FUJII, Hajime: New discography
(additions to Charles Delaunay's
New hot discography, 1948) in Hot
Jazz Club of Japan Bulletin, Vol.
7 (August 1954) to Vol. 8 (December 1955), and probably other
issues, various paginations;
PENSONEAULT, Ken, and Carl
SARLES: Additions and corrections
to New hot discography, by
Charles Delaunay in their Jazz
discography; additions and corrections. Jackson Heights, NY:
The Needle, 1944, 9-99 ((1, 2, 3,
4p, 7))

J91 Discographie in Jazz Hot, No. 322
(December 1975): 14, 18, 20, 22,
24, 26, 28, 30, 32, 34, 36, 38,
40, 42 ((—))

J92 Discography of the year in Metronome Yearbook, 1950 to 1954, various paginations [note: issues
after 1954 also have article with
same title, but these are based
on record reviews] ((2))

J93 DUTTON, Frank, and Eric TOWNLEY:
Jazz discography 1958 in TRAILL,
Sinclair, and Gerald LASCELLES,
eds.: Just jazz 3. London: Lands-

borough [c1959], 111-347 ((2, 3,
6, 7))

J94 FEATHER, Leonard: Discography of
the year in MILLER, Paul Eduard,
ed.: Esquire's 1945 jazz book.
New York: Barnes, 1945, 51-54
[large-format edition]; also New
York: Barnes, 1945 [small-format
edition], reprinted New York:
DaCapo, 1979, and New York: Editions for the Armed Services,
pagination unknown ((2, 7d))

J95 FEATHER, Leonard: Discography of
the year in MILLER, Paul Eduard,
ed.: Esquire's 1946 jazz book.
New York: Smith & Durrell, 1946,
88-90 [large-format edition];
also New York: Barnes, 1946
[small-format edition], reprinted
New York: DaCapo, 1979, 190-201
((2))

J96 Jazz: ASCAP music on records. New
York: American Society of Composers, Authors, and Publishers,
n.d., 100 pp. ((8))

J97 Jazz catalogue. Vol. 1-11: 1960-
1971. London (Vols. 1 to 8) or
Sevenoaks, Kent: Jazz Journal,
1961-1972. 11 v. in 10 (Vols. 9
and 10 bound together), annual;
additions and corrections in
BIELDERMANN, Gerard; Don TARRANT;
and Richard HALTREE: Additions
and corrections to the Jazz catalogues in Jazz Journal, Vol. 25
(August 1972): 19 ((2, 3, 6, 7))

J98 Jazz classique. [Tournai, Bel-
gium]: Casterman [1971], 259 pp.
(2, 7))

J99 JEPSEN, Jorgen Grunnet: Jazz records; a discography. Copenhagen
or Holte, Denmark: Knudsen (Vols.
1 to 4, 7 and 8) or Copenhagen:
Nordisk Tidskrift (Vols. 5 and
6), 1963-1970, 11 v. (Vol. 4 divided into 4 sub-volumes; covers
recordings from 1942; upper cut-
off date varies from 1962 to
1969); additions and corrections
in Diskofilspalten column in Orkester Journalen, various issues
and paginations; FONTEYNE, Andre,
and Yvon FOURNIER: J.-G. Jepsen,
"Jazz records 1942-1969": corrections et addenda in Point du
Jazz, various issues and paginations to No. 14 (June 1978);
FOURNIER, Yvon: Rectifications à
la disco Jepsen in Point du Jazz,
No. 15 (July 1979): 146-148 (to
be continued?); FOURNIER, Yvon,

and Andre FONTEYNE: Jazzologie in Point du Jazz, various issues and paginations; in various short items in Journal of Jazz Discography, all issues, various paginations; MORGAN, Alun: Collectors forum in Discographical Forum, No. 19 (July 1970): 7-8, and GARDNER, Mark: [additions and corrections to Vol. 8] in Discographical Forum, No. 21 (November 1970): 19 ((1, 2, 3, 6, 7))

J100 JEWSON, Ron; Derek HAMILTON-SMITH; and Ray WEBB: Horst H. Lange's The fabulous fives revised. [Chigwell, Essex: Storyville, c1978], 150 pp. [rev. ed. of next entry] ((2, 3, 4p, 4r, 6, 7, 8))

J101 LANGE, Horst H.: The fabulous fives; the "six big fives" of early white New York-jazz; a full discography of the Original Dixieland Jazz Band, Earl Fuller's Famous Jazz Band, Louisiana Five, New Orleans Jazz Band, Original Memphis Five, Original Indiana Five [Lübeck, W. Germany: Uhle & Kleimann, c1959], 30 pp. ((2, 3, 6, 7))

J102 [[LANGE, Horst H.: Die GJC-Disco. Berlin: 1951-1953, 3 v.]]

J103 McCARTHY, Albert J.: Discography of the year's recordings in his PL yearbook of jazz 1946. [London]: Editions Poetry London [1946], 182-188 ((2, 3, 7d))

J104 McCARTHY, Albert J.: Jazz discography I; an international discography of recorded jazz including blues, gospel and rhythm and blues, for the year January-December 1958. London: Cassell [1960] [no further volumes published] ((2, 3, 6, 7))

J105 MILLER, William H.: A discography of the "little" recording companies. Toorak, Vic., Australia: 1943, 20 pp. ((2, 4p))

J106 MILLER, William H.: The little discography. Melbourne: 1945, 61 pp. [rev. ed. of previous entry]; additions and corrections in Reprints and Reflections, No. 12 (February 1946): 6 ((2, 4p))

J107 MOHR, Kurt: Concert recordings & discographical classification in Discophile, No. 16 (February 1951): 7, 12; additions and corrections in Discophile, No. 18 (June 1951): 14; No. 19 (August 1951): 10 ((2, 3, 7))

J108 Musicians' bio-discographies in MILLER, Paul Eduard, ed.: Esquire's jazz book. Chicago: Books Inc., 1944, 59-74, 83-86 (also New York: Barnes, 1944, reprinted New York: DaCapo, 1979; and New York: Editions for the Armed Services, 1944, paginations unknown) ((—))

J109 Musicians' bio-discographies in MILLER, Paul Eduard, ed.: Esquire's 1945 jazz book. New York: Barnes, 1945, 59-74, 83-89 [large-format edition] (also New York: Barnes, 1945 [small-format edition], reprinted New York: DaCapo, 1977; and New York: Editions for the Armed Services, 1945, paginations unknown) ((—))

J110 PENSONEAULT, Ken, and Carl SARLES: Jazz discography; additions and corrections. Jackson Heights, NY: The Needle, 1944, 145 pp. ((2, 4p))

J111 [[RABEN, Erik: discografia in Musica Jazz, Vol. 21 (October 1965): 44-46]]

J112 Répertoire des disques de jazz édités en France in Annuaire du Jazz 1951, supplement to Jazz Hot, No. 52 (February 1951): 125-219 ((—))

J113 RUSSELL, Ross: Discography in his Jazz style in Kansas City and the southwest. Berkeley: Univ. of California Pr., 1971, 263-269 ((—))

J114 RUST, Brian A. L.: Jazz records A-Z, 1897-1931. [Hatch End, Middlesex: 1961], 884 sheets, looseleaf ((2, 3, 6, 7))

J115 RUST, Brian A. L.; Jazz records A-Z, 1897-1931. [2d ed. Hatch End, Middlesex: c1962]; with separate index by Richard GRANDORGE. [Hatch End, Middlesex: 1963], 736 + 62 pp., additions and corrections in: FLEISCHMAN, Hank: Canadian alternate take syndrome in IAJRC Journal, Vol.7, No. 1 (n.d.): 13-15; MILLER, Gene: Canada discophile in IAJRC Journal, Vol. 3 (October 1970); Vol. 4 (April 1971); (October 1971); Vol. 6 (January 1973); (summer 1973), various pagina-

tions; RAICHELSON, Dick: in IAJRC
Journal, Vol. 2 (January 1969):
11; KENDZIORA, Carl: Behind the
cobwebs in Record Research, No.
70 (August 1965); WHYATT, Bert:
Notes on Brian Rust's Jazz records 1897-1931 in 78 Quarterly,
Vol. 1, No. 2 (n.d.): 49-53 ((2,
3, 4p, 6, 7))

J116 RUST, Brian A. L.: Jazz records
A-Z, 1932-1942. [Hatch End, Middlesex: 1964], 680 pp. ((2, 3,
4p, 6, 7))

J117 RUST, Brian A. L.: Jazz records
A-Z 1897-1942. rev. ed. London:
Storyville, 1969, 2 v.; additions
and corrections in FONTEYNE,
Andre: Brian Rust "Jazz records
1897-1942"--quelques corrections
et additions (title varies) in
Point du Jazz, No. 6 (March 1972)
to date, various paginations;
FRASE, Bill: Filling in discographically [column] in Record
Research, various issues and paginations; There'll be some
changes made [column] in Storyville, various issues and paginations ((1, 2, 3, 4p, 6, 7))

J118 RUST, Brian A. L.: Jazz records
1897-1942; 4th rev. & enl. ed.
New Rochelle, NY: Arlington House
[1978], 2 v.; additions and corrections in CUMMINGS, Ross: Disco-
graphics in IAJRC Journal, Vol.
12 (October 1979): 10-12 (possibly to be continued) ((1, 2,
3, 4p, 4t, 6, 7))

J119 SCHLEMAN, Hilton R.: Rhythm on
record; a who's who and register
of recorded dance music, 1905-
1936. London: Melody Maker, 1936
(also Westport, CT: Greenwood,
1977?), 333 pp. ((2))

J120 SHAPIRO, Nat, and Nat HENTOFF:
The jazz makers. New York: Rine-
hart, 1957 (also New York: Grove
Press, 1958; London: Peter Davies,
1958; New York: DaCapo [1979,
c1957]), xii, 368 pp.; discographies at ends of chapters ((—))

J121 VENABLES, Ralph G. V.: A discography of the Cotton Pickers,
Tennessee Tooters and allied
groups in Jazz Forum (UK), No.
4 (April 1947): 30-31 ((2, 3, 7p))

J122 WILSON, John Steuart: Jazz from
abroad; a discography of jazz...
birth in High Fidelity, Vol. 8
(August 1958): 65-72 ((—))

J123 WOODWARD, Woody: Discography in
his Jazz Americana. [Los Angeles:
Trend Books, c1956], 104-127 ((—))

Additions and Corrections
See also JAZZ MUSIC (Pensoneault,
Ken)

J124 Afterthoughts [column] in Storyville, various issues and paginations, No. 2 (Dec. 1966-to date)

J125 BACKENSTO, Woody: Small change in
Record Research, various issues
and paginations, to May 1971.

J126 BADROCK, Arthur, and Derek
SPRUCE: Junkshoppers' column in
Matrix, various issues and pag-
inations.

J127 Collectors corner [column] in
Jazz (New York), various issues
and paginations.

J128 Collectors corner [column] in
Melody Maker, ca. 1942 to early
50s?, various issues and paginations.

J129 DAVIES, John, and G. F. GRAY-
CLARKE: Behind the label in Jazz
Magazine (UK), Vol. 3, No. 2
(n.d.), various issues and paginations.

J130 Discographical additions in Jazz
Monthly (September 1963): 26.

J131 Discomania [column] in Jazz Hot,
No. 249 (April 1969) to No. 267
(December 1970), most issues,
various paginations.

J132 Discophilie in Jazz Hot, No. 3
(December 1945).

J133 Diskofilspalten [column] in Orkester Journalen, various issues
and paginations.

J134 EYLE, Wim van: Plaatvraagbaak in
Jazz Press, 1977, most issues,
various paginations.

J135 Filling in discographically [col-
umn] in Record Research, Vol. 1
(February 1955) to date, various
paginations.

J136 GODRICH, John or Bob DIXON: I
believe I'll make a change in
Storyville, various issues and
paginations.

J137 GORDON, Jim: Notes on Crosby ex
Bobcats in IAJRC Journal, Vol. 9
(fall 1976): 30.

J138 Jazz information [column] in Jazz Journal, various issues and paginations.

J139 The jazz mine [column] in Jazz Notes (Australia), various issues and paginations (1940s).

J140 Jazz records in Jazz Monthly, Vol. 8 (June 1962) to (September 1962); [as tear-out supplement] Vol. 10 (June 1964) to (October 1964), various issues and paginations.

J141 Jazz research in Jazz Monthly, various issues and paginations; also in Jazz & Blues (successor to Jazz Monthly), various issues and paginations.

J142 Jazzologie [column] in Point du Jazz, No. 1 (September 1969) to date, various issues and paginations.

J143 Jazzwereldresearch [column] in Jazz Wereld, various issues and paginations.

J144 Journal of Jazz Discography (1977-1979), various paginations.

J145 KENDZIORA, Carl: Behind the cobwebs in Record Changer, Vol. 8 (April 1949) to Vol. 9 (December 1950), various paginations.

J146 KENNEDY, John, and William HAESLER or George HULME: In the wax [column] in Matrix, No. 1 (July 1954) and various issues and paginations.

J147 KINKLE, Roger D.: List of misc. recordings denoting solos and vocalists of special interest, most of which are not shown in the various discographies now available in his Check sheet (Project #1): 9-18; Check Sheet (Project #2): 8-16. [Evansville, IN?: n.d.]

J148 LAING, Ralph: The specialist labels; a listing in Jazz Journal, Vol. 29 (January 1976) to (July 1976), various paginations.

J149 LANGE, Horst H.: Disco courier [column] in Jazz Echo, various issues and paginations.

J150 Liste des éditions phonographiques aux États-Unis (or Les nouveautés phonographiques aux États-Unis) in Les Cahiers du Jazz, No. 1 (1959) to No. 14 (1965), back of each issue.

J151 LOWEY, Hal: Disc data digest in Recordiana, Vol. 1 (1944), various paginations.

J152 McCARTHY, Albert: Discographical forum [column] in Jazz Monthly, Vol. 5 (March 1959 to date), various issues and paginations.

J153 Microsolco USA [column] in Jazz di Ieri e di Oggi, various issues and paginations.

J154 MOHR, Kurt, and Otto FLUCKIGER: Discographical supplement in Jazz Bulletin, No. 1 (January 1953) to Vol. 4 (January 1955), various issues and paginations.

J155 MORGAN, Alun: Collectors notes [column] in Jazz Monthly, (November 1964) to (1971), most issues, various paginations; continued in Jazz & Blues, Vol. 3 (January 1973) and various issues and paginations.

J156 MORGAN, Alun: Modern forum [column] in Discographical Forum, No. 1 (May 1960) to No. 14, various issues and paginations.

J157 PENSONEAULT, Ken, and Carl SARLES: Collectors corner [column] in Jazz Session, various issues and paginations.

J158 PORTER, Bob: Modern eyes-zing in Record Research, various issues and paginations.

J159 Recently issued [column] in Discographical Forum, No. 4 (January 1961 - to date), various issues and paginations.

J160 Record Research. Supplements, No. 1 (June 30, 1955) to No. 18 (August 7, 1965), various paginations.

J161 Recorded Americana; bulletin of Record Research (later titled Record Research Bulletin), No. 1 (January 1958) to No. 12 (1960), various paginations.

J162 Research miscellany [column] in Discographical Forum, No. 1 (May 1960 - to date), various paginations.

J163 Some of the latest [column] in Jazz Statistics, No. 1 (April 1956) to No. 4 (November 1956), various paginations.

J164 STEINER, John: Beyond the impression [column] in Record Research, Vol. 3 (June-July 1957); (August-September 1957); No. 22 (April-May 1959); No. 24 (September-October 1959) to No. 49 (March 1963); No. 56 (November 1963); No. 62 (August 1964); No. 67 (April 1965) to No. 70 (August 1965); No. 99 (July 1969), various paginations.

J165 WALKER, Malcolm: Forum Notes in Discographical Forum, No. 11-to date, various issues and paginations.

J166 WYLER, Mike, and Albert McCARTHY: Collectors notes in Jazz Monthly, Vol. 1 (March 1955) to Vol. 2 (May 1956), various paginations.

Australia

J167 DRUST, Eduardo: Conjuntos australianos; discografia in Hot Jazz Club, No. 18 (June 1948): 13, 27; No. 26 (September 1950): 4-6, 8, 18, 23-28 ((1, 2, 3, 7))

J168 HARRIS, H. Meunier: A discography of Australian jazz in Jazzfinder, Vol. 1 (October 1948): 3-8 ((2, 3, 7))

J169 MITCHELL, Jack: Australian discography. Melbourne: Australian Jazz Quarterly, 1950, 16 pp.; additions and corrections in KENNEDY, John: Jazz ... Australia in Matrix, No. 1 (July 1954) to No. 75 (February 1968), various paginations ((2, 3, 6, 7))

Austria

J170 KRANER, Dietrich Heinz, and Klaus SCHULZ: Discography in their Jazz in Austria; historische Entwicklung und Diskographie des Jazz in Osterreich. Graz, Austria: Universal Edition, 1972, 33-95 ((2, 3, 4p, 6, 7))

Avant-Garde
See also JAZZ MUSIC--GREAT BRITAIN (Carr, Ian)

J171 Brief discography of new music in JONES, Leroi: Black music. New York: Morrow [c1967], 213-214 ((—))

J172 BURKE, Patrick: Modern forum: the new music in Discographical Forum, No. 10 (January 1969):

7-9; No. 12 (May 1969): 9-10 ((2, 7))

J173 Discography of free jazz 1958-1973 in Off Jazz, Vol. 7 (1974?): 5-16 ((2, 7))

J174 GERVAIS, Raymond, and Michel DITORRE: Musique; y-a-t-il place pour de la musique au Quebec? in Mediart, Vol. 18 (October 1973): 9-11 ((—))

J175 RABEN, Erik: Free jazz. Copenhagen: Knudsen [c1969], 38 pp. [Albert Ayler, Don Cherry, Ornette Coleman, Pharoah Sanders, Archie Shepp, Cecil Taylor] ((1, 2, 3, 7))

Bebop
See also JAZZ MUSIC--FRANCE (Burns, Jim); JAZZ MUSIC--GREAT BRITAIN (Burns, Jim); VIBRAPHONE MUSIC (JAZZ) (Dean, Roger)

J176 RUSSELL, Ross: Bop horn; a discography in Record Changer, Vol. 8 (February 1949): 10 ((—))

J177 RUSSELL, Ross: Bop rhythm; discography in Record Changer, Vol. 7 (July 1948): 28 ((—))

Belgium

J178 DEVOGHELAERE, Mon: Discografie Belgische jazz-geschiedenis in EYLE, Wim van, ed.: Jazz & geimproviseerde muziek in Nederland. Utrecht: Spectrum, 1978, 61 ((—))

J179 PERNET, Robert: Belgian compositions in his Jazz in little Belgium. Brussels: Sigma, 1967, 2d section, xii-xiv ((8))

J180 PERNET, Robert: Discography 1895-1966 in his Jazz in little Belgium. Brussels: Sigma, 1967, 2d section; xxx, 338, xi pp. ((2, 3, 4p, 6, 7))

Canada

J181 Jazz Canada in Matrix, No. 17 (April 1958): 6; No. 18 (July 1958): 6-8 [Mike White, Milt Sealey] ((1, 2, 7))

Chicago Style

J182 BAKKER, Dick M.: Chicago style in Micrography, No. 6 (October 1969): 10-11 ((7d))

Czechoslovakia

J183 EDWARDS, Marv: Recorded jazz in
Czechoslovakia in Hip, Vol. 7
(January 1970) to (March 1970),
various paginations ((—))

J184 Jazz na standardnich, a dluhohra-
jicich deskach, vydanych v letech
1945-1967 in DORUZKA, Lubomir,
and Ivan POLEDNAK: Ceskosloven-
sky jazz; minulost a pritomnost.
Prague: Supraphon, 1967, 259-293
((2, 3, 7d))

Denmark
See also JAZZ MUSIC--SCANDINAVIA

J185 DENMARK. NATIONALE DISKOTEKET.
Dansk jazz. [Copenhagen]: Nation-
almuseet, 1961, 4 v. ((1, 3, 4t,
8))

J186 MØLLER, Borje J. C.: Dansk jazz-
discography. [Copenhagen]: Artum,
1945, 94 pp. ((3, 7d, 8))

England
See JAZZ MUSIC--GREAT BRITAIN

Europe
See also BELL, GRAEME (Harris, H.
Meunier) and (Venables, Ralph G.
V.); NOBLE, RAY (Ray Noble Euro-
pean discography); REDMAN, DON
(The Redman band in Europe);
WEBSTER, BEN (Kauling, Bent)

J187 FLAKSER, Harold: Continental
disc-ology in Record Research,
Vol. 1 (February 1955) to No. 29
(August 1960); No. 34 (April
1961), various paginations ((2,
3, 6, 7))

Europe, Eastern

J188 CONRAD, Gerhard: Americans on
East European records in Jazz
Bazaar, No. 1 (April 1969) to No.
6 (June 1970), most issues, various paginations ((2, 3, 7))

J189 CONRAD, Gerhard: Die Disco-Ecke
in Jazzfreund, No. 1 (27) (September 1962) to date [serialized
alphabetically; by December 1979
it reached Ignatev] ((2, 3, 7))

Finland

J190 Discography; jazz records made in
Finland in GRANHOLM, Ake, ed.:
Finnish jazz; history, musicians,
discography. [Helsinki]: Finnish
Music Information Centre, 1974,
36-39 ((—))

J191 [[Finnish jazz discography in
Rytmi, May 1964-1965]]

J192 GRONOW, Pekka: Jazz on Finnish
labels in Record Research, No. 72
(November 1965): 3; No. 74 (March
1966): 4-5 ((—))

J193 WESTERBERG, Hans: Suomalaiset
jazzlevytykset 1932-1976; 45
Americans, 92 Europeans and hun-
dreds of Finns; a Finnish jazz
discography 1932-1976. [Hel-
sinki]: Suomen Jazzliitto, 1977,
104 pp. ((1, 2, 3, 4p, 4t, 7))

France
See also ARMSTRONG, LOUIS
(Simons, Sim); JAZZ MUSIC (Réper-
toire des disques de jazz édités
en France); SMITH, WILLIE "THE
LION" (Wiedemann, Erik); THOMP-
SON, LUCKY (Mohr, Kurt); WIGGINS,
GERALD (Wiedemann, Erik)

J194 BURNS, Jim: Boppin' in Paris in
Jazz Journal, Vol. 26 (January
1973): 17 ((—))

J195 DEPUTIER, Ivan: [Discography,
1904-1932] in Jazz Hot, No. 246
(January 1969): 37 ((—))

Germany
See also JAZZ MUSIC (Bielefelder
Katalog); STEWART, REX (Conrad,
Gerhard)

J196 CONRAD, Gerhard: Let's play happy
music; traditioneller Jazz in der
Bundesrespublik in Jazzfreund,
Vol. 16 (September 1974): 9-10
((—))

J197 LANGE, Horst H.: Die deutsche
Jazz Discographie; eine
geschichte der Jazz auf Schallplatten von 1902 bis 1955.
Berlin: Bote und G. Bock [1955],
651 pp.; additions and corrections in his Corrections of the
more important mistakes and
printing errors in Discophile,
No. 44 (October 1955): 9-11 ((2,
3, 4p, 7))

J198 LANGE, Horst H.: Die deutsche
"78-er" Discographie der Jazz-und
Hot-Dance-Musik 1903-1958. Berlin: Colloquium [c1966], 775, 4
pp. ((2, 3, 6, 7))

J199 [[LANGE, Horst H.: Die Deutsche
"78-er" Discographie der Jazz-
und Hot-Dance-Musik 1903-1958.
Berlin: Colloquium, 1978? [rev.
ed. of previous entry] ((2, 3, 6,
7))]]

J200 LANGE, Horst H.: Discographie in his Jazz in Deutschland; die deutsche Jazz-Chronik 1900-1960. Berlin: Colloquium [c1966], 183-202 ((—))

J201 LANGE, Horst H.: Die Geschichte des Jazz in Deutschland; die Entwicklung von 1910 bis 1960 mit Discographie. Lübeck, W. Germany: Uhle & Kleimann [c1960], 172 pp.; additions and corrections in SAGAWE, Harm, and Arthur BADROCK: Additions and corrections to Lange: Deutscher 78-er Discographie in R.S.V.P., No. 20 (January 1967); No. 21 (February 1967); No. 24 (May 1967); No. 37 (June 1968); No. 38 (July 1968), various paginations ((2, 3, 6, 7))

Germany, Eastern

J202 CONRAD, Gerhard: Iron curtain jazz; a survey of some recent German issues in Matrix, No. 35/36 (September 1961): 27-28; additions in Matrix, No. 37 (November 1961): 19 ((2, 3, 7))

J203 Diskographie in Jazz Podium, Vol. 28 (July 1979): 8 ((—))

Great Britain
See also AIRSHOTS (Flucker, Jack); JAZZ MUSIC (Cherrington, George) and (Coller, Derek) and (Dutton, Frank) and (Jazz catalogue)

J204 BOULTON, David: A selected discography in his Jazz in Britain. London: W.H. Allen, 1958 (also London: Jazz Book Club, 1959), 176-192 ((2, 4p, 7d))

J205 BURNS, Jim: My baby likes to be-bop; notes toward a history of British bop in Jazz & Blues, Vol. 1 (December 1971): 8 ((—))

J206 CARR, Ian: Discography in his Music outside; contemporary jazz in Britain. London: Latimer New Dimensions [1973], 149-173 ((2))

J207 [[GREEN, Benny: Jazz decade; ten years at Ronnie Scott's. London: Kings Road, 1969, 36 pp.]]

J208 WALKER, Edward S.: Discography--early English jazz in Jazz Journal, Vol. 21 (July 1968): 19, 22 ((2, 3, 6, 7))

Greece

J209 [[Greek jazz discography in Tzaz, Vol. 1 (No. 1, 1978)]]

Influenced by Classical Music
See CLASSICAL MUSIC--INFLUENCE ON JAZZ; SERIAL MUSIC AND JAZZ

Italy

J210 BARAZZETTA, Giuseppe; Enzo FRESIA; and Oscar MOIRAGHI: Discografia italiana in TESTONI, Gian Carlo: Enciclopedia del jazz. Milan: Messagerie Musicali, 1953, 333-487 ((2, 3, 7))

J211 BARAZZETTA, Giuseppe: Italian sessions in 1953 in Discophile, No. 34 (February 1954): 6-8; additions and corrections in Discophile, No. 35 (April 1954): 14 ((2, 3, 7))

J212 BARAZZETTA, Giuseppe: Jazz inciso in Italia. Milan: Messagerie Musicali [1960], 189 pp.; additions and corrections in his Spigolatura discografiche; addenda a "Jazz inciso in Italia" in Musica Jazz, Vol. 21 (May 1965): 33-34 ((2, 3, 4p, 6, 7))

J213 BARAZZETTA, Giuseppe; Enzo FRESIA; and Oscar MOIRAGHI: Jazz italiano in TESTONI, Gian Carlo: Enciclopedia del jazz. Milan: Messagerie Musicali, 1953, 487-495 ((2, 3, 7))

J214 Discografia in LEVI, Ezio: Introduzione alla vera musica di jazz. Milan: Magazzino Musicale, 1938, 49-106 ((2, 8))

J215 Incisioni d'orchestre hot italiane in LEVI, Ezio: Introduzione alla vera musica di jazz. Milan: Magazzino Musicale, 1938, 107-110 ((2, 8))

Japan
See also JAZZ AT THE ASAHIKODO

J216 CLOSE, Albert B.: Japanese jazz discography (1948-1953) in Record Research, No. 76 (May 1966): 8, 10; additions and corrections in Record Research, No. 98 (May 1969): 6 ((—))

J217 Discography of Japanese jazzmen Vol. 1 & Vol. 2 in Swing Journal,

Vol. 26 (May 1972): 226-233 ((2, 7d))

J218 GARDNER, Mark: Japanese forum in Discographical Forum, No. 19 (July 1970); No. 20 (September 1970); No. 24 (May 1971), various paginations ((2, 7))

J219 Ni hon no jazz discography in Swing Journal, Vol. 30 (January 1976): 305 ((2, 3, 7d))

Modern Style
See also CLARINET MUSIC (JAZZ); JAZZ MUSIC (Bruyninckx, Walter) and (Jepsen, Jorgen Grunnet); PIANO MUSIC (JAZZ) (Edwards, Ernie)

J220 Discografia in DONATI, William: Jazz americano del dopoguerra. [Milan]: Schwarz [c1958], 169-235 ((—))

J221 GARDNER, Mark: Discographical data [column] in Jazz Journal, Vol. 20 (March 1967) to (September 1967), various paginations ((2, 7))

J222 Jazz moderne. [Tournai, Belgium]: Casterman [1971], 255 pp. ((—))

Netherlands

J223 EYLE, Wim van: Een lijst Lp's die een indruk geedt van de Nederlandse jazz in his Jazz & geimproviseerde muziek in Nederland. Utrecht: Spectrum, 1978, 162 ((—))

J224 MAK, Jim: Dutch dixieland, a listing in Discophile, No. 54 (June 1957): 18-19, 13 ((2, 3, 6, 7))

New Orleans
See also NICHOLAS, WOODEN JOE (Bakker, Dick M.)

J225 BAKKER, Dick M. Dixieland--New Orleans 1917-1928 in Micrography, No. 45 (September 1977): 9-17 ((6, 7))

New Orleans Style
See also BRASS BANDS; COLUMBIA label (Davis, John: New Orleans jazz); TRUMPET MUSIC (JAZZ) (Tonks, Eric S.)

J226 CHARTERS, Samuel B.: Discographical appendix; the New Orleans recordings in his Jazz: New Orleans; an index to the Negro

musicians of New Orleans. New York: Oak [1963], 132-147 ((2, 3, 6, 7))

J227 CHARTERS, Samuel B.: Discographical listing of the recordings of the New Orleans revival in his Jazz: New Orleans 1885-1957; an index to the Negro musicians of New Orleans. Belleville, NJ: Walter C. Allen, 1958, 144-152 (Jazz monographs, No. 2) ((2, 3, 4p, 4t, 6, 7))

J228 STAGG, Tom, and Charlie CRUMP: New Orleans, the revival; a tape and discography of Negro traditional jazz recorded in New Orleans or by New Orleans bands 1937-1972. Dublin: Bashall Eaves, 1973, vi, 332 pp.; additions and corrections in Footnote, various issues and paginations ((1, 2, 3, 4p, 6, 7))

New York City
See also JAZZ MUSIC (Jewson, Ron) and (Lange, Horst H.) and (Venables, Ralph G. V.); VILLAGE VANGUARD (Night club in New York)

J229 SHAW, Arnold: 52nd Street music in his The street that never slept; New York's fabled 52nd St. New York: Coward McCann & Geoghegan [c1971] (also retitled 52nd Street; the Street of jazz. New York: Da Capo [1977, c1971]), 362-363 ((—))

Newport, Rhode Island
See NEWPORT JAZZ FESTIVAL

Norway
See also JAZZ MUSIC--SCANDINAVIA

J230 BERGH, Johs: Diskografi over norske jazzplater in ANGELL, Olav; Jan Erik VOLD; and Einar ØKLAND, eds.: Jazz i Norge. [Oslo]: Gyldendal [1976], 214-240; additions and corrections in his Additions to the discography published in the book Jazz i Norge in Jazz Nytt, Vol. 2 (No. 1, 1977): 15-18; Vol. 2 (May 1977): 15-18 ((2, 3, 6, 7))

J231 [[BERGH, Johs, and Knut AARFLOT: Norsk jazzdiskografi in Jazzbladet (February 1960)]]

J232 FORNO, Birger: Norwegian jazz discography in Jazz Monthly, Vol. 1 (November 1955): 26, 31; (December 1955): 26; additions and corrections in Jazz Monthly, Vol. 1 (February 1956): 26; (January 1957): 30-31 ((2, 3, 7))

Poland

J233 CABANOWSKI, Marek; Henryk CHOLIN-SKI; and Andrzej KARPINSKI: Dys-kografia in RADLINSKI, Jerzy: Obywatel jazz. [Warsaw]: Polskie Wydawnictwo Muzyczne [1967], 233-252 ((2, 4p 7))

J234 CABANOWSKI, Marek: Polska dysko-grafia jazzowa in Jazz (Poland) No. 81 (May 1963): 10 (part 7; probably in other issues) ((2, 3, 7))

J235 CABANOWSKI, Marek, and Henryk CHOLINSKI: Polska dyskografia jazzowa 1955-1972. Warsaw: n.p., 1974, 187 pp. ((2, 4p, 4t, 7))

St. Louis

J236 Une page d'histoire: Saint-Louis in Jazz Hot, No. 95 (January 1955): 15 ((2, 3, 6, 7d))

Scandinavia

J237 WALKER, Malcolm: Jazz from Scan-dinavia in Discographical Forum, No. 33 (1974): 6, 19 ((2, 7))

Sweden
See also ACCORDION MUSIC (JAZZ); ELDRIDGE, ROY (Rehnberg, Bert); JAZZ MUSIC--SCANDINAVIA; RAGTIME MUSIC (Englund, Bjorn); TIGER RAG (tune title) (Englund, Bjorn)

J238 [[[Discography of Swedish jazz] in Doctor Jazz, No. 54]]; addi-tions and corrections in Doctor Jazz, No. 62 (October-November 1973): 28 (to be continued)

J239 ENGLUND, Bjorn: Early Swedish jazz on records and cylinder in Jazz & Blues, Vol. 1 (September-October 1971): 15 ((2, 3, 6, 7))

J240 ENGLUND, Bjorn: Svenska skivbolag in Orkester Journalen, Vol. 35 (March 1967) to Vol. 39 (November 1971), various paginations ((2, 3, 6, 7))

J241 NICOLAUSSON, Harry: Svensk jazz-diskografi. Stockholm: Nordiska Musikforlaget [c1953], 115 pp. ((2, 3, 4p, 7d))

J242 A selective discography; a selec-tion of Swedish jazz records from 1976 to 1979 in Music in Sweden, No. 2 (May 1979): 8 ((—))

J243 Svenska jazzskivor 1971 in Orkes-ter Journalen, Vol. 38 (December 1971): 4-5; continued by Svensk jazz pa skiva in Orkester Jour-nalen, Vol. 40 (December 1972), thereafter in each year's Decem-ber issue to date, various pagin-ations ((—))

J244 WESTERBERG, Hans: Svenska musiker i finska jazzinspelningar in Or-kester Journalen, Vol. 46 (Janu-ary 1978): 21, 30 ((2, 7))

Switzerland
See also MONTREUX JAZZ FESTIVAL

J245 Helvetica discographica acta [column] in Jazz + Classic, No. 1 (February-March 1979- to date) and in Swiss Music Dial, No. 13 (April 1978) and possibly other issues, various paginations ((2, 7))

J246 HIPPENMEYER, Jean Roland: Discog-raphie 1930-1970 in his Le jazz en Suisse, 1930-1970. Yverdon, Switzerland: de la Thiele [1971], 133-223 ((1, 2, 4p, 7))

J247 HIPPENMEYER, Jean Roland: Swiss jazz disco. Yverdon, Switerland: de la Thiele [c1977], 216 pp. ((1, 2, 3, 4p, 6, 7))

J248 [[Jazz in Willisau: Discographie in Jazz 360, No. 12 (November 1978): 10-11]]

J249 MOHR, Kurt: Discographie du jazz. Geneva: R. Vuagnat, 1945, 84 pp. ((2, 4p, 7))

J250 SCHWANNINGER, A., and A. GUR-WITSCH: Swing discographie. Geneva: Ch. Grasset [1945], 200 pp. ((2, 7))

West Coast (U.S.)

J251 RAICHELSON, Dick: West coast labels in IAJRC Journal, Vol. 11 (spring 1978) to Vol. 12 (July 1979), various paginations, in 5 parts ((3, 6))

JAZZ-O-HARMONISTS (musical group)

J252 The Jazz-O-Harmonists--discogra-phy in Record Research, Vol. 1 (June 1955): 7 ((3))

JAZZ RECORD SOCIETY label

J253 DUTTON, Frank, and John GODRICH: Jazz Record Society; a label listing in Matrix, No. 40 (April 1962): 7-9; additions and corrections in Matrix, No. 49 (October 1963): 16 ((3, 6, 7))

JAZZ-ROCK MUSIC

J254 PICKERING, Dan: Selected discography in CORYELL, Julie, and Laura FRIEDMAN: Jazz rock fusion. New York: Delta, c1978, 265-297 ((—))

JAZZ SCENE (British broadcast series)
See AIRSHOTS (Flucker, Jack)

JAZZ SOCIETY label (French)

J255 DUTTON, Frank, and John GODRICH: Jazz Society; a label discography in Matrix, No. 39 (February 1962): 3-19; additions and corrections in Matrix, No. 47 (June 1963): 12; No. 49 (October 1963): 14-15; No. 68 (December 1966): 14 ((3, 6, 7))

J256 STEPHENSON, Allan: Jazz Society; a numerical catalogue of the long playing issues in Discophile, No. 53 (April 1957): 2-4; additions and corrections in Discophile, No. 60 (June 1958): 16-17 ((2))

JAZZ STAR label (Swedish)

J257 Discography of Jazz Star records in Jazzfinder, Vol. 1 (October 1948): 15 ((2, 3))

JAZZ STUDIO series
See DECCA label (Fresia, Enzo)

JAZZ WEST COAST label

J258 JEPSEN, Jorgen Grunnet: Disko-filspalten in Orkester Journalen, Vol. 27 (April 1959): 25; (May 1959): 21, 30 ((2, 3, 7d))

JAZZART label

J259 HAESLER, William, and John KENNEDY: The Jazzart catalogue in Matrix, No. 3 (November 1954): 9-12, 19 ((2, 3, 7d))

JAZZIN' BABY BLUES (tune title)
See TIN ROOF BLUES

JAZZOLOGY label

J260 The Jazzology, Progressive & G.H.B. labels; a numerical listing in Matrix, No. 65 (June 1966): 3-18; additions and corrections in Matrix, No. 75 (February 1968): 12-13 ((2, 3, 6, 7))

JEFFERSON, BLIND LEMON, 1897-1929?
guitar, vocal

J261 BAKKER, Dick M.: Blind Lemon Jefferson in Micrography, No. 5 (August 1969): 10 ((7d))

J262 BAKKER, Dick M.: Blind Lemon Jefferson in Micrography, No. 22 (October 1972): 8 ((7d))

J263 BAKKER, Dick M.: Discographie in Blues Notes, Vol. 7 (1970?): 12 ((7d))

J264 RUST, Brian; Andre GILLET; and Serge TONNEAU: Discography of Blind Lemon Jefferson in Rhythm & Blues Panorama, No. 22 (No. 1, 1963): 10-14 ((2, 3, 6, 7))

J265 STEWART-BAXTER, Derrick: Blind Lemon Jefferson in Jazz Journal, Vol. 7 (February 1954): 21, 23 ((2, 3, 6))

J266 STEWART-BAXTER, Derrick: Blind Lemon Jefferson; a new discography in Jazz Journal, Vol. 7 (May 1954): 15, 14 ((2, 3, 6, 7d))

JENKINS, GUS, 1931-
piano, vocal

J267 LEADBITTER, Mike: Frank Patt/Gus Jenkins--discographical details in Blues Unlimited, No. 40 (January 1967): 18 ((2, 3, 7))

JENKINS, LEROY, 1932-
violin

J268 Selected discography, on jacket of [phonodisc] India Navigation IN1028. New York: India Navigation [c1977] ((—))

J269 Selected Jenkins discography in Down Beat, Vol. 45 (November 16, 1978): 24 ((—))

JEWEL label

J270 DEMETRE, Jacques: Jewel records in Soul Bag, No. 21 (November-December 1972): 15-19, 29 ((3, 5))

J271 EAGLE, Bob, and Ken KEATING: Jewel listing in Alley Music, Vol. 1 (first quarter 1968): 11 [continued in later issues] ((—))

JOB label

J272 LOBSTEIN, Patrick: Job listing in Soul Bag, No. 68 (1978): 7; additions in Soul Bag, No. 69/70 (November-December 1978): 2 ((3))

JOHANSSON, JAN, 1931-
piano, guitar

J273 REHNBERG, Bert: Jan Johansson; a draft discography for 1956-1962 in Matrix, No. 55 (October 1964): 6-9; additions and corrections in Matrix, No. 63 (February 1966): 12 ((2, 7))

JOHN, MABLE
vocal

J274 [[Discography in Soul Bag, No. 9/10]]

JOHN, (LITTLE) WILLIE (John Davenport), d. 1968
vocal

J275 MOHR, Kurt: Discography of Little Willie John in Jazz Statistics, No. 9 (March 1959): 2-3; additions and corrections from Jorgen Grunnet JEPSEN in Jazz Statistics, No. 12 (September 1959): 8; [from Michel VOGLER] No. 17 (1960): 5 ((2, 3, 7))

JOHNNY AND JONES (musical group)

J276 [[OPENNEER, Herman: Two kids and a guitar; Johnny & Jones in Doctor Jazz, No. 84 (June 1978): 24-31]]

JOHNSON, ALPHONSO, 1952-
bass guitar

J277 Alphonso Johnson discography in Down Beat, Vol. 43 (January 29, 1976): 14 ((—))

JOHNSON, BUDD (Albert J. Johnson), 1910-
tenor saxophone
See also SAXOPHONE MUSIC (JAZZ) (Evensmo, Jan: The tenor saxophones of Budd Johnson...)

J278 [Discography] in Jazz Statistics, No. 18 (1960): 2 [1947-1959 recordings] ((2, 3, 7))

JOHNSON, BUDDY (Woodrow Wilson Johnson), 1915-
piano, vocal

J279 MOHR, Kurt: Disques publiés en France in Jazz Hot, No. 120 (April 1957): 15 ((—))

JOHNSON, BUNK (Willie Geary Johnson), 1880-1949
trumpet

J280 BAKKER, Dick M.: Bunk Johnson on A.M. in Micrography, No. 37 (July 1975): 7 ((3, 7d))

J281 Bunk discography in Down Beat, Vol. 16 (August 26, 1949): 6 ((2, 3, 7))

J282 CLARK, Clyde: Bunk Johnson on record in Jazz Notes (Australia), No. 86 (August 1948): 3-8 ((1, 2, 3, 6, 7))

J283 HULME, George: Bunk Johnson; a discography in Jazz Journal, Vol. 9 (January 1956): 8-9; (February 1956): 32-33 ((1, 2, 3, 6, 7))

J284 [[HULME, George: A Bunk Johnson discography. n.p. (England): Bunk Johnson Appreciation Society, 1954, 14 pp.]]

J285 RUSSELL, Tony: Bunk Johnson addenda in Discophile, No. 2 (October 1948): 3-4; additions and corrections from Clyde CLARK in Discophile, No. 3 (December 1948): 5-6 [lists sides recorded by Bunk Johnson without Jim Robinson] ((1, 2, 3, 6, 7))

J286 SONNIER, Austin M.: Discography in his Willie Geary "Bunk" Johnson; the New Iberia years. Boston: Crescendo [c1977], 27-37 ((2, 3, 6, 7))

J287 STEWART-BAXTER, Derrick: A discography of Bunk Johnson in Melody Maker, Vol. 25 (July 30, 1949): 11; (August 6, 1949): 11;

(August 13, 1949): 11 ((1, 2, 3, 7))

JOHNSON, CHARLIE, 1891-1959
piano
See also SMITH, JABBO (Bakker, Dick M.)

J288 DAVIES, John R. T., and Laurie WRIGHT: Charlie Johnson in Storyville, No. 35 (June-July 1971): 184-185 ((2, 3, 6, 7, 8, 9))

J289 [[DELDEN, Ate van: [Listing] in Doctor Jazz (March 1966)]]

JOHNSON, DINK (Oliver Johnson), 1892-1954
piano

J290 Discographie de Dink Johnson in Jazz Hot, No. 49 (November 1950): 30 ((2, 7))

J291 GRUT, Harald: Dink Johnson discography in Jazz Music, Vol. 4 (No. 7, 1951): 7 ((2, 3, 7p))

JOHNSON, EDDIE
tenor saxophone

J292 MOHR, Kurt: Eddie Johnson in Soul Bag, No. 45 (January 1975): 30 ((2, 3, 7))

JOHNSON, FRANK
trumpet

J293 DAVIS, William A.: Discography in Australian Jazz Quarterly, No. 22 (June 1954): 8-10 ((2, 3, 6, 7))

JOHNSON, J. J. (James Louis Johnson), 1924-
trombone
See also WINDING, KAI

J294 FINI, Francesco: The Jay Jay Johnson complete discography with biographical notes. Imola, Italy: 1962, 25 pp. ((1, 2, 3, 6, 7))

J295 JEPSEN, Jorgen Grunnet: Jay & Kai diskografi in Orkester Journalen, Vol. 25 (November 1957): 50 ((2, 3, 7d))

JOHNSON, JAMES P., 1891-1953
piano
See also DePARIS, SIDNEY (Sidney DeParis & James P. Johnson Blue Note sessions)

J296 Disques de James P. Johnson (actuellement en vente en France) in Jazz Hot, No. 39 (December 1949): 14 ((—))

Piano Rolls

J297 MONTGOMERY, Mike: James P. Johnson rollography in Record Research, No. 20 (November-December 1958): 16 ((5))

J298 Piano roll-ography in Record Research, Vol. 1 (April 1955): 19; additions and corrections in Record Research, Vol. 1 (June 1955): 1 ((8))

JOHNSON, LEROY
guitar, vocal

J299 LEADBITTER, Mike: Leroy "Country" Johnson in Blues Unlimited, No. 33 (May-June 1966): 7 ((3, 7))

JOHNSON, LONNIE (Alonzo Johnson), 1889-1970
guitar, vocal

J300 BROWN, Ken, and Brian RUST: Lonnie Johnson discography in Jazz Tempo, No. 19 (n.d.): 56-59 ((2, 3, 7d))

J301 Lonnie Johnson; a name listing for the period from 1943 in Matrix, No. 79 (October 1968): 3-12; additions and corrections in Matrix, No. 87 (February 1970): 13 ((2, 3, 6, 7))

J302 ROBERTS, Don W.: Discography in Pieces of Jazz (1970): 46-47 ((7d))

JOHNSON, PETE, 1904-1967
piano

J303 FAIRCHILD, Rolph: Pete Johnson discography in Jazz Report (California), Vol. 2 (August 1962) to Vol. 3 (January-February 1963), various paginations, in 4 parts; additions and corrections in Music Memories, Vol. 4 (summer 1964): 4-5 ((2, 3, 7))

J304 FAIRCHILD, Rolph, and Hans J. MAUERER: Discography in MAUERER, Hans J., ed.: The Pete Johnson story. New York: 1965, 57-73 ((1, 2, 3, 6, 7))

J305 MAUERER, Hans J.: The Pete Johnson discography in Jazz Bazaar,

No. 1 (April 1969) to No. 10
(June 1971), various paginations.
[rev. ed. of J304] ((1, 2, 3, 6,
7))

JOHNSON, PLAS, 1931–
  tenor saxophone

J306 [[COLMAN, Stuart: Plas Johnson
discography in Blues Unlimited,
No. 133 (January–February 1979):
14–15]]

JOHNSON, ROBERT, ca. 1912–1938
  guitar, vocal

J307 BAKKER, Dick M.: Robert Johnson
in Micrography, No. 13 (February
1971): 9 ((7d))

J308 HUYTON, Trevor: Robert Johnson
discography in GROOM, Bob, ed.:
Robert Johnson. Knutsford, Cheshire: Blues World [1965], 21–24;
additions and corrections in
Blues World, Nos. 26, 28, 32, 34,
and 35, various paginations ((2,
3, 6, 7))

J309 MOORE, Dave: Discography in Blues
Unlimited, No. 121 (September–
October 1976): 20–21 ((2, 3, 6,
7, 9))

Compositions

J310 GROOM, Bob: Discographies of
various compositions of Robert
Johnson in his Standing at the
crossroads: Robert Johnson's recordings in Blues Unlimited, Nos.
118 to 121, various paginations
((—))

JOHNSON, STACEY
  vocal

J311 Stacey Johnson/Vernon Guy in Soul
Bag, No. 58 (October 1976): 18
((2, 3, 7))

JOHNSON, SYL
  guitar, vocal

J312 MOHR, Kurt: Syl Johnson in Soul
Bag, No. 45 (January 1975): 27–
29; additions and corrections in
Soul Bag, No. 46 (February 1976):
6 ((2, 3, 7))

JOHNSON, TOMMY, ca. 1896–1956
  guitar, vocal

J313 BAKKER, Dick M.: Tommy Johnson in
Micrography, No. 4 (June 1969): 9
((—))

J314 BAKKER, Dick M.: Tommy Johnson in
Micrography, No. 9 (February
1970): 7 [rev. ed. of previous
entry] ((—))

J315 EVANS, David: Discography in his
Tommy Johnson. [London]: Studio
Vista (also New York: Stein &
Day) [c1971], 111–112 ((3, 6))

JOHNSON, (BLIND) WILLIE, 1902–1949
  guitar, vocal

J316 GRAUER, Bill: Blind Willie Johnson in Record Changer, Vol. 8
(June 1949): 6 ((3))

JOLLY ROGER label
  See BOLLETINO, DANTE

JONES, DILL, 1923–
  piano

J317 MORGAN, Alun: Dill Jones: a name
listing in Discographical Forum,
No. 5 (March 1968): 7–8 ((2, 3,
7))

JONES, EDDIE, 1926–1959
  guitar, vocal

J318 HANSEN, Barry: Discography:
Guitar Slim on Specialty in R and
B Collector, Vol. 1 (March–April
1970): 13 ((2, 3, 7))

J319 MOHR, Kurt, and Marcel CHAUVARD:
Discography of Guitar Slim in
Jazz Statistics, No. 22 (June
1961): 8, 12; additions and corrections from Mike LEADBITTER in
Jazz Statistics, No. 24 (December
1961): JS8; [from Kurt MOHR] No.
25 (March 1962): 7 ((2, 3, 7))

J320 NIQUET, Bernard: Discographie de
Guitar Slim in Jazz Hot, No. 270
(March 1971): 22 ((2, 3, 7))

JONES, ELVIN, 1927–
  drums

J321 Elvin Jones in Swing Journal,
Vol. 30 (January 1976): 280–283
((2, 7d))

J322 Elvin Jones in Swing Journal,
Vol. 32 (April 1978): 290–297
((2, 7d))

J323 LUZZI, Mario: Discografia Elvin Jones in Musica Jazz, Vol. 31 (July 1975): 48 ((2, 7))

J324 RABEN, Erik: Diskofilspalten in Orkester Journalen, Vol. 36 (January 1968): 19 [1961-1965 recordings] ((2, 7))

JONES, FLOYD, 1917-
guitar, vocal

J325 MOHR, Kurt, and Mike ROWE: Discography in Blues Unlimited, No. 40 (January 1967): 10 ((2, 3, 7d))

JONES, HANK, 1918-
piano

J326 BLUME, Jerry: Discographie in Jazz Hot, No. 44 (May 1950): 11, 16 ((2, 3, 7d))

J327 Great jazz piano in Swing Journal, Vol. 31 (June 1977): 288-291 ((2, 7d))

JONES, JAB
jug, piano, vocal

J328 ARX, Rolf von: Jab Jones (appreciation and discography of an unknown) in Storyville, No. 19 (October-November 1968): 30-32 ((2, 3, 6, 7))

JONES, JIMMY, 1918-
piano

J329 Discographie de Jimmy Jones in Jazz Hot, No. 94 (December 1954): 18-19 ((2, 3, 6, 7))

JONES, JOHNNY, 1924-1964
harmonica, piano, vocal

J330 [[Discography in Soul Bag, No. 5]]

JONES, JONAH, 1908-
trumpet

J331 Discographie (publiés sous son nom, ou de disques publiés en France, depuis la guerre, et auxquels il participe) in Jazz Hot, No. 48 (October 1950): 14-15 ((2, 3, 7d))

J332 JEPSEN, Jorgen Grunnet, and Ernie EDWARDS: Discography of Jonah Jones in Jazz Statistics, No. 13

(November 1959): 3-5; additions from Michel VOGLER in Jazz Statistics, No. 17 (1960): 4-5 ((2, 3, 7))

JONES, PHILLY JOE, 1923-
drums

J333 Selected Jones discography in Down Beat, Vol. 43 (September 9, 1976): 53 ((—))

JONES, QUINCY, 1933-
trumpet

J334 RABEN, Erik: Quincy Jones--a discography (after part 1 titled Quincy Jones--a name discography) in Discographical Forum, No. 5 (March 1968) to No. 9 (November 1968), various paginations; additions and corrections in Discographical Forum, No. 7 (July 1968): 12-13; No. 13 (July 1969): 2; No. 17 (March 1970): 7; No. 19 (July 1970): 20 ((2, 3, 6, 7))

J335 RABEN, Erik: Quincy Jones diskografi in Orkester Journalen, Vol. 34 (November 1966) to Vol. 35 (March 1967), in 5 parts, various paginations ((2, 3, 7))

J336 Selected Jones discography in Down Beat, Vol. 42 (October 23, 1975): 15 ((—))

JONES, RICHARD M., 1889-1945
piano

J337 BAKKER, Dick M.: Richard M. Jones and recordings accompagnying [sic] vocalists in Micrography, No. 16 (December 1971): 2 ((7d))

J338 DAVIES, Ron: Discography in Hot Revue, No. 2 (1947): 15-16 ((2, 3, 7d))

J339 HARRIS, H. Meunier, and Ron DAVIES: A discography of Richard M. Jones in Melody Maker, Vol. 22 (March 30, 1946): 4; (April 6, 1946): 4 ((2, 3, 7))

JONES, SAM
See STOVEPIPE NO. 1

JONES, THAD, 1923-
trumpet

J340 Discographie in Jazz Hot, No. 296 (July-August 1973): 13 ((—))

J341 ENDRESS, Gudrun: For the love of music: Thad Jones in Jazz Podium, Vol. 23 (November 1974): 12 ((—))

J342 OCCHIOGROSSO, Peter: Thad Jones/ Mel Lewis discography in Different Drummer, Vol. 1 (June-July 1974): 30 ((—))

J343 Selected Thad Jones/Mel Lewis Orchestra discography in Down Beat, Vol. 46 (June 7, 1980): 15 ((—))

J344 SHERIDAN, Chris: The Thad Jones/ Mel Lewis Orchestra; a discography in Jazz Journal, Vol. 31 (June 1978): 22-23; additions in Jazz Journal, Vol. 31 (November 1978): 52 ((2, 7))

J345 SMITH, Arnold Jay: Thad Jones conducts an interview in Down Beat, Vol. 41 (December 5, 1975): 15 ((—))

J346 Thad Jones discography in Swing Journal, Vol. 28 (February 1974): 262-269 ((2, 7d))

J347 Thad Jones/Mel Lewis Orchestra discography in Jazz Forum (Poland), Vol. 44 (June 1976): 89 ((—))

J348 [[TOLLARA, Gianni: [Discography, 1951-1969] in Musica Jazz, Vol. 26 (August-September 1970)]]

JOPLIN, SCOTT, 1868-1917
composer, piano

J349 JASEN, David A.: Appendices: rollography of Joplin works; discography of 78rpm records of Joplin works; selective discography of 33-1/3 rpm records of Joplin works in Scott Joplin collected piano works, ed. Vera Brodsky Lawrence. New York: New York Public Library [1971]; 297-302 ((—))

JORDAN, DUKE, 1922-
piano

J350 Duke Jordan in Swing Journal, Vol. 30 (November 1976): 88-93 ((2, 7d))

J351 GARDNER, Mark: Duke Jordan discography (1952-1962) in Discographical Forum, No. 19 (July 1970) to No. 23 (March 1971): various paginations ((1, 2, 3, 6, 7))

J352 MORGAN, Alun: Duke Jordan discography in Jazz Monthly, Vol. 2 (January 1957): 28; (February 1957): 26-27 ((2, 3, 6, 7))

JORDAN, LOUIS, 1908-1975
alto saxophone, vocal

J353 BAKKER, Dick M.: Louis Jordan 1938-1954 in Micrography, No. 42 (October 1976): 23 ((6, 7d))

J354 [[BRUIN, W. L.: Louis Jordan. Groningen, Netherlands: Swingmaster [ca. 1976?], 11, 2 pp.]]

J355 [[[Discography] in Soul Bag, No. 6]]; additions and corrections from Bernard NIQUET in Jazz, Blues & Co., No. 38 (March 1980): 7-8 ((2, 7))

J356 SEROFF, Doug: Louis Jordan in Record Exchanger, Vol. 4 (No. 22, n.d.): 20-23 ((—))

JORDAN, SHEILA, 1929-
vocal

J357 Sheila Jordan discography in Jazz Forum (Poland), No. 60 (1979): 35 ((—))

J358 TEPPERMAN, Barry: Sheila Jordan-- a discography in Pieces of Jazz (1970): 110 ((1, 2, 7))

JOSIE label

J359 [[Listing in Soul Bag, No. 9/10]]

JUG BANDS

J360 BAKKER, Dick M.: More jug bands in Micrography, No. 42 (October 1976): 6-7 ((6, 7))

J361 RYE, Howard: The Louisville jug bands in Micrography, No. 42 (October 1976): 3-5 ((6, 7))

JUMP label

J362 WHYATT, Bert: Discography of the "Jump" label's originals in Discophile, No. 10 (February 1950): 2-5; additions and corrections in Discophile, No. 11 (April 1950): 5; No. 13 (August 1950): 11-12; No. 23 (April 1952): 12 ((2, 3, 6, 7))

K R C label

K1   GRENDYSA, Pete: KRC in R and B
     Magazine, No. 9 (March 1972):
     8-9 ((5))

KAMUCA, RICHIE, 1930-1977
     tenor saxophone

K2   MORGAN, Alun: Richie Kamuca; a
     name listing in Discographical
     Forum, No. 5 (March 1968): 8-9
     ((2, 7))

KANSAS CITY FIVE/SIX/SEVEN

K3   BAKKER, Dick M: Kansas City Five-
     Six-Seven in Micrography, No. 7
     (November 1969): 7 ((7d))

KAS-MO label

K4   ARMITAGE, Steve: Kas-Mo label in
     Hot Buttered Soul, No. 34 (Octo-
     ber 1974?): 7 ((3))

KATZ, DICK, 1924-
     cello

K5   Discographie in Jazz Hot, No. 108
     (March 1956): 21 ((—))

KEANE, SHAKE, 1927-
     trumpet

K6   MORGAN, Alun: Shake Keane in Jazz
     Monthly (December 1965): 26-27
     ((2, 3, 7))

KELLY, GEORGE, 1915-
     tenor saxophone

K7   BEETZ, Tom: Discografie George
     Kelly in Jazz Nu, Vol. 2 (March-
     April 1980): 237 ((2, 7))

KELLY, WYNTON, 1931-1971
     piano

K8   JEPSEN, Jorgen Grunnet: Wynton
     Kelly diskografi (skivor inspel-
     ade under eget namn) in Orkester
     Journalen, Vol. 28 (November
     1960): 11 ((2, 3, 7))

K9   LEVIN, Jean: Wynton Kelly 1931-
     1971 in Jazz Magazine (France),
     No. 189 (May 1971): 31 ((—))

K10 MOON, Pete: Wynton Kelly discog-
     raphy in Discographical Forum,
     No. 32 (1973) to No. 41 (1978?),
     various paginations ((1, 2, 3, 6,
     7))

KENTON, STAN, 1911-1979
     piano, leader

K11 Current discography in Different
     Drummer, Vol. 1 (January 1975):
     20 ((—))

K12 Disques de Stan Kenton Orch.
     [sic] publiés en France in Jazz
     Hot, No. 56 (June 1951): 16
     ((—))

K13 EDWARDS, Ernie; Richard A. FOX;
     and William D. CLANCY: Stan Ken-
     ton and his Orchestra; a discog-
     raphy. [Brande, Denmark: Debut
     Records, 1962], 2 v. ((1, 2, 3,
     6, 7))

K14 ENGELS, Jacques: Discographie
     sommaire de Stan Kenton in Point
     du Jazz, No. 4 (March 1971): 49-
     51 ((—))

K15 EYLE, Wim van: Stan Kenton on LP
     in Jazz Press, No. 45 (November
     1, 1977): 15, 16, 19; additions
     and corrections in KARTING, Paul
     L.: Stan Kenton on LP (vervolg)
     in Jazz Press, No. 47 (January 1,
     1978): 15, 22 ((—))

K16 HARTLEY, Jack: Discography in
     Melody Maker, Vol. 27 (September
     1, 1951) to (October 13, 1951),
     in 7 parts, various paginations
     ((1, 2, 3, 7))

K17 JEPSEN, Jorgen Grunnet: Discogra-
     phy of Stan Kenton. [Brande, Den-
     mark: Debut Records, c1959], 22
     leaves ((1, 2, 3, 7))

K18 [[JEPSEN, Jorgen Grunnet: Stan
     Kenton 1947-57; a discography.
     Copenhagen: 1957. 11 pp.]]

K19 [[LANGE, Horst H.: The Kenton
     discography. Berlin: New Jazz
     Circle Berlin, 1959, 40? pp. ((2,
     3, 7))]]

K20 PIRIE, Christopher A., and Sieg-
     fried MULLER: Artistry in Kenton;
     the bio-discography of Stan Ken-
     ton and his music. Vol. 1. Vienna:
     Siegfried Muller [c1969], 289 pp.
     ((1, 2, 3, 4p, 4t, 6, 7, 9))

K21 [[TEUBIG, Klaus: Stan Kenton Dis-
     cographie. Hamburg: 1963, 11 pp.
     ((1))]]

K22 [[VENUDOR, Pete, and Michael
     SPARKE: Kenton on Capitol; a dis-
     cography compiled with the co-

operation of Capitol Records,
Inc. Hounslow, UK: 1966, 134 pp.;
additions and corrections in Jazz
Monthly, Vol. 12 (December 1966):
26-27; Vol. 13 (March 1967): 31
((1, 2, 3, 6, 7, 8, 9))]]

K23   [[VENUDOR, Pete, and Michael
SPARKE: The standard Kenton discography; Vol. 1, 1937-1949. Amsterdam: Pete Venudor, 1968, 64
pp. [covers up to December 1948;
Vol. 2 (1950-1959) and 3 (1960-
1969) scheduled for publication,
1969] ((1, 4t))]]

Sidemen

K24   SPARKE, Michael: The great Kenton
arrangers--Vol. 1. Whittier, CA:
ErnGeoBil, 1968, 70 leaves (Dance
band series, MS-1) ((1, 2, 3, 6,
7, 8, 9))

KEPPARD, FREDDIE, 1889-1933
trumpet

K25   ALLEN, Walter C.: Freddie Keppard
discography in Hot Notes, Vol. 2
(May-June 1947): 4-5; additions
and corrections in Hot Notes,
Vol. 2 (October 1947): 6; Jazz
Music, Vol. 6 (No. 4, 1955): 9-
11; reprinted in Jazz Discounter,
Vol. 2 (April 1949): 5, 19; reprinted with corrections in Jazz
Music, Vol. 6 (No. 1, 1954): 9-11
((2, 3, 6, 7))

K26   BAKKER, Dick M.: Freddie Keppard
in Micrography, No. 3 (May 1969):
4; additions and corrections in
Micrography, No. 5 (August 1969):
12 ((7d))

K27   BAKKER, Dick M.: Freddie Keppard
in Micrography, No. 15 (September
1971): 3 [rev. ed. of previous
entry] ((7d))

KEYMEN label

K28   JAFFIER, Patrick: Keymen label
listing in Soul Bag, No. 47
(March 1975): 9 ((3))

K29   WILSON, Jim: Keymen label listing
in Hot Buttered Soul, No. 11
(October 1972): 14 ((3))

KEYNOTE label
See also EMARCY label (Kwiecinski, Walter)

K30   FOURNIER, Yvon: Keynote in Point
du Jazz, No. 15 (July 1979): 53-
57 ((3, 7d))

K31   MORGAN, Alun: Keynote label listing in Jazz Monthly, No. 186
(August 1970): 27-28; No. 187
(September 1970): 28-31; additions and corrections in Jazz
Monthly, No. 190 (December 1970):
27-29 ((2, 3, 6, 7))

KHOURY, GEORGE
record producer

K32   LEADBITTER, Mike: Khoury's &
Lyric labels of Lake Charles,
Louisiana in Hot Buttered Soul,
No. 22 (September 1974): 2-6
((3))

KILLENS, REV

K33   EAGLE, Bob: I love the Lord--Rev.
Killens' story in Blues Link, No.
5 (1974): 35-36 ((3, 6, 7))

KING, AL (Al Smith), 1925-
vocal

K34   HILDEBRAND, Lee; Emmanuel CHOIS-
NEL; and Kurt MOHR: Discographie
d'Al King in Soul Bag, No. 22/23
(January-February 1973): 25-26
((2, 3, 7))

KING, ALBERT, 1923-

K35   MOHR, Kurt, and Pierre DAGUERRE:
Albert King in Soul Bag, No. 51
(January 1976): 12-16 ((2, 3, 6,
7, 9))

KING, B. B. (Riley B. King), 1925-
guitar, vocal

K36   B. B. King on singles in Blues
Unlimited, No. 2 (June 1963): 8-
9; additions and corrections in
Blues Unlimited, No. 12 (June
1964): suppl-3 ((2, 3))

K37   MOHR, Kurt: B. B. King in Soul
Bag, No. 32 (November 1973): 19-
25; additions and corrections in
Soul Bag, No. 47 (March 1975): 1
((2, 3, 7))

KING, BEN E. (Benny Nelson), 1938-
vocal

K38 MOHR, Kurt: Ben E. King in Soul
Bag, No. 35 (February 1974): 28-
33; additions and corrections in
Soul Bag, No. 45 (January 1975):
34 ((2, 3, 7))

KING, EARL, 1934-
guitar, vocal

K39 JONES, Tad, and Earl KING: Earl
King discography in Living Blues,
No. 41 (November-December 1978):
7; additions and corrections from
Tom STAGG and Guido van RIJN in
Living Blues, No. 44 (autumn
1979): 7 ((2, 3, 7))

KING, FREDDIE, 1934-1976
guitar, vocal

K40 Discographie de Freddy King in
Soul Bag, No. 15; No. 16 (1972?):
13-14 ((2, 3, 7))

K41 MOHR, Kurt, and François POSTIF:
Discographie in Jazz Hot No. 303
(March 1974): 9 ((2, 3, 7))

K42 MOHR, Kurt, and Jacques PERIN:
Freddie King discography in Soul
Bag, No. 58 (October 1976): 19-22
((2, 3, 6, 7))

KING, TEMPO, 1915-1939
vocal

K43 MARTIN, J. J., and Eric TONKS:
Tempo King and his Kings of Tempo
discography in Pickup, Vol. 1
(October 1946): 5-6 ((2, 7d))

KING label

K44 BARAZZETTA, Giuseppe: On Parlophone, from King in Discophile,
No. 60 (June 1958): 9-10 ((2, 3,
7))

K45 ROTANTE, Anthony: The "King" of
R & B labels in Record Research,
No. 22 (April-May 1959); No. 24
(September-October 1959); No. 25
(November-December 1959); No. 27
(March-April 1960); No. 29 (Au-
gust 1960); No. 30 (October
1960); No. 87 (December 1967);
No. 90 (May 1968) to No. 94 (De-
cember 1968); No. 98 (May 1969),
various paginations ((3, 6))

KING JAZZ label
See MEZZROW, MEZZ (Lambert,
Eddie) and (Phythian, Les)

KINSEY, TONY, 1927-
drums

K46 MORGAN, Alun: Tony Kinsey--a name
listing in Discographical Forum,
No. 1 (May 1960): 11-13; additions and corrections from Charles
FOX in Discographical Forum, No.
3 (September 1960): 16 ((2, 3, 6,
7))

KIRBY, JOHN, 1908-1952
bass violin

K47 BAKKER, Dick M.: John Kirby 1938-
42 in Micrography, No. 29 (December 1973): 3; additions and corrections in Micrography, No. 30
(April 1974): 1 ((1, 7d))

K48 CROSBIE, Ian: The biggest little
band in Jazz Journal, Vol. 25
(March 1972): 28 ((1, 2, 3, 6, 7))

K49 HOEFER, George: John Kirby discography in Down Beat, Vol. 29
(October 11, 1962): 27 ((1, 2, 3,
7))

KIRK, ANDY, 1898-
leader

K50 BAKKER, Dick M.: Andy Kirk 1936-
42 in Micrography, No. 24 (February 1973): 7; additions and corrections in Micrography, No. 26
(1973): 1 ((—))

K51 BAKKER, Dick M.: Early Andy Kirk
in Micrography, No. 37 (July
1975): 6 ((6, 7d))

K52 McCARTHY, Albert: Andy Kirk and
his Clouds of Joy in Jazz &
Blues, Vol. 1 (December 1971): 23
((—))

KIRK, EDDIE
See KIRKLAND, EDDIE

KIRK, ROLAND, 1936-1977
saxophones

K53 MOHR, Kurt, and François POSTIF:
Discographie de Roland Kirk in
Jazz Hot, No. 193 (December
1963): 56 ((2, 3, 7))

K54 Roland Kirk discography in Swing
Journal, Vol. 30 (October 1976):
80-83 ((2, 7d))

K55 [[TARRANT, Don: Roland Kirk discography. Southsea, UK: 1970, 9,
2 pp. ((1))]]

KIRKEBY, ED, 1891–
    leader
    See also CALIFORNIA RAMBLERS

K56 HURLOCK, Frank: Record research in Vintage Jazz Mart, (August 1963): 6 ((3, 6))

KIRKLAND, EDDIE, 1928–
    guitar, harmonica, vocal

K57 ROWE, Mike: [Discography] in Blues Unlimited, No. 44 (June–July 1967): 11 ((2, 3, 7))

KITTRELL, CHRISTINE
    vocal

K58 ROTANTE, Anthony: The discography of Christine Kittrell (exploratory) in Record Research, No. 69 (July 1965): 8 ((3, 8))

KLEMMER, JOHN, 1946–
    tenor saxophone

K59 POSTIF, François: Complétant l'interview de L. V. Mialy, voici la discographie de Johnny Klemmer in Jazz Hot, No. 259 (March 1970): 30 ((2, 7, 9))

KLUGH, EARL, 1955–
    guitar

K60 Selected Klugh discography in Down Beat, Vol. 47 (March 1980): 21 ((—))

KNIGHT, GLADYS
    vocal

K61 [[[Discography of Gladys Knight and the Pips] in Soul Bag, No. 11]]

KNIGHT, MARIE, ca. 1920–
    See also THARPE, ROSETTA (Jorgensen, Jorgen)

K62 GRUT, Harald: Marie Knight discography in Jazz Music, Vol. 4 (No. 6, 1951): 27–28 ((2, 3, 7))

K63 ROTANTE, Anthony: Marie Knight in Record Research, Vol. 1 (February 1955): 3; (April 1955): 3–4 ((2, 3, 6, 7d))

KNIGHT label

K64 [[Listing in Soul Bag, No. 15]]

K65 SHAW, Greg, and Ray TOPPING: Knight label listing in Shout, No. 82 (December 1972): 5–6 ((3, 5))

KOHLMAN, FREDDIE, 1915–
    drums

K66 STAGG, Tom: Freddie Kohlman; a "name" discography in Footnote, Vol. 2 (April–May 1977): 10–11 ((2, 7))

KOLAX, KING, 1918–
    trumpet

K67 MOHR, Kurt: Discographie in Jazz Hot, No. 120 (April 1957): 14 ((3))

KOLLER, HANS, 1921–
    saxophones

K68 KRANER, Dietrich H.: Die Hans Koller Discographie 1947–1966. Graz, Austria: Modern Jazz Series, c1967, 12, vi pp. ((1, 2, 3, 6, 7))

K69 LANGE, Horst: Hans Koller; a discography in Discophile, No. 41 (April 1955): 3–5; additions and corrections in Discophile, No. 42 (June 1955): 16; No. 45 (December 1955): 16; No. 53 (February 1957): 11 ((2, 3, 7))

KONITZ, LEE, 1927–
    alto saxophone
    See also MULLIGAN, GERRY (Jepsen, Jorgen Grunnet: Discography of Gerry Mulligan & Lee Konitz)

K70 BLUME, Jerry: Discographie de Lee Konitz in Jazz Hot, No. 53 (March 1951): 30 ((2, 3, 7))

K71 DELMAS, Jean: Discographie: Lee Konitz in Jazz Hot, No. 343 (November 1977): 28–31; No. 344 (December 1977): 32–35 ((1, 2, 3, 6, 7))

K72 Lee Konitz discography in Swing Journal, Vol. 27 (October 1973): 274–279 ((2, 7d))

K73 MORGAN, Alun, and Jorgen Grunnet JEPSEN: Lee Konitz discography in Jazz Monthly, Vol. 5 (August 1959): 24–25; (September 1959): 25–26; (October 1959): 28 ((2, 3, 7))

K74 Selected Konitz discography in Down Beat, Vol. 47 (January 1980): 18 ((—))

KOSZ, MIECZYSLAW, d.1973
    piano

K75 ROSZCZUK, Antoni: Mieczyslaw Kosz in Jazz Press, No. 29 (January 7, 1977): 2 ((—))

KRAL, ROY, 1921–
    vocal
    See CAIN, JACKIE

KRC label
    See K R C label

KRESS, CARL, 1907–1965
    guitar

K76 ROBERTS, Don W.: Discography in Pieces of Jazz (1971): 2 ((7d))

KROG, KARIN, 1937–
    vocal

K77 BERGH, Johs, and Mark GARDNER: Discography in Jazz & Blues, Vol. 2 (November 1972): 22 ((2, 6, 7))

K78 Karin Krog pa skiva in Orkester Journalen, Vol. 44 (October 1976): 15 ((—))

KRUPA, GENE, 1909–1973
    drums

K79 EDWARDS, Ernie; George HALL; and Bill KORST: A discography of the 1938–1951 Gene Krupa Orchestra. Whittier, CA: ErnGeoBil, 1968, 36 leaves (Dance band series, K-1A) ((1, 2, 3, 6, 7, 8))

K80 HALL, George, ed.: Gene Krupa and his Orchestra. Laurel, MD: Jazz Discographies Unlimited, 1975, ii, 90 pp. ((1, 2, 3, 4p, 4t, 6, 7))

K81 SHAW, Arnold: Gene Krupa discography in his Gene Krupa; first authentic life story of America's ace drummer man. New York: Pin Up Press, 1945, 26–27 ((—))

    Soundtracks
    See RICH, BUDDY--Soundtracks

KUHN, JOACHIM, 1944–
    piano

K82 Interview, Joachim Kuhn in Jazz Hot, No. 306 (June 1974): 22 ((—))

K83 TERCINET, Alain: Discographie de Joachim Kuhn in Jazz Hot, No. 273 (June 1971): 8 ((1, 2, 7))

KUHN, ROLF, 1929–
    clarinet, alto saxophone

K84 LANGE, Horst H.: Discography in Jazz Monthly, Vol. 4 (June 1958): 26–27 ((2, 3, 7))

L. A. FOUR (musical group)

L1 Eléments de disco de L. A. 4 in Jazz, Blues & Co., No. 30 (May-June 1979): 8 ((—))

LABELLE, PATTI
    vocal

L2 MOHR, Kurt: Patti Labelle & the Bluebelles in Hot Buttered Soul, No. 15 (February 1973): 2–5 ((3, 7))

LACY, STEVE, 1934–
    soprano saxophone

L3 EIGO, Jim: Steve Lacy discography in Down Beat, Vol. 47 (May 1980): 22 ((—))

L4 HARDY, Alain-Rene: Steve Lacy face à face in Jazz Magazine (France), No. 246 (August 1976): 14–15 ((2, 7))

L5 TERCINET, Alain: Discographie de Steve Lacy in Jazz Hot, No. 271 (April 1971): 10–11 ((1, 2, 7))

L6 WALKER, Malcolm: Discography in Jazz Monthly, Vol. 12 (March 1966): 12–13; additions and corrections in Jazz Monthly, Vol. 12 (April 1966): 26 ((2, 3, 7))

LADNIER, TOMMY, 1900–1939
    trumpet
    See also MEZZROW, MEZZ (Bakker, Dick M.)

L7 HILLMAN, J. C.: A discography in Jazz Journal, Vol. 18 (August 1965): 9–10, 40 ((2, 3, 6, 7))

L8 KEARTLAND, Eric F.: Discography of Tommy Ladnier in Jazz Forum (UK), No. 3 (January 1947): 17–20; additions and corrections in Jazz Forum (UK), No. 4 (April 1947): 24 ((2, 3, 6, 7))

L9   KEARTLAND, Eric F.: Tommy Ladnier diskografi in Orkester Journalen, Vol. 15 (March 1947): 16-17 [part 1, to October 1926; continued in later issue(s)] ((2, 3, 7))

LaFARO, SCOTT, 1936-1961
   bass violin

L10   MONTI, Pierre Andre: Discographie de Scott LaFaro in Jazz 360, No. 21 (October 1979): 9-13; reprinted in Jazzophone, No. 4 (October-December 1979): 12-13 ((2, 3, 7))

LAFITTE, GUY, 1927-
   tenor saxophone

L11   Discographie sommaire de Lafitte in Jazz Magazine (France), No. 56 (February 1960): 33 ((—))

L12   LAFARGUE, Pierre: A Guy Lafitte discography in Jazz Monthly, Vol. 9 (August 1963): 10-11; (September 1963): 24-25; (October 1963): 27 ((2, 3, 7))

LAINE, BOB, 1910-
   piano

L13   JONASSON, Stig: Spotlight on Bob Laine in Discophile, No. 2 (October 1948): 5-6; additions and corrections in Discophile, No. 3 (December 1948): 6 [1947 Swedish recordings] ((2, 3, 7))

LAINE, CLEO (Clementina Dinah Campbell), 1927-

L14   SIDERS, Harvey: Cleo Laine/Johnny Dankworth in Different Drummer, Vol. 1 (October 1974): 15 ((—))

LAMP, BUDDY
   vocal

L15   MOHR, Kurt: Buddy Lamp discography in Hot Buttered Soul, No. 44 (February-March 1976): 2 ((3, 5, 7, 8))

LANCE, MAJOR
   vocal

L16   MOHR, Kurt: Major Lance in Soul Bag, No. 45 (January 1975): 9-11; additions and corrections in Soul Bag, No. 47 (March 1975): 1 ((2, 3, 7))

LANG, EDDIE (Salvatore Massaro), 1902-1933
   guitar
   See also VENUTI, JOE (Bakker, Dick M.)

L17   HIGGINS, Jack: Eddie Lang on Parlophone in Jazz News, (February 27, 1959): 8 ((—))

L18   VENABLES, Ralph G. V.: Ed Lang on race records in Jazz (US), Vol. 1 (December 1943): 6 ((3))

L19   VENABLES, Ralph G. V.: A feature for the connoisseur in Discography (January 1943): 3-2 [recordings where he accompanies "race" artists] ((3))

LANIN, SAM
   leader

L20   BACKENSTO, Woody, and Bert WHYATT: Sam Lanin Okeh recordings in Record Research, No. 96/97 (April 1969): 4-8, 18 ((3, 6, 9))

LANKCHAN, HIP, 1936-
   guitar, vocal

L21   BAKER, Cary: Discography in Blue Flame, No. 14 (n.d.): 13 ((7))

LARKIN, BILLY
   organ

L22   NIQUET, Bernard: Billy Larkin in Soul Bag, No. 61 (June 1977): 28 ((2, 7))

L23   NIQUET, Bernard: Billy Larkin & the Delegates in Point du Jazz, No. 3 (August 1970): 75-76 ((2, 7))

LARKINS, ELLIS, 1923-
   piano

L24   Larkins op elpee in Jazz Press, No. 46 (December 1, 1977): 4 ((—))

LaROCCA, NICK, 1889-1961
   cornet

L25   [[LANGE, Horst H.: Nick LaRocca. Wetzlar, W. Germany: Pegasus, 1960, 64 pp. ((2, 3, 6, 7))]]

LASALLE label

L26   BAKER, Cary: LaSalle/Fay/Planet
      label listing in Hot Buttered
      Soul, No. 13 (December 1972): 7
      ((3, 6))

LATEEF, YUSEF (William Evans), 1921-
      saxophones

L27   COOKE, Ann: Yusef Lateef; a name
      discography in Jazz Monthly, Vol.
      9 (July 1963): 16-17 ((2, 3, 7))

L28   [[RABEN, Erik: [Discography] in
      Orkester Journalen, Vol. 36 (No-
      vember 1968), (December 1968)]]

LATTIMORE, BENNY

L29   [[Discography in Soul Bag, No.
      9/10]]

LATTIMORE, HARLAN, 1908-
      vocal

L30   CROSBY, Barney: Harlan Lattimore
      discography in International Dis-
      cophile, No. 2 (fall 1955): 7;
      additions and corrections in In-
      ternational Discophile, No. 3
      (spring 1956): 16 ((3, 6, 7d))

LAVETTE, BETTY
      vocal

L31   Betty Lavette in Soul Bag, No. 48
      (June 1975): 23, 25; additions and
      corrections in Soul Bag, No. 51
      (January 1976): 32 ((2, 3, 7))

LAWRANCE, BRIAN
      vocal

L32   HULME, George: Jazz Australia in
      Matrix, No. 45 (February 1963): 3-
      6; additions and corrections in
      Matrix, No. 53 (June 1964): 18;
      No. 54 (August 1964): 15 ((2, 3,
      6, 7))

LAWRENCE, AZAR, 1953-
      tenor saxophone
      See also GROSSMAN, STEVE

L33   Selected Lawrence discography in
      Down Beat, Vol. 43 (October 7,
      1976): 16 ((—))

LAWRENCE, BABY, 1921-
      tap-dancing

L34   NIQUET, Bernard: Baby Lawrence in
      Jazz, Blues & Co., No. 18/19/20
      (summer 1978): 8 ((2, 7))

LAWRENCE, ELLIOT, 1925-
      leader, piano

L35   GARROD, Charles: Elliott Lawrence
      and his Orchestra. Spotswood, NJ:
      Joyce Music, 1973, 18, 7 leaves.
      ((1, 2, 3, 4t, 6, 7))

L36   JEPSEN, Jorgen Grunnet: Disko-
      filspalten in Orkester   Journalen,
      Vol. 25 (January 1957): 21; (Feb-
      ruary 1957): 23 [1955-56 record-
      ings] ((2))

LAWS, HUBERT, 1939-
      flute

L37   Selected Laws discography in Down
      Beat, Vol. 44 (May 19, 1977): 17
      ((—))

LAWSON, YANK (John R. Lawson), 1911-
      trumpet

L38   WHYATT, Bert: The Yank Lawson
      band; a "name" discography in
      Discophile, No. 9 (December
      1949): 8-9; additions and correc-
      tions in Discophile, No. 10 (Feb-
      ruary 1950): 10 ((1, 2, 3, 7))

LAWYER HOUSTON
      See HOUSTON, LAWYER

LAZAR, SAM, 1933-
      organ

L39   NIQUET, Bernard: Qui connait Sam
      Lazar? in Point du Jazz, No. 13
      (June 1977): 140-141 ((2, 7))

LAZY LESTER (Lester Johnson), 1933-
      harmonica, vocal

L40   BROVEN, John J.: Discography of
      Lazy Lester (Lester Johnson), in
      Blues Statistics, No. 2 (March
      1963): 3 ((3))

LEADBELLY (Huddie Ledbetter), 1889-
      1949
      guitar, vocal

L41   CHMURA, Helene F.: Lead Belly's
      American Record Company record-
      ings in Discophile, No. 47 (April
      1956): 4-5; additions and correc-

tions in Discophile, No. 49 (August 1956): 11 ((2, 3, 7))

L42 HARVEY, Charles: Songs by Leadbelly in Jazzology. London: American Jazz Society [1946?], 2 different booklets, page 7 in one and page 14 in the other ((7))

L43 Leadbelly (Huddie Ledbetter) on Musicraft in Country Directory, No. 3 (1962): 36 ((2, 3, 7))

L44 RAMSEY, Frederic, and Albert J. McCARTHY: Huddie Ledbetter discography in JONES, Max, and Albert McCARTHY, eds.: A tribute to Huddie Ledbetter. London: Jazz Music Books, 1946, 9-14; additions and corrections in Jazz Music, Vol. 3 (No. 9, 1948): 20 ((1, 2, 3, 6, 7))

L45 RIJN, Guido van: Pre-war blues reissues: Huddie Ledbetter (Leadbelly) in Boogie Woogie & Blues Collector, No. 89 (1979): 4 ((3, 6, 7d))

L46 WIEDEMANN, Erik: Discographie de Leadbelly in Jazz Hot, No. 40 (January 1950): 28-29 ((2, 3, 7))

L47 WIEDEMANN, Erik: Lead Belly up to date in Discophile, No. 15 (December 1950): 7-8; additions and corrections in Discophile, No. 16 (February 1951): 9-11; No. 17 (April 1951): 15 [supplements L44; covers 1935-1946] ((2, 3, 6, 7))

L48 WYLER, Mike, and Albert McCARTHY: Huddie Ledbetter in Jazz Monthly, Vol. 2 (April 1956): 26 ((2, 3, 7))

LEAVILL, OTIS
vocal

L49 MOHR, Kurt: Otis Leavill in Soul Bag, No. 45 (January 1975): 31; additions and corrections in Soul Bag, No. 51 (January 1976): 32 ((2, 3, 7))

LEDBETTER, HUDDIE
See LEADBELLY

LEE, FRANKIE
vocal

L50 MOHR, Kurt, and Lee HILDEBRAND: Discographie de Little Frankie Lee in Soul Bag, No. 41 (September 1974): 23 ((3, 7))

LEE, JULIA, 1902-1958
piano, vocal

L51 DEXTER, Dave; Albert McCARTHY; and Erik WIEDEMANN: Discography of Julia Lee in Discophile, No. 16 (February 1951): 13-15; additions and corrections in Discophile, No. 17 (April 1951): 15 ((2, 3, 6, 7))

LEECAN AND COOKSEY (musical group)

L52 ALLEN, Walter C.: Leecan and Cooksey in Jazz Journal, Vol. 9 (September 1956): 8 ((2, 3, 7))

LENOIR, J. B., 1929-1967
guitar, vocal

L53 LEADBITTER, Mike; Kurt MOHR; and Marcel CHAUVARD: J. B. Lenoir discography in Blues Unlimited, No. 15 (September 1964): 6-7; additions and corrections in Blues Unlimited, No. 22 (May 1965): 10 ((2, 3, 7))

L54 MOHR, Kurt, and Marcel CHAUVARD: Discography of J. B. Lenoir in Jazz Statistics, No. 28 (December 1962): BLUES-5 to BLUES-7; additions and corrections from Mike LEADBITTER in Blues Statistics, No. 2 (March 1963): 2 ((2, 3, 7))

LENORE, J. B.
See LENOIR, J. B.

LEONARD, HARLAN, 1905-
leader, saxophones

L55 SIMMEN, Johnny: Harlan Leonard discography in Jazz Journal, Vol. 16 (August 1963): 6 ((2, 3, 7, 9))

LEVALLET, DIDIER, ca. 1945-
bass violin

L56 Discographie in Jazz Hot, No. 359 (March 1979): 15 ((—))

LEVY, LOU, 1928-
piano

L57 MORGAN, Alun: Lou Levy; a name listing in Discographical Forum, No. 10 (January 1969): 9-10; additions and corrections from Ernie EDWARDS in Discographical Forum, No. 14 (September 1969): 3-4 ((2, 7))

LEWIS, BARBARA
    vocal

L58 MOHR, Kurt: Discographie de Bar-
     bara Lewis in Soul Bag, No. 35
     (February 1974): 11-14; additions
     and corrections in Soul Bag, No.
     45 (January 1975): 34 ((2, 3, 7))

LEWIS, BOBBY

L59 [[Discography in Soul Music Month-
     ly, (December 1966)]]

LEWIS, FURRY (Walter Lewis), 1893-
    guitar, vocal

L60 BAKKER, Dick M.: Furry Lewis in
     Micrography, No. 9 (February
     1970): 8 ((—))

LEWIS, GEORGE, 1900-1968
    clarinet

L61 BAKKER, Dick M.: George Lewis on
     A.M. in Micrography, No. 37 (July
     1975): 8 ((3, 6))

L62 Discography of George Lewis in
     Second Line, Vol. 7 (January-
     February 1956): 8, 10-12 ((1, 7))

L63 Discography of George Lewis in
     Swing Journal, issue 9 of 1958:
     42; issue 10 of 1958: 36 ((—))

L64 [[George Lewis; a biography,
     appreciation, record survey and
     discography. London: National Jazz
     Federation, 1958, 16 pp.]]

L65 A George Lewis discography in
     Jazz Report (St. Louis), Vol. 2
     (February 1954): 4-5 ((1, 7))

L66 A George Lewis discography in
     BETHELL, Tom: George Lewis; a
     jazzman from New Orleans. Berkeley:
     Univ. of California Pr. [c1977],
     291-363 ((1, 2, 3, 6, 7))

L67 HARRIS, H. Meunier: George Lewis
     discography in Hot Club Magazine,
     No. 12 (December 1946): 5-6 ((1,
     2, 3, 7d))

L68 HULME, George: George Lewis on
     "Circle" Records in Discophile,
     No. 60 (June 1958): 11-12; addi-
     tions and corrections in Disco-
     phile, No. 61 (December 1958): 18;
     Matrix, No. 37 (November 1961):
     19 ((2, 3, 6, 7))

L69 JEPSEN, Jorgen Grunnet: George
     Lewis diskografi in Orkester
     Journalen, Vol. 27 (March 1959):

46-47; (April 1959): 46-47 ((2,
3, 6, 7d))

L70 [[KOHNO, Ryuji, ed.: The George
     Lewis discography including Bunk
     Johnson's. Fujisawa, Kanagawa: The
     Dixieland Academy, 1966, 40 pp.]]

L71 STENBECK, Lennart: George Lewis
     diskografi in Orkester Journalen,
     Vol. 33 (June 1965): 28; (July-
     August 1965): 30; (September
     1965): 40 ((2, 7))

LEWIS, GUITAR
    See LEWIS, PETE "GUITAR"

LEWIS, JIMMY, 1918-
    guitar, vocal

L72 MOHR, KURT: Discography in Jazz
     Statistics, No. 10 (May 1959):
     2-4; additions from Michel VOGLER
     in Jazz Statistics, No. 17 (1960):
     8 ((2, 3, 6, 7))

LEWIS, JOHN, 1920-
    piano

L73 JEPSEN, Jorgen Grunnet: John Lewis
     diskografi in Orkester Journalen,
     Vol. 27 (January 1959): 39 ((2,
     3, 7d))

L74 John Lewis & MJQ discography in
     Swing Journal, Vol. 28 (March
     1974): 266-271 ((2, 7d))

LEWIS, MEADE LUX, 1905-1964
    piano

L75 Discography of Meade Lux Lewis in
     Jazz Guide, No. 8 (December 1964);
     No. 12 (April 1965) [and possibly
     other issues], various pagina-
     tions. ((2, 3, 6, 7))

L76 DUTTON, Frank: Meade Lux Lewis; a
     discography in Melody Maker, Vol.
     27 (February 3, 1951): 9 ((2, 3,
     6, 7))

L77 JEPSEN, Jorgen Grunnet: Diskofil-
     spalten in Orkester Journalen,
     Vol. 33 (January 1965): 19, 30
     ((2, 3, 6, 7))

LEWIS, MEL, 1929-
    drums
    See also JONES, THAD

L78 MORGAN, Alun: Mel Lewis; a name
     listing in Discographical Forum,
     No. 5 (March 1968): 7; additions

and corrections in Discographical
Forum, No. 7 (July 1968): 1; No.
9 (November 1968): 1 ((2, 7))

LEWIS, PETE "GUITAR"
guitar, harmonica

L79 MOHR, Kurt: Pete "Guitar" Lewis
in Soul Bag, No. 20 (July-August
1972): 23-24 ((2, 3, 7))

LEWIS, SABBY (William Sebastian Lewis),
1914-
piano, arranger

L80 PORTER, Bob: Sabby Lewis discography in Jazz Journal, Vol. 20
(February 1967): 9; additions and
corrections from Mark GARDNER in
Jazz Journal, Vol. 20 (July 1967):
17 ((2, 3, 7))

LEWIS, SAMMY, 1925-
vocal

L81 ROTANTE, Anthony: Singing Sammy
Lewis in Record Research, No. 35
(June 1961): 19 ((2, 7))

LEWIS, SMILEY (Overton Amos Lemons),
1920-1966
piano, vocal

L82 LEADBITTER, Mike, and Mike VER-
NON: Discography in Jazz Monthly,
Vol. 13 (May 1967): 15-17 ((2, 3,
7))

L83 ROTANTE, Anthony, and Dan MAHONY:
Smiley Lewis (Overton Lemon) in
Record Research, Vol. 1 (August
1955): 2 ((3, 8))

LEWIS, STEVE, 1896-ca. 1941
piano

L84 TIUG, R. A.: Discography of Steve
Lewis in Second Line, Vol. 3
(September-October 1952): 11
((3))

LEWIS, TED (Theodore Leopold
Friedman), 1892-1971
clarinet, vocal

L85 BAKKER, Dick M.: Ted Lewis in
Micrography, No. 19 (April 1972):
5 ((—))

L86 CLOUGH, R.: Is everybody happy?
in R.S.V.P., No. 29 (October
1967): 25-26; No. 38 (November

1967): 25-26; No. 32 (January
1968) ((2, 3, 6, 7))

LIBRARY OF CONGRESS label
See also LEADBELLY (Harvey,
Charles); MORTON, JELLY ROLL
(Valenti, Jerry)

L87 ALLEN, Walter C.: Library of Congress recordings in Discophile,
No. 19 (August 1951): 14-15 ((2,
3))

L88 BENJAMIN, Sam: The Library of
Congress records in Discophile,
No. 30 (June 1953): 14-17, 19;
additions and corrections in Discophile, No. 31 (August 1953): 15
((2, 3))

L89 GROOM, Bob: The Library of Congress blues and gospel recordings
in Blues World, No. 45 (1973): 9
[Detroit area recordings, 2472-
2486] ((7d))

L90 RUARK, George: Library of Congress recordings in Country Directory, No. 1 (November 1960):
6-19; No. 3 (1962): 36 ((3))

LIEBMAN, DAVE, 1946-
saxophones

L91 Dave Liebman talks with Gene
Perla in Coda, Vol. 11 (January
1974): 27 ((—))

L92 GICKING, Jim: Dave Liebman's
discography in booklet with
[phonodisc] Artists House AH8.
New York: Artists House Records,
c1979 ((7d))

L93 Selected Liebman discography in
Down Beat, Vol. 43 (April 8,
1976): 15 ((—))

LIGGINS, JIMMY and JOE
vocal

L94 HANSEN, Barry: Jimmy & Joe Liggins in R and B Magazine, Vol. 1
(November 1970-February 1971):
10-14 ((2, 3, 7d))

LIGHTFOOT, PAPA (Alexander Lightfoot),
1924-1971
harmonica, vocal

L95 LEADBITTER, Mike: Papa Lightfoot
in Blues Unlimited, No. 34 (July
1966): 6 ((3, 7))

LIGHTNIN' SLIM (Otis Hicks), 1913-1974
   guitar, vocal

L96   BROVEN, J. J.: Discography of
      Lightnin' Slim in Jazz Statis-
      tics, No. 28 (December 1962):
      BLUES-4 to BLUES-5; additions and
      corrections from Mike LEADBITTER
      in Blues Statistics, No. 2 (March
      1963): 2 ((2, 3, 7))

LINCOLN, ABBEY, 1930-
   vocal

L97   KOOPMANS, Rudy: Discografie in
      Jazz Nu, Vol. 2 (January 1980):
      162 ((—))

LINDBERG, NILS, 1933-
   piano

L98   Nisse Lindberg pa skiva in Orkes-
      ter Journalen, Vol. 44 (December
      1976): 13 ((—))

LINDSTROM label

L99   LANGE, Horst H.: Lindstrom-Amer-
      ican Record (Lindstrom-Beka-Par-
      lophon, German) (LAR-A.4000-
      series) 1922-1929 in R.S.V.P. No.
      24 (May 1967) to No. 30 (November
      1967); No. 32 (January 1968); No.
      35 (April 1968); No. 38 (July
      1968), various paginations ((3,
      8))

L100 SAGAWE, Harm: Lindstrom in
      R.S.V.P., No. 5 (1965) to No. 13
      (June 1966), various paginations
      ((3))

LITTLE, BOOKER, 1938-1961
   trumpet

L101 EYLE, Wim van: Booker Little disco
      in Jazz Press, No. 26 (November
      12, 1976): 5-6, 14 ((2, 3, 7))

L102 KRANER, Dietrich H.: Booker Little
      discography in Journal of Jazz
      Discography, No. 5 (September
      1979): 2-9 ((2, 3, 7))

L103 LUZZI, Mario: Discografia Booker
      Little in Musica Jazz, Vol. 31
      (November 1975): 52-54 ((2, 7))

L104 [[TOLLARA, Gianni: Discography in
      Musica Jazz, Vol. 23 (January
      1967)]]

L105 WALKER, Malcolm: Booker Little in
      Jazz Monthly, Vol. 12 (July 1966):
      13-14; additions and corrections

in Jazz Monthly, Vol. 12 (October
1966): 26; Vol. 13 (April 1967):
27 ((2, 3, 7))

LITTLE AL (Al Gunter)
   guitar, vocal

L106 Discography in Jazz Statistics,
      No. 28 (December 1962): BLUES-7;
      additions and corrections from
      Mike LEADBITTER in Blues Statis-
      tics, No. 2 (March 1963): 3 ((2,
      3, 7))

LITTLE ESTHER
   See PHILLIPS, ESTHER

LITTLE JOE BLUE (Joe Vallery), 1934-
   vocal

L107 HILDEBRAND, Lee, and Kurt MOHR:
      Little Joe Blue's disco in Soul
      Bag, No. 31 (October 1973): 2, 9;
      additions and corrections in Soul
      Bag, No. 51 (January 1976): 32
      ((3, 7))

LITTLE MACK (Mack Simmons), 1934-
   harmonica, vocal

L108 BAKER, Cary: Little Mack Simmons
      in Shout, No. 77 (June 1972): 1-3
      ((3, 7))

L109 PATERSON, Neil, and Mike LEAD-
      BITTER: Discography in Blues Un-
      limited, No. 9 (January 1967): 7
      ((2, 3, 7))

L110 PATERSON, Neil, and Mike LEAD-
      BITTER: Discography in Blues Un-
      limited Collectors Classics, No.
      8 (July 1965): 10 [rev. ed. of
      previous entry] ((2, 3, 7))

LITTLE MILTON (Milton Campbell), 1934-
   guitar, vocal

L111 MOHR, Kurt; Emmanuel CHOISNEL;
      and Joel DUFOUR: Little Milton
      discography in Soul Bag, No. 51
      (January 1976): 7-11 ((2, 3, 6,
      7, 9))

LITTLE RICHARD (Richard Penniman),
   1935-
   piano, vocal

L112 Little Richard discographie in
      Soul Bag, No. 61 (June 1977): 18-
      23 ((2, 3, 6, 7))

L113 MOONOOGIAN, George A.: Blues classics revisited; Little Richard discography in Whiskey, Women and..., No. 3 (n.d.): 16-18 ((7))

LITTLE WALTER (Marion Walter Jacobs), 1930-1968
harmonica

L114 GREENSMITH, Bill: Little Walter discography in Blues Unlimited, No. 120 (July-August 1976): 12-14; additions and corrections in Blues Unlimited, No. 127 (November-December 1977): 12 ((2, 3, 7))

L115 ROTANTE, Anthony: [Discography of Checker/Chance/Herald recordings] in Record Research, Vol. 1 (April 1955): 4 ((2, 3))

L116 [[SLAVEN, Neil: [Discography]. Blues Unlimited booklet, 1964 or 1965?]]

LITTLE WILLIE JOHN
See JOHN, (LITTLE) WILLIE

LITTLEFIELD, WILLIE, 1931-
guitar, piano, vocal

L117 MOHR, Kurt: Little Willie Little-field in Blues Unlimited, No. 34 (July 1966): 10 ((2, 3, 7))

LITTLEJOHN, JOHNNY, 1931-
guitar, vocal

L118 LEADBITTER, Mike: Discographies: Johnnny Little John in Alley Music, No. 1 (first quarter 1971): 19-20 ((2, 7))

LIVINGSTON, FUD (Joseph Anthony Livingston), 1906-1957
clarinet, saxophones

L119 VENABLES, Ralph: [Additions to listing in Delaunay's Hot discography] in Jazz Information, Vol. 1 (May 24, 1940): 2

LLOYD, CHARLES, 1938-
saxophones

L120 FRESIA, Enzo: Discografia di Charles Lloyd (dischi editi sotto su nome) in Musica Jazz, Vol. 22 (August-September 1966): 20 ((2, 7))

L121 WILBRAHAM, Roy J.: Charles Lloyd in Jazz Monthly, Vol. 12 (December 1966): 24-26; additions and corrections in Jazz Monthly, No. 153 (November 1967): 28 ((2, 7))

LOEVENDIE, THEO, 1930-
saxophones

L122 Discography in Key Notes, No. 5 (1977): 40 ((—))

LOFTON, CLARENCE, 1887-1957
piano

L123 BAKKER, Dick M.: Cripple Clarence Lofton 27-43 in Micrography, No. 31 (1974): 9 ((7d))

L124 HALL, Bob, and Richard NOBLETT: [Discography of his recordings as a sideman] in Blues Unlimited, No. 113 (May-June 1975): 14-15 ((2, 3, 6, 7, 9))

L125 McCARTHY, Albert: Discography in Jazz Monthly, Vol. 3 (November 1957): 31-32; additions and corrections from George HULME in Jazz Monthly, Vol. 3 (February 1958): 32 ((2, 3, 6, 7))

L126 McCARTHY, Albert: Discography in Jazz Music, No. 1/2/3 (1943): 25 ((2, 3, 7p))

L127 OLDEREN, Martin van: Cripple Clarence Lofton in Boogie Woogie & Blues Collector, No. 24 (January 1973): 5-6 ((3, 6, 7))

LOMA label

L128 MOHR, Kurt, and Peter GIBBON: Loma label listing in Soul, No. 3 (April 1966): 25-26 [nos. 2001-2011] ((3))

L129 PETARD, Gilles: The Loma singles in Soul Bag, No. 59 (March 1977): 3-6 [nos. 2001-2006] ((3, 5))

LONDON, MEL
record producer

L130 Discography: first discography of Mel London and latter day labels in Blue Flame, No. 17/18 (n.d.): 26 ((3))

L131 TURNER, Bez: Mel London's labels in Blues Unlimited, No. 125 (July-August 1977): 13-15; additions and corrections in Blues Unlimited, No. 126 (September-October 1977): 17 ((3))

LONDON label (British)

L132 HAESLER, WILLIAM J.: London--Jazz
Archive series in Matrix, No. 2
(September 1954) to No. 6 (May
1955); No. 8 (September 1955);
No. 9 (December 1955), various
paginations ((2, 3, 6, 7))

LONDON JAZZ label (British)
See LYTTELTON, HUMPHREY (Carey,
Dave)

LONESOME SUNDOWN (Cornelius Green),
1928-
guitar, piano, vocal

L133 BROVEN, J. J.: Discography of
Lonesome Sundown in Jazz Statistics, No. 28 (December 1962):
BLUES-7; additions and corrections from Mike LEADBITTER in
Blues Statistics, No. 2 (March
1963): 2-3 ((2, 3, 7))

LOUISIANA FIVE
See JAZZ MUSIC (Jewson, Ron) and
(Lange, Horst H.)

LOUISIANA RED (Red Minter), 1936-
guitar, harmonica

L134 Louisiana Red LP-listing in Jazz
Press, No. 38 (May 13, 1977): 15
((—))

LOUISIANA RHYTHM KINGS

L135 WATERS, Howard J.: The Louisiana
Rhythm Kings in Record Research,
No. 44 (July 1962): 5-7 ((2, 3,
6, 7))

LOUISVILLE SERENADERS
See HENDRICKSON, HENNY

LOVE, PRESTON
alto saxophone

L136 MOHR, Kurt: Discography of Preston Love in Jazz Statistics, No.
6 (October 1957): 9-10 ((2, 3, 7))

LOVE, WILLIE, 1911-1957
piano, vocal

L137 LEADBITTER, Mike: The southern
blues singers 2...Willie Love in
Blues Unlimited, No. 6 (November
1963): 4-5 ((2, 3, 7))

LOVE WITH A FEELING (tune title)
See BLUES MUSIC (Groom, Bob)

LOWERY, ENNIS
See DALE, LARRY

LUCAS, BILL, 1918-
guitar, vocal

L138 Lazy Bill Lucas discography in
Whiskey, Women and..., No. 6
(March 1974): 22 ((2, 7))

LUCKY label (Japanese)

L139 NISHIJIMA, Tony, and Ed RESKE:
The Lucky discography in IAJRC
Journal, Vol. 2 (January 1969):
12-13; (July 1969): 14-15 ((—))

LUNCEFORD, JIMMIE, 1902-1947
leader

L140 BAKKER, Dick M: Jimmie Lunceford
'27-'46 in Micrography, No. 38
(October 1975): 5-7 ((1, 6, 7d))

L141 BAKKER, Dick M: Jimmie Lunceford
Voc/Col 33-40 in Micrography, No.
45 (September 1977): 6 ((7d))

L142 DEMEULDRE, Leon: Disques de Jimmie
Lunceford actuellement achetables
en Belgique in Point du Jazz, No.
1 (September 1969): 13 ((—))

L143 Disques de Jimmie Lunceford actuellement disponibles en France
in Jazz Magazine, No. 29 (July-
August 1957): 33 ((—))

L144 [[DUTTON, Frank, and Leon
DEMEULDRE: Discography of the
Jimmy Lunceford Orchestra.
Brussels: 1961, 9 leaves]]

L145 DUTTON, Frank: Jimmie Lunceford;
the broadcasts and transcriptions
in Matrix, No. 86 (December 1969):
3-10 ((1, 2, 7, 9))

L146 EDWARDS, Ernie; George HALL; and
Bill KORST, eds.: Jimmie Lunceford. Whittier, CA: Jazz Discographies Unlimited, 1965, 12 leaves
((1, 2, 3, 6, 7))

L147 FLUCKIGER, Otto: Discography of
Jimmie Lunceford-Eddie Wilcox
concerning with 1945 in Jazz
Statistics, No. 15 (March 1960):
7-10; additions and corrections
from Michel VOGLER in Jazz Statistics, No. 17 (1960): 6; No. 22
(June 1961): 3 ((1, 2, 3, 7))

L148 FRESIA, Enzo: Discografia italiana di Jimmie Lunceford in Musica Jazz, Vol. 18 (July–August 1962): 31 ((2, 3, 7))

L149 HALL, Bill; Klaus STRATEMANN; and Dick M. BAKKER: Jimmie Lunceford broadcasts-transcriptions & film-tracks in Micrography, No. 42 (October 1976): 14-17 ((1, 7d))

L150 Jimmie Lunceford and his Orchestra; a disco/solography in Matrix, No. 66/67 (September 1966): 3-27; additions and corrections in Matrix, No. 75 (February 1968): 13-14, 19; No. 78 (August 1968): 13; No. 83 (June 1969): 10; No. 85 (October 1969): 14 ((1, 2, 3, 6, 7, 9))

L151 Lunceford discography in Down Beat, Vol. 14 (July 20, 1947): 12-13 ((—))

LUNIVERSE label

L152 Luniverse Records in R and B Magazine, Vol. 1 (November 1970–February 1971): 37 ((3))

LUTCHER, NELLIE, 1915–
piano, vocal

L153 WIEDEMANN, Erik, and Dave DEXTER: Discographie de Nellie Lutcher in Jazz Hot, No. 46 (July–August 1950): 12 ((2, 3, 7))

LUTER, CLAUDE, 1923–
clarinet

L154 PASCOLI, Daniel: Discography of the band in Jazzfinder, Vol. 1 (July 1948): 6; additions and corrections in Discophile, No. 2 (October 1948): 9 ((1, 2, 3, 6, 7d))

L155 WHITTON, Doug: Claude Luter and his Orchestra in Discophile, No. 1 (August 1948): 10; additions and corrections in Discophile, No. 2 (October 1948): 9; No. 4 (February 1949): 8 ((2, 7))

LYONS, LONNIE (deceased)
piano, vocal

L156 LEADBITTER, Mike, and Kurt MOHR: Lonnie Lyons in Blues Unlimited, No. 37 (October 1966): 13 ((2, 3, 7))

LYRIC label
See KHOURY, GEORGE

LYTTELTON, HUMPHREY, 1921–
trumpet

L157 CAREY, Dave: Humphrey Lyttelton and his band; a discography of his "London Jazz" recordings in Discophile, No. 6 (June 1949): 13; additions and corrections in DAVIES, Ron, and Dave CAREY: Humphrey Lyttelton and his band in Discophile, No. 7 (August 1949): 8; No. 23 (April 1952): 8-9; No. 24 (June 1952): 12 [additions/corrections also add other labels] ((2, 3, 7))

L158 McSWAN, D. Norman: Discography in LYTTELTON, Humphrey: Second chorus. London: Macgibbon and Kee, 1958 (also London: Jazz Book Club, 1960), 179-198 ((2, 7))

L159 McSWAN, Norman, and Frank DUTTON: Humphrey Lyttelton; a discography in Matrix, No. 29/30 (August 1960): 3-29; additions and corrections in Matrix, No. 37 (November 1961): 14-15; No. 46 (April 1963): 12; No. 47 (June 1963): 11; No. 49 (October 1963): 14 ((1, 2, 3, 6, 7))

L160 STEWART-BAXTER, Derrick: A discography of Humphrey Lyttelton in Jazz Notes (Australia), No. 97 (October–November 1949): 13-15 ((1, 2, 3, 7))

M J R label

M1 LAING, Ralph: The specialist labels; a listing--Master Jazz Recordings in Jazz Journal, Vol. 29 (May 1976): 22-23 ((2, 7))

MPS label
See SABA/MPS label

M-PAC label

M2 MOHR, Kurt: M-Pac label listing in Shout, No. 85 (April 1973): 7-8 ((3, 5))

MABON, WILLIE, 1925–
piano

M3 MOHR Kurt, and Emmanuel CHOISNEL: Willie Mabon disco in Soul Bag,

No. 27 (June 1973): 3-5; additions and corrections in Soul Bag, No. 43/44 (November-December 1974): 13 ((2, 3, 7))

M4   Willie Mabon--discography in Blues Unlimited, No. 11 (April-May 1964): 5. ((2, 3, 7))

MAC
    See also Mc

MACEO, BIG
    See BIG MACEO

MACGREGOR TRANSCRIPTIONS
    See NICHOLS, RED (Backensto, Woody: The meandering Macgregors)

MACY'S label

M5   ROTANTE, Anthony: Macy's 5000 series in Discophile, No. 34 (February 1954): 10; additions and corrections in Discophile, No. 35 (April 1954): 14 ((3))

MADAME TUSSAUD'S DANCE ORCHESTRA

M6   The Madame Tussaud's Dance Orchestra in Matrix, No. 49 (October 1963): 8-9; additions and corrections in Matrix, No. 54 (August 1964): 16; No. 56 (December 1964): 12 ((2, 3, 6, 7))

MADISON, LOUIS "KID SHOTS," 1899-1948
    trumpet

M7   Louis "Kid Shots" Madison; a discography in Matrix, No. 18 (July 1958): 3-5 ((2, 3, 6, 7))

MAGIC SAM (Sam Maghett), 1937-1969
    guitar, vocal

M8   CHOISNEL, Emmanuel: Discographie de Magic Sam in Soul Bag, No. 18/19 (1972?): 6-8 ((2, 3, 7))

M9   PATERSON, Neil, and Mike LEADBITTER: A discography in Blues Unlimited, No. 7 (December 1963): 10 ((2, 3, 7))

M10   PATERSON, Neil: [Discography] in Blues Unlimited Collectors Classics, No. 8 (July 1965): 8 ((2, 3, 7))

M11   [[STRACHWITZ, Chris: [Discography]. Blues Unlimited booklet]]

MAGNIFICENTS (musical group)

M12   [[Discography in Soul Bag, No. 11]]

MAJESTIC label

M13   PORTER, Bob: Modern eyes-zing in Record Research, No. 159/160 (December 1978) to No. 167/168 (October 1979), various paginations [may also be in other issues] ((3))

MAKOWICZ, ADAM, 1940-
    piano

M14   Adam Makowicz selected discography in Jazz Forum (Poland), No. 45 (1977): 44 ((—))

M15   Discography in Jazz Forum (Poland), No. 32 (December 1974): 39 ((—))

MALTESE label

M16   WILSON, Jim: Maltese label discography in Hot Buttered Soul, No. 13 (December 1972): 6 ((—))

MANGIONE, CHUCK, 1940-
    flugelhorn

M17   DEVOGHELAERE, Mon: Chuck Mangione: deel 2 in Swingtime (Belgium), No. 41 (July 1979): 11-17 ((—))

M18   Mangione discography in Down Beat, Vol. 42 (May 8, 1975): 13 ((—))

MANNE, SHELLY, 1920-
    drums

M19   JEPSEN, Jorgen Grunnet: Shelly Manne diskografi (skivor inspelade under eget namn) in Orkester Journalen, Vol. 28 (March 1960): 30; (April 1960): 38 ((2, 3, 7))

MANONE, WINGY (Joseph Manone), 1904-
    trumpet

M20   AVAKIAN, George: Discography in MANONE, Wingy: Trumpet on the wing. Garden City, NY: Doubleday, 1948 (also London: Jazz Book Club, 1964): 240-256 ((2, 3, 7))

M21   Mannone [sic] discography in Jazz Notes (Australia), Vol. 1 (January 1, 1941): 11-12 ((2, 3, 7))

M22 TONKS, Eric: Wingy Mannone's [sic] records for Victor in Jazz Record (UK), No. 10 (February 1944): 4-6 ((2, 3, 7d))

M23 VENABLES, Ralph, and Eric TONKS: Wingy Manone on records; complete discography of Manone records, compiled by two of Britain's leading critics in Jazz Record (US), No. 25 (October 1944): 4-6, 11; additions and corrections in Jazz Record (US), No. 28 (January 1945): 7 ((2, 3, 7d))

M24 WHYATT, Bert: Discography of Joseph "Wingy" Mannone [sic] in Jazz Journal, Vol. 3 (September 1950): 18-19; (October 1950): 15, 19; additions and corrections in Jazz Journal, Vol. 4 (May 1951): 17 ((2, 3, 6, 7))

M25 Wingy Manone recordings for Gilt Edge in Matrix, No. 49 (October 1963): 17-18; additions and corrections in Matrix, No. 51 (February 1964): 18; No. 57 (February 1965): 21 ((2, 3, 7))

MAPLE LEAF RAG (tune title)

M26 MITCHELL, Bill: Maple Leaf Rag on records in Rag Times, Vol. 1 (September 1967): 6-7; additions in More maple leaves in Rag Times, Vol. 1 (January 1968): 6; Vol. 2 (July 1968): 10; Vol. 3 (July-August 1969): 4, 11 (title varies) ((—))

MAR-V-LUS label

M27 MOHR, Kurt: Mar-V-Lus label list in Shout, No. 85 (April 1973): 6-7 ((3, 5))

MARABLE, FATE, 1890-1947
piano, leader

M28 The (incomplete) story of Fate Marable's orchestras in Jazz Statistics, No. 8 (January 1959): 2, 4-5, 7 ((2, 3, 6, 7))

MARIANO, TOSHIKO
See AKIYOSHI, TOSHIKO

MARMAROSA, DODO (Michael M. Marmarosa), 1925-
piano

M29 GIBSON, Frank: Dodo Marmarosa discography in Jazz Journal, Vol. 18 (May 1965): 37; (June 1965): 25-26; additions and corrections in Jazz Journal, Vol. 18 (December 1965): 43; [from Ken CRAWFORD] Vol. 19 (June 1966): 25-26 ((1, 2, 3, 6, 7))

MARSH, WARNE, 1927-
tenor saxophone
See also TRISTANO, LENNIE (Lennie Tristano & Warne Marsh)

M30 BLOMBERG, Lennart: Warne Marsh diskografi in Orkester Journalen, Vol. 37 (February 1969): 30 ((2, 3, 7))

M31 DELMAS, Jean: [Discography] in Jazz Hot, No. 326 (April 1976): 14-16 ((1, 2, 3, 7))

M32 EYLE, Wim van: Warne Marsh discografie in Jazz Press, No. 10 (January 21, 1976): 2; No. 11 (February 4, 1976): 2; No. 14 (March 17, 1976): 12; additions and corrections in Jazz Press, No. 29 (January 7, 1977): 6 ((1, 2, 7))

M33 EYLE, Wim van: Warne Marsh discography in Journal of Jazz Discography, No. 1 (November 1976): 5-10; additions and corrections in Journal of Jazz Discography, No. 2 (June 1977): 2-3 ((2, 3, 7))

M34 MORGAN, Alun: Discography in Jazz Monthly, Vol. 7 (June 1961): 8-9 ((2, 3, 7))

M35 Warne Marsh pa skiva in Orkester Journalen, Vol. 44 (January 1976): 6 ((—))

M36 WIEDEMANN, Erik: Discographie de Warne Marsh in Jazz Hot, No. 100 (June 1955): 16 ((2, 3, 7))

MARSHALL, JACK, 1921-1973
guitar

M37 Jack Marshall on Capitol in Different Drummer, Vol. 1 (February 1974): 14 ((—))

MARTERRY label
See ARGO label

MARTIN, JOE, 1904-
guitar, vocal

M38   EVANS, David: Discography in
       Blues World, No. 20 (July 1968):
       5 [excludes recordings with Mem-
       phis Minnie] ((3, 7))

MARTIN, SARA, 1884-1955
       vocal

M39   Sara Martin discography in Dis-
       cophile, No. 43 (August 1955):
       10-15; additions and corrections
       in Discophile, No. 45 (December
       1955): 16; No. 47 (April 1956):
       12; No. 49 (August 1956): 11 ((2,
       3, 6, 7))

MARTINO, PAT, 1944-
       guitar

M40   Selected Martino discography in
       Down Beat, Vol. 42 (October 9,
       1975): 16 ((—))

MASON, TONY, 1906-1976
       alto saxophone, clarinet

M41   ENGLUND, Bjorn: Tony Mason pa
       skiva in Orkester Journalen, Vol.
       37 (April 1969): 17 ((—))

MASTER JAZZ RECORDINGS
       See MJR label

MATHISEN, LEO, 1906-
       piano

M42   [[JØRGENSEN, Birger: Leo Mathisen.
       Copenhagen: Erichsen, 1962, 76
       pp.]]

MATTHEWS, DAVE, 1911-
       saxophones, arranger

M43   [[ELLIOTT, Bill, and Jeff ALDAM:
       [Discography] in Melody Maker
       [issue(s) unknown]; additions and
       corrections from Carlo KRAHMER and
       O. H. BRYCE in Melody Maker, Vol.
       18 (August 1, 1942): 6]]

MATTHEWS, SHIRLEY

M44   [[Discography in Soul Bag, No. 5]]

MAUPIN, BENNIE, 1946-
       tenor saxophone

M45   Bennie Maupin discography in Down
       Beat, Vol. 42 (May 22, 1975): 18
       ((—))

MAYFIELD, PERCY, 1920-
       piano, vocal

M46   MOHR, Kurt, and Bernard NIQUET:
       Discographie in Jazz Hot, No. 273
       (June 1971): 19 ((2, 7))

M47   MOHR, Kurt, and Bernard NIQUET:
       Essai de discographie de Percy
       Mayfield in Point du Jazz, No. 14
       (June 1978): 69-71 ((2, 3, 7))

McBOOKER, CONNIE
       piano, vocal

M48   LEADBITTER, Mike: Connie McBooker
       discography in Blues Unlimited,
       No. 33 (May-June 1966): 6 ((3, 7))

McCAIN, JERRY, 1930-
       guitar, harmonica, vocal

M49   LEADBITTER, Mike: Jerry "Boogie"
       McCain in Blues Unlimited, No. 35
       (August 1966): 9 ((3, 7))

McCALL, CASH (Maurice Dollison)
       guitar, vocal

M50   MOHR, Kurt: Cash McCall in Soul
       Bag, No. 45 (January 1975): 25;
       additions and corrections in Soul
       Bag, No. 46 (February 1975): 6
       ((2, 3, 7))

McCANN, LES, 1935-
       piano

M51   Current discography in Different
       Drummer, Vol. 1 (January 1975):
       30 ((—))

McCLENNAN, TOMMY, 1908-ca. 1960?
       guitar, vocal

M52   BAKKER, Dick M.: Tommy McClennon
       [sic] in Micrography, No. 7 (No-
       vember 1969): 11 ((7d))

M53   FORMAN, E. C.: A discography of
       Tommy McClennon [sic], blues
       singer in Discophile, No. 40
       (February 1955): 3; additions and
       corrections in Discophile, No. 45
       (December 1955): 16-17; No. 47
       (April 1956): 12 ((2, 3, 6, 7))

McCLENNON, GEORGE, 1891-1937
       clarinet

M54   Discography--George McClennon in
       Record Research, No. 66 (February
       1965): 5, 9 ((2, 3, 7))

McCOY, JOE, 1905-1950
guitar, vocal

M55 OLIVER, Paul: [Discography] in Discographical Forum, No. 4 (January 1961): 17 ((2, 3, 6, 7))

McCOY, LEE
harmonica

M56 OLIVER, Paul: Lee McCoy (harmonica); a provisional listing in Discographical Forum, No. 2 (July 1960): 4-6; additions and corrections in Discographical Forum, No. 3 (September 1960): 15 ((2, 3, 6, 7))

McCRACKLIN, JIMMY, 1921-
piano, vocal

M57 LEADBITTER, Mike; Kurt MOHR; and Marcel CHAUVARD: Discography of Jimmy McCracklin in Jazz Statistics, No. 23 (December 1962): BLUES-1 to BLUES-4; additions and corrections in Blues Statistics, No. 2 (March 1963): 1-2 ((2, 3, 6, 7))

McCRAE, DARLENE, GEORGE, and GWEN
vocal

M58 MOHR, Kurt: Discographie de George McCrae, etc. in Soul Bag, No. 43/44 (November-December 1974): 4-5 ((2, 3, 7))

McDONOUGH, DICK, 1904-1938
guitar

M59 WHITE, Bozy: Dick McDonough and his Orchestra in Discophile, No. 21 (December 1951): 11-12, 19; additions and corrections in Discophile, No. 45 (December 1955): 17; [from Albert McCARTHY] in Jazz Monthly, Vol. 5 (July 1959): 22 ((—))

McFADDEN, CHARLIE
saxophones

M60 McCARTHY, Albert J.: Discography of Charlie McFadden in Discographical Forum, No. 3 (September 1960): 7-8; additions and corrections from Paul OLIVER in Discographical Forum, No. 4 (January 1961): 15 ((2, 3, 6, 7))

McGHEE, BROWNIE (Walter Brown McGhee), 1915-
guitar, vocal

M61 COLLER, Derek: A discography of Brownie McGhee in Jazz Notes (Australia), No. 88 (October-November 1948): 8 ((2))

M62 ROTANTE, Anthony: Brownie McGhee; a discography in Discophile, No. 28 (February 1953): 9-13; additions and corrections in Discophile, No. 29 (May 1953): 15-16; No. 30 (June 1953): 10; No. 34 (February 1954): 12; No. 35 (April 1954): 14-15; No. 45 (December 1955): 17; No. 61 (December 1958): 4-7, 20 ((2, 3, 7))

McGHEE, HOWARD, 1918-
trumpet

M63 [[BOENZLI, Richard E.: Discography of Howard McGhee. Basel: 1961, 32 pp.]]

M64 HOEFER, George: Early McGhee recordings in Down Beat, Vol. 30 (August 15, 1963): 34 [1942-1943] ((2, 3, 7))

M65 MORGAN, Alun: Howard McGhee--a name discography in Jazz Journal, Vol. 19 (January 1966): 14; (February 1966): 29; additions and corrections in Jazz Journal, Vol. 19 (November 1966): 38; [from Mark GARDNER] Vol. 20 (May 1967): 24 ((2, 3, 6, 7))

M66 MORGAN, Alun: Howard McGhee--a name listing in Discographical Forum, No. 3 (September 1960): 2-6, 18; additions and corrections in Discographical Forum, No. 4 (January 1961): 10 ((2, 3, 6, 7))

M67 URBAN, Georgia: Howard McGhee in Different Drummer, Vol. 1 (September 1974): 20 ((—))

McGHEE, STICKS (Granville H. McGhee), 1918-1961
guitar, vocal

M68 MITCHELL, Stuart, and Mike LEADBITTER: The unheralded Sticks McGhee in Blues Unlimited, No. 31 (March 1966): 7-8 ((2, 3, 7))

McGREGOR, CHRIS, 1936–
     piano

M69   Chris McGregor selected discography in Jazz Forum (Poland), No. 46 (1977): 43 ((—))

McINTYRE, HAL, 1914–1959
     leader

M70   GARROD, Charles: Hal McIntyre and his Orchestra. Spotswood, NJ: Joyce Music, 1974, 19, 3 leaves ((1, 2, 3, 4t, 6, 7))

McKAY, MARION, 1898–
     leader

M71   PLATH, Warren K.: Marion McKay and his Orchestra in Storyville, No. 60 (August–September 1975): 204–207 ((2, 3, 6, 7))

McKENNA, DAVE, 1930–
     piano

M72   [[MIDDLETON, Tony: [Discography] in Jazz Guide, January 1969]]

McKENZIE, RED (William McKenzie), 1899–1948
     kazoo, vocal
     See also MOUND CITY BLUE BLOWERS

M73   BAKKER, Dick M: Red McKenzie and the Mound City Blue Blowers in Micrography, No. 49 (December 1978): 20 ((—))

M74   CAREY, Dave: Red McKenzie in Jazz Journal, Vol. 17 (March 1964): 38 ((2, 3, 6, 7))

McKINLEY, BILL
     See GILLUM, JAZZ

McKINLEY, RAY, 1910–
     drums
     See also BRADLEY, WILL

M75   EDWARDS, Ernie, ed.: Ray McKinley Orchestra. Whittier, CA: ErnGeo-Bil, 1967, 19 leaves ((1, 2, 3, 6, 7))

McKINNEY'S COTTON PICKERS

M76   BAKKER, Dick M.: McKinney's Cotton Pickers 1928–31 in Micrography, No. 11 (September 1970): 5 ((7d))

M77   BAKKER, Dick M.: McKinney's Cotton Pickers 1928–31 in Micrography, No. 22 (October 1972): 4 [rev. ed. of previous entry] ((7d))

M78   CHILTON, John: [Discography] in his McKinney's music; a bio-discography of McKinney's Cotton Pickers. London: Bloomsbury Book Shop, 1978, 56–62 ((2, 3, 6, 7, 9))

M79   CHILTON, John; John R. T. DAVIES; and Laurie WRIGHT: McKinney's in Storyville, No. 32 (December 1970–January 1971): 63–64; No. 33 (February–March 1971): 98–103 ((2, 3, 6, 7, 8, 9))

McLAUGHLIN, JOHN 1942–
     guitar

M80   DELORME, Michel, and Alain TERCINET: Discographie de John McLaughlin in Jazz Hot, No. 269 (February 1971): 14 ((2, 7))

M81   Selected McLaughlin discography in Down Beat, Vol. 45 (June 15, 1978): 14 ((—))

McLAUGHLIN'S MELODIANS
     See BUFFALODIANS

McLEAN, JACKIE (John Lenwood McLean), 1932–
     alto saxophone

M82   ATKINS, Ronald, and Michael JAMES: Jackie McLean discography in Jazz Monthly, Vol. 5 (January 1960): 24–26 ((2, 3, 7))

M83   JEPSEN, Jorgen Grunnet: Jackie McLean discography in Jazz Statistics, No. 5 (April 1957): 2–3 ((2, 3, 7d))

M84   Selected discography in Jazz Forum (Poland), No. 61 (1979): 37 ((—))

M85   Selected McLean discography in Down Beat, Vol. 42 (April 10, 1975): 32 ((—))

M86   [[WILBRAHAM, Roy J.: Jackie McLean, a biography and discography. London: 1968, ii, 16 pp. ((2, 3, 7))]]

McNEELY, JAY, 1928?–
     alto and tenor saxophones

M87 ROTANTE, Anthony: A discography of Big Jay McNeely in Discophile, No. 32 (October 1953): 11, 10; additions and corrections in Discophile, No. 35 (April 1954): 15; No. 39 (December 1954): 17-18 ((3))

McPARTLAND, JIMMY, 1907–
    trumpet

M88 TEALDO ALIZIERI, Carlos L.: Discografia de Jimmy McPartland in Jazz Magazine (Argentina), No. 5 (January 1946): 16-20 ((2))

McPHEE, JOE
    tenor saxophone

M89 [[Discographie de Joe McPhee in Jazz 360, No. 9 (June 1978): 4-6]]

M90 Discographie Joe McPhee in Jazz Magazine (France), No. 275 (May 1979): 60 ((2))

M91 Joe McPhee discography/Discographie de Joe McPhee in Jazz Hot, No. 329 (July 1976): 31 ((—))

McPHERSON, CHARLES, 1939–
    alto saxophone

M92 GARDNER, Mark: Charles McPherson discography in Jazz Monthly, No. 183 (May 1970): 25-27; additions and corrections in Jazz Monthly, No. 185 (July 1970): 26 ((2, 6, 7))

McSHANN, JAY, 1909–
    piano
    See also PARKER, CHARLIE (Hoefer, George)

M93 Discographie "33t 30cm" de Jay McShann in Jazz Hot, No. 235 (October 1967): 25 ((2, 7))

McTELL, BLIND WILLIE, 1901-1959
    guitar, vocal

M94 BAKKER, Dick M.: Blind Willie McTell 27-35 in Micrography, No. 4 (June 1969): 11; additions and corrections in Micrography, No. 5 (August 1969): 12 ((—))

M95 BAKKER, Dick M.: Blind Willie McTell 1927-1956 in Micrography, No. 32 (1974): 11 [rev. ed. of previous entry] ((7d))

M96 CHARTERS, Samuel B.: The blues of Blind Willie McTell in Record Research, No. 23 (June-July 1959): 11-12; supplemented in his Blind Willie McTell--a last session in Record Research, No. 37 (August 1961): 20; additions and corrections in Recorded Americana (Record Research Bulletin), No. 10 (1959): 1; No. 11 (n.d.): 1 ((2, 3, 7))

M97 DAVIS, John, and C. G. GRAY-CLARKE: Blind Willie McTell; a discography in Jazz Journal, Vol. 3 (August 1950): 6 ((3))

M98 LP listing van Blind Willie McTell in Jazz Press, No. 39 (May 27, 1977): 9 ((—))

McVEA, JACK, 1914–
    tenor and alto saxophones

M99 MOHR, Kurt: Jack McVea--his discography in Discophile, No. 13 (August 1950): 14-17; additions and corrections in Discophile, No. 23 (April 1952): 6-7; No. 24 (June 1952): 12 ((2, 3, 7))

MEL or MEL-LON label
    See LONDON, MEL

MELLOWS (musical group)

M100 The Mellows in Quartette, No. 2 (March 1970): 26 ((3))

MELODISC label (British)

M101 HULME, G. W. George: A discography of "Melodisc" records in Discophile, No. 27 (December 1952): 6-10 ((2, 3, 7))

MELODY MAKER ALL STARS

M102 EVANS, CHRIS: Melody Maker All Stars in Journal of Jazz Discography, No. 3 (March 1978): 6; additions and corrections in Journal of Jazz Discography, No. 4 (January 1979): 18-19 ((2, 3, 7))

MELOTONE label
    See BANNER label (Complete numerical of Banner Melotone Oriole Perfect Romeo, 1935-1938)

MELROSE, FRANK, 1907-1941
piano

M103 EDELSTEIN, Sanford M., and Morty
NOVICK: Frank Melrose discography
in Jazz Record (US), No. 45 (June
1946): 11, 18 ((2, 3, 6, 7))

M104 STEINER, John: Discography in
McCARTHY, Albert J., and Max
JONES, eds.: Piano Jazz No. 1.
London: Jazz Sociological So-
ciety, 1945, 9-10 ((3, 6))

MELROSE label

M105 WIEDEMANN, Erik: Melrose records;
a label discography in Discophile, No. 22 (February 1952): 9
((2, 3, 7))

MEMPHIS JUG BAND

M106 ALLEN, Walter C.: Discography of
Memphis Jug Band and allied
groups in Jazz Monthly, Vol. 4
(February 1959): 4-5, 31; Vol. 5
(March 1959): 24-25, 30 [also
includes Cannon's Jug Stompers]
((2, 3, 6, 7))

M107 BAKKER, Dick M.: Memphis Jug Band
in Micrography, No. 2 (February
1969): 9; additions and corrections in Micrography, No. 5 (August 1969): 12 ((—))

MEMPHIS MINNIE (neé Lizzie Douglas;
later Lizzie McCoy), 1897-1973
guitar, vocal

M108 BAKKER, Dick M.: Memphis Minnie
in Micrography, No. 3 (May 1969):
8; additions and corrections in
Micrography, No. 5 (August 1969):
12 ((—))

M109 [[MOODY, Peter: Memphis Minnie.
Bristol: 1968, ca. 22 pp.]]

MEMPHIS SLIM (Peter Chatman), 1915-
piano, vocal

M110 Discography of Memphis Slim.
Basel: Jazz-Publications, 1962,
12 pp. (Discographical notes,
Vol. 2) ((2, 3, 6, 7))

M111 KNIGHT, Brian: Discography in
Jazz Journal, Vol. 15 (April
1962): 6-7; (May 1962): 18-19
((2, 3, 6, 7))

M112 ROTANTE, Anthony: A discography
of Peter Chatman alias Memphis

Slim in Discophile, No. 26 (October 1952): 11-13; additions and
corrections in Discophile, No. 27
(December 1952): 16; No. 29 (May
1953): 14 ((2, 3, 6, 7))

M113 ROTANTE, Anthony, and Marcel
CHAUVARD: Memphis Slim--Peter
Chatman; revised discography in
Record Research, No. 40 (January
1962): 12; No. 41 (February 1962):
9 [recordings to ca. 1952] ((2,
3, 7))

M114 ROTANTE, Anthony: A name discography of Peter Chatman, alias
Memphis Slim in Discophile, No.
53 (April 1957): 5-8; additions
and corrections in Discophile,
No. 59 (April 1958): 8; in
BRUYNOGHE, Yannick: Recording the
blues: Memphis Slim in Vintage
Jazz Mart, No. 1 (February 1961):
9-10 ((2, 3, 6, 7))

MERCER, MAE

M115 [[VERNON, Mike: [Discography] in
R and B Monthly, No. 10 (November
1964)]]

MERCER label

M116 JACOBS, Irving L.: Mercer; a discography of the original recordings in Discophile, No. 27 (December 1952): 18-21; additions
and corrections in Discophile,
No. 29 (May 1953): 9 ((2, 3, 7))

M117 SIMONS, Sim: Mercer label in
Swingtime (Belgium), No. 25 (November 1977): 6-12; No. 28 (February 1978): 12-15 ((2, 3, 7, 9))

MERCURY label

M118 MOHR, Kurt: Mercury Records; some
information on this label's
lesser known artists in Discophile, No. 54 (June 1957): 11-13
((2, 3, 7))

M119 SEROFF, Doug: Professor Longhair
and Duke Burrell with George
Miller and his Mid-Driffs; the
Mercury session in Living Blues,
No. 43 (summer 1979): 5 ((3, 6))

MERCY DEE (Mercy Dee Walton), 1915-1962
piano, vocal

M120 ROTANTE, Anthony: The records of
Mercy Dee Walton in Record Re-

search, No. 32 (January 1961):
9 ((3, 8))

MERITT label

M121 RANDOLPH, John: A discography of
Meritt records in Jazz Journal,
Vol. 10 (February 1957): 11 ((3))

METCALF, LOUIS, 1905-
trumpet

M122 KUNSTADT, Len: Provisional discography (from 1955) in Record
Research, No. 86 (September 1967):
4 ((2, 3, 7))

METERS (musical group)

M123 [[[Discography] in Soul Bag, No.
9/10]]

M124 MOHR, Kurt, and Gilles PETARD:
Meters' discography in Soul Bag,
No. 26 (May 1973): 13-15 ((2, 3,
7))

METHENY, PAT, 1955?-
guitar

M125 Pat Metheny discography in Jazz
Forum (Poland), No. 54 (1978):
42 ((—))

METRONOME label (Swedish)
See also ARNOLD, HARRY

M126 NYSTROM, Borje: A discography of
the Swedish company Metronome in
Discophile, No. 15 (December
1950): 9-11; additions and corrections in Discophile, No. 16
(February 1951): 11; No. 17
(April 1951): 17 ((2, 3, 7d))

METRONOME ALL STARS

M127 ALVAREZ, Horacio: Discografia de
las "All Star Bands" in Jazz
Magazine (Argentina), No. 36 (November-December 1952): 6-8 ((2,
3, 6, 7d))

M128 [[EVANS, Chris: Metronome All
Stars in Journal of Jazz Discography, No. 1 (November 1976): 14;
additions and corrections in
Journal of Jazz Discography, No.
2 (June 1977): 4]]

M129 [[HEIN, Walther: [Discography,
1938-1950] in Jazz Podium, Vol.
14 (January 1965)]]

M130 KRANER, Dietrich: The Metronome
All Star bands; a listing in Matrix, No. 76 (April 1968): 3-6;
additions and corrections in Matrix, No. 83 (June 1969): 10-11;
No. 90 (December 1970): 14 ((2,
3, 6, 7))

METTOME, DOUG, 1925-1964
trumpet

M131 BURNS, Jim: Records in Jazz Journal, Vol. 28 (June 1975): 22
((—))

MEZZROW, MEZZ (Milton Mesirow), 1899-
1972
clarinet

M132 BAKKER, Dick M.: Mezz Mezzrow-
Tommy Ladnier-Frankie Newton
Victor recording in Micrography,
No. 25 (March 1973): 10 ((7d))

M133 LAMBERT, Eddie: King Jazz in Jazz
& Blues, Vol. 2 (August 1972) to
(November 1972), various paginations [1945-1947 recordings] ((2,
3, 6, 7))

M134 PHYTHIAN, Les: Mezzrow-Bechet on
King Jazz; a provisional listing
in Melody Maker, Vol. 27 (January
27, 1951): 9; additions and corrections in Melody Maker, Vol. 27
(February 3, 1951): 9 ((2, 3, 7))

M135 TONKS, Eric: Discography of Mezz
Mezzrow in New Orleans & Chicago
jazz; a pamphlet published for
the Discographical Society. London: Clifford Jones, 1944, 19-22
((2, 3, 7))

M136 TOWNLEY, Eric P.: Mezz Mezzrow
discography in Jazz Monthly, Vol.
2 (August 1956): 27-29; (September 1956): 26-28 ((1, 2, 3, 6, 7))

MICHALL, KID ERNEST, d. 1930
clarinet

M137 GERT ZUR HEIDE, Karl: Clyde, Mike
& the Whitman sisters in Footnote,
Vol. 8 (February-March 1977): 16-
21 ((2, 3, 7))

MICKLE, ELMON, 1919-
harmonica, vocal

M138 VESTINE, Henry, and Bruce BROM-
BERG: Driftin' Slim discography
in Blues Unlimited, No. 40 (January 1967): 8 ((2, 3, 7))

MIDNIGHTERS (musical group)
See ROYALS

MIKIM label

M139 SIMONDS, Roy, and Ian SLATER:
Mikim label listing in Hot Buttered Soul, No. 30 (May 1974): 15
((3))

MILENBURG JOYS (tune title)
See also TIGER RAG (tune title)
(Madison, Joseph: Most up-to-date
Tiger rag-Milenburg joys listing)

M140 MADISON, Joe: A suggested discography of Milenburg joys in Jazz
Discounter, Vol. 2 (July 1949): 3
((—))

MILES, LIZZIE (nee Elizabeth Mary
Landreaux, later Pajaud), 1895-
1963
vocal

M141 DAVIES, Ron: Discography of
Lizzie Miles in Jazz Music, Vol.
3 (No. 3, 1946): 15-16; additions
and corrections in Jazz Music,
Vol. 3 (No. 8, 1948): 18; Vol. 3
(No. 9, 1948): 19; Vol. 4 (No. 1,
1949): 13 ((2))

M142 WHYATT, Bert, and Derek COLLER:
Discography of Lizzie Miles in
Jazz Music, Vol. 5, No. 4 (n.d.):
5-7; Vol. 5, No. 8 (1954): 23-26;
additions and corrections in Jazz
Music, Vol. 6, No. 3 (1955): 31;
Vol. 6, No. 4 (1955): 9 [rev. ed.
of previous entry] ((2, 3, 7d))

MILEY, BUBBER (James Wesley Miley),
1903-1932
trumpet

M143 HELLIWELL, Geoffrey, and Peter
TAYLOR: A discography of Bubber
Miley in Jazz Journal, Vol. 3
(August 1950): 13-14 ((2, 3, 6,
7))

MILLER, EDDIE, 1911-
tenor saxophone

M144 COLLER, Derek; Ralph VENABLES;
and Bert WHYATT: Discography of
the Eddie Miller Orchestra in
Discophile, No. 5 (April 1949):
8-10; additions and corrections
in Discophile, No. 10 (February
1950): 10 ((2, 3, 7))

MILLER, GEORGE
See MERCURY label (Seroff, Doug)

MILLER, HARRY, 1941-
bass violin

M145 Discography in Impetus, No. 8
(1978): 366 ((—))

M146 LEEUWEN, Frans van: Discografie:
Harry Miller in Jazz Nu, Vol. 1
(September 1979): 567 ((7d))

MILLER, PUNCH (Ernest Miller), 1894-
1971
trumpet

M147 ALLEN, Walter C.: Punch Miller
discography in Hot Notes, Vol. 2
(July-August 1947): 3-5 ((2, 3,
6, 7))

M148 DAVIES, Ron: Punch Miller discography in Pickup, Vol. 1 (June
1946): 8; additions and corrections in Pickup, Vol. 1 (July
1946): 10 ((—))

M149 KELLEY, L. A., and Keith JOHNSON:
Ernest "Kid Punch" Miller—a draft
discography in Melody Maker, Vol.
26 (July 22, 1950): 9; additions
and corrections [from Brian RUST]
in Melody Maker, Vol. 26 (August
12, 1950): 9; [from Bert HARPER]
(August 19, 1950): 9 ((2, 3, 7d))

M150 LAVINE, Steve: Punch Miller 1925-
30 in Micrography, No. 41 (May
1976): 8-9 ((6, 7d))

MILLER, SODARISSA
vocal

M151 DAVIS, Brian G.: Gabbin' blues in
Jazz Report (California), Vol. 1
(April 1961): w13; additions and
corrections from Jack PARSONS,
John GODRICH, and Paul OLIVER in
Jazz Report (California), Vol. 1
(July 1961): 1 (pink section)
((2, 3, 6))

MILLER, TAPS, 1915-
tap dancing, vocal

M152 NIQUET, Bernard: Taps Miller in
Jazz, Blues & Co., No. 18/19/20
(summer 1978): 7 ((3, 7d))

MILLERS (musical group)

M153 [[ZWARTENKOT, Henk: De Millers
disco in Doctor Jazz, No. 85

(September 1978): 39-41; No. 86
(December 1978): 18-21]]

MILLINDER, LUCKY (Lucius Millinder),
1900-1966
leader

M154 Discography of Lucky Millinder.
Basel: Jazz-Publications, 1962,
26 pp. ((2, 3, 7))

MILLS, IRVING, 1894-
leader

M155 BAKKER, Dick M.: Irving Mills and
his Hotsy-Totsy Gang 1928-1930 in
Micrography, No. 10 (May 1970):
12 ((7d))

M156 VENABLES, Ralph, ed.: Irving Mills
miscellany; previously unpublished
data on some obscure Variety and
Master sessions of 1936-37 in Discophile, No. 11 (April 1950): 2-4,
13 ((2, 3, 7d))

MILLS BLUE RHYTHM BAND

M157 BAKKER, Dick M.: Mill's [sic]
Blue Rhythm Band 1931-36 in Micrography, No. 22 (October 1972):
2-3 ((7d))

M158 BAKKER, Dick M.: Mills Blue Rhythm
Band 1931-1937 in Micrography, No.
43 (March 1977): 10-11 ((6, 7d))

MILLS BROTHERS

M159 DAVIES, John R. T.: The Mills
Brothers 1931-1934 in Storyville,
No. 6 (August-September 1966):
14-15 ((2, 3, 6, 7))

MILTON, ROY, 1907-
drums, vocal

M160 Discography in Jazz Statistics,
No. 18 (1960): 7-10; additions
and corrections from Michel VOGLER
in Jazz Statistics, No. 22 (June
1961): 4 ((2, 3, 6, 7))

M161 HANSEN, Barry: Roy Milton on
Specialty in R and B Magazine,
Vol. 1 (July-October 1970): 9-13
((2, 7))

M162 MOHR, Kurt, and Bernard NIQUET:
Discographie de Roy Milton in
Point du Jazz, No. 7 (October
1972): 121-126; additions and
corrections in Point du Jazz, No.
8 (April 1973): 126-127; No. 10

(October 1974): 111-112 ((2, 3,
6, 7))

M163 SEROFF, Doug: Roy Milton and Mil-
tone Records in Blues Unlimited,
No. 115 (September-October 1975):
10-17 ((—))

MINGUS, CHARLES, 1922-1979
bass violin
See also NORVO, Red (Kraner,
Dietrich H.)

M164 COSS, Bill: The music in Charles
Mingus. New York: BMI, c1961 ((2))

M165 Discography of Charles Mingus.
Basel: Jazz-Publications, 1962,
8 pp. (Discographical Notes, Vol.
5) ((2, 3, 7))

M166 Diskographie/Charles Mingus
übersicht in Blues Notes, No.
1&2/79 (1979): 78; No. 3/79
(1979): 55-56 ((—))

M167 EYLE, Wim van: Charles Mingus op
de plaat in Jazz Nu, Vol. 1 (February 1979): 248-249 ((—))

M168 Farewell to Mingus in Swing Journal, Vol. 33 (March 1979): 68-71
((2, 7d))

M169 KRANER, Dietrich H.: Private recordings: Mingus in Europe 1964;
a list of private recordings in
Discographical Forum, No. 10 (January 1969): 11 ((1, 2, 7, 9))

M170 RUPPLI, Michel: Discographie de
Charles Mingus in Jazz Hot, No.
337 (May 1977): 26-29; No. 338
(June 1977): 20-23; additions and
corrections in Jazz Hot, No. 342
(October 1977): 30 ((1, 2, 3, 7))

M171 Selected Mingus discography in
Down Beat, Vol. 42 (February 27,
1975): 13 ((—))

M172 WALKER, Malcolm: Charlie Mingus
discography in Jazz Monthly, Vol.
6 (April 1960): 26-27, 30; (May
1960): 24-25, 30-31; (June 1960):
24; additions and corrections
from Erik RABEN in Jazz Monthly,
Vol. 6 (November 1960): 31 ((2,
3, 6, 7))

M173 WILBRAHAM, Roy J.: Charles Mingus;
a discography with brief biography. London: 1967, iv, 28 pp.
((1, 2, 3, 6, 7))

M174 WILBRAHAM, Roy J.: Charles Mingus;
a discography with brief biography. rev. ed. London: 1970?, 35,
4 pp. ((1, 2, 3, 6, 7))

MINIT label

M175 [[[Listing] in Soul Bag, No. 14
    and 15]]

MIRWOOD label

M176 PETARD, Gilles: Mirwood label
    listing in Soul Bag, No. 16
    (1972?): 12, 14 ((3))

MISS RHAPSODY (Viola Gertrude Wells
    Underhill), 1902-
    vocal

M177 ROTANTE, Anthony: Miss Rhapsody
    in Record Research, No. 33 (March
    1961): 14 ((2, 3))

MISSOURIANS (musical group)

M178 FLUCKIGER, Otto: Interviewing
    Wendell Culley in Jazz Statis-
    tics, No. 4 (November 1956): 7-8
    [selective discography of Missour-
    ians and Cab Calloway 1929-1931]
    ((2, 3, 6, 9))

M179 SILVESTRI, Edgardo M.: The Mis-
    sourians in Jazz Magazine (Ar-
    gentina), No. 51 (December 1954):
    16; translated in Jazz Music,
    Vol. 10 (January-February 1959):
    7-8 ((2, 3, 6, 7d))

M180 TOWNLEY, Eric: Jazz Monthly, Vol.
    4 (July 1958): 32 ((2, 3, 6, 7))

MITCHELL, BILLY
    vocal

M181 ROTANTE, Anthony: The recordings
    of Billy Mitchell in Record Re-
    search, No. 36 (July 1961): 10
    [recordings on Blu label, 1949]
    ((—))

MITCHELL, BLUE (Richard Mitchell),
    1930-
    trumpet

M182 MOHR, Kurt: [Discography] in Jazz
    Statistics, No. 10 (May 1959):
    4-5 ((2, 3, 7))

M183 Selected Mitchell discography in
    Down Beat, Vol. 43 (May 20, 1976):
    19 ((—))

MITCHELL, BOBBY
    vocal

M184 HITE, Richard: Bobby Mitchell &
    the Toppers in R and B Magazine,
    No. 9 (March 1972): 16-17 ((3))

MITCHELL, FREDDIE
    tenor saxophone

M185 ROTANTE, Anthony: Some notes on
    Freddie Mitchell and others in
    Discophile, No. 37 (August 1954):
    11-13; additions and corrections
    in Discophile, No. 39 (December
    1954): 18 ((3))

MITCHELL, GEORGE, 1899-1972
    cornet

M186 ALLEN, Walter C.: George Mitchell
    discography in Hot Notes, Vol. 2
    (January 1947): 3-5; additions
    and corrections in Hot Notes,
    Vol. 2 (May-June 1947): 17 ((2,
    3, 6, 7))

M187 CABLE, Dave: A discography of
    George Mitchell in Jazz Journal,
    Vol. 3 (June 1950): 18; additions
    and corrections from Eric P.
    TOWNLEY in Jazz Journal, Vol. 3
    (August 1950): 16 ((2, 3, 6, 7))

MITCHELL, LOUIS, 1885-1957
    drums, leader

M188 CONTE, Gerard: Discographie;
    Mitchell's Jazz Kings in Jazz
    Hot, No. 244 (November 1968): 36
    ((2, 3))

M189 [[GILLET, Andre V.: The European
    recordings by Louis A. Mitchell.
    Brussels: 1957, 8 pp.]]

M190 [[GILLET, Andre V.: The European
    recordings by Louis A. Mitchell.
    2d ed. Brussels: 1957, 10 pp.]]

M191 [[GILLET, Andre V.: Louis A.
    Mitchell; bio-disco-bibliographie
    (alternate title: The Mitchell's
    Jazz Kings--discographie cri-
    tique). Brussels: 1966, 20 pp.]]

MITCHELL, McKINLEY

M192 MOHR, Kurt: McKinley Mitchell
    discography in Hot Buttered Soul,
    No. 12 (November 1972): 12 ((3,
    7))

MITCHELL, ROSCOE, 1940-
    saxophones

M193 SMITH, Bill, and John NORRIS:
Discography in Coda, No. 141
(September 1975): 9-10 ((2, 7))

MJR label
See M J R label

MO SOUL label

M194 JAFFIER, Patrick: Mo Soul label
listing in Soul Bag, No. 47
(March 1975): 9 ((3))

MOBLEY, HANK, 1930-
tenor saxophone

M195 FLUCKIGER, Otto: Discography of
Hank Mobley in Jazz Statistics,
No. 2 (June 1956): 7-8 ((2, 7, 9))

M196 JEPSEN, Jorgen Grunnet: Hank Mobley diskografi in Orkester Journalen, Vol. 26 (May 1958): 47
((2, 3, 7d))

M197 WILBRAHAM, Roy J.: Hank Mobley
discography in Discographical
Forum, No. 11 (March 1969) to No.
16 (January 1970): various paginations; additions and corrections
in Discographical Forum, No. 16
(January 1970): 2; No. 17 (March
1970): 2; No. 21 (November 1970):
2 ((2, 3, 6, 7))

MODE label

M198 EDWARDS, Ernie: The Mode label in
Matrix, No. 42 (August 1962): 3-
10; additions and corrections in
Matrix, No. 52 (April 1964): 16
[also includes Interlude reissues]
((2, 7))

MODEL T SLIM
See MICKLE, ELMON

MODERN JAZZ
See JAZZ MUSIC--Modern Style

MODERN JAZZ QUARTET
See also JACKSON, MILT; LEWIS,
JOHN (John Lewis & MJQ discogra-
phy)

M199 Discographie du Modern Jazz Quartet in Jazz Hot, No. 92 (October
1954): 9 ((2, 3, 7))

M200 Discophilia; the Modern Jazz Quartet in Jazz Up, No. 1, and other

unknown issues (one part in No.
3 (November 1965)) ((2, 7))

M201 FRESIA, Enzo: Discografia completa
del Modern Jazz Quartet in Musica
Jazz, Vol. 8 (June-July 1957): 41-
43 ((2, 3, 6, 7))

M202 JEPSEN, Jorgen Grunnet: Modern
Jazz Quartet diskografi in Orkester Journalen, Vol. 26 (January
1958): 46 ((2, 3, 7d))

M203 Modern Jazz Quartet pa skiva in
Orkester Journalen, Vol. 43 (January 1975): 10 ((—))

M204 OWENS, Thomas: Discography in
Journal of Jazz Studies, Vol. 4
(fall 1976): 45-46 [recordings of
their fugues] ((2, 7d))

M205 [[STIASSI, Ruggero: [Discography,
1956-1960] in Musica Jazz, Vol.
22 (July 1966)]]

MOLE, MIFF (Irving Milfred Mole),
1898-1961
trombone

M206 BAKKER, Dick M.: Miff Mole's
Little Molers in Micrography, No.
10 (May 1970): 7 ((7d))

MOMENTS (musical group)

M207 BRYANT, Steve: The Moment's [sic]
albums in Hot Buttered Soul, No.
41 (October 1975?): 11-13 ((5,
7d))

MONCUR, GRACHAN, 1937-
trombone
See TROMBONE MUSIC (JAZZ)

MONK, THELONIOUS, 1917-
piano

M208 EDWARDS, Marv: Thelonious Sphere
Monk: a selected discography in
Jazz Blast (October 1969): 3-4
((—))

M209 JEPSEN, Jorgen Grunnet: A discography of Thelonious Monk/Bud
Powell. Copenhagen: Knudsen
[c1969], 44 leaves ((1, 2, 3, 6,
7))

M210 JEPSEN, Jorgen Grunnet: Discography of Thelonious Monk/Sonny
Rollins. [Brande, Denmark: Debut
Records, c1960], 12, 26 leaves
((2, 3, 6, 7))

M211 [[KUHNE, Peter: Thelonious Monk auf unveröffentlichen Tonbandern in Jazz + Classic, Vol. 5 (December 1978): 21 ((1))]]

M212 LANGE, Horst H.: Discophilia; Thelonius [sic] Monk in Jazzmania, Vol. 3 (September 1959) [reprinted from Schlagzeug, unknown issue(s)] ((2, 3, 6, 7))

M213 LP-Monkografie in Jazz Wereld, No. 29 (May 1970): 19 ((—))

M214 Microsolco di Thelonious Monk pubblicati in Italia in Jazz di Ieri e di Oggi, Vol. 2 (June 1960): 16-17 ((—))

M215 Monk '41 to '59 in Kord, Vol. 1, No. 1 (n.d., ca. 1970?): 14 ((—))

M216 RAAY, Wytze van der, and Wim van EYLE: Thelonious Monk discografie in Jazz Press, No. 32 (February 18, 1977): 8-9; No. 33 (March 4, 1977): 8-9; additions and corrections in Jazz Press, No. 43 (September 2, 1977): 6 ((1, 2, 3, 6, 7))

M217 RUPPLI, Michael: Discographie de Thelonious Monk in Jazz Hot, No. 331 (October 1976): 22-25, 29 ((1, 2, 3, 6, 7))

M218 Les soli de piano enregistrés par Thelonius [sic] Monk in Jazz Hot, No. 306 (June 1974): 11 ((2, 7))

M219 Thelonious Monk in Swing Journal, Vol. 29 (November 1975): 252-259 ((2, 7d))

MONKEY JOE (Jesse Coleman)

M220 COLLER, Derek: Recording the blues; Monkey Joe in Vintage Jazz Mart, No. 11 (September 1962): 7-8 ((2, 3, 6, 7))

MONSBOURGH, ADE, 1917–
multi-instrumentalist

M221 HULME, G. W. George: Lazy Ade Monsbourgh; a name listing in Matrix, No. 6 (May 1953): 17-19, 10; additions and corrections in Matrix, No. 21 (January 1959): 21; No. 35/36 (September 1961): 37; No. 42 (August 1962): 18 ((2, 3, 6, 7))

MONTEROSE, J. R. (Frank Anthony Monterose Jr.), 1927–
tenor saxophone

M222 GARDNER, Mark: J. R. Monterose in Jazz Monthly, No. 157 (March 1968): 7-8 ((2, 3, 7))

MONTGOMERY, LITTLE BROTHER (Eurreal Montgomery), 1906–
piano, vocal

M223 BAKKER, Dick M.: Little Brother Montgomery in Micrography, No. 14 (May 1971): 11 ((7d))

M224 GERT ZUR HEIDE, Karl: Discography in his Deep south piano; the story of Little Brother Montgomery. [London]: Studio Vista (also New York: Stein & Day) [c1970], 104-107 ((2, 3, 6, 7))

M225 McCARTHY, Albert J.: Collectors' notes; discography of Little Brother Montgomery in JONES, Max, and Albert J. McCARTHY, eds.: Jazz review. London: Jazz Music Books, 1945, 8-9 ((2, 3, 7))

MONTGOMERY, MONK, 1921–
bass violin

M226 Selected Montgomery discography in Down Beat, Vol. 42 (April 24, 1975): 17 ((—))

MONTGOMERY, TAMMY
vocal

M227 [[Tammy Montgomery disco in Soul, No. 2 (1966)]]; additions and corrections in Soul, No. 3 (April 1966): 28; No. 4 (June 1966): 13

MONTGOMERY, WES, 1928–1968
guitar

M228 Wes Montgomery in Swing Journal, Vol. 32 (July 1978): 314-317 ((2, 7d))

M229 Wes Montgomery discography in Swing Journal, Vol. 27 (June 1973): 272-277 ((2, 7d))

MONTOLIU, TETE (Vincente Montoliu), 1933–
piano

M230 SAFANE, Clifford Jay: Tete Montoliu: a selected discography in Contemporary Keyboard, Vol. 6 (September 1980): 26 ((—))

MONTRELL, ROY, 1928–
guitar

M231 VERNON, Mike: Discography in Jazz Monthly, Vol. 13 (June 1967): 3 ((2, 7))

MONTREUX JAZZ FESTIVAL

M232 DENOREAZ, Michel: Le spectacle du jazz et le disque in Montreux jazz. [Lausanne: de la Tour, c1976], 122-123 ((—))

MONTROSE, JACK, 1928–
tenor saxophone

M233 Jack Montrose--a name listing in Discographical Forum, No. 2 (July 1960): 17, 19 ((2, 3, 7))

MOODY, JAMES, 1925–
saxophones

M234 [[KUHN, Raymond: Discography of James Moody. Neu-Allschwil, Switzerland: 1961?; also Basel: Jazz-Publications, 1960, with supplement of 1 sheet, 1961, 16 pp.]]

M235 A "name" discography of James Moody in Discophile, No. 35 (April 1954): 10-14; additions and corrections in Discophile, No. 39 (December 1954): 18-19; No. 40 (February 1955): 15-16 ((2, 3, 6, 7))

M236 WALKER, Malcolm, and Frank GIBSON: James Moody; a discography in Discographical Forum, No. 20 (September 1970) to No. 25 (July 1971), various paginations ((1, 2, 3, 6, 7))

MOONEY, JOE, 1911-1975
vocal
See also SUNSHINE BOYS

M237 MORGAN, Alun: Joe Mooney; a name listing in Discographical Forum, No. 25 (July 1971): 5-6 ((2, 3, 7))

M238 SALEMANN, Dieter: Joe Mooney 1911-1975, a sunshine boy? in Point du Jazz, No. 15 (July 1979): 29-43 ((1, 2, 3, 6, 7))

MOONSONG label

M239 SLATER, Ian: Moonsong label in Hot Buttered Soul, No. 34 (October 1974?): 7 ((3))

MOORE, ALEX, 1899–
harmonica, piano, vocal

M240 Whistlin' Alex Moore discography in Living Blues, No. 35 (November-December 1977): 10 ((7))

MOORE, ALICE
vocal

M241 McCARTHY, Albert J.: A discography of Alice Moore in Discophile, No. 6 (June 1949): 2-3; additions and corrections in Discophile, No. 7 (August 1949): 3; No. 10 (February 1950): 10 ((2, 3, 7))

MOORE, BILL
tenor saxophone

M242 MOHR, Kurt: Discography of Wild Bill Moore in Jazz Statistics, No. 8 (January 1959): 8, 10; additions and corrections from Jorgen Grunnet JEPSEN in Jazz Statistics, No. 12 (September 1959): 8; [from Michel VOGLER] No. 17 (1960): 6 ((2, 3, 7))

MOORE, BREW (Milton A. Moore), 1924–1973
tenor saxophone

M243 DAVIS, Brian: Discography of Brew Moore in Discographical Forum, No. 9 (November 1968): 7-10; No. 10 (January 1969): 3-4; additions and corrections in Discographical Forum, No. 11 (March 1969): 2, 9; No. 12 (May 1969): 2; No. 14 (September 1969): 2 ((1, 2, 3, 6, 7))

MOORE, JAMES
See SLIM HARPO

MOORE, JOHNNY
vocal

M244 MOHR, Kurt: Johnny Moore in Soul Bag, No. 45 (January 1975): 15 ((2, 3, 7))

MOORE, MERRILL

M245 [[[Discography] in Jazzspiegel, April 1964]]

MORAND, HERB, 1905-1952
trumpet
See HARLEM HAMFATS

MOREIRA, AIRTO
See AIRTO

MORGAN, SAM, 1895-1936
trumpet

M246 TEALDO ALIZIERI, Carlos L.: [Dis-
cography] in Jazz Magazine (Argentina), No. 15 (August-September
1950): 11 ((2, 3, 7d))

MORGANFIELD, McKINLEY
See MUDDY WATERS

MORRIS, JOE, 1922-1958
trumpet

M247 GRENDYSA, Peter A.: Joe Morris in
Record Exchanger, Vol. 4 (December 1975): 13-14 ((5))

M248 MOHR, Kurt: Joe Morris discogra-
phy in Jazz Statistics, No. 5
(April 1957): 5-6; additions and
corrections from Jorgen Grunnet
JEPSEN in Jazz Statistics, No. 12
(September 1959): 8 ((2, 3, 7))

MORRIS, THOMAS, 1898-1949?
cornet

M249 ALLEN, Walter C.: Thomas Morris
and his Seven Hot Babies in Discophile, No. 32 (October 1953):
16 ((2, 3, 6, 7))

M250 BAKKER, Dick M.: A partial listing of Thomas Morris on Victor in
Micrography, No. 35 (March 1975):
11 ((6, 7d))

M251 BAKKER, Dick M.: Thomas Morris
1923-26 in Micrography, No. 39
(January 1976): 4 [rev. ed. of
previous entry] ((6, 7d))

MORRISON, GEORGE, 1891-
guitar, violin

M252 RYE, Howard: The one that got
away...George Morrison on record
in Storyville, No. 90 (August-
September 1980): 219 ((2, 3, 6,
7))

MORTON, JELLY ROLL (Ferdinand Joseph
Morton), 1885-1941
piano

M253 BAKKER, Dick M.: Jelly Roll Morton
1923-1940 in Micrography, No. 49
(December 1978): 6-18 ((3, 6, 7d))

M254 BAKKER, Dick M.: Jelly Roll Morton
on the labels Gennett & Paramount
& Autograph 1923-1925 only in
Micrography, No. 19 (April 1972):
2 ((7d))

M255 BAKKER, Dick M.: Jelly Roll Morton's Victors in Micrography, No.
5 (August 1969): 6-7; additions
and corrections in Micrography,
No. 21 (September 1972): 2
((7d))

M256 BAKKER, Dick M.: Jelly's Victor's
[sic] in Micrography, No. 20
(June 1972): 6-7 ((7d))

M257 BROWN, Ken: Jelly Roll Morton:
Ken Brown gives corrections and
additions to Delaunay's Hot discography in Discography (December 1942): 6-7; (March 1943): 2;
(April 1943): 2 (title varies;
last part has Albert McCARTHY as
author)

M258 CAREY, DAVE: Frank DUTTON; and
George HULME: Jelly Roll's Victor
jazz in Jazz Journal, Vol. 15
(June 1962): 8-10; (July 1962):
9-10; (August 1962): 35-36; additions and corrections from Frank
DUTTON in Jazz Journal, Vol. 16
(July 1963): 27 [1926-1939 recordings as a sideman] ((3, 6,
7))

M259 [[CUSACK, Thomas: Jelly Roll
Morton; an essay in discography.
London: Cassell, 1952, viii, 40
pp.]]

M260 DAVIES, John R. T., and Laurie
WRIGHT: Morton's music. London:
Storyville, 1968, 36 pp.; additions and corrections in Storyville, No. 17 (June-July 1968):
29-30 ((2, 3, 6, 7, 9))

M261 Discografia di J. R. Morton in
Jazz di Ieri e di Oggi, Vol. 2
(January-February 1960): 19-23
((1, 2, 7))

M262 GAZÈRES, P.: Discographie des
principaux enregistrements
réédités au cours des derniers
années in Jazz Hot, No. 35 (July-
August 1949): 24; No. 36 (September 1949): 26 ((—))

M263 JEPSEN, Jorgen Grunnet: Discography of Jelly Roll Morton.
[Brande, Denmark: Debut Records,
c1959], 2 v. ((2, 3, 6, 7))

M264 LOMAX, Alan: The records in his
Mister Jelly Roll; the fortunes
of Jelly Roll Morton, New Orleans

Creole and inventor of jazz. New York: Duell, Sloane & Pierce, 1950 (also New York: Grosset & Dunlap, 1950; London: Jazz Book Club, 1956; Berkeley: Univ. of California Pr., 1973): 300-318; (also possibly London: Cassell, 1952; New York: Grove Press, 1956; London: Pan Books, 1959; and (translations) Stockholm: Raben & Sjogren, 1954; Copenhagen: Gyldendal, 1958; Paris: Flammarion, 1964; Zurich: Ex Libris, 1964; Zurich: Sanssouci, 1960, paginations unknown) ((2, 7))

M265 McCARTHY, Albert: Jelly Roll Morton discography in Jazz Music, Vol. 2 (February-March 1944): 102-106 ((2, 3, 6, 7))

M266 PAUTASSO, Oscar: Discografia in Hot Jazz Club, No. 15 (September 1947): 8, 50-52; No. 16 (December 1947): 24 [1939-1940 and Circle recordings] ((2, 3, 7))

M267 POSTIF, François: [Discography of records issued in France since 1945] in Jazz Hot, No. 102 (September 1955): 19 ((2, 7))

M268 Random notes on Jelly Roll in Matrix, No. 28 (April 1960): 11-12 [additions and corrections to various discographies]

M269 RICHARD, Roger: Jelly Roll news in Point du Jazz, No. 9 (December 1973): 121-123; No. 13 (June 1977): 133-134 [additions and corrections to various discographies]

M270 RUST, Brian: Ferdinand Jelly-Roll Morton; a discography in Jazz Journal, Vol. 2 (August 1949): 6; (September 1949): 12; (October 1949): 12, 14 ((2, 3, 6, 7))

M271 SPEAR, Horace L.: Some notes on Jelly Roll in Storyville, No. 33 (February-March 1971): 88-89 [additions and corrections to various discographies]

M272 VALENTI, Jerry: Jelly-Roll Morton and the Library of Congress; a discography in Jazz Record (US), No. 42 (March 1946): 17-18; additions in Jazz Record (US), No. 43 (April 1946): 13 ((2, 3, 6))

M273 WILLIAMS, Martin T.: Selected records in his Jelly Roll Morton. London: Cassell, 1962 (also New York: Barnes, 1962), 77-85 (Kings of Jazz, 11) ((2, 3, 6, 7))

M274 [[WRIGHT, Laurie: Mr. Jelly Lord. Chigwell, Essex: Storyville, 1980, 256 pp. ((1, 2, 3, 4p, 4r, 4t, 6, 7, 8, 9))]]

Compositions

M275 [Discographies of tunes by Jelly Roll Morton] in Jazz giants; "Jelly Roll" Morton blues, stomps & ragtime. New York: Edwin H. Morris [c1949] (also New York: Hansen [c1973]), 48 pp. ((—))

M276 [Discographies of tunes by Morton] in Just jazz, blues and stomps. New York: Hansen [c1973], 64 pp. ((—))

Piano Rolls

M277 The Jelly Roll Morton piano-rollography in Record Research, Vol. 1 (December 1955): 11; additions and corrections in Record Research, Vol. 2 (February 1956): 9; (May-June 1956): 10; (January-February 1957): 23 ((7d, 8))

M278 MONTGOMERY, Mike: More rolls by Morton in Record Research, No. 49 (March 1963): 6 ((5))

M279 SIMONE, Rodney: Jelly Roll Morton rollography in Matrix, No. 51 (February 1964): 14-17; additions and corrections in Matrix, No. 56 (December 1964): 19; No. 68 (December 1966): 14 ((5))

M280 SPEAR, Horace L.: Jelly rolls in Storyville, No. 32 (December 1970-January 1971): 50 ((5))

MOSEHOLM, ERIK, 1930-
bass violin

M281 [[THOMSEN, Jens Schoustrup: Erik Moseholm. Copenhagen: Erichsen, 1962, 64 pp.]]

MOSELY, SNUB (Lawrence Leo Mosely), 1909-
trombone

M282 MOHR, Kurt: Discography of Snub Mosely in Jazz Statistics, No. 26/27 (June-September 1962): 2-3 ((2, 3, 6, 7))

M283 WIEDEMANN, Erik: Discography of Snub Mosely in Jazz Music, Vol. 4 (No. 4, 1950): 21-22; additions in Jazz Music, Vol. 4 (No. 5, 1951): 21-22 ((2, 3, 7))

MOTEN, BENNIE, 1894-1935
     piano, leader

M284 BAKKER, Dick M.: Bennie Moten in
     Micrography, No. 4 (June 1969): 4
     ((7d))

M285 BAKKER, Dick M.: Bennie Moten
     1923-1932 in Micrography, No. 24
     (February 1973): 2-3; additions
     and corrections in Micrography,
     No. 26 (1973): 1 ((7d))

M286 DRIGGS, Frank: Benny Moten dis-
     cography (corrections) in Jazz
     Statistics, No. 7 (1958?): 9-10
     [corrections to various discogra-
     phies]

M287 TRAILL, Sinclair: Discography in
     Pickup, Vol. 1 (December 1946):
     10-11 ((2, 3, 7d))

MOTION PICTURES
     See SOUNDTRACKS

MOULDIE FYGGE label

M288 MAHONY, Dan: The Mouldie Fygge
     and Rampart labels in Matrix, No.
     40 (April 1962): 3-6; additions
     and corrections in Matrix, No. 49
     (October 1963): 15 ((3, 5, 6, 7d))

MOUND CITY BLUE BLOWERS
     See also McKENZIE, RED

M289 VENABLES, R. G. V.: Discography
     of the Mound City Blue Blowers in
     Jazz Forum (UK), No. 3 (January
     1947): 20-21 ((2, 3, 7))

MOUZON, ALPHONSE, 1948-
     drums

M290 Selected Mouzon discography in
     Down Beat, Vol. 42 (December 4,
     1975): 15 ((—))

MOVING PICTURES
     See SOUNDTRACKS

MUDDY WATERS (McKinley Morganfield)
     1915-
     guitar, vocal
     See also BLUES MUSIC (Guralnick,
     Peter)

M291 COLOMBATO, Donatello: Discography
     in Blues Power, Vol. 1 (No. 4,
     1974): 13-14 ((—))

M292 Discographie in Blues Notes, No.
     3 (1969): 8 ((—))

M293 LEADBITTER, Mike: Discography;
     all known sessions in Blues Un-
     limited Collectors Classics, No.
     B1 (March 1964): 8-15; additions
     and corrections in Blues Unlimit-
     ed Collectors Classics, No. 12
     (June 1964): suppl-3, 5 ((2, 3,
     6, 7))

M294 ROONEY, James: Discography/Muddy
     Waters in his Bossmen; Bill Mon-
     roe and Muddy Waters. New York:
     Dial (also New York: Hayden),
     1971, 17-18 ((—))

M295 ROTANTE, Anthony, and François
     POSTIF: Discographie de Muddy
     Waters in Jazz Hot, No. 101 (sum-
     mer 1955): 21 ((2, 3, 7p))

M296 ROTANTE, Anthony: A discography
     of Muddy Waters in Discophile,
     No. 24 (June 1952): 9-10; addi-
     tions and corrections in Disco-
     phile, No. 29 (May 1953): 17-19;
     No. 53 (April 1957): 11; No. 59
     (April 1958): 9-10 ((2, 3))

M297 Selected Waters discography in
     Down Beat, Vol. 42 (February 27,
     1975): 22 ((—))

M298 STRACHWITZ, Chris: The records of
     Muddy Waters in Jazz Report
     (California), Vol. 1 (June 1961);
     Vol. 2 (October 1961), in unpaged
     Blues Report section ((2, 3, 7))

MUELLER, GUS, 1890-1965
     clarinet

M299 Discographical data in Second
     Line, Vol. 17 (January-February
     1966): 8, 13 [taken from Black-
     stone's Index to jazz] ((—))

MULLIGAN, GERRY, 1927-
     baritone saxophone

M300 Discography of Gerry Mulligan in
     Swing Journal, issue 9 of 1959:
     44; issue 10 of 1959: 32 ((2, 7d))

M301 JEPSEN, Jorgen Grunnet: Discogra-
     phy of Gerry Mulligan & Lee Ko-
     nitz. [Brande, Denmark: Debut
     Records, 1960], 20, 13 leaves
     ((1, 2, 3, 6, 7))

M302 [[JEPSEN, Jorgen Grunnet: Gerry
     Mulligan; a discography. Copen-
     hagen: 1957, 10 leaves]]

M303 JEPSEN, Jorgen Grunnet: Gerry Mulligan discography in Orkester Journalen, Vol. 25 (June 1957): 42; (July-August 1957): 53 ((2, 3, 7d))

M304 [[MORGAN, Alun: Gerry Mulligan; a biography, appreciation, record survey and discography. London: National Jazz Federation [1958], 16 pp.]]

M305 Selected Mulligan discography in Down Beat, Vol. 43 (July 15, 1976): 13 ((—))

M306 TERCINET, Alain: Discographie de Gerry Mulligan in Jazz Hot, No. 335 (March 1977): 25-29; No. 336 (April 1977): 21-23 ((1, 2, 3, 6, 7))

M307 WILLARD, Patricia: Mulligan full steam ahead in Down Beat, Vol. 41 (October 24, 1974): 19 ((—))

MULLIGAN, MICK
trumpet

M308 A discography of Mick Mulligan in Jazz Music, Vol. 6 (No. 4, 1955): 2 ((2, 3, 7))

MUNIAK, JANUSZ, 1941-
saxophones

M309 Janusz Muniak's selected discography in Jazz Forum (Poland), No. 49 (1977): 43 ((—))

MURPHY, MARK, 1932-
vocal

M310 INGERSOLL, Chuck: Mark Murphy in Different Drummer, Vol. 1 (March 1974): 20 ((—))

M311 Plattenhinweise in Jazz Podium, Vol. 29 (January 1980): 17 ((—))

MURRAY, DON, d. 1949
saxophones

M312 LINEHAN, Norman: Listen to Don Murray; his records in Jazz Notes (Australia), No. 84 (June 1948): 13-16; additions and corrections in VENABLES, Ralph: Additional data on Don Murray in Jazz Notes (Australia), No. 88 (October-November 1948): 3-5 ((2, 3, 7))

MURRAY, SUNNY (James Marcellus Arthur Murray), 1937-
drums

M313 COOKE, Jack: Sonny [sic] Murray in Paris in Jazz & Blues, Vol. 3 (January 1973): 17 ((2, 7))

M314 GROS-CLAUDE, Paul: Sunny Murray le tambour 71 in Jazz Magazine (France), No. 189 (May 1971): 48 ((2, 7))

M315 RABEN, Erik: Diskofilspalten in Orkester Journalen, Vol. 37 (November 1969): 19 ((2, 7))

MUSICRAFT label
See LEADBELLY (Leadbelly...on Musicraft)

MUZA label (Polish)
See JAZZ MUSIC--Poland

MY BABY IT'S GONE (tune title)
See BLUES MUSIC (Groom, Bob)

NAMYSLOWSKI, ZBIGNIEW, 1939-
alto saxophone

N1 Discography Zbigniew Namyslowski in Jazz Forum (Poland), No. 1 (August 1967): 63 ((—))

N2 Zbigniew Namyslowski discography in Jazz Forum (Poland), No. 36 (April 1975): 41 ((—))

NAPOLEON, PHIL (Filippo Napoli), 1901-
trumpet

N3 Phil Napoleon; a "name" listing in Discophile, No. 28 (February 1953): 3-6; additions and corrections in Discophile, No. 29 (May 1953): 9-10; No. 36 (June 1954): 9 ((2, 3, 6, 7d))

NATIONAL label
See also EMARCY label (Kwiecinski, Walter)

N4 PORTER, Bob: Modern eyes-zing, in Record Research, No. 151/152 (January 1978) to No. 155/156 (July 1978), various paginations [to master no. 675] ((3))

A NATURAL HIT label

N5 EAGLE, Bob: A Natural Hit! records; preliminary listing in Record Research, No. 121 (March 1973): 5 ((2, 8))

NAVARRO, FATS (Theodore Navarro),
   1923-1950
   trumpet

N6   JEPSEN, Jorgen Grunnet: Discogra-
      phie Fats Navarro et Clifford
      Brown in Les Cahiers du Jazz, No.
      2 (February 1960?): 84-96 ((1, 2,
      3, 6, 7))

N7   JEPSEN, Jorgen Grunnet: Discogra-
      phy of Fats Navarro/Clifford
      Brown. [Brande, Denmark: Debut
      Records, c1960], 14, 12 leaves
      ((1, 2, 3, 6, 7))

N8   [[JEPSEN, Jorgen Grunnet: Fats
      Navarro; a discography. Copen-
      hagen: 1957, 11 pp.]]

N9   MORGAN, Alun: Theodore Navarro,
      1923-1950; a discography in Melody
      Maker, Vol. 28 (July 5, 1952): 4;
      (July 12, 1952): 4; (July 19,
      1952): 4 ((2, 3, 7))

N10   NEVERS, Daniel: Discographie de
      Fats Navarro in Jazz Hot, No. 328
      (June 1976): 26-29 ((1, 2, 3, 6,
      7))

N11   WIEDEMANN, Erik: Discographie in
      Jazz Hot, No. 47 (September 1950):
      13, 16 ((2, 3, 6, 7))

NELSON, BENNY
      See KING, BEN E.

NELSON, OLIVER, 1932-1975
      alto saxophone

N12   Oliver Nelson in Swing Journal,
      Vol. 30 (February 1976): 262-265
      ((2, 7d))

N13   Selected Nelson discography in
      Down Beat, Vol. 42 (April 24,
      1975): 11 ((—))

NELSON, RED
      See RED NELSON

NEW ORLEANS JAZZ BAND
      See also JAZZ MUSIC (Jewson, Ron)
      and (Lange, Horst H.)

N14   New Orleans Jazz Band in Record
      Research, Vol. 1 (August 1955):
      10; additions and corrections in
      Record Research, Vol. 1 (October
      1955): 21; (December 1955): 12;
      Vol. 2 (February 1956): 14; (Jan-
      uary-February 1957): 23 ((2, 3,
      6, 7d))

NEW ORLEANS OWLS

N15   TONKS, Eric S.: Discography of
      the New Orleans Owls in Disco-
      phile, No. 1 (August 1948): 7
      ((2, 3, 7))

NEW ORLEANS RHYTHM KINGS

N16   BAKKER, Dick M.: N.O.R.K. 1922-
      1925 in Micrography, No. 19 (April
      1972): 4 ((7d))

N17   TONKS, Eric: N.O.R.K. discography
      in ASMAN, James, and Bill KINNELL,
      eds.: Jazz on record. Chilwell,
      Nottinghamshire: Jazz Apprecia-
      tion Society [ca. 1946], 13-14
      ((2, 3, 6, 7d))

NEW PRINCE'S TORONTO BAND
      See CAPLAN, DAVE

NEWBORN, PHINEAS, 1931-
      piano

N18   MONTI, Pierre Andre: Discographie
      de Phineas Newborn in Jazz 360,
      No. 10 (September 1978): 6-8; No.
      12 (November 1978): 4-5; No. 13
      (December 1978): 8 ((2, 7))

NEWPORT JAZZ FESTIVAL

N19   Discography in GOLDBLATT, Burt:
      Newport Jazz Festival; the illus-
      trated history. New York: Dial
      [c1977], 259-261 ((7d))

N20   The Newport sessions in Swing
      Journal, Vol. 32, No. 6 (May 1978
      special issue): 238-243 ((2,
      7d))

NEWTON, FRANKIE, 1906-1954
      trumpet
      See also COLEMAN, BILL (Evensmo,
      Jan); MEZZROW, MEZZ (Bakker, Dick
      M.)

N21   BAKKER, Dick M.: Frankie Newton
      1936-39 in Micrography, No. 29
      (December 1973): 4-5 ((7d))

N22   KONOW, Albrekt von: Frankie Newton
      diskografi in Orkester Journalen,
      Vol. 42 (December 1974): 58; Vol.
      43 (January 1975): 35 ((2, 3, 6,
      7))

NICHOLAS, WOODEN JOE, 1883-1957
      clarinet, trumpet

N23   BAKKER, Dick M.: Wooden Joe/etc.
on A.M. in Micrography, No. 37
(July 1975): 8-10 ((3, 7d))

N24   HOLLAND, Bernard: Wooden Joe
Nicholas; a discography in Matrix, No. 17 (April 1958): 3-5
((2, 3, 7))

NICHOLS, HERBIE, 1919-1963
piano

N25   COOKE, Ann: Herbie Nichols discography in Jazz Monthly, Vol. 6
(November 1960): 30 ((2, 3, 7))

N26   EYLE, Wim van: Herbie Nichols
discografie in Jazz Press, No. 35
(April 1, 1977): 8; additions and
corrections in Jazz Press, No. 41
(July 8, 1977): 4 ((2, 3, 7))

N27   TARRANT, Don: Herbie Nichols discography in Journal of Jazz Discography, No. 5 (September 1979):
17-19 ((2, 3, 7))

NICHOLS, RED (Ernest Loring Nichols),
1905-1965
trumpet

N28   BACKENSTO, Woody: The meandering
Macgregors in Record Research,
No. 96/97 (April 1969): 11-13
((1))

N29   BACKENSTO, Woody: A modern Red
Nichols discography--since 1940
in Record Research, Vol. 2
(April-May 1957): 4-11 ((2, 3,
4p, 6, 7))

N30   BACKENSTO, Woody: A Red Nichols
discography since 1956 in Record
Research, No. 96/97 (April 1969):
15-16, 18 ((1, 2, 3, 7))

N31   BACKENSTO, Woody: Red Nichols
with Paul Whiteman in Record Exchange, Vol. 4 (October 1951): 3-
5 ((2, 3, 7d))

N32   BACKENSTO, Woody: Small change
[column of discographical information on Nichols] in Record Research, Vol. 2 (February 1956) to
No. 25 (November-December 1959);
No. 29 (August 1960) to No. 45
(August 1962); No. 55 (September
1963) to No. 56 (November 1963);
No. 60 (May-June 1964); No. 63
(September 1964) to No. 65 (December 1964); No. 68 (May 1965);
No. 70 (August 1965); No. 74
(March 1966); No. 79 (October
1966); No. 83 (April 1967); No.
85 (August 1967); No. 101 (Octo-

ber 1969) to No. 105 (May 1970),
various paginations ((2, 3, 6, 7))

N33   BAKKER, Dick M.: Red Nichols
Brunswick-recordings 1926-32 in
Micrography, No. 10 (May 1970): 7
((7d))

N34   BAKKER, Dick M.: Red Nichols
1926-31 in Micrography, No. 21
(September 1972): 8-9; additions
and corrections in Micrography,
No. 22 (October 1972): 1; No. 24
(February 1973): 1 ((7d))

N35   BAKKER, Dick M.: Red Nichols
1926-1932 in Micrography, No. 41
(May 1976): 3-7 ((6, 7d))

N36   DAVIES, John R. T.: Re-reminting
the Pennies in Storyville, No. 75
(February-March 1978) to No. 82
(April-May 1979), various paginations [to May 19, 1932] ((2, 3,
6, 7, 8, 9))

N37   HESTER, Stan: Red Nichols--his
records as a sideman in KINKLE,
Roger D.: Check sheet (Project
#4). [Evansville, IN?:] n.d., 1-
19; additions and corrections in
KINKLE, Roger D.: Check sheet
(Project #5). Evansville, IN:
[n.d.], 17-24 ((9))

N38   HESTER, Stan: Red Nichols recordings on Edison 1923-1928 in
Micrography, No. 46 (April 1978):
4-5 ((3, 6, 7d))

N39   HOEFER, George: Nichols discography in Down Beat, Vol. 18 (September 7, 1951): 16 ((—))

N40   LYTTON-EDWARDS, M.: Records by
Red in Swing Music, Vol. 1 (September 1935); (October 1935):
226-227 (and possibly other issues) ((—))

N41   [REID, John?]: [Discography].
n.p., n.d., 4 leaves [covers October 6, 1939, to October 26,
1927, in reverse chronological
order] ((2, 3, 7))

N42   VENABLES, Ralph G. V., and C. W.
Langston WHITE: A complete discography of Red Nichols and his
Five Pennies. Melbourne: Australian Jazz Quarterly [1946], 15
pp. (AJQ Handbook No. 2) ((2, 3,
7d))

N43   VENABLES, Ralph G. V., and C. W.
Langston WHITE: Re-minting the
Pennies; a complete discography
of Red Nichols and his Five
Pennies. [Tilford, Surrey]: 1942,
8 pp. ((2, 3, 7d))

NICKERSON, BOZO
piano

N44   McCARTHY, Albert J.: Blues pian-
ists: no. 4, Bozo Nickerson in
Jazz Notes (Australia), No. 62
(March 1946): 17 ((2))

NIEHAUS, LENNIE, 1929-
alto saxophone

N45   JEPSEN, Jorgen Grunnet: Lennie
Niehaus diskografi (skivor inspelade under eget namn) in Orkester Journalen, Vol. 28 (May
1960): 50 ((2, 7d))

NIGHTHAWK, ROBERT (Robert McCullum),
1909-1967
guitar, harmonica, vocal

N46   Discographie de Robert Nighthawk
in Soul Bag, No. 53 (May 1976):
6-10 ((2, 3, 6, 7d))

NIGHTINGALES (Musical group)

N47   HAYES, Cedric: The Nightingales;
a provisional listing in Matrix,
No. 71 (June 1967): 5-7; additions
and corrections in Matrix, No. 75
(February 1968): 19 ((2, 3, 7))

NILSSON, ALICE
See BABS, ALICE

NIX, WILLIE, 1922-
drums, guitar, vocal

N48   [[Willie Nix discography in Living
Blues, No. 43 (summer 1979): 13]];
additions and corrections from
Joseph DIETZGEN in Living Blues,
No. 45/46 (spring 1980): 5 ((2, 3,
6, 7))

NIXON, ELMORE, 1933-ca. 1975?
drums, piano, vocal

N49   BASTIN, Bruce, and Mike LEAD-
BITTER: Elmore Nixon--a name discography in Blues Unlimited, No.
33 (May-June 1966): 5 ((2, 3, 7))

NOBLE, RAY, 1903-1978
leader

N50   AVERY, Harry E.: Ray Noble; a
discography in Record Changer
(June 1951): 9-10, 20-22 ((2, 3,
7d))

N51   BAKKER, Dick M., and Helmut
GLUCKMANN-WEISSKIRCHEN: Ray Noble
1928-1934 in Micrography, No. 20
(June 1972): 8-9 ((7d))

N52   HEARNE, Will Roy: History of Ray
Noble's English and United States
records in Good Diggin' (annual
issue 1948): 61-70 ((—))

N53   Ray Noble European discography in
Clef, Vol. 1 (May 1946): 25-27
((—))

NOCTURNE label

N54   MORGAN, Alun: The Nocturne label
in Discographical Forum, No. 1
(May 1960): 13-16, 18 ((2, 3))

NOONE, JIMMY, 1895-1944
clarinet

N55   BAKKER, Dick M.: Jimmie Noone
1928-1941 in Micrography, No. 23
(January 1973): 2-3 ((7d))

N56   BAKKER, Dick M.: Jimmie Noone
1928-1944 in Micrography, No. 38
(October 1975): 11-12 ((6, 7d))

N57   JEPSEN, Jorgen Grunnet: Discographie de Jimmie Noone in Les
Cahiers du Jazz, No. 8 (1963?):
93-98 ((2, 3, 6, 7))

N58   NEFF, Wesley M.: Discography of
Jimmie Noone in Jazz Information,
Vol. 2 (November 8, 1940): 15-22
((2, 3))

NOORDIJK, PIET, 1932-
alto saxophone, clarinet

N59   Piet Noordijk op platen in Jazz
Wereld, No. 4 (January 1966): 118
((2, 7))

NORGRAN label
See GILLESPIE, DIZZY (Jepsen,
Jorgen Grunnet: Dizzy Gillespie
diskografi pa Clef-Norgran-Verve);
GRANZ, NORMAN

NORMANN, ROBERT, 1916-
guitar
See CHRISTIAN, CHARLIE (Evensmo,
Jan)

NORTH BAY label

N60   SLATER, Ian; Steve BRYANT; and
Chris SAVORY: North Bay label

listing in Hot Buttered Soul,
No. 35 (November 1974?): 4 ((3))

NORVO, RED (Kenneth Norville), 1908-
xylophone

N61 HOEFER, George: Norvo discography
in Down Beat, Vol. 17 (August 11,
1950) to (September 22, 1950),
various paginations, in 4 parts
((3, 7))

N62 KRANER, Dietrich H.: The Red
Norvo Trio with Tal Farlow and
Charles Mingus in Journal of Jazz
Discography, No. 2 (June 1977):
6-9 ((1, 2, 3, 6, 7))

N63 Selected Norvo discography in
Down Beat, Vol. 44 (November 3,
1977): 17 ((—))

NOVI SINGERS

N64 Novi Singers discography in Jazz
Forum (Poland), No. 39 (January
1976): 44 ((—))

O F C label

O1 BETTINELLI, Norberto R.: O.F.C.;
a label listing in Matrix, No. 89
(September 1970): 3-14 ((3, 6,
7d))

O'BRIEN, FLOYD, 1904-1968
trombone

O2 VENABLES, Ralph G. V.: Complete
Floyd O'Brien discography in Jazz
Forum (UK), No. 2 (September
1946): 27-28 ((2, 3, 6, 7d))

O'BRYANT, JIMMIE, d. 1928
saxophones

O3 BAKKER, Dick M.: Jimmie O'Bryant
1923-26 in Micrography, No. 44
(May 1977): 14-18 ((6, 7d))

ODEN, JIMMY, 1903-1977
piano, vocal

O4 COLLER, Derek, ed.: A discography
of St. Louis Jimmy (1944-1963) in
Blues Unlimited, No. 21 (April
1965): 12; No. 22 (May 1965): 6;
additions and corrections in Blues
Unlimited, No. 23 (June 1965): 11
((2, 3, 6, 7, 8))

O5 STEWART-BAXTER, Derrick: [Complete
discography] in Jazz Journal, Vol.
3 (July 1950): 3 ((2, 3, 6, 7d))

ODEON label (German)

O6 SAGAWE, Harm: The German Odeon
Swing-Music-Series in Storyville,
No. 25 (October-November 1969):
15-18 ((3, 6))

ODEON label (Italian)

O7 BARAZZETTA, Giuseppe, and Attilio
ROTA: Discografia italiana; la
serie "Italian Jazz Stars" in
Musica Jazz, Vol. 20 (February
1964): 44-45 ((—))

OFC label
See O F C label

OKEH label
See also ABRAMS, IRWIN; BASIE,
COUNT (Bakker, Dick M.: Count
Basie Vocalion-Okeh's [sic] (36-
42); DORSEY BROTHERS (Okeh Dor-
sey); ELLINGTON, DUKE (Bakker,
Dick M.: Duke Ellington on Colum-
bia/Okeh/Harmony 1927-30): GOOD-
MAN, BENNY (Benny Goodman's Okeh
period); GOOFUS FIVE; OLIVER, KING
JOE (Allen, Walter C.)

O8 NEILL, Billy: Okeh catalogue race
series (nos. 8053-8114) in JONES,
Max, and Albert McCARTHY, eds.:
Jazz review. London: Jazz Music
Books, 1945: 23; (nos. 8073-8187)
in McCARTHY, Albert, and Max
JONES, eds.: Jazz folio. London:
Jazz Sociological Society, 1944:
23-24; (nos. 8192-8269) in Mc-
CARTHY, Albert, and Max JONES,
eds.: Jazz miscellany. London:
Jazz Sociological Society [ca.
1946]: 25-26 ((—))

O9 Okeh label listing (nos. 6800-7337)
in Hot Buttered Soul, No. 40 (September 1975?) to No. 43 (December
1975), various paginations ((3))

O10 RUST, Brian: Okeh-Columbia discography in Jazz Tempo [issue unknown];
additions and corrections in Jazz
Tempo, Vol. 2 (November 8, 1943): 8

O11 SCOTT, Brian: Okeh 8000 race series
in Vintage Jazz Mart, No. 5 (September 1961) to (March 1969), various paginations, most issues [to
no. 8966] ((3))

OLD TIMERS (musical group)

O12 Old Timers discography in Jazz Forum
(Poland), No. 46 (1977): 56 ((—))

OLIVER, KING JOE, 1885-1938
cornet

013 ALLEN, Walter C., and Brian RUST: Discography in their King Joe Oliver. Belleville, NJ: 1955, 65-162 (also issued separately; also London: Jazz Book Club, 1957 and London: Sidgwick & Jackson, 1958, 73-223)); partly reprinted in A discography of King Oliver's 1923 Okeh recordings in Journal of Jazz Studies, Vol. 3 (spring 1976): 46 (Jazz monographs, No. 1) ((2, 3, 4p, 4r, 4t, 5, 6, 7, 8, 9))

014 BAKKER, Dick M.: King Joe Oliver in Micrography, No. 8 (January 1970): 5-8 ((7d))

015 BAKKER, Dick M.: King Oliver 1926-1931 Voc/Br in Micrography, No. 39 (January 1976): 3 ((6, 7d))

016 BAKKER, Dick M.: King Oliver on Victor in Micrography, No. 35 (March 1975): 2 ((6, 7d))

017 BAKKER, Dick M.: King Oliver on Victors in Micrography, No. 21 (September 1972): 2 ((—))

018 BAKKER, Dick M.: King Oliver's Brunswick/Vocalions 1926-1931 in Micrography, No. 23 (January 1973): 3; additions and corrections in Micrography, No. 24 (February 1973): 1 ((7d))

019 Discografia di King Oliver in Jazz di Ieri e di Oggi, Vol. 1 (October 1959): 18-21 ((2, 7))

020 Discography in Mississippi Rag, Vol. 4 (January 1977): 7 ((—))

021 Disques de King Oliver actuellement disponibles en France in Jazz Magazine (France), No. 26 (April 1957): 22 ((—))

022 GRUT, Harald: King Oliver's Creole Jazz Band; a discography in Jazz Music, Vol. 4 (No. 2, 1949): 19-20; additions and corrections [from Brian RUST] in Jazz Music, Vol. 4 (No. 2, 1949): 21; Vol. 4 (No. 4, 1950): 23-24 ((2, 3, 7))

023 HAESLER, William J.: King Oliver's Creole Jazz Band; a revision in Matrix, No. 1 (July 1954): 9-12; additions and corrections in ALLEN, Walter C., and William J. HAESLER: The King Oliver banjoist and other theories in Matrix, No. 5 (March 1955): 6-9; [other corrections] No. 7 (July 1955): 14 ((2, 3, 6, 7))

024 NEVERS, Daniel: Discographie de King Oliver in Jazz Hot, No. 333 (December 1976): 36-39 ((2, 3, 6, 7))

025 WILLIAMS, Eugene: King Oliver and his Dixie Syncopators; notes for a discography in Record Changer, Vol. 3 (September 1944): 49-51 ((2, 3, 6, 7))

026 WILLIAMS, Martin T.: Discography: King Oliver on microgroove in his King Oliver. London: Cassell, 1960 (also New York: Barnes, 1961 [c1960]): 89-90 (Kings of Jazz, 8) (also in translations, Stuttgart: Hatje, 1960; Stockholm; Horsta, 1960; Milan: Ricordi, 1961; Teufen, Switzerland: Arthur Niggli, 1960, paginations unknown) ((—))

OM (musical group)

027 Om discography in Jazz Forum (Poland), No. 48 (1977): 47 ((—))

ONE HUNDRED PROOF (musical group)

028 HUGHES, Rob: 100 Proof (aged in soul) discography in Hot Buttered Soul, No. 46 (June-July 1976): 8 ((2, 3, 7, 8))

ONLY FOR COLLECTORS label
See O F C label

ONYX label

029 HORLICK, Richard: Onyx in R and B Magazine, Vol. 1 (November 1970-February 1971): 27 [nos. 501-520] ((—))

OREGON (musical group)

030 Oregon discography in Down Beat, Vol. 46 (March 8, 1979): 13 ((—))

ORIGINAL DIXIELAND JAZZ BAND
See also JAZZ MUSIC (Jewson, Ron) and (Lange, Horst H.)

031 BAKKER, Dick M.: ODJB in Micrography, No. 14 (May 1971): 5 ((7d))

032 BRUNN, Harry Otis: Recordings of the Original Dixieland Jazz Band in his Story of the Original Dixieland Jazz Band. [Baton

Rouge]: Louisiana State Univ. Pr. [c1960] (also London: Sidgwick and Jackson, 1961; London, Jazz Book Club, 1963; New York: DaCapo, 1977): 102-103, 131, 148-149, 218-219, 242 ((2, 5, 7d))

033 DELAUNAY, Charles: Extraits empruntés à "Essai de discographie hot" in Jazz Hot, No. 3 (May-June 1935): 8-9 ((2, 7d))

034 RUST, Brian: The Original Dixieland Jazz Band in Jazz Tempo, No. 17 (n.d.): 24-25; reprinted, with Australian issues added by Ray MARGINSON, in Jazz Notes and Blue Rhythm, No. 46 (November 1944): 4-5 ((2, 3, 7))

035 TONKS, Eric S.: Discography of the Original Dixieland Jazz Band in Jazz Forum (UK), No. 1 (n.d.): 28-29 ((3, 7))

ORIGINAL FIVE BLIND BOYS OF MISSISSIPPI

036 Original Five Blind Boys of Mississippi discography in R and B Magazine, No. 8 (fall 1971): 10-11 ((2, 3, 7d))

ORIGINAL INDIANA FIVE
      See also JAZZ MUSIC (Jewson, Ron) and (Lange, Horst H.)

037 MILLER, William H.: The jazz mine; the Original Indiana Five in Jazz Notes (Australia), No. 64 (May 1946): 12-13 ((3))

038 RUST, Brian: The Original Indiana Five; a discography in Jazz Music, Vol. 10 (July-August 1959): 29, 34, 35; Vol. 11 (January 1960): 21-22 ((2, 3, 6, 7))

ORIGINAL MEMPHIS FIVE
      See also JAZZ MUSIC (Jewson, Ron) and (Lange, Horst H.)

039 DAVIES, John R. T.: The Original Memphis Five; an uncritical and incomplete listing in Discophile, No. 14 (October 1950): 3-12 ((3, 6))

040 STEINER, John: Discography: related recordings of Shake it and break it/Aunt Hagar's (children's) blues in Second Line, Vol. 7 (July/August 1956): 18-19 ((3, 6, 8))

ORIGINAL RAMBLERS

041 EYLE, Wim van: Het 1929 platen repertoire op LP in Doctor Jazz, No. 87 (March 1979): 12 ((2, 7))

ORIGINAL TEDDIES

042 FLUCKIGER, Otto: Discografie: Teddy Stauffer und seine Original Teddies in Jazz + Classic, No. 4 (1979): 13-15 (part 1, 1940-1941, to be continued) ((2, 3, 6, 7))

ORIOLE label
      See also BANNER label (Complete numerical of Banner Melotone Oriole Perfect Romeo, 1935-1938)

043 [[[Listing] in Melody Maker, Vol. 22 (February 2, 1946)]] additions and corrections in Melody Maker, Vol. 22 (February 16, 1946): 5 [listing and corrections possibly in other issues]

044 WRIGHT, Laurie: The Oriole 1000 series in Storyville, No. 6 (August-September 1966): 27 ((3, 8))

ORY, KID (Edward Ory), 1886-1973 trombone

045 BAKKER, Dick M.: A shortened discography of Kid Ory 1944-1956 in Micrography, No. 3 (May 1969): 9 ((—))

046 CHOQUART, Loys: Discographie du "Kid Ory's Creole Jazz Band" in Hot Revue, No. 2 (1947): 26 ((2, 3, 7))

047 COLLER, Derek: Kid Ory's Creole Jazz Band; a discography in Discophile, No. 2 (October 1948): 10-11; additions and corrections in Discophile, No. 3 (December 1948): 7 ((1, 2, 3, 6, 7))

048 Discographie: Kid Ory in Jazz Hot, No. 85 (February 1954): 31 [1949 AFRS transcriptions] ((1, 3, 7))

049 [[DIXON, Robert M. W., and GILTRAP: Kid Ory; a biography, appreciation, record survey and discography. London: National Jazz Federation [1958], 20 pp.]]

050 HOEFER, George: Kid Ory discography in Down Beat, Vol. 18 (August 10, 1951): 16 ((—))

051   [[JEPSEN, Jorgen Grunnet: Kid Ory.
      Copenhagen: 1957]]

052   MOHR, Kurt: Discographie de Kid
      Ory in Jazz Hot, No. 113 (Septem-
      ber 1956): 19, 35 ((2, 3, 6, 7))

053   TURNER, C. Ian: A discography of
      Kid Ory in Jazz Notes (Australia),
      No. 60 (January 1946): 13-18; re-
      printed as Discografia de Kid
      Ory in Jazz Magazine (Argentina),
      No. 10 (July 1946): 23-27; addi-
      tions and corrections in TEALDO
      ALIZIERI, Carlos L.: Comentarios
      sobre la discografia de Kid Ory
      in Jazz Magazine (Argentina), No.
      11 (August 1946): 24-26 ((2, 3,
      6, 7))

OTHERS BROTHERS (musical group)

054   MOHR, Kurt, and Emmanuel CHOIS-
      NEL: Discographie des Others
      Brothers in Soul Bag, No. 16
      (1972?): 4 ((3, 6, 7))

OTIS, JOHNNY, 1921–
      drums

055   ALLEN, Mike: Johnny Otis discog-
      raphy in Jazz Register, Vol. 2,
      No. 2 (issue No. 6, n.d.): 12
      ((2, 3, 6, 7))

OTIS, SHUGGIE, 1955?–
      guitar, vocal

056   NIQUET, Bernard: Discographie in
      Jazz Hot, No. 261 (May 1970): 21
      ((2, 7d))

OUWERCKX, JOHN
      piano

057   [[RAY, Harry: Les grandes figures
      du jazz. John Ouwerx, sa carrière,
      ses oeuvres, ses souvenirs.
      Bruxelles: Les Cahiers Selection,
      1945, 26 or 46 pp.]]

OZONE label
      See also ROSE, BORIS

058   DAVIS, Brian; Mike BOYLE; and
      Brian THOMAS: LP information:
      Ozone--a complete listing in Dis-
      cographical Forum, No. 33 (1974):
      3-5; additions and corrections in
      Discographical Forum, No. 36
      (1976): 12-14, 19; No. 40 (spring
      1978): 1 ((1, 2, 7))

059   WINTHER-RASMUSSEN, Nils: Ozone
      Records in Orkester Journalen,
      Vol. 41 (May 1973): 17, 34 [to
      no. 10] ((1, 2, 7))

PAAKKUNAINEN, SEPPO, 1943–
      baritone saxophone

P1   Seppo "Baron" Paakkunainen dis-
      cography in Jazz Forum (Poland),
      No. 36 (April 1975): 43 ((—))

PACIFIC JAZZ label

P2   Pacific Jazz; an artist listing
      of all releases on all speeds by
      the Pacific Jazz Record Company
      (winter 1953) in Discophile, No.
      34 (February 1954): 14-15; addi-
      tions and corrections in Disco-
      phile, No. 40 (February 1955): 4-
      7; No. 42 (June 1955): 16-17 ((2,
      3, 7d))

PACKERS (musical group)

P3   [[[Discography] in Soul Bag, No.
      4]]

PAGE, HOT LIPS (Oran Page), 1908-1954
      trumpet

P4   Hot Lips Page. Basel: Jazz-Publi-
      cations, 1961, 30, 1 p. ((2, 3,
      6, 7, 9))

P5   MORGENSTERN, Dan, and Michael
      SHERA, eds.: Hot Lips Page on
      record in Jazz Journal, Vol. 15
      (November 1962): 13-15; (December
      1962): 17-18 ((1, 2, 3, 6, 7))

P6   TONKS, Eric: Hot Lips Page dis-
      cography in Jazz Record (UK), No.
      11 (March 1944): 8-9 ((2, 7d))

PALM label (French)

P7   DOYLE, Mike: Palm label listing
      in Discographical Forum, No. 10
      (January 1969): 19-20; No. 11
      (March 1969): 19-20; No. 12 (May
      1969): 5-6; additions and correc-
      tions in Discographical Forum,
      No. 14 (September 1969): 4 ((1,
      2, 7))

PALM CLUB label (French)

P8   FRESART, Iwan: Out of nowhere in
      Point du Jazz, No. 3 (August
      1970): 77-87 ((1, 2, 7))

PALMER, ROY, 1892-1964
trombone

P9   ALLEN, Walter C.: Roy Palmer dis-
      cography in Hot Notes, No. 14
      (1948): 3-4 ((2, 3, 6, 7))

P10   BAKKER, Dick M.: Roy Palmer in
      Micrography, No. 9 (February
      1970): 3 ((7d))

PALMER, SYLVESTER
piano, vocal

P11   HALL, Bob, and Richard NOBLETT:
      [Discography] in Blues Unlimited,
      No. 112 (March-April 1975): 18
      ((2, 3, 6, 7, 9))

PANACHORD label (British)

P12   MITCHELL, Ray: The Panachord label
      in Matrix, No. 68 (December 1966)
      to No. 71 (June 1967); No. 74
      (December 1967) to No. 88 (June
      1970); No. 90 (December 1970);
      No. 91 (February 1971), various
      paginations ((3, 6))

PANAMA (tune title)

P13   RUGGLES, Happy: Panama; a sug-
      gested complete listing of this
      great tune in Jazz Discounter,
      Vol. 2 (April 1949): 17 ((—))

PAPA BUE (Arne Jensen)
trombone

P14   [[BENDIX, Ole: Papa Bue. Copen-
      hagen: Erichsen, 1962, 72 pp.]]

PAPA LIGHTFOOT
See LIGHTFOOT, PAPA

PARADOX label
See BOLLETINO, DANTE

PARAMOUNT label
See also MORTON, JELLY ROLL
(Bakker, Dick M.: Jelly Roll Morton on the labels Gennett & Paramount...)

P15   DAVIS, John, and G. F. GRAY-
      CLARKE: Paramount 12000 series in
      Jazz Journal, Vol. 4 (April 1951)
      to Vol. 5 (February 1952), various
      paginations, in 10 parts ((3, 6))

P16   HULME, George, and John STEINER:
      The Paramount label; a survey of
      the microgroove issues in Matrix,
      No. 20 (November 1958): 3-14; ad-
      ditions and corrections in Matrix,
      No. 33 (March 1961): 15 ((2, 3,
      7))

P17   MAHONY, Dan, and Walter ALLEN:
      Paramount; numerical listings of
      reissues in Discophile, No. 54
      (June 1957): 3-6; additions and
      corrections in Matrix, No. 37
      (November 1961): 18 ((3))

P18   VREEDE, Max: Paramount 12000
      13000. London: Storyville, c1971,
      240 pp. ((3, 4p, 5, 6))

P19   WYLER, Michael: The Paramount
      story in Jazz Monthly, Vol. 1
      (April 1955) to Vol. 2 (October
      1956); Vol. 2 (December 1956) to
      Vol. 3 (September 1957); Vol. 3
      (November 1957); (January 1958);
      Vol. 4 (March 1958); (May 1958);
      (July 1958); (October 1958); (Feb-
      ruary 1959); Vol. 5 (April 1959),
      various paginations; additions and
      corrections in Record Research
      Bulletin, No. 12 (1960): 6-7 [nos.
      12000-13066] ((3))

PARAMOUNT ORKESTER

P20   ENGLUND, Bjorn: Paramountorkes-
      terns diskografi in Orkester
      Journalen, Vol. 36 (December
      1968): 44 ((2, 3, 7))

PARAMOUNT SERENADERS

P21   Paramount Serenaders 1923-1926 in
      Storyville, No. 68 (December 1976-
      January 1977) to No. 70 (April-May
      1977); No. 72 (August-September
      1977) to No. 74 (December 1977-
      January 1978), various paginations
      ((2, 3, 6, 7, 8, 9))

P22   SUYKERBUYK, Eugen: Paramount Ser-
      enaders 1923-1926 in Swingtime
      (Belgium), No. 17 (January 1977):
      8-11 (deel 3; other parts in other
      issues) ((2, 3, 6, 7))

PARENTI, TONY, 1900-1972
clarinet

P23   MORSER, Roy, and Frank GILLIS:
      Tony Parenti discography July
      1928/May 1941 in Record Research,
      No. 28 (May-June 1960): 12 [only

lists records auditioned by
Parenti which have solos by him]
((3))

P24 MORSER, Roy, and Leon D. VOGEL:
Parenti on record in Playback,
Vol. 4 (February 1952): 3-5 ((2,
3, 6, 7))

PARHAM, TINY (Hartzell Strathdene
Parham), 1900-1947
piano

P25 BAKKER, Dick M.: Tiny Parham 1926-
1940 in Micrography, No. 11 (September 1970): 3 ((7d))

P26 BAKKER, Dick M.: Tiny Parham's
Victors in Micrography, No. 23
(January 1973): 5 ((7d))

P27 RUST, Brian?: Tiny Parham and his
musicians (Victor records) in
Pickup, Vol. 1 (November 1946):
5-6 ((2, 3, 7))

P28 RUST, Brian: Tiny Parham and his
musicians in Melody Maker, Vol.
26 (August 12, 1950): 9 ((2, 3,
6, 7))

PARKER, CHARLIE, 1920-1955
alto saxophone

P29 [[BETTONVILLE, Andre, and Andre
V. GILLET: The Dial Records long
playing discography of Charlie
Parker. Brussels: 1957, 18 folded
sheets]]

P30 BLUME, Jerry; Erik WIEDEMANN; and
Charles DELAUNAY: Discographie de
Charlie Parker in Jazz Hot, No.
39 (December 1949): 31-32; additions and corrections in Jazz Hot,
No. 43 (April 1950): 30 ((2, 3,
6, 7d))

P31 Charlie Parker on Dial in Jazz
Monthly, Vol. 1 (September 1955):
9-10 ((2, 3, 6, 7))

P32 Charlie Parker's discography in
Metronome, Vol. 67 (September
1951): 12 ((—))

P33 CHOLYNSKI, Henryk: Charlie Parker
discography in Jazz Forum (Poland), No. 35 (March 1975): 52-
54; No. 36 (April 1975): 51-53;
No. 37 (May 1975): 58-61 ((2, 7d))

P34 DELORME, Michel: Discographie com-
mentée des enregistrements publics
de Charlie Parker in Jazz Hot, No.
207 (March 1965): 30-35, 73-74;
additions and corrections in Jazz
Hot, No. 208 (April 1965): 42 ((1,
2, 7))

P35 [[Discography of Charlie Parker.
Basel: Jazz-Publications, 1962, 9
pp. (Discographical notes, No. 5)]]

P36 Disques de Parker parus en France
in Jazz Hot, No. 33 (May 1949): 9
((2, 3, 7d))

P37 [[EDWARDS, Ernie; George HALL; and
Bill KORST, eds.: Charlie Parker.
Whittier, CA: ErnGeoBil, 1965]]

P38 FLUCKIGER, Otto: Charlie Parker
alternate masters on Dial in Jazz
Statistics, No. 3 (August 1956):
7-9 ((3, 6, 7d))

P39 FLUCKIGER, Otto: Charlie Parker;
alternate masters on Savoy in Jazz
Statistics, No. 2 (June 1956): 9-
10; additions and corrections in
Jazz Statistics, No. 3 (August
1956): 9 ((2, 3, 6))

P40 FLUCKIGER, Otto: Charlie Parker
(Langspielplatten-Verzeichnis) in
Jazz Statistics, No. 1 (April
1956): 8-10 ((—))

P41 GARDNER, Mark: Discography--
Charlie Parker on cut-price labels
in Jazz Journal, Vol. 20 (June
1967): 9-11; additions and corrections in Jazz Journal, Vol. 22
(April 1969): 12; (May 1969): 40;
(July 1969): 38; (August 1969):
19; (September 1969): 39; (November 1969): 10; Vol. 23 (January
1970): 39 ((2, 3, 6, 7))

P42 GARDNER, Mark, and Frank GIBSON:
A discography of the studio recordings of Charlie Parker in Jazz
Journal, Vol. 17 (May 1964): 26-
27; (June 1964): 29; (July 1964):
25; additions and corrections in
Jazz Journal, Vol. 18 (January
1965): 17; Vol. 19 (September
1966): 17 ((2, 6, 7))

P43 [[GILLET, Andre V.: Essay in discography of Charlie Parker. Brussels: 1957, 42 pp.]]

P44 HOEFER, George: Parker with Mc-
Shann in Down Beat, Vol. 29 (April
12, 1962): 41 ((2, 3, 7))

P45 [[JEPSEN, Jorgen Grunnet: Charlie
Parker diskografi in Orkester
Journalen, Vol. 23 (April 1955)
to (August 1955), various pagina-
tions]]

P46 JEPSEN, Jorgen Grunnet: Discography of Charlie Parker. [Brande,
Denmark: Debut Records, c1959],
29 leaves ((1, 2, 3, 6, 7))

P47   JEPSEN, Jorgen Grunnet: Discography of Charlie Parker. Copenhagen: Knudsen [c1968], 38 leaves ((1, 2, 3, 6, 7))

P48   JEPSEN, Jorgen Grunnet: Diskofilspalten in Orkester Journalen, Vol. 25 (March 1957): 23; (April 1957): 21 [unauthorized recordings] ((1, 2, 7d))

P49   KOCH, Lawrence O.: A numerical listing of Charlie Parker's recordings in Journal of Jazz Studies, Vol. 2 (June 1975): 86-95 ((3, 6, 7d, 9))

P50   KOPELOWICZ, Guy, and François POSTIF: Discographie de Charlie Parker in Jazz Hot, No. 132 (May 1958) to No. 134 (Setpember 1958): various paginations ((1, 2, 3, 6, 7))

P51   KORTEWEG, Simon, and Piet KOSTER: Charlie Parker op Dial in Jazz Wereld, No. 26 (October-November 1969): 20-23 ((2, 3, 6, 7))

P52   KOSTER, Piet, and Dick M. BAKKER: Charlie Parker. Alphen aan de Rijn, Netherlands: Micrography, 1974-1976, 4 v. ((1, 2, 3, 4p, 4t, 6, 7, 8, 9))

P53   [[OLSSON, Jan: Charlie Parker. Kopparberg, Sweden: 1967, 51 pp.]]

P54   OWENS, Thomas: Annotated discography in his Charlie Parker; techniques of improvisation. Ph.D. (Music) dissertation, University of California at Los Angeles, 1974 (available from University Microfilms, Ann Arbor, MI; order no. 75-1992), Vol. 1: 291-385 ((1, 2, 6, 7, 9))

P55   RUSSELL, Ross: Charlie Parker performances/Running discography of principal Parker performances on record in his Bird lives! the high life and hard times of Charlie (Yardbird) Parker. New York: Charterhouse [1973], 385, 387-388 ((7d))

P56   WIEDEMANN, Erik: Charlie Parker discography in Melody Maker, Vol. 27 (January 5, 1952); (January 12, 1952); (February 2, 1952) plus unknown earlier issues possibly starting Vol. 26 (November 10, 1951), various paginations; additions in Melody Maker, Vol. 31 (June 25, 1955); 5 [and possibly other issues] ((1, 2, 3, 6, 7))

P57   WIEDEMANN, Erik: Discography in REISNER, Robert George, ed.: Bird; the legend of Charlie Parker. New York: Citadel, 1962 (also New York: Bonanza, 1962; London: Macgibbon and Kee, 1963; London: Quartet Books, 1974; New York: DaCapo, 1975), 241-256 and London: Jazz Book Club, 1965, 202-217 ((2, 3, 6, 7))

P58   WILLIAMS, Tony: Charlie Parker discography in Discographical Forum, No. 8 (September 1968) to No. 17 (January 1970), various paginations, in 9 parts; additions and corrections in Discographical Forum, No. 18 (1970) to No. 20 (September 1970), various paginations ((1, 2, 3, 6, 7, 9))

P59   WILLIAMS, Tony: Charlie Parker discography in RUSSELL, Ross: Bird lives! the high life and hard times of Charlie (Yardbird) Parker. London: Quartet Books, [1976, c1972], 384-388 ((7d))

Compositions
See SUPERSAX

Influences

P60   RUSSELL, Ross: Charlie Parker's sources, musical references, and companions in his Bird lives! the high life and hard times of Charlie (Yardbird) Parker. New York: Charterhouse [1973], 386-387 ((——))

CHARLIE PARKER label
See EGMONT label

PARKER, EVAN, 1944-
tenor and soprano saxophones

P61   Evan Parker discography in Jazz Forum (Poland), No. 51 (1978): 41 ((——))

PARKER, JUNIOR (Herman Parker), 1932-1971
harmonica

P62   BROVEN, John J.: Little Junior Parker in Blues Unlimited, No. 1 (April 1963): 8-9; additions and corrections in Blues Unlimited, No. 2 (June 1963): 11 ((2, 3, 6, 7d))

P63 BROVEN, John J.: Little Junior
Parker in Blues Unlimited, undated
supplement to Nos. 1-6: 4-5; additions and corrections in Blues
Unlimited, No. 12 (June 1964):
suppl-4 to suppl-5 [rev. ed. of
previous entry] ((2, 3, 6, 7d))

P64 DEMETRE, Jacques: Notes discographiques sur les enregistrements
de Little Junior Parker in Jazz
Hot, No. 122 (June 1957): 12 ((2,
3, 7d))

P65 MOHR, Kurt, and Emmanuel CHOISNEL:
Junior Parker in Soul Bag, No. 41
(September 1974): 14-19; additions
and corrections in Soul Bag, No.
43/44 (November-December 1974):
13 ((2, 3, 5, 7))

PARKER, LEO, 1925-1962
    baritone saxophone
    See also SMITH, Jimmy (Discogra-
    phy of Jimmy Smith-Leo Parker)

P66 EDWARDS, Ernie: Leo Parker discography in Discographical Forum,
No. 11 (March 1969): 3-6; No. 12
(May 1969): 3-5; additions and
corrections in Discographical
Forum, No. 14 (September 1969):
2; No. 15 (November 1969): 2-3;
No. 16 (January 1970): 1, 2; No.
17 (March 1970): 2; No. 21 (November 1970): 20 ((2, 3, 6, 7))

P67 JEPSEN, Jorgen Grunnet: Leo Parker
diskografi in Orkester Journalen,
Vol. 30 (April 1962): 34; (May
1962): 34 ((2, 3, 6, 7))

P68 ROTANTE, Anthony: A "name" discography of Leo Parker in Discophile, No. 38 (October 1954): 9-
10; additions and corrections in
Discophile, No. 40 (February
1955): 16; No. 46 (February
1956): 12 ((2, 3, 7))

PARKER, ROBERT, 1930-
    tenor saxophone

P69 [[[Discography] in Soul Bag, No.
2; additions and corrections in
Soul Bag, No. 21 (November-December 1972): 9]]

PARKER, SONNY, 1925-1957
    drums, vocal

P70 CHAUVARD, Marcel, and Kurt MOHR:
Discography of Sonny Parker in
Jazz Statistics, No. 26/27 (June-
September 1962): 8 ((2, 3, 7))

P71 MOHR, Kurt: Discographie de Sonny
Parker in Jazz Hot, No. 120 (April
1957): 12 ((2, 3, 7))

P72 TONNEAU, Serge: Discographie de
Sonny Parker in Point du Jazz, No.
2 (February 1970): 30-32 ((1, 2,
3, 6, 7))

PARLOPHON label (German)
    See LINDSTROM label (Lange, Horst
    H.)

PARLOPHONE label (British)
    See also BOSTIC, EARL (Friedrich,
    Heinz); KING label (Barazzetta,
    Giuseppe); LANG, EDDIE (Higgins,
    Jack)

P73 BROWN, Ken: Around the turntable
in Jazz Record (UK), No. 8 (October 1943): 8-9; additions and
corrections in GRAY-CLARKE, G. F.:
An appendix to the Parlophone
"race" discography in Jazz Record
(UK), No. 10 (February 1944): 10-
12 [nos. R3254-E5670] ((3, 7d))

P74 [[HAYES, Jim: English Parlophone,
F 100 to 999. Liverpool: 1969, 24
pp.]]

P75 LANGE, Horst H.: (Parlophone) New
Style Swing Series in R.S.V.P.,
No. 52 (January-February 1970):
25 ((2, 3, 6, 7d))

P76 [[MØLLER, Børge J. C.: Parlophone
bio-diskografi. Copenhagen: L.
Irich's Bogtrikkeri, 1946, 64
pp.]]

P77 MYLNE, Dave, and Bill LLOYD: The
Negro and his music (the Parlophone race series discography) in
Jazz Journal, Vol. 2 (January
1949): 5 ((3, 6))

PARROT label

P78 BRYMER, George: The "Parrot"
label; a provisional listing in
Discophile, No. 43 (July 1955):
17; additions and corrections in
ROTANTE, Anthony: The "Parrot"
label; some further notes in Discophile, No. 48 (June 1956): 7-8;
No. 50 (October 1956): 16 ((—))

PASS, JOE (Joseph Anthony Passalaqua),
1929-
    guitar

P79   JAMES, Burnett, and Chris SHERI-
DAN: Joe Pass discography in Jazz
Journal, Vol. 29 (May 1976): 13,
24; (June 1976): 24-25; additions
and corrections from Chris SHERI-
DAN in Jazz Journal, Vol. 29 (November 1976): 22 ((1, 2, 7))

P80   Joe Pass discography in Swing
Journal, Vol. 29 (May 1975): 238-
241 ((2))

P81   Selected Pass discography in Down
Beat, Vol. 42 (March 13, 1975):
15 ((—))

P82   Selected Pass discography in Down
Beat, Vol. 45 (April 6, 1978): 17
((—))

PASTOR, TONY, 1907-1969
   tenor saxophone, vocal

P83   GARROD, Charles: Tony Pastor and
his Orchestra. Spotswood, NJ:
Joyce Music, 1973, 1, 23, 9 leaves
((1, 2, 3, 4t, 6, 7))

PASTORIUS, JACO, 1951-
   bass guitar

P84   Jaco Pastorius discography in Down
Beat, Vol. 44 (January 27, 1977):
13 ((—))

P85   Jaco Pastorius discography in Jazz
Forum (Poland), No. 48 (1977): 38
((—))

PATE, JOHNNY, 1923-
   bass violin

P86   MOHR, Kurt: Discography of Johnny
Pate in Jazz Statistics, No. 9
(March 1959): 2; additions and
corrections from Michel VOGLER in
Jazz Statistics, No. 17 (1960):
6-7 ((2, 3, 7))

PATHE label
   See ACTUELLE label; CRESCENT
   label; SYNCO JAZZ BAND

PATT, FRANK, 1928-
   bass violin, guitar, vocal
   See JENKINS, GUS

PATTON, CHARLIE, 1887-1934
   guitar, vocal

P87   BAKKER, Dick M.: Charlie Patton in
Micrography, No. 4 (June 1969):

9; additions and corrections in
Micrography, No. 5 (August 1969):
12 [also supplements next entry]
((—))

P88   [[EVANS, David: Charlie Patton.
Knutsford, Cheshire: Blues World,
1969, 20 pp.]]

P89   FAHEY, John: A discography of
Charley Patton, Henry Sims,
Bertha Lee, Willie Brown, Louise
Johnson, and Walter (Buddy Boy)
Hawkins in his Charley Patton.
London: Studio Vista (also New
York: Stein & Day), [c1971], 108-
111 ((2, 3, 6, 7))

P90   STEWART-BAXTER, Derrick: [Discog-
raphy of Paramount issues] in Jazz
Journal, Vol. 2 (August 1949): 5
((—))

PAUL, LES, 1916-
   guitar

P91   BENNETT, Bill: Les Paul (guitar
genius); towards a discography
(later titled Research: Les Paul
or Les Paul Research) in Record
Research, No. 153/154 (April
1978); No. 155/156 (July 1978);
No. 161/162 (February-March 1979);
No. 163/164 (May-June 1979); No.
167/168 (December 1979), various
paginations ((3))

PAX label
   See BOLLETINO, DANTE

PAYNE, CECIL, 1922-
   baritone saxophone

P92   GARDNER, Mark: Cecil Payne in
Jazz Monthly, Vol. 10 (May 1964):
5-8; (June 1964): 5-7; (July
1964): 7-9 ((1, 2, 3, 7))

PEACOCK, GARY, 1935-
   bass violin

P93   Plattenhinweise in Jazz Podium,
Vol. 26 (September 1977): 16
((—))

P94   Sélection discographique in Jazz
Hot, No. 290 (January 1973): 17
((2, 7))

PEACOCK label
   See also BROWN, CLARENCE "GATE-
   MOUTH" (Mohr, Kurt)

P95 EAGLE, Bob; Fred WETHERELD; and Gary RICHARDS: Peacock 3000 gospel series in Alley Music, Vol. 1 (winter 1968): 13 ((3))

P96 HAYES, Cedric J.: Listing in Blues Research, No. 2 (January 1960): unpaged, on 8 pages; continued in his Gospel in Jazz Statistics, No. 28 (1962): BLUES-8; additions and corrections from Lenny GILL in Blues Statistics, No. 2 (March 1963): 6 ((—))

PEARSON, DUKE, 1932-1980
piano

P97 GARDNER, Mark: Duke Pearson in Jazz Monthly, No. 175 (September 1969): 29-30 ((2, 3, 7))

PECORA, SANTO (Santo J. Pecoraro), 1902-
trombone

P98 Discography of Santo Pecora in ROWE, John, ed.: Trombone jazz. London: Jazz Tempo, 1945: 17 ((2, 3, 7))

PENGUINS (musical group)

P99 BOLDEN, Don: Penguins discography in R and B Collector, Vol. 1 (March-April 1970): 10 ((—))

P100 PUTNEY, Bill: Spotlighting the Penguins in Rhythm & Blues Train, Vol. 1 (November 1964): 4-5 ((—))

PENNSYLVANIA SYNCOPATORS

P101 LANGE, Horst H.: The Pennsylvania Syncopators in Discophile, No. 37 (August 1954): 3-4; additions and corrections in Discophile, No. 41 (April 1955): 15-16 ((3))

PEPPER, ART, 1925-
alto saxophone

P102 Art Pepper in Swing Journal, Vol. 34 (January 1980): 162-167 ((2, 7d))

P103 Art Pepper discography in Swing Journal, Vol. 27 (May 1973): 262-267 ((2, 7d))

P104 EDWARDS, Ernie: Art Pepper discography. Whittier, CA: Jazz Discographies Unlimited, 1965, 22 leaves (Spotlight series, Vol. 4) ((2, 3, 7))

P105 EDWARDS, Ernie, and John C. IRWIN, eds.: The new revised Art Pepper discography. Whittier, CA: Ern-GeoBil, 1969, 20 leaves ((2, 3, 6, 7, 9))

P106 JEPSEN, Jorgen Grunnet: Art Pepper diskografi in Orkester Journalen, Vol. 26 (June-July 1958): 58 ((2, 3, 6, 7d))

P107 MORGAN, Alun: Art Pepper, a name listing in Discographical Forum, No. 4 (January 1961): 5-7 ((2, 3, 6, 7))

P108 SELBERT, Todd: Art Pepper discography in PEPPER, Art, and Laurie PEPPER: Straight life; the story of Art Pepper. New York: Schirmer Books [c1979], 477-507 ((1, 2, 3, 6, 7, 9))

P109 Selected Art Pepper discography in Down Beat, Vol. 46 (December 1979): 19 ((—))

P110 Selected Pepper discography in Down Beat, Vol. 42 (June 5, 1975): 17 ((—))

P111 SIDERS, Harvey: Art Pepper in Different Drummer, Vol. 1 (July 1974): 28 ((—))

PERCUSSION MUSIC (JAZZ)
See also DRUM MUSIC (JAZZ)

P112 Percussion profiles; Diskographie eines Jazzreignisses in Blues Notes, No. 3/79 (1979): 35-39 ((—))

PERFECT label
See also BANNER label (Complete numerical of Banner Melotone Oriole Perfect Romeo, 1935-1938)

P113 GODRICH, John: The Perfect 100 race series in 78 Quarterly, Vol. 1 (No. 1, 1967): 56-58 ((3, 5, 8))

P114 KENDZIORA, Carl, and Perry ARMAGNAC: Perfect dance and race catalog (1922-1930) in Record Research, No. 51/52 (May-June 1963), whole issue (48 pp.) ((3, 5, 6, 7d))

PERKINS, CARL, 1928-1958
piano

P115 MONTI, Pierre Andre: Discographie de Carl Perkins in Jazz 360, No. 18 (May 1979): 6-9; No. 20 (September 1979): 5 ((2, 7))

P116 MORGAN, Alun: Discography in Jazz Monthly, Vol. 8 (July 1962): 13-

15; additions and corrections in
Jazz Monthly, Vol. 12 (June 1966):
28 ((2, 7))

PERRY, KING

P117 MOHR, Kurt: King Perry; a name
discography in Discophile, No. 60
(June 1958): 8, 10 ((2, 3, 7))

PERSON, HOUSTON, 1934–
tenor saxophone

P118 PORTER, Bob: Houston Person in
Different Drummer, Vol. 1 (April
1974): 28 ((—))

PETERSON, OSCAR, 1925–
piano

P119 FRESIA, Enzo: Oscar Peterson 1961–
1963; Oscar Peterson Trio in
Musica Jazz, Vol. 20 (February
1964): 42–43 ((2, 7))

P120 JEPSEN, Jorgen Grunnet: Diskofilspalten in Orkester Journalen,
Vol. 31 (January 1963): 19; Victor recordings ((2, 3, 6, 7))

PETTIS, JACK, 1902–
tenor saxophone

P121 VENABLES, Ralph G. V.: A discography of Jack Pettis and his Orchestra in Jazzfinder, Vol. 1 (November 1948): 5–6; additions and
corrections in his On Jack Pettis
and some others in Jazzfinder,
Vol. 2 (June 1949): 32–33 ((2, 3,
7))

PHANTASIE CONCERT label

P122 KENDZIORA, Carl: Behind the cobwebs in Record Research, No. 65
(December 1964): 6–7 ((3, 6))

PHELPS, JIMMY
See The DU-ETTES

PHILIPS label (British)

P123 HAYES, Jim: Philips 10" LP series
BBR8000, a numerical catalogue
check listing in R.S.V.P., No. 16
(September 1966); No. 18 (November 1966); No. 20 (January 1967);
No. 22 (March 1967), various paginations ((7d))

PHILLIPS, ESTHER, 1935–
vocal

P124 HESS, Norbert: "Little Esther"
Phillips discography in Soul Bag,
No. 40 (July-August 1974): 8–15;
additions and corrections in Soul
Bag, No. 43/44 (November-December
1974): 3; No. 47 (March 1975): 1;
No. 51 (January 1976): 32; No. 54
(July 1976): 1 ((2, 3, 7))

P125 MOHR, Kurt: Little Esther on
Federal in Jazz Statistics, No.
12 (September 1959): 7 ((2, 3, 6,
7))

PHONOCYLINDERS
See RAGTIME MUSIC (Walker,
Edward)

PIANO MUSIC (JAZZ)
See also PIANO ROLLS; RAGTIME
MUSIC

P126 Disques de piano-blues in Jazz
Hot, No. 305 (May 1974): 9 ((—))

P127 EDWARDS, Ernie; George HALL; and
Bill KORST: Modern jazz piano Vol.
1: Joe Albany, Al Haig, Gene Di-
Novi, Argonne Thornton (Sadik
Hakim). Whittier, CA: ErnGeoBil,
1966, 2, 17, 5, 5 pp. (Spotlight
series, Vol. 5) ((1, 2, 3, 6, 7))

P128 KRISS, Eric: Part II--general
piano (discography of currently-
available piano blues) in his Six
blues-roots pianists. New York:
Oak, 1973, 100–104 ((—))

P129 WILSON, John Steuart: Jazz pianists, a discography in High Fidelity, Vol. 7 (August 1957): 65–72
((—))

PIANO RED (Willie Perryman), 1911–
piano, vocal

P130 ALLEN, Walter C.: A discography of
Piano Red in Melody Maker, Vol.
27 (August 4, 1951): 9 ((2, 3, 7))

P131 ALLEN, Walter C.: Piano Red Willie
Perryman; a discography in Discophile, No. 41 (April 1955): 6–7;
additions and corrections in Discophile, No. 44 (October 1955):
13; No. 50 (October 1956): 16–17
((2, 3, 6, 7))

PIANO ROLLS
See also BLAKE, EUBIE--Piano
Rolls; BLYTHE, JIMMY (Berg, Arne)

and (Kunstadt, Len); DAVENPORT,
COW COW (Montgomery, Mike); HAYES,
EDGAR; JOHNSON, JAMES P.--Piano
Rolls; JOPLIN, SCOTT; MORTON,
JELLY ROLL--Piano Rolls; RAGTIME
MUSIC (A list of player-piano
rolls...); ROBBINS, EVERETT;
ROBERTS, LUCKY; WALLER, FATS--
Piano Rolls

P132 KUNSTADT, Len: Piano-rollography;
an exploratory piano-rollography
check list of blues-jazz rolls
issued in 1921 by leading music
roll artists in Record Research,
Vol. 3 (June-July 1957): 8 ((5))

P133 KUNSTADT, Len: Piano-rollography
blues-jazz music rolls of 1922--
exploratory in Record Research,
Vol. 3 (January-February 1958): 9
((5, 8))

P134 WALKER, Edward S.: Piano roll
discography in Jazz Report (California), Vol. 6, No. 5 (n.d.):
unpaged, on 4 pages; additions
and corrections from Mike MONTGOM-
ERY in Jazz Report, Vol. 6, No.
6 (n.d.): unpaged, on 2 pages ((8))

PICK-UP label

P135 MAHONY, Dan: The Pick-Up and Swan
labels in Matrix, No. 28 (April
1960): 3-5 ((7d, 8))

PICKETT, CHARLIE
    guitar, vocal

P136 OLIVER, Paul: Charlie Pickett in
Jazz Monthly, Vol. 7 (July 1961):
18 ((2, 3, 6, 7d))

PICKETT, DAN
    guitar, vocal

P137 LOWRY, Pete: [Discography] in
Blues Unlimited, No. 45 (August
1967): 18 ((3))

PICKETT, WILSON,
    vocal

P138 MOHR, Kurt: Wilson Pickett in Soul
Bag, No. 35 (February 1974):
4-10; additions and corrections in
Soul Bag, No. 38 (May 1974): 46;
No. 44 (January 1975): 34 [reprint-
ed from Rock & Folk Magazine, No.
zero (July 1966)] ((2, 3, 7))

PICOU, ALPHONSE, 1878-1961
    clarinet

P139 MILLS, Ken Grayson: Discography
of Alphonse Picou in Jazz Report
(California), Vol. 1 (April 1961):
3-5 ((1, 2, 3, 7))

PIERCE, CHARLES, d. 1938?
    alto saxophone

P140 [Discography to be added to Delaunay's Hot discography] in Jazz
Information, Vol. 2 (November
1940): 87 ((2, 3, 7d))

PIERCE, DE DE (Joseph DeLacrois
    Pierce), 1904-1973
    cornet, trumpet

P141 De De's discography in Mississippi
Rag, Vol. 1 (January 1974): 2 ((2,
7))

PINKETT, WARD, 1906-1937
    trumpet, vocal

P142 McCARTHY, Albert J.: Discography
in Jazz Forum (UK), No. 2 (September 1946): 25-27 ((2, 3, 6, 7))

P143 McCARTHY, Albert J.: A discography
of Ward Pinkett in Record Changer,
Vol. 8 (March 1949): 16, 18 ((2,
3, 6, 7))

PIRATE label (Swedish)

P144 Pirate Records; an editorial feature in Matrix, No. 59 (June
1965): 15-17; No. 60 (August
1965): 15-16; No. 62 (December
1965): 12-13; additions and corrections in Matrix, No. 70 (April
1967): 14 ((3, 6, 7d))

PIRON, ARMAND J., 1888-1943
    violin

P145 BAKKER, Dick M.: Armand J. Piron's
recordings 1923-1925 in Micrography,
No. 25 (March 1973): 4; additions and corrections in Micrography, No. 26 (1973): 1; No. 29
(December 1973): 1 ((7d))

P146 Discography of Armand J. Piron in
Second Line, Vol. 3 (January-
February 1952): 18 ((2, 3, 7d))

P147 WARD, Alan: The Armand J. Piron
reissues in Footnote, Vol. 5
(June-July 1974): 23 ((—))

P148 WHYATT, Bert: Numerical natter;
Armand J. Piron in Vintage Jazz
Mart, Vol. 5 (February 1958): 3
((2, 3, 6, 7))

PIZZI, RAY, 1943–
saxophones

P149 Selected Pizzi discography in Down
Beat, Vol. 44 (October 20, 1977):
18 ((—))

PLANET label
See LASALLE label

PLAZA MUSIC COMPANY
See also BANNER label

P150 KENDZIORA, Carl: Plaza 5000 series
masters in Record Research, No.
36 (July 1961) to date, various
paginations [No. 173/174 (June
1980) reached matrix 8699] ((3))

PLEASURE, KING (Clarence Beeks), 1922–
vocal

P151 Discography, King Pleasure & Betty
Carter in Jazz Statistics, No. 7
(1958?): 8; additions by Jorgen
Grunnet JEPSEN in Jazz Statistics,
No. 12 (September 1959): 8 ((2))

P152 [[TARRANT, Don: King Pleasure
discography in Journal of Jazz
Discography, No. 1 (November
1976): 12-14]]; additions and
corrections in Journal of Jazz
Discography, No. 2 (June 1977):
3-4 ((3, 7d))

PLYMOUTH label

P153 FLUCKIGER, Otto: Notes to the
"Plymouth" longplaying records in
Jazz Statistics, No. 2 (June
1956): 5-6 ((—))

PM label (Canadian)

P154 PM Records in Canada--a discography in Jazz Forum, No. 53 (1978):
51 ((2, 7))

POLLACK, BEN, 1903-1971
leader, drums

P155 BAKKER, Dick M.: Ben Pollack 1926-
1933 in Micrography, No. 13 (February 1971): 4 ((7d))

P156 BAKKER, Dick M.: Ben Pollack 1926-
1933 in Micrography, No. 27 (September 1973): 4 [rev. ed. of previous entry] ((7d))

P157 NAPOLEON, Art, and John R. T.
DAVIES: A discography in Storyville, No. 36 (August-September
1971): 222-225 ((2, 3, 6, 7, 8,
9))

P158 VENABLES, Ralph G. V.: Discography; a feature for the connoisseur
in Discography (October 1943):
3-5; additions and corrections in
Discography (November 1943): 14
((2, 3, 7d))

P159 VENABLES, Ralph G. V.: Full discography of Ben Pollack and band
in Down Beat, Vol. 13 (January 14,
1946): 19 ((2, 3, 7d))

POLLARD, TOMMY, 1923-1960
piano, vibraphone

P160 MORGAN, Alun: Provisional discography in Jazz Monthly, Vol. 6
(December 1960): 8-9 ((2, 3, 7))

POLYDOR label (Australian)
See BRIGGS, ARTHUR (Grossman,
Ernst)

PONTY, JEAN LUC, 1942–
violin

P161 Plattenhinweise in Jazz Podium,
Vol. 28 (August 1979): 6 ((—))

P162 Selected Ponty discography in
Down Beat, Vol. 42 (December 4,
1975): 17 ((—))

P163 Selected Ponty discography in Down
Beat, Vol. 44 (December 1, 1977):
12 ((—))

PORTENA JAZZ BAND

P164 Portena Jazz Band in Anuario de
Jazz Caliente (1972): 10 ((2, 7))

PORTER, KING
trumpet

P165 FLUCKIGER, Otto: Discography of
King Porter in Jazz Statistics,
No. 14 (January 1960): 7; additions and corrections from Michel
VOGLER in Jazz Statistics, No. 22
(June 1961): 4 [1948-1949 recordings; this is not the same trumpeter as James "King" Porter who
recorded with Jelly Roll Morton]
((2, 3, 6, 7))

POST label

P166 [[[Listing] in Soul Bag, No. 15]]

P167 SHAW, Greg, and Ray TOPPING: Post label listing in Shout, No. 82 (December 1972): 6 ((3, 5))

POWELL, BUD (Earl Powell), 1924-1966
    piano
    See also MONK, THELONIOUS (Jepsen, Jorgen Grunnet: A discography of Thelonious Monk/Bud Powell); TATUM, ART (Jepsen, Jorgen Grunnet: Discography of Art Tatum/Bud Powell)

P168 BLUME, Jerry: Discographie in Jazz Hot, No. 44 (May 1950): 14, 16 ((2, 3, 7d))

P169 [Discography] in Swing Journal, Vol. 31 (November 1977): 298-303 ((2, 7d))

P170 GARDNER, Mark: Bud Powell on record in Jazz Monthly, Vol. 13 (July 1967): 28-30; additions and corrections in Jazz Monthly, No. 153 (November 1967): 27 ((2, 3, 6, 7))

P171 HOEFER, George: Early Powell discography in Down Beat, Vol. 30 (February 28, 1963): 38 [1944 recordings only] ((2, 3, 7))

P172 JEPSEN, Jorgen Grunnet: Bud Powell; a complete discography in Down Beat Music '69 (14th Yearbook): 45-52 ((1, 2, 3, 6, 7))

P173 [[STIASSI, Ruggero: [Discography 1946-1966] in Musica Jazz, Vol. 24 (November 1968)]]

P174 WIEDEMANN, Erik: Bud Powell--a discography in Discophile, No. 37 (August 1954): 5-7; additions and corrections in Discophile, No. 41 (April 1955): 16 ((2, 3, 6, 7))

POWELL, CHRIS
    vocal

P175 MOHR, Kurt, and Helene F. CHMURA: Chris Powell and his Five Blue Flames in Jazz Statistics, No. 4 (November 1956): 3; No. 9 (195?): 2; additions and corrections from M. VOGLER in Jazz Statistics, No. 17 (1960): 7 ((2, 3, 7))

POWELL, JESSE, 1924-
    tenor saxophone

P176 MOHR, Kurt: [Discography] in Jazz Statistics, No. 11 (July 1959): 4; additions and corrections from Michel VOGLER in Jazz Statistics,

No. 22 (June 1961): 6 ((2, 3, 6, 7))

P177 NIQUET, Bernard: Jesse Powell in Point du Jazz, No. 11 (June 1975): 44-47 ((2, 3, 7))

POWELL, TEDDY, ca. 1905-
    leader
    See also CHESTER, BOB

P178 CROSBIE, Ian: Selected recordings in Jazz Monthly, No. 165 (November 1968): 11 ((2, 3, 6, 7))

POWELL, TINY
    vocal

P179 CHOISNEL, Emmanuel: Discographie de Tiny Powell in Soul Bag, No. 22/23 (January-February 1973): 27-28 ((2, 3, 7))

PRATT, ALFRED, 1908-1960
    tenor saxophone, clarinet, vocal

P180 ORTIZ ODERIGO, Nestor R.: Discography of Al Pratt in Playback, Vol. 2 (August 1949): 6 ((—))

PREACHER ROLLO (Rollo Laylan)
    drums

P181 MORSER, Roy: Preacher Rollo & the Five Saints in Discophile, No. 23 (April 1952): 13; [[additions and corrections in Discophile, No. 24?]] ((2, 3, 7))

PRESTIGE label

P182 JEPSEN, Jorgen Grunnet: Prestige matrice numbers in Jazz Statistics, No. 6 (October 1957): 2-4 [nos. 757-978] ((7d))

P183 KRANER, Dietrich H.: The Prestige 16 rpm series in Journal of Jazz Discography, No. 5 (September 1979): 13-16 ((2, 3, 6, 7))

P184 PORTER, Bob: Discomania in Jazz Hot, No. 261 (May 1970): 30-31; No. 262 (June 1970): 31 [1969 recordings] ((2, 7))

P185 RUPPLI, Michel: Prestige jazz records 1949-1969; a discography. [Soisy-sous-Montmorency, France: 1972], 339, 2, 3, 3 pp. ((2, 3, 4p, 6, 7))

P186 RUPPLI, Michael, and Bob PORTER: The Prestige label; a discography.

Westport, CT: Greenwood [c1980],
xiii, 377 pp. [rev. ed. of previous entry] ((2, 3, 4p, 4r, 6,
7))

PRESTON, JIMMY
alto saxophone, vocal

P187 MOHR, Kurt: Discography of Jimmy
Preston in Jazz Statistics, No. 21
(March 1961): 11; additions and
corrections from Michel VOGLER in
Jazz Statistics, No. 22 (June
1961): 4 ((2, 3, 7))

PREVIN, ANDRE, 1929-
piano

P188 Discografia "Contemporary" di
Andre Previn in Jazz di Ieri e di
Oggi, Vol. 2 (December 1960): 43-
44 ((2, 7))

P189 WALKER, Malcolm: Discography in
GREENFIELD, Edward: Andre Previn.
New York: Drake [1973], 93-96
((2))

PRICE, SAMMY, 1908-
piano

P190 Discographie de Sammy Price parus
en France in Jazz Hot, No.107
(February 1956): 15 ((2, 3, 7d))

P191 Discographies in Jazz Hot, No. 38
(November 1949): 31; additions
and corrections in Jazz Hot, No.
39 (December 1949): 32 ((2, 3, 7))

PRICE, WALTER, 1917-
piano, vocal

P192 LEADBITTER, Mike: Big Walter
Price; a discography in Blues
Unlimited, No. 19 (February 1965):
9 ((2, 3, 7))

P193 LEADBITTER, Mike: Discography of
Big Walter Price in Blues Statistics, No. 2 (March 1963): 5-6
((3, 7))

PRIVATE RECORDINGS
See also ADDERLEY, JULIAN "CANNON-
BALL" (Adkins, Tony); AMMONS, GENE
(Walker, Malcolm); ARMSTRONG,
LOUIS (Norris, John); COLTRANE,
JOHN (Goddet, Laurent) and (Raben,
Erik: Diskofilspalten) and (Win-
ther-Rasmussen, Nils); DAVIS,
MILES (Lohmann, Jan); ELLINGTON,
DUKE (Aasland, Benny H.: Duke och

piraterna); GETZ, STAN (Adkins,
Tony); HOLIDAY, BILLIE (Millar,
Jack: Billie Holiday--a selected
discography of airshots...);
MINGUS, CHARLES (Kraner, Dietrich
H.); MONK, THELONIOUS (Kuhne,
Peter); MORTON, JELLY ROLL
(Gazères, P.); PARKER, CHARLIE
(Jepsen, Jorgen Grunnet: Disko-
filspalten); TERRY, CLARK (Adkins,
Tony)

P194 ADKINS, Tony, and Malcolm WALKER:
Private recordings in Discographical Forum, No. 25 (July 1971)
to No. 30/31 (1972), various paginations ((1, 2, 7, 9))

P195 FLUCKIGER, Otto: Private recordings in Jazz Statistics, No. 22
(June 1961): 9-10; No. 23 (September 1961): JS4-JS8; No. 24
(December 1961): JS4-JS6 ((1, 2,
7, 9))

P196 WALKER, Malcolm, and Tony WIL-
LIAMS: Private recordings in Discographical Forum, No. 5 (March
1968) to No. 9 (November 1968):
various paginations ((1, 2, 7, 9))

PROFESSOR LONGHAIR
See BYRD, ROY

PROGRESSIVE label
See JAZZOLOGY label

PROJECT label (British)

P197 The "Project" label in Matrix,
No. 66/67 (September 1966): 39
((3, 6))

PRYOR, SNOOKY (James Edward Pryor),
1921-
drums, harmonica, vocal

P198 LEADBITTER, Mike: James Snooky
Pryor, discography in Blues Unlimited, No. 31 (March 1966): 14-
15 ((2, 3, 7))

PRYSOCK, RED
tenor saxophone

P199 MOHR, Kurt: Red Prysock discographie in Soul Bag, No. 65 (January
1978): 9-11 ((2, 3, 7))

PULLEN, DON, 1944-
piano

P200 LUZZI, Mario: Discografia in
Musica Jazz, Vol. 23 (April 1977):
15-16 ((2, 7))

P201 Plattenhinweise in Jazz Podium,
Vol. 25 (April 1976): 12 ((—))

P202 RENSEN, Jan: Don Pullen; ik heb
Cecil Taylor altijd bewust gemeden
in Jazz Nu, Vol. 2 (October 1979):
21-25 ((2, 7))

PUMIGLIO, PETE
alto saxophone

P203 VENABLES, Ralph G. V.: A feature
for the connoisseur in Discography
(February 1943): 6 ((2, 3))

P204 VENABLES, Ralph G. V.: Pete Pumiglio in Jazz Notes and Blue Rhythm,
Vol. 3 (October 11, 1943): 7-8
((3))

PURDIE, PRETTY (Bernard Lee Purdie),
1939-
drums, vocal

P205 NIQUET, Bernard: Discographie de
Bernard Lee Purdie in Jazz Hot,
No. 241 (May-July 1968): 30 ((2,
7))

P206 NIQUET, Bernard: Essai de discographie critique in Point du Jazz,
No. 7 (October 1972): 9-12 ((2,
7))

PURIM, FLORA, 1942-
vocal
See also AIRTO

P207 Selected Purim discography in Down
Beat, Vol. 41 (December 19, 1974):
18 ((—))

PURIST label (British)

P208 HULME, G. W. George: The Purist
label in Discophile, No. 47 (April
1956): 18 ((1, 2, 7))

PURVIS, JACK, 1906-1962
multi-instrumentalist

P209 KELLEY, Peter L. A.: Discography
of Jack Purvis in Discophile, No.
4 (February 1949): 2-3 ((2, 3,
7d))

P210 KELLY, Peter: Jack Purvis discography in Jazz Journal, Vol. 20
(October 1967): 18-19, 22 ((2, 3,
6, 7)) [Note: authors' spellings

for previous 2 entries are as
given in the discographies; probably same person]

QRS label
See also WILLIAMS, CLARENCE
(Bakker, Dick M.: Clarence Williams' QRS-recordings and some
related sessions)

Q1   Listing of QRS records in Storyville, No. 7 (October-November
1966): 21-25 ((3))

Q2   SALT, Colin: Numerical catalogue
of the QRS label in Discophile,
No. 29 (May 1953): 2-6; additions
and corrections in Discophile, No.
31 (August 1953): 16-17; No. 32
(October 1953): 14; No. 33 (December 1953): 16; No. 34 (February
1954): 13; No. 50 (October 1956):
17 ((3))

QUILLAN, BEN, 1907- and QUILLAN, RUFUS,
1900-1946
piano, vocal
See BLUE HARMONY BOYS

QUINICHETTE, PAUL, 1921-
tenor saxophone

Q3   EDWARDS, Ernie: A name discography
of Paul Quinichette in Discophile,
No. 43 (August 1955): 5-6; additions and corrections in Discophile, No. 46 (February 1956):
12-13 ((2, 3, 6, 7))

Q4   JEPSEN, Jorgen Grunnet: A discography of Paul Quinichette in Jazz
Journal, Vol. 13 (October 1960):
15-16; additions and corrections
[from Jim HAYES] in Jazz Journal,
Vol. 13 (November 1960): 39-40;
[from Brian GLADWELL] (December
1960): 40; [from Mike SHERA] Vol.
14 (June 1961): 39 ((2, 3, 7))

QUINTET OF THE HOT CLUB OF ROTTERDAM

Q5   [[MALE, Dick van: Discography
"Quintet of the Hotclub of Rotterdam: 1970?, 13 pp.]]

QUINTETTE DU HOT CLUB DE FRANCE
See also REINHARDT, DJANGO

Q6   DELAUNAY, Charles: Discographie
du Quintette du Hot Club de
France, extrait de Hot discography
in Django Reinhardt and Stephane

Grappelly: Quintette du Hot Club de France. [Paris]: Jazz Hot [1937], 12-13 ((2, 3, 7))

RCA VICTOR label
See also ROLLINS, SONNY (Raben, Erik); VICTOR label

R1   [[MOONOOGIAN, George A.: The giant that started it all; RCA and the 50-000 series in Record Exchanger, No. 19 (n.d.): 26-29]]

RA, SUN
See SUN RA

RADCLIFFE, JIMMY
vocal

R2   HUGHES, Rob: Jimmy Radcliffe disco in Hot Buttered Soul, No. 42 (November 1975): 3 ((3, 7))

RAEBURN, BOYD, 1913-1966
bass saxophone, leader

R3   DALLEYWATER, Roger: Boyd Raeburn discography in Jazz Guide, No. 9 (January 1965): 6-7 ((2, 3, 7))

R4   EDWARDS, Ernie: Boyd Raeburn and his Orchestra; a complete discography. Whittier, CA: ErnGeoBil, 1966, iv, 16 leaves (Big Band series, R-1A) [also of Johnny Bothwell and George Handy, as is the next entry] ((1, 2, 3, 4r, 6, 7))

R5   HALL, George I., ed.: Boyd Raeburn and his Orchestra. rev. ed. Laurel, MD: Jazz Discographies Unlimited, 1972, iv, 22, 5 leaves ((1, 2, 3, 4t, 6, 7))

R6   HOEFER, George: Boyd Raeburn discography in Down Beat, Vol. 29 (April 26, 1962): 25 ((2, 3, 7))

R7   JACKSON, Arthur: Discography in Jazz Monthly, Vol. 12 (November 1966): 7-8; additions and corrections from Michael SPARKE in Jazz Monthly, Vol. 12 (January 1967): 28-29 ((2, 3, 7))

RAELETS (musical group)

R8   DUFOUR, Joel: The Raelets in Soul Bag, No. 39 (June 1974): 2-4 [also of members Mary Ann Fisher and Margie Hendricks, under their own names] ((2, 3, 7))

RAGGING THE SCALE (tune title)

R9   MONTGOMERY, Mike: [discography of most of the piano rolls issued of this tune, 1915-1919] in Ragtime Society Bulletin, Vol. 2 (May-June 1963): 7 ((—))

RAGTIME MUSIC

R10   CAREY, Dave: A listing of ragtime recordings in Jazz Journal, Vol. 3 (February 1950): 6-7 ((—))

R11   ENGLUND, Bjorn: Ragtime comes to far north in Ragtimer (May-June 1979): 8-9 [Swedish HMV recordings] ((3, 6, 7, 8))

R12   JASEN, David A.: Recorded ragtime 1897-1958. [Hamden, CT]: Archon Books, 1973, viii, 155 pp. ((4p, 5, 8))

R13   JASEN, David A.: 33 1/3 r.p.m. long playing microgroove records in BLESH, Rudi, and Harriet JANIS: They all played ragtime. 4th ed. New York: Oak, 1971, 343-347 ((—))

R14   A list of player-piano rolls/a selected list of phonograph records in BLESH, Rudi, and Harriet JANIS: They all played ragtime. 3d ed. New York: Oak, 1966 (also 4th ed. New York: Oak, 1971), 326-343 ((—))

R15   MANSKLEID, Felix: Discographie in Jazz Hot, No. 52 (February 1951): 14-15 ((—))

R16   MOE, Phil: A ragtime discography in Mississippi Rag, Vol. 6 (January 1979): 7-10 ((—))

R17   Ragtime on record; a classic rag discography in Mississippi Rag, Vol. 1 (March 1974): 8-9 ((—))

R18   ROGERS, Charles Payne: Discography of ragtime recordings in Jazz Forum (UK), No. 4 (April 1947): 7-8 ((8))

R19   Selected discography; collections of instrumental ragtime and "novelty" music which shows some transitions between ragtime and jazz in Mississippi Rag, Vol. 3 (August 1976): 11 ((—))

R20   WALDO, Terry: A selected discography in his This is ragtime. New York: Hawthorn [1976], 209-223 ((—))

R21   WALKER, Edward: Ragtime and jazz
on cylinder in Jazz Monthly, No.
190 (December 1970): 30-31; No.
191 (January 1971): 25 ((7))

Great Britain

R22   [[WALKER, Edward S.: English
ragtime. North Chesterfield,
UK: 1971, 110 pp.]]; additions and corrections from
Dave CUNNINGHAM in Rhythm
Rag, No. 4 (spring 1977):
22-23 ((3))

Orchestrations

R23   Selected discography in Mississippi Rag, Vol. 3 (February 1976):
9 ((—))

RAINEY, MA (née Gertrude Malissa Nix
Pridgett), 1886-1939
vocal

R24   BAKKER, Dick M.: Ma Rainey in
Micrography, No. 6 (October 1969):
9 ((7d))

R25   BAKKER, Dick M.: Ma Rainey listing
in Micrography, No. 35 (March
1975): 6-7 ((6, 7d))

R26   LOVE, William C.: Ma Rainey discography in Jazz Information, Vol.
2 (September 6, 1940): 9-14 ((2,
3))

RAMBLIN' THOMAS
See THOMAS, RAMBLIN'

RAMPART label
See MOULDIE FYGGE label

RANEY, JIMMY, 1927-
guitar

R27   MORGAN, Alun: Jimmy Raney--a name
listing in Discographical Forum,
No. 4 (January 1961): 7-9 ((2, 3,
7))

RAPPOLO, LEON
See ROPPOLO, LEON

RAVA, ENRICO, 1944-
trumpet

R28   Selected Rava discography in Down
Beat, Vol. 45 (February 9, 1978):
17 ((—))

RAYMOND RASPBERRY SINGERS

R29   HAYES, Cedric: The Raymond Raspberry Singers; a provisional listing in Matrix, No. 74 (December
1967): 5-6 ((3))

RCA VICTOR label
See RCA VICTOR label; VICTOR label

REARDON, CASPER
harp

R30   VENABLES, Ralph: Discography of
Casper Reardon in Jazz Tempo, No.
18 (n.d.): 40-41 ((2, 3, 7d))

RED NELSON (Nelson Wilborn), 1907-
piano, vocal

R31   OLIVER, Paul: A discography of
Nelson Wilborn (Red Nelson) in
Discographical Forum, No. 1 (May
1960): 6-8 ((2, 3, 7))

RED ONION JAZZ BAND (later called RED
ONIONS)

R32   Discography in Jazz Down Under,
Vol. 1 (March-April 1975): 24
((—)) [Australian; not US band
with same name]

REDDING, OTIS, d. 1967
vocal

R33   DAGUERRE, Pierre: Discographie de
Otis Redding in Soul Bag, No. 68
(1978): 14-23 ((2, 3, 7))

R34   [[Discography in Soul Bag, No.
9/10]]; additions and corrections
in Soul Bag, No. 27 (June 1973): 4

R35   [[Otis Redding's albums in
SCHIESEL, Jane: The Otis Redding
story. Garden City, NY: Doubleday,
1973, 139-143]]

REDMAN, DEWEY, 1931-
tenor saxophone

R36   Selected Redman discography in
Down Beat, Vol. 42 (November 6,
1975): 16 ((—))

REDMAN, DON, 1900-1964
arranger, multi-instrumentalist

R37   BAKKER, Dick M.: Don Redman 1931-
1940 in Micrography, No. 23 (January 1973): 4 ((7d))

R38   The Redman band in Europe--a discography in Jazz Forum (UK), No. 5 (autumn 1947): 14-15 ((2, 3, 7))

REECE, DIZZY (Alphonso Son Reece), 1931-
trumpet

R39   COOKE, Ann: Dizzy Reece discography in Jazz Monthly, Vol. 5 (October 1959): 26-27 ((2, 3, 7))

REED, A. C.
tenor saxophone, vocal

R40   SISCOE, John: A. C. Reed Chicago blues in Blue Flame, No. 14 (n.d.): 12 ((3))

REED, JIMMY, 1925-1976
guitar, harmonica, vocal

R41   BALFOUR, Alan: I'm the man down there--Jimmy Reed sorted out in Talking Blues, No. 5 (April-June 1977): 11-13 ((3, 7d))

R42   CHAUVARD, Marcel, and Kurt MOHR: Jimmy Reed on Vee-Jay in Jazz Statistics, No. 14 (January 1960): 9-10; additions and corrections from Michel VOGLER in Jazz Statistics, No. 22 (June 1961): 4-5 ((2, 3, 7))

R43   [[Discography. Blues Unlimited booklet]]

REED, WAYMON, 1940-
trumpet

R44   REED, Waymon: Discography selected by Waymon Reed in booklet to accompany [phonodisc] Artists House AH10. New York: Artists House Records, c1979 ((7d))

REGAL label

R45   ROTANTE, Tony, and Dan MAHONY: Regal 3230 through 3329--the modern Regal catalogue in Record Research, Vol. 1 (June 1955): 2-5; additions and corrections in Record Research, Vol. 2 (July-August 1956): 11 ((3))

REGAL label (British)

R46   [[HAYES, Jim: English Regal/Regal Zonophone MR 1 series. Liverpool: 1969, 28 pp.]]

REGAL ZONOPHONE label (British)

R47   HAYES, Jim: English Regal Zonophone Popular Jazz Series in R.S.V.P., No. 15 (August 1966): 33 ((3, 6, 7d))

REICHEL, HANS
guitar
See CARL, RUDIGER

REINHARDT, DJANGO (Jean Baptiste Reinhardt), 1910-1953
guitar
See also QUINTETTE DU HOT CLUB DE FRANCE

R48   ABRAMS, Max: The book of Django. Los Angeles: 1973, iii, 188 pp. ((1, 3, 4t, 6, 7, 9))

R49   BAJO, John: Djangology. Chicago: 1958, 91 leaves ((3, 6))

R50   DELAUNAY, Charles: Discography in his Django Reinhardt. London: Cassell [c1961] (also London: Jazz Book Club, 1963), 163-241; additions and corrections in EVANS, Chris: Django Reinhardt in Jazz Monthly, No. 162 (August 1968): 30-31; No. 163 (September 1968): 31; [from Iwan FRESART and Charles DELAUNAY] No. 171 (May 1969): 26 ((1, 2, 3, 6, 7))

R51   Discographie in Jazz Hot, No. 14 (1947): 11; No. 15 (1947): 22 ((2, 3, 7))

R52   [[[Discography] in DELAUNAY, Charles: Django Reinhardt, souvenirs. Paris: Jazz Hot, 1954]]

R53   HAYES, Jim: Djangology [column] in R.S.V.P., No. 15 (August 1966) to No. 17 (November 1966); No. 19 (December 1966), various paginations [additions and corrections to various discographies]

R54   NEILL, Billy, and E. GATES: Discography of the recorded works of Django Reinhardt and the Quintette du Hot Club de France. [London: Clifford Essex Music, 1944], 24 pp. ((2, 3, 7))

R55   Selected Django discography in Down Beat, Vol. 43 (February 26, 1976): 15 ((—))

REMUE, CHARLES, 1903-
clarinet, leader

R56   PERNET, Robert: A la recherche du jazz perdu...Charles Remue in Point du Jazz, No. 3 (August 1970): 35-53 ((2, 3, 6, 7))

R57   PERNET, Robert: Chas. Remue in Jazz Monthly, Vol. 13 (March 1967): 4-7 ((2, 3, 6, 7))

RENAUD, HENRI, 1925-
   piano

R58   MORGAN, Alun, and Ny RENAUD: Henri Renaud discography in Jazz Monthly, Vol. 4 (April 1958): 23-26; (May 1958): 26; additions and corrections from Jack HARTLEY in Jazz Monthly, Vol. 4 (August 1958): 32 ((2, 3, 7))

RENDELL, DON, 1926-
   tenor saxophone

R59   MORGAN, Alun: Don Rendell discography in Jazz Monthly, Vol. 3 (May 1957): 26-27, 32; (June 1957): 27-28 ((2, 3, 6, 7))

REPRISE label
   See ELLINGTON, DUKE (Fresia, Enzo: Ellington su Reprise)

RESER, HARRY, d. 1965
   banjo
   See also SEVEN LITTLE POLAR BEARS; SIX JUMPING JACKS

R60   [[LANGE, Horst H.: Discography in Jazz Podium, Vol. 13 (January 1964); (March 1964)]]

R61   TRIGGS, W. W.: The great Harry Reser. London: Henry G. Waker, 1978, ix, 200 pp. ((3, 6, 7))

REVELATION label

R62   JAMES, Michael: Discography in Jazz Monthly, No. 179 (January 1970): 15 ((2, 7))

R63   POSTIF, François: Les disques Revelation in Jazz Hot, No. 258 (February 1970): 29 ((2, 7))

REVUE label

R64   [[[Listing] in Soul Bag, No. 12]]

REX label (British)

R65   [[HAYES, Jim: Rex artist catalogue, 8001 to 8999. Liverpool: 1969, 26 pp.]]

RHAPSODY, MISS
   See MISS RHAPSODY

RHODES, TODD, 1900-1965
   piano

R66   [Discography] in Jazz Statistics, No. 17 (1960): 9-11; additions and corrections from Michel VOGLER in Jazz Statistics, No. 22 (June 1961): 5 ((2, 3, 6, 7))

R67   ROTANTE, Anthony: Todd Rhodes records in Record Research, Vol. 3 (March-April 1958): 9-10 [1947-1957 recordings] ((2, 3, 7d, 8))

RHYTHM label

R68   Rhythm in Quartette, No. 2 (March 1970): 38-39 ((3))

RHYTHM AND BLUES
   See also BLUES MUSIC (Rotante, Anthony); BLUES MUSIC--Additions and Corrections (Rotante, Anthony); JAZZ MUSIC (Bruyninckx, Walter) and (Carey, Dave) and (McCarthy, Albert J: Jazz discography I)

R69   CHAUVARD, Marcel, and Kurt MOHR: Some small discographies in Jazz Statistics, No. 24 (December 1961): JS2-JS3; additions from Kurt MOHR in Jazz Statistics, No. 25 (March 1962): 7 ((2, 3, 6, 7))

R70   [[Discographical reprints; amended discographies of Jimmy Reed, Little Walter Jacobs, Rufus Thomas, Little Richard, Johnny "Guitar" Watson, Larry Williams, T. Bone Walker, Fats Domino. Kenley, UK: R and B Monthly, 1967?, 55 pp.]]

R71   FERLINGERE, Robert D.: A discography of rhythm & blues and rock 'n roll vocal groups 1945 to 1965. [Pittsburg, CA: c1976], unpaged ((2, 3, 5))

R72   FLUCKIGER, Otto: Miscellaneous in Jazz Statistics, No. 14 (January 1960): 8 ((2, 3, 6, 7))

R73 GONZALEZ, Fernando L.: Disco-file; the discographical catalog of American rock & roll and rhythm & blues vocal harmony groups. 2d ed., 1902 to 1976. Flushing, NY: [c1974, 1977], vii, 447, 8, 33 pp. ((3, 7d))

R74 Groupography in Quartette, No. 1 (January 1970): 12-16; No. 2 (March 1970): 34-36; continued in R and B Magazine, Vol. 1 (July-October 1970): 17 [A to BEAU] ((3, 5))

R75 HARALAMBOS, Michael: Discography in his Right on: from blues to soul in black America. London: Eddison [c1974] (also New York: DaCapo, 1979), 179-181 ((—))

R76 LEICHTER, Albert: A discography of rhythm & blues and rock & roll circa 1946-1964. Supplement 1. [Staunton, VA: c1978], 87 leaves [supplements his 1975 ed.] ((7d))

R77 [[McCUTCHEON, Lynn Ellis: Rhythm and blues; an experience and adventure in its origin and development. Arlington, VA: Beatty, 1971, xi, 305 pp.]]

R78 MOHR, Kurt: Dans les archives de Kurt Mohr; listings in Soul Bag, No. 22/23 (January-February 1973): 48-50 ((3))

R79 MOHR, Kurt: Miscellaneous in Jazz Statistics, No. 11 (July 1959): 5-6; No. 12 (September 1959): 10; No. 13 (November 1959): 6 ((2, 3, 6, 7))

R80 MOHR, Kurt: Rhythm and blues forum [column] in Discographical Forum, No. 5 (March 1968) to No. 7 (July 1968), various paginations ((2, 3, 5, 7))

R81 MOHR, Kurt: Some small discographies in Jazz Statistics, No. 29 (October 1963): JS4-JS5 ((2, 3, 6, 7))

Additions and Corrections

See also BLUES MUSIC--Additions and Corrections (Rotante, Anthony)

R82 NIQUET, Bernard: Des souris et des chattes [column] in Soul Bag, various issues and paginations.

Cleveland

R83 MOHR, Kurt: Cleveland schtomp in Soul Bag, No. 32 (November 1973): 8-12 ((2, 3, 7))

Detroit

R84 [Discographies of various Detroit R & B artists and labels] in Soul Bag, No. 29 (August 1973): 4-12, 15-25, 27, 29, 31-34; No. 30 (September 1973): 3-5; No. 31 (October 1973): 5-7 ((2, 3, 7))

R85 FOSTER, Bob: Detroit label listings in Hot Buttered Soul, No. 47 (August-September 1976): 2-3, 6-12, 14-21 ((3))

R86 ROTANTE, Anthony, and Paul SHEATSLEY: Detroit research in Record Research, No. 129/130 (October-November 1974): 12, 14-16 ((—))

Michigan

R87 MOHR, Kurt: Les villes de Michigan in Soul Bag, No. 32 (November 1973): 3-6 ((2, 3, 7))

Ohio

R88 MOHR, Kurt: Les villes de l'Ohio in Soul Bag, No. 32 (November 1973): 7-8 ((2, 3, 7))

RHYTHM MAKERS

R89 CRAWFORD, Ken: Uncloaking the Rhythm Makers in Record Research, No. 50 (April 1963): 3-11 [Thesaurus transcriptions] ((1, 2, 3, 6, 7))

R90 CRAWFORD, Ken: Uncloaking the Rhythmakers in IAJRC Record, Vol. 1 (April 1968): 4½ unpaged pages; Vol. 1 No. 3 (n.d.): 5½ unpaged pages [Thesaurus transcriptions] ((1, 2, 3, 7))

RHYTHMAKERS
See BANKS, BILLY

RIC TIC label

R91 LYNSKY, Phil: Ric Tic label listing in Hot Buttered Soul, No. 44 (February-March 1976): 10-13; additions and corrections in Hot Buttered Soul, No. 45 (April-May 1976): 15 ((3, 8))

RICH, BUDDY (Bernard Rich), 1917-
drums

R92 [[COOPER, David J.: Buddy Rich discography. Blackburn, Lancashire: 1974]]

R93 MERIWETHER, Doug: The Buddy Rich orchestra and small groups. Spotswood, NJ: Joyce Music, 1974, 32, 9 pp. ((1, 2, 3, 4t, 6, 7))

Soundtracks

R94 [[STRATEMANN, Klaus: The Buddy Rich/Gene Krupa filmo-discography. Menden, W. Germany: Jazzfreund, 1980, 76 pp.]]

RICHARDSON, JOE

R95 [[[Discography] in Soul Bag, No. 15]]

RISTIC label (British)

R96 GODRICH, John, and Leslie HEWITT: The Ristic label in Matrix, No. 38 (December 1961): 3-7; additions and corrections in Matrix, No. 46 (April 1963): 13 ((3, 6))

RIVERS, SAM, 1930–
tenor saxophone

R97 Discographie de Sam Rivers in Jazz Hot, No. 321 (November 1975): 7 ((2, 7))

R98 JACCHETTI, Renato: Discografia Sam Rivers in Musica Jazz, Vol. 32 (August-September 1976): 46-47 ((2, 7))

R99 Sam Rivers discography in Swing Journal, Vol. 27 (November 1973): 119 ((2, 7d))

R100 Selected Rivers discography in Down Beat, Vol. 42 (February 13, 1975): 13 ((—))

RIVERSIDE label

R101 JEPSEN, Jorgen Grunnet: Diskofil-spalten in Orkester Journalen, Vol. 24 (July 1956): 18; (December 1956): 38-39, 70; Vol. 25 (September 1957): 24-25 ((2, 3, 7d))

R102 SHERA, Mike: Riverside label listing (title varies) in Discographical Forum, No. 19 (July 1970) to No. 35 (1976), various paginations ((2, 7))

ROACH, MAX, 1925–
drums

R103 [Album listing] in Down Beat, Vol. 35 (March 21, 1968): 21 ((—))

R104 COOKE, Ann: Max Roach; a name discography in Jazz Monthly, Vol. 9 (June 1963): 15-18 ((2, 3, 7))

R105 COOKE, Jack: Discography in Jazz Monthly, Vol. 8 (July 1962): 3-4 [covers 1958-1960] ((2, 7))

R106 [Discography] in Swing Journal, Vol. 31 (September 1977): 288-293 ((2, 7d))

R107 LUZZI, Mario: Discografia del quintetto Roach-Brown in Musica Jazz, Vol. 32 (April 1976): 15 ((1, 2, 7))

R108 A selected Max Roach discography in Coda, No. 172 (April 1980): 6 ((—))

ROBBINS, EVERETT, 1899-1926
piano

R109 KUNSTADT, Len: His piano rolls; his phonograph records in Record Research, No. 61 (July 1964): 8-10 ((5))

ROBERTS, LUCKY (Charles Luckeyth Roberts), 1887-1968
piano

R110 MONTGOMERY, Mike: Luckey Roberts rollography in Record Research, No. 30 (October 1960): 2 ((5, 8))

ROBERTSON, DICK, 1903–
vocal

R111 MORGAN, Cody: Dick Robertson discography in Jazz Journal, Vol. 21 (August 1968): 20-21; additions and corrections in Jazz Journal, Vol. 21 (November 1968): 18 ((2, 3, 6, 7d))

R112 VENABLES, Ralph G. V.: Discography of Dick Robertson in JONES, Clifford, ed.: Hot jazz. London: Discographical Society [ca. 1944], 13-16 ((2, 3))

ROBINSON, ALVIN
vocal

R113 MOHR, Kurt, and Peter GIBBON: Alvin Robinson discography in Soul, No. 3 (April 1966): 13-14 ((2, 3, 7d))

R114 WILSON, Jim: Searchin' for: Alvin Robinson in Hot Buttered Soul, No. 13 (December 1972): 8-9 ((3, 7))

ROBINSON, ELIZADIE
vocal

R115 STEWART-BAXTER, Derrick: Elizadie
Robinson discography in Jazz Journal, Vol. 17 (April 1964): 14 ((2,
3, 6, 7))

ROBINSON, FENTION (or FENTON), 1935–
guitar, vocal

R116 CHOISNEL, Emmanuel, and Kurt
MOHR: Fenton Robinson's discography in Soul Bag, No. 38 (May
1974): 23-24 ((2, 3, 7))

R117 [[LIBERGE, Luigi: Fention Robinson; elements de disco in Jazz,
Blues & Co., No. 17 (May–June
1978): 13]]

R118 PATERSON, Neil: Fention Robinson;
bio/disco in Blues Unlimited, No.
18 (January 1965): 7 ((2, 3, 6,
7))

ROBINSON, HUBERT
vocal

R119 MOHR, Kurt, and Bruce BASTIN:
Hubert Robinson discography in
Blues Unlimited, No. 35 (August
1966): 9 ((3, 7))

ROBINSON, (BANJO) IKEY, 1904–
banjo

R120 ENGLUND, Bjorn: Discography in
Jazz Monthly, Vol. 8 (December
1962): 10-12 ((2, 3, 6, 7))

ROBINSON, JIM, 1892-1976
trombone

R121 STEWART-BAXTER, Derrick: Discography of Jim Robinson in Jazz
Music, Vol. 3, No. 6 (1947): 17-
21; additions and corrections in
Jazz Music, Vol. 3, No. 8 (1948):
19 ((2, 3, 7d))

ROBINSON, JIMMY LEE, 1931–
guitar, vocal

R122 PATERSON, Neil: Jimmy Lee Robinson in Blues Unlimited, No. 14
(August 1964): 7 ((3, 7))

ROBINSON, L. C. "GOOD ROCKIN," 1915–
1976
guitar, harmonica, vocal

R123 Discography in Living Blues, No.
22 (July-August 1975): 21 ((—))

ROCKIN' SIDNEY (Sidney Semien), 1938–
guitar, vocal

R124 LEADBITTER, Mike: Rockin' Sidney
biography/discography in Blues
Unlimited, No. 34 (July 1966):
6 ((2, 3, 7))

ROCKO and ROCKET labels
See ZYNN label

RODNEY, RED (Robert Chudnick), 1927–
trumpet

R125 GIBSON, Frank: Red Rodney; a discography in Jazz Journal, Vol. 16
(October 1963): 10-12; additions
and corrections in Jazz Journal,
Vol. 17 (January 1964): 39-40 ((1,
2, 3, 7))

ROGERS, JIMMY, 1924–
guitar, harmonica, vocal

R126 BROVEN, John, and Mike LEADBITTER:
Discography of Jimmy Rogers in
Blues Unlimited, No. 23 (June
1965): 5-6 ((2, 3, 7))

R127 Jimmy Rogers Discography in Whiskey, women and..., No. 3 (n.d.):
14-15 ((3, 7))

ROGERS, SHORTY (Milton M. Rajonsky),
1924–
trumpet

R128 [[Shorty Rogers diskografi in
Orkester Journalen, Vol. 22 (November 1954): 33]]

ROLAND, WALTER
piano, vocal

R129 COLLER, Derek: Recording the blues
no. 4—Walter Roland in Vintage
Jazz Mart, Vol. 6 (April 1959):
3-4 ((2, 3, 6, 7))

ROLLINI, ADRIAN, 1912–
bass saxophone

R130 GLUECKMANN, Helmut: Adrian Rollini—1924-1927 in Micrography,
No. 48 (September 1978): 5-9
((7d))

R131 VENABLES, Ralph G. V.: Discography; a feature for the connoisseur in Discography (September 15, 1943): 2-5 ((2, 3, 7d))

R132 VENABLES, Ralph G. V.: A discography of Adrian Rollini in Jazz Notes and Blue Rhythm, No. 40 (May 1944): 1-2 ((2, 3, 7d))

ROLLINS, DEBBIE

R133 MOHR, Kurt: Debbie Rollins discography in Shout, No. 77 (June 1972): 10; additions and corrections from Hiroshi SUZUKI in Shout, No. 82 (December 1972): 6 ((3, 5, 7))

ROLLINS, SONNY (Theodore Walter Rollins), 1929-
tenor saxophone
See also MONK, THELONIOUS (Jepsen, Jorgen Grunnet: Discography of Thelonious Monk/Sonny Rollins)

R134 BLANCQ, Charles Clement: Discography (Rollins's) in his Melodic improvisation in American jazz; the style of Theodore "Sonny" Rollins, 1951-1962. Ph.D. (Music) dissertation, Tulane University (New Orleans), 1977 (also available from University Microfilms, Ann Arbor, MI; order no. 78-590): 247-250 ((7d))

R135 JEPSEN, Jorgen Grunnet: Sonny Rollins diskografi in Orkester Journalen, Vol. 25 (July-August 1957): 58; (September 1957): 54; (October 1957): 54 ((2, 3, 6, 7))

R136 MOON, Pete: A provisional discography of Sonny Rollins post-1960 recordings in Pieces of Jazz, No. 5 (1969): 41-45 ((2, 3, 7))

R137 MOON, Pete, and Don TARRANT: Sonny Rollins; a discography in Discographical Forum, No. 39 (1977): 4-6; No. 40 (spring 1978): 9-12; No. 41 (1978?): 11-12, 19-20 (to be continued) ((1, 2, 3, 6, 7))

R138 POSTIF, François: Discographie de Sonny Rollins in Jazz Hot, No. 116 (December 1956): 17, 39 ((2, 3, 7d))

R139 RABEN, Erik: Sonny Rollins su R.C.A. in Musica Jazz, Vol. 21 (July 1965): 37 ((2, 3, 7))

R140 Selected Rollins discography in Down Beat, Vol. 44 (April 7, 1977): 14 ((—))

R141 Sonny Rollins in Swing Journal, Vol. 33 (January 1979): 220-225 ((2, 7d))

R142 A Sonny Rollins discography in Down Beat, Vol. 41 (February 14, 1974): 15 ((—))

R143 Sonny Rollins discography in Swing Journal, Vol. 27 (February 1973): 262-267 ((2, 7d))

R144 [[TERCINET, Alain: Discographie: Sonny Rollins in Jazz Hot, No. 351/352 (summer 1978): 53-57]]

R145 Traditions et contradictions de Theodore Walter "Sonny" Rollins in Jazz Hot, No. 307 (July-August 1974): 17 [1972-1973 recordings] ((2, 7))

ROLLO, PREACHER
See PREACHER ROLLO

ROMAN NEW ORLEANS JAZZ BAND

R146 [Complete discography] in Jazztime, Vol. 1 (March 31-April 30, 1952): 1 ((2, 7))

R147 MAZZOLETTI, Adriano: Roman New Orleans Jazz Band discography in Jazz Music, Vol. 8 (March-April 1957): 19-20; additions in Jazz Music, Vol. 9 (January-February 1958): 22 ((2, 3, 7))

ROMEO label
See BANNER label (Complete numerical of Banner Melotone Oriole Perfect Romeo, 1935-1938)

ROOST label
See GETZ, STAN (Edwards, Ernie: Stan Getz on "Roost")

ROPPOLO (or RAPPOLO), LEON, 1902-1943
clarinet

R148 HOEFER, George: Leon Rappolo discography in Jazz Quarterly, Vol. 1 (spring 1944): 7-13 ((2, 3, 6, 7, 8))

R149 REEVES, Adrian: A discography of Leon Rappolo in GEE, Jack C., ed.: That's a plenty. Hemel Hempstead, UK: Society for Jazz Appreciation for the Younger Generation, 1945, 16-18 ((2, 3, 7))

R150 WEBB, Leslie: Rappolo discography in Pickup, Vol. 1 (August 1946): 11-12 ((2, 3))

ROSE, BORIS
    record producer

R151 MINER, Bill: Sub rosa stuff in
    Jazz Digest (Virginia), Vol. 2
    (November-December 1973): 13-18
    [lists various labels including
    Alto, Ozone, Session] ((1, 7))

ROSENGREN, BERNT, 1927-
    tenor saxophone

R152 Bernt Rosengren selected discog-
    raphy in Jazz Forum (Poland), No.
    43 (May 1976): 26 ((—))

R153 HANSSON, Lars: Bernt Rosengren
    diskografi in Orkester Journalen,
    Vol. 36 (July-August 1968): 2;
    additions and corrections in
    Orkester Journalen, Vol. 38 (No-
    vember 1968): 30 ((2, 3, 7))

ROSOLINO, FRANK, 1926-1978
    trombone

R154 Selected Rosolino discography in
    Down Beat, Vol. 44 (November 17,
    1977): 18 ((—))

ROSS, ANNIE, 1930-
    vocal

R155 COOPER, Reg, and Don TARRANT:
    Annie Ross discography in Journal
    of Jazz Discography, No. 4 (Janu-
    ary 1979): 9-18; additions and
    corrections in Journal of Jazz
    Discography, No. 5 (September
    1979): 1-2 ((2, 3, 6, 7))

ROSS, ISAIAH, 1925-
    guitar, vocal

R156 ROSS, Isaiah; Simon NAPIER; and
    Mike LEADBITTER: Doctor Ross dis-
    cography in Blues Unlimited, No.
    27 (November 1965): 12, 19 ((2,
    3, 7, 8))

ROSTAING, HUBERT, 1918-
    clarinet, alto saxophone

R157 MOHR, Kurt: Earl Cadillac, his
    alto sax and his orchestra in
    Discophile, No. 43 (August 1955):
    16-17; additions and corrections
    in Discophile, No. 45 (December
    1955): 13 ((2, 3, 7))

ROYAL, ERNIE, 1921-
    trumpet

R158 Discographie (des disques publiés
    en France) in Jazz Hot, No. 47
    (September 1950): 11 ((2, 7d))

ROYALE label

R159 ROTANTE, Anthony: Royale-Allegro-
    Elite labels, a preliminary ex-
    amination in Record Research, Vol.
    2 (January-February 1957): 11-12
    ((—))

ROYALS (musical group)

R160 MILLER, Mike, and Eddie ADLER:
    Spotlight on Royals/Midnighters
    in Rhythm & Blues Train, Vol. 1
    (November 1964): 7 ((7d))

R161 MOHR, Kurt, and Marcel CHAUVARD:
    The Royals later to become the
    Midnighters; all King issues as
    by Hank Ballard & the Midnighters
    in Jazz-Disco, Vol. 1 (July 1960):
    2-5 ((2, 3, 7))

RUDD, ROSWELL, 1935-
    trombone
    See also TROMBONE MUSIC (JAZZ)

R162 THOMPSON, Keith G.: Roswell Rudd
    discography in Discographical
    Forum, No. 20 (November 1970) to
    No. 22 (January 1971), various
    paginations ((1, 2, 3, 6, 7))

RUSH, BOBBY
    guitar, vocal

R163 MOHR, Kurt: Bobby Rush in Soul
    Bag, No. 45 (January 1975): 12
    ((2, 3, 7))

RUSH, OTIS, 1934-
    guitar, vocal

R164 CHAUVARD, Marcel; Kurt MOHR; and
    Willie DIXON: A discography of
    Otis Rush in Blues Unlimited, No.
    2 (June 1963): 2; additions and
    corrections in Blues Unlimited,
    No. 12 (June 1964): suppl-3 ((2,
    3, 7))

R165 O'NEAL, Jim, and Dick SHURMAN:
    Otis Rush discography in Living
    Blues, No. 28 (July-August 1976):
    22-23 ((2, 3, 7))

R166 PATERSON, Neil; Marcel CHAUVARD;
    and Kurt MOHR: Otis Rush discog-
    raphy in Blues Unlimited, No. 22
    (May 1965): 5-6 ((2, 3, 7))

R167 Selected Rush discography in Down
Beat, Vol. 44 (April 7, 1977): 17
((—))

RUSHEN, PATRICE, 1955-
piano

R168 Selected Rushen discography in
Down Beat, Vol. 45 (March 9,
1978): 17 ((—))

RUSHING, JIMMY, 1903-1972
vocal

R169 COWLYN, Martin: The blues shouters, part 2--Jimmy Rushing in
Blues Link, No. 5 (1974): 20-22
((7))

R170 ROTANTE, Anthony: Jimmy Rushing;
a "name" discography in Discophile, No. 55 (August 1957): 7-9;
additions and corrections in Discophile, No. 56 (October 1957):
18; No. 60 (June 1958): 18-19; No.
61 (December 1958): 18-19 ((2, 3,
7))

RUSSELL, GEORGE, 1923-
composer, leader

R171 FRESIA, Enzo: Discografia di
George Russell in Musica Jazz,
Vol. 21 (May 1965): 19 ((2,
7))

R172 KRANER, Dietrich: George Russell;
a discography in Matrix, No. 69
(February 1957): 3-8 ((2, 3,
7))

RUSSELL, JOHNNY, 1909-
tenor saxophone
See SAXOPHONE MUSIC (JAZZ)
(Evensmo, Jan: The tenor saxophones of Henry Bridges...)

RUSSELL, LUIS, 1902-1963
piano

R173 BAKKER, Dick M.: Luis Russell
band 1926-34 in Micrography, No.
20 (June 1972): 2-3 ((7d))

R174 BAKKER, Dick M.: Luis Russell
1926-1934 in Micrography, No. 6
(October 1969): 4 ((7d))

R175 [[BRYCE, Owen: [Discography] in
Jazz Tempo]] [unknown issue]; additions and corrections in Jazz
Tempo, Vol. 2 (November 8, 1943):
6-7

R176 TEALDO ALIZIERI, Carlos L., and
Edgardo M. SILVESTRI: Discografia
de Luis Russell in Jazz Magazine
(Argentina), No. 59 (1956); No.
61 (September-December 1956): 16-
19; additions and corrections
in Jazz Magazine (Argentina),
No. 63 (1957): 16 ((2, 3, 6,
7))

RUSSELL, PEE WEE (Charles Ellsworth
Russell), 1906-1969
clarinet

R177 HARRIS, H. Meunier: Discography
of Pee Wee Russell in Jazz Notes
(Australia), No. 76 (August 1947)
to No. 78 (October-November 1947),
various paginations; additions and
corrections in Jazz Notes (Australia), No. 80 (January 1948):
13-14 ((2, 3, 7d))

R178 SCHENCK, John T.: Pee Wee Rus-
sell--discography in Jazz Session, No. 3 (November 1944): 15-
18; No. 4 (December 1944): 11-14
((2, 3))

R179 VENABLES, Ralph: Russell on record in Discography (February
1944): 7-10; additions and corrections in Discography (March
1944): 15 ((2, 3, 7))

RYPDAL, TERJE, 1947-
guitar

R180 Résumé discographique in Jazz
Hot, No. 361 (May 1979): 33
((—))

SABA/MPS label (German)

S1   KRANER, Dietrich H.: Saba/MPS
label listing in Discographical
Forum, No. 13 (July 1969) to No.
18 (May 1970), various paginations; additions and corrections
in Discographical Forum, No. 18
(May 1970): 20; No. 19 (July
1970): 20 ((2, 7))

SABRE label
See CHANCE label

SACCO, TONY, 1908-
composer

S2   CAIRNS, Grant: Update: Tony Sacco
in IAJRC Journal, Vol. 10 (summer
1977): 5 ((—))

SAIN, OLIVER
    tenor saxophone

S3 MOHR, Kurt; Jacques PERIN; and
    Gilles PETARD: Oliver Sain in Soul
    Bag, No. 51 (January 1976): 21-22
    ((2, 3, 6, 7))

SAINT LOUIS BLUES (tune title)

S4 PENNY, Howard E.: Feelin' tomorrow
    like I feel today; a record his-
    tory of the St. Louis blues in
    Jazzfinder, Vol. 1 (January 1948)
    to (March 1948), various pagina-
    tions, in 3 parts ((2, 3, 6))

S5 PENNY, Howard E.: Saint Louis
    blues discography in Good Diggin',
    Vol. 2 (January 31, 1948): various
    pages throughout; (annual issue
    1948): 35-41, 44-51 ((2, 3, 7d))

SAINT LOUIS JIMMY
    See ODEN, JIMMY

SAINT LOUIS MAC
    See LITTLE MACK

SAMSON AND DELILAH (musical group)

S6 CHOISNEL, Emmanuel, and Kurt MOHR:
    Discographie de Samson and Delilah
    in Soul Bag, No. 16 (1972?): 11
    ((2, 3, 6, 7))

SAN (tune title)

S7 KUHLMAN, Gus: "San"--a discography
    in Record Research, Vol. 1 (Octo-
    ber 1955): 11-12 ((3, 6, 7d))

SANDERS, PHAROAH (Farrell Sanders),
    1940-
    tenor saxophone
    See also JAZZ MUSIC--Avant-Garde
    (Raben, Erik)

S8 LUZZI, Mario: Discografia Pharoah
    Sanders in Musica Jazz, Vol. 30
    (October 1974): 45-47 ((2, 7))

S9 SIMONS, Sim: Upper and lower
    Egypt; vijf jaar Pharoah Sanders
    in Swingtime (Belgium), No. 41
    (July 1979): 3-10 [1964-1969 re-
    cordings] ((2, 7))

S10 TEPPERMAN, Barry: Pharoah
    Sanders--a discography in Pieces
    of Jazz (1970): 24-26, 60 ((1, 2,
    3, 7))

SANDMAN label

S11 BAKER, Cary: Sandman label list-
    ing in Hot Buttered Soul, No. 16
    (March 1973): 9 ((3))

SANDPEBBLES (musical group)

S12 HUGHES, Rob: Sandpebbles/C & The
    Shells discography in Soul Bag,
    No. 54 (September 1976): 2 ((2,
    3, 7d))

SARAVAH label (French)

S13 POSTIF, François: Saravah in Jazz
    Hot, No. 267 (December 1970): 41
    ((2, 7))

SARMANTO, HEIKKI, 1939-
    piano

S14 The Heikki Sarmanto discography
    in Jazz Forum (Poland), No. 32
    (December 1974): 41 ((—))

SATO, MASAHIKO, 1941-
    piano

S15 [Discography] in Swing Journal,
    Vol. 32 (December 1978): 340-345
    ((2, 7d))

SAUNDERS, GERTRUDE
    vocal

S16 Gertrude Saunders discography in
    Record Research, No. 74 (March
    1966): 3 ((2, 3, 7))

SAUNDERS, RED (Theodore Saunders),
    1912-
    drums, vibraphone

S17 MOHR, Kurt: Red Saunders in Soul
    Bag, No. 45 (January 1975): 19-20
    ((2, 3, 7))

S18 RYE, Howard W.: Red Saunders Col-
    umbia and Okeh sessions in Journal
    of Jazz Discography, No. 5 (Sep-
    tember 1979): 9-11 ((3, 6, 7))

SAURY, MAXIM, 1928-
    clarinet

S19 LAFARGUE, Pierre: Maxim Saury--a
    name discography in Discographical
    Forum, No. 3 (September 1960):
    10-13 ((2, 7))

SAUTER-FINEGAN ORCHESTRA

S20   MORGAN, Alun: Sauter-Finegan in
      Jazz Monthly, Vol. 12 (August
      1966): 14-16 ((2, 3, 7))

SAVITT, JAN, 1913-1948
      leader

S21   HALL, George, ed.: Jan Savitt and
      his Orchestra. Spotswood, NJ:
      Joyce Music, 1974, 22, 4 leaves
      ((1, 2, 3, 4t, 6, 7))

S22   HALL, George, ed.: Jan Savitt and
      his Top Hatters. Laurel, MD: Jazz
      Discographies Unlimited, 1971, 16
      leaves ((1, 2, 3, 4t, 6, 7))

SAVOY label (Chicago)

S23   ALLEN, Walter C.: Savoy Records
      in Discophile, No. 42 (June 1955):
      5; additions and corrections in
      Discophile, No. 45 (December 1955):
      18 ((—))

SAVOY label (Newark, NJ)
      See also PARKER, CHARLIE (Fluck-
      iger, Otto: Charlie Parker; alter-
      nate masters on Savoy)

S24   JEPSEN, Jorgen Grunnet: Diskofil-
      spalten in Orkester Journalen,
      Vol. 28 (January 1960): 17, 34;
      (February 1960): 17, 42 [9000
      series] ((2, 3, 7d))

S25   ROWE, Mike: [listing of unissued
      sides recorded in Atlanta] in
      Blues Unlimited, No. 36 (September
      1966): 5 ((—))

S26   RUPPLI, Michel, and Bob PORTER:
      The Savoy label/a discography.
      Westport, CT: Greenwood [c1980],
      xix, 442 pp. ((2, 3, 4p, 4r, 6,
      7))

S27   WIEDEMANN, Erik: The Savoy 5500
      race series; an attempted listing
      in Melody Maker, Vol. 27 (July 21,
      1951): 9 ((3))

SAVOY BANDS

S28   RUST, Brian: A discography of the
      Savoy bands of the twenties in
      Recorded Sound, No. 25 (January
      1967): 150-157; No. 26 (April
      1967): 193-195 [Savoy Havana Band,
      Savoy Orpheans, and Sylvians] ((2,
      3, 6, 7))

SAXOPHONE MUSIC (JAZZ)
      See also CLARINET MUSIC (JAZZ)

S29   EVENSMO, Jan: The tenor saxophones
      of Budd Johnson, Cecil Scott,
      Elmer Williams, Dick Wilson 1927-
      1942. [Hosle, Norway: 1977], 11,
      9, 7, 15 pp. (Jazz solography
      series, Vol. 7) ((1, 2, 3, 6, 7,
      9))

S30   EVENSMO, Jan: The tenor saxo-
      phones of Henry Bridges, Robert
      Carroll, Herschel Evans, Johnny
      Russell. [Hosle, Norway: 1976],
      3, 10, 13, 6 pp. (Jazz solography
      series, Vol. 2) ((1, 2, 3, 6, 7,
      9))

S31   EVENSMO, Jan: The tenor saxophon-
      ists of the period 1930-1942;
      presenting Leon Chu Berry, Her-
      schel Evans, Coleman Hawkins, Ben
      Webster, Lester Young, with a
      critical assessment of all their
      known recordings and broadcasts.
      Oslo: 1969, v, 35, 11, 29, 33, 29
      pp. (Jazz solography series [old],
      Vol. 1) ((1, 2, 3, 6, 7, 9))

SAYLES, JOHNNY
      vocal

S32   MOHR, Kurt: Johnny Sayles in Soul
      Bag, No. 45 (January 1975): 33
      ((2, 3, 7))

SCALA label (British)

S33   FLAKSER, Harold: A selective ma-
      trix chronology of Scala derived
      recordings in jazz vein part 1,
      1937-1939 in Jazz-Disco, Vol. 1
      (July 1960): 9-10 ((3, 6, 7d))

SCALA label (Swedish)

S34   ELFSTROM, Mats: Scala. Stockholm:
      Kungliga Biblioteket, 1967, 79 pp.
      (Nationalfonotekets diskografier,
      2) ((3, 4p, 7, 8))

SCHIØPFFE, WILLIAM, 1926-
      drums

S35   [[MOSEHOLM, Erik: William
      Schiøpffe. Copenhagen: Erichsen,
      1962, 62 pp.]]

SCHLIPPENBACH, ALEXANDER von, 1938-
      piano

S36 PIACENTINO, Giuseppe: Discografia di Schlippenbach in Musica Jazz, Vol. 32 (July 1976): 25 ((—))

SCHROEDER, GENE, 1915–
piano

S37 HUBNER, Alma: Schroeder on wax in Jazz Notes (Australia), No. 62 (March 1946): 9–10, 19 ((2, 7d))

SCOBEY, BOB, 1916–1963
trumpet

S38 GOGGIN, Jim: Bob Scobey; a bibliography and discography. [San Leandro, CA]: 1977, 2, 13, 1, 13 pp. ((1, 2, 7))

SCOTT, CECIL, 1905–1964
tenor saxophone
See SAXOPHONE MUSIC (JAZZ) (Evensmo, Jan: The tenor saxophones of Budd Johnson...)

SCOTT, LONNIE or LANNIE
piano, vocal

S39 LEADBITTER, Mike: Discography of Sonny Boy & Lonnie in Blues Unlimited, No. 29 (January 1966): 14; additions and corrections in Blues Unlimited, No. 32 (April 1966): 12 ((—))

SCOTT, MABEL, 1920–
vocal

S40 MOHR, Kurt: Discography of Mabel Scott in Jazz Statistics, No. 21 (March 1961): 8; additions and corrections from Michel VOGLER in Jazz Statistics, No. 22 (June 1961): 5–6 ((2, 3, 7))

SEALEY, MILT, 1928–
piano
See JAZZ MUSIC--Canada

SEALS, SON (Frank Junior Seals), 1942–
guitar, vocal

S41 Son Seals disco in Jazz, Blues & Co., No. 31 (July 1979): 13 ((—))

SEARS, AL, 1910–
tenor saxophone

S42 MOHR, Kurt: Al Sears; discographie des enregistrements publiés sous son nom in Jazz Hot, No. 126 (November 1957): 24 ((2, 3, 7))

S43 MOHR, Kurt: Discographie de Al Sears in Soul Bag, No. 65 (January 1978): 8–9 ((2, 3, 7))

S44 MOHR, Kurt: Discography of Al Sears in Jazz Statistics, No. 12 (September 1959): 3–4; additions and corrections from Michel VOGLER in Jazz Statistics, No. 17 (1960): 7 ((2, 3, 7))

SEBESKY, DON, 1937–
arranger, composer

S45 SMITH, Arnold Jay: Date with Sebesky in Down Beat, Vol. 41 (November 21, 1974): 17 ((—))

SEIFERT, ZBIGNIEW, 1947–1979
violin

S46 BATESON, Matthew: Selected discography in Jazz Journal, Vol. 32 (July 1979): 27 ((2))

S47 Selected Seifert discography in Jazz Forum (Poland), No. 59 (1979): 44 ((—))

SELLERS, JOHN, 1924–
guitar, vocal

S48 ROTANTE, Anthony, and John SELLERS: Brother John Sellers; a revised discography in Record Research, No. 39 (November 1961): 8–9, 20 ((2, 3, 7d))

S49 ROTANTE, Anthony, and Derek COLLER: A discography of Brother John Sellers in Discophile, No. 59 (April 1958): 2–5; additions and corrections in Discophile, No. 61 (December 1958): 19; Matrix, No. 37 (November 1961): 18 ((2, 3, 7))

SELMER label

S50 PASCOLI, Daniel: Selmer: a new name in records in Playback, Vol. 2 (May 1949): 19 ((2, 3, 7))

SELS, JACK, 1922–1970
tenor saxophone

S51 PERNET, Robert: Discographie de
     Jack Sels in Point du Jazz, No. 3
     (August 1970): 70-72 ((1, 2, 3,
     7))

S52 PERNET, Robert: Jack Sels discog-
     raphy in Rhythm and Blues Pano-
     rama, No. 19 to No. 22 (1963) and
     possibly other issues, various
     paginations ((1, 2, 3, 7))

SELVIN, BEN, ca. 1900-
     leader

S53 [[BACKENSTO, Woody: A Ben Selvin
     discography. Woodbury, NJ: 1954,
     53 pp. ((3, 7d))]]

S54 KINKLE, Roger D.: Co numerical
     list of Ben Selvin recordings--
     complete from 2014-D thru 18000-D,
     with some earlier ones added--and
     listing soloists and vocalists
     where important in his Check sheet
     (Project #1). [Evansville, IN?:
     n.d.], 8 ((9))

SEMIEN, SIDNEY
     See ROCKIN' SIDNEY

SENSATION label

S55 ROTANTE, Anthony: Sensation Rec-
     ords in Record Research, Vol. 3
     (July-August 1958): 13 ((3))

SENTER, BOYD, 1899-
     clarinet

S56 LANGE, Horst H.: Boyd Senter dis-
     cography in Jazz Music, Vol. 9
     (September-October 1958): 6, 8-10
     ((2, 3, 6, 7))

S57 MILLER, William H.: Boyd Senter
     and his Senterpedes; a discography
     in Jazz Notes (Australia), Vol. 1
     (January 20, 1941): 6-7 ((2, 3,
     7d))

S58 VENABLES, Ralph: Discography of
     Boyd Senter and his Senterpedes
     in Jazz Notes (Australia), No. 89
     (December 1948): 17-18 ((2, 3, 7d))

S59 WILCOX, Sibley: Boyd Senter dis-
     cography in Good Diggin' (1948
     annual): 72 ((—))

SEPIA label

S60 MOHR, Kurt: Sepia label listing
     in Hot Buttered Soul, No. 30 (May
     1974?): 17 ((3))

SEPT BOOGIES
     See CINQ BOOGIES

SERIAL MUSIC AND JAZZ
     See also CLASSICAL MUSIC--
     INFLUENCE ON JAZZ

S61 HARRISON, Max: [Record listing] in
     Jazz Monthly (Oct. 1965): 17 ((—))

SERRANO, PAUL
     trumpet

S62 MOHR, Kurt: Paul Serrano in Soul
     Bag, No. 45 (January 1975): 32
     ((2, 3, 7))

SESAC label

S63 PRIESTLEY, Brian, and Steve VOCE:
     Sesac; discography of a transcrip-
     tion label in Jazz & Blues, Vol.
     2 (May 1972) to (June 1972), var-
     ious paginations ((1, 2, 7, 9))

SESSION label (Chicago)

S64 Session; a label listing in Ma-
     trix, No. 70 (April 1967): 10-11;
     additions and corrections in
     Matrix, No. 75 (February 1968):
     19; No. 78 (August 1968): 13; No.
     83 (June 1969): 10 ((3))

SESSION label (New York)
     See also ROSE, BORIS

S65 DAVIS, Brian; Bill MINER; and Don
     TARRANT: Session Disc--a complete
     listing in Discographical Forum,
     No. 34 (1976) to No. 36 (1976),
     various paginations; additions and
     corrections in Discographical
     Forum, No. 36 (1976): 12-14, 19;
     No. 41 (1978?): 1-2 ((1, 2, 7))

SEVEN LITTLE POLAR BEARS
     See also RESER, HARRY

S66 BACKENSTO, Woody: The Seven Little
     Polar Bears; a discography in
     Record Exchange, Vol. 5 (September
     1952); additions and corrections
     in Record Exchange, Vol. 5 (Octo-
     ber 1952): 9; reprinted in Disco-
     phile, No. 37 (August 1954): 10,
     9; additions and corrections in
     Discophile, No. 41 (April 1955):
     16; No. 46 (February 1956): 13
     ((2, 3, 6))

SEVEN SOULS (musical group)

S67   MOHR, Kurt, and Emmanuel CHOISNEL:
Discographie des Seven Souls in
Soul Bag, No. 16 (1972?): 4 ((3,
6, 7))

SEW CITY label

S68   FOSTER, Bob, and Jim WILSON: Sew
City label listing in Hot Buttered
Soul, No. 22 (September 1973): 10
((3, 6))

SHANDAR label (French)

S69   RABEN, Erik: Diskofilspalten in
Orkester Journalen, Vol. 39 (December 1971): 29 ((2, 7))

SHARPE, RAY
      guitar, vocal

S70   MOHR, Kurt: Discographie de Ray
Sharpe in Soul Bag, No. 36 (March
1974): 6; additions and corrections in Soul Bag, No. 38 (May
1974): 46; No. 45 (January 1975):
34 ((2, 3, 7))

SHAW, ARTIE (Arthur Arshawsky), 1910–
      clarinet

S71   BLANDFORD, Edmund L.: Artie Shaw/
a bio-discography. Hastings, Sussex: Castle Books, c1973, 229 pp.
((1, 2, 3, 7d))

S72   HOEFER, George: Shaw discography
in Down Beat, Vol. 18 (June 29,
1951): 18 ((—))

S73   JEPSEN, Jorgen Grunnet: Diskofilspalten in Orkester Journalen,
Vol. 27 (July–August 1959): 25
[1938–1945 Victor recordings] ((2,
3, 7d))

S74   KORST, Bill, and Charles GARROD:
Artie Shaw and his Orchestra.
Spotswood, NJ: Joyce Music, 1974,
45, 5 leaves ((1, 2, 3, 4t, 6,
7))

S75   LANGE, Horst H.: Discophilia:
Artie Shaw in Schlagzeug, Vol. 8
(April 1958): inside back cover
[part 1, 1936–January 1939; probably continued in other issues]
((2, 3, 7))

S76   ROBERTSON, Alastair: Artie Shaw
'36-'55. [Edinburgh: 1971], 25
pp.; additions and corrections
from Claude Bosseray in Point du

Jazz, No. 6 (March 1972): 111–112
((1, 2, 3, 6, 7))

S77   SIMOSKO, Vladimir: Artie Shaw and
his Gramercy Fives in Journal of
Jazz Studies, Vol. 1 (October
1973): 53–56 ((1, 2, 3, 7))

SHAW, CLARENCE "GENE," 1926–
      trumpet

S78   COOKE, Jack: Discography in Jazz
Monthly, Vol. 10 (September 1964):
12 ((2, 7))

S79   MOON, Pete: Gene Shaw--a discography in Pieces of Jazz, No. 7
(1969): 39–40; additions in Pieces
of Jazz, (1971): 8 ((2, 3, 7))

SHAW, THOMAS, 1908–
      guitar, vocal

S80   SCOTT, Frank: Thomas Shaw's born
in Texas in Boogie Woogie & Blues
Collector, No. 30/31 (August
1973): 12 ((7))

SHEARING, GEORGE, 1919–
      piano

S81   George Shearing in Swing Journal,
Vol. 32 (March 1978): 294–299 ((2,
7d))

S82   McCARTHY, Albert: George Shearing;
a name discography in Discophile,
No. 18 (June 1951): 15–18, 21;
additions and corrections in Discophile, No. 19 (August 1951): 11
((2, 3, 7))

SHEPP, ARCHIE, 1937–
      tenor saxophone
      See also JAZZ MUSIC--Avant-Garde
      (Raben, Erik)

S83   Discographie d'Archie Shepp in
Jazz Hot, No. 210 (June 1965): 26
((2, 7))

S84   Discographie Impulse d'Archie
Shepp in Jazz Hot, No. 238 (January 1968): 15 ((2, 7d))

S85   [Discography] in Swing Journal,
Vol. 31 (April 1977): 276–281 ((2,
7d))

S86   EYLE, Wim van: Archie Shepp discografie in Jazz Press, No. 4
(October 1975) to No. 6 (November
26, 1975), various paginations;
additions and corrections in Jazz
Press, No. 24 (October 15, 1976):

8-9, 13; No. 26 (November 12, 1976): 4 ((2, 7))

S87 JACCHETTI, Renato: Discografia Archie Shepp in Musica Jazz, Vol. 31 (May 1975): 47-48; (June 1975): 46-48 ((2, 7))

S88 LITWEILER, John B.: Shepp; an old schoolmaster in a brown suit in Down Beat, Vol. 41 (November 7, 1974): 17 ((—))

S89 POSTIF, François, and Guy KOPE-LOWICZ: Discographie d'Archie Shepp in Jazz Hot, No. 210 (June 1965): 26 ((2, 3, 7))

S90 RABEN, Erik: Diskofilspalten in Orkester Journalen, Vol. 35 (May 1967): 17; (September 1967): 23 ((2, 3, 7))

S91 [[RISSI, Mathias: Archie Shepp; discography. Adliswil, Switzerland: 1977, 21 pp.]]

S92 SMIDS, Peter: Discografie Archie Shepp in Jazz Wereld, No. 7 (July 1966): 241 ((2, 7, 8))

S93 [[STIASSI, Ruggero: [Discography 1960-1965] in Musica Jazz, Vol. 23 (January 1967)]]

S94 WALKER, Malcolm: Archie Shepp in Jazz Monthly, Vol. 12, (June 1966): 30-31 ((2, 3, 7))

SHERWOOD, BOBBY, 1914-
     guitar, trumpet

S95 MORSER, Roy: Bobby Sherwood listing in Jazz Discounter, Vol. 2 (February 1949): 6 ((—))

S96 NEU, Robert J.: Bobby Sherwood; a name discography in Discophile, No. 29 (May 1953): 12-13; additions and corrections in Discophile, No. 31 (August 1953): 17; No. 32 (October 1953): 15; No. 34 (February 1954): 12; No. 41 (April 1955): 17; No. 50 (October 1956): 17 ((2, 3, 7))

SHILKRET, NAT, 1895-
     leader

S97 MAGNUSSON, Tor: The Shilkret's Rhyth-Melodists sessions in Matrix, No. 90 (December 1970): 3-5 ((2, 3, 6, 7))

SHINES, JOHNNY, 1915-
     guitar, vocal
     See also BLUES MUSIC (Guralnick, Peter)

S98 LECUYER, Claude: Les disques de Johnny Shines in Soul Bag, No. 38 (May 1974): 6, 29 ((—))

SHIRLEY AND LEE (Shirley Goodman and Leonard Lee)

S99 HITE, Richard: Discography: Shirley & Lee in R and B Collector, Vol. 1 (January-February 1970): 13-14; additions and corrections in R and B Collector, Vol. 1 (March-April 1970): 4 ((2, 3, 6, 7))

SHOBEY, EL

S100 MOHR, Kurt: El Shobey & Co. in Soul Bag, No. 45 (January 1975): 12 ((2, 3, 7))

SHOFFNER, BOB, 1900-
     trumpet

S101 DURR, Claus Uwe: Bob Shoffner (in the 1920's) in Record Research, No. 64 (November 1964): 3 [excludes King Joe Oliver sessions] ((2, 3, 6, 7))

SHY, JEAN
     vocal

S102 MOHR, Kurt: Jean Shy in Soul Bag, No. 45 (January 1975): 11 ((2, 3, 7))

SIGNATURE label

S103 GODRICH, John: The Signature 900 series in Matrix, No. 78 (August 1968): 3; additions and corrections in Matrix, No. 83 (June 1969): 12 ((3, 6))

S104 PORTER, Bob.: Modern eyes-zing in Record Research, No. 171/172 (March 1980): 11 [H-1 to SRC101] ((3))

SILVA, ALAN, 1939-
     bass violin

S105 Discographie complète in Jazz Hot, No. 247 (February 1969): 23 ((—))

SILVER, HORACE, 1928-
     piano

S106 GARDNER, Mark: Horace Silver discography with a brief biography.

[Droitwich, Worcestershire: 1967], 21 pp. ((1, 2, 3, 6, 7))

S107 Horace Silver discography in Swing Journal, Vol. 27 (September 1973): 264-269 ((2, 7d))

S108 POSTIF, François: Discographie d'Horace Silver in Jazz Hot, No. 117 (January 1957): 15 ((2, 7))

S109 Selected Silver discography in Jazz Forum (Poland), No. 51 (1978): 37 ((—))

S110 TAYLOR, J. R.: A Horace Silver discography in Radio Free Jazz (March 1977): 21-27 ((1, 2, 7d))

SILVER FOX label

S111 JAFFIER, Patrick: Silver Fox label listing in Soul Bag, No. 46 (February 1975): 7 ((3))

SILVERTON label (Swedish)
    See DIXI label

SILVERTONE label

S112 GODRICH, John, and John MACKENZIE: Silvertone 3500 series in Matrix, No. 56 (December 1964): 3-9; additions and corrections in Matrix, No. 68 (December 1966): 14-15 [to no. 3577] ((3, 6))

SIMEON, OMER, 1902-1959
    clarinet

S113 KEARTLAND, Eric: Omer Simeon discography in Hot Notes, Vol. 2 (October 1947): 14-20 ((2, 3, 6, 7))

S114 OPENNEER, H.: Omer Simeon in Doctor Jazz, No. 43 (August-September 1970): 4-7 [covers 1929-1935; other parts possibly in other issues]; additions and corrections in Doctor Jazz, No. 45 (December 1970-January 1971): 25 ((7d))

SIMMON or SIMMONS, MACK
    See LITTLE MACK

SIMMONS, NORMAN, 1929-
    piano

S115 OLSSON, Jan: [Discography] in Orkester Journalen, Vol. 47 (December 1979): 9 ((—))

SIMPSON, CASSINO, 1909-1952
    piano

S116 SHIPMAN, J. S.: Tentative discography in Jazz Journal, Vol. 8 (November 1955): 2 ((3, 6))

SIMS, GERALD
    guitar, vocal

S117 MOHR, Kurt: Gerald Sims in Soul Bag, No. 45 (January 1975): 18 ((2, 3, 7))

SIMS, ZOOT (John Haley Sims), 1925-
    tenor saxophone
    See also COHN, AL (Al & Zoot)

S118 ASTRUP, Arne: The John Haley Sims (Zoot Sims) discography. Lyngby, Denmark: Danish Discographical Publishing [c1980], 103 pp. ((1, 2, 3, 6, 7))

S119 [Discography of 1973-1974 recordings] in Jazz Hot (July-August 1975): 13 ((2, 7))

S120 ENTWHISTLE, Algernon (pseud. for Alun MORGAN?): Sims on record in Jazz Monthly, No. 164 (October 1968): 13-15 ((—))

S121 MORGAN, Alun: Zoot Sims discography in Jazz Monthly, Vol. 2 (June 1956): 27-29, 31; (July 1956): 26-28 ((2, 3, 6, 7))

S122 Selected Sims discography in Down Beat, Vol. 43 (December 2, 1976): 13 ((—))

S123 Zoot Sims in Swing Journal, Vol. 30 (June 1976): 82-87 ((2, 7))

SINCOPA Y RITMO label (Argentine)

S124 TOSCANO POUCHAN, Mario A.: South of the border; the cats join in in Jazzfinder, Vol. 1 (November 1948): 12 ((2, 3, 7d))

SINGLETON, CHARLIE
    tenor saxophone, vocal

S125 MOHR, Kurt: A discography of Charlie Singleton in Discophile, No. 47 (April 1956): 13-15; additions and corrections in Discophile, No. 52 (February 1957): 11 ((2, 3, 7))

SINGLETON, ZUTTY (Arthur James Singleton), 1898-1975
    drums

S126 DUPONT, J.: Discographie de Zutty Singleton in Jazz Hot, No. 93 (November 1954): 17 ((2, 3, 7))

SISSLE, NOBLE, 1899-1975
vocal, leader
See BLAKE, EUBIE (Montgomery, Michael)

SISTERS' LOVE (musical group)

S127 MOHR, Kurt, and Emmanuel CHOIS-NEL: The Sisters' Love discography in Soul Bag, No. 25 (April 1973): 6 ((2, 3, 7))

SIX JUMPING JACKS
See also RESER, HARRY

S128 BACKENSTO, Woody: The Six Jumping Jacks in Discophile, No. 32 (October 1953): 4-7; additions and corrections in Discophile, No. 33 (December 1953): 16-17; No. 37 (August 1954): 13; No. 38 (October 1954): 15; No. 44 (October 1955): 13 ((2, 3, 6, 7))

SJOBLOM, ALICE
See BABS, ALICE

SLACK, FREDDIE, 1910-1965
piano

S129 EDWARDS, Ernie: Freddie Slack; a complete discographie [sic]. Whittier, CA: Jazz Discographies Unlimited, 1965, 17 leaves (Spotlight series, Vol. 3) ((1, 2, 3, 4p, 6, 7))

S130 [[Freddie Slack-Discographie in Jazz Echo (April 1958)]] [and possibly other issues]; additions and corrections in Jazz Echo (May 1958): 49 ((2))

SLIM HARPO (James Moore), 1924-1970
harmonica, vocal

S131 BROVEN, John J.: Discography of Slim Harpo (James Moore) in Blues Statistics, No. 2 (March 1963): 5 ((3, 7p))

S132 [[BRUYKER, Paul de: [Discography] in Jazzspiegel (April 1967)]]

SMITH, AL
See KING, AL

SMITH, BEN, 1905-
alto saxophone, clarinet

S133 FLUCKIGER, Otto: Biography and discography of Ben Smith in Jazz Statistics, No. 21 (March 1961): 9-10; additions and corrections from Kurt MOHR and Anthony ROTANTE in Jazz Statistics, No. 23 (September 1961): JS9; No. 24 (December 1961): JS8 ((2, 3, 6, 7))

SMITH, BESSIE, 1895-1937
vocal

S134 ALBERTSON, Chris: Selected discography in his Bessie. New York: Stein & Day [c1972] (also London: Barrie & Jenkins, 1973), 239-242 ((—))

S135 AVAKIAN, George: Bessie Smith on records in Jazz Record (US), No. 58 (September 1947): 5, 25-27 ((2, 3, 7))

S136 BAKKER, Dick M.: Bessie Smith in Micrography, No. 9 (February 1970): 4-5 ((7d))

S137 MOORE, Carman: Selected discography in his Somebody's angel child; the story of Bessie Smith. New York: Crowell [1970], 112-114 ((7d))

S138 OLIVER, Paul: Selected discography in his Bessie Smith. London: Cassell [1959] (also New York: Barnes [1961]?, 75-83 (Kings of Jazz, 3) ((2, 3, 6, 7))

S139 RUST, Brian: The discography of Bessie Smith in ROWE, John, ed.: Vocal jazz. London: Jazz Tempo [1946?], 8-11; reprinted in Jazz Notes (Australia), No. 65?; No. 69 (December 1946): 16-17 [part 2]; No. 71 (February 1947): 13-15 [conclusion] ((2, 3, 7))

SMITH, BUSTER (Henry Smith), 1904-
alto saxophone

S140 DRIGGS, Frank: Buster Smith on records in Jazz Review, Vol. 3 (February 1960): 16 ((2, 3, 7))

SMITH, CLARA, 1894-1935
vocal

S141 McCARTHY, Albert: Clara Smith discography in Discophile, No. 13 (August 1950): 5-10; additions and corrections in Discophile, No. 14

(October 1950): 16–17; No. 15
(December 1950): 18–19; No. 19
(August 1951): 11; No. 21 (December 1951): 18 ((2, 3, 6, 7))

SMITH, CLARENCE
See SMITH, PINE TOP

SMITH, DEREK, 1931–
piano

S142 MORGAN, Alun: Derek Smith in Jazz
Monthly, Vol. 9 (December 1963):
26 ((2, 3, 7))

SMITH, DRIFTIN'
See MICKLE, ELMON

SMITH, GEORGE, 1924–
harmonica, vocal

S143 LEADBITTER, Mike, and Bruce BROM-
BERG: Little George Smith discog-
raphy in Blues Unlimited, No. 39
(December 1966): 8 ((3, 7))

SMITH, HARL
drums, leader

S144 ALLEN, Walter C.: Harl Smith in
Jazz Journal, Vol. 8 (February
1955): 26 ((2, 3, 5, 6))

SMITH, HELENE

S145 [[[Discography] in Soul Bag, No.
9/10]]

SMITH, JABBO (Cladys Smith), 1908–
trumpet

S146 BAKKER, Dick M.: Jabbo Smith and
Charlie Johnson in Micrography,
No. 1 (December 1968): 3 ((6))

S147 CABLE, Dave: Jabbo Smith in Discophile, No. 18 (June 1951): 3–5;
additions and corrections in
Discophile, No. 19 (August 1951):
12; No. 21 (December 1951): 18
((2, 3, 7))

S148 [[DAUBRESSE, Jean Pierre: Les
trompettes fous: Cladys "Jabbo"
Smith in Jazz Hot, No. 356/357
(December 1978–January 1979):
43–46]]

S149 Discography of Jabbo Smith. Basel:
[Jazz-Publications], 1962, 8 pp.
(Discographical index, Vol. 3)
((2, 3, 7))

S150 STEANE, Ed: The discography in
Hip, Vol. 5 (September–October
1966): 1–2 ((3, 6, 7d))

S151 STEWART-BAXTER, Derrick: Jabbo
Smith; a discography in Jazz Jour-
nal, Vol. 6 (July 1953): 23–24;
(August 1953): 24 ((2, 3, 6, 7))

SMITH, JAMES L.
guitar, vocal

S152 SHIRLEY, Ralph: James L. Smith in
Alley Music, Vol. 1 (May 1970):
14–15 ((2, 3, 7))

SMITH, JIMMY, 1925–
organ

S153 COOKE, Ann: Jimmy Smith discography in Jazz Monthly, Vol. 7 (February 1962): 30 ((2, 7))

S154 Discography of Jimmy Smith–Leo
Parker. Basel: Jazz-Publications,
1962, 8 pp. (Discographical notes,
Vol. 4) ((2, 3, 6, 7))

S155 Selected Smith discography in Down
Beat, Vol. 44 (December 15, 1977):
23 ((—))

S156 SIDERS, Harvey: Jimmy Smith in
Different Drummer, Vol. 1 (September 1974): 12 ((—))

S157 [[TOLLARA, Gianni: [Discography
1958–1968] in Musica Jazz, Vol.
25 (March 1969)]]

SMITH, JOHNNY, 1922–
guitar

S158 EDWARDS, Ernie; A name discography
of Johnny Smith in Discophile, No.
40 (February 1955): 17; additions
and corrections in Discophile, No.
41 (April 1955): 17 ((2, 3, 7))

SMITH, LEO, 1941–
trumpet

S159 SMITH, Bill: Discography in Coda,
No. 143 (November 1975): 9 ((—))

SMITH, LONNIE LISTON, 1940–
piano

S160 Selected Smith discography in Down
Beat, Vol. 43 (January 15, 1976):
13 ((—))

SMITH, LOUIS, 1931–
trumpet

S161 GARDNER, Mark: Louis Smith in
Jazz Journal, Vol. 21 (May 1968):
20 ((2, 7))

SMITH, MAMIE (Mamie Robinson), 1883–
1946
piano, vocal

S162 DAVIS, John, and C. F. GRAY-
CLARKE: Mamie Smith; a very tentative discography of her Okeh
recordings with the Rega Orchestra
in Jazz Journal, Vol. 3 (December
1950): 20 ((2, 6, 8))

S163 Mamie Smith; a provisional discography in Discophile, No. 51
(December 1956): 2–10, 15 ((2, 3,
6, 7))

S164 Mamie Smith; a provisional discography in Record Research,
No. 57 (January 1964): 9–12 ((2,
3, 6, 7))

SMITH, MAYBELLE, 1924–1972
vocal

S165 A discography of Big Maybelle
Smith in Record Research, No. 60
(May–June 1964): 8–9 ((2, 3, 6,
7d))

SMITH, PINE TOP (Clarence Smith),
1904–1929
piano

S166 BENTLEY, John: Discography in Jazz
Report (California), Vol. 2 (March
1962): 12 ((2, 7))

SMITH, STUFF (Hezekiah Leroy Gordon
Smith), 1909–
violin

S167 Discographie de Stuff Smith in
Jazz Hot, No. 94 (December 1954):
19 ((2, 3, 7d))

SMITH, TAB (Talmadge Smith), 1909–1971
alto saxophone

S168 MOHR, Kurt: Tab Smith; a name
discography in Discophile, No. 53
(April 1957): 16–19 ((2, 3, 7))

SMITH, WILLIE "THE LION," 1897–1973
piano

S169 Discography in SMITH, Willie:
Music on my mind; the memoirs of
an American pianist. New York:

Doubleday, 1964 (also London:
Macgibbon and Kee, 1965; London:
Jazz Book Club, 1966; New York:
DaCapo [1975, c1964]), 302–311
((2, 7))

S170 SIMMEN, Johnny: Le Lion sur
disques in Point du Jazz, No. 7
(October 1972): 102–103 ((—))

S171 WIEDEMANN, Erik: Willie "The Lion"
Smith's French recordings in Discophile, No. 25 (August 1952): 8;
additions and corrections in Discophile, No. 26 (October 1952):
10; No. 27 (December 1952): 17
((2, 3, 7))

SNOW, MICHAEL, 1929–
piano, trumpet

S172 Discographie in Michael Snow; une
exposition organisée par Alain
Sayag et par Pierre Theberge.
[Paris]: Centre Georges Pompidou,
1978, 77 ((2, 7))

SNOW, VALAIDA
See VALAIDA

SNOWDEN, ELMER, 1900–1973
banjo

S173 DEMEUSY, BERTRAND: Elmer Snowden
discography in Jazz Journal, Vol.
16 (April 1963): 15–16 ((2, 7))

SOLAL, MARTIAL, 1927–
piano

S174 Discographie sommaire de Martial
Solal in Jazz Magazine, No. 58
(April 1960): 31 ((—))

SOLITAIRES (musical group)

S175 [Discography] in Quartette, No. 1
(January 1970): 9; additions and
corrections in Quartette, No. 2
(March 1970): 30 ((7d))

SONATA label (Swedish)

S176 ENGLUND, Bjorn: Sonata. Stockholm:
Kungliga Biblioteket, 1968, 34 pp.
(Nationalfonotekets diskografier,
7) ((3, 4p, 8))

SONNY BOY AND LONNIE
See SCOTT, LONNIE or LANNIE

SONORA label (Swedish)

S177 ENGLUND, Bjorn: Sonora. Stockholm:
Kungliga Biblioteket, 1968, 3 v.
(Nationalfonotekets diskografier,
4, 5, 6) ((3, 4p, 5, 7d, 8))

SONY label
See C B S SONY label

SOUDERS, JACKIE, 1904-1968
trombone

S178 KUNSTADT, Len: Jackie Souders
discography in Record Research,
No. 109 (February 1971): 10 ((3,
6, 7d, 9))

SOUL label

S179 CALTA, Gary: Diggin' up discographies; Soul Records: Part 1 in
Goldmine, No. 18 (September 1977):
6; [part 2] No. 19 (October 1977):
13 ((—))

S180 MOHR, Kurt: Soul label listing in
Soul, No. 4 (June 1966): 17-18
((3, 5))

SOUL CITY label

S181 [[[Listing] in Soul Bag, No. 6]]

SOUL STIRRERS (musical group)

S182 HANSEN, Barry: Soul Stirrers in R
and B Collector, Vol. 1 (May-June
1970): 8-9 ((2, 3, 7d))

SOUL SURVIVORS (musical group)

S183 BRYANT, Steve: [Discography] in
Hot Buttered Soul, No. 45 (April-
May 1976): 10-12 ((3, 7, 8))

SOUNDCRAFT label

S184 Soundcraft jazz in Matrix, No. 21
January 1959): 23 ((2, 7))

SOUNDTRACKS
See also ARMSTRONG, LOUIS--Sound-
tracks; BASIE, COUNT--Soundtracks;
BLAKE, EUBIE--Soundtracks; ELLING-
TON, DUKE--Soundtracks; HOLIDAY,
BILLIE (Millar, Jack: Billie
Holiday--a selected discography
of airshots...); LUNCEFORD,
JIMMIE (Hall, Bill: Jimmie Lunce-

ford broadcasts-transcriptions &
filmtracks); RICH, BUDDY--Sound-
tracks

S185 DORIGNÉ, Michel: Quelques films
de jazz in his Jazz, culture, et
société, suivi du dictionnaire du
jazz. Paris: Ouvrieres [1967],
283-284 ((—))

S186 HIPPENMEYER, Jean Roland: Jazz sur
films; ou 55 années de rapports
jazz-cinéma vus à travers plus de
800 films tournés entre 1917 et
1972; filmographie critique. Yverdon, Switzerland: de la Thiele,
1972, 125 pp.; additions and corrections in TERJANIAN, Leon: Jazz
et cinéma in Point du Jazz, No.
13 (June 1977): 150-152 ((2, 4p,
5, 9))

S187 Jazz on film in Swing Journal,
Vol. 29 (August 1975): 72-77 ((2,
7d))

S188 MEEKER, David: Jazz in the movies;
a guide to jazz musicians 1917-
1977. London: Talisman (also New
Rochelle, NY: Arlington House),
[c1977], unpaged; 2239 films
listed [rev. ed. of next entry]
((2, 4p, 5, 9))

S189 MEEKER, David: Jazz in the movies--
a tentative index to the work of
jazz musicians for the cinema.
London: British Film Institute,
1972, 89 pp. ((2, 4p, 5, 9))

S190 SMITH, Ernie: Hot filmography; a
limited listing in Record Research, No. 29 (August 1960): 6,
11 ((2, 5, 9))

SOUSA BAND

S191 SMART, James R.: The Sousa Band;
a discography. Washington, DC:
Library of Congress, 1970, v, 123
pp. ((3, 4p, 6, 7, 8))

SOUTH, EDDIE, 1904-1962
violin

S192 NIQUET, Bernard: Les derniers
disques de Eddie South in Point
du Jazz, No. 5 (September 1971):
106-107 ((2, 7))

SOUTHERN JAZZ GROUP (musical group)

S193 CROSBY, Barney: Southern Jazz
Group of Australia discography in
Theme, Vol. 1 (December 1953-
January 1954): 17 ((2))

SOUTHLAND label

S194 KNUDSEN, Karl Emil, and Allan STEPHENSON: Southland; a chronological listing of "Southland" releases in Discophile, No. 60 (June 1958): 2-7; additions and corrections in Discophile, No. 61 (December 1958): 19-20; Matrix, No. 37 (November 1961): 18-19 ((2, 7, 9))

SPAND, CHARLIE, ca. 1905–
piano

S195 HALL, Bob, and Richard NOBLETT: A handful of keys; a man trying to get away--Charlie Spand in Blues Unlimited, No. 117 (January-February 1976): 22-23 ((2, 3, 6, 7, 9))

SPANIELS (musical group)

S196 HORLICK, Richard A.: The Spaniels in R and B Magazine, Vol. 1 (July-October 1970): 47-50 ((2, 3, 7d))

SPANIER, MUGGSY (Francis Joseph Spanier), 1906-1967
cornet

S197 BAKKER, Dick M.: Muggsy Spanier '24-31 in Micrography, No. 31 (1974?): 2 ((7d))

S198 DAVIES, Ron: Muggsy Spanier; sa vie et ses disques in Hot Club Magazine, No. 7 (July 1946) to No. 10 (October 1946), various paginations ((2, 3, 7d))

S199 HOEFER, George: Spanier discography in Down Beat, Vol. 18 (May 4, 1951): 16 ((—))

S200 MAHONY, Daniel L.: Muggsy up to date; a complete listing of Spanier's recordings in Playback, Vol. 2 (February 1949): 5-10, 19-23 ((1, 2, 3, 6, 7))

S201 OST, N. R.: Muggsy Spanier's Ragtime Band; a discography in Jazz Notes and Blue Rhythm, No. 44 (September 1944), 5 ((2, 3, 7d))

S202 PENNY, Howard E.: Muggsy Spanier discography in Good Diggin', Vol. 1 (November 1, 1947) to Vol. 2 (December 1948), various paginations, in 3 parts ((2, 3, 7d))

S203 PENNY, Howard E.: Muggsy Spanier discography in Good Diggin' (1948 annual): 8-23 ((1, 2, 3, 7d))

S204 Recordings by Muggsy Spanier's Ragtime Band in Jazzology (UK), No. 4 new series (April 1946): 5 ((—))

S205 VENABLES, Ralph G. V.: Complete discography of Muggsy Spanier in Discography (November 1943): 6-9; additions and corrections in HARRIS, Rex, and Max JONES, eds.: Collectors corner [column] in Melody Maker, Vol. 21 (December 1, 1945): 4; Vol. 22 (May 11, 1946): 4; (May 25, 1946): 4 [and possibly other issues] ((1, 2, 3, 7d))

S206 WARD, Edgar: Muggsy Spanier discography in Jazz Register, Vol. 1 (April-June 1965) to Vol. 2 (January 1966), various paginations, in 4 parts ((1, 2, 3, 6, 7))

SPANN, OTIS, 1930-1970
piano, vocal

S207 BROVEN, John J.: Name discography; Otis Spann in Blues Unlimited, No. 10 (March 1964): 5 ((2, 7))

SPECIAL EDITIONS label

S208 HALL, George: The Special Editions series in IAJRC Journal, Vol. 3 (October 1970): 19 ((3, 6, 7d))

S209 MAHONY, Dan: Special Editions in Discophile, No. 9 (December 1949): 12-13 ((3, 6, 7d))

S210 TROLLE, Frank H.: The short life of a record label in IAJRC Journal, Vol. 13 (April 1980): 13-14 ((—))

SPECIALTY label

S211 Specialty complete catalogue in R and B Collector, Vol. 1 (March-April 1970): 4; (May-June 1970): 18 ((—))

SPECKLED RED (Rufus Perryman), 1892-1973
piano, vocal

S212 ENGLUND, Bjorn: A discography of Speckled Red (Rufus Perryman) in Matrix, No. 41 (June 1962): 7-11; additions and corrections in Matrix, No. 49 (October 1963): 16 ((2, 3, 6, 7, 9))

S213 KOESTER, Bob: Speckled Red in Record Changer, Vol. 14 (No. 4, 1955): 9, 16 ((2, 3, 7))

S214 McCARTHY, Albert J.: Blues pianists; 1. Speckled Red in Jazz Notes and Blue Rhythm, No. 50 (March 1945): 1-2 ((2, 3, 7))

S215 McCARTHY, Albert J.: [Discography] in Jazz Forum (UK), No. 1 (n.d.): 26 ((2, 3, 7))

S216 Speckled Red discography in Jazz Report (St. Louis), Vol. 3 (January 1955): 5 ((2, 3, 7d))

SPIRES, ARTHUR, 1912–
guitar, vocal

S217 WELDING, Pete: Discography in Blues Unlimited, No. 28 (December 1965): 5; additions and corrections in Blues Unlimited, No. 29 (January 1966): 10 ((—))

SPIRIT OF MEMPHIS (musical group)

S218 DEMETRE, Jacques: Discographie française du Spirit of Memphis in Jazz Hot, No. 255 (November 1969): 21 ((2, 3, 7))

SPIRITS OF RHYTHM (musical group)
See also WATSON, LEO

S219 WHYATT, Bert: The Spirits of Rhythm; a discography in Matrix, No. 75 (February 1968): 3-4; additions and corrections in Matrix, No. 80 (December 1968): 19; No. 82 (April 1969): 14 ((2, 3, 6, 7))

SPIRITUALS
See GOSPEL MUSIC

SPIVAK, CHARLIE, 1906–
leader

S220 GARROD, Charles: Charlie Spivak and his Orchestra. Spotswood, NJ: Joyce Music, 1974, 26, 4 leaves ((1, 2, 3, 4t, 6, 7))

S221 HALL, George I., ed.: Charlie Spivak and his Orchestra. Laurel, MD: Jazz Discographies Unlimited, 1972, 33 leaves ((1, 2, 3, 4t, 6, 7))

SPIVEY, VICTORIA, 1906-1976
vocal

S222 ROTANTE, Anthony: Victoria Spivey discography in Record Research,

Vol. 2 (May-June 1956): 5-6; additions and corrections in Record Research, Vol. 2 (November-December 1956): 13; (January-February 1957): 23; Recorded Americana, No. 3 (1958): 1 ((2, 3, 6, 7))

SPRIGGS, WALTER
vocal

S223 MOHR, Kurt: Discography of Walter Spriggs in Jazz Statistics, No. 13 (November 1959): 7; additions and corrections from Mike LEADBITTER in Jazz Statistics, No. 24 (December 1961): JS8 ((2, 3, 7))

SPRING label

S224 MOHR, Kurt: Listing Spring in Soul Bag, No. 27 (June 1973): 5 ((3, 5))

STACY, JESS, 1904–
piano

S225 MAHONY, Dan: A "name" discography of Jess Stacy in Discophile, No. 54 (June 1957): 14-17; additions and corrections in Discophile, No. 56 (October 1957): 19; No. 60 (June 1958): 19 ((2, 3, 6, 7))

STAFFORD, MARY
vocal

S226 Mary Stafford discography in Record Research, Vol. 1 (June 1955): 8 ((2, 3, 6, 8))

STANKO, TOMASZ, 1942–
trumpet

S227 Tomasz Stanko discography in Jazz Forum (Poland), No. 33 (January 1975): 43 ((—))

STAPLE SINGERS

S228 HAYES, Cedric J.: The Staple Singers in Blues Unlimited, No. 1 (April 1963): 10-11; additions and corrections in Blues Unlimited, No. 2 (June 1963): 13; undated supplement to Nos. 1-6: 5-6 ((2, 3, 7))

STAR DUST (tune title)

S229 ELDER, Warren E.: Compilation of "Star Dust" recordings in Good

Diggin', Vol. 2 (October 1948):
14-17; additions in BALLARD, Carl
C.: That tune...Star Dust in Good
Diggin', Vol. 2 (December 1948):
27-28 ((—))

S230 SCHULTZ, Allen W.: Star Dust; a
suggested complete listing of one
of the most popular of all in Jazz
Discounter, Vol. 2 (March 1949):
3-4; [titled More Stardust list-
ings] (June 1949): 7-8 ((1))

STARR, BOB (Carl Tate), 1932–
drums, vocal

S231 GREENSMITH, Bill: Carl Tate/Bob
Starr discography in Blues Unlimited, No. 119 (May-June 1976):
10 ((2, 3, 7))

STARR, KAY, 1922–
vocal

S232 TANNER, Peter: A discography of
Kay Starr in Discophile, No. 16
(February 1951): 3-6 ((2, 3, 7))

STARR GENNETT label (Canadian)
See also GENNETT label (Robertson,
Alex)

S233 NELSON, John R.: [Listing] in
Record Exchange, Vol. 3 (January
1950): 3-4 ((3, 6))

STATE STREET RAMBLERS

S234 BAKKER, Dick M.: State Street
Ramblers 1927-1931 in Micrography,
No. 26 (1973): 4 ((7d))

STATES label
See also BASCOMB, PAUL; UNITED
label

S235 BRYMER, George, and Anthony
ROTANTE: A catalogue of "States"
records in Discophile, No. 32
(October 1953): 3 ((—))

STATESIDE label

S236 [[Stateside label listing in Soul,
No. 2 (1966)]]; additions and
corrections in Soul, No. 3 (April
1966): 27

STAUFFER, TEDDY, 1907–
leader
See ORIGINAL TEDDIES

STAX label

S237 [[[Listing] in Soul Bag, Nos. 1
and 2]]

STEEPLECHASE label (Danish)

S238 LAING, Ralph: The specialist
labels; a listing: SteepleChase
in Jazz Journal, Vol. 29 (April
1976): 22-23 ((2, 7))

STEIG, JEREMY, 1942–
flute

S239 Plattenhinweise in Jazz Podium,
Vol. 28 (May 1979): 16 ((—))

STEINER-DAVIS label

S240 GODRICH, John, and Frank DUTTON:
The Steiner-Davis 100 (reissue)
series in Matrix, No. 71 (June
1967): 3 ((3, 6))

S241 STEINER, John: The Steiner-Davis
Christmas records in Matrix, No.
21 (January 1959): 14; additions
and corrections in Matrix, No.
29/30 (August 1960): 34 ((1, 2,
7))

STEWART, JEB
See STUART, JEB

STEWART, REX, 1907-1967
trumpet

S242 CONRAD, Gerhard: Rex Stewart in
Berlin in Jazz Journal, Vol. 24
(March 1971): 14 [July 1948 re-
cordings] ((2, 3, 7))

S243 [[LANGE, Horst H.: [Discography]
in Jazz Podium, Vol. 9 (August
1960) to (October 1960)]]

S244 [[LANGE, Horst H.: [Discography]
in Schlagzeug (February 1960)]]

S245 [REID, John?]: Rex Stewart discography. n.p., n.d., 7 leaves
[to 1937] ((2))

S246 Rex Stewart--a reissue discography in Hip, Vol. 2 (November
1967): 7-12; Vol. 3 (January
1968): 1-8 ((3, 6, 7d))

S247 SCHENCK, John T.: Rex Stewart
discography in Jazz Session, No.
1 (September 1944); No. 2 (October 1944): 16-20 ((2))

STEWART, SAMMY, 1890-1960
  piano

S248 GULLIVER, Ralph: The band from
  Columbus; Sammy Stewart and his
  Orchestra in Storyville, No. 48
  (August-September 1973): 229 ((2,
  3, 6, 7))

S249 Sammy Stewart--the recordings,
  Paramount series in IAJRC Journal,
  Vol. 10 (summer 1977): 14 ((2, 3,
  6, 7))

STEWART, SLAM (Leroy Stewart), 1914-

S250 BORROMEO, Filippo: Slam Stewart
  discography in Discographical
  Forum, No. 21 (November 1970) to
  No. 30/31 (1972), various paginations, in 10 parts; additions and
  corrections from Andreas MASEL in
  Discographical Forum, No. 36
  (1976): 1 ((1, 2, 3, 6, 7))

S251 [[THEURER, Johann A.: [Discogra-
  phy] in Swing Collectors Club Jazz
  News (Austria), August to December
  1972]]

STITT, SONNY (Edward Stitt), 1924-
  alto saxophone

S252 BLUME, Jerry: Discographie de
  Sonny Stitt in Jazz Hot, No. 54
  (April 1951): 30 ((2, 3, 7d))

STOKES, FRANK, 1888-1955
  guitar, vocal

S253 RUST, Brian: [Discography] in Jazz
  Journal, Vol. 10 (January 1957): 8
  ((2, 3, 6, 7))

STONE, JESSE, 1901-
  piano

S254 MOHR, Kurt: Jesse Stone and his
  Orchestra in Discophile, No. 54
  (June 1957): 2; additions and
  corrections in Discophile, No. 56
  (October 1957): 19 ((2, 3, 7))

STORK TOWN DIXIE KIDS

S255 BIELDERMAN, Gerard: Discografie
  Stork Town Dixie Kids in Jazz
  Press, No. 50 (April 1, 1978): 8
  ((2, 7))

STOVALL, BABE (Jewell Stovall), 1907-
  1974
  guitar, vocal

S256 [[BROVEN, John: [Discography].
  Blues Unlimited booklet, 1965]]

S257 PICKUP, Brian, and Chris SMITH:
  Babe Stovall discography in Talking Blues, No. 4 (January-March
  1977); No. 5 (April-June 1977):
  16 ((1, 2, 7))

S258 PICKUP, Brian; Bob GROOM; and
  Bruce BASTIN: Babe Stovall; a
  revised discography in Talking
  Blues, No. 9/10 (1979): 21-23
  ((1, 2, 7))

STOVEPIPE No. 1 (Sam Jones)
  guitar, harmonica, vocal

S259 BARCLAY, Ian: A discography of
  Sam Jones (Stovepipe No. 1) in
  Discographical Forum, No. 1 (May
  1960): 8, 18; additions and corrections in Discographical Forum,
  No. 2 (July 1960): 8-9 ((2, 3, 6,
  7))

STRICKLER, BENNY, ca. 1917-1946
  trumpet

S260 OPENNEER, Herman: Benny Strickler
  disco in Doctor Jazz, No. 89
  (September 1979): 17-19 ((2, 3,
  6, 7))

STROZIER, FRANK, 1937-
  alto saxophone

S261 EYLE, Wim van: Disco Frank
  Strozier in Jazz Press, No. 29
  (January 7, 1977): 6 [1967-1975
  recordings] ((2, 7))

S262 GARDNER, Mark: Frank Strozier
  discography in Discographical
  Forum, No. 8 (July 1968): 8-9;
  No. 9 (September 1968): 6-9; additions and corrections in Discographical Forum, No. 10 (November 1968): 4-5; No. 14 (September
  1969): 4; No. 15 (November 1969):
  4 ((2, 3, 7))

STUART, JEB
  vocal

S263 Jeb Stewart in Hot Buttered Soul,
  No. 34 (October 1974?): 11 ((2,
  3, 7))

SUGAR FOOT STOMP (tune title)

S264 SALES, Bob: Sugarfoot stomp-Dipper
  mouth in Jazz Discounter, Vol. 2
  (May 1949): 3 ((—))

SULIEMAN, IDREES (Leonard Graham),
1923–
trumpet

S265 JEPSEN, Jorgen Grunnet: Idrees
Sulieman (Leonard Graham) diskografi in Orkester Journalen, Vol.
32 (December 1964): 46; Vol. 33
(January 1965): 30; (February
1965): 27–28 ((2, 3, 7))

SULLIVAN, IRA, 1931–
trumpet, saxophones

S266 SPITZER, David B.: Ira Sullivan;
living legend in Down Beat, Vol.
39 (February 17, 1972): 15 ((—))

SULLIVAN, JOE, 1906–1971
piano

S267 Australian releases featuring Joe
Sullivan in Jazz Notes (Australia), No. 67 (September 1946): 15
((—))

S268 GENTIEU, Norman P.: [Discography]
in his Notes for a bio-discography
of Joe Sullivan. Part I: Chicago,
1906–1928 in Journal of Jazz
Studies, Vol. 4 (summer 1977):
40–41 ((2, 3, 6, 7))

SUMMIT label
See EGMONT label

SUN label
See also BLUES MUSIC (Guralnick,
Peter)

S269 ESCOTT, Colin, and Martin HAWKINS:
The complete Sun label session
files (revised). Ashford, Kent:
Martin Hawkins, 1975, 64 pp. ((2,
3, 7)) [rev. ed. of next entry]

S270 VERNON, Paul: The Sun legend.
[London: Steve Lane, 1969], 64
pp. ((3, 4p))

SUN RA (Herman Blount), ca. 1915–
piano

S271 BUZELIN, Jean, and Alain Rene
HARDY: Disco Sun Ra in Jazz Hot,
No. 361 (May 1979): 15–18; No.
362 (June 1979): 23–25 ((2, 7))

S272 FLUCKIGER, Otto: Discography of
Sun Ra in Jazz Statistics, No. 21
(March 1961): 4–6; additions and
corrections from Michel VOGLER in
Jazz Statistics, No. 22 (June
1961): 6 ((2, 3, 7))

S273 GANT, Dave: [Discography of ESP
recordings] in Jazz Studies, Vol.
1, No. 4 (1967): 65 ((2, 7))

S274 RABEN, Erik: Diskofilspalten in
Orkester Journalen, Vol. 38 (September 1970): 23; (October 1970):
21 ((2, 3, 7))

S275 [[STIASSI, Ruggero: [Discography
1965–1966] in Musica Jazz, Vol.
25 (June 1969)]]

S276 VEIN, Julian: Sun Ra on Saturn &
Savoy in Jazz Journal, Vol. 20
(November 1967): 19, 22 ((2, 7p))

S277 VUYSJE, Bert: Sun Ra op de plaat
in Jazz Wereld, No. 19 (August
1968): 8–9 ((2, 7))

SUNNYLAND SLIM (Albert Luandrew), 1907–
piano, vocal

S278 ROTANTE, Anthony: Discography of
Sunnyland Slim, Dr. Clayton's
Buddy (Albert Luandrew) in Record
Research, Vol. 1 (February 1955):
4–5; additions and corrections in
Record Research, Vol. 1 (April
1955): 2; (June 1955): 4; Vol. 2
(July–August 1956): 11 ((2, 3, 8))

S279 SHEATSLEY, Paul B., and Derek
COLLER: Discography of "Sunnyland
Slim" (Albert Luandrew) in Blues
Unlimited, No. 15 (October 1964):
9–10 ((2, 3, 7))

SUNSET label
See also HOLLYWOOD label

S280 MORGAN, Alun: Sunset Records; a
listing in Discographical Forum,
No. 2 (July 1960): 2–3, 19; additions and corrections from Kurt
MOHR in Discographical Forum, No.
3 (September 1960): 16 ((2, 3, 6,
7))

SUNSHINE BOYS (Joe and Dan Mooney)
See also MOONEY, JOE

S281 VENABLES, Ralph: Sunshine Boys
discography in Jazz Tempo, No. 16
(n.d.): 16 ((2, 3, 7d))

SUPERIOR label

S282 KAY, George W.: The Superior
catalog in Record Research, No.
37 (August 1961) to No. 39 (November 1961); No. 41 (February
1962) to No. 43 (May 1962); No.
47 (November 1962); No. 48 (Janu-

ary 1963), various paginations
((3, 8))

SUPERSAX (musical group)

S283 TOWNLEY, Ray, and Tim HOGAN:
Supersax; the genius of Bird
x Five in Down Beat, Vol. 41
(November 21, 1974): 15 ((——))

SUPRAPHON label (Czech)
See JAZZ MUSIC--Czechoslovakia

SUSSEX label

S284 WILSON, Jim: Sussex label listing
in Hot Buttered Soul, No. 16
(March 1973): 14 ((——))

SUTTON, RALPH, 1922–
piano

S285 COLLER, Derek; Frank DUTTON; and
Bert WHYATT; a
"name" discography in Matrix, No.
38 (December 1961): 11-13; additions and corrections in Matrix,
No. 46 (April 1963): 13; No. 47
(June 1963): 11; No. 49 (October
1963): 14 ((2, 3, 7))

S286 SHACTER, James D.: Discography in
his Piano man; the story of Ralph
Sutton. Chicago: Jaynar, 1975:
209-238 ((1, 2, 3, 6, 7))

SWAGGIE label (Australian)

S287 SHERBURN, Neville: Swaggie jazz
collector series in Matrix, No.
81 (February 1969) to No. 88 (June
1970), various paginations; additions and corrections in Matrix,
No. 88 (June 1970): 13 ((3, 6))

S288 SHERBURN, Neville, and George
HULME: The Swaggie label in Matrix, No. 23 (May 1959); No. 24
(July 1959); No. 27 (February
1960); No. 29/30 (August 1960);
No. 35/36 (September 1961), various paginations ((1, 2, 3, 6, 7))

SWAMP DOGG (Jerry Williams)
piano, vocal

S289 MOHR, Kurt; Gilles PETARD; and
J. P. ARNIAC: Swamp Dogg in Soul
Bag, No. 49 (July-August 1975?):
2-3; additions and corrections in
Soul Bag, No. 51 (January 1976):
32 ((2, 3, 7))

SWAN label
See also PICK-UP label

S290 VENABLES, Ralph: Discography of
the Swan sessions in Melody Maker,
Vol. 24 (March 27, 1948): 6 ((2,
3, 7))

SWEATMAN, WILBUR C., 1882-1961
clarinet

S291 KUNSTADT, Len, and Bob COLTON: A
discography of Wilbur Sweatman in
Discophile, No. 40 (February
1955): 10-13; additions and corrections in Discophile, No. 42
(June 1955): 17; No. 52 (February
1957: 14; Jazz Journal, Vol. 11
(January 1958): 9 ((1, 2, 3, 6,
7))

SWEET GEORGIA BROWN (tune title)

S292 SCHULTZ, Allen W.: Sweet Georgia
Brown in Jazz Discounter, Vol. 2
(November 1949): 2 ((——))

SWING label (French)

S293 BAKKER, Dick M.: Pre-war Swing-
label on micro in Micrography,
No. 4 (June 1969): 3 [omits Django
Reinhardt titles] ((7d))

S294 FRESART, Iwan: Discographie des
sessions organisées par Charles
Delaunay pour la marque "Swing"
aux U.S.A. en 1946 in Point du
Jazz, No. 5 (September 1971): 18-
20 ((2, 3, 6, 7))

S295 [[FRESART, Iwan: 78 rpm Swing
label discography. Brussels: 1965,
16 pp.]]

S296 FRESART, Iwan: Swing; a numerical
listing of the 78 rpm issues in
Matrix, No. 62 (December 1965) to
No. 64 (April 1966); No. 66/67
(September 1966) to No. 71 (June
1967); No. 74 (December 1967) to
No. 79 (October 1968), various
paginations ((3, 6))

S297 PASCOLI, Daniel: Postwar French
Swing issues in Jazzfinder, Vol.
1 (October 1948): 12-14 ((2, 3,
7))

SYKES, ROOSEVELT, 1906–
piano, vocal

S298 COLLER, Derek: Recording the blues
no. 6--Roosevelt Sykes in Vintage
Jazz Mart, Vol. 6 (June 1959): 4,

42; (July-August 1959): 4; Vol. 7 (July 1960): 4 [supplements next entry] ((2, 3, 6, 7))

S299 WIEDEMANN, Erik: Rossevelt [sic] Sykes discography in Discophile, No. 17 (April 1951): 8-12; additions and corrections in Discophile, No. 18 (June 1951): 14; No. 19 (August 1951): 12; No. 21 (December 1951): 18-19; No. 22 (February 1952): 12; No. 23 (April 1952): 5; No. 24 (June 1952): 13; No. 29 (May 1953): 19 ((2, 3, 7))

SYLVIANS
　　See SAVOY BANDS

SYNCO JAZZ BAND

S300 The Pathe label and the Synco Jazz Band in Playback, Vol. 2 (May 1949): 18 ((3))

SZUKALSKI, TOMASZ, 1948-
　　tenor saxophone

S301 Tomasz Szukalski selected discography in Jazz Forum (Poland), No. 41 (March 1976): 53 ((—))

TDS label
　　See DUD SOUND label

TABACKIN, LEW, 1940-
　　tenor saxophone
　　See AKIYOSHI, TOSHIKO

TAILGATE label

T1　BELLAMY, Ken: A discography of the "Tailgate" label in Discophile, No. 12 (June 1950): 7, 15 ((2, 3, 7))

TALBERT, ELMER, 1900-1950
　　trumpet

T2　STAGG, Tom: The recordings of Elmer Talbert in Footnote, Vol. 3 (February 1972): 12-15 ((2, 6, 7d))

TALENT label

T3　McCORMICK, Mack: The Talent label in Blues Unlimited, No. 41 (February 1967): 13 ((3))

TALLAHASSEE TIGHT (probably Louis Washington)
　　guitar, vocal

T4　COLLER, Derek, and Paul OLIVER: Tallahassee Tight in Discographical Forum, No. 4 (January 1961): 15-16 ((2, 3, 7))

TAMLA label

T5　CALTA, Gary: Diggin' up discographies: Tamla Records, Detroit, Michigan, part 2 in Goldmine, No. 17 (July-August 1977): 6 ((—))

TAMPA RED (Hudson Whittaker), 1900?-

T6　PARRY, Bill, and Derek COLLER: Tampa Red (Hudson Whittaker); a discography of his Victor and Bluebird recordings in Matrix, No. 37 (November 1961): 3-11; additions and corrections in Matrix, No. 45 (February 1963): 15 ((2, 3, 6, 7))

TATE, CARL
　　See STARR, BOB

TATE, ERSKINE, 1898-
　　leader

T7　MOHR, Kurt: The (incomplete) story of Erskine Tate's orchestra in Jazz Statistics, No. 9 (March 1959): 6 ((2, 3, 7))

TATUM, ART, 1910-1956
　　piano

T8　HOEFER, George: Early Tatum discography in Down Beat, Vol. 30 (October 24, 1963): 39 ((2, 3, 7))

T9　JEPSEN, Jorgen Grunnet: Art Tatum; a discography in Discophile, No. 36 (June 1954): 4-8; additions and corrections in Discophile, No. 41 (April 1955): 17-19; No. 53 (April 1957): 11 ((2, 3, 6, 7))

T10　[[JEPSEN, Jorgen Grunnet: Art Tatum; a discography. Copenhagen: 1957, 10 leaves]]

T11　JEPSEN, Jorgen Grunnet: Discographie d'Art Tatum in Les Cahiers du Jazz, No. 5 (1960-1961?): 76-84 ((1, 2, 3, 6, 7))

T12 JEPSEN, Jorgen Grunnet: Discography of Art Tatum/Bud Powell. [Brande, Denmark: Debut Records, c1961], 28 leaves ((1, 2, 3, 6, 7))

T13 SPENCER, Ray: An Art Tatum discography in Jazz Journal, Vol. 19 (August 1966): 9-10; (September 1966): 13-16; (October 1966): 13-16; additions and corrections in Jazz Journal (December 1966): 31 ((1, 2, 3, 6, 7))

T14 [[SPORTIS, Felix: Art Tatum--essai. Marseille: Jazz Club Aix-Marseille, 1968, 15 pp.]]

TAYLOR, BILLY, 1921-
piano

T15 Selected Billy Taylor discography in Down Beat, Vol. 47 (May 1980): 25 ((—))

TAYLOR, CECIL, 1933-
piano
See also JAZZ MUSIC--Avant-Garde (Raben, Erik)

T16 Cecil Taylor; a selected discography in Contemporary Keyboard, Vol. 5 (January 1979): 42 ((—))

T17 Cecil Taylor discography in Coda, No. 136 (March 1975): 8 ((2, 7))

T18 CERUTTI, Gustave: Discographie de Cecil Taylor in Jazz 360, No. 22 (November 1979): 9-14 ((2, 7))

T19 Discographie de Cecil Taylor in Jazz Hot, No. 248 (March 1969): 35 ((2, 7))

T20 Discographie de Cecil Taylor in Jazz Hot, No. 296 (July-August 1973): 21 ((2, 7))

T21 HARDY, Alain Rene: Les faces de Cecil Taylor; essai d'inventaire discographique in Jazz Magazine (France), No. 260 (December 1977): 34-35 ((2, 7))

T22 JACCHETTI, Renato: Discografia Cecil Taylor in Musica Jazz, Vol. 32 (May 1976): 47-48 ((1, 2, 7))

T23 JEPSEN, Jorgen Grunnet: Cecil Taylor diskografi in Orkester Journalen, Vol. 30 (December 1962): 48 ((2, 7))

T24 Selected Taylor discography in Down Beat, Vol. 42 (April 10, 1975): 13 ((—))

T25 [[STIASSI, Ruggero: [Discography] in Musica Jazz, Vol. 25 (April 1969)]]

TAYLOR, COCOA
See TAYLOR, KOKO

TAYLOR, EDDIE, 1923-
guitar, vocal

T26 CHAUVARD, Marcel, and Jacques DEMETRE: A discography of Eddie Taylor in Blues Unlimited, No. 17 (November-December 1964): 10; additions and corrections in Blues Unlimited, No. 22 (May 1965): 10 ((2, 3, 7))

TAYLOR, EVA, 1896-197?
vocal

T27 WILE, Ray: Eva Taylor on Edison in Record Research, No. 142 (September 1976): 7 ((3, 6, 7))

TAYLOR, HOUND DOG (Theodore Roosevelt Taylor), 1917-1975
guitar, vocal

T28 PERIN, Jacques, and Jacques DEMETRE: Hound Dog Taylor in Soul Bag, No. 52 (March 1976): 5 ((2, 7))

TAYLOR, KOKO (nee Cora Walton), 1935-
vocal

T29 [[[Discography] in Australian Blues Society Progress, ca. spring 1967]]

T30 MOHR, Kurt; Emmanuel CHOISNEL; and Willy LEISER: Koko Taylor in Soul Bag, No. 50 (September 1975): 6-7; additions and corrections in Soul Bag, No. 51 (January 1976): 32 ((2, 3, 7))

TAYLOR, TED
vocal

T31 LeBLANC, Eric S.; Jim O'NEAL; and Robert PRUTER: Ted Taylor discography in Living Blues, No. 32 (May-June 1977): 5 ((—))

TCHICAI, JOHN, 1936-
alto saxophone

T32 BARNETT, Anthony: Published recordings in Jazz Monthly, No. 164
(October 1968): 5 ((7))

T33 Discographie in Jazz Hot, No. 272
(May 1971): 11 ((7))

T34 [[HAMES, Michael: John Tchicai on
disc and tape. Wimborne, Dorset:
1976 ((1))]]

T35 RABEN, Erik: Diskofilspalten in
Orkester Journalen, Vol. 38 (January 1970): 16-17; (February
1970): 17 ((2, 3, 7))

TDS label
See DUD SOUND label

TEAGARDEN, CHARLIE, 1913-
trumpet

T36 SHOWLER, Joe: [Selected list of
recordings and soundtracks] in
IAJRC Journal, Vol. 9 (fall 1976):
8-9 ((7d))

TEAGARDEN, JACK, 1905-1964
trombone

T37 BAKKER, Dick M.: Jack Teagarden
1939 in Micrography, No. 38 (October 1975): 10 ((6, 7d))

T38 BAKKER, Dick M.: Teagarden 1927-
1933 in Micrography, No. 27 (September 1973): 5-8; additions and
corrections in Micrography, No.
29 (December 1973): 1 ((6, 7d))

T39 HOEFER, George: Teagarden discography in Down Beat, Vol. 18 (March
9, 1951): 18 ((—))

T40 [[SMITH, Jay D.: Big Gate, a
chronological listing of the recorded works of Jack Teagarden
from 1928 to 1950. Washington,
DC: 1951, 36 pp. ((2, 3, 6, 7))]]

T41 SMITH, Jay D., and Len GUTTRIDGE:
Selected discography in their Jack
Teagarden; the story of a jazz
maverick. London: Cassell [c1960]
(also London: Jazz Book Club,
1962; New York: DaCapo, 1976),
185-200 ((2, 7d))

T42 WATERS, Howard J.: Jack Teagarden's music; his career and recordings. Stanhope, NJ: Walter C.
Allen, c1960, ix, 222 pp. (Jazz
Monographs, No. 3) ((1, 2, 3, 4p,
4r, 4t, 6, 7, 9))

TELEFUNKEN label (Swedish)

T43 ENGLUND, Bjorn: A glimpse into
the past; Telefunken's wartime
Swedish jazz recordings in Storyville, No. 76 (April-May 1978):
134-136 ((3, 7))

TELEVOX label (German)

T44 LANGE, Horst H.: The Televox-
Special Record story in R.S.V.P.,
No. 45 (February 1969): 32; No.
47 (April 1969): 15 ((3, 6))

TEMPLE, JOHNNIE, 1906-1968
guitar, piano, vocal

T45 McCARTHY, Albert J.: Preliminary
discography of Johnnie Temple in
Record Changer, Vol. 5 (August
1946): 23 ((2, 3, 7))

T46 WHYATT, Bert, and Derek COLLER:
Investigation department; Johnnie
Temple in Jazz Music, Vol. 7
(January-February 1956): 9-12;
additions and corrections from
Hugues PANASSIE in Jazz Music,
Vol. 7 (July-August 1956): 22
((2, 3, 7))

TEMPLE label

T47 A bootleg label listing; Temple
in Discophile, No. 45 (December
1955): 8-9, 20; additions and
corrections in Discophile, No. 46
(February 1956): 14; No. 52 (February 1957): 14 ((1, 3))

TEMPO label (British)

T48 DAVIES, Ron: A discography of
"Tempo" records in Discophile, No.
7 (August 1949): 1-2 ((2, 3, 7))

T49 HULME, George, and Bernard HOL-
LAND: Tempo in Matrix, No. 44
(December 1962) to No. 47 (June
1963), various paginations; additions and corrections in Matrix,
No. 52 (April 1964): 18-19; No.
53 (June 1964): 18; No. 55 (October 1964): 17; No. 59 (June 1965):
18-19 ((2, 3, 5, 6, 7))

TENNESSEE TOOTERS
See JAZZ MUSIC (Venables, Ralph
G. V.)

TERRELL, TAMMI
    See MONTGOMERY, TAMMY

TERRITORY BANDS

T50   BAKKER, Dick M.: The territory
      bands on record in Micrography,
      No. 14 (May 1971): 2-4 ((7d))

T51   BAKKER, Dick M.: Territory bands
      till 1931 in Micrography, No. 37
      (July 1975): 3-6 ((6, 7d))

TERRY, CLARK, 1920-
    trumpet

T52   ADKINS, Tony, and Malcolm WALKER:
      Private recordings; Clark Terry-
      Bob Brookmeyer in Discographical
      Forum, No. 12 (May 1969): 6 ((1,
      2, 7, 9))

T53   JEPSEN, Jorgen Grunnet: Clark
      Terry diskografi (skivor inspelade
      under eget namn) in Orkester
      Journalen, Vol. 28 (July-August
      1960): 50 ((1, 2, 3, 7))

T54   [[RADZITSKY, Carlos de: Clark
      Terry, a 1960-1967 discography
      with biographical notes. Antwerp:
      1968, 48 pp.]] [excludes Duke
      Ellington sessions]; additions
      and corrections in Jazz Journal,
      Vol. 21 (October 1968): 39; Vol.
      22 (January 1969): 17

T55   WALKER, Malcolm: Clark Terry dis-
      cography (1947-1960) in Jazz
      Monthly, Vol. 7 (December 1961)
      to Vol. 8 (April 1962),
      various paginations, in 5 parts
      ((1, 2, 3, 6, 7))

TERRY, SONNY, 1911-
    harmonica, vocal

T56   JAVORS, Robert: Discography in
      TERRY, Sonny: The harp styles of
      Sonny Terry (note: latest printing
      has title Sonny Terry's country
      blues harmonica). New York: Oak
      [c1975], 114-124; additions and
      corrections from Kip LORNELL in
      Living Blues, No. 27 (May-June
      1976): 45 ((2, 7))

T57   ROTANTE, Anthony: Sonny Terry in
      Jazz Music, Vol. 5, No. 5 (n.d.):
      6-9; additions and corrections in
      Jazz Music, Vol. 5, No. 8 (1954):
      26; Vol. 6, No. 3 (1955): 31-32;
      No. 4 (1955): 9, 26; Vol. 6, No.
      5 (n.d.): 10; [from Jacques DE-
      METRE and Paul OLIVER] in Disco-

phile, No. 61 (December 1958):
3-4 ((2, 3, 6, 7))

TESCHEMACHER, FRANK, 1906-1932
    clarinet

T58   AVAKIAN, George: The unissued
      Teschemachers in Jazz Informa-
      tion, Vol. 2 (March 21, 1941): 2
      ((2, 3, 6, 7d))

T59   DELLERNIA, Gaspare: Discografia
      in Musica Jazz, Vol. 19 (May
      1963): 42-43 ((2, 3, 6, 7))

T60   Discographie de Frank Teschmaker
      [sic]; voici une liste de tous les
      disques où, a notre conaissance,
      Teschmaker a joué des solos in
      Jazz Hot, No. 8 (May 1936): 9
      ((—))

T61   SIMOSKO, Vladimir: Frank Tesche-
      macher discography in Journal of
      Jazz Studies, Vol. 2 (fall 1975):
      51-53 ((2, 3, 6, 7))

T62   TEALDO ALIZIERI, Carlos L.: Dis-
      cografia de Frank Teschemacher in
      Jazz Magazine (Argentina), No. 30
      (March 1952): 19-21, 26 ((2, 3,
      6, 7d))

T63   TOSCANO POUCHAN, Mario A.: Dis-
      cografia in Hot Jazz Club, No. 15
      (September 1947): 30, 34, 36;
      additions and corrections in Hot
      Jazz Club, No. 16 (December 1947):
      13, 27 ((2, 3, 7d))

T64   VENABLES, Ralph: Discography of
      the late Frank Teschemacher in
      Jazz (Belgium), No. 5 (1945):
      15-16 ((2, 3, 7d))

T65   VENABLES, Ralph: Discography of
      the late Frank Teschemacher in
      Jazz Forum (UK), No. 1 (n.d.):
      27-28 ((2, 3, 7d))

TEST PRESSINGS
    See BLUES MUSIC (Bastin, Bruce);
    COLUMBIA label (Colton, Bob)

TEX, JOE

T66   [[[Discography] in Soul Bag, No.
      1]]

THARPE, ROSETTA, 1921-1973
    vocal

T67   HAYES, C. J.: Sister Rosetta
      Tharpe; a discography in Matrix,
      No. 77 (June 1968): 3-14; addi-

tions and corrections in Matrix, No. 83 (June 1969): 11-12; No. 85 (October 1969): 19 ((1, 2, 3, 6, 7))

T68   JORGENSEN, Jorgen: Rosetta Tharpe and Marie Knight; discography 1947-1952 in Melody Maker, Vol. 28 (September 6, 1952); (September 13, 1952); (October 11, 1952); (October 18, 1952); (October 25, 1952), various paginations ((2, 3, 7d))

T69   McCARTHY, Albert: Discography of Rosetta Tharpe in Jazz Music, Vol. 3, No. 5 (1947): 15-16 ((2, 3, 7))

T70   NIQUET, Bernard: Au revoir Rosetta in Soul Bag, No. 16 (1972?): 20-21 [1966-1969 recordings] ((7))

T71   PEDERSEN, Hans Jorgen: Sister Rosetta Tharpe; a discography in Jazz Music, Vol. 4, No. 5 (1951): 15-17 ((3, 7))

THAT'S A PLENTY (tune title)

T72   RUGGLES, Happy: That's a plenty in Jazz Discounter, No. 12 (December 1948): 10; [by Edward KINSEL] No. ? (August-September 1949): 3-6 ((—)) [part 1]; ((2, 3, 6, 7d)) [part 2]

THELIN, EJE, 1938-
     trombone

T73   Eje Thelin diskografi in Orkester Journalen, Vol. 41 (January 1973): 11 ((2, 7d))

T74   Eje Thelin in the 70s; a selected discography in Jazz Forum (Poland), No. 49 (1977): 39 ((—))

T75   HANSSON, Lars: Eje Thelin diskografi in Orkester Journalen, Vol. 35 (December 1967): 48 ((2, 3, 7))

THESAURUS TRANSCRIPTIONS
     See RHYTHM MAKERS

THIELEMANS, TOOTS (Jean Thielemans), 1922-
     harmonica

T76   JEPSEN, Jorgen Grunnet: Toots Thielemans diskografi in Orkester Journalen, Vol. 29 (July-August 1961): 38-39; (September 1961): 38; (October 1961): 34 ((2,3, 7))

T77   Selected Thielemans discography in Down Beat, Vol. 45 (August 10, 1978): 25 ((—))

THIS IS JAZZ (radio broadcast series)
     See AIRSHOTS (Litchfield, Jack)

THOMAS, ELLA
     vocal

T78   CHOISNEL, Emmanuel: Discographie d'Ella Thomas in Soul Bag, No. 22/23 (January-February 1973): 25 ((2, 3, 7))

THOMAS, HARRY, 1890-1941
     piano

T79   MILLER, Gene: Harry Thomas at the piano in IAJRC Journal, Vol. 5 (July 1972): 7-8 ((7))

THOMAS, HERSAL, ca. 1907-1926
     piano

T80   Hersal Thomas discography in Jazzology (UK), No. 6 new series (June 1946): 21 ((2, 3, 7d))

THOMAS, JAMES
     vocal, bongos

T81   MOHR, Kurt; Emmanuel CHOISNEL; and Lionel ROUCHEZ: James Thomas disco in Soul Bag, No. 21 (November-December 1972): 28-29 ((2, 3, 7))

THOMAS, JOE (Joseph Lewis Thomas), 1909-
     trumpet

T82   ANGELL, Olav: Discography in Swingtime (Sweden), No. 1 (December 1960): 10 (to be continued) ((2, 3, 7))

T83   NIQUET, Bernard: Les Joe Thomas in Point du Jazz, No. 8 (April 1973): 76-96 ((2, 3, 7))

T84   TROLLE, Frank H., and William COVERDALE: Joseph Lewis Thomas; a discography and short biography in IAJRC Journal, Vol. 12 (April 1979): 12-18 ((1, 2, 3, 6, 7))

THOMAS, JOE (Joseph Vankert Thomas), 1909-
     tenor saxophone

T85 CRESSANT, Pierre: Discographie de Joe Thomas depuis la formation de son nouvel orchestre in Jazz Hot, No. 49 (November 1950): 15 ((2))

T86 MOHR, Kurt: Discography of Joe Thomas in Jazz Statistics, No. 22 (June 1961): 11-12 [1945-1951 recordings] ((2, 3, 7))

THOMAS, KID
See VALENTINE, KID THOMAS

THOMAS, LAFAYETTE
guitar, vocal

T87 CHOISNEL, Emmanuel: Lafayette Thomas in Soul Bag, No. 22/23 (January-February 1973): 39 ((2, 3, 7))

THOMAS, RAMBLIN' (George Willard Thomas)
guitar, vocal

T88 BAKKER, Dick M.: Ramblin' Thomas in Micrography, No. 2 (February 1969): 10 ((7d))

T89 GILLET, Andre, and Serge TONNEAU: George Willard "Ramblin'" Thomas in Rhythm and Blues Panorama, No. 22 (1963): 14-15 ((2, 3, 6, 7))

THOMAS, RENÉ, 1927-1975
guitar

T90 LAFARGUE, Pierre: René Thomas; quelques éléments discographiques in Jazz Hot, No. 313 (February 1975): 12-13 ((2, 3, 7))

T91 VANDE VELDE, Paul: René Thomas discography in Discographical Forum, No. 25 (July 1971) to No. 27 (November 1971): various paginations ((1, 2, 3, 7))

THOMAS, RUFUS, 1917-
vocal

T92 Rufus Thomas' 1950's records in Living Blues, No. 29 (September-October 1976): 12 ((—))

THOMPSON, DICKIE, 1917-
guitar, vocal

T93 MOHR, Kurt: Discographie in Jazz, Blues & Co., No. 25/26 (January 1979): 11 ((2, 3, 7))

THOMPSON, DON, 1940-
bass violin, piano

T94 Selected Thompson discography in Jazz Forum (Poland), No. 58 (1979): 36 ((—))

THOMPSON, LUCKY (Eli Thompson), 1924-
tenor saxophone

T95 MOHR, Kurt: Lucky Thompson in Paris; a listing in Discophile, No. 48 (June 1956): 10-12, 14-15; additions and corrections in Discophile, No. 49 (August 1956): 11 ((2, 3, 7))

T96 POSTIF, François: La discographie française de Lucky Thompson in Jazz Magazine (France), No. 18 (June 1956): 14 ((2, 3, 7))

T97 [[WILLIAMS, Tony: Eli "Lucky" Thompson discography; part 1, 1944-1951; a discography and biography. London: 1967, vi, 23 pp.]]

THOMPSON, SONNY
piano

T98 MOHR, Kurt: Sonny Thompson; a name discography in Discophile, No. 61 (December 1958): 12-16 ((2, 3, 6, 7))

THORNHILL, CLAUDE, 1909-1965
leader

T99 CROSBIE, Ian: Prophet without honour (part 2) in Jazz Journal, Vol. 24 (April 1971): 31 ((2, 3, 6, 7))

T100 EDWARDS, Ernie: Claude Thornhill and his Orchestra. Whittier, CA: ErnGeoBil [1967], v, 20 leaves (Dance band series, T-1) ((1, 2, 3, 6, 7, 9))

T101 EDWARDS, Ernie: A Claude Thornhill discography in Jazz Monthly, Vol. 8 (January 1963): 13-14; Vol. 9 (March 1963): 16-17 ((1, 2, 3, 6, 7))

T102 GARROD, Charles: Claude Thornhill and his Orchestra. Zephyrhills, FL: Joyce Music, 1975, 25, 3 leaves ((1, 2, 3, 4t, 6, 7))

T103 HALL, George I., ed.: Claude Thornhill and his Orhcestra. rev. ed. Laurel, MD: Jazz Discographies Unlimited, 1971, v, 20, 4 leaves ((1, 2, 3, 4t, 6, 7))

THORNTON, ARGONNE, 1921–
    piano
    See PIANO MUSIC (JAZZ) (Edwards,
    Ernie)

THORNTON, BIG MAMA (Willie Mae
    Thornton), 1926–
    vocal

T104 MOHR, Kurt: A discography of
    Willie Mae Thornton in Jazz Sta-
    tistics, No. 7 (1958?): 4-5 ((2,
    3, 7))

THORNTON, CLIFFORD, 1936–
    trombone

T105 LUZZI, Mario: Discografia di
    Clifford Thornton in Musica Jazz,
    Vol. 30 (August-September 1974):
    15-16 ((2, 7))

T106 Selected Thornton discography in
    Down Beat, Vol. 42 (June 19, 1975):
    20 ((—))

THREE RIFFS (musical group)
    See ATLANTIC label (Grendysa,
    Peter A.: Atlantic's early groups)

TIGER label

T107 GIBBON, Peter: Tiger label listing
    in Soul, No. 3 (April 1966): 31
    ((3))

TIGER RAG (tune title)

T108 ENGLUND, Bjorn: Tiger rag pa
    svenska in Orkester Journalen,
    Vol. 40 (December 1972): 21 ((3,
    7d))

T109 LANGE, Horst H.: Discophilia;
    Tiger rag in Schlagzeug, No. 14
    (October 1958?) (part 5 to 7 in
    February, March, and June 1959
    issues; possibly in other issues,
    various paginations) ((2, 3, 6,
    7))

T110 MADISON, Joseph W.: A compilation
    of all Tiger rags ever issued in
    any country in Good Diggin', Vol.
    1 (November 1, 1947): 9-13; addi-
    tions in Good Diggin', Vol. 2
    (January 31, 1948): 6-7; (March
    1948): 9; (July 1, 1948): 19-20.
    ((—))

T111 MADISON, Joseph: Discography of
    Tiger rag in Record Changer (April
    1949): 21-22 ((1))

T112 MADISON, Joseph: Most up-to-date
    Tiger rag-Milenburg joys listing
    in Jazz Discounter, Vol. 2 (De-
    cember 1949) to Vol. 3 (April
    1950), various paginations; pos-
    sibly continued in other issues
    (issues shown cover A to Q) ((3,
    6))

TILLMAN, WILBER, 1898-1967
    sousaphone, tuba

T113 DASH, Terry: The Wilber Tillman
    discography in Footnote, Vol. 8
    (December 1976-January 1977): 28-
    30 ((2, 7))

TIMMONS, BOBBY, 1935–
    piano

T114 Bobby Timmons discography in Swing
    Journal, Vol. 28 (May 1974): 252-
    257 ((2, 7d))

T115 JEPSEN, Jorgen Grunnet: Bobby
    Timmons diskografi in Orkester
    Journalen, Vol. 29 (January 1961):
    42; (February 1961): 38; (March
    1961): 36-37 ((2, 3, 7))

TIN ROOF BLUES (tune title)

T116 McGEAGH, Michael R.: A discography
    of Tin roof blues/Jazzin' baby
    blues in Jazz Journal, Vol. 2
    (December 1949): 18; Vol. 3 (Feb-
    ruary 1950): 20-19 ((2, 3, 7))

TINY TOPSY
    vocal

T117 MOHR, Kurt: [Discography] in Jazz
    Statistics, No. 11 (July 1959): 5
    ((2, 3, 7))

TIPPETT, KEITH, 1947–
    piano

T118 RENSEN, Jan: Geselecteerde dis-
    cografie in Jazz Nu, Vol. 1 (June
    1979): 407 ((2, 7))

TOGASHI, MASAHIKO, 1940–
    drums

T119 [Discography] in Swing Journal,
    Vol. 31 (February 1977): 266-
    271 ((2, 7d))

TOLBERT, JOHNNY
    vocal, guitar

T120 CHOISNEL, Emmanuel: Discographie
de Johnny Tolbert in Soul Bag, No.
22/23 (January-February 1973): 20
((2, 3, 7))

TOLBERT, SKEETS

T121 McCARTHY, Albert J.: Discography
of Skeets Tolbert in Discographical Forum, No. 2 (July 1960):
12-13 ((2, 3, 7))

TOLLIVER, KIM

T122 [[[Discography] in Soul Bag, No.
9/10]]

TOP NOTES (musical group)

T123 MOHR, Kurt: Discographie des Top
Notes in Soul Bag, No. 35 (February 1974): 26; additions and corrections in Soul Bag, No. 45
(January 1975): 34 ((2, 3, 7))

TOPSY, TINY
See TINY TOPSY

TORNER, GOSTA
trumpet

T124 ENGLUND, Bjorn: Gosta Torner diskografi in Orkester Journalen,
Vol. 36 (January 1968) to (May
1968), various paginations, in 5
parts ((2, 3, 6, 7))

TOSCANO, ELI
record producer
See ABCO label

TOSHIKO-TABACKIN band
See AKIYOSHI, TOSHIKO

TOUSAN, AL
See TOUSSAINT, ALLEN

TOUSSAINT, ALLEN, 1938-
piano, vocal

T125 MOHR, Kurt: Allen Toussaint's
discography in Soul Bag, No. 26
(May 1973): 10-11 ((2, 3, 7))

TOWER label (British)

T126 BADROCK, Arthur: Tower in Collecta, No. 7 (September-October
1969): 19-23 ((3))

TOWLES, NAT, 1905-1963
bass violin, leader

T127 MOHR, Kurt: The (incomplete) story
of Nat Towles Orchestra in Jazz
Statistics, No. 10 (May 1959): 8-9
((2, 3, 7))

TOWNER, RALPH, 1940-
guitar

T128 Selected Towner discography in
Down Beat, Vol. 42 (June 19,
1975): 17 ((—))

TRACEY, STAN, 1926-
piano

T129 MORGAN, Alun: Stan Tracey--a name
listing in Discographical Forum,
No. 30/31 (1972): 19-21; additions
and corrections in Discographical
Forum, No. 33 (1974): 1, 19 ((2,
3, 7))

T130 Stan Tracey discography in Jazz
Forum (Poland), No. 46 (1977): 45
((—))

TRANSCRIPTIONS
See also ARMED FORCES RADIO SER-
VICE; ELLINGTON, DUKE--Transcrip-
tions; LUNCEFORD, JIMMIE (Dutton,
Frank) and (Hall, Bill: Jimmie
Lunceford broadcasts-transcrip-
tions & filmtracks); NICHOLS, RED
(Backensto, Woody: The meandering
Macgregors); RHYTHM MAKERS; SESAC
label; V DISC label; WORLD PROGRAM
SERVICE; YOUNG, LESTER (Schroeder,
Harry)

T131 [HEIDER, Wally]: Transcography; a
discography of jazz and "pop"
music issued on 16" transcriptions. n.p. [ca. 1956?], 105 pp.
((—))

TRANSITION label
See CANDID label (Candid & Transition)

TREMBLE KIDS (musical group)

T132 A swingin' reunion--the Tremble
Kids are back! in Jazz Podium,
Vol. 23 (April 1974): 19 ((—))

TRENDS (musical group)

T133 MOHR, Kurt: The Trends in Soul
Bag, No. 45 (January 1975): 32
((2, 3, 7))

TRICE, WILLIE, 1910-1976
guitar, vocal

T134 BASTIN, Bruce: Willie Trice: North
Carolina blues man in Talking
Blues, No. 9/10 (1979): 12-17 ((2,
3, 6, 7))

TRIPLE B label

T135 FOSTER, Bob and Jim WILSON: Triple
B label listing in Hot Buttered
Soul, No. 30 (May 1974?): 5 ((3))

TRISTANO, LENNIE, 1919-1979
piano

T136 DELMAS, Jean: [Discography] in
Jazz Hot, No. 326 (April 1976):
16-17 ((1, 2, 3, 7))

T137 Discography in Down Beat, Vol. 46
(August 9, 1979): 16 ((—))

T138 Diskographie in Jazz Podium, Vol.
28 (February 1979): 15 ((1, 2, 7))

T139 Lennie Tristano & Warne Marsh in
Swing Journal, Vol. 30 (August
1976): 78-83 ((2, 7d))

T140 McKINNEY, John F.: Discography in
his The pedagogy of Lennie Tristano. D. Ed. dissertation, Fair-
leigh Dickinson University, 1978
(also available from University
Microfilms, Ann Arbor, MI; order
no. 78-24880): 191-197 ((1, 2, 3,
6, 7))

T141 MERCERON, Gerald: Discography in
Jazz Hot, No. 214 (November 1956):
21 ((—))

T142 MOON, Pete: Discography in The
Professional, No. 3 (March 1974):
4-9 ((1, 2, 3, 6, 7))

T143 MOON, Pete: Lennie Tristano; a
discography in Pieces of Jazz,
No. 4 (fall 1968): 37-40; additions and corrections in Pieces
of Jazz, No. 5 (1969): 3; No. 6
(1969): 23 ((1, 2, 3, 7))

T144 PORTALEONI, Sergio: Discografia
Lennie Tristano in Musica Jazz,
Vol. 30 (February 1974): 46-47
((2, 7))

T145 WIEDEMANN, Erik: Lennie Tristano;
a discography in Discophile, No.
54 (June 1957): 8-10; additions
and corrections in Discophile, No.
56 (October 1957): 20 ((1, 2, 3,
6, 7))

TRIX label

T146 MARTIN, ?: Trix records in Boogie
Woogie & Blues Collector, No. 30/
31 (August 1973): 6 ((—))

TROMBONE MUSIC (JAZZ)

T147 TEPPERMAN, Barry: Rudd, Moncur &
some other stuff in Coda, Vol. 10
(August 1971): 11 ((—))

TROY, DORIS
vocal

T148 MOHR, Kurt: Doris Troy discography in Soul Bag, No. 63 (August
1977): 6-7 ((2, 3, 7))

TRUMBAUER, FRANKIE, 1901-1956
C melody saxophone
See BEIDERBECKE, BIX (Discographie
de Bix et Trumbauer)

TRUMPET MUSIC (JAZZ)
See also JAZZ MUSIC--Bebop
(Russell, Ross: Bop horn)

T149 TONKS, Eric S.: Some New Orleans
trumpet players; a discography in
Jazz Magazine (UK), Vol. 3, No. 3
(n.d.), whole issue ((2, 3, 7))

TRUNK, PETER, 1936-1973
bass violin

T150 SCHEFFNER, Manfred: Peter Trunk
Diskographie in Jazz Podium, Vol.
23 (October 1974): 37-38 ((2, 7))

TRUSOUND label

T151 [[[Listing] in Soul Bag, Nos. 12
and 13]]

TUCKER, GEORGE, 1927-
bass violin

T152 FRIEDMAN, Peter S.: George Tucker in Jazz Monthly, No. 163 (September 1968); No. 166 (December 1968); No. 167 (January 1969), various paginations ((2, 3, 7))

TUCKER, TOMMY, 1933–
organ, vocal

T153 LEE, Chris: Tommy Tucker discography in Jazz Journal, Vol. 30 (November 1977): 31 ((2, 3, 7))

TURNER, BRUCE, 1922–
alto saxophone, clarinet

T154 CLUTTEN, Michael N.: A Bruce Turner discography. South Harrow, Middlesex: British Institute of Jazz Studies, 1972, 19 pp.; supplemented by his Supplement to discography. Leicester, UK: 1979?, 10 pp. ((1, 2, 3, 6, 7))

TURNER, IKE, 1931–
guitar, piano

T155 DAGUERRE, Pierre; Kurt MOHR; and Jacques PERIN: Ike & Tina Turner discography in Soul Bag, No. 55 (October 1976): 19-29 ((2, 3, 7))

T156 POSTIF, François: Discographie (33 t.) de Ike et Tina Turner in Jazz Hot, No. 270 (March 1971): 11 ((—))

TURNER, JOE, 1911–
vocal

T157 BENJAMIN, Sam: Joe Turner/a discography in Discophile, No. 35 (April 1954): 16-19; additions and corrections in Discophile, No. 37 (August 1954): 18-19; No. 41 (April 1955): 19, 13 ((2, 3, 7))

TURNER, TINA, 1939–
vocal
See TURNER, IKE

TURRENTINE, STANLEY, 1934–
tenor saxophone

T158 Selected Turrentine discography in Down Beat, Vol. 42 (November 6, 1975): 12 ((—))

TUSSAUD'S DANCE ORCHESTRA
See MADAME TUSSAUD'S DANCE ORCHESTRA

TWARDZIK, DICK, 1931–1955
piano

T159 [[EYLE, Wim van: Disco: Richard "Dick" Twardzick [sic] (1931-1955) in Swingtime (Belgium), No. 28 (February 1978): 11]]

T160 MORGAN, Alun: Dick Twardzik in Jazz Monthly, Vol. 9 (November 1963): 27 ((2, 3, 6, 7))

TWIN STACKS label

T161 BRYANT, Steve: Twin Stacks label listing in Hot Buttered Soul, No. 40 (September 1975?): 3 ((3, 8))

TYLER, ALVIN "RED," 1925–
tenor saxophone

T162 MOHR, Kurt: Discographie de Alvin "Red" Tyler in Soul Bag, No. 26 (May 1973): 8 ((2, 3, 7))

TYNER, McCOY, 1938–
piano

T163 BOURNE, Michael A.: McCoy Tyner in Down Beat, Vol. 40 (December 6, 1973): 15 ((—))

T164 GARDNER, Mark: McCoy Tyner; a discography in Jazz Journal, Vol. 20 (August 1967): 34; (September 1967): 26-28 ((2, 3, 7))

T165 LUZZI, Mario: Discografia McCoy Tyner in Musica Jazz, Vol. 31 (December 1975) to Vol. 32 (March 1976), various paginations, in 4 parts; additions and corrections in Musica Jazz, Vol. 33 (March 1977): 48 ((1, 2, 7))

T166 McCoy Tyner discography in Swing Journal, Vol. 26 (November 1972): 244-249 ((2, 7d))

T167 Selected McCoy Tyner discography in Jazz Forum (Poland), No. 33 (January 1975): 41 ((—))

T168 Selected Tyner discography in Down Beat, Vol. 42 (September 11, 1975): 14 ((—))

T169 THOMPSON, Vern: McCoy Tyner in Different Drummer, Vol. 1 (September 1974): 17 ((—))

TYNES, MARIA
   vocal

T170   MOHR, Kurt: Maria Tynes in Soul
   Bag, No. 45 (January 1975): 15
   ((2, 3, 7))

UHCA label

U1   MAHONY, Dan: United Hot Clubs of
   America; a numerical catalogue of
   the UHCA label in Discophile, No.
   52 (February 1957): 5-10 ((3))

UKULELE IKE
   See EDWARDS, CLIFF

ULTRA label

U2   DIEZ, Jerry, and Dave ANTRELL:
   Dig/Ultra in R and B Collector,
   Vol. 1 (January-February 1970):
   6-7 ((3))

U3   GREENSMITH, Bill: Ultra/Dig in
   Blues Unlimited, No. 131/132
   (September-December 1978): 9-10
   ((3))

ULTRAPHON label (Swedish)

U4   ELFSTROM, Mats, and Bjorn ENG-
   LUND: Ultraphon. Stockholm:
   Kungliga Biblioteket, 1968, 14 pp.
   (Nationalfonoteket diskografier,
   3) ((3, 4p, 7d, 8))

U5   ELFSTROM, Mats, and Bjorn ENGLUND:
   Ultraphon. rev. ed. Stockholm:
   Kungliga Biblioteket, 1976, 20 pp.
   (Nationalfonoteket diskografier,
   19) ((3, 4p, 7d, 8))

UNITED label
   See also FORREST, JIMMY (Hartmann,
   Dieter)

U6   KOESTER, Bob: The United/States
   masters in Blues Unlimited, No.
   123 (January-February 1977): 14-
   22; additions and corrections in
   Blues Unlimited, No. 124 (1978),
   11 ((3, 7))

UNITED HOT CLUBS OF AMERICA
   See UHCA label

UPSETTERS (musical group)

U7   MOHR, Kurt, and Emmanuel CHOISNEL:
   The Upsetters discography in Soul

Bag, No. 18/19 (1972?): 25-26 ((2,
3, 7))

V DISC label
   See also GOODMAN, BENNY (Benny
   Goodman...some revisions...) and
   (Bosseray, Claude); WALLER, FATS
   (Bakker, Dick M.: Thomas "Fats"
   Waller)

V1   [[BARAZZETTA, Giuseppe: Indice-
   discografia dei V-Discs in Musica
   Jazz, Vols. 4 to 5 (1948-1949),
   unknown issues]]; additions and
   corrections in Vol. 5 (February
   1949): 23-24

V2   DENIS, Jacques: V Disc on LP's in
   Point du Jazz, No. 9 (December
   1973): 47-53; additions and corrections in Point du Jazz, No. 10
   (October 1974): 112-113 ((1, 7d))

V3   MYLNE, Dave: V Disc catalogue in
   Jazz Journal, Vol. 1 (June 1948)
   to Vol. 2 (February 1949); (May
   1949) to (July 1949); (October
   1949); (November 1949); Vol. 3
   (January 1950) to (April 1950),
   various paginations, in 18 parts
   ((1))

V4   POTTIER, Denis, and Jean DENIS:
   L'aventure des V-Disc in Point du
   Jazz, No. 9 (December 1973): 33-
   46 ((1, 2, 7))

V5   ROBBERECHTS, Henri: L'aventure des
   V-Disc in Point du Jazz, No. 11
   (June 1975): 105-107 ((1))

V6   TEUBIG, Klaus: "V" Disc catalogue;
   discography (No. 500-904). Berlin:
   Bibliotheksverband Arbeitsstelle
   für das Bibliothekwesen, 1976,
   155 pp. (Musikbibliothek aktuell,
   Beitrage 5) ((1, 2, 3, 4p, 6, 7))

V7   V-Disc on LP in Swing Journal,
   Vol. 29 (January 1975): 266-273
   ((—))

V8   WANTE, Stephen, and Walter de
   BLOCK: V-Disc catalogue. Antwerp:
   n.d., 83 pp. [covers nos. 1 to
   500; continued by V6, which indexes the personnel in this work
   as well] ((2, 3, 7))

VJR label
   See VINYLITE JAZZ REISSUES

VALAIDA (Valaida Snow), 1900-1956
   trumpet

V9 MOHR, Kurt: A discography of Valaida Snow in Discophile, No. 49 (August 1956): 12-13; additions and corrections in Discophile, No. 56 (October 1956): 18 ((2, 3, 6, 7))

VALENTINE, KID THOMAS, 1896-
trumpet

V10 BETHELL, Tom: Kid Thomas; his recordings in Jazz Times, Vol. 4 (June 1967) to (September 1967), unpaged, in 4 parts ((1, 2, 7))

V11 BETHELL, Tom: Kid Thomas Valentine; a discography in Jazz Report (California), Vol. 5, Nos. 4 and 5 (n.d.), unpaged ((1, 2, 7))

V12 BETHELL, Tom: The recordings in Jazz Digest (New Orleans), Vol. 1 (February 1966): 15-21; additions and corrections in Jazz Digest (New Orleans), Vol. 1 (March 1966): 8 ((1, 2, 7))

V13 STENBECK, Lennart: Kid Thomas Valentine diskografi in Orkester Journalen, Vol. 31 (February 1962): 34; (March 1962): 34 ((2, 3, 7))

VAN HOVE, FRED
See HOVE, FRED van

VANGUARD label

V14 McCARTHY, Albert J.: Vanguard jazz discography in Discophile, No. 50 (October 1956): 5-8 ((2, 7d))

V15 SELCHOW, Manfred: Mainstream auf Vanguard in Jazzfreund, No. 96 (December 1979): 14; No. 97 (March 1980): 12-13 ((2, 7))

VANT'HOFF, JASPER
See HOFF, JASPER VAN'T

VARSITY label

V16 STEWART-BAXTER, Derrick: Varsity in Jazz Journal, Vol. 3 (August 1950) to Vol. 4 (April 1951), various paginations, in 9 parts [6000 series] ((3, 6))

V17 The Varsity 6000 "race" series in Matrix, No. 32 (January 1961): 3-19; additions and corrections in Matrix, No. 40 (April 1962): 17-18; No. 54 (August 1964): 15 ((3, 7))

VAUGHAN, SARAH, 1924-
vocal

V18 DELAUNAY, Charles, and Erik WIEDEMANN: Discographie de Sarah Vaughan in Jazz Hot, No. 64 (March 1952): 9, 30-32 ((1, 2, 3, 7))

V19 [Discography] in Jazz Statistics, No. 25 (March 1962): 6 [1944-1945 recordings] ((2, 3, 6, 7))

V20 GARDNER, Mark: Sarah Vaughan on the cheap labels; a discographical guide in Jazz Journal, Vol. 20 (January 1967): 10 ((2, 3, 7))

V21 JAMES, Johnny: Hot discography [sic] de Sarah Vaughan in Revue du Jazz, No. 4 (April 1949): 118 ((2, 7d))

V22 Sarah Vaughan in Swing Journal, Vol. 34 (April 1980): 178-183 ((2, 7d))

V23 Selected Vaughan discography in Down Beat, Vol. 44 (May 5, 1977): 17 ((—))

VEE JAY label
See also HOOKER, JOHN LEE (Chauvard, Marcel); REED, JIMMY (Chauvard, Marcel)

V24 CHAUVARD, Marcel: Vee-Jay traditional and modern sessions in Jazz Statistics, No. 21 (March 1961): 12-14 ((2, 3, 7))

V25 ROTANTE, Anthony: Vee Jay catalogue in Record Research, Vol. 2 (May-June 1956): 11-12 ((4p))

V26 TURNER, Bez: Vee-Jay Records in Blues Unlimited, No. 135/136 (July-September 1979): 21-27; additions and corrections from Peter GIBBON in Blues Unlimited, No. 137/138 (spring 1980): 26 ((3))

VEEP label

V27 FOSTER, Bob; Chris SAVORY; and Jim WILSON: Veep label listing in Hot Buttered Soul, No. 45 (April-May 1976): 2-6 ((3, 5))

VELVET TONE label
See also HARMONY label (Bedoian, Jim)

V28 DAVIS, John, and [G. F.] GRAY-CLARKE: The Velvet Tone 7000-V series in Discophile, No. 1 (August 1948): 8-10 ((3))

VENNIK, DICK, 1940–
tenor saxophone
See GRAAFF, REIN de

VENTURA, RAY, 1908–
leader

V29 LAPLACE, Michel: Ray Ventura disco in Jazz Press, No. 49 (March 1, 1978): 10-11 ((1, 2, 3, 6, 7))

VENUTI, JOE, 1899-1978
violin

V30 BAKKER, Dick M.: Venuti-Lang and friends in Micrography, No. 5 (August 1969): 3-5 ((—))

V31 HOEFER, George: Joe Venuti discography in Down Beat, Vol. 17 (December 1, 1950): 18 ((—))

VERBEKE, HARRY, 1923–
tenor saxophone

V32 EYLE, Wim van; Gerard BIELDERMAN; and Jan MULDER: Harry Verbeke disco in Jazz Press, No. 48 (February 1, 1978): 30-32 ((2, 7))

VERVE label
See also GILLESPIE, DIZZY (Jepsen, Jorgen Grunnet: Dizzy Gillespie diskografi pa Clef-Norgran-Verve); GRANZ, NORMAN

V33 RIJN, Guido van: Verve in Boogie Woogie & Blues Collector, No. 30/31 (August 1973): 10-11 ((—))

VIBRAPHONE MUSIC (JAZZ)

V34 DEAN, Roger: Jazz vibes; bebop and after in Jazz Journal, Vol. 30 (April 1977): 6 ((—))

V35 TEPPERMAN, Barry: Vibes in motion [with discographies of Earl Griffith and Walt Dickerson] in Coda, Vol. 10 (December 1971): 9 ((—))

VICK, HAROLD, 1936–
tenor saxophone

V36 GARDNER, Mark: Harold Vick; a name listing in Jazz Monthly, No. 171 (May 1969): 9 ((2, 3, 7))

VICTOR label
See also ALLEN, HENRY "RED" (Davies, John R. T.); BECHET,

SIDNEY (Bakker, Dick M.: Victor recording: Sidney Bechet); BEIDERBECKE, BIX (Bakker, Dick M.: Bix Beiderbecke on Victor's [sic]); BERIGAN, BUNNY [Reid, John D.?]; CALLOWAY, CAB (Bakker, Dick M.: Cab Calloway--Victors); DODDS, JOHNNY (Bakker, Dick M.: Johnny Dodds except the Oliver-Hot Five/Seven...) and (Bakker, Dick M.: Johnny Dodds on Victor-sessions); ELLINGTON, DUKE (Bakker, Dick M.: Duke Ellington Victor's [sic]) and (Bakker, Dick M.: on Victor 1940-42) and (Reid, John D.); GOODMAN, BENNY (Bakker, Dick M.); HENDERSON, FLETCHER (Bakker, Dick M.: Fletcher Henderson on Victors) and (Bakker, Dick M.: Henderson on Victor 27-36); MEZZROW, MEZZ (Bakker, Dick M.); MORTON, JELLY ROLL (Bakker, Dick M.: Jelly Roll Morton's Victors) and (Bakker, Dick M.: Jelly's Victors) and (Carey, Dave); OLIVER, KING JOE (Bakker, Dick M.: King Oliver on Victor); PARHAM, TINY (Bakker, Dick M.: Tiny Parham's Victors) and ([Rust, Brian?]: Tiny Parham and his musicians in Pickup); RCA VICTOR label; WALLER, FATS (Bakker, Dick M.: Thomas "Fats" Waller); WHITEMAN, PAUL (Bakker, Dick M.: Whiteman's Victors)

V37 GODRICH, John, and Bob DIXON: Victor race issues listing in Vintage Jazz Mart (August 1963): 9-10; (July 1964): 10-11; (December 1964): 3-4 ((—))

V38 GODRICH, John: The Victor race series in Blues Unlimited, No. 10 (March 1964) to No. 17 (November-December 1964): most issues, various paginations ((3, 6))

V39 RUST, Brian: The Victor master book Vol. 2 (1925-1936). Hatch End, Middlesex: 1969 (also Highland Park, NJ: Walter C. Allen, c1969), 776 pp. [other volumes never published] ((2, 3, 4p, 4r, 4t, 6, 7))

VICTORY label (British)

V40 From Banner to the Victory; American Plaza recordings on English Victory in Collecta, No. 3 (January-February 1969): 26-28 ((7d))

VILLAGE VANGUARD (night club in New York)

V41 Village Vanguard sessions in Swing
     Journal, Vol. 31 (No. 14, 1978):
     66-69 ((2, 7))

VINSON, EDDIE, 1917-
     alto saxophone, vocal

V42 Selected Vinson discography in
     Down Beat, Vol. 42 (May 8, 1975):
     16 ((—))

VINYLITE JAZZ REISSUES

V43 MILLAR, Jack: Catalogue of Vinyl-
     ite Jazz Reissues in Discophile,
     No. 24 (June 1952): 5-6; additions
     and corrections in Discophile, No.
     26 (October 1952): 10; No. 28
     (February 1953): 8; No. 56 (Octo-
     ber 1957): 20 ((—))

VOCAL MUSIC (JAZZ)

V44 ANDERSON, Doug: Discography of
     vocal jazz groups in Jazz Maga-
     zine (US), Vol. 3 (fall 1978): 39
     ((—))

VOCALION label
     See also BASIE, COUNT (Bakker,
     Dick M.: Count Basie Vocalion-
     Okeh's [sic] 36-42); BLUES MUSIC
     (Colton, Bob); ELLINGTON, DUKE
     (Bakker, Dick M.: Ellington-
     Brunswick-Voc-Col-listing 1926-
     35); HOLIDAY, BILLIE (Bakker,
     Dick M.); LUNCEFORD, JIMMIE
     (Bakker, Dick M.: Jimmie Lunceford
     Voc/Col. 33-40); OLIVER, KING JOE
     (Bakker, Dick M.: King Oliver
     1926-1931 Voc/Br)

V45 KINER, Larry F.: Okeh-Vocalion
     numerical check list in Interna-
     tional Discophile, 1st series,
     (summer 1955) to (spring 1956),
     various paginations, in 3 parts
     [to no. 1299] ((3))

VOCALION label (British)
     See also DECCA label (British)

V46 COX, A. G.: Discography of the
     Vocalion swing series, 1936 to
     1940 in Jazz Journal, Vol. 19
     (March 1966) to (June 1966),
     various paginations, in 4 parts
     ((2, 7d))

V47 FRY, John: Swing Vocalion series
     in R.S.V.P., No. 1 (May 1965) to
     No. 11 (April 1966), various
     paginations ((3, 6))

V48 PARRY, William Hewitt: The English
     Vocalion Continental series in
     Discophile, No. 18 (June 1951):
     6-7; additions and corrections in
     Discophile, No. 19 (August 1951):
     12-13; No. 52 (February 1957): 12;
     No. 53 (April 1957): 11 ((3, 6,
     7d))

VOGUE label

V49 BROOKS, Tim: Vogue discography in
     Record Research, No. 151/152
     (January 1978): 5-10; additions
     and corrections in Record Re-
     search, No. 153/154 (April 1978):
     10 ((3, 5, 6))

VOGUE label (French)
     See BYAS, DON (Mohr, Kurt: Don
     Byas on "Vogue" Records)

VOLA, LOUIS
     bass violin

V50 GONZÁLEZ VIZCAÍNO, Carlos M.:
     Discografía de Louis Vola (regis-
     tros efectuados en la Argentina)
     in Jazz Magazine (Argentina), No.
     33 (July-August 1952): 8-9 ((2,
     7))

VON EICHWALD, HAKAN
     See EICHWALD, HAKAN von

VON SCHLIPPENBACH, ALEXANDER
     See SCHLIPPENBACH, ALEXANDER von

WADE, JIMMY, ca. 1895-1933
     leader, trumpet

W1   GULLIVER, Ralph: Jimmy Wade in
     Storyville, No. 56 (December 1974-
     January 1975): 68 ((2, 3, 6, 7))

WALDRON, MAL, 1926-
     piano

W2   Discography: Mal Waldron in Swing
     Journal, issue 6 of 1958: 23
     ((—))

W3   Mal Waldron in Swing Journal,
     Vol. 32 (September 1978): 286-291
     ((2, 7d))

WALKER, BIG MOOSE (John Mayon Walker),
     1929-
     organ, piano, vocal

W4 MOHR, Kurt, and Emmanuel CHOISNEL: Big Moose Walker in Soul Bag, No. 38 (May 1974): 30; additions and corrections in Soul Bag, No. 43 (November-December 1974): 13 ((2, 3, 7))

WALKER, T-BONE (Aaron Walker), 1910-1975
guitar, vocal

W5 [[MOHR, Kurt, and others: [Discography]. Blues Unlimited booklet, 1964/1965]]

W6 ROTANTE, Anthony: Aaron "T-Bone" Walker; a discography in Discophile, No. 27 (December 1952): 3-5; additions and corrections in Discophile, No. 29 (May 1953): 16-17 ((2, 3, 7))

WALLACE, SIPPIE (née Belulah Thomas), 1898-
piano, vocal

W7 ROTANTE, Anthony: Sippie Wallace in Record Research, No. 76 (May 1966): 9-10 ((2, 3, 8))

WALLACE, WESLEY, d. ca. 1959
piano

W8 HALL, Bob, and Richard NOBLETT: [Discography] in Blues Unlimited, No. 112 (March-April 1975): 18 ((2, 3, 6, 7, 9))

WALLER, FATS (Thomas Wright Waller), 1904-1943
piano, vocal

W9 BAKKER, Dick M.: Fats Waller in Micrography, No. 3 (May 1969): 6; additions and corrections in Micrography, No. 5 (August 1969): 12 [to 1929] ((—))

W10 BAKKER, Dick M.: Thomas "Fats" Waller; all Victor-sessions + one Columbia-session + one V-Disc session in Micrography, No. 16 (December 1971): 5-9 ((1, 7d))

W11 DAVIES, John R. T. as "Ristic": Discography of the late Thomas "Fats" Waller in Jazz Journal, Vol. 1 (May 1948) to (September 1948), various paginations, in 5 parts; additions and corrections in Jazz Journal, Vol. 2 (April 1949): 6-7 ((2, 3, 7d))

W12 DAVIES, John R. T.: A discography of Thomas "Fats" Waller in his The music of Thomas "Fats" Waller with complete discography. London: J. J. Publications, 1950, 7-28 ((1, 2, 3, 6, 7))

W13 DAVIES, John R. T. and R. M. COOKE: A discography of Thomas "Fats" Waller in DAVIES, John R. T.: The music of Thomas "Fats" Waller with complete discography. rev. ed. London: Friends of Fats, 1953, 8-34 ((1, 2, 3, 4t, 6, 7))

W14 DAVIES, John R. T., and Bob KUMM: The music of Thomas "Fats" Waller in Storyville, No. 2 (December 1965) to No. 12 (August-September 1967), various paginations ((1, 2, 3, 6, 7))

W15 FEATHER, Leonard: ...And his rhythm; a discographical survey of Fats Waller in Swing Music, Vol. 1, No. 9 (November? 1935): 244-246 ((—))

W16 FOX, Charles: Discography in his Fats Waller. London: Cassell, 1960 (also New York: Barnes [c1961]), 84-87 (Kings of Jazz, 7) ((—))

W17 [[MAGNUSSON, Tor: An almost complete Thomas "Fats" Waller discography. Stockholm?: 1964, pages numbered to no. 41]]

W18 The music of Thomas "Fats" Waller; a selective discography in KIRKEBY, Ed: Ain't misbehavin'; the story of Fats Waller. London: Peter Davies [1966] (also New York: Dodd Mead, 1966; London: Jazz Book Club, 1967; New York: DaCapo, 1975), 233-248 ((1, 2, 3, 6, 7))

Piano Rolls

W19 BAKKER, Dick M.: Fats Waller--piano rolls--1923-1931 in Micrography, No. 25 (March 1973): 6 ((—))

W20 MAGNUSSON, Tor: The piano rolls by Thomas Waller and by Fats Waller; a compilation in Matrix, No. 106 (February 1975): 1-8 [includes rolls played by J. Lawrence Cook which were issued as by Waller] ((7d))

W21 MONTGOMERY, Mike: Thomas Waller rollography in Record Research, Vol. 3 (July-August 1958): 11 [with appendix of J. Lawrence Cook rolls] ((5))

WALLINGTON, GEORGE (Giorgio Figlia),
1924–
piano

W22 Discographie de George Wallington
in Jazz Hot, No. 68 (July–August
1952): 16; No. 83 (December 1953):
12 ((2, 3, 6, 7d))

W23 GIBSON, Frank: George Wallington;
a discography in Jazz Journal,
Vol. 17 (September 1964): 22–23;
additions and corrections in Jazz
Journal, Vol. 18 (June 1965): 38
((2, 3, 6, 7))

W24 GOODWIN, Jack: George Wallington;
a discography of known recordings
in Jazz Journal, Vol. 27 (February 1974): 56–58 ((1, 2, 3, 6, 7))

W25 MORGAN, Alun: George Wallington;
a name discography in Jazz Monthly, Vol. 9 (November 1963): 25,
27 ((2, 3, 6, 7))

WALTERS, EDDIE
ukulele, vocal

W26 VENABLES, Ralph G. V.: R.G.V.V.
gives a brief discography of Eddie
Walters in Jazz Tempo, Vol. 2
(November 8, 1943): 4 ((2, 3))

WALTON, CEDAR, 1934–
piano

W27 MOON, Pete: [Discography] in
Pieces of Jazz (1971): 25–37 ((2,
3, 7))

WALTON, MERCY DEE
See MERCY DEE

WALTON, WADE, 1923–
guitar, harmonica, vocal

W28 HAYNES, Jessie: Wade Walton discography in Living Blues, No. 29
(Sept.–Oct. 1976): 25 ((2, 7))

WARD, CARLOS, 1940–
alto saxophone

W29 Selected Ward discography in Down
Beat, Vol. 42 (July 17, 1975): 39
((—))

WARD SINGERS

W30 ROTANTE, Anthony: The famous Ward
singers in Discophile, No. 56
(October 1957): 5–8 ((2, 3, 6))

WARLOP, MICHEL, 1911–1947
violin

W31 Michel Warlop in Jazz Hot, No. 13
(1947): 9 ((2))

WARNER, ALBERT, 1890–
trombone

W32 MILLS, Ken: Discography of Albert
Warner (small group recordings)
in Jazz Report (California), Vol.
2 (Jan.–Feb. 1963): 10 ((2, 7))

WARREN, BABY BOY (Robert Henry Warren),
1919–1977
guitar, vocal

W33 LEADBITTER, Mike: R. "Baby Boy"
Warren in Blues Unlimited, No. 32
(April 1966): 10, 12 ((2, 3, 7))

W34 ROTANTE, Anthony: Baby Boy Warren
in Record Research, No. 33 (March
1961): 15 ((2, 3, 7d))

WASHBOARD RHYTHM KINGS

W35 BAKER, John H.: The Washboard
Rhythm Kings; hot discana in
Record Research, No. 22 (April–May
1959): 6–7; additions and correc-
tions in DRIGGS, Frank: WashBoard
Rhythm Kings research in Record
Research, No. 29 (August 1960): 7
((3, 7, 8))

WASHBOARD SAM (Robert Brown), 1910–1966
vocal

W36 Discography of Washboard Sam in
Jazz Journal, Vol. 8 (October
1955): 2–3 ((2, 3, 6, 7))

WASHBOARD SERENADERS

W37 HURLOCK, Frank: [Discography] in
Jazz Music, Vol. 7 (March–April
1946): 7–8 ((2, 3, 7))

WASHINGTON, GROVER, 1943–
tenor saxophone

W38 Current discography in Different
Drummer, Vol. 1 (January 1975):
17 ((—))

W39 Selected Washington discography
in Down Beat, Vol. 42 (July 17,
1975): 15 ((—))

WASHINGTON, LOUIS
See TALLAHASSEE TIGHT

WATERLAND ENSEMBLE

W40 Discography in Disk in the World,
Vol. 1 (July 1980): 31 ((—))

WATERS, BENNY, 1902-
clarinet, tenor saxophone

W41 TARRANT, Don, and Reg COOPER:
Benny Waters discography in Journal of Jazz discography, No. 2
(June 1977): 11-22; additions and
corrections in Journal of Jazz
Discography, No. 3 (March 1978):
2-4 ((1, 2, 3, 6, 7))

WATERS, ETHEL, 1896-1977
vocal

W42 DAVIES, Ron; Dan MAHONY; and H.
Meunier HARRIS: The records of
Ethel Waters in Playback, Vol. 2
(June 1949): 26-29; additions and
corrections in Jazz Journal, Vol.
10 (April 1958) ((2, 3, 7d))

W43 DAVIS, Ken: Ethel Waters; a discography in Discographer, Vol. 1
(third quarter 1968): 1-227 to
1-234a ((3))

W44 NEVERS, Daniel: Discographie in
Jazz Hot, No. 345/346 (February
1978): 45 ((—))

W45 NIQUET, Bernard: Discographie L.P.
de Ethel Waters in Point du Jazz,
No. 6 (March 1972): 12-18 ((2, 3,
6, 7))

WATERS, MUDDY
See MUDDY WATERS

WATKINS, VIOLA

W46 ROTANTE, Anthony: Viola Watkins in
Discophile, No. 37 (August 1954):
14 ((2, 3))

WATSON, JOHNNY "GUITAR," 1935-
guitar, vocal

W47 [[[Discography] in Jefferson, No.
24 (January 1974)]]

W48 MOHR, Kurt, and Joel DUFOUR: Discographie de Johnny Guitar Watson
in Soul Bag, No. 58 (October
1976): 15-18 ((2, 3, 6, 7))

WATSON, LEO, 1898-1950
vocal
See also SPIRITS OF RHYTHM

W49 DAVISON, Martin: Leo Watson discography in Discographical Forum,
No. 33 (1974): 17-18; No. 34
(1976); additions and corrections
from Andreas MASEL in Discographical Forum, No. 36 (1976): 1 ((2,
3, 6, 7))

W50 MAGNUSSON, Tor: Leo "Scat" Watson
diskografi. Goteborg, Sweden:
1967, 8 pp.; additions and corrections in Orkester Journalen, Vol.
36 (March 1968): 11 ((1, 2, 3, 6,
7))

WATTERS, LU, 1911-
trumpet

W51 HULME, G. W. George: Lu Watters,
a discography in Matrix, No. 24
(July 1959): supp. i-xiii; No.
35/36 (September 1961): 35 [rev.
ed. of next entry] ((2, 3, 7))

W52 HULME, G. W. George: Lu Watters &
the Yerba Buena Jazz Band; a discography in Matrix, No. 1 (July
1954): 3-8; additions and corrections in Matrix, No. 7 (July
1955): 14; No. 16 (May 1957): 18;
No. 21 (January 1959): 22 ((2, 3,
7))

W53 Lu Watters 1949-50 in Micrography,
No. 32 (1974): 10 ((7d))

WATTS, TREVOR, 1939-
alto and soprano saxophones

W54 RENSEN, Jan: Disco Trevor Watts
in Jazz Press, No. 26 (November
12, 1976): 13-14 ((2, 7))

WAX SHOP label
See BOLLETINO, DANTE

WAYNE, JAMES "WEE WILLIE"
vocal

W55 ROTANTE, Anthony: James Wayne
(Waynes) in Record Research, No.
72 (November 1965): 9 ((3))

WEATHER REPORT (musical group)

W56 Discografia del Weather Report
in Musica Jazz, Vol. 31 (March
1975): 12 ((2, 7))

W57 Discographie in Jazz Hot, No. 296
(July–August 1973): 14 ((2))

W58 Weather Report discography in
Jazz Forum (Poland), No. 42 (April
1976): 42 ((—))

WEATHERFORD, TEDDY, 1903–1945
piano

W59 DARKE, K. Peter: Teddy Weatherford's Indian recording sessions
1941–45 in Matrix, No. 107/108
(December 1975): 3–6 ((2, 3, 6,
7))

WEATHERS label

W60 In the wax in Matrix, No. 33
(March 1961): 16–17 ((2))

WEAVER, SYLVESTER
guitar, vocal

W61 PARRY, William Hewitt: Sylvester
Weaver; a provisional discography
in Discophile, No. 18 (June 1951):
11–13; additions and corrections
in Discophile, No. 19 (August
1951): 12 ((2, 3, 6, 7))

WEBB, CHICK (William Webb), 1909?–1939
drums

W62 BAKKER, Dick M.: Chick Webb 1928–
1939 in Micrography, No. 31
(1974?): 4–5 ((7d))

W63 BAKKER, Dick M.: Chick Webb on
microgroove in Micrography, No. 2
(February 1969): 3 ((—))

WEBB, GEORGE
piano

W64 Discography of George Webb's
Dixielanders in Pickup, Vol. 1
(May 1946): 5 ((2, 3, 7))

WEBER, EBERHARD, 1940–
bass violin

W65 Discography in Impetus, No. 7
(1978): 299 ((—))

W66 PANKE, Werner: Eberhard Weber in
Jazz Podium, Vol. 23 (February
1974): 19 ((—))

W67 Selected Weber discography in Jazz
Forum (Poland), No. 59 (1979): 37
((—))

WEBSTER, BEN, 1909–1973
tenor saxophone
See also SAXOPHONE MUSIC (JAZZ)
(Evensmo, Jan: The tenor saxo-
phonists of the period 1930–1942)

W68 Ben Webster discography in Swing
Journal, Vol. 27 (December 1973):
278–285 ((2, 7d))

W69 EVENSMO, Jan: The tenor saxophone
of Ben Webster 1931–1943 [Hosle,
Norway: 1978], 50 pp. Jazz solography series, Vol. 6 ((1, 2, 3,
6, 7, 9))

W70 JEPSEN, Jorgen Grunnet: Ben
Webster discography in Jazz
Monthly, Vol. 6 (November 1960);
(January 1961) to Vol. 7 (March
1961); (June 1961) to (August
1961), various paginations, in 7
parts; additions and corrections
from Warren SKERO in Discographical Forum, No. 4 (January 1961):
11 ((1, 2, 3, 6, 7))

W71 KAULING, Bent: Ben Webster (European discography). [Copenhagen]:
1973?, 5 leaves ((2, 7))

W72 KAULING, Bent: The Ben Webster
European discography in Coda, No.
145 (March 1976): 8–9 ((2, 7))

WEBSTER, FREDDIE, 1916–1947
trumpet

W73 EDWARDS, Ernie: Freddie Webster
discography in Discographical
Forum, No. 15 (November 1969):
5–6; No. 16 (January 1970): 3–5;
additions and corrections in Discographical Forum, No. 20 (September 1970): 2 ((2, 3, 6, 7))

W74 HOEFER, George: Selected discography in Down Beat, Vol. 29 (January 4, 1962): 42 ((2, 3, 7))

WEE WILLIE (Willie Armour)
vocal

W75 MOHR, Kurt: Discographie de Wee
Willie in Soul Bag, No. 32 (November 1973): 14 ((2, 3, 7))

WEGLINSKI, HELMUT
violin

W76 [[KAYSER, Erhard: [Discography]
in Jazz Podium, Vol. 10 (June
1961)]]

WEINTRAUB, STEFAN, 1897–
drums

W77 BERGMEIER, Horst: The Weintraub
     story in Doctor Jazz, No. 87
     (March 1979): 27-32 [to September
     1929; to be continued] ((2, 3, 7))

WELDON, CASEY BILL (Will Weldon), 1909-
     guitar, vocal

W78 GODRICH, John, and Robert M. W.
     DIXON: Kansas City Bill Wheldon
     [sic]--see B.U. 3--ARC/discography
     in Blues Unlimited, undated sup-
     plement to Nos. 1-6: 7-8 ((2, 3,
     6, 7))

W79 PANASSIÉ, Hugues: The BlueBird
     [sic] recordings of Casey Bill in
     Discophile, No. 43 (August 1944):
     19; additions and corrections in
     Discophile, No. 44 (October 1955):
     12 ((2, 3, 7))

WELLS, JUNIOR (Amos Wells), 1934-
     harmonica, vocal

W80 KENT, Don; Kurt MOHR; and Neil
     PATERSON: Discography in Blues
     Unlimited, No. 7 (December 1963):
     6-7; additions and corrections in
     Blues Unlimited, No. 12 (June
     1964): suppl-3, 5 ((2, 3, 7))

W81 KENT, Don; Kurt MOHR; and Neil
     PATERSON: Discography in Blues
     Unlimited Collectors Classics,
     No. 8 (July 1965): 6-7 ((2, 3, 7))

W82 ROTANTE, Anthony: The records of
     Junior Wells in Record Research,
     No. 37 (August 1961): 11 ((3))

W83 [[STRACHWITZ, Chris: [Discography].
     Blues Unlimited booklet, 1966]]

WELLS, VIOLA
     See MISS RHAPSODY

WENDT, GEORGE, 1909-1974
     trumpet

W84 RAICHELSON, Dick: George Wendt; a
     sideman's world in IAJRC Journal,
     Vol. 7 (spring 1974): 8 [to 1931]
     ((2, 3, 6, 7))

WESTBROOK, MIKE, 1936-
     leader, composer

W85 Diskographie in Jazz Podium, Vol.
     28 (November 1979): 12 ((2, 7p))

W86 Mike Westbrook discography in Jazz
     Forum (Poland), No. 39 (January
     1976): 40 ((—))

WESTON, RANDY, 1926-
     piano

W87 EYLE, Wim van: Randy Weston dis-
     cografie in Jazz Press, No. 25
     (October 29, 1976): 13-14; addi-
     tions and corrections in Jazz
     Press, No. 44 (October 1, 1977): 6
     ((2, 7))

W88 GARDNER, Mark: Discography in
     Jazz Monthly, Vol. 12 (January
     1967): 4-6; additions and correc-
     tions in Jazz Monthly, Vol. 12
     (April 1967): 27 ((2, 7))

W89 Selected Weston discography in
     Down Beat, Vol. 46 (September 6,
     1979): 19 ((—))

WHATNAUTS (musical group)

W90 MOHR, Kurt: Whatnauts discography
     in Hot Buttered Soul, No. 32 (July
     1974?): 2-3 ((2, 3, 7))

WHEATSTRAW, PEETIE (William Bunch),
     1902-1941
     guitar, vocal

W91 GARON, Paul: Discography in his
     the Devil's Son-in-Law [London]:
     Studio Vista [c1971]: 107-111
     ((2, 3, 7, 8))

W92 McCARTHY, Albert: Tentative dis-
     cography in Melody Maker, Vol. 22
     (January 12, 1946): 4; continued
     in unknown issues; additions and
     corrections in Melody Maker, Vol.
     22 (April 27, 1946): 4, and pos-
     sibly other issues ((2, 3, 7d))

W93 PARSONS, Jack: Peetie Wheatstraw
     discography in Jazz Monthly, Vol.
     5 (June 1959): 23-24; (July 1959):
     23; additions and corrections from
     Olav ANGELL in Discographical
     Forum, No. 2 (July 1960): 6-7, 9
     ((2, 3, 6, 7))

WHEELER, KENNY, 1930-
     trumpet

W94 Selected Wheeler discography in
     Down Beat, Vol. 47 (April 1980):
     24 ((—))

WHEELSVILLE label

W95 FOSTER, Bob, and Jim WILSON:
     Wheelsville label listing in Hot
     Buttered Soul, No. 33 (August
     1974?): 6-7 ((3))

WHIRLIN' DISC label

W96 Whirlin' Disc in Quartette, No. 2
(March 1970): 30 ((3))

WHITE, ANDREW, 1942–
saxophones

W97 INGERSOLL, Chuck: Andrew White in
Different Drummer, Vol. 1 (September 1974): 14 ((—))

WHITE, BUKKA (Booker T. Washington
White), 1906–1977
guitar, vocal

W98 BAKKER, Dick M.: Bukka White in
Micrography, No. 4 (June 1969):
11; additions and corrections in
Micrography, No. 5 (August 1969):
12 [to 1940] ((—))

W99 [[[Discografia completa] in Blues
Power, issue after Vol. 1 (No. 4,
1974)]]

W100 DOERING, Teddy: Blues aus erster
Hand; Bukka White in Jazz Podium,
Vol. 20 (October 1971): 351 ((—))

WHITE, CALVIN
See SANDPEBBLES

WHITE, DANNY

W101 [[[Discography] in Soul Bag, No.
8]]

WHITE, GEORGIA, 1903–
piano, vocal

W102 McCARTHY, Albert: Georgia White
in Discophile, No. 25 (August
1952): 4–6; additions and corrections in Discophile, No. 27 (December 1952): 17; No. 29 (May
1953): 10 ((2, 3, 7))

WHITE, JOSH, 1915–1969
guitar, vocal

W103 COLLER, Derek, and Bert WHYATT,
eds.: Josh White discography.
Barking, Essex: Discophile, 1951,
13 pp. (The Discophile, No. 20);
additions and corrections in Discophile, No. 21 (December 1951):
19 ((1, 2, 3, 6, 7))

W104 COLLER, Derek: Josh White on ABC-
Paramount in Matrix, No. 29/30
(August 1960): 41 ((2, 7))

W105 CRESSANT, Pierre: Discographie
des disques de Josh White édités
en France in Jazz Hot, No. 48
(October 1950): 12 ((2, 3, 7))

W106 Josh White—a discography in Discophile, No. 8 (October 1949):
2–7; additions and corrections in
Discophile, No. 9 (December 1949):
15, 9; No. 11 (April 1950): 11–13;
No. 12 (June 1950): 9; No. 13
(August 1950): 12–13; No. 15 (December 1950): 19 ((1, 2, 3, 6,
7d))

W107 WIEDEMANN, Erik: Josh White as an
accompanist in Melody Maker, Vol.
27 (November 3, 1951): 9 ((2, 3,
7))

WHITE, MIKE
trumpet
See JAZZ MUSIC—CANADA

WHITEMAN, PAUL, 1890–1967
leader
See also NICHOLS, RED (Backensto,
Woody: Red Nichols with Paul
Whiteman)

W108 BAKKER, Dick M.: Paul Whiteman in
Micrography, No. 43 (March 1977):
8 ((6, 7d))

W109 BAKKER, Dick M.: Whiteman's Columbia's [sic] 1928–30 in Micrography, No. 19 (April 1972): 7
((7d))

W110 BAKKER, Dick M.: Whiteman's Victors in Micrography, No. 19 (April
1972): 6 ((7d))

W111 RUST, Brian: Paul Whiteman; a
discography in Recorded Sound, No.
27 (July 1967): 219–228; No. 28
(October 1967): 255–258 ((2, 3,
6, 7))

WHITMAN SISTERS
See MICHALL, KID ERNEST

WHITTLE, TOMMY, 1926–
tenor saxophone, clarinet

W112 MORGAN, Alun: Tommy Whittle in
Jazz Monthly, Vol. 9 (December
1963): 26–27 ((2, 3, 6, 7))

WHOOPEE MAKERS

W113 BAKKER, Dick M.: Whoopee Makers
in Micrography, No. 2 (February
1969): 6 ((6))

W114 BAKKER, Dick M.: Whoopee Makers
1928-29 in Micrography, No. 20
(June 1972): 4 ((6, 7d))

W115 NÚÑEZ, Eduardo L.: Los Whoopee
Makers in Hot Jazz Club, No. 22
(June 1949): 4-6, 8 ((—))

WHYTE, ZACH, 1898-1967
leader

W116 DEMEUSY, Bertrand, and Otto
FLUCKIGER: The (incomplete) band
story of Zach Whyte in Jazz Statistics, No. 29 (October 1963):
JS6 ((2, 3, 6, 7))

WIGGINS, GERALD, 1922-
piano

W117 CRESSANT, Pierre: Discographie in
Jazz Hot, No. 52 (February 1951):
16 ((—))

W118 WIEDEMANN, Erik: Jerry Wiggins'
French recordings in Discophile,
No. 24 (June 1952): 10 ((2, 3, 7))

WIGGINS, JAMES, d. ca. 1930
vocal

W119 HALL, Bob, and Richard NOBLETT:
[Discography] in Blues Unlimited,
No. 114 (July-August 1975): 14-15
((2, 3, 6, 7, 9))

WIGGS, JOHNNY, 1899-
cornet

W120 HABY, Peter R.: Johnny Wiggs;
discography in Footnote, Vol. 9
(October-November 1977): 8-14 ((2,
3, 6, 7))

WILBER, BOB, 1907-
soprano saxophone, clarinet

W121 Discography; Bob Wilber and his
Wildcats in Discophile, No. 1
(August 1948): 4; additions and
corrections in Discophile, No. 4
(February 1949): 8 ((2, 3, 6, 7d))

WILCOX, EDDIE, 1907-1968
piano, arranger
See LUNCEFORD, JIMMIE (Fluckiger,
Otto)

WILEY, LEE, 1915-
vocal

W122 NELSON, John R.: Lee Wiley; a
provisional discography in Discophile, No. 56 (October 1957): 11-
16; additions and corrections in
Matrix, No. 37 (November 1961):
18 ((2, 3, 7))

WILKINS, ROBERT, 1896-
guitar, vocal

W123 BAKKER, Dick M.: Robert Wilkins
1928-35 in Micrography, No. 18
(February 1972): 10 ((—))

W124 [[[Discography] in Soul Bag, No.
5]]

W125 DIXON, Robert M. W.: Wilkins
Brothers--discography and biogra-
phy in Eureka, Vol. 1 (September-
October 1960): 8 ((2, 3, 7))

WILKINS, TIMOTHY, 1908-
guitar, vocal
See WILKINS, ROBERT (Dixon, Robert
M. W.)

WILLIAMS, ANDRE, ca. 1936-
vocal

W126 LEADBITTER, Mike, and Dick HOR-
LICK: Andre Williams in Blues Unlimited, No. 14 (August 1964): 8
((2, 3, 7p))

WILLIAMS, CLARENCE, 1893-1964
piano, composer

W127 BAKKER, Dick M.: Clarence Williams
1923-33 in Micrography, No. 17
(February 1972): 5-8 ((7d))

W128 BAKKER, Dick M.: Clarence Williams
on microgroove 1923 1931 in Micrography, No. 6 (October 1969):
5-8 ((7d))

W129 BAKKER, Dick M.: Clarence Williams' QRS-recordings and some
related sessions in Micrography,
No. 22 (October 1972): 5 ((—))

W130 BORRETTI, Raffaele: Clarence
Williams; a list of reissues
available to-day (1971) in booklet to accompany [phonodisc] Right
Keyhole RK-2001. [Cosenza, Italy:
1971], 6 pp. ((—))

W131 [[BORRETTI, Raffaele: L'opera di
Clarence Williams in Musica Jazz,
Vol. 17 (June 1961): 22-26]]

W132 BRYCE, Owen: Clarence Williams'
discography in Jazz Magazine (UK),

Vol. 3, No. 1 (n.d.): 22-23; No. 2 (n.d.): 21 [to October 1924] ((2, 3, 7d))

W133 DAVIES, Ron: Clarence Williams--a suggested discography in Jazz-finder, Vol. 1 (June 1948) to (August 1948), various pagina-tions, in 3 parts; additions and corrections in BAKER, John H.: Further Clarence Williams docu-mentation in Playback, Vol. 2 (January 1949): 21-22 ((2, 3, 6, 7d))

W134 DAVIES, Ron; George AVAKIAN; and Charles DELAUNAY: Discography of Clarence Williams in Record Changer, Vol. 5 (December 1946): 23-25; additions and corrections in RUST, Brian: Elegy on a Clar-ence Williams discography in Pickup, Vol. 2 (February-March 1947): 14-17; (August 1947): 1 [excludes Louis Armstrong and Bessie Smith sessions] ((2, 3, 7d))

W135 GOLDMAN, Elliott: Clarence Wil-liams, discography. London: Jazz Music Books [1947], 27 pp.; addi-tions and corrections in MOULTON, Desmond, and Eric KEARTLAND: Ad-ditions to Clarence Williams dis-cography in Hot Notes, Vol. 2 (March 1947): 16-17; [from Dolf RERINK] (May-June 1947): 17-18 ((2, 3, 7d))

W136 LORD, Tom, ed.: Clarence Williams; discography in Storyville, No. 13 (October-November 1967) to No. 30 (August-September 1970), various paginations ((2, 3, 6, 7, 8))

W137 LORD, Tom: Clarence Williams. [Chigwell, Essex: Storyville, 1976], xiii, 625 pp.; supplemented by BAKKER, Dick M.: Clarence Williams on microgroove. Alphen aan de Rijn, Netherlands: Microg-raphy [1976], 44 pp. ((2, 3, 4p, 4r, 4t, 5, 6, 7, 8, 9))

W138 [[MØLLER, Borge J. C.: Clarence Williams discography in Orkester Journalen, Vol. 13 (June 1945): 18]]

W139 [[SILVESTRI, Edgardo M.: Discog-raphy in Boletin del Hot Club de Buenos Aires, Nos. 1/2 (1960)]]

WILLIAMS, COOTIE (Charles Melvin Williams), 1910-
trumpet

W140 BAKKER, Dick M.: Cootie Williams and his Rug Cutters 1937-1940 plus the Gotham Stompers 25-3-37 in Micrography, No. 16 (December 1971): 1 ((—))

W141 HARTMANN, Dieter: Discography of Cootie Williams 1942-1959 in Jazz Statistics, No. 16 (1960): 2-9; additions and corrections from Michel VOGLER in Jazz Statistics, No. 17 (1960): 8-9 ((2, 3, 6, 7))

W142 JEPSEN, Jorgen Grunnet: Cootie Williams diskografi (fran ten tid han etablerade sig som egen kapell-mastare) in Orkester Journalen, Vol. 26 (August 1958): 46-47 ((2, 3, 7d))

WILLIAMS, EARL

W143 [[[Discography] in Soul Bag, No. 1]]

WILLIAMS, ELMER, 1905-1962
tenor saxophone
See SAXOPHONE MUSIC (JAZZ)
(Evensmo, Jan: The tenor saxo-phones of Budd Johnson...)

WILLIAMS, JERRY
See SWAMP DOGG

WILLIAMS, JOE LEE, 1903-
guitar, vocal

W144 BAKKER, Dick M.: Big Joe Williams 35-52 in Micrography, No. 7 (No-vember 1969): 10-11 ((7d))

W145 A discography of Joe Williams in Discophile, No. 47 (April 1956): 16; additions and corrections in Discophile, No. 52 (February 1957): 15; No. 53 (April 1957): 19 ((—))

W146 Diskografie in Jazz Wereld, No. 29 (May 1970): 10 ((—))

W147 HOLLAND, Bernard: A discography of Joe Lee Williams--blues singer in Matrix, No. 34 (June 1961): 9-17; additions and corrections in Ma-trix, No. 43 (October 1962): 18-19; No. 44 (December 1962): 9 ((2, 3, 6, 7))

WILLIAMS, JOHN, 1929-
piano

W148 MORGAN, Alun: A John Williams discography in Jazz Monthly, (October 1962): 4-5; (November 1962): 13-14; additions and corrections in Jazz Monthly, (June 1966): 28; (October 1966): 27 ((2, 3, 6, 7))

WILLIAMS, L. C., 1930-1960
  drums, vocal

W149 ROTANTE, Anthony: L. C. Williams in Record Research, No. 34 (April 1961): 11 ((2, 3, 7))

WILLIAMS, LESTER, 1920-
  guitar, vocal

W150 LEADBITTER, Mike: Lester Williams discography in Blues Unlimited, No. 33 (May-June 1966): 7 ((3, 7))

WILLIAMS, MARY LOU, 1910-
  piano

W151 Current discography in Different Drummer, Vol. 1 (January 1975): 13 ((—))

W152 Mary Lou Williams (disques publiés en France) in Jazz Hot, No. 44 (May 1950): 16 ((2, 3, 7d))

WILLIAMS, PAUL
  alto and baritone saxophones

W153 MOHR, Kurt: Discography of Paul Williams in Jazz Statistics, No. 26/27 (June-September 1962): 3-7 ((2, 3, 6, 7))

WILLIAMS, RICHARD, 1931-
  trumpet
  See also CHERRY, DON (Ioakimidis, Demetre)

W154 KLEINHOUT, Henk: Geselecteerde LP-lijst Richard Williams in Jazz Nu, Vol. 2 (Oct. 1979): 20 ((—))

WILLIAMS, ROBERT PETE, 1914-
  guitar, vocal
  See also BLUES MUSIC (Guralnick, Peter)

W155 [[LIBERGE, Luigi: Disco: Robert Pete Williams in Jazz, Blues & Co., No. 16 (April 1978): 15]]

WILLIAMS, TONI
  vocal

W156 CHOISNEL, Emmanuel, and Kurt MOHR: Miss Toni Williams in Soul Bag, No. 16 (1972?): 7-8 ((2, 3, 6, 7))

WILLIAMS, TONY, 1945-
  drums
  See also CARTER, RON [Discography of Ron Carter and Tony Williams]

W157 Selected Williams discography in Down Beat, Vol. 43 (January 29, 1976): 18 ((—))

W158 Selected Williams discography in Down Beat, Vol. 46 (June 21, 1979): 21 ((—))

W159 TONGEREN, Teo van: Zeer onvolledige discografie in Jazz Nu, Vol. 1 (July 1979): 445 ((—))

WILLIAMSON, CLAUDE, 1926-
  piano

W160 [Discography] in Swing Journal, Vol. 28 (June 1974): 153 ((2, 7))

WILLIAMSON, "HOMESICK" JAMES, 1910-
  guitar, harmonica, vocal

W161 Homesick James Williamson; a discography in Blues Unlimited Collectors Classics, No. 7 (May 1965): 9-10 ((2, 3, 7))

W162 PATERSON, Neil; Marcel CHAUVARD; and Kurt MOHR: A discography in Blues Unlimited, No. 6 (November 1963): 9; additions and corrections in Blues Unlimited, No. 12 (June 1964): suppl-6 ((2, 3, 7d))

WILLIAMSON, SONNY BOY (né Aleck Ford, later Alex "Rice" Miller), 1899-1965
  harmonica, vocal

W163 CHAUVARD, Marcel, and Kurt MOHR: Discography of Sonny Boy Williamson in Jazz Statistics, No. 16 (1960): 10-11; additions and corrections from Michel VOGLER in Jazz Statistics, No. 17 (1960): 8; No. 22 (June 1961): 6; [from Wolfie BAUM] No. 24 (December 1961): JS8 ((2, 3, 6, 7))

W164 Discography in Record Research, Vol. 2 (July-Aug. 1956): 11 ((3))

W165 MOHR, Kurt: Discography in Blues Unlimited, No. 8 (January 1964): 5-8; additions and corrections in Blues Unlimited, No. 12 (June 1964): suppl-5 ((2, 3, 7))

WILLIAMSON, SONNY BOY (John Lee
Williamson), 1914-1948
harmonica, vocal

W166 BAKKER, Dick M.: Sonny Boy Williamson in Micrography, No. 7
(November 1969): 9-11 ((7d))

W167 PANASSIÉ, Hugues: Discography of
Sonny Boy Williamson in Jazz
Journal, Vol. 8 (April 1955): 2
((2, 3, 7))

WILLIS, CHUCK, 1928-1958
vocal

W168 CHOISNEL, Emmanuel: Discographie
de Chuck Willis in Soul Bag, No.
22/23 (January-February 1973): 45
((2, 3, 7))

W169 NIQUET, Bernard: Essai de discographie de Chuck Willis in Jazz
Hot, No. 271 (April 1971): 19;
additions and corrections in Jazz
Hot, No. 272 (May 1971): 17 ((2,
3, 6, 7d))

WILLIS, LITTLE SON (Aaron Willis),
1932-
guitar, harmonica, vocal

W170 CHAUVARD, Marcel, and Jacques
DEMETRE: Little Son Willis in
Blues Unlimited, No. 14 (August
1964): 7 ((2, 3, 7))

WILLIS, RALPH
guitar, vocal

W171 ROTANTE, Anthony: A discography of
Ralph Willis in Discophile, No. 39
(December 1954): 10; additions and
corrections in Discophile, No. 52
(February 1957): 15 ((2, 3))

WILLIS, TIMMY, 1948-
vocal

W172 CHOISNEL, Emmanuel, and Kurt MOHR:
Discographie Timmy Willis in Soul
Bag, No. 16 (1972?): 9-10 ((2, 3,
6, 7))

WILSON, DICK, 1911-1941
tenor saxophone
See SAXOPHONE MUSIC (JAZZ) (Evensmo, Jan: The tenor saxophones of
Budd Johnson...)

WILSON, EDITH, 1906-
vocal

W173 ALLEN, Walter C.: Edith Wilson on
Columbia Records in Record Research, No. 73 (January 1966): 3-
4 ((2, 3, 6, 7, 8))

WILSON, GARLAND, 1909-1954
piano

W174 STEWART-BAXTER, Derrick: Garland
Wilson discography in Hot Club
Magazine, No. 18 (June 15, 1947):
14 ((7p))

W175 STEWART-BAXTER, Derrick: A Garland
Wilson discography in Jazz Notes
(Australia), No. 92 (April 1949):
5-6; additions and corrections
from John DAVIS in Jazz Notes
(Australia), No. 99 (January-
February 1950): 15 ((2, 3, 7))

WILSON, HOP (Harding Wilson), 1921-
1975
guitar, harmonica, vocal

W176 LEADBITTER, Mike: Hop Wilson; a
discography in Blues Unlimited,
No. 31 (March 1966): 14 ((2, 3,
7))

WILSON, JACK, 1936-
piano

W177 Selected Wilson discography in
Down Beat, Vol. 45 (March 9,
1978): 18 ((—))

WILSON, JIMMY
vocal

W178 CHAUVARD, Marcel; Kurt MOHR; and
Mike LEADBITTER: Discography of
Jimmy Wilson in Jazz Statistics,
No. 29 (October 1963): BS1-BS2
((2, 3, 7))

W179 ROTANTE, Anthony: The recordings
of Jimmy Wilson in Record Research, No. 35 (June 1961): 19
((—))

WILSON, SOCKS
vocal
See GRANT, COOT

WILSON, TEDDY, 1912-
piano

W180 BAKKER, Dick M.: Billie & Teddy on
microgroove 1932-1944. Alphen aan
de Rijn, Netherlands: Micrography,
1975, 52 pp. ((1, 2, 3, 4p, 4t,
6, 7))

W181 [Discography] in booklet to accompany [phonodisc] CBS-Sony
SONP-50332/3. Tokyo: CBS-Sony
Records [1971?], 8-10 ((2, 3, 6,
7))

W182 Disques de Teddy Wilson actuellement en vente en France in Jazz
Hot, No. 42 (March 1950): 24
((—))

W183 Selected Wilson discography in
Down Beat, Vol. 44 (February 24,
1977): 18 ((—))

WINDING, KAI, 1922-
trombone
See also JOHNSON, J. J. (Jepsen,
Jorgen Grunnet)

W184 FRESIA, Enzo: Discografia di Kai
Winding & J. J. Johnson in Musica
Jazz, Vol. 8 (May 1957): 39;
(June-July 1957): 47 ((2, 3, 7d))

WINGATE label

W185 FOSTER, Bob, and Jim WILSON: Wingate label listing in Hot Buttered
Soul, No. 32 (July 1974?): 7 ((3))

WINSTON, EDNA
vocal

W186 DAVIS, John, and G. F. GRAY-
CLARKE: Edna Winston; a discography in Jazz Journal, Vol. 3 (August 1950): 6 ((3, 7))

WINTER, PAUL, 1939-
soprano and alto saxophones

W187 Selected Winter discography in
Down Beat, Vol. 45 (May 4, 1978):
19 ((—))

WINTERS, RUBY
vocal

W188 MOHR, Kurt: Ruby Winters discography in Hot Buttered Soul, No.
45 (April-May 1976): 17 ((3, 5,
7))

WIRGES, BILL, 1894-
piano, arranger

W189 BACKENSTO, Woody: Bill Wirges and
his Orchestra in Discophile, No.
34 (February 1954): 9, 12; additions and corrections in Discophile, No. 36 (June 1954): 10 ((2,
3, 6, 7))

WITHERSPOON, JIMMY, 1923-
vocal

W190 COWLYN, Martin: The blues shouters,
part 1--Jimmy Witherspoon in Blues
Link, No. 4 (1974): 5-7 ((7))

W191 JEPSEN, Jorgen Grunnet: Jimmy
Witherspoon in Discophile, No. 36
(June 1954): 17-19 ((2, 3, 6))

W192 MOHR, Kurt: Jimmy Witherspoon on
Federal in Jazz Statistics, No. 5
(April 1957): 3-4 ((2, 3, 7))

W193 ROTANTE, Anthony: Jimmy Witherspoon discography in Record Research, No. 62 (August 1964) to
No. 68 (May 1965), various paginations; additions and corrections
in Record Research, No. 71 (October 1965): 10 ((2, 3, 6, 7, 8))

WOODING, SAM, 1895-
piano

W194 BETTONVILLE, Albert: Sam Wooding
and his Chocolate Dandies in Hot
Club Magazine, No. 7 (July 1946):
8 ((2, 3))

WOODS, OSCAR, 1900?-ca. 1956
guitar, vocal

W195 OLIVER, Paul: Discography of Oscar
Woods in Discographical Forum, No.
4 (January 1961): 14-15 ((2, 3,
6, 7))

WOODS, PHIL, 1931-
alto saxophone

W196 Phil Woods discography in Swing
Journal, Vol. 27 (July 1973):
276-283 ((2, 7d))

W197 Phil Woods diskografi (skivor
inspelade under eget namn) in
Orkester Journalen, Vol. 28 (June
1960): 34 ((2, 7d))

W198 Selected discography in Jazz
Magazine (US), Vol. 2 (summer
1978): 40 ((—))

WORLD PROGRAM SERVICE

W199 KRESSLEY, David: Catalog of World
transcriptions (1933 to 1963) in
Record Research, No. 89 (March
1968) to No. 94 (December 1968);
No. 98 (May 1969), various paginations ((—))

WORLD SAXOPHONE QUARTET

W200 Selected World Saxophone Quartet
discography in Down Beat, Vol. 46
(October 1979): 29 ((—))

WORLD'S GREATEST JAZZ BAND

W201 LOMBARDI, Giorgio: Discografia in
Musica Jazz, Vol. 34 (December
1978): 46-47 ((2, 7))

WRIGHTSMAN, STAN, 1910-1975
piano

W202 HEERMANS, Jerry: Stanley Wrightsman discography in Good Diggin',
Vol. 2 (October 1948): 10-13
((7d))

WYNNE, BILLY
drums, leader

W203 BACKENSTO, Woody: Billy Wynne in
Record Research, No. 100 (August
1969): 3-4 ((2, 3, 5, 6, 9))

X label

X1   ALLEN, Walter C., and Carl
KENDZIORA: "X" Vault Originals;
data in Matrix, No. 11/12 (June
1956) to No. 19 (September 1958),
various paginations, in 8 parts;
additions and corrections in Matrix, No. 21 (January 1959): 15-
17; No. 22 (March 1959): 18-20;
No. 29/30 (August 1960): 36; No.
33 (March 1961): 19 ((2, 3, 6, 7))

X2   WHITE, Bozy, and Tony NISHIJIMA:
"X" Vault Originals reborn...in
Japan in Matrix, No. 64 (April
1966): 3-11; additions and corrections in Matrix, No. 74 (December 1967): 12; No. 75 (February 1968): 12; No. 82 (April
1969): 14 ((2, 3, 6, 7))

XX label (Australian)

X3   BAKER, Frank Owen: XX Records in
Music Maker, Vol. 46 (May 1951):
38; Vol. 47 (April 1952): 38
((—))

X4   HAESLER, William J., and M. John
KENNEDY: XX catalogue in Matrix,
No. 2 (September 1954): 20-21
((3, 6))

YAMASHITA, YOSUKE, 1942-
piano

Y1   WEBER, Horst: Discographie in
Jazz Magazine (France), No. 253
(April 1977): 40 ((2, 7))

YAMBO label

Y2   BAKER, Cary: Yambo label listing
in Hot Buttered Soul, No. 12 (November 1972): 11 ((3, 6))

Y3   TOHLEMONT, Marc: Yambo listing in
Soul Bag, No. 38 (May 1974): 37-
38 ((3, 6))

YANCEY, JIMMY, ca. 1894-1951
piano
See also YANCEY FAMILY

Y4   BAKKER, Dick M.: Jimmy Yancey
1939-1943 in Micrography, No. 31
(1974?): 8 ((3, 7d))

Y5   FUJII, H.: Yancey discography
(complete) in Hot Jazz Club Bulletin, Vol. 4 (November 1951): 9
((7d))

Y6   HARRIS, Rex, and Max JONES: Discography in Melody Maker, Vol. 21
(February 10, 1945): 6 ((2, 3, 7))

Y7   HOEFER, George: Yancey discography
in Down Beat, Vol. 18 (November
2, 1951): 4 ((—))

Y8   HOLLEY, John: Jimmie Yancey, a
discography in Matrix, No. 95:
3-7; additions and corrections in
Matrix, No. 105 (November 1974):
17 ((2, 3, 6, 7))

Y9   McCARTHY, Albert J.: Discography
in Jazz Notes and Blue Rhythm,
No. 52 (May 1945): 1-2 ((2, 3))

Y10 McCARTHY, Albert J.: Discography;
piano solos by Jimmy Yancey in
Jazz Music (September 1943): 6
((2))

Y11 POSTIF, François: Discographie de
Jimmy Yancey in Jazz Hot, No. 102
(September 1955): 13 ((2, 3, 7))

Y12 TEALDO ALIZIERI, Carlos L.: Discografia de Jimmy Yancey in Jazz
Magazine (Argentina), No. 27 (November 1951): 5 ((2, 3, 6, 7))

YANCEY FAMILY

Y13 ALLEN, Walter C.: Discography of
the Yancey Family in Record Research, Vol. 2 (February 1956):
4-6 ((2, 3, 6, 7, 9))

YERBA BUENA JAZZ BAND
  See WATTERS, LU

YOUNG, (MIGHTY) JOE, 1927-
  guitar, vocal

Y14 CHOISNEL, Emmanuel: Mighty Joe
     Young in Soul Bag, No. 38 (May
     1974): 21-22 ((2, 3, 7))

Y15 Discography Mighty Joe Young in
     Living Blues, No. 3 (autumn 1970):
     25 ((2, 3, 7))

YOUNG, JOHNNY, 1918-1974
  guitar, vocal

Y16 LEADBITTER, Mike A.: Johnny
     Young--a discography in Blues Un-
     limited, No. 26 (October 1965):
     11 ((2, 7))

YOUNG, LESTER, 1909-1959
    tenor saxophone
    See also HOLIDAY, BILLIE (Shera,
    Michael G.); KANSAS CITY FIVE/SIX/
    SEVEN; SAXOPHONE MUSIC (JAZZ)
    (Evensmo, Jan: The tenor saxo-
    phonists of the period 1930-1942)

Y17 Disques de Lester Young recemment
     publiés en France in Jazz Hot, No.
     35 (July-August 1949): 9 ((2, 3,
     7d))

Y18 EVENSMO, Jan: The tenor saxophone
     and clarinet of Lester Young 1936-
     1942 [Hosle, Norway: 1977], 36 pp.
     (Jazz solography series, Vol. 5)
     ((1, 2, 3, 6, 7, 9))

Y19 HOEFER, George: Selected Lester
     Young discography in Down Beat,
     Vol. 29 (March 1, 1962): 19, 43
     [to 1944] ((2, 3, 7))

Y20 JEPSEN, Jorgen Grunnet: Discogra-
     phie de l'oeuvre de Lester Young
     in Les Cahiers du Jazz, No. 1
     (November 1959): 128-144 ((1, 2,
     3, 6, 7))

Y21 JEPSEN, Jorgen Grunnet: Discogra-
     phy of Lester Young. [Brande,
     Denmark: Debut Records, c1959], 26
     leaves; additions and corrections
     from Olav ANGELL in Discographical
     Forum, No. 2 (July 1960): 9-10
     ((1, 2, 3, 6, 7))

Y22 JEPSEN, Jorgen Grunnet: A discog-
     raphy of Lester Young. Copenhagen:
     Knudsen [c1968], 45 leaves; addi-
     tions and corrections in Point du
     Jazz, No. 10 (October 1974): 107-
     108 ((1, 2, 3, 6, 7))

Y23 [[JEPSEN, Jorgen Grunnet: Lester
     Young. Copenhagen: 1957]]

Y24 JEPSEN, Jorgen Grunnet: Lester
     Young diskografi in Orkester
     Journalen, Vol. 27 (April 1959)
     to (July-August 1959), various
     paginations, in 4 parts ((2, 3,
     6, 7))

Y25 JEPSEN, Jorgen Grunnet: Lester
     Young; records for Norman Granz,
     a listing in Jazz Journal, Vol.
     13 (August 1960): 15-16 ((2, 3,
     6, 7))

Y26 KORST, Bill: Big Bill's waxworks
     in IAJRC Record, un-numbered 1969
     issue, at bottom of unpaged page
     [additions and corrections to
     various discographies]

Y27 Lester Young on Aladdin; discog-
     raphy in Jazz Monthly, Vol. 2
     (December 1956): 10 ((2, 3, 7))

Y28 MORGAN, Alun: Lester Young on
     Clef--a name listing in Jazz
     Monthly, Vol. 2 (December 1956):
     26, 31 ((2, 3, 6, 7))

Y29 MORGENSTERN, Dan: Lester Young
     discography. Part 1: 1936-1945 in
     Down Beat Music '71 (16th annual
     yearbook): 73-83 [later parts not
     published] ((1, 2, 3, 6, 7))

Y30 PORTER, Lewis Robert: Title dis-
     cography in his The jazz impro-
     visations of Lester Young. MA
     dissertation, Tufts University,
     1979, 151-204 ((6, 7))

Y31 RABEN, Erik: Lester Young discog-
     raphy in Jazz Journal, Vol. 21
     (January 1968): 28-29; (February
     1968): 21-22; (March 1968): 17-
     19, 22 ((1, 2, 3, 6, 7))

Y32 SCHROEDER, Harry: Lester Young
     1937-1942 in Micrography, No. 42
     (October 1976): 21-22 ((1, 7d))

Y33 SCHROEDER, Harry: Lester Young
     1943-44 in Micrography, No. 44
     (May 1977): 19 ((1))

Y34 SCHROEDER, Harry: Lester Young
     1946-1957 in Micrography, No. 41
     (May 1976): 21-23 ((1, 7d))

Y35 SCHROEDER, Harry: Lester Young
     1946-58 in Micrography, No. 48
     (September 1978): 16-18 ((1, 7))

Y36 STIASSI, Ruggero: Discografia
     Lester Young in Musica Jazz, Vol.
     31 (January 1975): 44-48; (Feb-
     ruary 1975): 47-48; (March 1975):
     47-48 ((2, 7))

Y37   WIEDEMANN, Erik: Lester Young on
      records in Jazz Review, Vol. 2
      (September 1959): 10–11 [from
      July 15, 1942] ((1, 2, 3, 6,
      7))

ZAWINUL, JOE, 1932–
      piano

Z1   Selected Zawinul discography in
      Down Beat, Vol. 42 (January 30,
      1975): 17 ((—))

ZEITLIN, DENNY, 1938–
      piano

Z2   Denny Zeitlin discography in Down
      Beat, Vol. 46 (May 17, 1979): 17
      ((—))

Z3   FRESIA, Enzo: Discografia di Denny
      Zeitlin in Musica Jazz, Vol. 22
      (August–September 1966): 27 ((2,
      7))

ZYNN label

Z4   "BIG AL" (pseud.): Zynn Records of
      Crowley, Louisiana, in SMG, Vol. 6
      (September 1977): 20 ((—))

Z5   LEADBITTER, Mike: Zynn/Feature/
      Rocko/Rocket label listings in
      Hot Buttered Soul, No. 16 (March
      1973): 2–5 ((3))

SMALL PUBLISHERS CITED

Note: Names of small publishers cited in the text are not included in this list if their books are known to be out of print.

Walter C. Allen
  Box 929 Adelaide Station
  Toronto, Ontario M5C 2K3
  Canada

Gerard Bieldermann
  Leie 18
  7000 Zwolle
  Netherlands

Raffaele Borretti
  C.P. 394
  Cosenza
  Italy

Walter Bruyninckx
  Lange Nieuwstraat 135
  Mechelen
  Belgium

Gerhard Conrad. See Jazzfreund

Vince Danca
  2418 Barrington Pl.
  Rockford, IL 61107

Danish Discographical Publishing
  Klintevej 25
  2800 Lyngby
  Denmark

Jan Evensmo
  Granveien 54
  1360 Nesbru
  Norway

Leslie Fancourt
  11 Front Brents
  Faversham, Kent
  England

Otto Fluckiger
  Talackerstr. 7
  4153 Reinach
  Switzerland

Jim Goggin
  Box 7
  San Leandro, CA 94577

Edwin Harkins
  617 Canyon Pl.
  Solana Beach, CA 92075

Jaynar Press
  Box 3141
  Merchandise Mart Plaza
  Chicago, IL 60654

Jazzfreund
  Von-Stauffenbergstr. 24
  D-5750 Menden
  West Germany

Daniel Koechlin
  1 rue Desire-Laigre
  76160 Darnetal
  France

Ashley Mark Publishing Co.
  Saltmeadows Road
  Gateshead NE8 3AJ
  England

Micrography
  Stevinstraat 14
  2405CP Alphen aan de Rijn
  Netherlands

Raretone
  c/o Liborio Pusateri
  Box 947
  I-20100 Milano
  Italy

Matthias Rissi
  Haldenstr. 23
  CH8134 Adliswil
  Switzerland

Alex Robertson
  163 Broadview Ave.
  Pointe Claire, Quebec H9R 3Z5
  Canada

Storyville Publications
  66 Fairview Dr.
  Chigwell, Essex IG7 6HS
  England

Suomen Jazzliitto
  c/o Hans Westerberg

Harvarvagen 11c
SF-00390 Helsinki 39
Finland

Willie Timner
  285 Grosvenor Ave.
  Beaconsfield, Quebec H9W 1S6
  Canada

Wildmusic
  Box 2138
  Ann Arbor, MI 48106

PERIODICALS CITED

Addresses and latest frequency of publication are not given for those periodicals known to be out-of-print. Since the availability and addresses of current periodicals in jazz and related music are subject to change, it is suggested that the user consult the latest issue of Jazz Index; Bibliography of Jazz Literature in Periodicals and Collections (available from Norbert Ruecker, Box 4106, D-6000 Frankfurt 1, West Germany) for up-to-date information. Bibliographic information, such as years of publication and frequency, is given for all periodicals if known.

After Beat (US). Vol. 1, No. 1, October 1970-

Alley Music; Australia's Blues Magazine. Vol. 1, 1967?- . Irreg.

American Music Lover

Annals of Internal Medicine

Anschlaege; Zeitschrift des Archivs für Populäre Musik. 1978?- . Quarterly. Archiv für Populäre Musik, Ostertorsteinweg 3, D-2800 Bremen, West Germany. ISSN 0344-2667

Anuario de Jazz Caliente (Chile)

Australian Blues Society Progress

Australian Jazz Quarterly; a magazine for the connoisseur of hot music. Melbourne, No. 1 (May 1946) to No. 31 (April 1957). Irreg. Available on microfilm from Greenwood Press

The Big Beat

Billboard (US). 1894- . (Formerly Billboard Music Week.) Weekly. Billboard Publications, 9000 Sunset Blvd., Los Angeles, CA 90069

Bixography (US). 4? issues, 1943

Blue Flame (Chicago). No. 1 (May 1970) to No. 17/18 (n.d.). Irreg.

Blues Life; Deutschsprachiges Bluesmagazin (Austria). 1978?- . Quarterly. Kegelgasse 40/1/17, A-1030 Vienna, Austria

Blues Magazine (Toronto). Vol. 1, No. 1 (February 1975)- .. (defunct)

Blues Notes; erstes deutschsprachiges Blues- und Jazzmagazin (Austria). No. 1, 1969- . Irreg. Wienerstr. 81, A-4020 Linz, Austria

Blues Power (Varese, Italy). Vol. 1, 1974-

Blues Research (Brooklyn). No. 1 (May 1959) to No. 16 (January 1970). Irreg.

Blues Statistics (Reinach, Switzerland). No. 2, March 1963. Other issues published as part of Jazz Statistics

Blues Unlimited (England). No. 1, April 1963- . Irreg. 36 Belmont Park, Lewisham, London SE13 5DB, England

Blues Unlimited Collectors Classics (Bexhill-on-Sea, Sussex). No. 1 (March 1964) to No. 14 (October 1966), except No. 6 never published. Irreg.

Blues World (Knutsford, England). No. 1, 1965-No. 50? (1974). Monthly

Boletín del Hot Club de Buenos Aires (Argentina)

Boogie Woogie & Blues Collector (Netherlands). Irreg. Martin van Olderen, Maasdrielhof 175, NL-1106NG Amsterdam, Netherlands

Bulletin du Hot Club de France. Monthly. Jacques Pescheux, 28 rue Saint-Caprais, F-91770 Saint-Vrain, France

les Cahiers du Jazz (Paris, France). No. 1 (1959) to No. 16/17 (1968?). Available on microfilm from Greenwood Press

Change (US)

Coda; the jazz magazine (Toronto). No. 1, 1958- . Bimonthly. Box 87 Station J, Toronto, Ontario M4J 4X8, Canada. ISSN CN 0010-017X

Collecta (England). No. 1 (1968)- .
Irreg.

Contemporary Keyboard (US). Vol. 1,
1975- . Monthly. GPI Publications,
20605 Lazaneo, Cupertino, CA 95014.
ISSN 0361-5820

Country Directory (US). No. 1 (November 1960)-

Different Drummer (Rochester, NY).
Vol. 1, No. 1 (September-October
1973) to Vol. 1, No. 15 (January
1975)

Disc-ribe (US). 1980- . Wildmusic,
Box 2138, Ann Arbor, MI 48106

Discographical Forum (England). No. 1,
1960- . Irreg. Malcolm Walker, 44
Belleville Rd., London SW11 6QT,
England

Discography (London, England). Monthly, October 1942 to April 1944;
thereafter irreg. to 1947, when it
merged with Jazz Music

Discophile; the magazine for record
information (London, England). No. 1
(August 1948) to No. 61 (December
1958), when it merged with Matrix.
Available on microfilm from Greenwood Press

Disk in the World (Japan). Vol. 1, No.
1, July 1980- . Disk Union, 2-13-1
Iidabashi, Chiyoda-ku, Tokyo 102,
Japan

Doctor Jazz (Netherlands). Quarterly.
Jan Taris, van Lynden van Sanden-
burglaan 5, Utrecht, Netherlands

Down Beat; the contemporary music
magazine. Vol. 1, 1934- . Monthly.
222 West Adams St., Chicago, IL
60606. ISSN 0012-5768

Down Beat Yearbook (Chicago). No. 1,
1956- . Annual. Same address as
previous periodical. ISSN 0077-
2372

Eureka; the bi-monthly magazine of New
Orleans jazz (England). Vol. 1, No.
1 (January-February 1960) to Vol. 2,
No. 1 (n.d.)

Footnote; dedicated to New Orleans
music (England). Vol. 1, No. 1,
December 1969- . Bimonthly. 44 High
St., Meldreth, Royston, Herts.
SG8 6JU, England

Goldmine (US)

Good Diggin' (Portland, OR). Vol. 1
(1947?)-1948. Irreg.

Hip; the Milwaukee jazz letter. Vol. 1
(old series) (1962) to Vol. 10, No.
6 (new series) (December 1971), when
it merged with Jazz Digest (Vir-
ginia). Available on microfilm from
Greenwood Press

Hot Buttered Soul (England)

Hot Club Magazine (Brussels, Belgium).

No. 1 (January 1946) to No. 29
(August 1948). Monthly. Incorporated
into Jazz Hot

Hot Jazz Club (Sastre, Argentina). No.
1, 1944- . Quarterly

Hot Jazz Club Bulletin (Japan)

Hot Jazz Info (West Germany). 1973?- .
Monthly. Gesellschaft fur Forderung
des New Orleans Jazz e.V., Austr.
43, D-6050 Offenbach, West Germany

Hot Notes (Ireland). Vol. 1, No. 1
(March 1946)-Vol. 2, No. 14 (spring
1948). Bimonthly

Hot Revue (Switzerland). December 1945
to May 1947. Monthly. Incorporated
into Jazz Hot

IAJRC Journal (US). Vol. 1 (1968)- .
Quarterly. (First few issues called
IAJRC Record.) Bozy White, Box 10208,
Oakland, CA 94610

Impetus; new music (England). No. 1,
1978- . Irreg. Philpot Lane, London
EC3, England

International Discophile (Los Angeles).
No. 1 (summer 1955) to Vol. 1, No. 4
(May-June 1960)

Jazz (Belgium). No. 1 (March 1945) to
No. 13 (November 1945). Monthly.
Continued by Hot Club Magazine

Jazz (New York). Vol. 1, No. 1 (June
1942) to Vol. 1, No. 10 (December
1943); Vol. 1 (new series), No. 1
(December 1944) to No. 2 (January
1945)

Jazz (Poland). 1956-

Jazz (Switzerland). 1975?-

Jazz and Blues (London, England). Vol.
1 (April 1971) to December 1973,
when it was incorporated by Jazz
Journal

Jazz + Classic (Switzerland). No. 1
(February-March 1979)- . Bimonthly.
St. Jakobstr. 8, CH-4132 Muttenz,
Switzerland

Jazz Bazaar (West Germany). No. 1
(April 1969) to No. 12/13 (December
1971-January 1972). Quarterly

Jazz Blast (Mt. Ephraim, NJ). 1968?-
1973?

Jazz, Blues & Co. (France). No. 1,
1975- . Monthly. 1 rue Dalloz,
Paris, France

Jazz Bulletin (Basel, Switzerland).
Vol. 1 (1952?)- . Irreg.

Jazz di Ieri e di Oggi (Italy). Vol. 1
(1959)- . Monthly

Jazz Digest (New Orleans). Vol. 1, No.
1 (January 1966)-Vol. 1, No. 3
(March 1966). Monthly

Jazz Digest (McLean, VA). Vol. 1, No.
1 (January-February 1972) to Vol. 3,
No. 6 (June 1974). Irreg. Available
on microfilm from Greenwood Press

Jazz-Disco (Sweden). Vol. 1 (1960)-

Jazz Discounter (Evansville, IN). Vol. 1 (1948)-

Jazz Down Under (Sydney, Australia). No. 1 (1975) to No. 20 (1977). Monthly

Jazz Echo (Hamburg, West Germany). Issued as a supplement to Gondel Magazine. Monthly

Jazz Forum; the magazine of the European Jazz Federation (Warsaw, Poland). No. 1, February 1967- . Bimonthly. Jazz Forum Publications Distribution, 1697 Broadway, Suite 1203, New York, NY 10019. ISSN PL 0021-5635

Jazz Forum; quarterly review of jazz and literature (Fordingbridge, Hants., England). No. 1 (May 1946) to No. 5 (July 1947)

Jazz Guide (London, England). Vol. 1 (1964)- . Monthly

Jazz Hot (France). No. 1 (March 1935) to No. 32 (July 1939); No. 1 (new series) (March 1945-). Monthly except in summer. 14 rue Chaptal, F-75009 Paris, France. ISSN FR 0021-5643. Available on microfilm (to 1972) from Greenwood Press

Jazz Hot Club Bulletin (Tokyo, Japan). Formerly called Hot Club of Japan Bulletin. Vol. 1 (1948?)- . Monthly

Jazz Information (New York). Vol. 1 (September 12, 1939) to Vol. 2, No. 16 (November 1941). Irreg. Available on microfilm from Greenwood Press

Jazz Journal (England). Vol. 1, No. 1, May 1948- . Monthly. Pitman Periodicals, 41 Parker St., London WC2B 5PB, England

Jazz Magazine (Buenos Aires, Argentina). Vol. 1 (September 1945)- . Monthly

Jazz Magazine (Chilwell, Notts., England). September 1946 to Vol. 3 (Nos. 1-4, n.d.). Bimonthly

Jazz Magazine (France). No. 1, December 1954- . Monthly. Box 87-08, F-75360 Paris Cedex 8, France. ISSN FR 0021-566X

Jazz Magazine (US). Vol. 1, 1975- . Semiannual or quarterly. Box 212, Northport, NY 11768

Jazz Monthly (England). Vol. 1 (1954)-1971. Incorporated by Jazz and Blues

Jazz Music; the international jazz magazine (London, England). October 1942-Vol. 11, No. 4 (April 1960). Bimonthly. Continued by Jazz Times

Jazz News (London, England). 1956-1964. Fortnightly

Jazz Notes (Adelaide, Australia). Vol. 1, No. 1 (January 1941)- . Monthly.

Continued by Jazz Notes and Blue Rhythm

Jazz Notes (New Orleans). No. 1 (September 1951)-

Jazz Notes and Blue Rhythm (Melbourne, Australia). January 1940- No. 103? (October 1950). Monthly

Jazz Nu; maandblad voor aktuele geimproviseerde muziek (Netherlands). Vol. 1, 1978- . Monthly. Postbus 10217, NL-5000 Tilburg, Netherlands

Jazz Nytt (Norway). 5 issues per year. Norsk Jazzforbund, Boks 261, N-6401 Molde, Norway. ISSN NO 0332-7248

Jazz Panorama; the Canadian music scene (Toronto). Vol. 1 (December 1, 1946) to May 1948. Irreg.

Jazz Podium (West Germany). Vol. 1, 1952- . Monthly. Verlag Dieter Zimmerle, Vogelsangstr. 32, D-7000 Stuttgart 1, West Germany. ISSN GW 0021-5686

Jazz Press (Almelo, Netherlands). No. 1 (1975) to No. 53/54 (September 1978). Fortnightly to May 1977, then monthly

Jazz Quarterly (Kingsville, TX). Summer 1942-1945

Jazz Record; free bulletin of the Society for Jazz Appreciation (Chilwell, Notts., England). No. 1 (May 1943) to No. 12 (April 1944). Irreg. Incorporated by Jazz Magazine (England)

Jazz Record (New York). No. 1 (February 15, 1943) to No. 60 (December 1947). Monthly. Available on microfilm from Greenwood Press

Jazz Register (US). No. 1 (1965) to Vol. 2, No. 1? (January 1966)

Jazz Report (St. Louis, MO). Vol. 1 (1954) to Vol. 7, No. 3 (new series) (December 1959). Monthly

Jazz Report (Ventura, CA). Vol. 1, No. 1 (September 1960-). Irreg. Box 476, Ventura, CA 93001

Jazz Reprints (Portsmouth, England). Vol. 1, Nos. 1-3 (n.d.)

Jazz Review (New York). Vol. 1, No. 1 (November 1958) to Vol. 4, No. 1 (1961). Reprinted by Kraus Reprint Corp

Jazz Rhythm & Blues; schweizerische Jazz-Zeitschrift (Zurich). 1967-

Jazz Session (Chicago). September 1944 to July 1946. Monthly or bimonthly. Available on Microfilm from Greenwood Press

Jazz Statistics (Reinach or Basel, Switzerland). No. 1 (1958) to No. 29 (October 1963). Irreg.

Jazz Studies (England). Vol. 1 (1964?)-Vol.3 (March 1971?). Irreg.

Jazz Tempo (London, England). March 1943 to April 1944. Irreg. Incorporated by Jazz Music

Jazz 360 (Switzerland). 1978?- . Monthly. Gustave Cerutti, 8 Ave. du Marche, CH-3960 Sierre, Switzerland

Jazz Times; bulletin of the West London Jazz Society (England). Vol. 1, No. 1 (1964)-1972? Monthly

Jazz Up (Buenos Aires, Argentina)

Jazz Wereld; verschynt elke twee maanden (Netherlands). No. 1 (1965) to No. 43

Jazzbladet (Norway)

Jazzfinder (New Orleans). Vol. 1, No. 1 (January 1948) to January 1949. Incorporated by Playback

Jazzforschung (Austria). Vol. 1, 1969- . Annual. Internationale Gesellschaft für Jazzforschung, Leonhardstr. 15, A-8010 Graz, Austria

Jazzfreund; Mitteilungsblatt für Jazzfreunde in Ost und West (West Germany). No. 1, 1956- . Quarterly. Von-Stauffenbergstr. 24, D-5750 Menden, West Germany. ISSN GW 0021-5724

Jazzmanía (Buenos Aires, Argentina). Vol. 1, 1957?- . Irreg.

Jazzology (Columbia, SC)

Jazzology (London, England). 1944 to Vol. 2, No. 2 (new series) (February 1947). Monthly

Jazzophone (France). No. 1, 1978- . Quarterly. 83 bis, rue Doudeauville, F-75018 Paris, France

Jazzspiegel (Belgium)

Jazztime (Italy). Anno 1, No. 1-3 (1952)

Jefferson; nordisk tidskrift för Blues och Folkmusik (Sweden). Quarterly. Scandinavian Blues Association, c/o Tommy Löfgren, Skördvägen 7, S-18600 Vallentuna, Sweden. ISSN SW 0345-5653

JEMF Quarterly (Los Angeles). Vol. 1, 1974- . John Edwards Memorial Foundation, Folklore & Mythology Center, University of California, Los Angeles, CA 90024

Journal of Jazz Discography (Newport, Wales). No. 1 (1977) to No. 5 (1979). Irreg.

Journal of Jazz Studies (US). Vol. 1, No. 1, October 1973- . Irreg. Transaction Periodicals Consortium, Rutgers University, New Brunswick, NJ 08903. ISSN 0093-3686

Key Notes (Netherlands). No. 1, 1975-

Kord (US). Ca. 1970-1972? Quarterly

Living Blues (US). No. 1, spring 1970- . Bimonthly. 2615 North Wilton Ave., Chicago, IL 60614. ISSN 0024-5232

Matrix (London, England). No. 1 (July 1954) to No. 107/108 (December 1975). Irreg. Available on microfilm from Greenwood Press

Mediart (Montreal, Quebec)

Melody Maker (England). Vol. 1, 1926- . Weekly. IPC Business Press, Oakfield House, 35 Perrymount Rd., Haywards Heath, Sussex RH16 3DH, England. ISSN 0025-9012

Metronome (New York). 1885-1961. Monthly

Metronome Yearbook (New York). 1950-1951, 1953-1959. Annual

Micrography; jazz and blues on microgroove. No. 1 (December 1968)- . Irreg. Stevinstraat 14, Alphen aan de Rijn, Netherlands

Mississippi Rag; the voice of traditional jazz and ragtime (US). Vol. 1, No. 1, November 1973- . Monthly. 5644 Morgan Ave. S., Minneapolis, MN 55419

Music in Sweden. No. 1 (1979?)- . Rikskonserter, Box 1225, S-11182 Stockholm, Sweden

Music Maker (Sydney, Australia). Vol. 1 (1906?)-Vol. 49 (1954); Vol. 1 (new series) (1955)- . Monthly

Musica Jazz (Italy). Vol. 1, 1945- . Monthly. Via Quintiliano 40, I-20138 Milano, Italy. ISSN IT 0027-4542

Nuova Musica (Torino, Italy). No. 1 (1979?)-

Oh Play That Thing (San Francisco). Irreg.

Orkester Journalen; tidskrift for jazzmusik (Sweden). Vol. 1, 1933- . Monthly. Drottninggatan 14, S-11151 Stockholm, Sweden. ISSN SW 0030-5043

Paul's Record Magazine (US?)

Pieces of Jazz (England). No. 1 (January 1968) to No. 7 (1969), quarterly; 1970 and 1971, annual

Playback; the jazz record magazine (New Orleans). Vol. 2 (January 1949) to March/April 1952

Point du Jazz (Belgium). No. 1 (1969)- . Annual. Lucien Ravet, rue de la Commune 66, B-1030 Brussels, Belgium

The Professional (England). No. 1, 1974?-

Quartette (US). No. 1 (January 1970); No. 2 (March 1970); thereafter merged with R and B Collector

R and B Collector (Northridge, CA). Vol. 1, No. 1 (January-February 1970)- . Title changed to R and B Magazine with Vol. 1 (July-October 1970)

Radio Free Jazz (US). Vol. 1, 1961?- . Monthly. Title changed to Jazz Times,

June 1980. Ira Sabin, 3212 Pennsylvania Ave. SE, Washington, DC 20020

Rag Times (Los Angeles). Vol. 1 (May
15, 1967)- . Bimonthly. Maple Leaf
Club, 5560 W. 62 St., Los Angeles,
CA 90056

Ragtimer (Canada). Vol. 1, 1962- .
Bimonthly. Called Ragtime Society
Bulletin, Vols. 1-5. Box 520, Sta-
tion A, Weston, Ontario M9N 3N3,
Canada. ISSN CN 0033-8672

Record Changer (New York). Vol. 1
(1944) to Vol. 15, No. 2 (1957).
Irreg.

Record Exchange (Toronto). Vol. 1
(1948) to Vol. 5 (1952). Monthly.
Incorporated by Theme

Record Exchanger (Anaheim, CA). Vol. 1,
1971?-

Record Research (US). Vol. 1, No. 1
(February 1955)- . Bimonthly. 65
Grand Ave., Brooklyn, NY 11205.
ISSN 0034-1592

Record Research. Bulletin (US). No. 1
(January 1958) to No. 12. Irreg. Some
issues called Recorded Americana.
Same address as Record Research

Record Research. Supplements (US). No.
1 (June 30, 1955) to No. 18 (August
7, 1965). Irreg. Same address as
Record Research

Recorded Sound; journal of the British
Institute of Recorded Sound. No. 1
(1961)- . Quarterly. 29 Exhibition
Rd., London SW7, England

Recordiana (Norwich, CT). Vol. 1, No.
1 (May 1944) to Vol. 1, No. 3 (October 1944). Irreg.

Reprints and Reflections (Australia)

Rhythm and Blues Panorama; bulletin
periodique du Rhythm and Blues Club
(Belgium). No. 1, February 1960- .
Monthly or semimonthly

Rhythm and Blues Train (US). Vol. 1,
1964?-

Rhythm Rag

Rockrevue (Austria)

RSVP; the record collectors' journal
(London, England). No. 1, May 1965- .
Monthly

Sailor's Delight (England)

Schlagzeug (Berlin, West Germany)

Schwann-1 Record and Tape Guide (US).
1949- . Monthly. Title varies. 137
Newbury St., Boston, MA 02116

Second Line (US). Vol. 1, (1950)- .
Quarterly. New Orleans Jazz Club, 103

Verret St., New Orleans, LA 70114.
ISSN 0037-0576. Available on micro-
film (to 1976) from Greenwood
Press

Seventy-eight Quarterly (Brooklyn).
Vol. 1, No. 1 (1967) to Vol. 1, No.
3

Shout (Chislehurst, Kent, England).
1968-

SMG

Soul (Plymouth, England). 1966?-

Soul Bag (France). Ca. 1970- . Irreg.
C.L.A.R.B., 25 rue Frezel, F-92300
Levallois-Perret, France. ISSN FR
0398-9089

Soul Music Monthly (US)

Sounds 3

Storyville (England). No. 1, October
1965- . Bimonthly. 66 Fairview Dr.,
Chigwell, Essex IG7 6HS, England.
ISSN 0039-2030

Swing Collectors Club Jazz News
(Austria)

Swing Journal (Japan). Vol. 1, 1947- .
Monthly. 3-6-24, Shibakoen, Minato-
ku, Tokyo, Japan

Swing Music (London, England). Vol. 1,
No. 1 (March 1935) to No. 14 (fall
1936). Quarterly

Swing Shop Magazine (London, England).
September 1952 to summer 1955. Bimonthly

Swingtime; maandblad voor jazz en
blues (Belgium). Monthly. SWOJB,
Bruggestraat 26, B-8080 Ruiselede,
Belgium

Swingtime; the magazine with a swing
to it (Malmo, Sweden). No. 1, December 1960-

Swiss Music Dial (Switzerland)

Talking Blues (London, England). 1976-
1979

Theme (North Hollywood, CA). Vol. 1,
No. 1 (July 1953) to Vol. 4, No. 1
(fall 1957). Irreg.

Tzaz (Thessaloniki, Greece)

Universal Jazz (Reading, Berks., England). Vol. 1, May 1946 to late 1946.
Monthly

Vintage Jazz Mart (England). Vol. 1,
December 1953- . Irreg. Trevor
Benwell, 4 Hillcrest Gardens,
Dollis Hill, London NW2 6HZ,
England

Whiskey, women and... (Boston, MA).
No. 1 (n.d.) to No. 6? (March
1974). Irreg.

INDEX

Note: References are to entry numbers, not page numbers. Numbers in parentheses indicate the volume, number, or part in the series of that specific entry. An underlined entry number indicates a correction only, not a full discography. Only authors, distinctive titles, and names of series have been indexed.